THE LAST WISH

By Andrzej Sapkowski

The Last Wish
Sword of Destiny
Blood of Elves
The Time of Contempt
Baptism of Fire
The Tower of Swallows
The Lady of the Lake
Season of Storms

The Malady and Other Stories:
An Andrzej Sapkowski Sampler (e-only)

THE
LAST WISH

INTRODUCING
THE WITCHER

ANDRZEJ SAPKOWSKI

Translated by Danusia Stok

www.orbitbooks.net

Original text copyright © 1993 by Andrzej Sapkowski
English translation copyright © 2007 by Danusia Stok
Excerpt from *Sword of Destiny* copyright © 1993 by Andrzej Sapkowski
Excerpt from *The Tower of Fools* © 2002 by Andrzej Sapkowski

Cover design by Lauren Panepinto
Cover illustration by Bartłomiej Gaweł, Paweł Mielniczuk, Marcin Błaszczak, Arkadiusz Matyszewski, Marian Chomiak
Cover copyright © 2012 by Hachette Book Group, Inc.

Originally published in Polish as *Ostatnie Zyczenie*

Orbit
Hachette Book Group
1290 Avenue of the Americas
New York, NY 10104
orbitbooks.net

Published by arrangement with The Patricia Pasqualini Literary Agency

Originally published in mass market paperback and ebook by Orbit in May 2008
Originally published in hardcover by Gollancz in Great Britain in 2007

First Trade Paperback Edition: July 2017

Orbit is an imprint of Hachette Book Group.
The Orbit name and logo are trademarks of Little, Brown Book Group Limited.

The publisher is not responsible for websites (or their content) that are not owned by the publisher.

The Hachette Speakers Bureau provides a wide range of authors for speaking events. To find out more, go to www.hachettespeakersbureau.com or call (866) 376-6591.

Library of Congress Control Number: 2017939747

ISBNs: 978-0-316-43896-4 (trade paperback),
978-0-316-02918-6 (mass market paperback), 978-0-316-05508-6 (ebook)

Printed in the United States of America

LSC-C

Printing 12, 2021

THE LAST WISH

CHAPTER ONE

THE VOICE OF REASON

She came to him toward morning.

She entered very carefully, moving silently, floating through the chamber like a phantom; the only sound was that of her mantle brushing her naked skin. Yet this faint sound was enough to wake the witcher—or maybe it only tore him from the half-slumber in which he rocked monotonously, as though traveling through fathomless depths, suspended between the seabed and its calm surface amid gently undulating strands of seaweed.

He did not move, did not stir. The girl flitted closer, threw off her mantle and slowly, hesitantly, rested her knee on the edge of the large bed. He observed her through lowered lashes, still not betraying his wakefulness. The girl carefully climbed onto the bedclothes, and onto him, wrapping her thighs around him. Leaning forward on straining arms, she brushed his face with hair which smelled of chamomile. Determined, and as if impatient, she leaned over and touched his eyelids, cheeks, lips with the tips of her breasts. He smiled, very slowly, delicately, grasping her by the shoulders, and she straightened, escaping his fingers. She was radiant, luminous in the misty brilliance of dawn. He moved, but with pressure from both hands, she forbade him to change position and, with a light but decisive movement of her hips, demanded a response.

He responded. She no longer backed away from his hands; she threw her head back, shook her hair. Her skin was cool and surprisingly smooth. Her eyes, glimpsed when her face came close to his, were huge and dark as the eyes of a water nymph.

Rocked, he sank into a sea of chamomile as it grew agitated and seethed.

THE WITCHER

I

Later, it was said the man came from the north, from Ropers Gate. He came on foot, leading his laden horse by the bridle. It was late afternoon and the ropers', saddlers' and tanners' stalls were already closed, the street empty. It was hot but the man had a black coat thrown over his shoulders. He drew attention to himself.

He stopped in front of the Old Narakort Inn, stood there for a moment, listened to the hubbub of voices. As usual, at this hour, it was full of people.

The stranger did not enter the Old Narakort. He pulled his horse farther down the street to another tavern, a smaller one, called The Fox. Not enjoying the best of reputations, it was almost empty.

The innkeeper raised his head above a barrel of pickled cucumbers and measured the man with his gaze. The outsider, still in his coat, stood stiffly in front of the counter, motionless and silent.

"What will it be?"

"Beer," said the stranger. His voice was unpleasant.

The innkeeper wiped his hands on his canvas apron and filled a chipped earthenware tankard.

The stranger was not old but his hair was almost entirely white. Beneath his coat he wore a worn leather jerkin laced up at the neck and shoulders.

As he took off his coat those around him noticed that he carried a sword—not something unusual in itself, nearly every man in Wyzim carried a weapon—but no one carried a sword strapped to his back as if it were a bow or a quiver.

The stranger did not sit at the table with the few other guests. He remained standing at the counter, piercing the innkeeper with his gaze. He drew from the tankard.

"I'm looking for a room for the night."

"There's none," grunted the innkeeper, looking at the guest's boots, dusty and dirty. "Ask at the Old Narakort."

"I would rather stay here."

"There is none." The innkeeper finally recognized the stranger's accent. He was Rivian.

"I'll pay." The outsider spoke quietly, as if unsure, and the whole nasty affair began. A pockmarked beanpole of a man who, from the moment the outsider had entered had not taken his gloomy eyes from him, got up and approached the counter. Two of his companions rose behind him, no more than two paces away.

"There's no room to be had, you Rivian vagabond," rasped the pockmarked man, standing right next to the outsider. "We don't need people like you in Wyzim. This is a decent town!"

The outsider took his tankard and moved away. He glanced at the innkeeper, who avoided his eyes. It did not even occur to him to defend the Rivian. After all, who liked Rivians?

"All Rivians are thieves," the pockmarked man went on, his breath smelling of beer, garlic and anger. "Do you hear me, you bastard?"

"He can't hear you. His ears are full of shit," said one of the men with him, and the second man cackled.

"Pay and leave!" yelled the pocked man.

Only now did the Rivian look at him.

"I'll finish my beer."

"We'll give you a hand," the pockmarked man hissed. He knocked the tankard from the stranger's hand and simultaneously grabbing him by the shoulder, dug his fingers into the leather strap which ran diagonally across the outsider's chest. One of the men behind him raised a fist to strike. The outsider curled up on the spot, throwing the pockmarked man off balance. The sword hissed in its sheath and glistened briefly in the dim light. The place seethed. There was a scream, and one of the few remaining customers tumbled toward the exit. A chair fell with a crash and earthenware smacked hollowly against the floor. The innkeeper, his lips trembling, looked at the horribly slashed face of the pocked man, who, clinging with his fingers to the edge of the counter, was slowly sinking from sight. The other two were lying on the floor, one motionless, the other writhing and convulsing in a dark, spreading puddle. A woman's hysterical scream vibrated in the air, piercing the ears as the innkeeper shuddered, caught his breath, and vomited.

The stranger retreated toward the wall, tense and alert. He held the sword in both hands, sweeping the blade through the air. No one moved. Terror, like cold mud, was clear on their faces, paralyzing limbs and blocking throats.

Three guards rushed into the tavern with thuds and clangs. They must have been close by. They had truncheons wound with leather straps at the ready, but at the sight of the corpses, drew their swords. The Rivian pressed his back against the wall and, with his left hand, pulled a dagger from his boot.

"Throw that down!" one of the guards yelled with a

trembling voice. "Throw that down, you thug! You're coming with us!"

The second guard kicked aside the table between himself and the Rivian.

"Go get the men, Treska!" he shouted to the third guard, who had stayed closer to the door.

"No need," said the stranger, lowering his sword. "I'll come by myself."

"You'll go, you son of a bitch, on the end of a rope!" yelled the trembling guard. "Throw that sword down or I'll smash your head in!"

The Rivian straightened. He quickly pinned his blade under his left arm and with his right hand raised toward the guards, swiftly drew a complicated sign in the air. The clout-nails which studded his tunic from his wrists to elbows flashed.

The guards drew back, shielding their faces with their arms. One of the customers sprang up while another darted to the door. The woman screamed again, wild and earsplitting.

"I'll come by myself," repeated the stranger in his resounding, metallic voice. "And the three of you will go in front of me. Take me to the castellan. I don't know the way."

"Yes, sir," mumbled the guard, dropping his head. He made toward the exit, looking around tentatively. The other two guards followed him out backward, hastily. The stranger followed in their tracks, sheathing his sword and dagger. As they passed the tables the remaining customers hid their faces from the dangerous stranger.

II

Velerad, castellan of Wyzim, scratched his chin. He was neither superstitious nor fainthearted but he did not relish the thought of being alone with the white-haired man. At last he made up his mind.

"Leave," he ordered the guards. "And you, sit down. No, not there. Farther away, if you please."

The stranger sat down. He no longer carried his sword or black coat.

"I am Velerad, castellan of Wyzim," said Velerad, toying with a heavy mace lying on the table. "And I'm listening. What do you have to say to me, you brigand, before you are thrown into the dungeon? Three killed and an attempted spell-casting; not bad, not bad at all. Men are impaled for such things in Wyzim. But I'm a just man, so I will listen to you, before you are executed. Speak."

The Rivian unbuttoned his jerkin and pulled out a wad of white goat leather.

"You nail this crossways, in taverns," he said quietly. "Is what's written here true?"

"Ah." Velerad grunted, looking at the runes etched into the leather. "So that's it. And I didn't guess at once. Yes, it's true. It's signed by Foltest, King of Temeria, Pontar and Mahakam, which makes it true. A proclamation is a proclamation, witcher, but law is law—and I take care of law and order in Wyzim. I will not allow people to be murdered! Do you understand?"

The Rivian nodded to show he understood. Velerad snorted with anger.

"You carry the witcher's emblem?" The stranger reached into his jerkin once more and pulled out a round medallion on a silver chain. It pictured the head of a wolf, baring its fangs. "And do you have a name? Any name will do, it's simply to make conversation easier."

"My name is Geralt."

"Geralt, then. Of Rivia I gather, from your accent?"

"Of Rivia."

"Right. Do you know what, Geralt? This"—Velerad slapped the proclamation—"let it go. It's a serious matter. Many have tried and failed already. This, my friend, is not the same as roughing up a couple of scoundrels."

"I know. This is my job, Velerad. And that proclamation offers a three thousand oren reward."

"Three thousand." Velerad scowled. "And the princess as a wife, or so rumor says, although gracious Foltest has not proclaimed that."

"I'm not interested in the princess," Geralt said calmly. He was sitting motionless, his hands on his knees. "Just in the three thousand."

"What times," sighed the castellan. "What foul times! Twenty years ago who would have thought, even in a drunken stupor, that such a profession as a witcher would exist? Itinerant killers of basilisks; traveling slayers of dragons and vodniks! Tell me, Geralt, are you allowed beer in your guild?"

"Certainly."

Velerad clapped his hands.

"Beer!" he called. "And sit closer, Geralt. What do I care?"

The beer, when it arrived, was cold and frothy.

"Foul times," Velerad muttered, drinking deep from his tankard. "All sorts of filth has sprung up. Mahakam, in the mountains, is teeming with bogeymen. In the past it was just wolves howling in the woods, but now it's kobolds and spriggans wherever you spit, werewolves or some other vermin. Fairies and rusalkas snatch children from villages by the hundreds. We have diseases never heard of before; it makes my hair stand on end. And now, to top it all, this!" He pushed the wad of leather back across the table. "It's not surprising, Geralt, that you witchers' services are in demand."

"The king's proclamation, Castellan." Geralt raised his head. "Do you know the details?"

Velerad leaned back in his chair, locked his hands over his stomach.

"The details? Yes, I know them. Not firsthand perhaps, but from a good source."

"That's what I want."

"If you insist, then listen." Velerad drank some beer and lowered his voice. "During the reign of old Medell, his father, when our gracious king was still a prince, Foltest showed us what he was capable of, and he was capable of a great deal. We hoped he would grow out of it. But shortly after his coronation Foltest surpassed himself, jaw-droppingly: he got his own sister with child. Adda was younger and they were always together, but nobody suspected anything except, perhaps, the queen... To get to the point: suddenly there is Adda with a huge belly, and Foltest talking about getting wed to his sister. The situation was made even more tense because Vizimir of Novigrad wanted his daughter, Dalka, to marry Foltest and had already sent out his envoys. We had to restrain Foltest from insulting them, and lucky we did, or Vizimir would have torn our insides out. Then, not without Adda's help—for she influenced her brother—we managed to dissuade the boy from a quick wedding.

"Well, then Adda gave birth. And now listen, because this is where it all starts. Only a few saw what she bore, but one midwife jumped from the tower window to her death and the other lost her senses and remains dazed to this day. So I gather that the royal bastard—a girl—was not comely, and she died immediately. No one was in a hurry to tie the umbilical cord. Nor did Adda, to her good fortune, survive the birth.

"But then Foltest stepped in again. Wisdom dictated that the royal bastard should have been burned or buried in the wilderness. Instead, on the orders of our gracious king, she was laid to rest in a sarcophagus in the vaults beneath the palace."

"It's too late for your wisdom now." Geralt raised his head. "One of the Knowing Ones should have been sent for."

"You mean those charlatans with stars on their hats? Of course. About ten of them came running later, when it became known what lay in the sarcophagus. And what scrambled out of it at night. Though it didn't start manifesting straight away. Oh, no. For seven years after the funeral there was peace. Then one night—it was a full moon—there were screams in the palace, shouting and commotion! I don't have to tell you, this is your trade and you've read the proclamation. The infant had grown in the coffin—and how!—grown to have incredible teeth! In a word, she became a striga.

"Pity you didn't see the corpses, as I did. Had you, you'd have taken a great detour to avoid Wyzim."

Geralt was silent.

"Then, as I was saying," Velerad continued, "Foltest summoned a whole crowd of sorcerers. They all jabbered at the same time and almost came to blows with those staffs they carry—to beat off the dogs, no doubt, once they've been set loose on them. And I think they regularly are. I'm sorry, Geralt, if you have a different opinion of wizards. No doubt you do, in your profession, but to me they are swindlers and fools. You witchers inspire greater confidence in men. At least you are more straightforward."

Geralt smiled, but didn't comment.

"But, to the point." The castellan peered into his tankard and poured more beer for himself and the Rivian. "Some of the sorcerers' advice didn't seem so stupid. One suggested burning the striga together with the palace and the sarcophagus. Another advised chopping her head off. The rest were keen on driving aspen stakes into her body during the day, when the she-devil was asleep in her coffin, worn out by her night's delights. Unfortunately one, a jester with a pointed hat and a bald pate, a hunchbacked hermit, argued it was magic: the spell could be undone and the striga would turn into Foltest's little daughter, as pretty as a picture. Someone simply had to stay in the crypt throughout the night, and that would be that. After which—can you imagine such a fool?—he went to the palace for the night. Little of him was left in the morning, only, I believe, his hat and stick. But Foltest clung to his idea like a burr to a dog's tail. He forbade any attempt to kill the striga and brought in charlatans from all corners of Wyzim to reverse the spell and turn her into a princess. What colorful company! Twisted women, cripples, dirty and louse-ridden. It was pitiful.

"They went ahead and cast spells—mainly over a bowl and tankard. Of course some were quickly exposed as frauds by Foltest or the council. A few were even hung on the palisades, but not enough of them. I would have hung them all. I don't suppose I have to say that the striga, in the meantime, was getting her teeth into all sorts of people every now and again and paying no attention to the fraudsters and their spells. Or that Foltest was no longer living in the palace. No one lived there anymore."

Velerad paused, drank some beer, and the witcher waited in silence.

"And so it's been for seven years, Geralt, because she was born around fourteen years ago. We've had a few other worries, like war with Vizimir of Novigrad—fought for real, understandable reasons—over the border posts, not for some princess or marriage alliance. Foltest sporadically hints at marriage and looks over portraits from neighboring courts, which he then throws down the privy. And every now and then this mania seizes hold of him again, and he sends horsemen out to look for new sorcerers. His promised reward, the three thousand, has attracted any number of cranks, stray knights, even a shepherd known throughout the whole region as a cretin, may he rest in peace. But the striga is still doing well. Every now and again she gets her teeth into someone. You get used to it. And at least those heroes trying to reverse the spell have a use—the beast stuffs herself on the spot and doesn't roam beyond her palace. Foltest has a new palace, of course, quite a fine one."

"In seven years"—Geralt raised his head—"in seven years, no one has settled the matter?"

"Well, no." Velerad's gaze penetrated the witcher. "Because the matter can't be settled. We have to come to terms with it, especially Foltest, our gracious and beloved ruler, who will keep nailing these proclamations up at crossroads. Although there are fewer volunteers now. There was one recently, but he insisted on the three thousand in advance. So we put him in a sack and threw him in the lake."

"There is still no shortage of fraudsters, then."

"No, far from it," the castellan agreed without taking his eyes off the witcher. "That's why you mustn't demand gold in advance when you go to the palace. If you go."

"I'll go."

"It's up to you. But remember my advice. As we're talking of the reward, there has been word recently about the second part of it. I mentioned it to you: the princess for a wife. I don't know who made it up, but if the striga looks the way they say then it's an exceptionally grim joke. Nevertheless there's been no lack of fools racing to the palace for the chance of joining the royal family. Two apprentice shoemakers, to be precise. Why are shoemakers so foolish, Geralt?"

"I don't know. And witchers, Castellan? Have they tried?"

"There were a few. But when they heard the spell was to be lifted and the striga wasn't to be killed, they mostly shrugged and left. That's one of the reasons why my esteem for witchers has grown, Geralt. And one came along, younger than you—I forget his name, if he gave it at all. He tried."

"And?"

"The fanged princess spread his entrails over a considerable distance."

Geralt nodded. "That was all of them?"

"There was one other."

Velerad remained silent for a while, and the witcher didn't urge him on.

"Yes," the castellan said finally. "There was one more. At first, when Foltest threatened him with the noose if he killed or harmed the striga, he laughed and started packing his belongings. But then"—Velerad leaned across the table, lowered his voice to almost a whisper—"then he undertook the task. You see, Geralt, there are some wise men in Wyzim, in high positions, who've had enough of this whole affair. Rumor has it these men persuaded the witcher, in secret, not to fuss around with spells but to batter the striga to death and tell the king the spell had failed, that his dear daughter had been killed in self-defense—an accident at work. The king, of course, would be furious and refuse to pay an oren in reward. But that would be an end to it. The witty witcher replied we could chase strigas ourselves for nothing. Well, what could we do? We collected money, bargained . . . but nothing came of it."

Geralt raised his eyebrows.

"Nothing," repeated Velerad. "The witcher didn't want to try that first night. He trudged around, lay in wait, wandered about the neighborhood. Finally, they say, he saw the striga in action, as she does not clamber from her crypt just to stretch her legs. He saw her and scarpered that night. Without a word."

Geralt's expression changed a little, in what was probably supposed to be a smile.

"Those wise men," he said, "they still have the money, no doubt? Witchers don't take payment in advance."

"No doubt they still do," said Velerad.

"Does the rumor say how much they offer?"

Velerad bared his teeth in a smile. "Some say eight hundred—"

Geralt shook his head.

"Others," murmured the castellan, "talk of a thousand."

"Not much when you bear in mind that rumor likes to exaggerate. And the king is offering three thousand."

"Don't forget about the betrothal," Velerad mocked. "What are you talking about? It's obvious you won't get the three thousand."

"How's it obvious?"

Velerad thumped the table. "Geralt, do not spoil my impression of witchers! This has been going on for more than seven years! The striga is finishing off up to fifty people a year, fewer now people are avoiding the palace. Oh no, my friend, I believe in magic. I've seen a great deal and I believe, to a certain extent, in the abilities of wizards and witchers. But all this nonsense about lifting the spell was made up by a hunchbacked, snotty old man who'd lost his mind on his hermit's diet. It's nonsense which no one but Foltest believes. Adda gave birth to a striga because she slept with her brother. That is the truth, and no spell will help. Now the striga devours people—as strigas do—she has to be killed, and that is that. Listen: two years ago peasants from some godforsaken hole near Mahakam were plagued by a dragon devouring their sheep. They set out together, battered the dragon to death with stanchions, and did not even think it worth boasting about. But we in Wyzim are waiting for a miracle and bolting our doors every full moon, or tying our criminals to a stake in front of the palace, praying the beast stuffs herself and returns to her sarcophagus."

"Not a bad method." The witcher smiled. "Are there fewer criminals?"

"Not a bit of it."

"Which way to the palace, the new one?"

"I will take you myself. And what about the wise men's suggestion?"

"Castellan," said Geralt, "why act in haste? After all, I really could have an accident at work, irrespective of my intentions. Just in case, the wise men should be thinking about how to save me from the king's anger and get those fifteen hundred orens, of which rumor speaks, ready."

"It was to be a thousand."

"No, Lord Velerad," the witcher said categorically. "The witcher who was offered a thousand ran at the mere sight of the striga, without bargaining. So the risk is greater than a thousand. Whether it is greater than one and a half remains to be seen. Of course, I will say goodbye beforehand."

"Geralt?" Velerad scratched his head. "One thousand two hundred?"

"No. This isn't an easy task. The king is offering three, and sometimes it's easier to lift a spell than to kill. But one of my predecessors would have done so, or killed the striga, if this were simple. You think they let themselves be devoured out of fear of the king?"

"Then, witcher"—Velerad nodded wistfully—"our agreement stands. But a word of advice—say nothing to the king about the danger of an accident at work."

III

Foltest was slim and had a pretty—too pretty—face. He was under forty, the witcher thought. The king was sitting on a dwarf-armchair carved from black wood, his legs stretched out toward the hearth, where two dogs were warming themselves. Next to him on a chest sat an older, powerfully built man with a beard. Behind the king stood another man, richly dressed and with a proud look on his face. A magnate.

"A witcher from Rivia," said the king after the moment's silence which fell after Velerad's introduction.

"Yes, your Majesty." Geralt lowered his head.

"What made your hair so gray? Magic? I can see that you are not old. That was a joke. Say nothing. You've had a fair amount of experience, I dare presume?"

"Yes, your Majesty."

"I would love to hear about it."

Geralt bowed even lower. "Your Majesty, you know our code of practice forbids us to speak of our work."

"A convenient code, witcher, very convenient. But tell me, have you had anything to do with spriggans?"

"Yes."

"Vampires, leshys?"

"Those too."

Foltest hesitated. "Strigas?"

Geralt raised his head, looking the king in the eyes. "Yes."

Foltest turned his eyes away. "Velerad!"

"Yes, Gracious Majesty?"

"Have you given him the details?"

"Yes, your Gracious Majesty. He says the spell cast on the princess can be reversed."

"I have known that for a long time. How, witcher? Oh, of course, I forgot. Your code of practice. All right. I will make one small comment. Several witchers have been here already. Velerad, you have told him? Good. So I know that your speciality is to kill, rather than to reverse spells. This isn't an option. If one hair falls from my daughter's head, your head will be on the block. That is all. Ostrit, Lord Segelen, stay and give him all the information he requires. Witchers always ask a lot of questions. Feed him and let him stay in the palace. He is not to drift from tavern to tavern."

The king rose, whistled to his dogs and made his way to the door, scattering the straw covering the chamber floor. At the door he paused.

"If you succeed, witcher, the reward is yours. Maybe I will add something if you do well. Of course, the nonsense spread by common folk about marrying the princess carries not a word of truth. I'm sure you don't believe I would give my daughter's hand to a stranger?"

"No, your Majesty. I don't."

"Good. That shows you have some wisdom."

Foltest left, closing the door behind him. Velerad and the magnate, who had been standing all the while, immediately sat at the table. The castellan finished the king's half-full cup, peered into the jug and cursed. Ostrit, who took Foltest's chair, scowled at the witcher while he stroked the carved armrests. Segelin, the bearded man, nodded at Geralt.

"Do sit, witcher, do sit. Supper will soon be served. What would you like to know? Castellan Velerad has probably already told you everything. I know him, he has sooner told you too much than too little."

"Only a few questions."

"Ask."

"The castellan said that, after the striga's appearance, the king called up many Knowing Ones."

"That's right. But don't say striga, say princess. It makes it easier to avoid making a mistake in the king's presence—and any consequent unpleasantness."

"Was there anyone well-known among the Knowing Ones? Anyone famous?"

"There were such, then and later. I don't remember the names. Do you, Lord Ostrit?"

"I don't recall," said the magnate. "But I know some of them enjoyed fame and recognition. There was much talk of it."

"Were they in agreement that the spell can be lifted?"

"They were far from any agreement"—Segelin smiled—"on any subject. But such an opinion was expressed. It was supposed to be simple, not even requiring magical abilities. As I understand it, it would suffice for someone to spend the night—from sunset to the third crowing of the cock—by the sarcophagus."

"Simple indeed," snorted Velerad.

"I would like to hear a description of the ... the princess."

Velerad leapt up from his chair. "The princess looks like a striga!" he yelled. "Like the most strigish striga I have heard of! Her Royal Highness, the cursed royal bastard, is four cubits high, shaped like a barrel of beer, has a maw which stretches from ear to ear and is full of dagger-like teeth, has red eyes and a red mop of hair! Her paws, with claws like a wild cat's, hang down to the ground! I'm surprised we've yet to send her likeness to friendly courts! The princess, plague choke her, is already fourteen. Time to think of giving her hand to a prince in marriage!"

"Hold on, Velerad." Ostrit frowned, glancing at the door. Segelin smiled faintly.

"The description, although vivid, is reasonably accurate, and that's what you wanted, isn't it, witcher? Velerad didn't mention that the princess moves with incredible speed and is far stronger for her height and build than one would expect. And she is fourteen years old, if that is of any importance."

"It is," said the witcher. "Do the attacks on people only occur during the full moon?"

"Yes," replied Segelin, "if she attacks beyond the old palace.

Within the palace walls people always die, irrespective of the moon's phase. But she only ventures out during the full moon, and not always then."

"Has there been even one attack during the day?"

"No."

"Does she always devour her victims?"

Velerad spat vehemently on the straw.

"Come on, Geralt, it'll be supper soon. Pish! Devours, takes a bite, leaves aside, it varies—according to her mood, no doubt. She only bit the head from one, gutted a couple, and a few more she picked clean to the bone, sucked them dry, you could say. Damned mother's—!"

"Careful, Velerad," snarled Ostrit. "Say what you want about the striga but do not insult Adda in front of me, as you would not dare in the king's presence!"

"Has anyone she's attacked survived?" the witcher asked, apparently paying no special attention to the magnate's outburst.

Segelin and Ostrit looked at each other.

"Yes," said the bearded man. "At the very beginning, seven years ago, she threw herself at two soldiers standing guard over the crypt. One escaped—"

"And then," interrupted Velerad, "there was another, the miller she attacked near the town. You remember...?"

IV

The following day, late in the evening, the miller was brought to the small chamber above the guardhouse allocated to the witcher. He was led in by a soldier in a hooded coat.

The conversation did not yield any significant results. The miller was terrified; he mumbled and stammered, and his scars told the witcher more than he did. The striga could open her jaws impressively wide and had extremely sharp teeth, including very long upper fangs—four of them, two on each side. Her claws were sharper than a wildcat's, but less curved. And it was only because of that the miller had managed to tear himself away.

Having finished his examination Geralt nodded to the miller and soldier, dismissing them. The soldier pushed the peasant through the door and lowered his hood. It was Foltest himself.

"Sit, do not get up," said the king. "This visit is unofficial. Are you happy with the interview? I heard you were at the palace this morning."

"Yes, your Majesty."

"When will you set about your task?"

"It is four days until the full moon. After that."

"You prefer to have a look at her yourself beforehand?"

"There is no need. But having had her fill the—the princess will be less active."

"Striga, master witcher, striga. Let us not play at diplomacy. She will be a princess afterward. And that is what I have come to talk about. Answer me unofficially, briefly and clearly: will it work or not? Don't hide behind your code."

Geralt rubbed his brow.

"I confirm, your Majesty, that the spell might be reversed. And, unless I am mistaken, it can be done by spending the night at the palace. The third crowing of the cock, as long as it catches the striga outside her sarcophagus, will end the spell. That is what is usually done with strigas."

"So simple?"

"It is not simple. First you have to survive the night. Then there are exceptions to the rule, for example, not one night but three. Consecutively. There are also cases which are . . . well . . . hopeless."

"Yes," Foltest bristled. "I keep hearing that from some people. Kill the monster because it's an incurable case. Master witcher, I am sure they have already spoken to you. Am I right? Hack the man-eater to death without any more fuss, at the beginning, and tell the king nothing else could be done. I won't pay, but they will. Very convenient. And cheap. Because the king will order the witcher beheaded or hanged and the gold will remain in their pockets."

"The king unconditionally orders the witcher to be beheaded?" Geralt grimaced.

Foltest looked the Rivian in the eyes for a long while.

"The king does not know," he finally said. "But the witcher should bear such an eventuality in mind."

Geralt was silent for a moment. "I intend to do what is in my power," he said. "But if it goes badly I will defend my life. Your Majesty, you must also be prepared for such an eventuality."

Foltest got up. "You do not understand me. It's obvious you'll kill her if it becomes necessary, whether I like it or not. Because otherwise she'll kill you, surely and inevitably. I won't punish anyone who kills her in self-defense. But I will not allow her to be killed without trying to save her. There have already been attempts to set fire to the old palace. They shot at her with arrows, dug pits and set traps and snares, until I hung a few of her attackers. But that is not the point. Witcher, listen!"

"I'm listening."

"After the third crowing of the cock, there will be no striga, if I understand correctly. What will there be?"

"If all goes well, a fourteen-year-old girl."

"With red eyes? Crocodile's teeth?"

"A normal fourteen-year-old. Except that..."

"Well?"

"Physically."

"I see. And mentally? Every day, a bucket of blood for breakfast? A little girl's thigh?"

"No. Mentally... There is no telling. On the level, I think, of a three- or four-year-old child. She'll require loving care for a long while."

"That's obvious. Witcher?"

"I'm listening."

"Can it happen to her again? Later on?"

Geralt was silent.

"Aha," said the king. "It can. And what then?"

"Should she die after a long swoon lasting several days, her body will have to be burned. Quickly."

Foltest grew gloomy.

"I do not think it will come to that," added Geralt. "Just to be sure, I will give you some instructions, your Majesty, to lessen the danger."

"Right now? Is it not too soon, master witcher? And if—"

"Right now," interrupted the Rivian. "Many things may happen, your Majesty. It could be that you'll find a princess in the morning, the spell already broken, and my corpse."

"Even so? Despite my permission to defend yourself? Which, it seems, wasn't that important to you."

"This is a serious matter, your Majesty. The risk is great. That is why you must listen: the princess should always wear a sapphire around her neck, or better, an inclusion, on a silver chain. Day and night."

"What is an inclusion?"

"A sapphire with a pocket of air trapped within the stone.

Aside from that, every now and then you should burn juniper, broom and aspen in the fireplace of her chamber."

Foltest grew pensive. "I thank you for your advice, witcher. I will pay heed if—And now listen to me carefully. If you find the case is hopeless, kill her. If you undo the spell but the girl is not...normal. If you have a shadow of a doubt as to whether you have been entirely successful, kill her. Do not worry, you have nothing to fear from me. I'll shout at you in front of others, banish you from the palace and the town, nothing more. Of course I won't give you the reward, but maybe you'll manage to negotiate something from you know who."

They were both quiet for a while.

"Geralt." For the first time Foltest called the witcher by his name.

"Yes."

"How much truth is there in the rumor that the child is as she is because Adda was my sister?"

"Not much. A spell has to be cast, they don't cast themselves. But I think your congress with your sister was the reason the spell was cast, and this is the result."

"As I thought. That is what some of the Knowing Ones said, although not all of them. Geralt? Where do such things come from? Spells, magic?"

"I don't know, your Majesty. Knowing Ones study the causes of such phenomena. For us witchers the knowledge that concentrated will can cause such phenomena is enough. That and the knowledge to fight them."

"And kill them?"

"Usually. Besides, that is what we're usually paid for. Only a few demand the reversal of spells, your Majesty. As a rule, people simply want to defend themselves from danger. If the monster has men on its conscience then revenge can also come into play."

The king got up, took a few paces across the chamber, and stopped in front of the witcher's sword hanging on the wall.

"With this?" he asked, not looking at Geralt.

"No. That is for men."

"So I heard. Do you know what, Geralt? I'm going to the crypt with you."

"Out of the question."

Foltest turned, his eyes glinted. "Do you know, sorcerer, that I have not seen her? Neither after she was born, nor later. I was afraid. I may never see her, am I not right? At least I have the right to see my daughter while you're murdering her."

"I repeat, it's out of the question. It is certain death. For me as well as you. If my attention, my will falters—No, your Majesty."

Foltest turned away, started toward the door. For a moment Geralt thought he would leave without a word, without a parting gesture, but the king stopped and looked at him.

"You inspire trust," he said, "although I know what a rogue you are. I was told what happened at the tavern. I'm sure you killed those thugs solely for word to spread, to shock people, to shock me. It's obvious that you could have dealt with them without killing. I'm afraid I'll never know whether you are going there to save my daughter, or to kill her. But I agree to it. I have to agree. Do you know why?"

Geralt did not reply.

"Because I think," said the king, "I think that she is suffering. Am I not right?"

The witcher fixed his penetrating eyes on the king. He didn't confirm it, didn't nod, didn't make the slightest gesture, but Foltest knew. He knew the answer.

V

Geralt looked out of the palace window for the last time. Dusk was falling rapidly. Beyond the lake the distant lights of Wyzim twinkled. There was a wilderness around the old palace—a strip of no-man's land with which, over seven years, the town had cut itself off from this dangerous place, leaving nothing but a few ruins, rotten beams and the remains of a gap-toothed palisade which had obviously not been worth dismantling and moving. As far away as possible—at the opposite end of the settlement—the king had built his new residence. The stout tower of his new palace loomed black in the distance, against the darkening blue of the sky.

In one of the empty, plundered chambers, the witcher returned to the dusty table at which he was preparing, calmly and meticulously. He knew he had plenty of time. The striga would not leave her crypt before midnight.

On the table in front of him he had a small chest with metal fittings. He opened it. Inside, packed tightly in compartments lined with dried grass, stood small vials of dark glass. The witcher removed three.

From the floor, he picked up an oblong packet thickly wrapped in sheep's skins and fastened with a leather strap. He unwrapped it and pulled out a sword with an elaborate hilt, in a black, shiny scabbard covered with rows of runic signs and symbols. He drew the blade, which lit up with a pure shine of mirror-like brightness. It was pure silver.

Geralt whispered an incantation and drank, one after the other, the contents of two vials, placing his left hand on the blade of the sword after each sip. Then, wrapping himself tightly in his black coat, he sat down on the floor. There were no chairs in the chamber, or in the rest of the palace.

He sat motionless, his eyes closed. His breathing, at first

even, suddenly quickened, became rasping and tense. And then stopped completely. The mixture which helped the witcher gain full control of his body was chiefly made up of veratrum, stramonium, hawthorn and spurge. The other ingredients had no name in any human language. For anyone who was not, like Geralt, inured to it from childhood, it would have been lethal poison.

The witcher turned his head abruptly. In the silence his hearing, sharpened beyond measure, easily picked out a rustle of footsteps through the courtyard overgrown with stinging nettles. It could not be the striga. The steps were too light. Geralt threw his sword across his back, hid his bundle in the hearth of the ruined chimney-place and, silent as a bat, ran downstairs.

It was still light enough in the courtyard for the approaching man to see the witcher's face. The man, Ostrit, backed away abruptly; an involuntary grimace of terror and repulsion contorted his lips. The witcher smiled wryly—he knew what he looked like. After drinking a mixture of banewart, monk's hood and eyebright the face takes on the color of chalk, and the pupils fill the entire iris. But the mixture enables one to see in the deepest darkness, and this is what Geralt wanted.

Ostrit quickly regained control.

"You look as if you were already a corpse, witcher," he said. "From fear, no doubt. Don't be afraid. I bring you reprieve."

The witcher did not reply.

"Don't you hear what I say, you Rivian charlatan? You're saved. And rich." Ostrit hefted a sizeable purse in his hand and threw it at Geralt's feet. "A thousand orens. Take it, get on your horse and get out of here!"

The Rivian still said nothing.

"Don't gawp at me!" Ostrit raised his voice. "And don't waste my time. I have no intention of standing here until midnight. Don't you understand? I do not wish you to undo the spell. No, you haven't guessed. I am not in league with Velerad and Segelin. I don't want you to kill her. You are simply to leave. Everything is to stay as it is."

The witcher did not move. He did not want the magnate to realize how fast his movements and reactions now were. It was quickly growing dark. A relief, as even the semi-darkness of dusk was too bright for his dilated pupils.

"And why, sir, is everything to remain as it is?" he asked, trying to enunciate each word slowly.

"Now, that"—Ostrit raised his head proudly—"should really be of damn little concern to you."

"And what if I already know?"

"Go on."

"It will be easier to remove Foltest from the throne if the striga frightens the people even more? If the royal madness completely disgusts both magnates and common folk, am I right? I came here by way of Redania and Novigrad. There is much talk there that there are those in Wyzim who look to King Vizimir as their savior and true monarch. But I, Lord Ostrit, do not care about politics, or the successions to thrones, or revolutions in palaces. I am here to accomplish my task. Have you never heard of a sense of responsibility and plain honesty? About professional ethics?"

"Careful to whom you speak, you vagabond!" Ostrit yelled furiously, placing his hand on the hilt of his sword. "I have had enough of this. I am not accustomed to hold such discussions! Look at you—ethics, codes of practice, morality?! Who are you to talk? A brigand who's barely arrived before he starts murdering men? Who bends double to Foltest and behind his back bargains with Velerad like a hired thug? And you dare to turn your nose up at me, you serf? Play at being a Knowing

One? A Magician? You scheming witcher! Be gone before I run the flat of my sword across your gob!"

The witcher did not stir. He stood calmly.

"You'd better leave, Lord Ostrit," he said. "It's growing dark."

Ostrit took a step back, drew his sword in a flash.

"You asked for this, you sorcerer. I'll kill you. Your tricks won't help you. I carry a turtle-stone."

Geralt smiled. The reputation of turtle-stone was as mistaken as it was popular. But the witcher was not going to lose his strength on spells, much less expose his silver sword to contact with Ostrit's blade. He dived under the whirling blade and, with the heel of his hand and his silver-studded cuff, hit him in the temple.

VI

Ostrit quickly regained consciousness and looked around in the total darkness. He noticed that he was tied up. He did not see Geralt standing right beside him. But he realized where he was and let out a prolonged, terrifying howl.

"Keep quiet," said the witcher. "Otherwise you'll lure her out before her time."

"You damned murderer! Where are you? Untie me immediately, you louse! You'll hang for this, you son of a bitch!"

"Quiet."

Ostrit panted heavily.

"You're leaving me here to be devoured by her! Tied up?" he asked, quieter now, whispering a vile invective.

"No," said the witcher. "I'll let you go. But not now."

"You scoundrel," hissed Ostrit. "To distract the striga?"

"Yes."

Ostrit didn't say anything. He stopped wriggling and lay quietly.

"Witcher?"

"Yes."

"It's true that I wanted to overthrow Foltest. I'm not the only one. But I am the only one who wanted him dead. I wanted him to die in agony, to go mad, to rot alive. Do you know why?"

Geralt remained silent.

"I loved Adda. The king's sister. The king's mistress. The king's trollop. I loved her—Witcher, are you there?"

"I am."

"I know what you're thinking. But it wasn't like that. Believe me, I didn't cast any spells. I don't know anything about magic. Only once in anger did I say... Only once. Witcher? Are you listening?"

"I am."

"It's his mother, the old queen. It must be her. She couldn't watch him and Adda—It wasn't me. I only once, you know, tried to persuade them but Adda—Witcher! I was besotted, and said... Witcher? Was it me? Me?"

"It doesn't matter anymore."

"Witcher? Is it nearly midnight?"

"It's close."

"Let me go. Give me more time."

"No."

Ostrit did not hear the scrape of the tomb lid being moved aside, but the witcher did. He leaned over and, with his dagger, cut the magnate's bonds. Ostrit did not wait for the word. He jumped up, numb, hobbled clumsily, and ran. His eyes had grown accustomed enough to the darkness for him to see his way from the main hall to the exit.

The slab blocking the entrance to the crypt opened and fell

to the floor with a thud. Geralt, prudently behind the staircase balustrade, saw the misshapen figure of the striga speeding swiftly and unerringly in the direction of Ostrit's receding footsteps. Not the slightest sound issued from the striga.

A terrible, quivering, frenzied scream tore the night, shook the old walls, continued rising and falling, vibrating. The witcher couldn't make out exactly how far away it was—his sharpened hearing deceived him—but he knew that the striga had caught up with Ostrit quickly. Too quickly.

He stepped into the middle of the hall, stood right at the entrance to the crypt. He threw down his coat, twitched his shoulders, adjusted the position of his sword, pulled on his gauntlets. He still had some time. He knew that the striga, although well fed after the last full moon, would not readily abandon Ostrit's corpse. The heart and liver were, for her, valuable reserves of nutrition for the long periods spent in lethargic sleep.

The witcher waited. By his count, there were about three hours left until dawn. The cock's crow could only mislead him. Besides, there were probably no cocks in the neighborhood.

He heard her. She was trudging slowly, shuffling along the floor. And then he saw her.

The description had been accurate. The disproportionately large head set on a short neck was surrounded by a tangled, curly halo of reddish hair. Her eyes shone in the darkness like an animal's. The striga stood motionless, her gaze fixed on Geralt. Suddenly she opened her jaws—as if proud of her rows of pointed white teeth—then snapped them shut with a crack like a chest being closed. And leapt, slashing at the witcher with her bloodied claws.

Geralt jumped to the side, spun a swift pirouette. The striga rubbed against him, also spun around, slicing through the air with her talons. She didn't lose her balance and attacked anew, mid-spin, gnashing her teeth fractions of an inch from Geralt's chest. The Rivian jumped away, changing the direction of his spin with a fluttering pirouette to confuse the striga. As he leapt away he dealt a hard blow to the side of her head with the silver spikes studding the knuckles of his gauntlet.

The striga roared horribly, filling the palace with a booming echo, fell to the ground, froze and started to howl hollowly and furiously.

The witcher smiled maliciously. His first attempt, as he had hoped, had gone well. Silver was fatal to the striga, as it was for most monsters brought into existence through magic. So there was a chance: the beast was like the others, and that boded well for lifting the spell, while the silver sword would, as a last resort, assure his life.

The striga was in no hurry with her next attack. She approached slowly, baring her fangs, dribbling repulsively. Geralt backed away and, carefully placing his feet, traced a semi-circle. By slowing and quickening his movements he distracted the striga, making it difficult for her to leap. As he walked, the witcher unwound a long, strong silver chain, weighted at the end.

The moment the striga tensed and leapt the chain whistled through the air and, coiling like a snake, twined itself around the monster's shoulders, neck and head. The striga's jump became a tumble, and she let out an ear-piercing whistle. She thrashed around on the floor, howling horribly with fury or from the burning pain inflicted by the despised metal. Geralt was content—if he wanted he could kill the striga without great difficulty. But the witcher did not draw his sword. Nothing in the striga's behavior had given him reason to think she might be an incurable case. Geralt moved to a safer distance and, without letting the writhing shape on the floor out of his sight, breathed deeply, focused himself.

The chain snapped. The silver links scattered like rain in all directions, ringing against the stone. The striga, blind with fury, tumbled to the attack, roaring. Geralt waited calmly and, with his raised right hand, traced the Sign of Aard in front of him.

The striga fell back as if hit by a mallet but kept her feet, extended her talons, bared her fangs. Her hair stood on end and fluttered as if she were walking against a fierce wind. With difficulty, one rasping step at a time, she slowly advanced. But she did advance.

Geralt grew uneasy. He did not expect such a simple Sign to paralyze the striga entirely but neither did he expect the beast to overcome it so easily. He could not hold the Sign for long, it was too exhausting, and the striga had no more than ten steps to go. He lowered the Sign suddenly, and sprung aside. The striga, taken by surprise, flew forward, lost her balance, fell, slid along the floor and tumbled down the stairs into the crypt's entrance, yawning in the floor.

Her infernal scream reverberated from below.

To gain time Geralt jumped on to the stairs leading to the gallery. He had not even climbed halfway up when the striga ran out of the crypt, speeding along like an enormous black spider. The witcher waited until she had run up the stairs after him, then leapt over the balustrade. The striga turned on the stairs, sprang and flew at him in an amazing ten-meter leap. She did not let herself be deceived by his pirouettes this time; twice her talons left their mark on the Rivian's leather tunic. But another desperately hard blow from the silver spiked gauntlet threw the striga aside, shook her. Geralt, feeling fury building inside him, swayed, bent backward and, with a mighty kick, knocked the beast off her legs.

The roar she gave was louder than all the previous ones. Even the plaster crumbled from the ceiling.

The striga sprang up, shaking with uncontrolled anger and lust for murder. Geralt waited. He drew his sword, traced circles with it in the air, and skirted the striga, taking care that the movement of his sword was not in rhythm with his steps. The striga did not jump. She approached slowly, following the bright streak of the blade with her eyes.

Geralt stopped abruptly, froze with his sword raised. The striga, disconcerted, also stopped. The witcher traced a slow semi-circle with the blade, took a step in the striga's direction. Then another. Then he leapt, feigning a whirling movement with his sword above her head.

The striga curled up, retreated in a zigzag. Geralt was close again, the blade shimmering in his hand. His eyes lit up with an ominous glow, a hoarse roar tore through his clenched teeth. The striga backed away, pushed by the power of concentrated hatred, anger and violence which emanated from the attacking man and struck her in waves, penetrating her mind and body. Terrified and pained by feelings unknown to her she let out a thin, shaking squeak, turned on the spot and ran off in a desperate, crazy escape down the dark tangle of the palace's corridors.

Geralt stood quivering in the middle of the hall. Alone. It had taken a long time, he thought, before this dance on the edge of an abyss, this mad, macabre ballet of a fight, had achieved the desired effect, allowed him to psychically become one with his opponent, to reach the underlayers of concentrated will which permeated the striga. The evil, twisted will from which the striga was born. The witcher shivered at the memory of taking on that evil to redirect it, as if in a mirror, against the monster. Never before had he come across such a concentration of hatred and murderous frenzy, not even from basilisks, who enjoyed a ferocious reputation for it.

All the better, he thought as he walked toward the crypt

entrance and the blackness that spread from it like an enormous puddle. All the better, all the stronger, was the blow received by the striga. This would give him a little more time until the beast recovered from the shock. The witcher doubted whether he could repeat such an effort. The elixirs were weakening and it was still a long time until dawn. But the striga could not return to her crypt before first light, or all his trouble would come to nothing.

He went down the stairs. The crypt was not large; there was room for three stone sarcophagi. The slab covering the first was half pushed aside. Geralt pulled the third vial from beneath his tunic, quickly drank its contents, climbed into the tomb and stretched out in it. As he had expected, it was a double tomb—for mother and daughter.

He had only just pulled the cover closed when he heard the striga's roar again. He lay on his back next to Adda's mummified corpse and traced the Sign of Yrden on the inside of the slab. He laid his sword on his chest, stood a tiny hourglass filled with phosphorescent sand next to it and crossed his arms. He no longer heard the striga's screams as she searched the palace. He had gradually stopped hearing anything as the true-love and celandine began to work.

VII

When Geralt opened his eyes, the sand had passed through the hourglass, which meant his sleep had been even longer than he had intended. He pricked up his ears, and heard nothing. His senses were now functioning normally.

He took hold of his sword and, murmuring an incantation, ran his hand across the lid of the sarcophagus. He then moved the slab slightly, a couple of inches.

Silence.

He pushed the lid further, sat, holding his weapon at the ready, and lifted his head above the tomb. The crypt was dark but the witcher knew that outside dawn was breaking. He struck a light, lit a miniature lamp and lifted it, throwing strange shadows across the walls of the crypt.

It was empty.

He scrambled from the sarcophagus, aching, numb, cold. And then he saw her. She was lying on her back next to the tomb, naked and unconscious.

She was rather ugly. Slim with small pointed breasts, and dirty. Her hair—flaxen-red—reached almost to her waist. Standing the lamp on the slab, he knelt beside her and leaned over. Her lips were pale and her face was bloody where he had hit her cheekbone. Geralt removed his gloves, put his sword aside and, without any fuss, drew up her top lip with his finger. Her teeth were normal. He reached for her hand, which was buried in her tangled hair. Before he took it he saw her open eyes. Too late.

She swiped him across the neck with her talons, cutting him deeply. Blood splashed onto her face. She howled, striking him in the eyes with her other hand. He fell on her, grabbing her by the wrists, nailing her to the floor. She gnashed her teeth— which were now too short—in front of his face. He butted her in the face with his forehead and pinned her down harder. She had lost her former strength; she could only writhe beneath him, howling, spitting out blood—his blood—which was pouring over her mouth. His blood was draining away quickly. There was no time. The witcher cursed and bit her hard on the neck, just below the ear. He dug his teeth in and clenched them until her inhuman howling became a thin, despairing scream and then a choking sob—the cry of a hurt fourteen-year-old girl.

He let her go when she stopped moving, got to his knees,

tore a piece of canvas from his sleeve pocket and pressed it to his neck. He felt for his sword, held the blade to the unconscious girl's throat, and leaned over her hand. The nails were dirty, broken, bloodied but...normal. Completely normal.

The witcher got up with difficulty. The sticky-wet grayness of early morning was flooding in through the crypt's entrance. He made a move toward the stairs but staggered and sat down heavily on the floor. Blood was pouring through the drenched canvas onto his hands, running down his sleeve. He unfastened his tunic, slit his shirt, tore and ripped rags from it and tied them around his neck, knowing that he didn't have much time, that he would soon faint...

He succeeded. And fainted.

In Wyzim, beyond the lake, a cock, ruffling his feathers in the cold damp, crowed hoarsely for the third time.

VIII

He saw the whitened walls and beamed ceiling of the small chamber above the guardroom. He moved his head, grimacing with pain, and moaned. His neck was bandaged, thickly, thoroughly, professionally.

"Lie still, witcher," said Velerad. "Lie, do not move."

"My...sword..."

"Yes, yes. Of course, what is most important is your witcher's silver sword. It's here, don't worry. Both the sword and your little trunk. And the three thousand orens. Yes, yes, don't utter a word. It is I who am an old fool and you the wise witcher. Foltest has been repeating it over and over for the last two days."

"Two—"

"Oh yes, two. She slit your neck open quite thoroughly. One

could see everything you have inside there. You lost a great deal of blood. Fortunately we hurried to the palace straight after the third crowing of the cock. Nobody slept in Wyzim that night. It was impossible; you made a terrible noise. Does my talking tire you?"

"The prin...cess?"

"The princess is like a princess. Thin. And somewhat dull-witted. She weeps incessantly and wets her bed. But Foltest says this will change. I don't think it'll change for the worse, do you, Geralt?"

The witcher closed his eyes.

"Good. I take my leave now. Rest." Velerad got up. "Geralt? Before I go, tell me: why did you try to bite her to death? Eh? Geralt?"

The witcher was asleep.

CHAPTER TWO

THE VOICE OF REASON

I

"Geralt."

He raised his head, torn from sleep. The sun was already high and forced blinding golden rays through the shutters, penetrating the chamber with tentacles of light. The witcher shaded his eyes with his hand in an unnecessary, instinctive reflex which he had never managed to shake off—all he needed to do, after all, was narrow his pupils into vertical slits.

"It's late," said Nenneke, opening the shutters. "You've slept in. Off with you, Iola."

The girl sat up suddenly and leaned out of bed to take her mantle from the floor. Geralt felt a trickle of cool saliva on his shoulder, where her lips had been a moment ago.

"Wait..." he said hesitantly. She looked at him, quickly turned away.

She had changed. There was nothing of the water nymph in her anymore, nothing of the luminous, chamomile-scented apparition she had been at dawn. Her eyes were blue, not black. And she had freckles—on her nose, her neckline, her shoulders. They weren't unattractive; they suited her complexion and reddish hair. But he hadn't seen them at dawn, when she had been his dream. With shame he realized he felt resentment toward her, resentment that she hadn't remained a dream, and that he would never forgive himself for it.

"Wait," he repeated. "Iola...I wanted—"

"Don't speak to her, Geralt," said Nenneke. "She won't answer you anyway. Off with you, Iola."

Wrapped in her mantle, the girl pattered toward the door, her bare feet slapping the floor—troubled, flushed, awkward. No longer reminding him, in any way, of—

Yennefer.

"Nenneke," he said, reaching for his shirt. "I hope you're not annoyed that—You won't punish her, will you?"

"Fool," the priestess snorted. "You've forgotten where you are. This is neither a hermitage nor a convent. It's Melitele's temple. Our goddess doesn't forbid our priestesses anything. Almost."

"You forbade me to talk to her."

"I didn't forbid you. But I know it's pointless. Iola doesn't speak."

"What?"

"She doesn't speak. She's taken a vow. It's a sort of sacrifice through which...Oh, what's the point of explaining; you wouldn't understand anyway. You wouldn't even try to understand. I know your views on religion. No, don't get dressed yet. I want to check your neck."

She sat on the edge of the bed and skillfully unwound the linen bandages wrapped thickly around the witcher's neck. He grimaced in pain.

As soon as he had arrived in Ellander, Nenneke had removed the painfully thick stitches of shoemaker's twine with which they had stitched him in Wyzim, opened the wound and dressed it again. The results were clear: he had arrived at the temple almost cured, if perhaps a little stiff. Now he was sick again, and in pain. But he didn't protest. He'd known the priestess for years and knew how great was her knowledge of healing, how rich and comprehensive her pharmacy was. A course of treatment at Melitele's temple could do nothing but good.

Nenneke felt the wound, washed it and began to curse. He already knew this routine by heart. She had started on the very first day, and had never failed to moan when she saw the marks left by the princess of Wyzim's talons.

"It's terrible! To let yourself be slashed like this by an ordinary striga. Muscles, tendons—she only just missed your carotid artery! Great Melitele! Geralt, what's happening to you? How did she get so close to you? What did you want with her? To mount her?"

He didn't answer, and smiled faintly.

"Don't grin like an idiot." The priestess rose and took a bag of dressings from the chest of drawers. Despite her weight and low stature, she moved swiftly and gracefully. "There's nothing funny about it. You're losing your reflexes, Geralt."

"You're exaggerating."

"I'm not exaggerating at all." Nenneke spread a greenish mush smelling sharply of eucalyptus over the wound. "You shouldn't have allowed yourself to get wounded, but you did, and very seriously at that. Fatally even. And even with your exceptional powers of regeneration it'll be months before your neck is fully mobile again. I warn you, don't test your strength by fighting an agile opponent during that time."

"Thank you for the warning. Perhaps you could give me some advice, too: how am I supposed to live in the meantime? Rally a few girls, buy a cart and organize a traveling house of ill-repute?"

Nenneke shrugged, bandaging his neck with quick, deft movements. "Am I supposed to give you advice and teach you how to live? Am I your mother or something? Right, that's done. You can get dressed. Breakfast's waiting for you in the refectory. Hurry up or you'll have to make it yourself. I don't intend to keep the girls in the kitchen to midday."

"Where will I find you later? In the sanctuary?"

"No." Nenneke got up. "Not in the sanctuary. You're a welcome guest here, witcher, but don't hang around in the sanctuary. Go for a walk, and I'll find you myself."

"Fine."

II

Geralt strolled—for the fourth time—along the poplar alley which led from the gate to the dwellings by the sanctuary and main temple block, which merged into the sheer rock. After brief consideration he decided against returning to shelter, and turned toward the gardens and outbuildings. Umpteen priestesses, clad in gray working garments, were toiling away, weeding the beds and feeding the birds in the henhouses. The majority of them were young or very young, virtually children. Some greeted him with a nod or a smile in passing. He answered their greetings but didn't recognize any of them. Although he often visited the temple—once or even twice a year—he never saw more than three or four faces he knew. The girls came and went—becoming oracles in other temples, midwives and healers specializing in women's and children's diseases, wandering druids, teachers or governesses. But there was never a shortage of priestesses, arriving from all over, even the remotest regions. Melitele's temple in Ellander was well-known and enjoyed well-earned fame.

The cult of Melitele was one of the oldest and, in its day, one of the most widespread cults from time immemorial.

Practically every pre-human race and every primordial nomadic human tribe honored a goddess of harvest and fertility, a guardian of farmers and gardeners, a patroness of love and marriage. Many of these religions merged into the cult of Melitele.

Time, which was quite pitiless toward other religions and cults, effectively isolating them in forgotten, rarely visited little temples and oratories buried among urban buildings, had proved merciful to Melitele. She did not lack either followers or sponsors. In explaining the popularity of the goddess, learned men who studied this phenomenon used to hark back to the pre-cults of the Great Mother, Mother Nature, and pointed to the links with nature's cycle, with the rebirth of life and other grandiloquently named phenomena. Geralt's friend, the troubadour Dandelion, who enjoyed a reputation as a specialist in every possible field, looked for simpler explanations. Melitele's cult, he deduced, was a typical woman's cult. Melitele was, after all, the patroness of fertility and birth; she was the guardian of midwives. And a woman in labor has to scream. Apart from the usual cries—usually promising never to give herself to any bloody man ever again in her life—a woman in labor has to call upon some godhead for help, and Melitele was perfect. And since women gave birth, give birth and will continue to give birth, the goddess Melitele, the poet proved, did not have to fear for her popularity.

"Geralt."

"Nenneke. I was looking for you."

"Me?" The priestess looked at him mockingly. "Not Iola?"

"Iola, too," he admitted. "Does that bother you?"

"Right now, yes. I don't want you to get in her way and distract her. She's got to get herself ready and pray if something's to come of this trance."

"I've already told you," he said coldly, "I don't want any trance. I don't think a trance will help me in any way."

"While I"—Nenneke winced—"don't think a trance will harm you in any way."

"I can't be hypnotized. I have immunity. I'm afraid for Iola. It might be too great an effort for a medium."

"Iola isn't a medium or a mentally ill soothsayer. That child enjoys the goddess's favor. Don't pull silly faces, if you please. As I said, your view on religion is known to me, it's never particularly bothered me and, no doubt, it won't bother me in the future. I'm not a fanatic. You've a right to believe that we're governed by Nature and the Force hidden within her. You can think that the gods, including my Melitele, are merely a personification of this power invented for simpletons so they can understand it better, accept its existence. According to you, that power is blind. But for me, Geralt, faith allows you to expect what my goddess personifies from nature: order, law, goodness. And hope."

"I know."

"If you know that, then why your reservations about the trance? What are you afraid of? That I'll make you bow your head to a statue and sing canticles? Geralt, we'll simply sit together for a while—you, me and Iola—and see if the girl's talents will let her see into the vortex of power surrounding you. Maybe we'll discover something worth knowing. And maybe we won't discover anything. Maybe the power and fate surrounding you won't choose to reveal themselves to us, will remain hidden and incomprehensible. I don't know. But why shouldn't we try?"

"Because there's no point. I'm not surrounded by any vortex or fate. And if I were, why the hell would I delve into it?"

"Geralt, you're sick."

"Injured, you mean."

"I know what I mean. There's something not quite right with you. I can sense that. After all, I have known you ever since you were a youngster. When I met you, you came up to my waist. And now I feel that you're spinning around in some damned whirlpool, tangled up in a slowly tightening noose. I want to know what's happening. But I can't do it myself. I have to count on Iola's gifts."

"You want to delve too deeply. Why the metaphysics? I'll confide in you, if you like. I'll fill your evenings with tales of ever more astounding events from the past few years. Get a keg of beer so my throat doesn't dry up and we can start today. But I fear I'll bore you because you won't find any nooses or vortexes there. Just a witcher's ordinary tales."

"I'll willingly listen to them. But a trance, I repeat, would do no harm."

"Don't you think"—he smiled—"that my lack of faith makes such a trance pointless?"

"No, I don't. And do you know why?"

"No."

Nenneke leaned over and looked him in the eyes with a strange smile on her pale lips.

"Because it would be the first proof I've ever heard of that a lack of faith has any kind of power at all."

A GRAIN OF TRUTH

I

A number of black points moving against a bright sky streaked with mist drew the witcher's attention. Birds. They wheeled in slow, peaceful circles, then suddenly swooped and soared up again, flapping their wings.

The witcher observed the birds for a long time, then—bearing in mind the shape of the land, density of the wood, depth and course of the ravine which he suspected lay in his path—calculated the distance to them, and how long he would take to cover it. Finally he threw aside his coat and tightened the belt across his chest by two holes. The pommel and hilt of the sword strapped across his back peeked over his shoulder.

"We'll go a little out of our way, Roach," he said. "We'll take a detour from the highway. I don't think the birds are circling there for nothing."

The mare walked on, obedient to Geralt's voice.

"Maybe it's just a dead elk," said Geralt. "But maybe it's not. Who knows?"

There was a ravine, as he had suspected; the witcher scanned the crowns of the trees tightly filling the rift. But the sides of the gully were gentle, the riverbed dry and clear of blackthorns and rotting tree trunks. He crossed it easily. On the other side was a copse of birches, and behind it a large glade, heath and undergrowth, which threw tentacles of tangled branches and roots upward.

The birds, scared away by the appearance of a rider, soared higher, croaking sharply in their hoarse voices.

Geralt saw the first corpse immediately—the white of the sheepskin jacket and matt-blue of the dress stood out clearly against a yellowing clump of sedge. He didn't see the second corpse but its location was betrayed by three wolves sitting calmly on their haunches watching the witcher. His mare snorted and the wolves, as if at a command, unhurriedly trotted into the woods, every now and again turning their triangular heads to watch the newcomer. Geralt jumped off his horse.

The woman in the sheepskin and blue dress had no face or throat, and most of her left thigh had gone. The witcher, not leaning over, walked by her.

The man lay with his face to the ground. Geralt didn't turn the body over, seeing that the wolves and birds hadn't been idle. And there was no need to examine the corpse in detail—the shoulders and back of the woollen doublet were covered with thick black rivulets of dried blood. It was clear the man had died from a blow to the neck, and the wolves had only found the body afterward.

On a wide belt next to a short cutlass in a wooden sheath the man wore a leather purse. The witcher tore it off and, item by item, threw the contents on the grass: a tinderbox, a piece of chalk, sealing-wax, a handful of silver coins, a folding shaving-knife with a bone handle, a rabbit's ear, three keys and a talisman with a phallic symbol. Two letters, written on canvas, were damp with rain and dew, smudged beyond readability. The third, written on parchment, was also ruined by damp, but still legible. It was a credit note made out by the dwarves' bank in Murivel to a merchant called Rulle Asper, or Aspen. It wasn't for a large sum.

Bending over, Geralt lifted the man's right hand. As he had expected, the copper ring digging into the swollen, blue finger carried the sign of the armorers' guild: a stylized helmet with visor, two crossed swords and the rune "A" engraved beneath them.

The witcher returned to the woman's corpse. As he was turning the body over, something pricked him in the finger— a rose, pinned to the dress. The flower had withered but not lost its color: the petals were dark blue, very dark blue. It was the first time Geralt had seen such a rose. He turned the body over completely, and winced.

On the woman's bare and bloody neck were clear bite marks. And not those of a wolf.

The witcher carefully backed away to his horse. Without taking his eyes from the forest edge, he climbed into the saddle. He circled the glade twice and, leaning over, looked around, examining the ground closely.

"So, Roach," he said quietly, "the case is reasonably clear. The armorer and the woman arrived on horseback from the direction of the forest. They were on their way home from Murivel, because nobody carries an uncashed credit note for long. Why they were going this way and not following the highway? I don't know. But they were crossing the heath, side by side. And then—again, I don't know why—they both dismounted, or fell from, their horses. The armorer died instantly. The woman ran, then fell and died, and whatever attacked her—which didn't leave any tracks—dragged her along the ground, with her throat in its teeth. The horses ran off. This happened two or three days ago."

The mare snorted restlessly, reacting to his tone of voice.

"The thing which killed them," continued Geralt, watching

the forest's edge, "was neither a werewolf nor a leshy. Neither would have left so much for the scavengers. If there were swamps here I'd say it was a kikimora or a vypper...but there aren't any swamps here."

Leaning over, the witcher pulled back the blanket which covered the horse's side and uncovered another sword strapped to the saddlebag—one with a shining, ornate guard and black corrugated hilt.

"Well, Roach. We're taking a roundabout route; we'd better check why this armorer and woman were riding through the forest, not along the highway. If we pass by ignoring such incidents, we won't ever earn enough for your oats, will we?"

The mare obediently moved forward, across the heath, carefully sidestepping hollows.

"Although it's not a werewolf, we won't take any risks," the witcher continued, taking a bunch of dried monkshead from a saddlebag and hanging it by the bit. The mare snorted. Geralt unlaced his tunic a little and pulled out a medallion engraved with a wolf with bared jaws. The medallion, hanging on a silver chain, bobbed up and down in rhythm to the horse's gait, sparkling in the sun's rays like mercury.

II

He noticed the red tiles of the tower's conical roof from the summit of a hill as he cut across a bend in the faint trail. The slope, covered with hazel, dry branches and a thick carpet of yellow leaves, wasn't safe to descend on horseback. The witcher retreated, carefully rode down the incline and returned to the main path. He rode slowly, stopped the horse every now and again and, hanging from the saddle, looked out for tracks.

The mare tossed her head, neighed wildly, stamped and danced on the path, kicking up a storm of dried leaves. Geralt, wrapping his left arm around the horse's neck, swept his right hand—the fingers arranged in the Sign of Axii—over the mount's head as he whispered an incantation.

"Is it as bad as all that?" he murmured, looking around and not withdrawing the Sign. "Easy, Roach, easy."

The charm worked quickly but the mare, prodded with his heel, moved forward reluctantly, losing the natural springy rhythm of her gait. The witcher jumped nimbly to the ground and went on by foot, leading her by the bridle. He saw a wall.

There was no gap between the wall and the forest, no distinct break. The young trees and juniper bushes twined their leaves with the ivy and wild vines clinging to the stonework. Geralt looked up. At that same moment, he felt a prickle along his neck, as if an invisible, soft creature had latched on to his neck, lifting the hairs there.

He was being watched.

He turned around smoothly. Roach snorted; the muscles in her neck twitched, moved under her skin.

A girl was standing on the slope of the hill he had just climbed down, one arm resting on the trunk of an alder tree. Her trailing white dress contrasted with the glossy blackness of her disheveled hair, falling to her shoulders. She seemed to be smiling, but she was too far away to be sure.

"Greetings," he said, raising his hand in a friendly gesture. He took a step toward the girl. She turned her head a little, following his movements. Her face was pale, her eyes black and enormous. The smile—if it had been a smile—vanished from her face as though wiped away with a cloth. Geralt took another step, the leaves rustled underfoot, and the girl ran down the slope like a deer, flitting between the hazel bushes. She was no more than a white streak as she disappeared into the depths of the forest. The long dress didn't appear to restrict her ease of movement in the least.

Roach neighed anxiously, tossing her head. Geralt, still watching the forest, instinctively calmed her with the Sign again. Pulling the mare by the bridle, he walked slowly along the wall, wading through burdock up to the waist.

He came to a sturdy gate, with iron fittings and rusty hinges, furnished with a great brass knocker. After a moment's hesitation Geralt reached out and touched the tarnished ring. He immediately jumped back as, at that moment, the gate opened, squeaking, clattering, and raking aside clumps of grass, stones and branches. There was no one behind it—the witcher could only see a deserted courtyard, neglected and overgrown with nettles. He entered, leading Roach. The mare, still stunned by the Sign, didn't resist, but she moved stiffly and hesitantly after him.

The courtyard was surrounded on three sides by a wall and the remains of some wooden scaffolding. On the fourth side stood the mansion, its façade mottled by a pox of chipped plaster, dirty damp patches, and festooned with ivy. The shutters, with their peeling paint, were closed, as was the door.

Geralt threw Roach's reins over the pillar by the gate and slowly made his way toward the mansion, following the gravel path past a small fountain full of leaves and rubbish. In the center of the fountain, on a fanciful plinth, a white stone dolphin arched, turning its chipped tail upward.

Next to the fountain in what, a very long time ago, used to be a flowerbed, grew a rosebush. Nothing but the color of the flowers made this bush unique—but the flowers were exceptional: indigo, with a faint shade of purple on the tips of some of the petals. The witcher touched one, brought his face closer and inhaled. The flowers held the typical scent of roses, only a little more intense.

The door and all the shutters of the mansion flew open at the same instant with a bang. Geralt raised his head abruptly. Down the path, scrunching the gravel, a monster was rushing straight at him.

The witcher's right hand rose, as fast as lightning, above his right shoulder while his left jerked the belt across his chest, making the sword hilt jump into his palm. The blade, leaping from the scabbard with a hiss, traced a short, luminous semicircle and froze, the point aiming at the charging beast.

At the sight of the sword, the monster stopped short, spraying gravel in all directions. The witcher didn't even flinch.

The creature was humanoid, and dressed in clothes which, though tattered, were of good quality and not lacking in stylish and useless ornamentation. His human form, however, reached no higher than the soiled collar of his tunic, for above it loomed a gigantic, hairy, bear-like head with enormous ears, a pair of wild eyes and terrifying jaws full of crooked fangs in which a red tongue flickered like flame.

"Flee, mortal man!" the monster roared, flapping his paws but not moving from the spot. "I'll devour you! Tear you to pieces!" The witcher didn't move, didn't lower his sword. "Are you deaf? Away with you!" The creature screamed, then made a sound somewhere between a pig's squeal and a stag's bellowing roar, making the shutters rattle and clatter and shaking rubble and plaster from the sills. Neither witcher nor monster moved.

"Clear off while you're still in one piece!" roared the creature, less sure of himself. "Because if you don't, then—"

"Then what?" interrupted Geralt.

The monster suddenly gasped and tilted his monstrous head. "Look at him, isn't he brave?" He spoke calmly, baring his fangs and glowering at Geralt with bloodshot eyes. "Lower that iron, if you please. Perhaps you've not realized you're in my courtyard? Or maybe it's customary, wherever you come from, to threaten people with swords in their own courtyards?"

"It is customary," Geralt agreed, "when faced with people who greet their guests with a roar and the cry that they're going to tear you to pieces."

"Pox on it!" The monster got himself worked up. "And he'll insult me on top of it all, this straggler. A guest, is he? Pushes his way into the yard, ruins someone else's flowers, plays the lord and thinks that he'll be brought bread and salt. Bah!"

The creature spat, gasped and shut his jaws. The lower fangs protruded, making him look like a boar.

"So?" The witcher spoke after a moment, lowering his sword. "Are we going to carry on standing like this?"

"And what do you suggest instead? Lying down?" snorted the monster. "Put that iron away, I said."

The witcher nimbly slipped the weapon into its scabbard and, without lowering his arm, stroked the hilt which rose above his shoulder.

"I'd prefer you," he said, "not to make any sudden moves. This sword can always be drawn again, faster than you imagine."

"I noticed," rasped the monster. "If it wasn't for that, you'd have been out of this gate a long time ago, with my bootprint on your arse. What do you want here? How did you get here?"

"I got lost," lied the witcher.

"You got lost," repeated the monster, twisting his jaws in a menacing grin. "Well, unlose your way. Out of the gate, turn your left ear to the sun and keep walking and you'll soon get back to the highway. Well? What are you waiting for?"

"Is there any water?" asked Geralt calmly. "The horse is thirsty. And so am I, if that doesn't inconvenience you."

The monster shifted from one foot to the other and

scratched his ear. "Listen, you," he said. "Are you really not frightened of me?"

"Should I be?"

The monster looked around, cleared his throat and yanked up his baggy trousers.

"Pox on it, what's the harm of a guest in the house? It's not every day I meet someone who doesn't run away or faint at the sight of me. All right, then. If you're a weary but honest wanderer, I invite you in. But if you're a brigand or a thief, then I warn you: this house does what I tell it to. Within these walls I rule!"

He lifted his hairy paw. All the shutters clattered against the wall once more and deep in the dolphin's stone gullet, something rumbled.

"I invite you in," he repeated.

Geralt didn't move, scrutinizing him.

"Do you live alone?"

"What's that to do with you?" said the monster angrily, opening his jaws, then croaked loudly, "Oh, I see. No doubt you'd like to know whether I've got forty servants all as beautiful as me. I don't. Well, pox, are you going to make use of my generous invitation? If not, the gate's over there."

Geralt bowed stiffly. "I accept your invitation," he said formally. "I won't slight the right of hospitality."

"My house is your house," the monster said in return, just as formally, although a little offhandedly. "This way please, dear guest. And leave the horse here, by the well."

The interior was in need of extensive repair, although it was reasonably clean and tidy. The furniture had been made by skilled craftsmen, if a very long time ago. A pungent smell of dust hung in the dark rooms.

"Light!" growled the monster, and the torch in its iron bracket burst into flames and sooty smoke.

"Not bad," remarked the witcher.

The monster cackled. "That's it? I see you won't be amazed by any old trick. I told you this house obeys my commands. This way, please. Careful, the stairs are steep. Light!"

On the stairs, the monster turned. "What's that around your neck, dear guest?"

"Have a look."

The creature took the medallion in his paw, lifted it up to his eyes, tightening the chain around Geralt's neck a little.

"The animal has an unpleasant expression. What is it?"

"My guild's badge."

"Ah, you make muzzles, no doubt. This way, please. Light!"

The center of the large room, completely devoid of windows, was taken up by a huge oak table, empty apart from an enormous brass candlestick, slowly turning green and covered with trickles of hardened wax. At the monster's command, the candles lit and flickered, brightening the interior a little.

One wall was hung with weapons, compositions of round shields, crossed partisans, javelins and guisarmes, heavy sabers and axes. Half of the adjacent wall was taken up by an enormous fireplace, above which hung rows of flaking and peeling portraits. The wall facing the entrance was filled with hunting trophies—elks and stag antlers whose branching racks threw long shadows across the grinning mounted heads of wild boar, bear and lynx, over the ruffled and frayed wings of eagles and hawks. The place of honor was filled by a rock dragon's head, tainted brown, damaged and leaking stuffing. Geralt examined it more closely.

"My grandpa killed it," said the monster, throwing a huge log into the depths of the fireplace. "It was probably the last one in the vicinity when it got itself killed. Sit, my dear guest. You're hungry?"

"I won't deny it, dear host."

The monster sat at the table, lowered his head, clasped his hairy paws over his stomach, muttered something while twiddling his enormous thumbs, then suddenly roared, thumping the table with his paw. Dishes and platters rattled like pewter and silver, chalices jingled like crystal. There was a smell of roast meat, garlic, marjoram and nutmeg. Geralt did not show any surprise.

"Yes." The monster rubbed his hands. "This is better than servants, isn't it? Help yourself, dear guest. Here is some fowl, here some boar ham, here terrine of...I don't know what. Something. Here we have some hazel grouse. Pox, no, it's partridge. I got the spells muddled up. Eat up, eat up. This is proper, real food, don't worry."

"I'm not worried." Geralt tore the fowl in two.

"I forgot," snorted the monster, "that you're not timid. What shall I call you?"

"Geralt. And your name, dear host?"

"Nivellen. But they call me Degen or Fanger around here. And they use me to frighten children."

The monster poured the contents of an enormous chalice down his throat, after which he sank his fingers in the terrine, tearing half of it from the bowl in one go.

"Frighten children," repeated Geralt with his mouth full. "Without any reason, no doubt?"

"Of course not. Your health, Geralt!"

"And yours, Nivellen."

"How's the wine? Have you noticed that it's made from grapes and not apples? But if you don't like it, I'll conjure up a different one."

"Thank you, it's not bad. Are your magical powers innate?"

"No. I've had them since growing this. This trap, that is. I don't know how it happened myself, but the house does whatever I wish. Nothing very big; I can conjure up food, drink, clothes, clean linen, hot water, soap. Any woman can do that, and without using magic at that. I can open and close windows and doors. I can light a fire. Nothing very remarkable."

"It's something. And this...trap, as you call it, have you had it long?"

"Twelve years."

"How did it happen?"

"What's it got to do with you? Pour yourself some more wine."

"With pleasure. It's got nothing to do with me. I'm just asking out of curiosity."

"An acceptable reason," the monster said, and laughed loudly. "But I don't accept it. It's got nothing to do with you and that's that. But just to satisfy your curiosity a little, I'll show you what I used to look like. Look at those portraits. The first from the chimney is my father. The second, pox only knows. And the third is me. Can you see it?"

Beneath the dust and spiderwebs, a nondescript man with a bloated, sad, spotty face and watery eyes looked down from the painting. Geralt, who was no stranger to the way portrait painters tended to flatter their clients, nodded.

"Can you see it?" repeated Nivellen, baring his fangs.

"I can."

"Who are you?"

"I don't understand."

"You don't understand?" The monster raised his head; his eyes shone like a cat's. "My portrait is hung beyond the candlelight. I can see it, but I'm not human. At least, not at the moment. A human, looking at my portrait, would get up, go closer and, no doubt, have to take the candlestick with him. You didn't do that, so the conclusion is simple. But I'm asking you plainly: are you human?"

Geralt didn't lower his eyes. "If that's the way you put it," he answered after a moment's silence, "then, not quite."

"Ah. Surely it won't be tactless if I ask, in that case, what you are?"

"A witcher."

"Ah," Nivellen repeated after a moment. "If I remember rightly, witchers earn their living in an interesting way—they kill monsters for money."

"You remember correctly."

Silence fell again. Candle flames pulsated, flicked upward in thin wisps of fire, glimmering in the cut-crystal chalices. Cascades of wax trickled down the candlestick.

Nivellen sat still, lightly twitching his enormous ears. "Let's assume," he said finally, "that you draw your sword before I jump on you. Let's assume you even manage to cut me down. With my weight, that won't stop me; I'll take you down through sheer momentum. And then it's teeth that'll decide. What do you think, witcher, which one of us has a better chance if it comes to biting each other's throats?"

Geralt, steadying the carafe's pewter stopper with his thumb, poured himself some wine, took a sip and leaned back into his chair. He was watching the monster with a smile. An exceptionally ugly one.

"Yeeees," said Nivellen slowly, digging at the corner of his jaws with his claw. "One has to admit you can answer questions without using many words. It'll be interesting to see how you manage the next one. Who paid you to deal with me?"

"No one. I'm here by accident."

"You're not lying, by any chance?"

"I'm not in the habit of lying."

"And what are you in the habit of doing? I've heard about witchers—they abduct tiny children whom they feed with magic herbs. The ones who survive become witchers themselves, sorcerers with inhuman powers. They're taught to kill, and all human feelings and reactions are trained out of them. They're turned into monsters in order to kill other monsters. I've heard it said it's high time someone started hunting witchers, as there are fewer and fewer monsters and more and more witchers. Do have some partridge before it's completely cold."

Nivellen took the partridge from the dish, put it between his jaws and crunched it like a piece of toast, bones cracking as they were crushed between his teeth.

"Why don't you say anything?" he asked indistinctly, swallowing. "How much of the rumors about you witchers is true?"

"Practically nothing."

"And what's a lie?"

"That there are fewer and fewer monsters."

"True. There's a fair number of them." Nivellen bared his fangs. "One is sitting in front of you wondering if he did the right thing by inviting you in. I didn't like your guild badge right from the start, dear guest."

"You aren't a monster, Nivellen," the witcher said dryly.

"Pox, that's something new. So what am I? Cranberry pudding? A flock of wild geese flying south on a sad November morning? No? Maybe I'm the virtue that a miller's buxom daughter lost in spring? Well, Geralt, tell me what I am. Can't you see I'm shaking with curiosity?"

"You're not a monster. Otherwise you wouldn't be able to touch this silver tray. And in no way could you hold my medallion."

"Ha!" Nivellen roared so powerfully the candle flames fell horizontal for a moment. "Today, very clearly, is a day for revealing great and terrible secrets! Now I'm going to be told that I grew these ears because I didn't like milky porridge as a child!"

"No, Nivellen," said Geralt calmly. "It happened because of a spell. I'm sure you know who cast that spell."

"And what if I do?"

"In many cases a spell can be uncast."

"You, as a witcher, can uncast spells in many cases?"

"I can. Do you want me to try?"

"No. I don't." The monster opened his jaws and poked out his tongue, two span long, and very red. "Surprised you, hasn't it?"

"That it has," admitted Geralt.

The monster giggled and lounged in his armchair. "I knew that would," he said. "Pour yourself some more, get comfortable and I'll tell you the whole story. Witcher or not, you've got an honest face and I feel like talking. Pour yourself more."

"There's none left."

"Pox on it!" The monster cleared his throat, then thumped the table with his paw again. A large earthenware demijohn in a wicker basket appeared next to the two empty carafes, from nowhere. Nivellen tore the sealing wax off with his teeth.

"As no doubt you've noticed," he began, pouring the wine, "this is quite a remote area. It's a long way to the nearest human settlement. It's because, you see, my father, and my grandfather too, in his time, didn't make themselves particularly loved by our neighbors or the merchants using the highway. If anyone went astray here and my father spotted them from the tower, they lost—at best—their fortune. And a couple of the nearer settlements were burnt because Father decided the levies were being paid tardily. Not many people liked my father. Except for me, naturally. I cried awfully when what was left of my father after a blow from a two-handed sword was brought home on a cart one day. Grandpa didn't take part in robbery anymore because, ever since he was hit on the head with a morningstar, he had a terrible stutter. He dribbled and rarely made it to the privy on time. As their heir, I had to lead the gang.

"I was young at the time," Nivellen continued, "a real milksop, so the lads in the crew wound me around their little fingers in a flash. I was as much in command of them as a fat piglet is of a pack of wolves. We soon began doing things which Father would never have allowed, had he been alive. I'll spare you the details and get straight to the point. One day we took ourselves as far as Gelibol, near Mirt, and robbed a temple. A young priestess was there too."

"Which temple, Nivellen?"

"Pox only knows, but it must have been a bad one. There were skulls and bones on the altar, I remember, and a green fire was burning. It stank like nobody's business. But to the point. The lads overpowered the priestess and stripped her, then said I had to become a man. Well, I became a man, stupid little snot that I was, and while I was achieving manhood, the priestess spat into my face and screamed something."

"What?"

"That I was a monster in human skin, that I'd be a monster in a monster's skin, something about love, blood...I can't remember. She must have had the dagger, a little one, hidden in her hair. She killed herself and then—

"We fled from there, Geralt, I'm telling you—we nearly wore our horses out. It was a bad temple."

"Go on."

"Then it was as the priestess had said. A few days later, I woke up and as the servants saw me, they screamed and took to their heels. I went to the mirror... You see, Geralt, I panicked, had some sort of an attack, I remember it almost through a haze. To put it briefly, corpses fell. Several. I used whatever came to hand—and I'd suddenly become very strong. And the house helped as best it could: doors slammed, furniture flew in the air, fires broke out. Whoever could get out ran away in a panic: my aunt and cousin, the lads from the crew. What am I saying? Even the dogs howled and cowered. My cat, Glutton, ran away. Even my aunt's parrot kicked the bucket out of fear. I was alone, roaring, howling, going mad, smashing whatever came to hand, mainly mirrors."

Nivellen paused, sighed and sniffed.

"When the attack was over," he resumed after a while, "it was already too late. I was alone. I couldn't explain to anyone that only my appearance had changed, that although in this horrible shape, I was just a stupid youngster, sobbing over the servants' bodies in an empty manor. I was afraid they'd come back and kill me before I could explain. But nobody returned."

The monster grew silent for a moment and wiped his nose on his sleeve. "I don't want to go back to those first months, Geralt. It still leaves me shaking when I recall them. I'll get to the point. For a long time, a very long time, I sat in the manor, quiet as a mouse, not stirring from the place. If anyone appeared, which rarely happened, I wouldn't go out. I'd tell the house to slam the shutters a couple of times, or I'd roar through the gargoyle, and that was usually enough for the would-be guest to leave in a hurry. So that's how it was, until one day I looked out of the window one pale dawn and—what did I see? Some trespasser stealing a rose from my aunt's bush. And it isn't just any old rosebush: these are blue roses from Nazair. It was Grandfather who brought the seedlings. I flew into a fury and jumped outside.

"The fat trespasser, when he got his voice back—he'd lost it when he saw me—squealed that he only wanted a few flowers for his daughter, that I should spare him, spare his life and his health. I was just ready to kick him out of the main gate when I remembered something. Stories Lenka, my nanny—the old bag—used to tell me. Pox on it, I thought, if pretty girls turn

frogs into princes, or the other way round, then maybe...
Maybe there's a grain of truth in these stories, a chance...I
leapt four yards, roared so loud wild vines tumbled from the
wall, and I yelled, 'Your daughter or your life!' Nothing better
came to mind. The merchant, for he was a merchant, began
to weep, then confessed that his daughter was only eight. Are
you laughing?"

"No."

"I didn't know whether to laugh or cry over my shitty fate.
I felt sorry for the old trader. I couldn't watch him shake like
that. I invited him inside, made him welcome and, when he
was leaving, I poured gold and precious stones into his bag.
There was still a fair fortune in the cellar from Father's day. I
hadn't quite known what to do with it, so I could allow myself
this gesture. The merchant beamed and thanked me so profusely that he slobbered all over himself. He must have boasted
about his adventure somewhere because not two weeks had
gone by when another merchant appeared. He had a pretty
large bag ready with him. And a daughter. Also pretty large."

Nivellen extended his legs under the table and stretched
until the armchair creaked.

"I came to an understanding with the merchant in no time,"
he continued. "He'd leave her with me for a year. I had to help
him load the sack onto his mule; he wouldn't have managed
by himself."

"And the girl?"

"She had fits at the sight of me for a while. She really
thought I'd eat her. But after a month we were eating at the
same table, chatting and going for long walks. She was kind,
and remarkably smart, and I'd get tongue-tied when I talked
to her. You see, Geralt, I was always shy with girls, always
made a laughing stock of myself, even with wenches from the
cowshed with dung up to their knees, girls the lads from the

crew turned over this way and that at will. Even they made
fun of me. To say nothing of having a maw like this. I couldn't
even make myself say anything about why I had paid so dearly
for a year of her life. The year dragged like the stench following marauding troops until, at last, the merchant arrived and
took her away.

"I locked myself in the house, resigned, and didn't react
for several months to any of the guests who turned up with
daughters. But after a year spent with company, I realized how
hard it was to live without anyone to talk to." The monster
made a noise which was supposed to be a sigh but came out
more like a hiccup.

"The next one," he said after a while, "was called Fenne.
She was small, bright and chirpy, a real goldcrest. She wasn't
frightened of me at all. Once, on the anniversary of my first
haircut, my coming of age, we'd both drunk too much mead
and...ha, ha. Straight after, I jumped out of bed and ran to
the mirror. I must admit I was disappointed, and despondent.
The trap was the same as it ever was, if with a slightly more
stupid expression. And they say the wisdom of ages is to be
found in fairy tales. It's not worth a shit, wisdom like that,
Geralt.

"Well, Fenne quickly tried to make me forget my worries.
She was a jolly girl, I tell you. Do you know what she thought
up? We'd both frighten unwanted guests. Imagine: a guest
like that enters the courtyard, looks around, and then, with
a roar, I charge at him on all fours with Fenne, completely
naked, sitting on my back and blowing my grandfather's hunting horn!"

Nivellen shook with laughter, the white of his fangs flashing. "Fenne," he continued, "stayed with me for a year, then
returned to her family with a huge dowry. She was preparing
to marry a tavern owner, a widower."

"Carry on, Nivellen. This is interesting."

"You think so?" said the monster, scratching himself between the ears with a rasping sound. "All right. The next one, Primula, was the daughter of an impoverished knight. The knight, when he got here, had a skinny horse, a rusty cuirass and incredible debts. He was as hideous as cow dung, I tell you, Geralt, and spread a similar smell. Primula, I'd wager my right hand, was conceived while he was at war, as she was quite pretty. I didn't frighten her either, which isn't surprising, really, as compared to her parent I might have appeared quite comely. She had, as it turned out, quite a temperament and I, having gained some self-confidence, seized the moment by the horns. After two weeks Primula and I already had a very close relationship. She liked to pull me by the ears and shout, 'Bite me to death, you animal!' and 'Tear me apart, you beast!' and other equally idiotic things. I ran to the mirror in the breaks, but just imagine, Geralt, I looked at myself with growing anxiety. Less and less did I long to return to my former shape. You see, Geralt, I used to be a weakling and now I'd become a strapping fellow. I'd keep getting ill, I'd cough, my nose would run, but now I don't catch anything. And my teeth? You wouldn't believe how rotten my teeth had been! And now? I can bite through the leg of a chair. Do you want me to bite a chair leg?"

"No, I don't."

"Maybe that's good." The monster opened his mouth wide. "My showing-off used to amuse the girls and there aren't many whole chairs left in the house." Nivellen yawned, his enormous tongue rolling up into a tube.

"This talking has made me tired, Geralt. Briefly: there were two after Primula, Ilka and Venimira. Everything happened in the same way, to the point of boredom. First, a mixture of fear and reserve, then a thread of sympathy they reinforced by small but precious gifts, then 'Bite me, eat me up,' Daddy's return, a tender farewell and an increasingly discernible depletion of the treasury. I decided to take longer breaks to be alone. Of course, I'd long ago stopped believing that a virgin's kiss would transform the way I looked. And I'd come to terms with it. And, what's more, I'd come to the conclusion that things were fine as they were and that there wasn't any need for changes."

"Really? No changes, Nivellen?"

"It's true. I have a horse's health, which came with the way I look, for one. Secondly, my being different works on girls like an aphrodisiac. Don't laugh! I'm certain that as a human, I'd have to give a mighty good chase to get at a girl like, for example, Venimira, who was an extremely beautiful maid. I don't suppose she'd have glanced twice at the fellow in the portrait. And thirdly: safety. Father had enemies, and a couple of them had survived. People whom the crew, under my pitiful leadership, had sent to their graves, had relatives. There's gold in the cellar. If it wasn't for the fear inspired by me, somebody would come and get it, if only peasants with pitchforks."

"You seem quite sure," Geralt remarked, playing with an empty chalice, "that you haven't offended anyone in your present shape. No father, no daughter. No relative or daughter's betrothed—"

"Leave off, Geralt." Nivellen was indignant. "What are you talking about? The fathers couldn't contain themselves for joy. I told you, I was incredibly generous. And the daughters? You didn't see them when they got here in their dresses of sackcloth, their little hands raw from washing, their shoulders stooped from carrying buckets. Even after two weeks with me, Primula still had marks on her back and thighs from the strap her knightly father had beaten her with. They walked around like princesses here, carried nothing but a fan and didn't even know where the kitchen was. I dressed them up and covered them with trinkets. At the click of a finger, I'd conjure up hot water in the tin bath Father had plundered for my mother at Assengard. Can you imagine? A tin bath! There's hardly a regent, what am I saying, hardly a lord who's got a tin bath at home. This was a house from a fairy tale for them, Geralt. And as far as bed is concerned, well... Pox on it, virtue is rarer today than a rock dragon. I didn't force any of them, Geralt."

"But you suspected someone had paid me to kill you. Who would have?"

"A scoundrel who wanted the contents of my cellar but didn't have any more daughters," Nivellen said emphatically. "Human greed knows no limits."

"And nobody else?"

"And nobody else."

They both remained silent, gazing at the nervous flicker of the candle flames.

"Nivellen," said the witcher suddenly, "are you alone now?"

"Witcher," answered the monster after a moment's hesitation, "I think that, in principle, I ought to insult you, take you by the neck and throw you down the stairs. Do you know why? Because you treat me like a dimwit. I noticed how you've been cocking your ears and glancing at the door. You know perfectly well that I don't live alone. Am I right?"

"You are. I'm sorry."

"Pox on your apologies. Have you seen her?"

"Yes. In the forest, by the gate. Is she why merchants and daughters have been leaving here empty-handed for some time?"

"So you know about that too? Yes, she's the reason."

"Do you mind if I ask whether—"

"Yes, I do mind."

Silence again.

"Oh well, it's up to you," the witcher finally said, getting up. "Thanks for your hospitality, dear host. Time I was on my way."

"Quite right." Nivellen also got up. "For certain reasons, I can't offer you a room in the manor for the night, and I don't encourage you to spend the night in these woods. Ever since the area's been deserted, it's been bad at night here. You ought to get back to the highway before dusk."

"I'll bear that in mind, Nivellen. Are you sure you don't need my help?"

The monster looked at him askance. "You think you *could* help me? You'd be able to lift this from me?"

"I wasn't only thinking about that sort of help."

"You didn't answer my question. Although . . . you probably did. You wouldn't be able to."

Geralt looked him straight in the eyes. "You had some bad luck," he said. "Of all the temples in Gelibol and the Nimnar Valley, you picked the Church of Coram Agh Tera, the Lionheaded Spider. In order to lift the curse thrown by the priestess of Coram Agh Tera, you need knowledge and powers which I don't possess."

"And who does?"

"So you are interested after all? You said things were fine as they are."

"As they are, yes. But not as they might be. I'm afraid that—"

"What are you afraid of?"

The monster stopped at the door to the room and turned. "I've had enough of your questions, witcher, which you keep asking instead of answering mine. Obviously, you've got to be asked in the right way. Listen. For some time now I've had hideous dreams. Maybe the word 'monstrous' would be more accurate. Am I right to be afraid? Briefly, please."

"Have you ever had muddy feet after waking from such a dream? Conifer needles in your sheets?"

"No."

"And have—"

"No. Briefly, please."

"You're rightly afraid."

"Can anything be done about it? Briefly, please."

"No."

"Finally. Let's go. I'll see you out."

In the courtyard, as Geralt was adjusting the saddle-bags, Nivellen stroked the mare's nostrils and patted her neck. Roach, pleased with the caress, lowered her head.

"Animals like me," boasted the monster. "And I like them, too. My cat, Glutton, ran away at the beginning but she came back later. For a long time, she was the only living creature who kept me company in my misfortune. Vereena, too—" He broke off with a grimace.

Geralt smiled. "Does she like cats too?"

"Birds." Nivellen bared his teeth. "I gave myself away, pox on it. But what's the harm. She isn't another merchant's daughter, Geralt, or another attempt to find a grain of truth in old folk tales. It's serious. We love each other. If you laugh, I'll sock you one."

Geralt didn't laugh. "You know your Vereena," he said, "is probably a rusalka?"

"I suspected as much. Slim. Dark. She rarely speaks, and in a language I don't know. She doesn't eat human food. She disappears into the forest for days on end, then comes back. Is that typical?"

"More or less." The witcher tightened Roach's girth-strap. "No doubt you think she wouldn't return if you were to become human?"

"I'm sure of it. You know how frightened rusalkas are of people. Hardly anybody's seen a rusalka from up close. But Vereena and I... Pox on it! Take care, Geralt."

"Take care, Nivellen." The witcher prodded the mare in the side with his heel and made toward the gate. The monster shuffled along at his side.

"Geralt?"

"Yes."

"I'm not as stupid as you think. You came here following the tracks of one of the merchants who'd been here lately. Has something happened to one of them?"

"Yes."

"The last was here three days ago. With his daughter, not one of the prettiest, by the way. I commanded the house to close all its doors and shutters and give no sign of life. They wandered around the courtyard and left. The girl picked a rose from my aunt's rosebush and pinned it to her dress. Look for them somewhere else. But be careful; this is a horrible area. I told you that the forest isn't the safest of places at night. Ugly things are heard and seen."

"Thanks, Nivellen. I'll remember about you. Who knows, maybe I'll find someone who—"

"Maybe yes. And maybe no. It's my problem, Geralt, my life and my punishment. I've learned to put up with it. I've got used to it. If it gets worse, I'll get used to that too. And if it gets far worse, don't look for anybody. Come here yourself and put an end to it. As a witcher. Take care, Geralt."

Nivellen turned and marched briskly toward the manor. He didn't look round again.

III

The area was deserted, wild and ominously inhospitable. Geralt didn't return to the highway before dusk; he didn't want to take a roundabout route, so he took a shortcut through the forest. He spent the night on the bare summit of a high hill, his sword on his knees, beside a tiny campfire into which, every now and then, he threw wisps of monkshood. In the middle of the night he noticed the glow of a fire far away in the valley; he heard mad howling and singing and a sound which could only have been the screaming of a tortured woman. When dawn had barely broken, he made his way there to find nothing but a trampled glade and charred bones in still-warm ashes. Something sitting in the crown of an enormous oak shrieked and hissed. It could have been a harpy, or an ordinary wildcat. The witcher didn't stop to check.

IV

About midday, while Roach was drinking at a spring, the mare neighed piercingly and backed away, baring her yellow teeth and chewing her bit. Geralt calmed her with the Sign. Then he noticed a regular ring formed by the caps of reddish mushrooms peering from the moss.

"You're becoming a real hysteric, Roach," he said. "This is just an ordinary devil's ring. What's the fuss?"

The mare snorted, turning her head toward him. The witcher rubbed his forehead, frowned and grew thoughtful. Then he leapt into the saddle, turned the horse around and started back, following his own tracks.

"Animals like me," he muttered. "Sorry, Roach. It turns out you've got more brains than me!"

V

The mare flattened her ears against her skull and snorted, throwing up earth with her hooves; she didn't want to go. Geralt didn't calm her with the Sign; he jumped from the saddle and threw the reins over the horse's head. He no longer had his old sword in its lizard-skin sheath on his back; its place was filled with a shining, beautiful weapon with a cruciform and slender, well-weighted hilt, ending in a spherical pommel made of white metal.

This time the gate didn't open for him. It was already open, just as he had left it.

He heard singing. He didn't understand the words; he couldn't even identify the language. He didn't need to—the witcher felt and understood the very nature, the essence, of this quiet, piercing song which flowed through the veins in a wave of nauseous, overpowering menace.

The singing broke off abruptly, and then he saw her.

She was clinging to the back of the dolphin in the dried-up fountain, embracing the moss-overgrown stone with her tiny hands, so pale they seemed transparent. Beneath her storm of tangled black hair shone huge, wide-open eyes the color of anthracite.

Geralt slowly drew closer, his step soft and springy, tracing a semi-circle from the wall and blue rosebush. The creature glued to the dolphin's back followed him with her eyes, turning her petite face with an expression of longing, and full of charm. He could still hear her song, even though her thin, pale lips were held tight and not the slightest sound emerged from them.

The witcher halted at a distance of ten paces. His sword, slowly drawn from its black enameled sheath, glistened and glowed above his head.

"It's silver," he said. "This blade is silver."

The pale little face did not flinch; the anthracite eyes did not change expression.

"You're so like a rusalka," the witcher continued calmly, "that you could deceive anyone. All the more as you're a rare bird, black-haired one. But horses are never mistaken. They recognize creatures like you instinctively and perfectly. What are you? I think you're a moola, or an alpor. An ordinary vampire couldn't come out in the sun."

The corners of the pale lips quivered and turned up a little.

"Nivellen attracted you with that shape of his, didn't he? You evoked his dreams. I can guess what sort of dreams they were, and I pity him."

The creature didn't move.

"You like birds," continued the witcher. "But that doesn't stop you biting the necks of people of both sexes, does it? You and Nivellen, indeed! A beautiful couple you'd make, a monster and a vampire, rulers of a forest castle. You'd dominate the whole area in a flash. You, eternally thirsty for blood, and he, your guardian, a murderer at your service, a blind tool. But first he had to become a true monster, not a human being in a monster's mask."

The huge black eyes narrowed.

"Where is he, black-haired one? You were singing, so you've drunk some blood. You've taken the ultimate measure, which means you haven't managed to enslave his mind. Am I right?"

The black-tressed head nodded slightly, almost imperceptibly, and the corners of the mouth turned up even more. The tiny little face took on an eerie expression.

"No doubt you consider yourself the lady of this manor now?"

A nod, this time clearer.

"Are you a moola?"

A slow shake of the head. The hiss which reverberated through his bones could only have come from the pale, ghastly, smiling lips, although the witcher didn't see them move.

"Alpor?"

Denial.

The witcher backed away and clasped the hilt of his sword tighter. "That means you're—"

The corners of the lips started to turn up higher and higher; the lips flew open...

"A bruxa!" the witcher shouted, throwing himself toward the fountain.

From behind the pale lips glistened white, spiky fangs. The vampire jumped up, arched her back like a leopard and screamed.

The wave of sound hit the witcher like a battering ram, depriving him of breath, crushing his ribs, piercing his ears and brain with thorns of pain. Flying backward, he just managed to cross his wrists in the Sign of Heliotrop. The spell cushioned some of his impact with the wall but even so, the world grew dark and the remainder of his breath burst from his lungs in a groan.

On the dolphin's back, in the stone circle of the dried-up fountain where a dainty girl in a white dress had sat just a moment ago, an enormous black bat flattened its glossy body, opening its long, narrow jaws wide, revealing rows of needle-like white teeth. The membranous wings spread and flapped silently, and the creature charged at the witcher like an arrow fired from a crossbow.

Geralt, with the metallic taste of blood in his mouth, shouted a spell and threw his hand, fingers spread in the Sign of Quen, out in front of him. The bat, hissing, turned abruptly, then chuckled and veered up into the air before diving down vertically, straight at the nape of the witcher's neck. Geralt jumped aside, slashed, and missed. The bat, smoothly, gracefully drew in a wing, circled around him and attacked anew, opening its eyeless, toothed snout wide. Geralt waited, sword held with both hands, always pointed in the creature's direction. At the last moment, he jumped—not to the side but forward, dealing a swinging cut which made the air howl.

He missed. It was so unexpected that he lost his rhythm and dodged a fraction of a second too late. He felt the beast's talons tear his cheek, and a damp velvety wing slapped against his neck. He curled up on the spot, transferred the weight of his body to his right leg and slashed backward sharply, missing the amazingly agile creature again.

The bat beat its wings, soared up and glided toward the fountain. As the crooked claws scraped against the stone casing, the monstrous, slobbering snout was already blurring, morphing, disappearing, although the pale little lips which were taking its place couldn't quite hide the murderous fangs.

The bruxa howled piercingly, modulating her voice into a macabre tune, glared at the witcher with eyes full of hatred, and screamed again.

The sound wave was so powerful it broke through the Sign. Black and red circles spun in Geralt's eyes; his temples and the crown of his head throbbed. Through the pain drilling in his ears, he began to hear voices wailing and moaning, the sound of flute and oboe, the rustle of a gale. The skin on his face grew numb and cold. He fell to one knee and shook his head.

The black bat floated toward him silently, opening its toothy jaws. Geralt, still stunned by the scream, reacted instinctively. He jumped up and, in a flash, matching the tempo of his movements to the speed of the monster's flight, took three steps forward, dodged, turned a semi-circle and then, quick as a thought, delivered a two-handed blow. The blade met with no resistance…almost no resistance. He heard a scream, but this time it was a scream of pain, caused by the touch of silver. The wailing bruxa was morphing on the dolphin's back. On her white dress, slightly above her left breast, a red stain was visible beneath a slash no longer than a little finger. The witcher ground his teeth—the cut, which should have sundered the beast in two, had been nothing but a scratch.

"Shout, vampire," he growled, wiping the blood from his cheek. "Scream your guts out. Lose your strength. And then I'll slash your pretty little head off!"

You. You will be the first to grow weak, Sorcerer. I will kill you.

The bruxa's lips didn't move, but the witcher heard the words clearly; they resounded in his mind, echoing and reverberating as if underwater.

"We shall see," he muttered through his teeth as he walked, bent over, in the direction of the fountain.

I will kill you. I'll kill you. I'll kill you.

"We shall see."

"Vereena!" Nivellen, his head hanging low and both hands clinging to the doorframe, stumbled from the mansion. He staggered toward the fountain, waving his paws unsteadily. Blood stained the cuff of his tunic.

"Vereena!" he roared again.

The bruxa jerked her head in his direction. Geralt, raising his sword to strike, jumped toward her, but the vampire's reaction was much faster. A sharp scream and another sound wave knocked the witcher from his feet. He tumbled onto his back and scraped against the gravel of the path. The bruxa arched and tensed to jump, her fangs flashing like daggers. Nivellen, spreading his paws like a bear, tried to grab her but she screamed straight into his face, throwing him back against

75

the wooden scaffolding under the wall, which broke with a sharp crash and buried him beneath a stack of timber.

Geralt was already on his feet, running, tracing a semi-circle around the courtyard, trying to draw the bruxa's attention away from Nivellen. The vampire, fluttering her white dress, scurried straight at him, light as a butterfly, barely touching the ground. She was no longer screaming, no longer trying to morph. The witcher knew she was tired, and that she was still lethal. Behind Geralt's back, Nivellen was clattering under the scaffolding, roaring.

Geralt leapt to the left, executing a short moulinet with his sword to confuse the bruxa gliding toward him—white and black, windblown, terrible. He'd underestimated her. She screamed. He didn't make the Sign in time, flew backward until he thumped against the wall. The pain in his spine shot all the way to the tips of his fingers, paralyzed his shoulders, cut him down at the legs. He fell to his knees. The bruxa, wailing melodiously, jumped toward him.

"Vereena!" roared Nivellen.

She turned—and Nivellen forced the sharp broken end of a three-meter-long pole between her breasts. She didn't shout. She only sighed.

The witcher shook, hearing this sigh.

They stood there: Nivellen, on widespread legs, was wielding the pole in both hands, one end firmly secured under his arm.

The bruxa, like a white butterfly on a pin, hung on the other end of the stake, clutching it with both hands. The vampire exhaled excruciatingly and suddenly pressed herself hard against the stake.

Geralt watched a red stain bloom on her back, on the white dress through which the broken tip emerged in a geyser of blood: hideous, almost obscene. Nivellen screamed, took one step back, then another, retreating from her, but he didn't let go of the pole and dragged the bruxa behind him. One more step and he leaned back against the mansion. The end of the pole scraped against the wall.

Slowly, as if a caress, the bruxa moved her tiny hands along the stake, stretched her arms out to their full length, grasped the pole hard and pulled on it again. Over a meter of bloodied wood already protruded from her back. Her eyes were wide open, her head flung back. Her sighs became more frequent and rhythmic, turning into a ruckling wheeze.

Geralt stood but, fascinated by the scene, still couldn't make himself act. He heard words resounding dully within his skull, as if echoing around a cold, damp dungeon.

Mine. Or nobody's. I love you. Love you.

Another terrible, vibrating sigh, choking in blood. The bruxa moved further along the pole and stretched out her arms. Nivellen roared desperately and, without letting go of the stake, tried to push the vampire as far from himself as possible—but in vain. She pulled herself closer and grabbed him by the head. He wailed horrifically and tossed his hairy head. The bruxa moved along the pole again and tilted her head toward Nivellen's throat. The fangs flashed a blinding white.

Geralt jumped. Every move he made, every step, was part of his nature: hard-learned, automatic and lethally sure. Three quick steps, and the third, like a hundred such steps before, finished on the left leg with a strong, firm stamp. A twist of his torso and a sharp, forceful cut. He saw her eyes. Nothing could change now. He heard the voice. Nothing. He yelled, to drown the word which she was repeating. Nothing could change. He cut.

He struck decisively, like hundreds of times before, with the center of the blade, and immediately, following the rhythm of the movement, took a fourth step and half a turn. The blade, freed by the half-turn, floated after him, shining, drawing a fan of red droplets in its wake. The streaming raven-black hair floated in the air, *floated, floated, floated*...

The head fell onto the gravel.

There are fewer and fewer monsters?

And I? What am I?

Who's shouting? The birds?

The woman in a sheepskin jacket and blue dress?

The roses from Nazair?

How quiet!

How empty. What emptiness.

Within me.

Nivellen, curled up in a bundle, sheltering his head in his arms and shaking with twitches and shivers, was lying in the nettles by the manor wall.

"Get up," said the witcher.

The young, handsome, well-built man with a pale complexion lying by the wall raised his head and looked around. His eyes were vague. He rubbed them with his knuckles. He looked at his hands, felt his face. He moaned quietly and, putting his finger in his mouth, ran it along his gums for a long time. He grasped his face again and moaned as he touched the four bloody, swollen streaks on his cheek. He burst out sobbing, then laughed.

"Geralt! How come? How did this—Geralt!"

"Get up, Nivellen. Get up and come along. I've got some medicine in my saddlebags. We both need it."

"I've no longer got... I haven't, have I? Geralt? Why?"

The witcher helped him get up, trying not to look at the tiny hands—so pale as to be transparent—clenched around the pole stuck between the small breasts which were now plastered with a wet red fabric.

Nivellen moaned again. "Vereena—"

"Don't look. Let's go."

They crossed the courtyard, holding each other up, and passed the blue rosebush.

Nivellen kept touching his face with his free hand. "Incredible, Geralt. After so many years? How's it possible?"

"There's a grain of truth in every fairy tale," said the witcher quietly. "Love and blood. They both possess a mighty power. Wizards and learned men have been racking their brains over this for years, but they haven't arrived at anything except that—"

"That what, Geralt?"

"It has to be true love."

CHAPTER THREE

THE VOICE OF REASON

"I'm Falwick, Count of Moën. And this knight is Tailles, from Dorndal."

Geralt bowed cursorily, looking at the knights. Both wore armor and crimson cloaks with the emblem of the White Rose on their left shoulder. He was somewhat surprised as, so far as he knew, there was no Commandery of that Order in the neighborhood.

Nenneke, to all appearances smiling lightheartedly and at ease, noticed his surprise.

"These nobly born gentlemen," she said casually, settling herself more comfortably in her throne-like armchair, "are in the service of Duke Hereward, who governs these lands most mercifully."

"Prince." Tailles, the younger of the knights, corrected her emphatically, fixing his hostile pale blue eyes on the priestess. "Prince Hereward."

"Let's not waste time with details and titles." Nenneke smiled mockingly. "In my day, only those with royal blood were addressed as princes, but now, it seems, titles don't mean so much. Let's get back to our introductions, and why the Knights of the White Rose are visiting my humble temple. You know, Geralt, that the Chapter is requesting investitures for the Order from Hereward, which is why so many Knights of the Rose have entered his service. And a number of locals, like Tailles here, have taken vows and assumed the red cloak which becomes him so well."

"My honor." The witcher bowed once more, just as cursorily as before.

"I doubt it," the priestess remarked coldly. "They haven't come here to honor you. Quite the opposite. They've arrived demanding that you leave as soon as possible. In short, they're here to chase you out. You consider that an honor? I don't. I consider it an insult."

"The noble knights have troubled themselves for no reason." Geralt shrugged. "I don't intend to settle here. I'm leaving of my own accord without any additional incentives, and soon at that."

"Immediately," growled Tailles. "With not a moment's delay. The prince orders—"

"In this temple, I give the orders," interrupted Nenneke in a cold, authoritative voice. "I usually try to ensure my orders don't conflict too much with Hereward's politics, as far as those politics are logical and understandable. In this case they are irrational, so I won't treat them any more seriously than they deserve. Geralt, witcher of Rivia, is my guest. His stay is a pleasure to me. So he will stay in my temple for as long as he wishes."

"You have the audacity to contradict the prince, woman?" Tailles shouted, then threw his cloak back over his shoulder to reveal his grooved, brass-edged breastplate in all its splendor. "You dare to question our ruler's authority?"

"Quiet," Nenneke snapped, and narrowed her eyes. "Lower your voice. Have a care who you speak to like that."

"I know who I'm talking to!" The knight advanced a step. Falwick, the older knight, grabbed him firmly by the elbow

and squeezed until the armor-plated gauntlet grated. Tailles
yanked furiously. "And my words express the prince's will, the
lord of this estate! We have got soldiers in the yard, woman—"

Nenneke reached into the purse at her belt and took out
a small porcelain jar. "I really don't know," she said calmly,
"what will happen if I smash this container at your feet,
Tailles. Maybe your lungs will burst. Maybe you'll grow fur.
Or maybe both, who knows? Only merciful Melitele."

"Don't dare threaten me with your spells, priestess! Our
soldiers—"

"If any one of your soldiers touches one of Melitele's priestesses, they will hang, before dusk, from the acacias along
the road to town. And they know that very well. As do you,
Tailles, so stop acting like a fool. I delivered you, you shitty
brat, and I pity your mother, but don't tempt fate. And don't
force me to teach you manners!"

"All right, all right," the witcher butted in, growing bored.
"It looks as though I'm becoming the cause of a serious conflict and I don't see why I should. Sir Falwick, you look more
levelheaded than your companion who, I see, is beside himself
with youthful enthusiasm. Listen, Falwick, I assure you that I
will leave in a few days. I also assure you that I have no intention to work here, to undertake any commissions or orders. I'm
not here as a witcher, but on personal business."

Count Falwick met his eyes and Geralt realized his mistake. There was pure, unwavering hatred in the White Rose
knight's eyes. The witcher was sure that it was not Duke Hereward who was chasing him out, but Falwick and his like.

The knight turned to Nenneke, bowed with respect and
began to speak. He spoke calmly and politely. He spoke log-
ically. But Geralt knew Falwick was lying through his teeth.

"Venerable Nenneke, I ask your forgiveness, but Prince

Hereward will not tolerate the presence of this witcher on his lands. It is of no importance if he is hunting monsters or claims to be here on personal business—the prince knows that witchers do not undertake personal business. But they do attract trouble like a magnet filings. The wizards are rebelling and writing petitions, the druids are threatening—"

"I don't see why Geralt should bear the consequences of the unruliness of local wizards and druids," interrupted the priestess. "Since when has Hereward been interested in either's opinion?"

"Enough of this discussion." Falwick stiffened. "Have I not made myself sufficiently clear, venerable Nenneke? I will make it so clear as can't be clearer: neither the prince nor the Chapter of the Order will tolerate the presence of this witcher, Geralt, the Butcher of Blaviken, in Ellander for one more day."

"This isn't Ellander!" The priestess sprang from her chair. "This is the temple of Melitele! And I, Nenneke, the high priestess of Melitele, will not tolerate your presence on temple grounds a minute longer, sirs!"

"Sir Falwick," the witcher said quietly, "listen to the voice of reason. I don't want any trouble, nor do I believe that you particularly care for it. I'll leave this neighborhood within three days. No, Nenneke, don't say anything, please. It's time for me to be on my way. Three days. I don't ask for more."

"And you're right not to ask." The priestess spoke before Falwick could react. "Did you hear, boys? The witcher will remain here for three days because that's his fancy. And I, priestess of Great Melitele, will for those three days be his host, for that is my fancy. Tell that to Hereward. No, not Hereward. Tell that to his wife, the noble Ermellia, adding that if she wants to continue receiving an uninterrupted supply of aphrodisiacs from my pharmacy, she'd better calm her duke down. Let her curb his humors and whims, which look ever more like symptoms of idiocy."

"Enough!" Tailles shouted so shrilly his voice broke into a falsetto. "I don't intend to stand by and listen as some charlatan insults my lord and his wife! I will not let such an insult pass unnoticed! It is the Order of the White Rose which will rule here, now; it's the end of your nests of darkness and superstitions. And I, a Knight of the White Rose—"

"Shut up, you brat," interrupted Geralt, smiling nastily. "Halt your uncontrolled little tongue. You speak to a lady who deserves respect, especially from a Knight of the White Rose. Admittedly, to become one it's enough, lately, to pay a thousand Novigrad crowns into the Chapter's treasury, so the Order's full of sons of money-lenders and tailors—but surely some manners have survived? But maybe I'm mistaken?"

Tailles grew pale and reached to his side.

"Sir Falwick," said Geralt, not ceasing to smile. "If he draws his sword, I'll take it from him and beat the snotty-nosed little brat's arse with the flat of his blade. And then I'll batter the door down with him."

Tailles, his hands shaking, pulled an iron gauntlet from his belt and, with a crash, threw it to the ground at the witcher's feet.

"I'll wash away the insult to the Order with your blood, mutant!" he yelled. "On beaten ground! Go into the yard!"

"You've dropped something, son," Nenneke said calmly. "So pick it up; we don't leave rubbish here. This is a temple. Falwick, take that fool from here or this will end in grief. You know what you're to tell Hereward. And I'll write a personal letter to him; you don't look like trustworthy messengers to me. Get out of here. You can find your way out, I hope?"

Falwick, restraining the enraged Tailles with an iron grip, bowed, his armor clattering. Then he looked the witcher in the eyes. The witcher didn't smile. Falwick threw his crimson cloak over his shoulders.

"This wasn't our last visit, venerable Nenneke," he said. "We'll be back."

"That's just what I'm afraid of," replied the priestess coldly. "The displeasure's mine."

THE LESSER EVIL

I

As usual, cats and children noticed him first. A striped tomcat sleeping on a sun-warmed stack of wood, shuddered, raised his round head, pulled back his ears, hissed and bolted off into the nettles. Three-year-old Dragomir, fisherman Trigla's son, who was sitting on the hut's threshold doing his best to make dirtier an already dirty shirt, started to scream as he fixed his tearful eyes on the passing rider.

The witcher rode slowly, without trying to overtake the hay-cart obstructing the road. A laden donkey trotted behind him, stretching its neck and constantly pulling the cord tied to the witcher's pommel tight. In addition to the usual bags, the long-eared animal was lugging a large shape, wrapped in a saddlecloth, on its back. The gray-white flanks of the ass were covered with black streaks of dried blood.

The cart finally turned down a side street leading to a granary and harbor from which a sea breeze blew, carrying the stink of tar and ox's urine. Geralt picked up his pace. He didn't react to the muffled cry of the woman selling vegetables who was staring at the bony, taloned paw sticking out beneath the horse blanket, bobbing up and down in time with the donkey's

86

trot. He didn't look round at the crowd gathering behind him and rippling with excitement.

There were, as usual, many carts in front of the alderman's house. Gerald jumped from the saddle, adjusted the sword on his back and threw the reins over the wooden barrier. The crowd following him formed a semi-circle around the donkey.

Even outside, the alderman's shouts were audible.

"It's forbidden, I tell you! Forbidden, goddammit! Can't you understand what I say, you scoundrel?"

Gerald entered. In front of the alderman, small, podgy and red with rage, stood a villager holding a struggling goose by the neck.

"What—By all the gods! Is that you, Gerald? Do my eyes deceive me?" And turning to the peasant again: "Take it away, you boor! Are you deaf?"

"They said," mumbled the villager, squinting at the goose, "that a wee something must be given to his lordship, otherways—"

"Who said?" yelled the alderman. "Who? That I supposedly take bribes? I won't allow it, I say! Away with you! Greetings, Gerald."

"Greetings, Caldemeyn."

The alderman squeezed the witcher's hand, slapped him on the shoulder. "You haven't been here for a good two years, Gerald. Eh? You can never stay in one place for long, can you? Where are you coming from? Ah, dog's arse, what's the difference where? Hey, somebody bring us some beer! Sit down, Gerald, sit down. It's mayhem here because we've the market tomorrow. How are things with you, tell me!"

"Later. Come outside first."

The crowd outside had grown twofold but the empty space around the donkey hadn't grown any smaller. Gerald threw the horse blanket aside. The crowd gasped and pulled back. Caldemeyn's mouth fell open.

"By all the gods, Geralt! What is it?"

"A kikimora. Is there any reward for it?"

Caldemeyn shifted from foot to foot, looking at the spidery shape with its dry black skin, that glassy eye with its vertical pupil, the needle-like fangs in the bloody jaws.

"Where—From where—?"

"On the dyke, not some four miles from town. On the swamps. Caldemeyn, people must have disappeared there. Children."

"Well, yes, true enough. But nobody—Who could have guessed—Hey, folks, go home, get back to work! This isn't a show! Cover it up, Geralt. Flies are gathering."

Back inside, the alderman grabbed a large jug of beer without a word and drank it to the last drop in one draught. He sighed deeply and sniffed.

"There's no reward," he said gloomily. "No one suspected that there was something like that lurking in the salt marshes. It's true that several people have disappeared in those parts, but...Hardly anyone loitered on that dyke. And why were you there? Why weren't you taking the main road?"

"It's hard for me to make a living on main roads, Caldemeyn."

"I forgot." The alderman suppressed a belch, puffing out his cheeks. "And this used to be such a peaceful neighborhood. Even imps only rarely pissed in the women's milk. And here, right next to us, some sort of felispectre. It's only fitting that I thank you. Because as for paying you, I can't. I haven't the funds."

"That's a shame. I could do with a small sum to get through the winter." The witcher took a sip from his jug, wiped away the froth. "I'm making my way to Yspaden, but I don't know if

I'll get there before the snows block the way. I might get stuck in one of the little towns on the Lutonski road."

"Do you plan to stay long in Blaviken?"

"No. I've no time to waste. Winter's coming."

"Where are you going to stay? With me perhaps? There's an empty room in the attic. Why get fleeced by the innkeepers, those thieves. We'll have a chat and you can tell me what's happening in the big, wide world."

"Willingly. But what will Libushe have to say about it? It was quite obvious last time that she's not very keen on me."

"Women don't have a say in my house. But, just between us, don't do what you did during supper last time in front of her again."

"You mean when I threw my fork at that rat?"

"No. I mean when you hit it, even in the dark."

"I thought it would be amusing."

"It was. But don't do it in front of Libushe. And listen, this . . . what's it called . . . kiki—"

"Kikimora."

"Do you need it for anything?"

"What would I want it for? You can have them throw it in the cesspool if there's no reward for it."

"That's not a bad idea. Hey, Karelka, Borg, Carrypebble! Any of you there?"

A town guard entered with a halberd on his shoulder, the blade catching the doorframe with a crash.

"Carrypebble," said Caldemeyn. "Get somebody to help you and take the donkey with that muck wrapped up in the horse blanket, lead it past the pigsties and chuck the kikimora in the cesspool. Understood?"

"At your command. But . . . Alderman, sir—"

"What?"

"Maybe before we drown that hideous thing—"

"Well?"

"We could show it to Master Irion. It might be useful to him."

Caldemeyn slapped his forehead with his open palm.

"You're not stupid, Carrypebble. Listen, Geralt, maybe our local wizard will spare you something for that carcass. The fishermen bring him the oddest of fish—octopedes, clabaters or herrongs—many have made some money on them. Come on, let's go to the tower."

"You've got yourselves a wizard? Is he here for good or only passing?"

"For good. Master Irion. He's been living in Blaviken for a year. A powerful magus, Geralt, you'll see that from his very appearance."

"I doubt whether a powerful magus will pay for a kikimora," Geralt grimaced. "As far as I know, it's not needed for any elixirs. Your Irion will only insult me, no doubt. We witchers and wizards don't love each other."

"I've never heard of Master Irion insulting anyone. I can't swear that he'll pay you but there's no harm in trying. There might be more kikimoras like that on the marshes and what then? Let the wizard look at the monster and cast some sort of spell on the marshlands or something, just in case."

The witcher thought for a moment.

"Very well, Caldemeyn. What the heck, we'll risk a meeting with Master Irion. Shall we go?"

"We're off. Carrypebble, chase the kids away and bring the floppyears. Where's my hat?"

II

The tower, built from smoothly hewn blocks of granite and crowned by tooth-like battlements, was impressive, dominating the broken tiles of homesteads and dipping-roofed thatched cottages.

"He's renovated it, I see," remarked Geralt. "With spells, or did he have you working at it?"

"Spells, chiefly."

"What's he like, this Irion?"

"Decent. He helps people. But he's a recluse, doesn't say much. He rarely leaves the tower."

On the door, which was adorned with a rosace inlaid with pale wood, hung a huge knocker in the shape of a flat bulging-eyed fish-head holding a brass ring in its toothed jaws. Caldemeyn, obviously well-versed with the workings of its mechanics, approached, cleared his throat and recited:

"Alderman Caldemeyn greets you with a case for Master Irion. With him greets you Witcher Geralt, with respect to the same case."

For a long moment nothing happened; then finally the fish-head moved its toothed mandibles and belched a cloud of steam.

"Master Irion is not receiving. Leave, my good people."

Caldemeyn waddled on the spot and looked at Geralt. The witcher shrugged. Carrypebble picked his nose with serious concentration.

"Master Irion is not receiving," the knocker repeated metallically. "Go, my good—"

"I'm not a good person," Geralt broke in loudly. "I'm a witcher. That thing on the donkey is a kikimora, and I killed it not far from town. It is the duty of every resident wizard to look after the safety of the neighborhood. Master Irion does not have to honor me with conversation, does not have to receive me, if that is his will. But let him examine the kikimora and draw his own conclusions. Carrypebble, unstrap the kikimora and throw it down by the door."

"Geralt," the alderman said quietly. "You're going to leave but I'm going to have to—"

"Let's go, Caldemeyn. Carrypebble, take that finger out of your nose and do as I said."

"One moment," the knocker said in an entirely different tone. "Geralt, is that really you?"

The witcher swore quietly.

"I'm losing patience. Yes, it's really me. So what?"

"Come up to the door," said the knocker, puffing out a small cloud of steam. "Alone. I'll let you in."

"What about the kikimora?"

"To hell with it. I want to talk to you, Geralt. Just you. Forgive me, Alderman."

"What's it to me, Master Irion?" Caldemeyn waved the matter aside. "Take care, Geralt. We'll see each other later. Carrypebble! Into the cesspool with the monster!"

"As you command."

The witcher approached the inlaid door, which opened a little bit—just enough for him to squeeze through—and then slammed shut, leaving him in complete darkness.

"Hey!" he shouted, not hiding his anger.

"Just a moment," answered a strangely familiar voice.

The feeling was so unexpected that the witcher staggered and stretched out his hand, looking for support. He didn't find any.

The orchard was blossoming with white and pink, and smelled of rain. The sky was split by the many-colored arc of a rainbow, which bound the crowns of the trees to the distant, blue chain of mountains. The house nestled in the orchard, tiny and modest, was drowning in hollyhocks. Geralt looked down and discovered that he was up to his knees in thyme.

"Well, come on, Geralt," said the voice. "I'm in front of the house."

He entered the orchard, walking through the trees. He noticed a movement to his left and looked round. A fair-haired girl, entirely naked, was walking along a row of shrubs carrying a basket full of apples. The witcher solemnly promised himself that nothing would surprise him anymore.

"At last. Greetings, witcher."

"Stregobor!" Geralt was surprised.

During his life, the witcher had met thieves who looked like town councilors, councilors who looked like beggars, harlots who looked like princesses, princesses who looked like calving cows and kings who looked like thieves. But Stregobor always looked as, according to every rule and notion, a wizard should look. He was tall, thin and stooping, with enormous bushy gray eyebrows and a long, crooked nose. To top it off, he wore a black, trailing robe with improbably wide sleeves, and wielded a long staff capped with a crystal knob. None of the wizards Geralt knew looked like Stregobor. Most surprising of all was that Stregobor was, indeed, a wizard.

They sat in wicker chairs at a white marble-topped table on a porch surrounded by hollyhocks. The naked blonde with the apple basket approached, smiled, turned and, swaying her hips, returned to the orchard.

"Is that an illusion, too?" asked Geralt, watching the sway.

"It is. Like everything here. But it is, my friend, a first-class illusion. The flowers smell, you can eat the apples, the bee can sting you, and she"—the wizard indicated the blonde—"you can—"

"Maybe later."

"Quite right. What are you doing here, Geralt? Are you still toiling away, killing the last representatives of dying species for money? How much did you get for the kikimora? Nothing, I guess, or you wouldn't have come here. And to think that there are people who don't believe in destiny. Unless you knew about me. Did you?"

"No, I didn't. It's the last place I could have expected you. If my memory serves me correctly, you used to live in a similar tower in Kovir."

"A great deal has changed since then."

"Such as your name. Apparently, you're Master Irion now."

"That's the name of the man who created this tower. He died about two hundred years ago, and I thought it right to honor him in some way since I occupied his abode. I'm living here. Most of the inhabitants live off the sea and, as you know, my speciality, apart from illusions, is weather. Sometimes I'll calm a storm, sometimes conjure one up, sometimes drive schools of whiting and cod closer to the shores with the westerly wind. I can survive. That is," he added, miserably, "I could."

"How come 'I could'? Why the change of name?"

"Destiny has many faces. Mine is beautiful on the outside and hideous on the inside. She has stretched her bloody talons toward me—"

"You've not changed a bit, Stregobor." Geralt grimaced. "You're talking nonsense while making wise and meaningful faces. Can't you speak normally?"

"I can," sighed the wizard. "I can if that makes you happy. I made it all the way here, hiding and running from a monstrous being that wants to murder me. My escape proved in vain—it found me. In all probability, it's going to try to kill me tomorrow, or at the latest, the day after."

"Aha," said the witcher dispassionately. "Now I understand."

"My facing death doesn't impress you much, does it?"

"Stregobor," said Geralt, "that's the way of the world. One sees all sorts of things when one travels. Two peasants kill each other over a field which, the following day, will be trampled flat by two counts and their retinues trying to kill each other off. Men hang from trees at the roadside; brigands slash merchants' throats. At every step in town you trip over corpses in the gutters. In palaces they stab each other with daggers, and somebody falls under the table at a banquet every minute, blue from poisoning. I'm used to it. So why should a death threat impress me, and one directed at you at that?"

"One directed at me at that," Stregobor repeated with a sneer. "And I considered you a friend. Counted on your help."

"Our last meeting," said Geralt, "was in the court of King Idi of Kovir. I'd come to be paid for killing the amphisboena which had been terrorizing the neighborhood. You and your compatriot Zavist vied with each other to call me a charlatan, a thoughtless murdering machine and a scavenger. Consequently, not only didn't Idi pay me a penny, he gave me twelve hours to leave Kovir and, since his hourglass was broken, I barely made it. And now you say you're counting on my help. You say a monster's after you. What are you afraid of, Stregobor? If it catches up with you, tell it you like monsters, that you protect them and make sure no witcher scavenger ever troubles their peace. Indeed, if the monster disembowels and devours you, it'll prove terribly ungrateful."

The wizard turned his head away silently. Geralt laughed. "Don't get all puffed up like a frog, magician. Tell me what's threatening you. We'll see what can be done."

"Have you heard of the Curse of the Black Sun?"

"But of course. Except that it was called the Mania of Mad Eltibald after the wizard who started the lark and caused dozens of girls from good, even noble, families to be murdered or imprisoned in towers. They were supposed to have been possessed by demons, cursed, contaminated by the Black Sun, because that's what, in your pompous jargon, you called the most ordinary eclipse in the world."

"Eltibald wasn't mad at all. He deciphered the writing on Dauk menhirs, on tombstones in the Wozgor necropolises, and examined the legends and traditions of weretots. All of them spoke of the eclipse in no uncertain terms. The Black Sun was to announce the imminent return of Lilit, still honored in the East under the name of Niya, and the extermination of the human race. Lilit's path was to be prepared by 'sixty women wearing gold crowns, who would fill the river valleys with blood.'"

"Nonsense," said the witcher. "And what's more, it doesn't rhyme. All decent predictions rhyme. Everyone knows what Eltibald and the Council of Wizards had in mind at the time. You took advantage of a madman's ravings to strengthen your own authority. To break up alliances, ruin marriage allegiances, stir up dynasties. In a word: to tangle the strings of crowned puppets even more. And here you are lecturing me about predictions, which any old storyteller at the marketplace would be ashamed of."

"You can have your reservations about Eltibald's theories, about how the predictions were interpreted. But you can't challenge the fact that there have been horrendous mutations among girls born just after the eclipse."

"And why not? I've heard quite the opposite."

"I was present when they did an autopsy on one of them," said the wizard. "Geralt, what we found inside the skull and marrow could not be described. Some sort of red sponge. The internal organs were all mixed up, some were missing completely. Everything was covered in moving cilia, bluish-pink shreds. The heart was six-chambered, with two chambers practically atrophied. What do you say to that?"

"I've seen people with eagles' talons instead of hands, people with a wolf's fangs. People with additional joints, additional organs and additional senses. All of which were the effects of your messing about with magic."

"You've seen all sorts of mutations, you say." The magician raised his head. "And how many of them have you slaughtered for money, in keeping with your witcher's calling? Well? Because one can have a wolf's fangs and go no further than baring them at the trollops in taverns, or one can have a wolf's nature, too, and attack children. And that's just how it was with the girls who were born after the eclipse. Their outright insane tendency to cruelty, aggression, sudden bursts of anger and an unbridled temperament were noted."

"You can say that about any woman," sneered Geralt. "What are you driveling on about? You're asking me how many mutants I've killed. Why aren't you interested in how many I've extricated from spells, freed from curses? I, a witcher despised by you. And what have you done, you mighty magicians?"

"A higher magic was used. Ours and that of the priests, in various temples. All attempts ended in the girls' deaths."

"That speaks badly of you, not the girls. And so we've now got the first corpses. I take it the only autopsies were done on them?"

"No. Don't look at me like that; you know very well that there were more corpses, too. It was initially decided to eliminate all of them. We got rid of a few ... autopsies were done on all of them. One of them was even vivisected."

"And you sons of bitches have the nerve to criticize witchers? Oh, Stregobor, the day will come when people will learn, and get the better of you."

"I don't think a day like that will come soon," said the wizard caustically. "Don't forget that we were acting in the people's defense. The mutant girls would have drowned entire countries in blood."

"So say you magicians, turning your noses up, so high and mighty with your auras of infallibility. While we're on the subject, surely you're not going to tell me that in your hunt for these so-called mutants you haven't once made a mistake?"

"All right," said Stregobor after a long silence. "I'll be honest, although for my own sake I shouldn't. We did make a mistake—more than one. Picking them out was extremely difficult. And that's why we stopped... getting rid of them, and started isolating them instead."

"Your famous towers," snorted the witcher.

"Our towers. But that was another mistake. We underestimated them. Many escaped. Then some mad fashion to free imprisoned beauties took hold of princes, especially the younger ones, who didn't have much to do and still less to lose. Most of them, fortunately, twisted their necks—"

"As far as I know, those imprisoned in the towers died quickly. It's been said you must have helped them somewhat."

"That's a lie. But it is true that they quickly fell into apathy, refused to eat... What is interesting is that shortly before they died, they showed signs of the gift of clairvoyance. Further proof of mutation."

"Your proofs are becoming ever less convincing. Do you have any more?"

"I do. Silvena, the lady of Narok, whom we never managed to get close to because she gained power so quickly. Terrible things are happening in Narok now. Fialka, Evermir's daughter, escaped her tower using a homemade rope and is now terrorizing North Velhad. Bernika of Talgar was freed by an idiot prince. Now he's sitting in a dungeon, blinded, and the most common feature of the Talgar landscape is a set of gallows. There are other examples, too."

"Of course there are," said the witcher. "In Yamurlak, for instance, old man Abrad reigns. He's got scrofula, not a single tooth in his head, was probably born some hundred years before this eclipse, and can't fall asleep unless someone's being tortured to death in his presence. He's wiped out all his relatives and emptied half of the country in crazy—how did you put it?—attacks of anger. There are also traces of a rampant temperament. Apparently he was nicknamed Abrad Jack-up-the-Skirt in his youth. Oh, Stregobor, it would be great if the cruelty of rulers could be explained away by mutations or curses."

"Listen, Geralt—"

"No. You won't win me over with your reasons nor convince me that Eltibald wasn't a murdering madman, so let's get back to the monster threatening you. You'd better understand that, after the introduction you've given me, I don't like the story. But I'll hear you out."

"Without interrupting with spiteful comments?"

"That I can't promise."

"Oh well"—Stregobor slipped his hands into the sleeves of his robe—"then it'll only take longer. Well, the story begins in Creyden, a small principality in the north. The wife of Fredefalk, the Prince of Creyden, was Aridea, a wise, educated woman. She had many exceptional adepts of the magical arts in her family and—through inheritance, no doubt—she came into possession of a rare and powerful artifact. One of Nehalenia's Mirrors. They're chiefly used by prophets and oracles because they predict the future accurately, albeit intricately. Aridea quite often turned to the Mirror—"

"With the usual question, I take it," interrupted Geralt. "'Who is the fairest of them all?' I know; all Nehalenia's Mirrors are either polite or broken."

"You're wrong. Aridea was more interested in her country's fate. And the Mirror answered her questions by predicting a horrible death for her and for a great number of others by the hand, or fault, of Fredefalk's daughter from his first marriage. Aridea ensured this news reached the Council, and the Council sent me to Creyden. I don't have to add that Fredefalk's firstborn daughter was born shortly after the eclipse. I was quite discreet for a little while. She managed to torture a canary and two puppies during that time, and also gouged out a servant's eye with the handle of a comb. I carried out a few tests using curses, and most of them confirmed that the little one was a mutant. I went to Aridea with the news because Fredefalk's daughter meant the world to him. Aridea, as I said, wasn't stupid—"

"Of course," Geralt interrupted again, "and no doubt she wasn't head-over-heels in love with her stepdaughter. She preferred her own children to inherit the throne. I can guess what followed. How come nobody throttled her? And you, too, while they were at it."

Stregobor sighed, raised his eyes to heaven, where the rainbow was still shimmering colorfully and picturesquely.

"I wanted to isolate her, but Aridea decided otherwise. She sent the little one out into the forest with a hired thug, a trapper. We found him later in the undergrowth...without any trousers, so it wasn't hard to re-create the turn of events. She had dug a brooch-pin into his brain, through his ear, no doubt while his attention was on entirely different matters."

"If you think I feel sorry for him," muttered Geralt, "then you're wrong."

"We organized a manhunt," continued Stregobor, "but all traces of the little one had disappeared. I had to leave Creyden in a hurry because Fredefalk was beginning to suspect something. Then, four years later I received news from Aridea. She'd tracked down the little one, who was living in Mahakam with seven gnomes whom she'd managed to convince it was more profitable to rob merchants on the roads than to pollute their lungs with dust from the mines. She was known as Shrike because she liked to impale the people she caught on a sharp pole while they were still alive. Several times Aridea hired assassins, but none of them returned. Well, then it became hard to find anyone to try— Shrike had already become quite famous. She'd learned to use a sword so well there was hardly a man who could defy her. I was summoned, and arrived in Creyden secretly, only to learn that someone had poisoned Aridea. It was generally believed that it was the work of Fredefalk, who had found himself a younger, more robust mistress—but I think it was Renfri."

"Renfri?"

"That's what she was called. I said she'd poisoned Aridea. Shortly afterward, Prince Fredefalk died in a strange hunting accident, and Aridea's eldest son disappeared without a word. That must have been the little one's doing, too. I say 'little' but she was seventeen by then. And she was pretty well-developed.

"Meanwhile," the wizard picked up after a moment's break, "she and her gnomes had become the terror of the whole of Mahakam. Until, one day, they argued about something. I don't know what—sharing out the loot, or whose turn it was to spend the night with her—anyway, they slaughtered each other with knives. Only Shrike survived. Only her. And I was in the neighborhood at the time. We met face-to-face: she recognized me in a flash and knew the part I'd played in Creyden. I tell you, Geralt, I had barely managed to utter a curse—and my hands were shaking like anything—when that wildcat flew at me with a sword. I turned her into a neat slab of mountain crystal, six ells by nine. When she fell into a lethargy, I threw the slab into the gnomes' mine and brought the tunnels down on it."

"Shabby work," commented Geralt. "That spell could have been reversed. Couldn't you have burnt her to cinders? You know so many nice spells, after all."

"No. It's not my speciality. But you're right. I did make a hash of it. Some idiot prince found her, spent a fortune on a counter-curse, reversed the spell and triumphantly took her home to some out-of-the-way kingdom in the east. His father, an old brigand, proved to have more sense. He gave his son a hiding, and questioned Shrike about the treasures which she and the gnomes had seized and which she'd hidden. His mistake was to allow his elder son to assist him when he had her stretched out, naked, on the executioner's bench. Somehow, the following day, that same eldest son—now an orphan bereft of siblings—was ruling the kingdom, and Shrike had taken over the office of first favorite."

"Meaning she can't be ugly."

"That's a matter of taste. She wasn't a favorite for long. Up until the first coup d'état at the palace, to give it a grand name—it was more like a barn. It soon became clear that she hadn't forgotten about me. She tried to assassinate me three times in Kovir. I decided not to risk a fourth attempt and to wait her out in Pontar. Again, she found me. This time I escaped to Angren, but she found me there too. I don't know how she does it. I cover my traces well. It must be a feature of her mutation."

"What stopped you from casting another spell to turn her into crystal? Scruples?"

"No. I don't have any of those. She had become resistant to magic."

"That's impossible."

"It's not. It's enough to have the right artifact or aura. Or this could also be associated with her mutation, which is progressing. I escaped from Angren and hid here, in Arcsea, in Blaviken. I've lived in peace for a year, but she's tracked me down again."

"How do you know? Is she already in town?"

"Yes. I saw her in the crystal ball." The wizard raised his wand. "She's not alone. She's leading a gang, which shows that she's brewing something serious. Geralt, I don't have anywhere else to run. I don't know where I could hide. The fact that you've arrived here exactly at this time can't be a coincidence. It's fate."

The witcher raised his eyebrows. "What's on your mind?"

"Surely it's obvious. You're going to kill her."

"I'm not a hired thug, Stregobor."

"You're not a thug, agreed."

"I kill monsters for money. Beasts which endanger people. Horrors conjured up by spells and sorceries cast by the likes of you. Not people."

"She's not human. She's exactly a monster: a mutant, a cursed mutant. You brought a kikimora here. Shrike's worse than a kikimora. A kikimora kills because it's hungry, but Shrike does it for pleasure. Kill her and I'll pay you whatever sum you ask. Within reason, of course."

"I've already told you. I consider the story about mutations and Lilit's curse to be nonsense. The girl has her reasons for settling her account with you, and I'm not going to get mixed up in it. Turn to the alderman, to the town guards. You're the town wizard; you're protected by municipal law."

"I spit on the law, the alderman and his help!" exploded Stregobor. "I don't need defense. I need you to kill her! Nobody's going to get into this tower—I'm completely safe here. But what's that to me? I don't intend to spend the rest of my days here, and Shrike's not going to give up while I'm alive. Am I to sit here, in this tower, and wait for death?"

"They did. Do you know what, magician? You should have left that hunt for the girls to other, more powerful wizards. You should have foreseen the consequences."

"Please, Geralt."

"No, Stregobor."

The sorcerer was silent. The unreal sun in its unreal sky hadn't moved toward the zenith but the witcher knew it was already dusk in Blaviken. He felt hungry.

"Geralt," said Stregobor, "when we were listening to Eltibald, many of us had doubts. But we decided to accept the lesser evil. Now I ask you to make a similar choice."

"Evil is evil, Stregobor," said the witcher seriously as he got up. "Lesser, greater, middling, it's all the same. Proportions are negotiated, boundaries blurred. I'm not a pious hermit. I haven't done only good in my life. But if I'm to choose between one evil and another, then I prefer not to choose at all. Time for me to go. We'll see each other tomorrow."

"Maybe," said the wizard. "If you get here in time."

III

The Golden Court, the country town's elegant inn, was crowded and noisy. The guests, locals and visitors, were mostly engaged in activities typical for their nation or profession. Serious merchants argued with dwarves over the price of goods and credit interest. Less serious merchants pinched the backsides of the girls carrying beer, cabbage and beans. Local nitwits pretended to be well-informed. Harlots were trying to please those who had money while discouraging those who had none. Carters and fishermen drank as if there were no tomorrow. Some seamen were singing a song which celebrated the ocean waves, the courage of captains and the graces of mermaids, the latter graphically and in considerable detail.

"Exert your memory, friend," Caldemeyn said to the innkeeper, leaning across the counter in order to be heard over the din. "Six men and a wench, all dressed in black leather studded with silver in the Novigradian style. I saw them at the turnpike. Are they staying here or at The Tuna Fish?"

The innkeeper wrinkled his bulging forehead and wiped a tankard on his striped apron.

"Here, Alderman," he finally said. "They say they've come for the market but they all carry swords, even the woman. Dressed, as you said, in black."

"Well." The alderman nodded. "Where are they now? I don't see them here."

"In the lesser alcove. They paid in gold."

"I'll go in alone," said Geralt. "There's no point in making this an official affair in front of them all, at least for the time being. I'll bring her here."

"Maybe that's best. But be careful, I don't want any trouble."

"I'll be careful."

The seamen's song, judging by the growing intensity of obscene words, was reaching its grand finale. Geralt drew aside the curtain—stiff and sticky with dirt—which hid the entrance to the alcove.

Six men were seated at the table. Shrike wasn't with them.

"What d'you want?" yelled the man who noticed him first. He was balding and his face was disfigured by a scar which ran across his left eyebrow, the bridge of his nose and his right cheek.

"I want to see Shrike."

Two identical figures stood up—identical motionless faces and fair, disheveled, shoulder-length hair, identical tight-fitting black outfits glistening with silver ornaments. And with identical movements, the twins took identical swords from the bench.

"Keep calm, Vyr. Sit down, Nimir," said the man with the scar, leaning his elbows on the table. "Who d'you say you want to see, brother? Who's Shrike?"

"You know very well who I mean."

"Who's this, then?" asked a half-naked athlete, sweaty, girded crosswise with belts, and wearing spiked pads on his forearms. "D'you know him, Nohorn?"

"No," said the man with the scar.

"It's some albino," giggled a slim, dark-haired man sitting next to Nohorn. Delicate features, enormous black eyes and pointed ears betrayed him to be a half-blood elf. "Albino, mutant, freak of nature. And this sort of thing is allowed to enter pubs among decent people."

"I've seen him somewhere before," said a stocky, weather-beaten man with a plait, measuring Geralt with an evil look in his narrowed eyes.

"Doesn't matter where you've seen him, Tavik," said Nohorn. "Listen here. Civril insulted you terribly a moment ago. Aren't you going to challenge him? It's such a boring evening."

"No," said the witcher calmly.

"And me, if I pour this fish soup over your head, are you going to challenge me?" cackled the man sitting naked to the waist.

"Keep calm, Fifteen," said Nohorn. "He said no, that means no. For the time being. Well, brother, say what you have to say and clear out. You've got one chance to clear out on your own. You don't take it, the attendants will carry you out."

"I don't have anything to say to you. I want to see Shrike. Renfri."

"Do you hear that, boys?" Nohorn looked around at his companions. "He wants to see Renfri. And may I know why?"

"No."

Nohorn raised his head and looked at the twins as they took a step forward, the silver clasps on their high boots jangling.

"I know," the man with the plait said suddenly. "I know where I've seen him now!"

"What's that you're mumbling, Tavik?"

"In front of the alderman's house. He brought some sort of dragon in to trade, a cross between a spider and a crocodile. People were saying he's a witcher."

"And what's a witcher?" Fifteen asked. "Eh? Civril?"

"A hired magician," said the half-elf. "A conjurer for a fistful of silver. I told you, a freak of nature. An insult to human and divine laws. They ought to be burned, the likes of him."

"We don't like magicians," screeched Tavik, not taking his narrowed eyes off Geralt. "It seems to me, Civril, that we're going to have more work in this hole than we thought. There's more than one of them here and everyone knows they stick together."

"Birds of a feather." The half-breed smiled maliciously. "To think the likes of you walk the earth. Who spawns you freaks?"

"A bit more tolerance, if you please," said Geralt calmly, "as I see your mother must have wandered off through the forest alone often enough to give you good reason to wonder where you come from yourself."

"Possibly," answered the half-elf, the smile not leaving his face. "But at least I knew my mother. You witchers can't say that much about yourselves."

Geralt grew a little pale and tightened his lips. Nohorn, noticing it, laughed out loud.

"Well, brother, you can't let an insult like that go by. That thing that you have on your back looks like a sword. So? Are you going outside with Civril? The evening's so boring."

The witcher didn't react.

"Shitty coward," snorted Tavik.

"What did he say about Civril's mother?" Nohorn continued

monotonously, resting his chin on his clasped hands. "Something extremely nasty, as I understood it. That she was an easy lay, or something. Hey, Fifteen, is it right to listen to some straggler insulting a companion's mother? A mother, you son of a bitch, is sacred!"

Fifteen got up willingly, undid his sword and threw it on the table. He stuck his chest out, adjusted the pads spiked with silver studs on his shoulders, spat and took a step forward.

"If you've got any doubts," said Nohorn, "then Fifteen is challenging you to a fistfight. I told you they'd carry you out of here. Make room."

Fifteen moved closer and raised his fists. Geralt put his hand on the hilt of his sword.

"Careful," he said. "One more step and you'll be looking for your hand on the floor."

Nohorn and Tavik leapt up, grabbing their swords. The silent twins drew theirs with identical movements. Fifteen stepped back. Only Civril didn't move.

"What's going on here, dammit? Can't I leave you alone for a minute?"

Geralt turned round very slowly and looked into eyes the color of the sea.

She was almost as tall as him. She wore her straw-colored hair unevenly cut, just below the ears. She stood with one hand on the door, wearing a tight, velvet jacket clasped with a decorated belt. Her skirt was uneven, asymmetrical—reaching down to her calf on the left side and, on the right, revealing a strong thigh above a boot made of elk's leather. On her left side, she carried a sword; on her right, a dagger with a huge ruby set in its pommel.

"Lost your voices?"

"He's a witcher," mumbled Nohorn.

"So what?"

"He wanted to talk to you."

"So what?"

"He's a sorcerer!" Fifteen roared.

"We don't like sorcerers," snarled Tavik.

"Take it easy, boys," said the girl. "He wants to talk to me; that's no crime. You carry on having a good time. And no trouble. Tomorrow's market day. Surely you don't want your pranks to disrupt the market, such an important event in the life of this pleasant town?"

A quiet, nasty giggle reverberated in the silence which fell. Civril, still sprawled out carelessly on the bench, was laughing.

"Come on, Renfri," chuckled the half-blood. "Important... event!"

"Shut up, Civril. Immediately."

Civril stopped laughing. Immediately. Geralt wasn't surprised. There was something very strange in Renfri's voice—something associated with the red reflection of fire on blades, the wailing of people being murdered, the whinnying of horses and the smell of blood. Others must also have had similar associations—even Tavik's weather-beaten face grew pale.

"Well, white-hair," Renfri broke the silence. "Let's go into the larger room. Let's join the alderman you came with. He wants to talk to me too, no doubt."

At the sight of them, Caldemeyn, who was waiting at the counter, broke off his quiet conversation with the innkeeper, straightened himself and folded his arms across his chest.

"Listen, young lady," he said severely, not wasting time with banal niceties, "I know from this witcher of Rivia here what brings you to Blaviken. Apparently you bear a grudge against our wizard."

"Maybe. What of it?" asked Renfri quietly, in an equally brusque tone.

"Only that there are tribunals to deal with grudges like

that. He who wants to revenge a grudge using steel—here in Arcsea—is considered a common bandit. And also, that either you get out of Blaviken early in the morning with your black companions, or I throw you into prison, pre—How do you say it, Geralt?"

"Preventively."

"Exactly. Understood, young lady?"

Renfri reached into the purse on her belt and pulled out a parchment which had been folded several times.

"Read this, Alderman. If you're literate. And don't call me 'young lady.'"

Caldemeyn took the parchment, spent a long time reading it, then, without a word, gave it to Geralt.

"'To my regents, vassals and freemen subjects,'" the witcher read out loud. "'To all and sundry. I proclaim that Renfri, the Princess of Creyden, remains in our service and is well seen by us; whosoever dares maltreet her will incur our wrath. Audoen, King—' Maltreat is not spelled like that. But the seal appears authentic."

"Because it is authentic," said Renfri, snatching the parchment from him. "It was affixed by Audoen, your merciful lord. That's why I don't advise you to maltreat me. Irrespective of how you spell it, the consequences for you would be lamentable. You are not, honorable Alderman, going to put me in prison. Or call me 'young lady.' I haven't infringed any law. For the time being."

"If you infringe by even an inch"—Caldemeyn looked as if he wanted to spit—"I'll throw you in the dungeon together with this piece of paper. I swear on all the gods, young lady. Come on, Geralt."

"With you, witcher." Renfri touched Geralt's shoulder. "I'd still like a word."

"Don't be late for supper," the alderman threw over his shoulder, "or Libushe will be furious."

"I won't."

Geralt leaned against the counter. Fiddling with the wolf's head medallion hanging around his neck, he looked into the girl's blue-green eyes.

"I've heard about you," she said. "You're Geralt, the white-haired witcher from Rivia. Is Stregobor your friend?"

"No."

"That makes things easier."

"Not much. Don't expect me to look on peacefully."

Renfri's eyes narrowed.

"Stregobor dies tomorrow," she said quietly, brushing the unevenly cut hair off her forehead. "It would be the lesser evil if he died alone."

"If he did, yes. But in fact, before Stregobor dies, several other people will die too. I don't see any other possibility."

"Several, witcher, is putting it mildly."

"You need more than words to frighten me, Shrike."

"Don't call me Shrike. I don't like it. The point is, I see other possibilities. It would be worth talking it over...but Libushe is waiting. Is she pretty, this Libushe?"

"Is that all you had to say to me?"

"No. But you should go. Libushe's waiting."

IV

There was someone in his little attic room. Geralt knew it before he even reached the door, sensing it through the barely perceptible vibration of his medallion. He blew out the oil lamp which had lit his path up the stairs, pulled the dagger from his boot, slipped it into the back of his belt and pressed the door handle. The room was dark. But not for a witcher.

He was deliberately slow in crossing the threshold; he closed the door behind him carefully. The next second he dived at the person sitting on his bed, crushed them into the linen, forced his forearm under their chin and reached for his dagger. He didn't pull it out. Something wasn't right.

"Not a bad start," she said in a muffled voice, lying motionless beneath him. "I expected something like this, but I didn't think we'd both be in bed so quickly. Take your hand from my throat please."

"It's you."

"It's me. Now there are two possibilities. The first: you get off me and we talk. The second: we stay in this position, in which case I'd like to take my boots off at least."

The witcher released the girl, who sighed, sat up and adjusted her hair and skirt.

"Light the candle," she said. "I can't see in the dark, unlike you, and I like to see who I'm talking to."

She approached the table—tall, slim, agile—and sat down, stretching out her long legs in their high boots. She wasn't carrying any visible weapons.

"Have you got anything to drink here?"

"No."

"Then it's a good thing I brought something," she laughed, placing a traveling wineskin and two leather tumblers on the table.

"It's nearly midnight," said Geralt coldly. "Shall we come to the point?"

"In a minute. Here, have a drink. Here's to you, Geralt."

"Likewise, Shrike."

"My name's Renfri, dammit." She raised her head. "I will permit you to omit my royal title, but stop calling me Shrike!"

"Be quiet or you'll wake the whole house. Am I finally going to learn why you crept in here through the window?"

"You're slow-witted, witcher. I want to save Blaviken from slaughter. I crawled over the rooftops like a she-cat in March in order to talk to you about it. Appreciate it."

"I do," said Geralt. "Except that I don't know what talk can achieve. The situation's clear. Stregobor is in his tower, and you'd have to lay siege to it in order to get to him. If you do that, your letter of safe conduct won't help you. Audoen won't defend you if you openly break the law. The alderman, guards, the whole of Blaviken will stand against you."

"The whole of Blaviken would regret standing up to me." Renfri smiled, revealing a predator's white teeth. "Did you take a look at my boys? They know their trade, I assure you. Can you imagine what would happen in a fight between them and those dimwit guards who keep tripping over their own halberds?"

"Do you imagine I would stand by and watch a fight like that? I'm staying at the alderman's, as you can see. If the need arises, I should stand at his side."

"I have no doubt"—Renfri grew serious—"that you will. But you'll probably be alone, as the rest will cower in the cellars. No warrior in the world could match seven swordsmen. So, white-hair, let's stop threatening each other. As I said: slaughter and bloodshed can be avoided. There are two people who can prevent it."

"I'm all ears."

"One," said Renfri, "is Stregobor himself. He leaves his tower voluntarily, I take him to a deserted spot, and Blaviken sinks back into blissful apathy and forgets the whole affair."

"Stregobor may seem crazy, but he's not *that* crazy."

"Who knows, witcher, who knows. Some arguments can't

be denied, like the Tridam ultimatum. I plan to present it to
the sorcerer."

"What is it, this ultimatum?"

"That's my sweet secret."

"As you wish. But I doubt it'll be effective. Stregobor's teeth
chatter when he speaks of you. An ultimatum which would
persuade him to voluntarily surrender himself into your beautiful hands would have to be pretty good. So who's the other
person? Let me guess."

"I wonder how sharp you are, white-hair."

"It's you, Renfri. You'll reveal a truly princely—what am I
saying, *royal* magnanimity and renounce your revenge. Have
I guessed?"

Renfri threw back her head and laughed, covering her
mouth with her hand. Then she grew silent and fixed her
shining eyes on the witcher.

"Geralt," she said, "I used to be a princess. I had everything
I could dream of. Servants at my beck and call, dresses, shoes.
Cambric knickers. Jewels and trinkets, ponies, goldfish in a
pond. Dolls, and a doll's house bigger than this room. That
was my life until Stregobor and that whore Aridea ordered a
huntsman to butcher me in the forest and bring back my heart
and liver. Lovely, don't you think?"

"No. I'm pleased you evaded the huntsman, Renfri."

"Like shit I did. He took pity on me and let me go. After
the son of a bitch raped me and robbed me."

Geralt, fiddling with his medallion, looked her straight in
the eyes. She didn't lower hers.

"That was the end of the princess," she continued. "The
dress grew torn, the cambric grew grubby. And then there
was dirt, hunger, stench, stink and abuse. Selling myself to
any old bum for a bowl of soup or a roof over my head. Do you
know what my hair was like? Silk. And it reached a good foot

below my hips. I had it cut right to the scalp with sheep-shears when I caught lice. It's never grown back properly."

She was silent for a moment, idly brushing the uneven strands of hair from her forehead.

"I stole rather than starve to death. I killed to avoid being killed myself. I was locked in prisons which stank of urine, never knowing if they would hang me in the morning, or just flog me and release me. And through it all, my stepmother and your sorcerer were hard on my heels, with their poisons and assassins and spells. And you want me to reveal my magnanimity? To forgive him royally? I'll tear his head off, royally, first."

"Aridea and Stregobor tried to poison you?"

"With an apple seasoned with nightshade. I was saved by a gnome, and an emetic I thought would turn my insides out. But I survived."

"Was that one of the seven gnomes?" Renfri, pouring wine, froze holding the wineskin over the tumbler.

"Ah," she said. "You do know a lot about me. Yes? Do you have something against gnomes? Or humanoids? They were better to me than most people, not that it's your business."

"Stregobor and Aridea hunted me like a wild animal as long as they could. Until I became the hunter. Aridea died in her own bed. She was lucky I didn't get to her earlier—I had a special plan for her, and now I've got one for the sorcerer. Do you think he deserves to die?"

"I'm no judge. I'm a witcher."

"You are. I said that there were two people who could prevent bloodshed in Blaviken. The second is you. The sorcerer will let you into the tower. You could kill him."

"Renfri," said Geralt calmly, "did you fall from the roof onto your head on the way to my room?"

"Are you a witcher or aren't you, dammit? They say you

killed a kikimora and brought it here on a donkey to get a price
for it. Stregobor is worse than the kikimora. It's just a mindless
beast which kills because that's how the gods made it. Stregobor is a brute, a true monster. Bring him to me on a donkey
and I won't begrudge you any sum you care to mention."

"I'm not a hired thug, Shrike."

"You're not," she agreed with a smile. She leaned back on
the stool and crossed her legs on the table without the slightest
effort to cover her thighs with her skirt. "You're a witcher,
a defender of people from evil. And evil is the steel and fire
which will cause devastation here if we fight each other. Don't
you think I'm proposing a lesser evil, a better solution? Even
for that son of a bitch Stregobor. You can kill him mercifully,
with one thrust. He'll die without knowing it. And I guarantee
him quite the reverse."

Geralt remained silent.

Renfri stretched, raising her arms.

"I understand your hesitation," she said. "But I need an
answer now."

"Do you know why Stregobor and the king's wife wanted
to kill you?"

Renfri straightened abruptly and took her legs off the table.

"It's obvious," she snarled. "I am heir to the throne.
Aridea's children were born out of wedlock and don't have any
right to—"

"No."

Renfri lowered her head, but only for a moment. Her eyes
flashed. "Fine. I'm supposed to be cursed. Contaminated in
my mother's womb. I'm supposed to be..."

"Yes?"

"A monster."

"And are you?"

For a fleeting moment she looked helpless, shattered. And very sad.

"I don't know, Geralt," she whispered, and then her features hardened again. "Because how am I to know, dammit? When I cut my finger, I bleed. I bleed every month, too. I get a bellyache when I overeat, and a hangover when I get drunk. When I'm happy I sing and I swear when I'm sad. When I hate someone I kill them and when—But enough of this! Your answer, witcher."

"My answer is no."

"You remember what I said?" she asked after a moment's silence. "There are offers you can't refuse, the consequences are so terrible, and this is one of them. Think it over."

"I have thought carefully. And my suggestion was as serious."

Renfri was silent for some time, fiddling with a string of pearls wound three times around her shapely neck before falling teasingly between her breasts, their curves just visible through the slit of her jacket.

"Geralt," she said, "did Stregobor ask you to kill me?"

"Yes. He believed it was the lesser evil."

"Can I believe you refused him, as you have me?"

"You can."

"Why?"

"Because I don't believe in a lesser evil."

Renfri smiled faintly, an ugly grimace in the yellow candlelight.

"You don't believe in it, you say. Well you're right, in a way. Only Evil and Greater Evil exist and beyond them, in the shadows, lurks True Evil. True Evil, Geralt, is something you can barely imagine, even if you believe nothing can still surprise you. And sometimes True Evil seizes you by the throat and demands that you choose between it and another, slightly lesser, Evil."

"What's your goal here, Renfri?"

"Nothing. I've had a bit to drink and I'm philosophising. I'm looking for general truths. And I've found one: lesser evils exist, but we can't choose them. Only True Evil can force us to such a choice. Whether we like it or not."

"Maybe I've not had enough to drink." The witcher smiled sourly. "And in the meantime midnight's passed, the way it does. Let's speak plainly. You're not going to kill Stregobor in Blaviken because I'm not going to let you. I'm not going to let it come to a slaughter here. So, for the second time, renounce your revenge. Prove to him, to everyone, that you're not an inhuman and bloodthirsty monster. Prove he has done you great harm through his mistake."

For a moment Renfri watched the witcher's medallion spinning as he twisted the chain.

"And if I tell you, witcher, that I can neither forgive Stregobor nor renounce my revenge then I admit that he is right, is that it? I'd be proving that I am a monster cursed by the gods? You know, when I was still new to this life, a freeman took me in. He took a fancy to me, even though I found him repellent. So every time he wanted to fuck me, he had to beat me so hard I could barely move, even the following day. One morning I rose while it was still dark and slashed his throat with a scythe. I wasn't yet as skilled as I am now, and a knife seemed too small. And as I listened to him gurgle and choke, watched him kicking and flailing, I felt the marks left by his feet and fists fade, and I felt, oh, so great, so great that... I left him, whistling, sprightly, feeling so joyful, so happy. And it's the same each time. If it wasn't, who'd waste time on revenge?"

"Renfri," said Geralt. "Whatever your motives, you're not going to leave here joyful and happy. But you'll leave here alive, early tomorrow morning, as the alderman ordered. You're not going to kill Stregobor in Blaviken."

Renfri's eyes glistened in the candlelight, reflecting the flame; the pearls glowed in the slit of her jacket; the wolf medallion spinning round on its chain sparkled.

"I pity you," she said slowly, gazing at the medallion. "You claim a lesser evil doesn't exist. You're standing on a flagstone running with blood, alone and so very lonely because you can't choose, but you had to. And you'll never know, you'll never be sure, if you were right... And your reward will be a stoning, and a bad word. I pity you..."

"And you?" asked the witcher quietly, almost in a whisper.

"I can't choose, either."

"What are you?"

"I am what I am."

"Where are you?"

"I'm... cold..."

"Renfri!" Geralt squeezed the medallion tightly in his hand.

She tossed her head as if waking up, and blinked several times, surprised. For a very brief moment she looked frightened.

"You've won," she said sharply. "You win, witcher. Tomorrow morning I'll leave Blaviken and never return to this rotten town. Never. Now pass me the wineskin."

Her usual derisive smile returned as she put her empty tumbler back on the table. "Geralt?"

"I'm here."

"That bloody roof is steep. I'd prefer to leave at dawn than fall and hurt myself in the dark. I'm a princess and my body's delicate. I can feel a pea under a mattress—as long as it's not well-stuffed with straw, obviously. How about it?"

"Renfri"—Geralt smiled despite himself—"is that really befitting of a princess?"

"What do you know about princesses, dammit? I've lived as one and the joy of it is being able to do what you like. Do I have to tell you straight out what I want?"

Geralt, still smiling, didn't reply.

"I can't believe you don't find me attractive." Renfri grimaced. "Are you afraid you'll meet the freeman's sticky fate? Eh, white-hair, I haven't got anything sharp on me. Have a look for yourself."

She put her legs on his knees. "Pull my boots off. A high boot is the best place to hide a knife."

Barefoot, she got up, tore at the buckle of her belt. "I'm not hiding anything here, either. Or here, as you can see. Put that bloody candle out."

Outside, in the darkness, a cat yawled.

"Renfri?"

"What?"

"Is this cambric?"

"Of course it is, dammit. Am I a princess or not?"

V

"Daddy," Marilka nagged monotonously, "when are we going to the market? To the market, Daddy!"

"Quiet, Marilka," grunted Caldemeyn, wiping his plate with his bread. "So what were you saying, Geralt? They're leaving?"

"Yes."

"I never thought it would end so peacefully. They had me by the throat with that letter from Audoen. I put on a brave face but, to tell you the truth, I couldn't do a thing to them."

"Even if they openly broke the law? Started a fight?"

"Even if they did. Audoen's a very touchy king. He sends

people to the scaffold on a whim. I've got a wife, a daughter, and I'm happy with my office. I don't have to worry where the bacon will come from tomorrow. It's good news that they're leaving. But how, and why, did it happen?"

"Daddy, I want to go to the market!"

"Libushe! Take Marilka away! Geralt, I asked Centurion, the Golden Court's innkeeper, about that Novigradian company. They're quite a gang. Some of them were recognized."

"Yes?"

"The one with the gash across his face is Nohorn, Abergard's old adjutant from the so-called Free Angren Company—you'll have heard of them. That hulk they call Fifteen was one of theirs too and I don't think his nickname comes from fifteen good deeds. The half-elf is Civril, a brigand and professional murderer. Apparently, he had something to do with the massacre at Tridam."

"Where?"

"Tridam. Didn't you hear of it? Everyone was talking about it three... Yes, three years ago. The Baron of Tridam was holding some brigands in the dungeons. Their comrades—one of whom was that half-blood Civril—seized a river ferry full of pilgrims during the Feast of Nis. They demanded the baron set those others free. The baron refused, so they began murdering pilgrims, one after another. By the time the baron released his prisoners they'd thrown a dozen pilgrims overboard to drift with the current—and following the deaths the baron was in danger of exile, or even of execution. Some blamed him for waiting so long to give in, and others claimed he'd committed a great evil in releasing the men, in setting a pre—precedent or something. The gang should have been shot from the banks, together with the hostages, or attacked on the boats; he shouldn't have given an inch. At the tribunal the baron argued he'd had no choice, he'd chosen the lesser evil to save more than twenty-five people—women and children—on the ferry."

"The Tridam ultimatum," whispered the witcher. "Renfri—"

"What?"

"Caldemeyn, the marketplace."

"What?"

"She's deceived us. They're not leaving. They'll force Stregobor out of his tower as they forced the Baron of Tridam's hand. Or they'll force me to... They're going to start murdering people at the market; it's a real trap!"

"By all the gods—Where are you going? Sit down!"

Marilka, terrified by the shouting, huddled, keening, in the corner of the kitchen.

"I told you!" Libushe shouted, pointing to the witcher. "I said he only brings trouble!"

"Silence, woman! Geralt? Sit down!"

"We have to stop them. Right now, before people go to the market. And call the guards. As the gang leaves the inn, seize them and hold them."

"Be reasonable. We can't. We can't touch a hair of their heads if they've done nothing wrong. They'll defend themselves and there'll be bloodshed. They're professionals; they'll slaughter my people, and it'll be my head for it if word gets to Audoen. I'll gather the guards, go to the market and keep an eye on them there—"

"That won't achieve anything, Caldemeyn. If the crowd's already in the square, you can't prevent panic and slaughter. Renfri has to be stopped right now, while the marketplace is empty."

"It's illegal. I can't permit it. It's only a rumor the half-elf was at Tridam. You could be wrong, and Audoen would flay me alive."

"We have to take the lesser evil!"

"Geralt, I forbid it! As Alderman, I forbid it! Leave your sword! Stop!"

Marilka was screaming, her hands pressed over her mouth.

VI

Shading his eyes with his hand, Civril watched the sun emerge from behind the trees. The marketplace was coming to life. Wagons and carts rumbled past and the first vendors were already filling their stalls. A hammer was banging, a cock crowing and seagulls screeched loudly overhead.

"Looks like a lovely day," Fifteen said pensively.

Civril looked at him askance but didn't say anything.

"The horses all right, Tavik?" asked Nohorn, pulling on his gloves.

"Saddled and ready. But, there's still not many of them in the marketplace."

"There'll be more."

"We should eat."

"Later."

"Dead right. You'll have time later. And an appetite."

"Look," said Fifteen suddenly.

The witcher was approaching from the main street, walking between stalls, coming straight toward them.

"Renfri was right," Civril said. "Give me the crossbow, Nohorn." He hunched over and, holding the strap down with his foot, pulled the string back. He placed the bolt carefully in the groove as the witcher continued to approach. Civril raised the crossbow.

"Not one step closer, witcher!"

Geralt stopped about forty paces from the group.

123

"Where's Renfri?"

The half-blood's pretty face contorted. "At the tower. She's making the sorcerer an offer he can't refuse. But she knew you would come. She left a message for you."

"Speak."

"'I am what I am. Choose. Either me, or a lesser.' You're supposed to know what it means."

The witcher nodded, raised his hand above his right shoulder, and drew his sword. The blade traced a glistening arc above his head. Walking slowly, he made his way toward the group.

Civril laughed nastily, ominously.

"Renfri said this would happen, witcher, and left us something special to give you. Right between the eyes."

The witcher kept walking, and the half-elf raised the crossbow to his cheek. It grew very quiet.

The bowstring hummed, the witcher's sword flashed and the bolt flew upward with a metallic whine, spinning in the air until it clattered against the roof and rumbled into the gutter.

"He deflected it..." groaned Fifteen. "Deflected it in flight—"

"As one," ordered Civril. Blades hissed as they were drawn from sheaths, the group pressed shoulder to shoulder, bristling with blades.

The witcher came on faster; his fluid walk became a run— not straight at the group quivering with swords, but circling it in a tightening spiral.

As Geralt circled the group, Tavik's nerve failed. He rushed the witcher, the twins following him.

"Don't disperse!" Civril roared, shaking his head and losing sight of the witcher. He swore and jumped aside, seeing the group fall apart, scattering around the market stalls.

Tavik went first. He was chasing the witcher when he saw

Geralt running in the opposite direction, toward him. He skidded, trying to stop, but the witcher shot past before he could raise his sword. Tavik felt a hard blow just above his hip, fell to his knees and, when he saw his hip, started screaming.

The twins simultaneously attacked the black, blurred shape rushing toward them, mistimed their attack and collided with each other as Geralt slashed Vyr across the chest and Nimir in the temple, leaving one twin to stagger, head down, into a vegetable stall, and the other to spin in place and fall limply into the gutter.

The marketplace boiled with vendors running away, stalls clattering to the ground and screams rising in the dusty air. Tavik tried to stumble to his trembling legs and fell painfully to the ground.

"From the left, Fifteen!" Nohorn roared, running in a semi-circle to approach the witcher from behind.

Fifteen spun. But not quickly enough. He bore a thrust through the stomach, prepared to strike and was struck again in the neck, just below his ear. He took four unsteady steps and collapsed into a fish cart, which rolled away beneath him. Sliding over the slippery cargo, Fifteen fell onto the flagstones, silver with scales.

Civril and Nohorn struck simultaneously from both sides, the elf with a high sweeping cut, Nohorn from a kneeling position, low and flat. The witcher caught both, two metallic clangs merging into one. Civril leapt aside and tripped, catching himself against a stall as Nohorn warded off a blow so powerful it threw him backward to his knees. Leaping up, he parried too slowly, taking a gash in the face parallel to his old scar.

Civril bounced off the stall, jumping over Nohorn as he fell, missed the witcher and jumped away. The thrust was so sharp, so precise, he didn't feel it; his legs only gave way when he tried to attack again. The sword fell from his hand, the tendons severed above the elbow. Civril fell to his knees and shook his head, trying and failing to rise. His head dropped, and among the shattered stalls and market wares, the scattered fish and cabbages, his body stilled in the center of a growing red puddle.

Renfri entered the marketplace.

She approached slowly with a soft, feline step, avoiding the carts and stalls. The crowd in the streets and by the houses, which had been humming like a hornet's nest, grew silent. Geralt stood motionless, his sword in his lowered hand. Renfri came to within ten paces and stopped, close enough to see that, under her jacket, she wore a short coat of chain mail, barely covering her hips.

"You've made your choice," she said slowly. "Are you sure it's the right one?"

"This won't be another Tridam," Geralt said with an effort.

"It wouldn't have been. Stregobor laughed in my face. He said I could butcher Blaviken and the neighboring villages and he wouldn't leave his tower. And he won't let anyone in, not even you. Why are you looking at me like that? Yes, I deceived you. I'll deceive anyone if I have to; why should you be special?"

"Get out of here, Renfri."

She laughed. "No, Geralt." She drew her sword, quickly and nimbly.

"Renfri."

"No. You made a choice. Now it's my turn." With one sharp move, she tore the skirt from her hips and spun it in the air, wrapping the material around her forearm. Geralt retreated and raised his hand, arranging his fingers in the Sign.

Renfri laughed hoarsely. "It doesn't affect me. Only the sword will."

"Renfri," he repeated. "Go. If we cross blades, I—I won't be able—"

"I know," she said. "But I, I can't do anything else. I just can't. We are what we are, you and I."

She moved toward him with a light, swaying step, her sword glinting in her right hand, her skirt dragging along the ground from her left.

She leapt, the skirt fluttered in the air and, veiled in its tracks, the sword flashed in a short, sparing cut. Geralt jumped away; the cloth didn't even brush him, and Renfri's blade slid over his diagonal parry. He attacked instinctively, spinning their blades, trying to knock her weapon aside. It was a mistake. She deflected his blade and slashed, aiming for his face. He barely parried and pirouetted away, dodging her dancing blade and jumping aside again. She fell on him, threw the skirt into his eyes and slashed flatly from short range, spinning. Spinning with her, he avoided the blow. She knew the trick and turned with him, their bodies so close he could feel the touch of her breath as she ran the edge across his chest. He felt a twinge of pain, ignored it. He turned again, in the opposite direction, deflected the blade flying toward his temple, made a swift feint and attacked. Renfri sprang away as if to strike from above as Geralt lunged and swiftly slashed her exposed thigh and groin from below with the very tip of his sword.

She didn't cry out. Falling to her side, she dropped her sword and clutched her thigh. Blood poured through her fingers in a bright stream over her decorated belt, elk-leather boots, and onto the dirty flagstones. The clamor of the swaying crowd, crammed in the streets, grew as they saw blood.

Geralt put up his sword.

"Don't go..." she moaned, curling up in a ball.

He didn't reply.

"I'm...cold..."

He said nothing. Renfri moaned again, curling up tighter as her blood flowed into the cracks between the stones.

"Geralt...Hold me..."

The witcher remained silent.

She turned her head, resting her cheek on the flagstones and was still. A fine dagger, hidden beneath her body until now, slipped from her numb fingers.

After a long moment, the witcher raised his head, hearing Stregobor's staff tapping against the flagstones. The wizard was approaching quickly, avoiding the corpses.

"What slaughter," he panted. "I saw it, Geralt. I saw it all in my crystal ball..."

He came closer, bent over. In his trailing black robe, supported by his staff, he looked old.

"It's incredible." He shook his head. "Shrike's dead."

Geralt didn't reply.

"Well, Geralt." The wizard straightened himself. "Fetch a cart and we'll take her to the tower for an autopsy."

He looked at the witcher and, not getting any answer, leaned over the body.

Someone the witcher didn't know found the hilt of his sword and drew it. "Touch a single hair of her head," said the person the witcher didn't know, "touch her head and yours will go flying to the flagstones."

"Have you gone mad? You're wounded, in shock! An autopsy's the only way we can confirm—"

"Don't touch her!"

Stregobor, seeing the raised blade, jumped aside and waved his staff. "All right!" he shouted. "As you wish! But you'll never know! You'll never be sure! Never, do you hear, witcher?"

"Be gone."

"As you wish." The wizard turned away, his staff hitting the flagstones. "I'm returning to Kovir. I'm not staying in this hole another day. Come with me rather than rot here. These people don't know anything, they've only seen you killing. And you kill nastily, Geralt. Well, are you coming?"

Geralt didn't reply; he wasn't looking at him. He put his sword away. Stregobor shrugged and walked away, his staff tapping rhythmically against the ground.

A stone came flying from the crowd and clattered against the flagstones. A second followed, whizzing past just above Geralt's shoulder. The witcher, holding himself straight, raised both hands and made a swift gesture with them. The crowd heaved; the stones came flying more thickly but the Sign, protecting him behind an invisible oval shield, pushed them aside.

"Enough!" yelled Caldemeyn. "Bloody hell, enough of that!"

The crowd roared like a surge of breakers but the stones stopped flying. The witcher stood, motionless.

The alderman approached him.

"Is this," he said, with a broad gesture indicating the motionless bodies strewn across the square, "how your lesser evil looks? Is this what you believed necessary?"

"Yes," replied Geralt slowly, with an effort.

"Is your wound serious?"

"No."

"In that case, get out of here."

"Yes," said the witcher. He stood a moment longer, avoiding the alderman's eyes. Then he turned away slowly, very slowly.

"Geralt."

The witcher looked round.

"Don't come back," said Caldemeyn. "Never come back."

CHAPTER FOUR

THE VOICE OF REASON

"Let's talk, Iola.

"I need this conversation. They say silence is golden. Maybe it is, although I'm not sure it's worth that much. It has its price certainly; you have to pay for it.

"It's easier for you. Yes it is, don't deny it. You're silent through choice; you've made it a sacrifice to your goddess. I don't believe in Melitele, don't believe in the existence of other gods either, but I respect your choice, your sacrifice. Your belief. Because your faith and sacrifice, the price you're paying for your silence, will make you a better, a greater being. Or, at least, it could. But my faithlessness can do nothing. It's powerless.

"You ask what I believe in, in that case.

"I believe in the sword.

"As you can see, I carry two. Every witcher does. It's said, spitefully, the silver one is for monsters and the iron for humans. But that's wrong. As there are monsters which can be struck down only with a silver blade, so there are those for whom iron is lethal. And, Iola, not just any iron, it must come from a meteorite. What is a meteorite, you ask? It's a falling star. You must have seen them—short, luminous streaks in the night. You've probably made a wish on one. Perhaps it was one more reason for you to believe in the gods. For me, a meteorite is nothing more than a bit of metal, primed by the sun and its fall, metal to make swords.

"Yes, of course you can take my sword. Feel how light it— No! Don't touch the edge; you'll cut yourself. It's sharper than a razor. It has to be.

"I train in every spare moment. I don't dare lose my skill. I've come here—this furthest corner of the temple garden— to limber up, to rid my muscles of that hideous, loathsome numbness which has come over me, this coldness flowing through me. And you found me here. Funny, for a few days I was trying to find you. I wanted—

"I need to talk, Iola. Let's sit down for a moment.

"You don't know me at all, do you?

"I'm called Geralt. Geralt of—No. Only Geralt. Geralt of nowhere. I'm a witcher.

"My home is Kaer Morhen, Witcher's Settlement. It's...It was a fortress. Not much remains of it.

"Kaer Morhen...That's where the likes of me were produced. It's not done anymore; no one lives in Kaer Morhen now. No one but Vesemir. Who's Vesemir? My father. Why are you so surprised? What's so strange about it? Everyone's got a father, and mine is Vesemir. And so what if he's not my real father? I didn't know him, or my mother. I don't even know if they're still alive, and I don't much care.

"Yes, Kaer Morhen. I underwent the usual mutation there, through the Trial of Grasses, and then hormones, herbs, viral infections. And then through them all again. And again, to the bitter end. Apparently, I took the changes unusually well; I was only ill briefly. I was considered to be an exceptionally resilient brat...and was chosen for more complicated experiments as a result. They were worse. Much worse. But, as you see, I survived. The only one to live out of all those chosen for further trials. My hair's been white ever since. Total loss of pigmentation. A side effect, as they say. A trifle.

"Then they taught me various things until the day when I left Kaer Morhen and took to the road. I'd earned my medallion, the Sign of the Wolf's School. I had two swords: silver and iron, and my conviction, enthusiasm, incentive and...faith. Faith that I was needed in a world full of monsters and beasts, to protect the innocent. As I left Kaer Morhen, I dreamed of meeting my first monster. I couldn't wait to stand eye to eye with him. And the moment arrived.

"My first monster, Iola, was bald and had exceptionally rotten teeth. I came across him on the highway where, with some fellow monsters, deserters, he'd stopped a peasant's cart and pulled out a little girl, maybe thirteen years old. His companions held her father while the bald man tore off her dress, yelling it was time for her to meet a real man. I rode up and said the time had come for him, too—I thought I was very witty. The bald monster released the girl and threw himself at me with an axe. He was slow but tough. I hit him twice—not clean cuts, but spectacular, and only then did he fall. His gang ran away when they saw what a witcher's sword could do to a man....

"Am I boring you, Iola?

"I need this. I really do need it.

"Where was I? My first noble deed. You see, they'd told me again and again in Kaer Morhen not to get involved in such incidents, not to play at being knight errant or uphold the law. Not to show off, but to work for money. And I joined this fight like an idiot, not fifty miles from the mountains. And do you know why? I wanted the girl, sobbing with gratitude, to kiss her savior on the hands, and her father to thank me on his knees. In reality her father fled with his attackers, and the girl, drenched in the bald man's blood, threw up, became hysterical and fainted in fear when I approached her. Since then, I've only very rarely interfered in such matters.

"I did my job. I quickly learned how. I'd ride up to village enclosures or town pickets and wait. If they spat, cursed and threw stones, I rode away. If someone came out to give me a commission, I'd carry it out.

"I visited towns and fortresses. I looked for proclamations nailed to posts at the crossroads. I looked for the words 'Witcher urgently needed.' And then there'd be a sacred site, a dungeon, necropolis or ruins, forest ravine or grotto hidden in the mountains, full of bones and stinking carcasses. Some creature which lived to kill, out of hunger, for pleasure, or invoked by some sick will. A manticore, wyvern, fogler, aeschna, ilyocoris, chimera, leshy, vampire, ghoul, graveir, werewolf, giant scorpion, striga, black annis, kikimora, vypper . . . so many I've killed. There'd be a dance in the dark and a slash of the sword, and fear and distaste in the eyes of my employer afterward.

"Mistakes? Of course I've made them. But I keep to my principles. No, not the code. Although I have at times hidden behind a code. People like that. Those who follow a code are often respected and held in high esteem. But no one's ever compiled a witcher's code. I invented mine. Just like that. And keep to it. Always—

"Not always.

"There have been situations where it seemed there wasn't any room for doubt. When I should say to myself, 'What do I care? It's nothing to do with me. I'm a witcher.' When I should listen to the voice of reason. To listen to my instinct, even if it's fear, if not to what my experience dictates.

"I should have listened to the voice of reason that time . . .

"I didn't.

"I thought I was choosing the lesser evil. I chose the lesser

evil. Lesser evil! I'm Geralt! Witcher...I'm the Butcher of
Blaviken—

"Don't touch me! It might... You might see... and I don't
want you to. I don't want to know. I know my fate whirls about
me like water in a weir. It's hard on my heels, following my
tracks, but I never look back.

"A loop? Yes, that's what Nenneke sensed. What tempted
me, I wonder, in Cintra? How could I have taken such a risk
so foolishly—?

"No, no, no. I never look back. I'll never return to Cintra.
I'll avoid it like the plague. I'll *never* go back there.

"Heh, if my calculations are correct, that child would have
been born in May, sometime around the feast of Belleteyn. If
that's true, it's an interesting coincidence. Because Yennefer
was also born on Belleteyn's...

"Enough of this, we should go. It's already dusk.

"Thank you for talking to me. Thank you, Iola.

"No, nothing's wrong. I'm fine.

"Quite fine."

A QUESTION OF PRICE

I

The witcher had a knife at his throat.

He was wallowing in a wooden tub, brimful of soapsuds, his head thrown back against its slippery rim. The bitter taste of soap lingered in his mouth as the knife, blunt as a doorknob, scraped his Adam's apple painfully and moved toward his chin with a grating sound.

The barber, with the expression of an artist who is conscious that he is creating a masterpiece, scraped once more for form's sake, then wiped the witcher's face with a piece of linen soaked in tincture of angelica.

Geralt stood up, allowed a servant to pour a bucket of water over him, shook himself and climbed from the tub, leaving wet footmarks on the brick floor.

"Your towel, sir." The servant glanced curiously at his medallion.

"Thanks."

"Clothes," said Haxo. "Shirt, underpants, trousers and tunic. And boots."

"You've thought of everything. But can't I go in my own shoes?"

"No. Beer?"

"With pleasure."

He dressed slowly. The touch of someone else's coarse, unpleasant clothes against his swollen skin spoiled his relaxed mood.

"Castellan?"

"Yes, Geralt?"

"You don't know what this is all about, do you? Why they need me here?"

"It's not my business," said Haxo, squinting at the servants. "My job is to get you dressed—"

"Dressed up, you mean."

"—get you dressed and take you to the banquet, to the queen. Put the tunic on, sir. And hide the medallion beneath it."

"My dagger was here."

"It isn't anymore. It's in a safe place, like your swords and your possessions. Nobody carries arms where you're going."

The witcher shrugged, pulling on the tight purple tunic.

"And what's this?" he asked, indicating the embroidery on the front of his outfit.

"Oh yes," said Haxo. "I almost forgot. During the banquet, you will be the Honorable Ravix of Fourhorn. As guest of honor, you will sit at the queen's right hand, such is her wish, and that, on the tunic, is your coat of arms. A bear passant sable, damsel vested azure riding him, her hair loose and arms raised. You should remember it—one of the guests might have a thing about heraldry. It often happens."

"Of course I'll remember it," said Geralt seriously. "And Fourhorn, where's that?"

"Far enough. Ready? Can we go?"

"We can. Just tell me, Haxo, what's this banquet in aid of?"

"Princess Pavetta is turning fifteen and, as is the custom, contenders for her hand have turned up in their dozens.

Queen Calanthe wants her to marry someone from Skellige; an alliance with the islanders would mean a lot to us."

"Why them?"

"Those they're allied with aren't attacked as often as others."

"A good reason."

"And not the sole one. In Cintra women can't rule. King Roegner died some time ago and the queen doesn't want another husband: our Lady Calanthe is wise and just, but a king is a king. Whoever marries the princess will sit on the throne, and we want a tough, decent fellow. They have to be found on the islands. They're a hard nation. Let's go."

Geralt stopped halfway down the gallery surrounding the small inner courtyard and looked around.

"Castellan," he said under his breath, "we're alone. Quickly, tell me why the queen needs a witcher. You of all people must know something."

"For the same reasons as everyone else," Haxo grunted. "Cintra is just like any other country. We've got werewolves and basilisks and a manticore could be found, too, if you looked hard enough. So a witcher might also come in useful."

"Don't twist my words, Castellan. I'm asking why the queen needs a witcher in disguise as a bear passant, with hair loose at that, at the banquet."

Haxo also looked around, and even leaned over the gallery balustrade.

"Something bad's happening, Geralt," he muttered. "In the castle. Something's frightening people."

"What?"

"What usually frightens people? A monster. They say it's small, hunchbacked, bristling like an Urcheon. It creeps around the castle at night, rattles chains. Moans and groans in the chambers."

"Have you seen it?"

"No," Haxo spat, "and I don't want to."

"You're talking nonsense, Castellan," grimaced the witcher. "It doesn't make sense. We're going to an engagement feast. What am I supposed to do there? Wait for a hunchback to jump out and groan? Without a weapon? Dressed up like a jester? Haxo?"

"Think what you like," grumbled the castellan. "They told me not to tell you anything, but you asked. So I told you. And you tell me I'm talking nonsense. How charming."

"I'm sorry, I didn't mean to offend you, Castellan. I was simply surprised..."

"Stop being surprised." Haxo turned away, still sulking. "Your job isn't to be surprised. And I strongly advise you, witcher, that if the queen orders you to strip naked, paint your arse blue and hang yourself upside down in the entrance hall like a chandelier, you do it without surprise or hesitation. Otherwise you might meet with a fair amount of unpleasantness. Have you got that?"

"I've got it. Let's go, Haxo. Whatever happens, that bath's given me an appetite."

II

Apart from the curt, ceremonious greetings with which she welcomed him as "Lord of Fourhorn," Queen Calanthe didn't exchange a single word with the witcher. The banquet was about to begin and the guests, loudly announced by the herald, were gathering.

The table was huge, rectangular, and could seat more than forty men. Calanthe sat at the head of the table on a throne with a high backrest. Geralt sat on her right and, on her left, a gray-haired bard called Drogodar, with a lute. Two more chairs at the head of the table, on the queen's left, remained empty.

To Geralt's right, along the table, sat Haxo and a voivode whose name he'd forgotten. Beyond them were guests from the Duchy of Attre—the sullen and silent knight Rainfarn and his charge, the chubby twelve-year-old Prince Windhalm, one of the pretenders to the princess's hand. Further down were the colorful and motley knights from Cintra, and local vassals.

"Baron Eylembert of Tigg!" announced the herald.

"Coodcoodak!" murmured Calanthe, nudging Drogodar. "This will be fun."

A thin and whiskered, richly attired knight bowed low, but his lively, happy eyes and cheerful smirk belied his subservience.

"Greetings, Coodcoodak," said the queen ceremoniously. Obviously the baron was better known by his nickname than by his family name. "We are happy to see you."

"And I am happy to be invited," declared Coodcoodak, and sighed. "Oh well, I'll cast an eye on the princess, if you permit, my queen. It's hard to live alone, ma'am."

"Aye, Coodcoodak." Calanthe smiled faintly, wrapping a lock of hair around her finger. "But you're already married, as we well know."

"Aaahh." The baron was miffed. "You know yourself, ma'am, how weak and delicate my wife is, and smallpox is rife in the neighborhood. I bet my belt and sword against a pair of old slippers that in a year I'll already be out of mourning."

"Poor man, Coodcoodak. But lucky, too." Calanthe's smile grew wider. "Lucky your wife isn't stronger. I hear that last harvest, when she caught you in the haystack with a strumpet, she chased you for almost a mile with a pitchfork but couldn't catch you. You have to feed her better, cuddle her more and take care that her back doesn't get cold during the night. Then, in a year, you'll see how much better she is."

Coodcoodak pretended to grow doleful. "I take your point. But can I stay for the feast?"

"We'd be delighted, Baron."

"The legation from Skellige!" shouted the herald, becoming increasingly hoarse.

The islanders—four of them, in shiny leather doublets trimmed with seal fur and belted with checkered woolen sashes—strode in with a sprightly, hollow step. They were led by a sinewy warrior with a dark face and aquiline nose and, at his side, a broad-shouldered youth with a mop of red hair. They all bowed before the queen.

"It is a great honor," said Calanthe, a little flushed, "to welcome such an excellent knight as Eist Tuirseach of Skellige to my castle again. If it weren't for your well-known disdain for marriage, I'd be delighted to think you're here to court my Pavetta. Has loneliness got the better of you after all, sir?"

"Often enough, beautiful Calanthe," replied the dark-faced islander, raising his glistening eyes to the queen. "But my life is too dangerous for me to contemplate a lasting union. If it weren't for that...Pavetta is still a young girl, an unopened bud, but I can see..."

"See what?"

"The apple does not fall far from the tree." Eist Tuirseach smiled, flashing his white teeth. "Suffice it to look at you, my queen, to know how beautiful the princess will be when she reaches the age at which a woman can please a warrior. In the meantime, it is young men who ought to court her. Such as our King Bran's nephew here, Crach an Craite, who traveled here for exactly that purpose."

Crach, bowing his red head, knelt on one knee before the queen.

"Who else have you brought, Eist?"

A thickset, robust man with a bushy beard and a strapping fellow with bagpipes on his back knelt by Crach an Craite.

"This is the gallant druid Mousesack, who, like me, is a good friend and advisor to King Bran. And this is Draig Bon-Dhu, our famous skald. And thirty seamen from Skellige are waiting in the courtyard, burning with hope to catch a glimpse of the beautiful Calanthe of Cintra."

"Sit down, noble guests. Tuirseach, sir, sit here."

Eist took the vacant seat at the narrower end of the table, only separated from the queen by Drogodar and an empty chair. The remaining islanders sat together on the left, between Marshal Vissegerd and the three sons of Lord Strept, Tinglant, Fodcat and Wieldhill.

"That's more or less everyone." The queen leaned over to the marshal. "Let's begin, Vissegerd."

The marshal clapped his hands. The servants, carrying platters and jugs, moved toward the table in a long line, greeted by a joyful murmur from the guests.

Calanthe barely ate, reluctantly picking at the morsels served her with a silver fork. Drogodar, having bolted his food, kept strumming his lute. The rest of the guests, on the other hand, laid waste to the roast piglets, birds, fish and mollusks on offer—with the red-haired Crach an Craite in the lead. Rainfarn of Attre reprimanded the young Prince Windhalm severely, even slapping his hand when he reached for a jug of cider. Coodcoodak stopped picking bones for a moment and entertained his neighbors by imitating the whistle of a mud turtle. The atmosphere grew merrier by the minute. The first toasts were being raised, and already becoming less and less coherent.

Calanthe adjusted the narrow golden circlet on her curled ash-gray hair and turned to Geralt, who was busy cracking open a huge red lobster.

"It's loud enough that we can exchange a few words discreetly. Let us start with courtesies: I'm pleased to meet you."

"The pleasure's mutual, your Majesty."

"After the courtesies come hard facts. I've got a job for you."

"So I gathered. I'm rarely invited to feasts for the pleasure of my company."

"You're probably not very interesting company, then. What else have you gathered?"

"I'll tell you when you've outlined my task, your Majesty."

"Geralt," said Calanthe, her fingers tapping an emerald necklace, the smallest stone of which was the size of a bumblebee, "what sort of task do you expect, as a witcher? What? Digging a well? Repairing a hole in the roof? Weaving a tapestry of all the positions King Vridank and the beautiful Cerro tried on their wedding night? Surely you know what your profession's about?"

"Yes, I do. I'll tell you what I've gathered, your Majesty."

"I'm curious."

"I gathered that. And that, like many others, you've mistaken my trade for an altogether different profession."

"Oh?" Calanthe, casually leaning toward the lute-strumming Drogodar, gave the impression of being pensive and absent. "Who, Geralt, makes up this ignorant horde with whom you equate me? And for what profession do those fools mistake your trade?"

"Your Majesty," said Geralt calmly, "while I was riding to Cintra, I met villagers, merchants, peddlers, dwarves, tinkers and woodcutters. They told me about a black annis who has its hideout somewhere in these woods, a little house on a chicken-claw tripod. They mentioned a chimera nestling in the mountains. Aeschnes and centipedeanomorphs. Apparently a manticore could also be found if you look hard enough. So

THE LAST WISH

many tasks a witcher could perform without having to dress up in someone else's feathers and coat of arms."

"You didn't answer my question."

"Your Majesty, I don't doubt that a marriage alliance with Skellige is necessary for Cintra. It's possible, too, that the schemers who want to prevent it deserve a lesson—using means which don't involve you. It's convenient if this lesson were to be given by an unknown lord from Fourhorn, who would then disappear from the scene. And now I'll answer your question. You mistake my trade for that of a hired killer. Those others, of whom there are so many, are rulers. It's not the first time I've been called to a court where the problems demand the quick solutions of a sword. But I've never killed people for money, regardless of whether it's for a good or bad cause. And I never will."

The atmosphere at the table was growing more and more lively as the beer diminished. The red-haired Crach an Craite found appreciative listeners to his tale of the battle at Thwyth. Having sketched a map on the table with the help of meat bones dipped in sauce, he marked out the strategic plan, shouting loudly. Coodcoodak, proving how apt his nickname was, suddenly cackled like a very real sitting hen, creating general mirth among the guests, and consternation among the servants who were convinced that a bird, mocking their vigilance, had somehow managed to make its way from the courtyard into the hall.

"Thus fate has punished me with too shrewd a witcher." Calanthe smiled, but her eyes were narrowed and angry. "A witcher who, without a shadow of respect or, at the very least, of common courtesy, exposes my intrigues and infamous plans. But hasn't fascination with my beauty and charming personality clouded your judgment? Don't ever do that again,

Geralt. Don't speak to those in power like that. Few of them would forget your words, and you know kings—they have all sorts of things at their disposal: daggers, poisons, dungeons, red-hot pokers. There are hundreds, thousands, of ways kings can avenge their wounded pride. And you wouldn't believe how easy it is, Geralt, to wound some rulers' pride. Rarely will any of them take words such as 'No,' 'I won't,' and 'Never' calmly. But that's nothing. Interrupt one of them or make inappropriate comments, and you'll condemn yourself to the wheel."

The queen clasped her narrow white hands together and lightly rested her chin on them. Geralt didn't interrupt, nor did he comment.

"Kings," continued Calanthe, "divide people into two categories—those they order around, and those they buy—because they adhere to the old and banal truth that everyone can be bought. Everyone. It's only a question of price. Don't you agree? Ah, I don't need to ask. You're a witcher, after all; you do your job and take the money. As far as you're concerned, the idea of being bought has lost its scornful undertone. The question of your price, too, is clear, related as it is to the difficulty of the task and how well you execute it. And your fame, Geralt. Old men at fairs and markets sing of the exploits of the white-haired witcher from Rivia. If even half of it is true, then I wager your services are not cheap. So it would be a waste of money to engage you in such simple, trite matters as palace intrigue or murder. Those can be dealt with by other, cheaper hands."

"BRAAAK! Ghaaa-braaak!" roared Coodcoodak suddenly, to loud applause. Geralt didn't know which animal he was imitating, but he didn't want to meet anything like it. He turned his head and caught the queen's venomously green glance. Drogodar, his lowered head and face concealed by his curtain of gray hair, quietly strummed his lute.

"Ah, Geralt," said Calanthe, with a gesture forbidding a servant from refilling her goblet. "I speak and you remain silent. We're at a feast. We all want to enjoy ourselves. Amuse me. I'm starting to miss your pertinent remarks and perceptive comments. I'd also be pleased to hear a compliment or two, homage or assurance of your obedience. In whichever order you choose."

"Oh well, your Majesty," said the witcher, "I'm not a very interesting dinner companion. I'm amazed to be singled out for the honor of occupying this place. Indeed, someone far more appropriate should have been seated here. Anyone you wished. It would have sufficed for you to give them the order, or to buy them. It's only a question of price."

"Go on, go on." Calanthe tilted her head back and closed her eyes, the semblance of a pleasant smile on her lips.

"So I'm honored and proud to be sitting by Queen Calanthe of Cintra, whose beauty is surpassed only by her wisdom. I also regard it as a great honor that the queen has heard of me and that, on the basis of what she has heard, does not wish to use me for trivial matters. Last winter Prince Hrobarik, not being so gracious, tried to hire me to find a beauty who, sick of his vulgar advances, had fled the ball, losing a slipper. It was difficult to convince him that he needed a huntsman, and not a witcher."

The queen was listening with an enigmatic smile.

"Other rulers, too, unequal to you in wisdom, didn't refrain from proposing trivial tasks. It was usually a question of the murder of a stepson, stepfather, stepmother, uncle, aunt—it's hard to mention them all. They were all of the opinion that it was simply a question of price."

The queen's smile could have meant anything.

"And so I repeat"—Geralt bowed his head a little—"that I can't contain my pride to be sitting next to you, ma'am. And pride means a very great deal to us witchers. You wouldn't believe how much. A lord once offended a witcher's pride by proposing a job that wasn't in keeping with either honor or the witcher's code. What's more, he didn't accept a polite refusal and wished to prevent the witcher from leaving his castle. Afterward, everyone agreed this wasn't one of his best ideas."

"Geralt," said Calanthe, after a moment's silence, "you were wrong. You're a very interesting dinner companion."

Coodcoodak, shaking beer froth from his whiskers and the front of his jacket, craned his neck and gave the penetrating howl of a she-wolf in heat. The dogs in the courtyard, and the entire neighborhood, echoed the howl.

One of the brothers from Strept dipped his finger in his beer and touched up the thick line around the formation drawn by Crach an Craite.

"Error and incompetence!" he shouted. "They shouldn't have done that! Here, toward the wing, that's where they should have directed the cavalry, struck the flanks!"

"Ha!" roared Crach an Craite, whacking the table with a bone and splattering his neighbors' faces and tunics with sauce. "And so weaken the center? A key position? Ludicrous!"

"Only someone who's blind or sick in the head would miss the opportunity to maneuver in a situation like that!"

"That's it! Quite right!" shouted Windhalm of Attre.

"Who's asking you, you little snot?"

"Snot yourself!"

"Shut your gob or I'll wallop you—"

"Sit on your arse and keep quiet, Crach," called Eist Tuirseach, interrupting his conversation with Vissegerd. "Enough of these arguments. Drogodar, sir! Don't waste your talent! Indeed, your beautiful though quiet tunes should be listened to with greater concentration and gravity. Draig Bon-Dhu, stop scoffing and guzzling! You're not going to impress anyone here like that. Pump up your bagpipes and delight our ears with decent martial music. With your permission, noble Calanthe!"

"Oh mother of mine," whispered the queen to Geralt, raising her eyes to the vault for a moment in silent resignation. But she nodded her permission, smiling openly and kindly.

"Draig Bon-Dhu," said Eist, "play us the song of the battle of Hochebuz. It won't leave us in any doubt as to the tactical maneuvers of commanders—or as to who acquired immortal fame there! To the health of the heroic Calanthe of Cintra!"

"The health! And glory!" the guests roared, emptying their goblets and clay cups.

Draig Bon-Dhu's bagpipes gave out an ominous drone and burst into a terrible, drawn-out, modulated wail. The guests took up the song, beating out a rhythm on the table with whatever came to hand. Coodcoodak was staring avidly at the goatleather sack, captivated by the idea of adopting its dreadful tones in his own repertoire.

"Hochebuz," said Calanthe, looking at Geralt, "my first battle. Although I fear rousing the indignation and contempt of such a proud witcher, I confess that we were fighting for money. Our enemy was burning villages which paid us levies and we, greedy for our tributes, challenged them on the field. A trivial reason, a trivial battle, a trivial three thousand corpses pecked to pieces by the crows. And look—instead of being ashamed I'm proud as a peacock that songs are sung about me. Even when sung to such awful music."

Again she summoned her parody of a smile full of happiness and kindness, and answered the toast raised to her by lifting her own, empty, goblet. Geralt remained silent.

"Let's go on." Calanthe accepted a pheasant leg offered to her by Drogodar and picked at it gracefully. "As I said, you've aroused my interest. I've been told that witchers are an interesting caste, but I didn't really believe it. Now I do. When hit, you give a note which shows you're fashioned of pure steel, unlike these men molded from bird shit. Which doesn't, in any way, change the fact that you're here to execute a task. And you'll do it without being so clever."

Geralt didn't smile disrespectfully or nastily, although he very much wanted to. He held his silence.

"I thought," murmured the queen, appearing to give her full attention to the pheasant's thigh, "that you'd say something. Or smile. No? All the better. Can I consider our negotiations concluded?"

"Unclear tasks," said the witcher dryly, "can't be clearly executed."

"What's unclear? You did, after all, guess correctly. I have plans regarding a marriage alliance with Skellige. These plans are threatened, and I need you to eliminate the threat. But here your shrewdness ends. The supposition that I mistake your trade for that of a hired thug has piqued me greatly. Accept, Geralt, that I belong to that select group of rulers who know exactly what witchers do, and how they ought to be employed. On the other hand, if someone kills as efficiently as you do, even though not for money, he shouldn't be surprised if people credit him with being a professional in that field. Your fame runs ahead of you, Geralt; it's louder than Draig Bon-Dhu's accursed bagpipes, and there are equally few pleasant notes in it."

The bagpipe player, although he couldn't hear the queen's words, finished his concert. The guests rewarded him with an uproarious ovation and dedicated themselves with renewed zeal to the remains of the banquet, recalling battles and making rude jokes about womenfolk. Coodcoodak was making a series of loud noises, but there was no way to tell if these were yet another animal imitation, or an attempt to relieve his overloaded stomach.

Eist Tuirseach leaned far across the table. "Your Majesty," he said, "there are good reasons, I am sure, for your dedication to the lord from Fourhorn, but it's high time we saw Princess Pavetta. What are we waiting for? Surely not for Crach an Craite to get drunk? And even that moment is almost here."

"You're right as usual, Eist." Calanthe smiled warmly. Geralt was amazed by her arsenal of smiles. "Indeed, I do have important matters to discuss with the Honorable Ravix. I'll dedicate some time to you too, but you know my principle: duty then pleasure. Haxo!"

She raised her hand and beckoned the castellan. Haxo rose without a word, bowed, and quickly ran upstairs, disappearing into the dark gallery. The queen turned to the witcher.

"You heard? We've been debating for too long. If Pavetta has stopped preening in front of the looking glass, she'll be here presently. So prick up your ears because I won't repeat this. I want to achieve the ends which, to a certain degree, you have guessed. There can be no other solution. As for you, you have a choice. You can be forced to act by my command—I don't wish to dwell on the consequences of disobedience, although obedience will be generously rewarded—or you can render me a paid service. Note that I didn't say 'I can buy you,' because I've decided not to offend your witcher's pride. There's a huge difference, isn't there?"

"The magnitude of this difference has somehow escaped my notice."

"Then pay greater attention. The difference, my dear witcher, is that one who is bought is paid according to the buyer's whim, whereas one who renders a service sets his own price. Is that clear?"

"To a certain extent. Let's say, then, that I choose to serve. Surely I should know what that entails?"

"No. Only a command has to be specific and explicit. A paid service is different. I'm interested in the results, nothing more. How you achieve it is your business."

Geralt, raising his head, met Mousesack's penetrating black gaze. The druid of Skellige, without taking his eyes from the witcher, was crumbling bread in his hands and dropping it as if lost in thought. Geralt looked down. There on the oak table, crumbs, grains of buckwheat and fragments of lobster shell were moving like ants. They were forming runes which joined up—for a moment—into a word. A question.

Mousesack waited without taking his eyes off him. Geralt, almost imperceptibly, nodded. The druid lowered his eyelids and, with a stony face, swiped the crumbs off the table.

"Honorable gentlemen!" called the herald. "Pavetta of Cintra!"

The guests grew silent, turning to the stairs.

Preceded by the castellan and a fair-haired page in a scarlet doublet, the princess descended slowly, her head lowered. The color of her hair was identical to her mother's—ash-gray—but she wore it braided into two thick plaits which reached below her waist. Pavetta was adorned only with a tiara ornamented with a delicately worked jewel and a belt of tiny golden links which girded her long silvery-blue dress at the hips.

Escorted by the page, herald, castellan and Vissegerd, the princess occupied the empty chair between Drogodar and Eist Tuirseach. The knightly islander immediately filled her goblet and entertained her with conversation. Geralt didn't notice her answer with more than a word. Her eyes were permanently lowered, hidden behind her long lashes even during the noisy toasts raised to her around the table. There was no doubt her beauty had impressed the guests—Crach an Craite stopped shouting and stared at Pavetta in silence, even forgetting his tankard of beer. Windhalm of Attre was also devouring the princess with his eyes, flushing shades of red as though only a few grains in the hourglass separated them from their wedding night. Coodcoodak and the brothers from Strept were studying the girl's petite face, too, with suspicious concentration.

"Aha," said Calanthe quietly, clearly pleased. "And what do you say, Geralt? The girl has taken after her mother. It's even a shame to waste her on that red-haired lout, Crach. The only hope is that the pup might grow into someone with Eist Tuirseach's class. It's the same blood, after all. Are you listening, Geralt? Cintra has to form an alliance with Skellige because the interest of the state demands it. My daughter has to marry the right person. Those are the results you must ensure me."

"I have to ensure that? Isn't your will alone sufficient for it to happen?"

"Events might take such a turn that it won't be sufficient."

"What can be stronger than your will?"

"Destiny."

"Aha. So I, a poor witcher, am to face down a destiny which is stronger than the royal will. A witcher fighting destiny! What irony!"

"Yes, Geralt? What irony?"

"Never mind. Your Majesty, it seems the service you demand borders on the impossible."

"If it bordered on the possible," Calanthe drawled, "I would manage it myself. I wouldn't need the famous Geralt of Rivia. Stop being so clever. Everything can be dealt with—it's only a question of price. Bloody hell, there must be a figure on your witchers' pricelist for work that borders on the impossible. I can guess one, and it isn't low. You ensure me my outcome and I will give you what you ask."

"What did you say?"

"I'll give you whatever you ask for. And I don't like being told to repeat myself. I wonder, witcher, do you always try to dissuade your employers as strongly as you are me? Time is slipping away. Answer, yes or no?"

"Yes."

"That's better. That's better, Geralt. Your answers are much closer to the ideal. They're becoming more like those I expect when I ask a question. So. Discreetly stretch your left hand out and feel behind my throne."

Geralt slipped his hand under the yellow-blue drapery. Almost immediately he felt a sword secured to the leather-upholstered backrest. A sword well-known to him.

"Your Majesty," he said quietly, "not to repeat what I said earlier about killing people, you do realize that a sword alone will not defeat destiny?"

"I do." Calanthe turned her head away. "A witcher is also necessary. As you see, I took care of that."

"Your Maje—"

"Not another word, Geralt. We've been conspiring for too long. They're looking at us, and Eist is getting angry. Talk to the castellan. Have something to eat. Drink, but not too much. I want you to have a steady hand."

He obeyed. The queen joined a conversation between Eist, Vissegerd and Mousesack, with Pavetta's silent and dreamy participation. Drogodar had put away his lute and was making up for his lost eating time. Haxo wasn't talkative. The voivode with the hard-to-remember name, who must have heard something about the affairs and problems of Fourhorn, politely asked whether the mares were foaling well. Geralt answered yes, much better than the stallions. He wasn't sure if the joke had been well taken, but the voivode didn't ask any more questions.

Mousesack's eyes constantly sought the witcher's, but the crumbs on the table didn't move again.

Crach an Craite was becoming more and more friendly with the two brothers from Strept. The third, the youngest brother, was paralytic, having tried to match the drinking speed imposed by Draig Bon-Dhu. The skald had emerged from it unscathed.

The younger and less important lords gathered at the end of the table, tipsy, started singing a well-known song—out of tune—about a little goat with horns and a vengeful old woman with no sense of humor.

A curly-haired servant and a captain of the guards wearing the gold and blue of Cintra ran up to Vissegerd. The marshal, frowning, listened to their report, rose, and leaned down from behind the throne to murmur something to the queen. Calanthe glanced at Geralt and answered with a single word. Vissegerd leaned over even further and whispered something more; the queen looked at him sharply and, without a word, slapped her armrest with an open palm. The marshal bowed and passed the command to the captain of the guards. Geralt didn't hear it but he did notice that Mousesack wriggled uneasily and glanced at Pavetta—the princess was sitting motionless, her head lowered.

Heavy footsteps, each accompanied by the clang of metal striking the floor, could be heard over the hum at the table. Everyone raised their heads and turned.

The approaching figure was clad in armor of iron sheets and leather treated with wax. His convex, angular, black and blue breastplate overlapped a segmented apron and short thigh pads. The armor-plated brassards bristled with sharp, steel spikes and the visor, with its densely grated screen extending out in the shape of a dog's muzzle, was covered with spikes like a conker casing.

Clattering and grinding, the strange guest approached the table and stood motionless in front of the throne.

"Noble queen, honorable gentlemen," said the newcomer, bowing stiffly. "Please forgive me for disrupting your ceremonious feast. I am Urcheon of Erlenwald."

"Greetings, Urcheon of Erlenwald," said Calanthe slowly. "Please take your place at the table. In Cintra we welcome every guest."

"Thank you, your Majesty." Urcheon of Erlenwald bowed once again and touched his chest with a fist clad in an iron gauntlet. "But I haven't come to Cintra as a guest but on a matter of great importance and urgency. If your Majesty permits, I will present my case immediately, without wasting your time."

"Urcheon of Erlenwald," said the queen sharply, "a praiseworthy concern about our time does not justify lack of respect. And such is your speaking to us from behind an iron trellis. Remove your helmet, and we'll endure the time wasted while you do."

"My face, your Majesty, must remain hidden for the time being. With your permission."

An angry ripple, punctuated here and there with the odd curse, ran through the gathered crowd. Mousesack, lowering his head, moved his lips silently. The witcher felt the spell electrify the air for a second, felt it stir his medallion. Calanthe was looking at Urcheon, narrowing her eyes and drumming her fingers on her armrest.

"Granted," she said finally. "I choose to believe your motive is sufficiently important. So—what brings you here, Urcheon-without-a-face?"

"Thank you," said the newcomer. "But I'm unable to suffer the accusation of lacking respect, so I explain that it is a matter of a knight's vows. I am not allowed to reveal my face before midnight strikes."

Calanthe, raising her hand perfunctorily, accepted his explanation. Urcheon advanced, his spiked armor clanging.

"Fifteen years ago," he announced loudly, "your husband King Roegner lost his way while hunting in Erlenwald. Wandering around the pathless tracts, he fell from his horse into a ravine and sprained his leg. He lay at the bottom of the gully and called for help but the only answer he got was the hiss of vipers and the howling of approaching werewolves. He would have died without the help he received."

"I know what happened," the queen affirmed. "If you know it, too, then I guess you are the one who helped him."

"Yes. It is only because of me he returned to you in one piece, and well."

"I am grateful to you, then, Urcheon of Erlenwald. That gratitude is none the lesser for the fact that Roegner, gentleman of my heart and bed, has left this world. Tell me, if the implication that your aid was not disinterested does not offend another of your knightly vows, how I can express my gratitude."

"You well know my aid was not disinterested. You know, too, that I have come to collect the promised reward for saving the king's life."

"Oh yes?" Calanthe smiled but green sparks lit up her eyes. "So you found a man at the bottom of a ravine, defenseless, wounded, at the mercy of vipers and monsters. And only when he promised you a reward did you help? And if he didn't want to or couldn't promise you something, you'd have left him there, and, to this day, I wouldn't know where his bones lay? How noble. No doubt your actions were guided by a particularly chivalrous vow at the time."

The murmur around the hall grew louder.

"And today you come for your reward, Urcheon?" continued the queen, smiling even more ominously. "After fifteen years? No doubt you are counting the interest accrued over this period? This isn't the dwarves' bank, Urcheon. You say Roegner promised you a reward? Ah, well, it will be difficult to get him to pay you. It would be simpler to send you to him, into the other world, to reach an agreement over who owes what. I loved my husband too dearly, Urcheon, to forget that I could have lost him then, fifteen years ago, if he hadn't chosen to bargain with you. The thought of it arouses rather-ill feeling toward you. Masked newcomer, do you know that here in Cintra, in my castle and in my power, you are just as helpless and close to death as Roegner was then, at the bottom of the ravine? What will you propose, what price, what reward will you offer, if I promise you will leave here alive?"

The medallion on Geralt's neck twitched. The witcher caught Mousesack's clearly uneasy gaze. He shook his head a little and raised his eyebrows questioningly. The druid also shook his head and, with a barely perceptible move of his curly beard, indicated Urcheon. Geralt wasn't sure.

"Your words, your Majesty," called Urcheon, "are calculated to frighten me, to kindle the anger of the honorable gentlemen gathered here, and the contempt of your pretty daughter, Pavetta. But above all, your words are untrue. And you know it!"

"You accuse me of lying like a dog." An ugly grimace crept across Calanthe's lips.

"You know very well, your Majesty," the newcomer continued adamantly, "what happened then in Erlenwald. You know Roegner, once saved, vowed of his own will to give me whatever I asked for. I call upon every one to witness my words! When the king, rescued from his misadventure, reached his retinue, he asked me what I demanded and I answered. I asked him to promise me whatever he had left at home without knowing or expecting it. The king swore it would be so, and on his return to the castle he found you, Calanthe, in labor. Yes, your Majesty, I waited for fifteen years and the interest on my reward has grown. Today I look at the beautiful Pavetta and see that the wait has been worth it! Gentlemen and knights! Some of you have come to Cintra to ask for the princess's hand. You have come in vain. From the day of her birth, by the power of the royal oath, the beautiful Pavetta has belonged to me!"

An uproar burst forth among the guests. Some shouted, someone swore, someone else thumped his fist on the table and knocked the dishes over. Wieldhill of Strept pulled a knife out of the roast lamb and waved it about. Crach an Craite, bent over, was clearly trying to break a plank from the table trestle.

"That's unheard of!" yelled Vissegerd. "What proof do you have? Proof?"

"The queen's face," exclaimed Urcheon, extending his hand, "is the best proof!"

Pavetta sat motionless, not raising her head. The air was growing thick with something very strange. The witcher's medallion was tearing at its chain under the tunic. He saw the queen summon a page and whisper a short command. Geralt couldn't hear it, but he was puzzled by the surprise on the boy's face and the fact that the command had to be repeated. The page ran toward the exit.

The uproar at the table continued as Eist Tuirseach turned to the queen.

"Calanthe," he said calmly, "is what he says true?"

"And if it is," the queen muttered through her teeth, biting her lips and picking at the green sash on her shoulder, "so what?"

"If what he says is true"—Eist frowned—"then the promise will have to be kept."

"Is that so?"

"Or am I to understand," the islander asked grimly, "that you treat all promises this lightly, including those which have etched themselves so deeply in my memory?"

Geralt, who had never expected to see Calanthe blush deeply, with tears in her eyes and trembling lips, was surprised.

"Eist," whispered the queen, "this is different—"

"Is it, really?"

"Oh, you son of a bitch!" Crach an Craite yelled unexpectedly, jumping up. "The last fool who said I'd acted in vain was pinched apart by crabs at the bottom of Allenker bay! I didn't sail here from Skellig to return empty-handed! A suitor has turned up, some son of a trollop! Someone bring me a sword and give that idiot some iron! We'll soon see who—"

"Maybe you could just shut up, Crach?" Eist snapped scathingly, resting both fists on the table. "Draig Bon-Dhu! I render you responsible for his future behavior!"

"And are you going to silence me, too, Tuirseach?" shouted Rainfarn of Attre, standing up. "Who is going to stop me from washing the insult thrown at my prince away with blood? And his son, Windhalm, the only man worthy of Pavetta's hand and bed! Bring the swords! I'll show that Urcheon, or whatever he's called, how we of Attre take revenge for such abuse! I wonder whether anybody or anything can hold me back?"

"Yes. Regard for good manners," said Eist Tuirseach calmly. "It is not proper to start a fight here or challenge anyone without permission from the lady of the house. What is this? Is the throne room of Cintra an inn where you can punch each other's heads and stab each other with knives as the fancy takes you?"

Everybody started to shout again, to curse and swear and wave their arms about. But the uproar suddenly stopped, as if cut by a knife, at the short, furious roar of an enraged bison. "Yes," said Coodcoodak, clearing his throat and rising from his chair. "Eist has it wrong. This doesn't even look like an inn anymore. It's more like a zoo, so a bison should be at home here. Honorable Calanthe, allow me to offer my opinion."

"A great many people, I see," said Calanthe in a drawling voice, "have an opinion on this problem and are offering it even without my permission. Strange that you aren't interested in mine? And in my opinion, this bloody castle will sooner collapse on my head than I give my Pavetta to this crank. I haven't the least intention—"

"Roegner's oath—" Urcheon began, but the queen silenced him, banging her golden goblet on the table.

"Roegner's oath means about as much to me as last year's snows! And as for you, Urcheon, I haven't decided whether to allow Crach or Rainfarn to meet you outside, or to simply hang you. You're greatly influencing my decision with your interruption!"

Geralt, still disturbed by the way his medallion was quivering, looked around the hall. Suddenly he saw Pavetta's eyes, emerald green like her mother's. The princess was no longer hiding them beneath her long lashes—she swept them from Mousesack to the witcher, ignoring the others. Mousesack, bent over, was wriggling and muttering something.

Coodcoodak, still standing, cleared his throat meaningfully. "Speak." The queen nodded. "But be brief."

"As you command, your Majesty. Noble Calanthe and you, knights! Indeed, Urcheon of Erlenwald made a strange request of King Roegner, a strange reward to demand when the king offered him his wish. But let us not pretend we've never heard of such requests, of the Law of Surprise, as old as humanity itself. Of the price a man who saves another can demand, of the granting of a seemingly impossible wish. 'You will give me the first thing that comes to greet you.' It might be a dog, you'll say, a halberdier at the gate, even a mother-in-law impatient to holler at her son-in-law when he returns home. Or: 'You'll give me what you find at home yet don't expect.' After a long journey, honorable gentlemen, and an unexpected return, this could be a lover in the wife's bed. But sometimes it's a child. A child marked out by destiny."

"Briefly, Coodcoodak." Calanthe frowned.

"As you command. Sirs! Have you not heard of children marked out by destiny? Was not the legendary hero, Zatret Voruta, given to the dwarves as a child because he was the first person his father met on his return? And Mad Deï, who demanded a traveler give him what he left at home without knowing it? That surprise was the famous Supree, who later liberated Mad Deï from the curse which weighed him down. Remember Zivelena, who became the Queen of Metinna with the help of the gnome Rumplestelt, and in return promised him her firstborn? Zivelena didn't keep her promise when Rumplestelt came for his reward and, by using spells, she forced him to run away. Not long after that, both she and the child died of the plague. You do not dice with Destiny with impunity!"

"Don't threaten me, Coodcoodak." Calanthe grimaced. "Midnight is close, the time for ghosts. Can you remember any more legends from your undoubtedly difficult childhood? If not, then sit down."

"I ask your Grace"—the baron turned up his long whiskers—"to allow me to remain standing. I'd like to remind everybody of another legend. It's an old, forgotten legend— we've all probably heard it in our difficult childhoods. In this legend, the kings kept their promises. And we, poor vassals, are only bound to kings by the royal word: treaties, alliances, our privileges and fiefs all rely on it. And now? Are we to doubt all this? Doubt the inviolability of the king's word? Wait until it is worth as much as yesteryear's snow? If this is how things are to be, then a difficult old age awaits us after our difficult childhoods!"

"Whose side are you on, Coodcoodak?" hollered Rainfarn of Attre.

"Silence! Let him speak!"

"This cackler, full of hot air, insults her Majesty!"

"The Baron of Tigg is right!"

"Silence," Calanthe said suddenly, getting up. "Let him finish."

"I thank you graciously." Coodcoodak bowed. "But I have just finished."

Silence fell, strange after the commotion his words had caused. Calanthe was still standing. Geralt didn't think anyone else had noticed her hand shake as she wiped her brow.

"My lords," she said finally, "you deserve an explanation. Yes, this... Urcheon... speaks the truth. Roegner did swear to give him that which he did not expect. It looks as if our lamented king was an oaf as far as a woman's affairs are concerned, and couldn't be trusted to count to nine. He confessed the truth on his death-bed, because he knew what I'd do to him if he'd admitted it earlier. He knew what a mother, whose child is disposed of so recklessly, is capable of."

The knights and magnates remained silent. Urcheon stood motionless, like a spiked, iron statue.

"And Coodcoodak," continued Calanthe, "well, Coodcoodak has reminded me that I am not a mother but a queen. Very well, then. As queen, I shall convene a council tomorrow. Cintra is not a tyranny. The council will decide whether a dead king's oath is to decide the fate of the successor to the throne.

It will decide whether Pavetta and the throne of Cintra are to be given to a stranger, or to act according to the kingdom's interest." Calanthe was silent for a moment, looking askance at Geralt. "And as for the noble knights who have come to Cintra in the hope of the princess's hand... It only remains for me to express my deep regret at the cruel disrespect and dishonor they have experienced here, at the ridicule poured on them. I am not to blame."

Amid the hum of voices which rumbled through the guests, the witcher managed to pick out Eist Tuirseach's whisper.

"On all the gods of the sea," sighed the islander. "This isn't befitting. This is open incitement to bloodshed. Calanthe, you're simply setting them against each other—"

"Be quiet, Eist," hissed the queen furiously, "because I'll get angry."

Mousesack's black eyes flashed as—with a glance—the druid indicated Rainfarn of Attre who, with a gloomy, grimacing face, was preparing to stand. Geralt reacted immediately, standing up first and banging the chair noisily.

"Maybe it will prove unnecessary to convene the council," he said in ringing tones.

Everyone grew silent, watching him with astonishment. Geralt felt Pavetta's emerald eyes on him, he felt Urcheon's gaze fall on him from behind the lattice of his black visor, and he felt the Force surging like a flood-wave and solidifying in the air. He saw how, under the influence of this Force, the smoke from the torches and oil lamps was taking on fantastic forms. He knew that Mousesack saw it too. He also knew that nobody else saw it.

"I said," he repeated calmly, "that convening the council may not prove necessary. You understand what I have in mind, Urcheon of Erlenwald?"

The spiked knight took two grating steps forward.

"I do," he said, his words hollow beneath his helmet. "It would take a fool not to understand. I heard what the merciful and noble lady Calanthe said a moment ago. She has found an excellent way of getting rid of me. I accept your challenge, knight unknown to me!"

"I don't recall challenging you," said Geralt. "I don't intend to duel you, Urcheon of Erlenwald."

"Geralt!" called Calanthe, twisting her lips and forgetting to call the witcher Ravix, "don't overdo it! Don't put my patience to the test!"

"Or mine," added Rainfarn ominously. Crach an Craite growled, and Eist Tuirseach meaningfully showed him a clenched fist. Crach growled even louder.

"Everyone heard," spoke Geralt, "Baron Tigg tell us about the famous heroes taken from their parents on the strength of the same oath that Urcheon received from King Roegner. But why should anyone want such an oath? You know the answer, Urcheon of Erlenwald. It creates a powerful, indissoluble tie of destiny between the person demanding the oath and its object, the child-surprise. Such a child, marked by blind fate, can be destined for extraordinary things. It can play an incredibly important role in the life of the person to whom fate has tied it. That is why, Urcheon, you demanded the prize you claim today. You don't want the throne of Cintra. You want the princess."

"It is exactly as you say, knight unknown to me." Urcheon laughed out loud. "That is exactly what I claim! Give me the one who is my destiny!"

"That," said Geralt, "will have to be proved."

"You dare doubt it? After the queen confirmed the truth of my words? After what you've just said?"

"Yes. Because you didn't tell us everything. Roegner knew the power of the Law of Surprise and the gravity of the oath he took. And he took it because he knew law and custom have a power which protects such oaths, ensuring they are only fulfilled when the force of destiny confirms them. I declare, Urcheon, that you have no right to the princess as yet. You will win her only when—"

"When what?"

"When the princess herself agrees to leave with you. This is what the Law of Surprise states. It is the child's, not the parent's, consent which confirms the oath, which proves that the child was born under the shadow of destiny. That's why you returned after fifteen years, Urcheon, and that's the condition King Roegner stipulated in his oath."

"Who are you?"

"I am Geralt of Rivia."

"Who are you, Geralt of Rivia, to claim to be an oracle in matters of laws and customs?"

"He knows this law better than anyone else," Mousesack said in a hoarse voice, "because it applied to him once. He was taken from his home because he was what his father hadn't expected to find on his return. Because he was destined for other things. And by the power of destiny he became what he is."

"And what is he?"

"A witcher."

In the silence that reigned, the guardhouse bell struck, announcing midnight in a dull tone. Everyone shuddered and raised their heads. Mousesack watched Geralt with surprise. But it was Urcheon who flinched most noticeably and moved uneasily. His hands, clad in their armor gauntlets, fell to his sides lifelessly, and the spiked helmet swayed unsteadily.

The strange, unknown Force suddenly grew thicker, filling the hall like a gray mist.

"It's true," said Calanthe. "Geralt, present here, is a witcher. His trade is worthy of respect and esteem. He has sacrificed himself to protect us from monsters and nightmares born in the night, those sent by powers ominous and harmful to man. He kills the horrors and monsters that await us in the forests and ravines. And those which have the audacity to enter our dwellings." Urcheon was silent. "And so," continued the queen, raising her ringed hand, "let the law be fulfilled, let the oath which you, Urcheon of Erlenwald, insist should be satisfied, be satisfied. Midnight has struck. Your vow no longer binds you. Lift your visor. Before my daughter expresses her will, before she decides her destiny, let her see your face. We all wish to see your face."

Urcheon of Erlenwald slowly raised his armored hand, pulled at the helmet's fastenings, grabbed it by the iron horn and threw it against the floor with a crash. Someone shouted, someone swore, someone sucked in their breath with a whistle. On the queen's face appeared a wicked, very wicked, smile. A cruel smile of triumph.

Above the wide, semi-circular breastplate, two bulbous, black, button eyes looked out. Eyes set to either side of a blunt, elongated muzzle covered in reddish bristles and full of sharp white fangs. Urcheon's head and neck bristled with a brush of short, gray, twitching prickles.

"This is how I look," spoke the creature, "which you well knew, Calanthe. Roegner, in telling you of his oath, wouldn't have omitted describing me. Urcheon of Erlenwald to whom—despite my appearance—Roegner swore his oath. You prepared well for my arrival, queen. Your own vassals have pointed out your haughty and contemptuous refusal to keep Roegner's word. When your attempt to set the other suitors on me didn't succeed, you still had a killer witcher in reserve, ready at your right hand. And finally, common, low

165

deceit. You wanted to humiliate me, Calanthe. Know that it is yourself you have humiliated."

"Enough." Calanthe stood up and rested her clenched fist on her hip. "Let's put an end to this. Pavetta! You see who, or rather what, is standing in front of you, claiming you for himself. In accordance with the Law of Surprise and eternal custom, the decision is yours. Answer. One word from you is enough. Yes, and you become the property, the conquest, of this monster. No, and you will never have to see him again."

The Force pulsating in the hall was squeezing Geralt's temples like an iron vise, buzzing in his ears, making the hair on his neck stand on end. The witcher looked at Mousesack's whitening knuckles, clenched at the edge of the table. At the trickle of sweat running down the queen's cheek. At the breadcrumbs on the table, moving like insects, forming runes, dispersing and again gathering into one word: CAREFUL!

"Pavetta!" Calanthe repeated. "Answer. Do you choose to leave with this creature?"

Pavetta raised her head. "Yes."

The Force filling the hall echoed her, rumbling hollowly in the arches of the vault. No one, absolutely no one, made the slightest sound.

Calanthe very slowly collapsed into her throne. Her face was completely expressionless.

"Everyone heard," Urcheon's calm voice resounded in the silence. "You, too, Calanthe. As did you, witcher, cunning hired thug. My rights have been established. Truth and destiny have triumphed over lies and deviousness. What do you have left, noble queen, disguised witcher? Cold steel?" No one answered. "I'd like to leave with Pavetta immediately," continued Urcheon, his bristles stirring as he snapped his jaw shut, "but I won't deny myself one small pleasure. It is you,

Calanthe, who will lead your daughter here to me and place her white hand in mine."

Calanthe slowly turned her head in the witcher's direction. Her eyes expressed a command. Geralt didn't move, sensing that the Force condensing in the air was concentrated on him. Only on him. Now he understood. The queen's eyes narrowed, her lips quivered...

"What?! What's this?" yelled Crach an Craite, jumping up. "Her white hand? In his? The princess with this bristly stinker? With this... pig's snout?"

"And I wanted to fight him like a knight!" Rainfarn chimed in. "This horror, this beast! Loose the dogs on him! The dogs!"

"Guards!" cried Calanthe.

Everything happened at once. Crach an Craite seized a knife from the table and knocked his chair over with a crash. Obeying Eist's command, Draig Bon-Dhu, without a thought, whacked the back of his head with his bagpipes, as hard as he could. Crach dropped onto the table between a sturgeon in gray sauce and the few remaining arched ribs of a roast boar. Rainfarn leapt toward Urcheon, flashing a dagger drawn from his sleeve. Coodcoodak, springing up, kicked a stool under his feet which Rainfarn jumped agilely, but a moment's delay was enough—Urcheon deceived him with a short feint and forced him to his knees with a mighty blow from his armored fist. Coodcoodak fell to snatch the dagger from Rainfarn but was stopped by Prince Windhalm, who clung to his thigh like a bloodhound.

Guards, armed with guisarmes and lances, ran in from the entrance. Calanthe, upright and threatening, with an authoritative, abrupt gesture indicated Urcheon to them. Pavetta started to shout, Eist Tuirseach to curse. Everyone jumped up, not quite knowing what to do.

"Kill him!" shouted the queen.

Urcheon, huffing angrily and baring his fangs, turned to face the attacking guards. He was unarmed but clad in spiked steel, from which the points of the guisarmes bounced with a clang. But the blows knocked him back, straight onto Rainfarn, who was just getting up and immobilized him by grabbing his legs. Urcheon let out a roar and, with his iron elbow-guards, deflected the blades aimed at his head. Rainfarn jabbed him with his dagger but the blade slid off the breastplate. The guards, crossing their spear-shafts, pinned him to the sculpted chimney. Rainfarn, who was hanging onto his belt, found a chink in the armor and dug the dagger into it. Urcheon curled up.

"Dunyyyyyyy!" Pavetta shrilled as she jumped onto the chair.

The witcher, sword in hand, sprang onto the table and ran toward the fighting men, knocking plates, dishes and goblets all over the place. He knew there wasn't much time. Pavetta's cries were sounding more and more unnatural. Rainfarn was raising his dagger to stab again.

Geralt cut, springing from the table into a crouch. Rainfarn wailed and staggered to the wall. The witcher spun and, with the center of his blade, slashed a guard who was trying to dig the sharp tongue of his lance between Urcheon's apron and breastplate. The guard tumbled to the ground, losing his helmet. More guards came running in from the entrance.

"This is not befitting!" roared Eist Tuirseach, grabbing a chair. He shattered the unwieldly piece of furniture against the floor with great force and, with what remained in his hand, threw himself at those advancing on Urcheon.

Urcheon, caught by two guisarme hooks at the same time, collapsed with a clang, cried out and huffed as he was dragged along the floor. A third guard raised his lance to stab down and

Geralt cut him in the temple with the point of his sword. Those dragging Urcheon stepped back quickly, throwing down their guisarmes, while those approaching from the entrance backed away from the remnants of chair brandished by Eist like the magic sword Balmur in the hand of the legendary Zatreta Voruta.

Pavetta's cries reached a peak and suddenly broke off. Geralt, sensing what was about to happen, fell to the floor watching for a greenish flash. He felt an excruciating pain in his ears, heard a terrible crash and a horrifying wail ripped from numerous throats. And then the princess's even, monotonous and vibrating cry.

The table, scattering dishes and food all around, was rising and spinning; heavy chairs were flying around the hall and shattering against the walls; tapestries and hangings were flapping, raising clouds of dust. Cries and the dry crack of guisarme shafts snapping like sticks came from the entrance.

The throne, with Calanthe sitting on it, sprang up and flew across the hall like an arrow, smashing into the wall with a crash and falling apart. The queen slid to the floor like a ragged puppet. Eist Tuirseach, barely on his feet, threw himself toward her, took her in his arms and sheltered her from the hail pelting against the walls and floor with his body.

Geralt, grasping the medallion in his hand, slithered as quickly as he could toward Mousesack, miraculously still on his knees, who was lifting a short hawthorn wand with a rat's skull affixed to the tip. On the wall behind the druid, a tapestry depicting the siege and fire of Fortress Ortagar was burning with very real flames.

Pavetta wailed. Turning round and round, she lashed everything and everybody with her cries as if with a whip. Anyone who tried to stand tumbled to the ground or was flattened against the wall. An enormous silver sauceboat in the shape of a many-oared vessel with an upturned bow came whistling through the air in front of Geralt's eyes and knocked down the voivode with the hard-to-remember name just as he was trying to dodge it. Plaster rained down silently as the table rotated beneath the ceiling, with Crach an Craite flattened on it and throwing down vile curses.

Geralt crawled to Mousesack and they hid behind the heap formed by Fodcat of Strept, a barrel of beer, Drogodar, a chair and Drogodar's lute.

"It's pure, primordial Force!" the druid yelled over the racket and clatter. "She's got no control over it!"

"I know!" Geralt yelled back. A roast pheasant with a few striped feathers still stuck in its rump, fell from nowhere and thumped him in the back.

"She has to be restrained! The walls are starting to crack!"

"I can see!"

"Ready?"

"Yes!"

"One! Two! Now!"

They both hit her simultaneously, Geralt with the Sign of Aard and Mousesack with a terrible, three-staged curse powerful enough to make the floor melt. The chair on which the princess was standing disintegrated into splinters. Pavetta barely noticed—she hung in the air within a transparent green sphere. Without ceasing to shout, she turned her head toward them and her petite face shrunk into a sinister grimace.

"By all the demons—!" roared Mousesack.

"Careful!" shouted the witcher, curling up. "Block her, Mousesack! Block her or it's the end of us!"

The table thudded heavily to the ground, shattering its trestle and everything beneath it. Crach an Craite, who was lying on the table, was thrown into the air. A heavy rain of plates and remnants of food fell; crystal carafes exploded as they hit the ground. The cornice broke away from the wall, rumbling like thunder, making the floors of the castle quake.

"Everything's letting go!" Mousesack shouted, aiming his wand at the princess. "The whole Force is going to fall on us!"

Geralt, with a blow of his sword, deflected a huge double-pronged fork which was flying straight at the druid.

"Block it, Mousesack!"

Emerald eyes sent two flashes of green lightning at them. They coiled into blinding, whirling funnels from the centers of which the Force—like a battering ram which exploded the skull, put out the eyes and paralyzed the breath—descended on them. Together with the Force, glass, majolica, platters, candlesticks, bones, nibbled loaves of bread, planks, slats and smoldering firewood from the hearth poured over them. Crying wildly like a great capercaillie, Castellan Haxo flew over their heads. The enormous head of a boiled carp splattered against Geralt's chest, on the bear passant sable and damsel of Fourhorn.

Through Mousesack's wall-shattering curses, through his own shouting and the wailing of the wounded, the din, clatter and racket, through Pavetta's wailing, the witcher suddenly heard the most terrible sound.

Coodcoodak, on his knees, was strangling Draig Bon-Dhu's bagpipes with his hands, while, with his head thrown back, he shouted over the monstrous sounds emerging from the bag, wailed and roared, cackled and croaked, bawled and squawked in a cacophony of sounds made by all known, unknown, domestic, wild and mythical animals.

Pavetta fell silent, horrified, and looked at the baron with her mouth agape. The Force eased off abruptly.

"Now!" yelled Mousesack, waving his wand. "Now, witcher!"

They hit her. The greenish sphere surrounding the princess

burst under their blow like a soap bubble and the vacuum instantly sucked in the Force raging through the room. Pavetta flopped heavily to the ground and started to weep.

After the pandemonium, a moment's silence rang in their ears; then, with difficulty, laboriously, voices started to break through the rubble and destruction, through the broken furniture and the inert bodies.

"*Cuach op arse, ghoul y badraigh mal an cuach,*" spat Crach an Craite, spraying blood from his bitten lip.

"Control yourself, Crach," said Mousesack with effort, shaking buckwheat from his front. "There are women present."

"Calanthe. My beloved. My Calanthe!" Eist Tuirseach said in the pauses between kisses.

The queen opened her eyes but didn't try to free herself from his embrace.

"Eist. People are watching," she said.

"Let them watch."

"Would somebody care to explain what that was?" asked Marshal Vissegerd, crawling from beneath a fallen tapestry.

"No," said the witcher.

"A doctor!" Windhalm of Attre, leaning over Rainfarn, shouted shrilly.

"Water!" Wieldhill, one of the brothers from Strept, called, stifling the smoldering tapestry with his jacket. "Water, quickly!"

"And beer!" Coodcoodak croaked.

A few knights, still able to stand, were trying to lift Pavetta, but she pushed their hands aside, got up on her own and, unsteadily, walked toward the hearth. There, with his back resting against the wall, sat Urcheon, awkwardly trying to remove his blood-smeared armor.

"The youth of today," snorted Mousesack, looking in their direction. "They start early! They've only got one thing on their minds."

"What's that?"

"Didn't you know, witcher, that a virgin, that is one who's untouched, wouldn't be able to use the Force?"

"To hell with her virginity," muttered Geralt. "Where did she get such a gift anyway? Neither Calanthe nor Roegner—"

"She inherited it, missing a generation, and no mistake," said the druid. "Her grandmother, Adalia, could raise a drawbridge with a twitch of her eyebrows. Hey, Geralt, look at that! She still hasn't had enough!"

Calanthe, supported by Eist Tuirseach's arm, indicated the wounded Urcheon to the guards. Geralt and Mousesack approached quickly but unnecessarily. The guards recoiled from the semi-reclining figure and, whispering and muttering, backed away.

Urcheon's monstrous snout softened, blurred and was beginning to lose its contours. The spikes and bristles rippled and became black, shiny, wavy hair and a beard which bordered a pale, angular, masculine face, dominated by a prominent nose.

"What..." stammered Eist Tuirseach. "Who's that? Urcheon?"

"Duny," said Pavetta softly.

Calanthe turned away with pursed lips.

"Cursed?" murmured Eist. "But how—"

"Midnight has struck," said the witcher. "Just this minute. The bell we heard before was early. The bell-ringer's mistake. Am I right, Calanthe?"

"Right, right," groaned the man called Duny, answering instead of the queen, who had no intention of replying anyway. "But maybe instead of standing there talking, someone could help me with this armor and call a doctor. That madman Rainfarn stabbed me under the ribs."

"What do we need a doctor for?" said Mousesack, taking out his wand.

"Enough." Calanthe straightened and raised her head proudly. "Enough of this. When all this is over, I want to see you in my chamber. All of you, as you stand. Eist, Pavetta, Mousesack, Geralt and you... Duny. Mousesack?"

"Yes, your Majesty."

"That wand of yours... I've bruised my backbone. And thereabouts."

"At your command, your Majesty."

III

"...a curse," continued Duny, rubbing his temple. "Since birth. I never found a reason for it, or who did it to me. From midnight to dawn, an ordinary man, from dawn... you saw what. Akerspaark, my father, wanted to hide it. People are superstitious in Maecht; spells and curses in the royal family could prove fatal for the dynasty. One of my father's knights took me away from court and brought me up. The two of us wandered around the world—the knight errant and his squire, and later, when he died, I journeyed alone. I can't remember who told me that a child-surprise could free me from the curse. Not long after that, I met Roegner. The rest you know."

"The rest we know, or can guess." Calanthe nodded. "Especially that you didn't wait the fifteen years agreed upon with Roegner but turned my daughter's head before that. Pavetta! Since when?"

The princess lowered her head and raised a finger.

"There. You little sorceress. Right under my nose! Let me just find out who let him into the castle at night! Let me at the ladies-in-waiting you went gathering primroses with. Primroses, dammit! Well, what am I to do with you now?"

"Calanthe—" began Eist.

"Hold on, Tuirseach. I haven't finished yet. Duny, the matter's become very complicated. You've been with Pavetta for a year now, and what? And nothing. So you negotiated the oath from the wrong father. Destiny has made a fool of you. What irony, as Geralt of Rivia, present here, is wont to say."

"To hell with destiny, oaths and irony." Duny grimaced. "I love Pavetta and she loves me; that's all that counts. You can't stand in the way of our happiness."

"I can, Duny, I can, and how." Calanthe smiled one of her unfailing smiles. "You're lucky I don't want to. I have a certain debt toward you, Duny. I'd made up my mind...I ought to ask your forgiveness, but I hate doing that. So I'm giving you Pavetta and we'll be quits. Pavetta? You haven't changed your mind, have you?"

The princess shook her head eagerly.

"Thank you, your Majesty. Thank you." Duny smiled. "You're a wise and generous queen."

"Of course I am. And beautiful."

"And beautiful."

"You can both stay in Cintra if you wish. The people here are less superstitious than the inhabitants of Maecht and adjust to things quicker. Besides, even as Urcheon you were quite pleasant. But you can't count on having the throne just yet. I intend to reign a little longer beside the new king of Cintra. The noble Eist Tuirseach of Skellige has made me a very interesting proposition."

"Calanthe—"

"Yes, Eist, I accept. I've never before listened to a confession of love while lying on the floor amidst fragments of my own throne but...How did you put it, Duny? This is all that counts and I don't advise anyone to stand in the way of my happiness. And you, what are you staring at? I'm not as old as you think."

"Today's youth," muttered Mousesack. "The apple doesn't fall far—"

"What are you muttering, sorcerer?"

"Nothing, ma'am."

"Good. While we're at it, I've got a proposition for you, Mousesack. Pavetta's going to need a teacher. She ought to learn how to use her gift. I like this castle, and I'd prefer it to remain standing. It might fall apart at my talented daughter's next attack of hysteria. How about it, Druid?"

"I'm honored."

"I think"—the queen turned her head toward the window—"it's dawn. Time to—"

She suddenly turned to where Pavetta and Duny were whispering to each other, holding hands, their foreheads all but touching.

"Duny!"

"Yes, your Majesty?"

"Do you hear? It's dawn! It's already light. And you..."

Geralt glanced at Mousesack and both started laughing.

"And why are you so happy, sorcerers? Can't you see—?"

"We can, we can," Geralt assured her.

"We were waiting until you saw for yourself," snorted Mousesack. "I was wondering when you'd catch on."

"To what?"

"That you've lifted the curse. It's you who's lifted it," said the witcher. "The moment you said 'I'm giving you Pavetta,' destiny was fulfilled."

"Exactly," confirmed the druid.

"Oh gods," said Duny slowly. "So, finally. Damn, I thought I'd be happier, that some sort of trumpets would play or... Force of habit. Your Majesty! Thank you. Pavetta, do you hear?"

"Mhm," said the princess without raising her eyes.

"And so," sighed Calanthe, looking at Geralt with tired eyes, "all's well that ends well. Don't you agree, witcher? The curse has been lifted, two weddings are on their way, it'll take about a month to repair the throne-room, there are four dead, countless wounded and Rainfarn of Attre is half-dead. Let's celebrate. Do you know, witcher, that there was a moment when I wanted to have you—"

"I know."

"But now I have to do you justice. I demanded a result and got one. Cintra is allied to Skellige. My daughter's marrying the right man. For a moment I thought all this would have been fulfilled according to destiny anyway, even if I hadn't had you brought in for the feast and sat you next to me. But I was wrong. Rainfarn's dagger could have changed destiny. And Rainfarn was stopped by a sword held by a witcher. You've done an honest job, Geralt. Now it's a question of price. Tell me what you want."

"Hold on," said Duny, fingering his bandaged side. "A question of price, you say. It is I who am in debt; it's up to me—"

"Don't interrupt." Calanthe narrowed her eyes. "Your mother-in-law hates being interrupted. Remember that. And you should know that you're not in any debt. It so happens that you were the subject of my agreement with Geralt. I said we're quits and I don't see the sense of my having to endlessly apologize to you for it. But the agreement still binds me. Well, Geralt. Your price."

"Very well," said the witcher. "I ask for your green sash, Calanthe. May it always remind me of the color of the eyes of the most beautiful queen I have ever known."

Calanthe laughed, and unfastened her emerald necklace.

"This trinket," she said, "has stones of the right hue. Keep it, and the memory."

"May I speak?" asked Duny modestly.

"But of course, son-in-law, please do, please do."

"I still say I am in your debt, witcher. It is my life that Rainfarn's dagger endangered. I would have been beaten to death by the guards without you. If there's talk of a price, then I should be the one to pay. I assure you I can afford it. What do you ask, Geralt?"

"Duny," said Geralt slowly, "a witcher who is asked such a question has to ask to have it repeated."

"I repeat, therefore. Because, you see, I am in your debt for still another reason. When I found out who you were, there in the hall, I hated you and thought very badly of you. I took you for a blind, bloodthirsty tool, for someone who kills coldly and without question, who wipes his blade clean of blood and counts the cash. But I've become convinced that the witcher's profession is worthy of respect. You protect us not only from the evil lurking in the darkness, but also from that which lies within ourselves. It's a shame there are so few of you."

Calanthe smiled.

For the first time that night, Geralt was inclined to believe it was genuine.

"My son-in-law has spoken well. I have to add two words to what he said. Precisely two. Forgive, Geralt."

"And I," said Duny, "ask again. What do you ask for?"

"Duny," said Geralt seriously, "Calanthe, Pavetta. And you, righteous knight Tuirseach, future king of Cintra. In order to become a witcher, you have to be born in the shadow of destiny, and very few are born like that. That's why there are so few of us. We're growing old, dying, without anyone to pass our knowledge, our gifts, on to. We lack successors. And this world is full of Evil which waits for the day none of us are left."

"Geralt," whispered Calanthe.

"Yes, you're not wrong, queen. Duny! You will give me that

which you already have but do not know. I'll return to Cintra in six years to see if destiny has been kind to me."

"Pavetta." Duny opened his eyes wide. "Surely you're not—"

"Pavetta!" exclaimed Calanthe. "Are you . . . are you—?"

The princess lowered her eyes and blushed. Then replied.

CHAPTER FIVE

THE VOICE OF REASON

"Geralt! Hey! Are you there?"

He raised his head from the coarse, yellowed pages of *The History of the World* by Roderick de Novembre, an interesting if controversial work which he had been studying since the previous day.

"Yes, I am. What's happened, Nenneke? Do you need me?"

"You've got a guest."

"Again? Who's it this time? Duke Hereward himself?"

"No. It's Dandelion this time, your fellow. That idler, parasite and good-for-nothing, that priest of art, the bright-shining star of the ballad and love poem. As usual, he's radiant with fame, puffed up like a pig's bladder and stinking of beer. Do you want to see him?"

"Of course. He's my friend, after all."

Nenneke, peeved, shrugged her shoulders. "I can't understand that friendship. He's your absolute opposite."

"Opposites attract."

"Obviously. There, he's coming." She indicated with her head. "Your famous poet."

"He really is a famous poet, Nenneke. Surely you're not going to claim you've never heard his ballads."

"I've heard them." The priestess winced. "Yes, indeed. Well, I don't know much about it, but maybe the ability to jump from touching lyricism to obscenities so easily is a talent. Never mind. Forgive me, but I won't keep you company. I'm not in the mood for either his poetry or his vulgar jokes."

A peal of laughter and the strumming of a lute resounded in the corridor and there, on the threshold of the library, stood Dandelion in a lilac jerkin with lace cuffs, his hat askew. The troubadour bowed exaggeratedly at the sight of Nenneke, the heron feather pinned to his hat sweeping the floor.

"My deepest respects, venerable mother," he whined stupidly. "Praise be the Great Melitele and her priestesses, the springs of virtue and wisdom—"

"Stop talking bullshit," snorted Nenneke. "And don't call me mother. The very idea that you could be my son fills me with horror."

She turned on her heel and left, her trailing robe rustling. Dandelion, aping her, sketched a parody bow.

"She hasn't changed a bit," he said cheerfully. "She still can't take a joke. She's furious because I chatted a bit to the gatekeeper when I got here, a pretty blonde with long lashes and a virgin's plait reaching down to her cute little bottom, which it would be a sin not to pinch. So I did and Nenneke, who had just arrived... Ah, what the deuce. Greetings, Geralt."

"Greetings, Dandelion. How did you know I was here?"

The poet straightened himself and yanked his trousers up. "I was in Wyzim," he said. "I heard about the striga, and that you were wounded. I guessed where you would come to recuperate. I see you're well now, are you?"

"You see correctly, but try explaining that to Nenneke. Sit, let's talk."

Dandelion sat and peeped into the book lying on the

lectern. "History?" He smiled. "Roderick de Novembre? I've read him, I have. History was second on my list of favorite subjects when I was studying at the Academy in Oxenfurt."

"What was first?"

"Geography," said the poet seriously. "The atlas was bigger and it was easier to hide a demijohn of vodka behind it."

Geralt laughed dryly, got up, removed Lunin and Tyrss's *The Arcane Mysteries of Magic and Alchemy* from the shelf and pulled a round-bellied vessel wrapped in straw from behind the bulky volume and into the light of day.

"Oho." The bard visibly cheered up. "Wisdom and inspiration, I see, are still to be found in libraries. Oooh! I like this! Plum, isn't it? Yes, this is true alchemy. This is a philosopher's stone well worth studying. Your health, brother. Ooooh, it's strong as the plague!"

"What brings you here?" Geralt took the demijohn over from the poet, took a sip and started to cough, fingering his bandaged neck. "Where are you going?"

"Nowhere. That is, I could go where you're going. I could keep you company. Do you intend staying here long?"

"Not long. The local duke let it be known I'm not welcome."

"Hereward?" Dandelion knew all the kings, princes, lords and feudal lords from Jaruga to the Dragon Mountains. "Don't you give a damn. He won't dare fall foul of Nenneke, or Melitele. The people would set fire to his castle."

"I don't want any trouble. And I've been sitting here for too long anyway. I'm going south, Dandelion. Far south. I won't find any work here. Civilization. What the hell do they need a witcher here for? When I ask after employment, they look at me as if I'm a freak."

"What are you talking about? What civilization? I crossed Buina a week ago and heard all sorts of stories as I rode through the country. Apparently there are water sprites here, myriapodans, chimera, flying drakes, every possible filth. You should be up to your ears in work."

"Stories, well, I've heard them too. Half of them are either made up or exaggerated. No, Dandelion. The world is changing. Something's coming to an end."

The poet took a long pull at the demijohn, narrowed his eyes and sighed heavily. "Are you crying over your sad fate as a witcher again? And philosophizing on top of that? I perceive the disastrous effects of inappropriate literature, because the fact that the world is changing occurred even to that old fart Roderick de Novembre. The changeability of the world is, as it happens, the only thesis in this treatise you can agree with. But it's not so innovative you have to ply me with it and put on the face of a great thinker—which doesn't suit you in the least."

Instead of answering, Geralt took a sip from the demijohn.

"Yes, yes," sighed Dandelion anew. "The world is changing, the sun sets, and the vodka is coming to an end. What else, in your opinion, is coming to an end? You mentioned something about endings, philosopher."

"I'll give you a couple of examples," said Geralt after a moment's silence, "all from two months this side of the Buina. One day I ride up and what do I see? A bridge. And under that bridge sits a troll and demands every passerby pays him. Those who refuse have a leg injured, sometimes both. So I go to the alderman: 'How much will you give me for that troll?' He's amazed. 'What are you talking about?' he asks. 'Who will repair the bridge if the troll's not there? He repairs it regularly with the sweat of his brow, solid work, first rate. It's cheaper to pay his toll.' So I ride on, and what do I see? A forktail. Not very big, about four yards nose-tip to tail-tip. It's flying, carrying a sheep in its talons. I go to the village. 'How much,' I ask, 'will you pay me for the forktail?' The peasants fall on their knees. 'No!' they shout. 'It's our baron's youngest daughter's favorite dragon. If a scale falls from its back, the baron will burn our hamlet, and skin us.' I ride on, and I'm getting hungrier and hungrier. I ask around for work. Certainly it's there, but what work? To catch a rusalka for one man, a nymph for another, a dryad for a third . . . They've gone completely mad—the villages are teeming with girls but they want humanoids. Another asks me to kill a mecopteran and bring him a bone from its hand because, crushed and poured into a soup, it cures impotence—"

"That's rubbish," interrupted Dandelion. "I've tried it. It doesn't strengthen anything and it makes the soup taste of old socks. But if people believe it and are inclined to pay—"

"I'm not going to kill mecopterans. Nor any other harmless creatures."

"Then you'll go hungry. Unless you change your line of work."

"To what?"

"Whatever. Become a priest. You wouldn't be bad at it with all your scruples, your morality, your knowledge of people and of everything. The fact that you don't believe in any gods shouldn't be a problem—I don't know many priests who do. Become a priest and stop feeling sorry for yourself."

"I'm not feeling sorry for myself. I'm stating the facts."

Dandelion crossed his legs and examined his worn sole with interest. "You remind me, Geralt, of an old fisherman who, toward the end of his life, discovers that fish stink and the breeze from the sea makes your bones ache. Be consistent. Talking and regretting won't get you anywhere. If I were to find that the demand for poetry had come to an end, I'd hang up my lute and become a gardener. I'd grow roses."

"Nonsense. You're not capable of giving it up."

"Well," agreed the poet, still staring at his sole, "maybe not.

But our professions differ somewhat. The demand for poetry and the sound of lute strings will never decline. It's worse with your trade. You witchers, after all, deprive yourselves of work, slowly but surely. The better and the more conscientiously you work, the less work there is for you. After all, your goal is a world without monsters, a world which is peaceful and safe. A world where witchers are unnecessary. A paradox, isn't it?"

"True."

"In the past, when unicorns still existed, there was quite a large group of girls who took care of their virtue in order to be able to hunt them. Do you remember? And the ratcatchers with pipes? Everybody was fighting over their services. But they were finished off by alchemists and their effective poisons and then domesticated ferrets and weasels. The little animals were cheaper, nicer and didn't guzzle so much beer. Notice the analogy?"

"I do."

"So use other people's experiences. The unicorn virgins, when they lost their jobs, immediately popped their cherry. Some, eager to make up for the years of sacrifice, became famous far and wide for their technique and zeal. The rat-catchers... Well, you'd better not copy them, because they, to a man, took to drink and went to the dogs. Well, now it looks as if the time's come for witchers. You're reading Roderick de Novembre? As far as I remember, there are mentions of witchers there, of the first ones who started work some three hundred years ago. In the days when the peasants used to go to reap the harvest in armed bands, when villages were surrounded by a triple stockade, when merchant caravans looked like the march of regular troops, and loaded catapults stood on the ramparts of the few towns night and day. Because it was us, human beings, who were the intruders here. This land was ruled by dragons, manticores, griffins and amphisboenas, vampires and werewolves, striga, kikimoras, chimera and flying drakes. And this land had to be taken from them bit by bit, every valley, every mountain pass, every forest and every meadow. And we didn't manage that without the invaluable help of witchers. But those times have gone, Geralt, irrevocably gone. The baron won't allow a forktail to be killed because it's the last draconid for a thousand miles and no longer gives rise to fear but rather to compassion and nostalgia for times passed. The troll under the bridge gets on with people. He's not a monster used to frighten children. He's a relic and a local attraction—and a useful one at that. And chimera, manticores and amphisboenas? They dwell in virgin forests and inaccessible mountains—"

"So I was right. Something is coming to an end. Whether you like it or not, something's coming to an end."

"I don't like you mouthing banal platitudes. I don't like your expression when you do it. What's happening to you? I don't recognize you, Geralt. Ah, plague on it, let's go south as soon as possible, to those wild countries. As soon as you've cut down a couple of monsters, your blues will disappear. And there's supposed to be a fair number of monsters down there. They say that when an old woman's tired of life, she goes alone and weaponless into the woods to collect brushwood. The consequences are guaranteed. You should go and settle there for good."

"Maybe I should. But I won't."

"Why? It's easier for a witcher to make money there."

"Easier to make money." Geralt took a sip from the demijohn. "But harder to spend it. And on top of that, they eat pearl barley and millet, the beer tastes like piss, the girls don't wash and the mosquitoes bite."

Dandelion chuckled loudly and rested his head against the bookshelf, on the leather-bound volumes.

"Millet and mosquitoes! That reminds me of our first

expedition together to the edge of the world," he said. "Do you remember? We met at the fête in Gulet and you persuaded me—"

"You persuaded me! You had to flee from Gulet as fast as your horse could carry you because the girl you'd knocked up under the musicians' podium had four sturdy brothers. They were looking for you all over town, threatening to geld you and cover you in pitch and sawdust. That's why you hung on to me then."

"And you almost jumped out of your pants with joy to have a companion. Until then, you only had your horse for company. But you're right; it was as you say. I did have to disappear for a while, and the Valley of Flowers seemed just right for my purpose. It was, after all, supposed to be the edge of the inhabited world, the last outpost of civilization, the furthest point on the border of two worlds... Remember?"

"I remember."

THE EDGE OF THE WORLD

I

Dandelion came down the steps of the inn carefully, carrying two tankards dripping with froth. Cursing under his breath, he squeezed through a group of curious children and crossed the yard at a diagonal, avoiding the cowpats.

A number of villagers had already gathered round the table in the courtyard where the witcher was talking to the alderman. The poet set the tankards down and found a seat. He realized straight away that the conversation hadn't advanced a jot during his short absence.

"I'm a witcher, sir," Geralt repeated for the umpteenth time, wiping beer froth from his lips. "I don't sell anything. I don't go around enlisting men for the army and I don't know how to treat glanders. I'm a witcher."

"It's a profession," explained Dandelion yet again. "A witcher, do you understand? He kills strigas and specters. He exterminates all sorts of vermin. Professionally, for money. Do you get it, alderman?"

"Aha!" The alderman's brow, deeply furrowed in thought, grew smoother. "A witcher! You should have said so right away!"

"Exactly," agreed Geralt. "So now I'll ask you: is there any work to be found around here for me?"

"Aaaa." The alderman quite visibly started to think again. "Work? Maybe those...Well...werethings? You're asking are there any werethings hereabouts?"

The witcher smiled and nodded, rubbing an itching eyelid with his knuckles.

"That there are," the alderman concluded after a fair while. "Only look ye yonder, see ye those mountains? There's elves live there; that there is their kingdom. Their palaces, hear ye, are all of pure gold. Oh aye, sir! Elves, I tell ye. 'Tis awful. He who yonder goes, never returns."

"I thought so," said Geralt coldly. "Which is precisely why I don't intend going there."

Dandelion chuckled impudently.

The alderman pondered a long while, just as Geralt had expected.

"Aha," he said at last. "Well, aye. But there be other werethings here too. From the land of elves they come, to be sure. Oh, sir, there be many, many. 'Tis hard to count them all. But the worst, that be the Bane, am I right, my good men?"

The "good men" came to life and besieged the table from all sides.

"Bane!" said one. "Aye, aye, 'tis true what the alderman says. A pale virgin, she walks the cottages at daybreak, and the children, they die!"

"And imps," added another, a soldier from the watchtower. "They tangle up the horses' manes in the stables!"

"And bats! There be bats here!"

"And myriapodans! You come up all in spots because of them!"

The next few minutes passed in a recital of the monsters which plagued the local peasants with their dishonorable doings, or their simple existence. Geralt and Dandelion learned of misguids and mamunes, which prevent an honest peasant from finding his way home in a drunken stupor, of the flying drake which drinks milk from cows, of the head on spider's legs which runs around in the forest, of hobolds which wear red hats and about a dangerous pike which tears linen from women's hands as they wash it—and just you wait and it'll be at the women themselves. They weren't spared hearing that old Nan the Hag flies on a broom at night and performs abortions in the day, that the miller tampers with the flour by mixing it with powdered acorns and that a certain Duda believed the royal steward to be a thief and scoundrel.

Geralt listened to all this calmly, nodding with feigned interest, and asked a few questions about the roads and layout of the land, after which he rose and nodded to Dandelion.

"Well, take care, my good people," he said. "I'll be back soon; then we'll see what can be done."

They rode away in silence alongside the cottages and fences, accompanied by yapping dogs and screaming children.

"Geralt," said Dandelion, standing in the stirrups to pick a fine apple from a branch which stretched over the orchard fence, "all the way you've been complaining about it being harder and harder to find work. Yet from what I just heard, it looks as if you could work here without break until winter. You'd make a penny or two, and I'd have some beautiful subjects for my ballads. So explain why we're riding on."

"I wouldn't make a penny, Dandelion."

"Why?"

"Because there wasn't a word of truth in what they said."

"I beg your pardon?"

"None of the creatures they mentioned exist."

"You're joking!" Dandelion spat out a pip and threw the apple core at a patched mongrel. "No, it's impossible. I was watching them carefully, and I know people. They weren't lying."

"No," the witcher agreed. "They weren't lying. They firmly believed it all. Which doesn't change the facts."

The poet was silent for a while.

"None of those monsters...None? It can't be. Something of what they listed must be here. At least one! Admit it."

"All right. I admit it. One does exist for sure."

"Ha! What?"

"A bat."

They rode out beyond the last fences, on to a highway between beds yellow with oilseed and cornfields rolling in the wind. Loaded carts traveled past them in the opposite direction. The bard pulled his leg over the saddle-bow, rested his lute on his knee and strummed nostalgic tunes, waving from time to time at the giggling, scantily clad girls wandering along the sides of the road carrying rakes on their robust shoulders.

"Geralt," he said suddenly, "but monsters do exist. Maybe not as many as before, maybe they don't lurk behind every tree in the forest, but they are there. They exist. So how do you account for people inventing ones, then? What's more, believing in what they invent? Eh, famous witcher? Haven't you wondered why?"

"I have, famous poet. And I know why."

"I'm curious."

"People"—Geralt turned his head—"like to invent monsters and monstrosities. Then they seem less monstrous themselves. When they get blind-drunk, cheat, steal, beat their wives, starve an old woman, when they kill a trapped fox with an axe or riddle the last existing unicorn with arrows, they like to think that the Bane entering cottages at daybreak is more monstrous than they are. They feel better then. They find it easier to live."

"I'll remember that," said Dandelion, after a moment's silence. "I'll find some rhymes and compose a ballad about it."

"Do. But don't expect a great applause."

They rode slowly but lost the last cottages of the hamlet from sight. Soon they had climbed the row of forested hills.

"Ha." Dandelion halted his horse and looked around. "Look, Geralt. Isn't it beautiful here? Idyllic, damn it. A feast for the eyes!"

The land sloped gently down to a mosaic of flat, even fields picked out in variously colored crops. In the middle, round and regular like a leaf of clover, sparkled the deep waters of three lakes surrounded by dark strips of alder thickets. The horizon was traced by a misty blue line of mountains rising above the black, shapeless stretch of forest.

"We're riding on, Dandelion."

The road led straight toward the lakes alongside dykes and ponds hidden by alder trees and filled with quacking mallards, garganeys, herons and grebes. The richness of bird life was surprising alongside the signs of human activity—the dykes were well maintained and covered with fascines, while the sluice gates had been reinforced with stones and beams. The outlet boxes, which were not in the least rotten, trickled merrily with water. Canoes and jetties were visible in the reeds by the lakes and bars of set nets and fish-pots were poking out of the deep waters.

Dandelion suddenly looked around.

"Someone's following us," he said, excited. "In a cart!"

"Incredible," scoffed the witcher without looking around. "In a cart? And I thought that the locals rode on bats."

"Do you know what?" growled the troubadour. "The closer we get to the edge of the world, the sharper your wit. I dread to think what it will come to!"

They weren't riding fast and the empty cart, drawn by two piebald horses, quickly caught up with them.

"Woooooaaaaahhhh!" The driver brought the horses to a halt just behind them. He was wearing a sheepskin over his bare skin and his hair reached down to his brows. "The gods be praised, noble sirs!"

"We, too," replied Dandelion, familiar with the custom, "praise them."

"If we want to," murmured the witcher.

"I call myself Nettly," announced the carter. "I was watching ye speak to the alderman at Upper Posada. I know ye tae be a witcher."

Geralt let go of the reins and let his mare snort at the roadside nettles.

"I did hear," Nettly continued, "the alderman prattle ye stories. I marked your expression and 'twas nae strange to me. In a long time now I've nae heard such balderdash and lies."

Dandelion laughed.

Geralt was looking at the peasant attentively, silently.

Nettly cleared his throat. "Care ye nae to be hired for real, proper work, sir?" he asked. "There'd be something I have for ye."

"And what is that?"

Nettly didn't lower his eyes. "It be nae good to speak of business on the road. Let us drive on to my home, to Lower Posada. There we'll speak. Anyways, 'tis that way ye be heading."

"Why are you so sure?"

"As 'cos ye have nae other way here, and yer horses' noses be turned in that direction, not their butts."

Dandelion laughed again. "What do you say to that, Geralt?"

"Nothing," said the witcher. "It's no good to talk on the road. On our way, then, honorable Nettly."

"Tie ye the horses to the frame, and sit yerselves down in the cart," the peasant proposed. "It be more comfortable for ye. Why rack yer arses on the saddle?"

"Too true."

They climbed onto the cart. The witcher stretched out comfortably on the straw. Dandelion, evidently afraid of getting his elegant green jerkin dirty, sat on the plank. Nettly clucked his tongue at the horses and the vehicle clattered along the beam-reinforced dyke.

They crossed a bridge over a canal overgrown with water lilies and duckweed, and passed a strip of cut meadows. Cultivated fields stretched as far as the eye could see.

"It's hard to believe that this should be the edge of the world, the edge of civilization," said Dandelion. "Just look, Geralt. Rye like gold, and a mounted peasant could hide in that corn. Or that oilseed, look, how enormous."

"You know about agriculture?"

"We poets have to know about everything," said Dandelion haughtily. "Otherwise we'd compromise our work. One has to learn, my dear fellow, learn. The fate of the world depends on agriculture, so it's good to know about it. Agriculture feeds, clothes, protects from the cold, provides entertainment and supports art."

"You've exaggerated a bit with the entertainment and art."

"And booze, what's that made of?"

"I get it."

"Not very much, you don't. Learn. Look at those purple flowers. They're lupins."

"They's be vetch, to be true," interrupted Nettly. "Have ye nae seen lupins, or what? But ye have hit exact with one thing, sir. Everything seeds mightily here, and grows as to make the heart sing. That be why 'tis called the Valley of Flowers. That be why our forefathers settled here, first ridding the land of the elves."

"The Valley of Flowers, that's Dol Blathanna." Dandelion nudged the witcher, who was stretched out on the straw, with his elbow. "You paying attention? The elves have gone but their name remains. Lack of imagination. And how do you get on with the elves here, dear host? You've got them in the mountains across the path, after all."

"We nae mix with each other. Each to his own."

"The best solution," said the poet. "Isn't that right, Geralt?"

The witcher didn't reply.

II

"Thank you for the spread." Geralt licked the bone spoon clean and dropped it into the empty bowl. "A hundred thanks, dear host. And now, if you permit, we'll get down to business."

"Well, that we can," agreed Nettly. "What say ye, Dhun?"

Dhun, the elder of Lower Posada, a huge man with a gloomy expression, nodded to the girls who swiftly removed the dishes from the table and left the room, to the obvious regret of Dandelion, who had been grinning at them ever since the feast began, and making them giggle at his gross jokes.

"I'm listening," said Geralt, looking at the window from where the rapping of an axe and the sound of a saw drifted. Some sort of woodwork was going on in the yard and the sharp, resinous smell was penetrating the room. "Tell me how I can be of use to you."

Nettly glanced at Dhun.

The elder of the village nodded and cleared his throat. "Well, it be like this," he said. "There be this field hereabouts—"

Geralt kicked Dandelion—who was preparing to make a spiteful comment—under the table.

"—a field," continued Dhun. "Be I right, Nettly? A long time, that field there, it lay fallow, but we set it to the plough and now, 'tis on it we sow hemp, hops and flax. It be a grand piece of field, I tell ye. Stretches right up to the forest—"

"And what?" The poet couldn't help himself. "What's on that field there?"

"Well." Dhun raised his head and scratched himself behind the ear. "Well, there be a deovel prowls there."

"What?" snorted Dandelion. "A what?"

"I tell ye: a deovel."

"What deovel?"

"What can he be? A deovel and that be it."

"Devils don't exist!"

"Don't interrupt, Dandelion," said Geralt in a calm voice. "And go on, honorable Dhun."

"I tell ye: it's a deovel."

"I heard you." Geralt could be incredibly patient when he chose. "Tell me, what does he look like, where did he come from, how does he bother you? One thing at a time, if you please."

"Well"—Dhun raised his gnarled hand and started to count with great difficulty, folding his fingers over, one at a time—"one thing at a time. Forsooth, ye be a wise man. Well, it be like this. He looks, sir, like a deovel, for all the world like a deovel. Where did he come from? Well, nowhere. Crash, bang, wallop and there we have him: a deovel. And bother us, forsooth he doesnae bother us overly. There be times he even helps."

"Helps?" cackled Dandelion, trying to remove a fly from his beer. "A devil?"

"Don't interrupt, Dandelion. Carry on, Dhun, sir. How does he help you, this, as you say—"

"Deovel," repeated the freeman with emphasis. "Well, this be how he helps: he fertilizes the land, he turns the soil, he gets rid of the moles, scares birds away, watches over the turnips and beetroots. Oh, and he eats the caterpillars he does, they as do hatch in the cabbages. But the cabbages, he eats them too, forsooth. Nothing but guzzle, be what he does. Just like a deovel."

Dandelion cackled again, then flicked a beer-drenched fly at a cat sleeping by the hearth. The cat opened one eye and glanced at the bard reproachfully.

"Nevertheless," the witcher said calmly, "you're ready to pay me to get rid of him, am I right? In other words, you don't want him in the vicinity?"

"And who"—Dhun looked at him gloomily—"would care to have a deovel on his birthright soil? This be our land since forever, bestowed upon us by the king and it has nought to do with the deovel. We spit on his help. We've got hands ourselves, have we not? And he, sir, is nay a deovel but a malicious beast and has got so much, forgive the word, shite in his head as be hard to bear. There be no knowing what will come into his head. Once he fouled the well, then chased a lass, frightening and threatening to fuck her. He steals, sir, our belongings and victuals. He destroys and breaks things, makes a nuisance of himself, churns the dykes, digs ditches like some muskrat or beaver—the water from one pond trickled out completely and the carp in it died. He smoked a pipe in the haystack he did, the son-of-a-whore, and all the hay it went up in smoke—"

"I see," interrupted Geralt. "So he does bother you."

"Nay." Dhun shook his head. "He doesnae bother us. He be simply up to mischief, that's what he be."

Dandelion turned to the window, muffling his laughter.

The witcher kept silent.

"Oh, what be there to talk about," said Nettly who had been silent until then. "Ye be a witcher, nae? So do ye something about this deovel. It be work ye be looking for in Upper Posada. I heard so myself. So ye have work. We'll pay ye what needs be. But take note: we don't want ye killing the deovel. No way."

The witcher raised his head and smiled nastily. "Interesting," he said. "Unusual, I'd say."

"What?" Dhun frowned.

"An unusual condition. Why all this mercy?"

"He should nae be killed." Dhun frowned even more. "Because in this Valley—"

"He should nae and that be it," interrupted Nettly. "Only catch him, sir, or drive him off yon o'er the seventh mountain. And ye will nae be hard done by when ye be paid."

The witcher stayed silent, still smiling.

"Seal it, will ye, the deal?" asked Dhun.

"First, I'd like a look at him, this devil of yours."

The freemen glanced at each other.

"It be yer right," said Nettly, then stood up. "And yer will. The deovel he do prowl the whole neighborhood at night but at day he dwells somewhere in the hemp. Or among the old willows on the marshland. Ye can take a look at him there. We won't hasten ye. Ye be wanting rest, then rest as long as ye will. Ye will nae go wanting in comfort and food as befits the custom of hospitality. Take care."

"Geralt." Dandelion jolted up from his stool and looked out into the yard at the freemen walking away from the cottage. "I can't understand anything anymore. A day hasn't gone by since our chat about imagined monsters and you suddenly get yourself hired hunting devils. And everybody—except ignorant freemen obviously—knows that devils are an invention;

they're mythical creatures. What's this unexpected zeal of yours supposed to mean? Knowing you a little as I do, I take it you haven't abased yourself so as to get us bed, board and lodging, have you?"

"Indeed." Geralt grimaced. "It does look as if you know me a little, singer."

"In that case, I don't understand."

"What is there to understand?"

"There's no such things as devils!" yelled the poet, shaking the cat from sleep once and for all. "No such thing! To the devil with it, devils don't exist!"

"True." Geralt smiled. "But, Dandelion, I could never resist the temptation of having a look at something that doesn't exist."

III

"One thing is certain," muttered the witcher, sweeping his eyes over the tangled jungle of hemp spreading before them. "This devil is not stupid."

"How did you deduce that?" Dandelion was curious. "From the fact that he's sitting in an impenetrable thicket? Any old hare has enough brains for that."

"It's a question of the special qualities of hemp. A field of this size emits a strong aura against magic. Most spells will be useless here. And there, look, do you see those poles? Those are hops—their pollen has the same effect. It's not mere chance. The rascal senses the aura and knows he's safe here."

Dandelion coughed and adjusted his breeches. "I'm curious." He scratched his forehead beneath his hat. "How are you going to go about it, Geralt? I've never seen you work. I take it you know a thing or two about catching devils—I'm trying to recall some ballads. There was one about a devil and a woman. Rude, but amusing. The woman, you see—"

"Spare me, Dandelion."

"As you wish. I only wanted to be helpful, that's all. And you shouldn't scorn ancient songs. There's wisdom in them, accumulated over generations. There's a ballad about a farm-hand called Slow, who—"

"Stop wittering. We have to earn our board and lodging."

"What do you want to do?"

"Rummage around a bit in the hemp."

"That's original," snorted the troubadour. "Though not too refined."

"And you, how would you go about it?"

"Intelligently." Dandelion sniffed. "Craftily. With a hound-ing, for example. I'd chase the devil out of the thicket, chase him on horseback, in the open field, and lasso him. What do you think of that?"

"Interesting. Who knows, maybe it could be done, if you took part—because at least two of us are needed for an enter-prise like that. But we're not going hunting yet. I want to find out what this thing is, this devil. That's why I'm going to rummage about in the hemp."

"Hey!" The bard had only just noticed. "You haven't brought your sword!"

"What for? I know some ballads about devils, too. Neither the woman nor Slow the farmhand used a sword."

"Hmm…" Dandelion looked around. "Do we have to squeeze through the very middle of this thicket?"

"You don't have to. You can go back to the village and wait for me."

"Oh, no," protested the poet. "And miss a chance like this? I want to see a devil too, see if he's as terrible as they claim. I was asking if we have to force our way through the hemp when there's a path."

"Quite right." Geralt shaded his eyes with his hand. "There is a path. So let's use it."

"And what if it's the devil's path?"

"All the better. We won't have to walk too far."

"Do you know, Geralt," babbled the bard, following the witcher along the narrow, uneven path among the hemp. "I always thought the devil was just a metaphor invented for cursing: 'go to the devil', 'to the devil with it', 'may the devil.' Lowlanders say: 'The devils are bringing us guests,' while dwarves have 'Duvvel hoael' when they get something wrong, and call poor-blooded livestock devvelsheyss. And in the Old Language, there's a saying, 'A d'yaebl aep arse,' which means—"

"I know what it means. You're babbling, Dandelion."

Dandelion stopped talking, took off the hat decorated with a heron's feather, fanned himself with it and wiped his sweaty brow. The humid, stifling heat, intensified by the smell of grass and weeds in blossom, dominated the thicket. The path curved a little and, just beyond the bend, ended in a small clearing which had been stamped in the weeds.

"Look, Dandelion."

In the very center of the clearing lay a large, flat stone, and on it stood several clay bowls. An almost burnt-out tallow candle was set among the bowls. Geralt saw some grains of corn and broad beans among the unrecognizable pips and seeds stuck in the flakes of melted fat.

"As I suspected," he muttered. "They're bringing him offerings."

"That's just it," said the poet, indicating the candle. "And they burn a tallow candle for the devil. But they're feeding him seeds, I see, as if he were a finch. Plague, what a bloody pigsty. Everything here is all sticky with honey and birch tar. What—"

The bard's next words were drowned by a loud, sinister bleating. Something rustled and stamped in the hemp; then the strangest creature Geralt had ever seen emerged from the thicket.

The creature was about half a rod tall with bulging eyes and a goat's horns and beard. The mouth, a soft, busy slit, also brought a chewing goat to mind. Its nether regions were covered with long, thick, dark-red hair right down to the cleft hooves. The devil had a long tail ending in a brush-like tassel which wagged energetically.

"Uk! Uk!" barked the monster, stamping his hooves. "What do you want here? Leave! Leave or I'll ram you down. Uk! Uk!"

"Has anyone ever kicked your arse, little goat?" Dandelion couldn't stop himself.

"Uk! Uk! Beeeeee!" bleated the goathorn in agreement, or denial, or simply bleating for the sake of it.

"Shut up, Dandelion," growled the witcher. "Not a word."

"Blebleblebeeeee!" The creature gurgled furiously, his lips parting wide to expose yellow horse-like teeth. "Uk! Uk! Bleubeeeeubleuuuuubleeeeeeee!"

"Most certainly"—nodded Dandelion—"you can take the barrel-organ and bell when you go home—"

"Stop it, damn you," hissed Geralt. "Keep your stupid jokes to yourself—"

"Jokes!" roared the goathorn loudly and leapt up. "Jokes? New jokers have come, have they? They've brought iron balls, have they? I'll give you iron balls, you scoundrels, you. Uk! Uk! Uk! You want to joke, do you? Here are some jokes for you! Here are your balls!"

The creature sprang up and gave a sudden swipe with

his hand. Dandelion howled and sat down hard on the path, clasping his forehead. The creature bleated and aimed again. Something whizzed past Geralt's ear.

"Here are your balls! Brrreee!"

An iron ball, an inch in diameter, thwacked the witcher in the shoulder and the next hit Dandelion in the knee. The poet cursed foully and scrambled away, Geralt running after him as balls whizzed above his head.

"Uk! Uk!" screamed the goathorn, leaping up and down. "I'll give you balls! You shitty jokers!"

Another ball whizzed through the air. Dandelion cursed even more foully as he grabbed the back of his head. Geralt threw himself to one side, among the hemp, but didn't avoid the ball that hit him in the shoulder. The goathorn's aim was true and he appeared to have an endless supply of balls. The witcher, stumbling through the thicket, heard yet another triumphant bleat from the victorious goathorn, followed by the whistle of a flying ball, a curse and the patter of Dandelion's feet scurrying away along the path.

And then silence fell.

IV

"Well, well, Geralt." Dandelion held a horseshoe he'd cooled in a bucket to his forehead. "That's not what I expected. A horned freak with a goatee like a shaggy billy goat, and he chased you away like some upstart. And I got it in the head. Look at that bump!"

"That's the sixth time you've shown it to me. And it's no more interesting now than it was the first time."

"How charming. And I thought I'd be safe with you!"

"I didn't ask you to traipse after me in the hemp, and I did

ask you to keep that foul tongue of yours quiet. You didn't
listen, so now you can suffer. In silence, please, because they're
just coming."

Nettly and Dhun walked into the dayroom. Behind them
hobbled a gray-haired old woman, twisted as a pretzel, led by
a fair-haired and painfully thin teenage girl.

"Honorable Dhun, honorable Nettly," the witcher began
without introduction. "I asked you, before I left, whether you
yourselves had already tried to do something with that devil
of yours. You told me you hadn't done anything. I've grounds
to think otherwise. I await your explanation."

The villagers murmured among themselves, after which
Dhun coughed into his fist and took a step forward. "Ye be
right, sir. Asking forgiveness. We lied—it be guilt devours
us. We wanted to outwit the deovel ourselves, for him to go
away—"

"By what means?"

"Here in this Valley," said Dhun slowly, "there be monsters
in the past. Flying dragons, earth myriapodans, were-brawls,
ghosts, gigantous spiders and various vipers. And all the times
we be searching in our great booke for a way to deal with all
that vermin."

"What great book?"

"Show the booke, old woman. Booke, I say. The great
booke! I'll be on the boil in a minute! Deaf as a doorknob, she
be! Lille, tell the old woman to show the booke!"

The girl tore the huge book from the taloned fingers of the
old woman and handed it to the witcher.

"In this here great booke," continued Dhun, "which be in
our family clan for time immemorial, be ways to deal with
every monster, spell and wonder in the world that has been,
is, or will be."

Geralt turned the heavy, thick, greasy, dust-encrusted

volume in his hands. The girl was still standing in front of him, wringing her apron in her hands. She was older than he had initially thought—her delicate figure had deceived him, so different from the robust build of the other girls in the village. He lay the book down on the table and turned its heavy wooden cover. "Take a look at this, Dandelion."

"The first Runes," the bard worked out, peering over his shoulder, the horseshoe still pressed to his forehead. "The writing used before the modern alphabet. Still based on elfin runes and dwarves' ideograms. A funny sentence construction, but that's how they spoke then. Interesting etchings and illuminations. It's not often you get to see something like this, Geralt, and if you do, it's in libraries belonging to temples and not villages at the edge of the world. By all the gods, where did you get that from, dear peasants? Surely you're not going to try to convince me that you can read this? Woman? Can you read the First Runes? Can you read any runes?"

"Whaaaat?"

The fair-haired girl moved closer to the woman and whispered something into her ear.

"Read?" The crone revealed her toothless gums in a smile. "Me? No, sweetheart. 'Tis a skill I've ne'er mastered."

"Explain to me," said Geralt coldly, turning to Dhun and Nettly, "how do you use the book if you can't read runes?"

"Always the oldest woman knows what stands written in the booke," said Dhun gloomily. "And what she knows, she teaches some young one, when 'tis time for her to turn to earth. Heed ye, yerselves, how 'tis time for our old woman. So our old woman has taken Lille in and she be teaching her. But for now, 'tis the old woman knows best."

"The old witch and the young witch," muttered Dandelion.

"The old woman knows the whole book by heart?" Geralt asked with disbelief. "Is that right, Grandma?"

"Nae the whole, oh nae," answered the woman, again through Lille, "only what stands written by the picture."

"Ah." Geralt opened the book at random. The picture on the torn page depicted a dappled pig with horns in the shape of a lyre. "Well then—what's written here?"

The old woman smacked her lips, took a careful look at the etching, then shut her eyes.

"The horned aurochs or Taurus," she recited, "erroneously called bison by ignoramuses. It hath horns and useth them to ram—"

"Enough. Very good, indeed." The witcher turned several sticky pages. "And here?"

"Cloud sprites and wind sprites be varied. Some rain pour, some wind roar, and others hurl their thunder. Harvests to protect from them, takest thou a knife of iron, new, of a mouse's droppings a half ounce, of a gray heron's fat—"

"Good, well done. Hmm...And here? What's this?"

The etching showed a disheveled monstrosity with enormous eyes and even larger teeth, riding a horse. In its right hand, the monstrous being wielded a substantial sword, in its left, a bag of money.

"A witchman," mumbled the woman. "Called by some a witcher. To summon him is most dangerous, albeit one must; for when against the monster and the vermin there be no aid, the witchman can contrive. But careful one must be—"

"Enough," muttered Geralt. "Enough, Grandma. Thank you."

"No, no," protested Dandelion with a malicious smile. "How does it go on? What a greatly interesting book! Go on, Granny, go on."

"Eeee...But careful one must be to touch not the witchman, for thus the mange can one acquire. And lasses do from him hide away, for lustful the witchman is above all measure—"

"Quite correct, spot on," laughed the poet, and Lille, so it seemed to Geralt, smiled almost imperceptibly.

"—though the witchman greatly covetous and greedy for gold be," mumbled the old woman, half-closing her eyes, "giveth ye not such a one more than: for a drowner, one silver penny or three halves; for a werecat, silver pennies two; for a plumard, silver pennies—"

"Those were the days," muttered the witcher. "Thank you, Grandma. And now show us where it speaks of the devil and what the book says about devils. This time 'tis grateful I'd be to heareth more, for to learn the ways and meanes ye did use to deal with him most curious am I."

"Careful, Geralt," chuckled Dandelion. "You're starting to fall into their jargon. It's an infectious mannerism."

The woman, controlling her shaking hands with difficulty, turned several pages. The witcher and the poet leaned over the table. The etching did, in effect, show the ball-thrower: horned, hairy, tailed and smiling maliciously.

"The deovel," recited the woman. "Also called 'willower' or 'sylvan.' For livestock and domestic fowl, a tiresome and great pest is he. Be it your will to chase him from your hamlet, takest thou—"

"Well, well," murmured Dandelion.

"—takest thou of nuts, one fistful," continued the woman, running her finger along the parchment. "Next, takest thou of iron balls a second fistful. Of honey an utricle, of birch tar a second. Of gray soap a firkin; of soft cheese another. There where the deovel dwelleth, goest thou when 'tis night. Commenceth then to eat the nuts. Anon, the deovel who hath great greed, will hasten and ask if they are tasty indeed. Givest to him then the balls of iron—"

"Damn you," murmured Dandelion. "Pox take—"

"Quiet," said Geralt. "Well, Grandma. Go on."

"...having broken his teeth he will be attentive as thou eatest the honey. Of said honey will he himself desire. Givest him of birch tar, then yourself eateth soft cheese. Soon, hearest thou, will the deovel grumbleth and tumbleth, but makest of it as naught. Yet if the deovel desireth soft cheese, givest him soap. For soap the deovel withstandeth not—"

"You got to the soap?" interrupted Geralt with a stony expression, turning toward Dhun and Nettly.

"In no way," groaned Nettly. "If only we had got to the balls. But he gave us what for when he bit a ball—"

"And who told you to give him so many?" Dandelion was enraged. "It stands written in the book, one fistful to take. Yet ye gaveth of balls a sackful! Ye furnished him with ammunition for two years, the fools ye be!"

"Careful." The witcher smiled. "You're starting to fall into their jargon. It's infectious."

"Thank you."

Geralt suddenly raised his head and looked into the eyes of the girl standing by the woman. Lille didn't lower her eyes. They were pale and wildly blue. "Why are you bringing the devil offerings in the form of grain?" he asked sharply. "After all, it's obvious that he's a typical herbivore."

Lille didn't answer.

"I asked you a question, girl. Don't be frightened, you won't get the mange by talking to me."

"Don't ask her anything, sir," said Nettly, with obvious unease in his voice. "Lille...She...She be strange. She won't answer you; don't force her."

Geralt kept looking into Lille's eyes, and Lille still met his gaze. He felt a shiver run down his back and creep along his shoulders.

"Why didn't you attack the devil with stancheons and pitchforks?" He raised his voice. "Why didn't you set a trap for him? If you'd wanted to, his goat's head would already be spiked on a pole to frighten crows away. You warned me not to kill him. Why? You forbade it, didn't you, Lille?"

Dhun got up from the bench. His head almost touched the beams.

"Leave, lass," he growled. "Take the old woman and leave."

"Who is she, honorable Dhun?" the witcher demanded as the door closed behind Lille and the woman. "Who is that girl? Why does she enjoy more respect from you than that bloody book?"

"It be nae yer business." Dhun looked at him, and there was no friendliness in his eyes. "Persecute wise women in your own town, burn stakes in yer own land. There has been none of it here, nor will there be."

"You didn't understand me," said the witcher coldly.

"Because I did nae try," growled Dhun.

"I noticed," Geralt said through his teeth, making no effort to be cordial. "But be so gracious as to understand something, honorable Dhun. We have no agreement. I haven't committed myself to you in any way. You have no reason to believe that you've bought yourself a witcher who, for a silver penny or three halves, will do what you can't do yourselves. Or don't want to do. Or aren't allowed to. No, honorable Dhun. You have not bought yourself a witcher yet, and I don't think you'll succeed in doing so. Not with your reluctance to understand."

Dhun remained silent, measuring Geralt with a gloomy stare.

Nettly cleared his throat and wriggled on the bench, shuffling his rag sandals on the dirt floor, then suddenly straightened up.

"Witcher, sir," he said. "Do nae be enraged. We will tell ye, what and how. Dhun?"

The elder of the village nodded and sat down.

"As we be riding here," began Nettly, "ye did notice how everything here grows, the great harvests we have? There be nae many places ye see all grow like this, if there be any such. Seedlings and seeds be so important to us that 'tis with them we pay our levies and we sell them and use them to barter—"

"What's that got to do with the devil?"

"The deovel was wont to make a nuisance of himself and play silly tricks, and then he be starting to steal a great deal of grain. At the beginning, we be bringing him a little to the stone in the hemp, thinking his fill he'd eat and leave us in peace. Naught of it. With a vengeance he went on stealing. And when we started to hide our supplies in shops and sheds, well locked and bolted, 'tis furious he grew, sir, he roared, bleated. 'Uk! Uk!' he called, and when he goes 'Uk! Uk!' ye'd do best to run for yer life. He threatened to—"

"—screw," Dandelion threw in with a ribald smile.

"That too," agreed Nettly. "Oh, and he mentioned a fire. Talk long as we may, he could nae steal so 'tis levies he demanded. He ordered grain and other goods be brought him by the sackful. Riled we were then and intending to beat his tailed arse. But—" The freeman cleared his throat and lowered his head.

"Ye need nae beat about the bush," said Dhun suddenly. "We judged the witcher wrong. Tell him everything, Nettly."

"The old woman forbade us to beat the devil," said Nettly quickly, "but we know 'tis Lille, because the woman... The woman only says what Lille tell her to. And we... Ye know yerself, sir. We listen."

"I've noticed." Geralt twisted his lips in a smile. "The woman can only waggle her chin and mumble a text which she doesn't understand herself. And you stare at the girl, with gaping mouths, as if she were the statue of a goddess. You avoid her eyes but try to guess her wishes. And her wishes are your command. Who is this Lille of yours?"

"But ye have guessed that, sir. A prophetess. A Wise One. But say naught of this to anyone. We ask ye. If word were to get to the steward, or, gods forbid, to the viceroy—"

"Don't worry," said Geralt seriously. "I know what that means and I won't betray you."

The strange women and girls, called prophetesses or Wise Ones, who could be found in villages, didn't enjoy the favor of those noblemen who collected levies and profited from farming. Farmers always consulted prophetesses on everything and believed them, blindly and boundlessly. Decisions based on their advice were often completely contrary to the politics of lords and overlords. Geralt had heard of incomprehensible decrees—the slaughter of entire pedigree herds, the cessation of sowing or harvesting, and even the migration of entire villages. Local lords therefore opposed the superstition, often brutally, and freemen very quickly learned to hide the Wise Ones. But they didn't stop listening to their advice. Because experience proved the Wise Ones were always right in the long run.

"Lille did not permit us to kill the deovel," continued Nettly. "She told us to do what the booke says. As ye well know, it did nae work out. There has already been trouble with the steward. If we give less grain in levy than be normal, 'tis bawl he will, shout and fulminate. Thus we have nay even squeaked to him of the deovel, the reason being the steward be ruthless and knows cruelly little about jokes. And then ye happened along. We asked Lille if we could . . . hire ye—"

"And?"

"She said, through the woman, that she need first of all to look at ye."

"And she did."

"That she did. And accepted ye she has, that we know. We can tell what Lille accepts and what she doesnae."

"She never said a word to me."

"She ne'er has spoken word to anyone—save the old woman. But if she had not accepted ye, she would nay have entered the room for all in the world—"

"Hmm..." Geralt reflected. "That's interesting. A prophetess who, instead of prophesying, doesn't say a word. How did she come to be among you?"

"We nae know, witcher, sir," muttered Dhun. "But as for the old woman, so the older folk remember, it be like this. The old woman afore her took a close-tongued girl under her wing too, one as which came from no one knows. And that girl she be our old woman. My grandfather would say the old woman be reborn that way. Like the moon she be reborn in the sky and ever new she be. Do nae laugh—"

"I'm not laughing." Geralt shook his head. "I've seen too much to laugh at things like that. Nor do I intend to poke my nose into your affairs, honorable Dhun. My questions aim to establish the bond between Lille and the devil. You've probably realized yourselves that one exists. So if you're anxious to be on good terms with your prophetess, then I can give you only one way to deal with the devil: you must get to like him."

"Know ye, sir," said Nettly, "it be nae only a matter of the deovel. Lille does nae let us harm anything. Any creature."

"Of course," Dandelion butted in, "country prophetesses grow from the same tree as druids. And a druid will go so far as to wish the gadfly sucking his blood to enjoy its meal."

"Ye hits it on the head." Nettly faintly smiled. "Ye hits the nail right on the head. 'Twas the same with us and the wild boars that dug up our vegetable beds. Look out the window: beds as pretty as a picture. We have found a way, Lille doesnae even know. What the eyes do nay see, the heart will nae miss. Understand?"

"I understand," muttered Geralt. "And how. But we can't move forward. Lille or no Lille, your devil is a sylvan. An exceptionally rare but intelligent creature. I won't kill him; my code doesn't allow it."

"If he be intelligent," said Dhun, "go speak reason to him."

"Just so," Nettly joined in. "If the deovel has brains, that will mean he steals grain according to reason. So ye, witcher, find out what he wants. He does nae eat that grain, after all—not so much, at least. So what does he want grain for? To spite us? What does he want? Find out and chase him off in some witcher way. Will ye do that?"

"I'll try," decided Geralt. "But..."

"But what?"

"Your book, my friends, is out of date. Do you see what I'm getting at?"

"Well, forsooth," grunted Dhun, "not really."

"I'll explain. Honorable Dhun, honorable Nettly, if you're counting on my help costing you a silver penny or three halves, then you are bloody well mistaken."

V

"Hey!"

A rustle, an angry *Uk! Uk!* and the snapping of stakes, reached them from the thicket.

"Hey!" repeated the witcher, prudently remaining hidden. "Show yourself, willower."

"Willower yourself."

"So what is it? Devil?"

"Devil yourself." The sylvan poked his head out from the hemp, baring his teeth. "What do you want?"

"To talk."

"Are you making fun of me or what? Do you think I don't know who you are? The peasants hired you to throw me out of here, eh?"

"That's right," admitted Geralt indifferently. "And that's precisely what I wanted to chat to you about. What if we were to come to an understanding?"

"That's where it hurts," bleated the sylvan. "You'd like to get off lightly, wouldn't you? Without making an effort, eh? Pull the other one! Life, my good man, means competition. The best man wins. If you want to win with me, prove you're the best. Instead of coming to an understanding, we'll have competitions. The winner dictates the conditions. I propose a race from here to the old willow on the dyke."

"I don't know where the dyke is, or the old willow."

"I wouldn't suggest the race if you knew. I like competitions but I don't like losing."

"I've noticed. No, we won't race each other. It's very hot today."

"Pity. So maybe we'll pit ourselves against each other in a different way?" The sylvan bared his yellow teeth and picked up a large stone from the ground. "Do you know the game 'Who shouts loudest?' I shout first. Close your eyes."

"I have a different proposition."

"I'm all ears."

"You leave here without any competitions, races or shouting. Of your own accord, without being forced."

"You can shove such a proposition a *d'yeabl aep arse.*" The devil demonstrated his knowledge of the Old Language. "I won't leave here. I like it here."

"But you've made too much of a nuisance of yourself here. Your pranks have gone too far."

"*Duvvelsheyss* to you with my pranks." The sylvan, as it turned out, also knew the dwarves' tongue. "And your proposition is also worth as much as a duvvelsheyss. I'm not going anywhere unless you beat me at some game. Shall I give you a chance? We'll play at riddles if you don't like physical games. I'll give you a riddle in a minute and if you guess it, you win and I leave. If you don't, I stay and you leave. Rack your brains because the riddle isn't easy."

Before Geralt could protest, the sylvan bleated, stamped his hooves, whipped the ground with his tail and recited:

> *It grows in soft clay, not far from the stream,*
> *Little pink leaves, pods small and full,*
> *It grows in soft clay, not far from the stream,*
> *On a long stalk, its flower is moist,*
> *But to a cat, please show it not,*
> *'Cos if you do, he'll eat the lot.*

"Well, what is it? Guess."

"I haven't the faintest idea," the witcher said, not even trying to think it over. "Sweet pea, perhaps?"

"Wrong. You lose."

"And what is the correct answer? What has...hmm... moist pods?"

"Cabbage."

"Listen," growled Geralt. "You're starting to get on my nerves."

"I warned you," chuckled the sylvan, "that the riddle wasn't easy. Tough. I won, I stay. And you leave. I wish you, sir, a cold farewell."

"Just a moment." The witcher surreptitiously slipped a hand

into his pocket. "And my riddle? I have the right to a revenge match, haven't I?"

"No!" protested the devil. "I might not guess it, after all. Do you take me for a fool?"

"No." Geralt shook his head. "I take you for a spiteful, arrogant dope. We're going to play quite a new game shortly, one which you don't know."

"Ha! After all! What game?"

"The game is called," said the witcher slowly, "'don't do unto others what you would not have them do to you.' You don't have to close your eyes."

Geralt stooped in a lightning throw; the one-inch iron ball whizzed sharply through the air and thwacked the sylvan straight between the horns. The creature collapsed onto his back as if hit by a thunderbolt. Geralt dived between the poles and grabbed him by one shaggy leg. The sylvan bleated and kicked. The witcher sheltered his head with his arm, but to little effect. The sylvan, despite his mean posture, kicked with the strength of an enraged mule. The witcher tried and failed to catch a kicking hoof. The sylvan flapped, thrashed his hands on the ground and kicked him again in the forehead. The witcher cursed, feeling the sylvan's leg slip from his fingers. Both, having parted, rolled in opposite directions, kicked the poles with a crash and tangled themselves up in the creeping hemp.

The sylvan was the first to jump up, and, lowering his horned head, charged. But Geralt was already on his feet and effortlessly dodged the attack, grabbed the creature by a horn, tugged hard, threw him to the ground and crushed him with his knees. The sylvan bleated and spat straight into the witcher's eyes like a camel suffering from excess saliva. The witcher instinctively stepped back without releasing the devil's horns. The sylvan, trying to toss his head, kicked with both hooves at once and—strangely—hit the mark with both. Geralt swore nastily, but didn't release his grip. He pulled the sylvan up, pinned him to the creaking poles and kicked him in a shaggy knee with all his might; then he leaned over and spat right into his ear. The sylvan howled and snapped his blunt teeth.

"Don't do unto others..." panted the witcher, "...what you would not have them do to you. Shall we play on?" The sylvan gurgled, howled and spat fiercely, but Geralt held him firmly by the horns and pressed his head down hard, making the spittle hit the sylvan's own hooves, which tore at the ground, sending up clouds of dust and weeds.

The next few minutes passed in an intense skirmish and exchange of insults and kicks. If Geralt was pleased about anything, it was only that nobody could see him—for it was a truly ridiculous sight.

The force of the next kick tore the combatants apart and threw them in opposite directions, into the hemp thicket. The sylvan got up before the witcher and rushed to escape, limping heavily. Geralt, panting and wiping his brow, rushed in pursuit. They forced their way through the hemp and ran into the hops. The witcher heard the pounding of a galloping horse, the sound he'd been waiting for.

"Here, Dandelion! Here!" he yelled. "In the hops!"

He saw the mount breast right in front of him and was knocked over. He bounced off the horse as though it were a rock and tumbled onto his back. The world darkened. He managed to roll to the side, behind the hop poles, to avoid the hooves. He sprung up nimbly but another rider rode into him, knocking him down again. Then suddenly, someone threw themselves at him and pinned him to the ground.

Then there was a flash, and a piercing pain in the back of his head.

And darkness.

VI

There was sand on his lips. When he tried to spit it out, he realized he was lying facedown on the ground. And he was tied up. He raised his head a little and heard voices.

He was lying on the forest floor, by a pine tree. Some twenty paces away stood unsaddled horses. They were obscured behind the feathery fronds of ferns, but one of those horses was, without a doubt, Dandelion's chestnut.

"Three sacks of corn," he heard. "Good, Torque. Very good. You've done well."

"That's not all," said the bleating voice, which could only be the sylvan devil. "Look at this, Galarr. It looks like beans but it's completely white. And the size of it! And this, this is called oilseed. They make oil from it."

Geralt squeezed his eyes shut, then opened them again. No, it wasn't a dream. The devil and Galarr, whoever he was, were using the Old Language, the language of elves. But the words *corn, beans,* and *oilseed* were in the common tongue.

"And this? What's this?" asked Galarr.

"Flaxseed. Flax, you know? You make shirts from flax. It's much cheaper than silk, and more hardwearing. It's quite a complicated process as far as I know but I'll find out the ins and outs."

"As long as it takes root, this flax of yours; as long as it doesn't go to waste like the turnip," grumbled Galarr, in the same strange Volapuk. "Try to get some new turnip seedlings, Torque."

"Have no fear," bleated the sylvan. "There's no problem with that here. Everything grows like hell. I'll get you some, don't worry."

"And one more thing," said Galarr. "Finally find out what that three-field system of theirs is all about."

The witcher carefully raised his head and tried to turn around.

"Geralt..." He heard a whisper. "Are you awake?"

"Dandelion..." he whispered back. "Where are we...? What's happening?"

Dandelion only grunted quietly. Geralt had had enough. He cursed, tensed himself and turned on to his side.

In the middle of the glade stood the sylvan devil with—as he now knew—the sweet name of Torque. He was busy loading sacks, bags and packs on to the horses. He was being helped by a slim, tall man who could only be Galarr. The latter, hearing the witcher move, turned around. His hair was black with a distinct hint of dark blue. He had sharp features, big, bright eyes and pointed ears.

Galarr was an elf. An elf from the mountains. A pure-blooded Aen Seidhe, a representative of the Old People.

Galarr wasn't alone. Six more sat at the edge of the glade. One was busy emptying Dandelion's packs; another strummed the troubadour's lute. The remainder, gathered around an untied sack, were greedily devouring turnips and raw carrots.

"Vanadain, Toruviel," said Galarr, indicating the prisoners with a nod of his head. "Vedrai! Enn'le!"

Torque jumped up and bleated. "No, Galarr! No! Filavandrel has forbidden it! Have you forgotten?"

"No, I haven't forgotten." Galarr threw two tied sacks across the horse's back. "But we have to check if they haven't loosened the knots."

"What do you want from us?" the troubadour moaned as

one of the elves knocked him to the ground with his knee and checked the knots. "Why are you holding us prisoners? What do you want? I'm Dandelion, a poe—"

Geralt heard the sound of a blow. He turned around, twisted his head.

The elf standing over Dandelion had black eyes and raven hair, which fell luxuriantly over her shoulders, except for two thin plaits braided at her temples. She was wearing a short leather camisole over a loose shirt of green satin, and tight woollen leggings tucked into riding boots. Her hips were wrapped around with a colored shawl which reached halfway down her thighs.

"*Que glosse?*" she asked, looking at the witcher and playing with the hilt of the long dagger in her belt. "*Que l'en pavienn, ell'ea?*"

"*Nell'ea,*" he contested. "*T'en pavienn, Aen Seidhe.*"

"Did you hear?" The elf turned to her companion, the tall Seidhe who, not bothering to check Geralt's knots, was strumming away at Dandelion's lute with an expression of indifference on his long face. "Did you hear, Vanadain? The ape-man can talk! He can even be impertinent!"

Seidhe shrugged, making the feathers decorating his jacket rustle. "All the more reason to gag him, Toruviel."

The elf leaned over Geralt. She had long lashes, an unnaturally pale complexion and parched, cracked lips. She wore a necklace of carved golden birch pieces on a thong, wrapped around her neck several times.

"Well, say something else, ape-man," she hissed. "We'll see what your throat, so used to barking, is capable of."

"What's this? Do you need an excuse to hit a bound man?" The witcher turned over on his back with an effort and spat out the sand. "Hit me without any excuses. I've seen how you like it. Let off some steam."

The elf straightened. "I've already let off some steam on you, while your hands were free," she said. "I rode you down and swiped you on the head. And I'll also finish you off when the time comes."

He didn't answer.

"I'd much rather stab you from close up, looking you in the eyes," continued the elf. "But you stink most hideously, human, so I'll shoot you."

"As you wish." The witcher shrugged, as far as the knots let him. "Do as you like, noble Aen Seidhe. You shouldn't miss a tied-up, motionless target."

The elf stood over him, legs spread, and leaned down, flashing her teeth.

"No, I shouldn't," she hissed. "I hit whatever I want. But you can be sure you won't die from the first arrow. Or the second. I'll try to make sure you can feel yourself dying."

"Don't come so close." He grimaced, pretending to be repulsed. "You stink most hideously, Aen Seidhe."

The elf jumped back, rocked on her narrow hips and forcefully kicked him in the thigh. Geralt drew his legs in and curled up, knowing where she was aiming next. He succeeded, and got her boot in the hip, so hard his teeth rattled.

The tall elf standing next to her echoed each kick with a sharp chord on the lute.

"Leave him, Toruviel!" bleated the sylvan. "Have you gone mad? Galarr, tell her to stop!"

"*Thaesse!*" shrieked Toruviel, and kicked the witcher again. The tall Seidhe tore so violently at the strings that one snapped with a protracted whine.

"Enough of that! Enough, for gods' sake!" Dandelion yelled fretfully, wriggling and tumbling in the ropes. "Why are you bullying him, you stupid whore? Leave us alone! And you leave my lute alone, all right?"

Toruviel turned to him with an angry grimace on her cracked lips. "Musician!" she growled. "A human, yet a musician! A lutenist!"

Without a word, she pulled the instrument from the tall elf's hand, forcefully smashed the lute against the pine and threw the remains, tangled in the strings, on Dandelion's chest.

"Play on a cow's horn, you savage, not a lute."

The poet turned as white as death; his lips quivered. Geralt, feeling cold fury rising up somewhere within him, drew Toruviel's eyes with his own.

"What are you staring at?" hissed the elf, leaning over. "Filthy ape-man! Do you want me to gouge out those insect eyes of yours?"

Her necklace hung down just above him. The witcher tensed, lunged, and caught the necklace in his teeth, tugging powerfully, curling his legs in and turning on his side.

Toruviel lost her balance and fell on top of him.

Geralt wriggled in the ropes like a fish, crushed the elf beneath him, tossed his head back with such force that the vertebrae in his neck cracked and, with all his might, butted her in the face with his forehead. Toruviel howled and struggled.

They pulled him off her brutally and, tugging at his clothes and hair, lifted him. One of them struck him; he felt rings cut the skin over his cheekbone and the forest danced and swam in front of his eyes. He saw Toruviel lurch to her knees, blood pouring from her nose and mouth. The elf wrenched the dagger from its sheath but gave a sob, hunched over, grasped her face and dropped her head between her knees.

The tall elf in the jacket adorned with colorful feathers took the dagger from her hand and approached the witcher. He smiled as he raised the blade. Geralt saw him through a red haze; blood from his forehead, which he'd cut against Toruviel's teeth, poured into his eye sockets.

"No!" bleated Torque, running up to the elf and hanging on to his arm. "Don't kill him! No!"

"*Voe'rle, Vanadain,*" a sonorous voice suddenly commanded. "*Quess aen? Caelm, evellienn! Galarr!*"

Geralt turned his head as far as the fist clutching his hair permitted.

The horse which had just reached the glade was as white as snow, its mane long, soft and silky as a woman's hair. The hair of the rider sitting in the sumptuous saddle was identical in color, pulled back at the forehead by a bandana studded with sapphires.

Torque, bleating now and then, ran up to the horse, caught hold of the stirrup and showered the white-haired elf with a torrent of words. The Seidhe interrupted him with an authoritative gesture and jumped down from his saddle. He approached Toruviel, who was being supported by two elves, and carefully removed the bloodied handkerchief from her face. Toruviel gave a heartrending groan. The Seidhe shook his head and approached the witcher. His burning black eyes, shining like stars in his pale face, had dark rings beneath them, as if he had not slept for several nights in a row.

"You stink even when bound," he said quietly in unaccented common tongue. "Like a basilisk. I'll draw my conclusions from that."

"Toruviel started it," bleated the devil. "She kicked him when he was tied up, as if she'd lost her mind—"

With a gesture, the elf ordered him to be quiet. At his command, the other Seidhe dragged the witcher and Dandelion under the pine tree and fastened them to the trunk with belts. Then they all knelt by the prostrate Toruviel, sheltering her. After a moment Geralt heard her yell and fight in their arms.

"I didn't want this," said the sylvan, still standing next to them. "I didn't, human. I didn't know they'd arrive just when we—When they stunned you and tied your companion up, I asked them to leave you there, in the hops. But—"

"They couldn't leave any witnesses," muttered the witcher.

"Surely they won't kill us, will they?" groaned Dandelion. "Surely they won't..."

Torque said nothing, wiggling his soft nose.

"Bloody hell." The poet groaned. "They're going to kill us? What's all this about, Geralt? What did we witness?"

"Our sylvan friend is on a special mission in the Valley of Flowers. Am I right, Torque? At the elves' request he's stealing seeds, seedlings, knowledge about farming...What else, devil?"

"Whatever I can," bleated Torque. "Everything they need. And show me something they don't need. They're starving in the mountains, especially in winter. And they know nothing about farming. And before they've learned to domesticate game or poultry, and to cultivate what they can in their plots of land...They haven't got the time, human."

"I don't care a shit about their time. What have I done to them?" groaned Dandelion. "What wrong have I done them?"

"Think carefully," said the white-haired elf, approaching without a sound, "and maybe you can answer the question yourself."

"He's simply taking revenge for all the wrong that man has done the elves." The witcher smiled wryly. "It's all the same to him who he takes his revenge on. Don't be deluded by his noble bearing and elaborate speech, Dandelion. He's no different than the black-eyes who knocked us down. He has to unload his powerless hatred on somebody."

The elf picked up Dandelion's shattered lute. For a moment, he looked at the ruined instrument in silence, and finally threw it into the bushes.

"If I wanted to give vent to hatred or a desire for revenge," he said, playing with a pair of soft white leather gloves, "I'd storm the valley at night, burn down the village and kill the villagers. Childishly simple. They don't even put out a guard. They don't see or hear us when they come to the forest. Can there be anything simpler, anything easier, than a swift, silent arrow from behind a tree? But we're not hunting you. It is you, man with strange eyes, who is hunting our friend, the sylvan Torque."

"Eeeeee, that's exaggerating," bleated the devil. "What hunt? We were having a bit of fun—"

"It is you humans who hate anything that differs from you, be it only by the shape of its ears," the elf went on calmly, paying no attention to the sylvan. "That's why you took our land from us, drove us from our homes, forced us into the savage mountains. You took our Dol Blathanna, the Valley of Flowers. I am Filavandrel aen Fidhail of Silver Towers, of the Feleaorn family from White Ships. Now, exiled and hounded to the edge of the world, I am Filavandrel of the Edge of the World."

"The world is huge," muttered the witcher. "We can find room. There's enough space."

"The world is huge," repeated the elf. "That's true, human. But you have changed this world. At first, you used force to change it. You treated it as you treat anything that falls into your hands. Now it looks as if the world has started to fit in with you. It's given way to you. It's given in."

Geralt didn't reply.

"Torque spoke the truth," continued Filavandrel. "Yes, we are starving. Yes, we are threatened with annihilation. The sun shines differently, the air is different, water is not as it used to be. The things we used to eat, made use of, are dying, diminishing, deteriorating. We never cultivated the land. Unlike you humans, we never tore at it with hoes and ploughs.

To you, the earth pays a bloody tribute. It bestowed gifts on us. You tear the earth's treasures from it by force. For us, the earth gave birth and blossomed because it loved us. Well, no love lasts forever. But we still want to survive."

"Instead of stealing grain, you can buy it. As much as you need. You still have a great many things that humans consider valuable. You can trade."

Filavandrel smiled contemptuously. "With you? Never."

Geralt frowned, breaking up the dried blood on his cheek. "The devil with you, then, and your arrogance and contempt. By refusing to cohabit, you're condemning yourselves to annihilation. To cohabit, to come to an understanding, that's your only chance."

Filavandrel leaned forward, his eyes blazing.

"Cohabit on your terms?" he asked in a changed, yet still calm, voice. "Acknowledging your sovereignty? Losing our identity? Cohabit as what? Slaves? Pariahs? Cohabit with you from beyond the walls you've built to fence yourselves away in towns? Cohabit with your women and hang for it? Or look on at what half-blood children must live with? Why are you avoiding my eyes, strange human? How do you find cohabiting with neighbors from whom, after all, you do differ somewhat?"

"I manage." The witcher looked him straight in the eyes. "I manage because I have to. Because I've no other way out. Because I've overcome the vanity and pride of being different. I've understood that they are a pitiful defense against being different. Because I've understood that the sun shines differently when something changes, but I'm not the axis of those changes. The sun shines differently, but it will continue to shine, and jumping at it with a hoe isn't going to do anything. We've got to accept facts, elf. That's what we've got to learn."

"That's what you want, isn't it?" With his wrist, Filavandrel wiped away the sweat above his white brows. "Is that what you want to impose on others? The conviction that your time has come, your human era and age, and that what you're doing to other races is as natural as the rising and the setting of the sun? That everybody has to come to terms with it, to accept it? And you accuse me of vanity? And what are the views you're proclaiming? Why don't you humans finally realize that your domination of the world is as natural and repellant as lice multiplying in a sheepskin coat? You could propose we cohabit with lice and get the same reaction—and I'd listen to the lice as attentively if they, in return for our acknowledgment of their supremacy, were to agree to allow common use of the coat."

"So don't waste time discussing it with such an unpleasant insect, elf," said the witcher, barely able to control his voice. "I'm surprised you want to arouse a feeling of guilt and repentance in such a louse as me. You're pitiful, Filavandrel. You're embittered, hungry for revenge and conscious of your own powerlessness. Go on, thrust the sword into me. Revenge yourself on the whole human race. You'll see what relief that'll bring you. First kick me in the balls or the teeth, like Toruviel."

Filavandrel turned his head.

"Toruviel is sick," he said.

"I know that disease and its symptoms." Geralt spat over his shoulder. "The treatment I gave her ought to help."

"This conversation is senseless." Filavandrel stepped away. "I'm sorry we've got to kill you. Revenge has nothing to do with it; it's purely practical. Torque has to carry on with his task and no one can suspect who he's doing it for. We can't afford to go to war with you, and we won't be taken in by trade and exchange. We're not so naïve that we don't know your merchants are just outposts of your way of life. We know what follows them. And what sort of cohabitation they bring."

"Elf," Dandelion, who had remained silent until now, said quietly, "I've got friends. People who'll pay ransom for us. In the form of provisions, if you like, or any form. Think about it. After all, those stolen seeds aren't going to save you—"

"Nothing will save them anymore," Geralt interrupted him. "Don't grovel, Dandelion, don't beg him. It's pointless and pitiful."

"For someone who has lived such a short time"—Filavandrel forced a smile—"you show an astounding disdain for death, human."

"Your mother gives birth to you only once and only once do you die," the witcher said calmly. "An appropriate philosophy for a louse, don't you agree? And your longevity? I pity you, Filavandrel."

The elf raised his eyebrows.

"Why?"

"You're pathetic, with your little stolen sacks of seeds on pack horses, with your handful of grain, that tiny crumb thanks to which you plan to survive. And with that mission of yours which is supposed to turn your thoughts from imminent annihilation. Because you know this is the end. Nothing will sprout or yield crops on the plateau; nothing will save you now. But you live long, and you will live very long in arrogant isolation, fewer and fewer of you, growing weaker and weaker, more and more bitter. And you know what'll happen then, Filavandrel. You know that desperate young men with the eyes of hundred-year-old men and withered, barren and sick girls like Toruviel will lead those who can still hold a sword and bow in their hands, down into the valleys. You'll come down into the blossoming valleys to meet death, wanting to die honorably, in battle, and not in sickbeds of misery, where anemia, tuberculosis and scurvy will send you. Then, long-living Aen Seidhe, you'll remember me. You'll remember that I pitied you. And you'll understand that I was right."

"Time will tell who was right," said the elf quietly. "And herein lies the advantage of longevity. I've got a chance of finding out, if only because of that stolen handful of grain. You won't have a chance like that. You'll die shortly."

"Spare him, at least." Geralt indicated Dandelion with his head. "No, not out of lofty mercy. Out of common sense. Nobody's going to ask after me, but they are going to take revenge for him."

"You judge my common sense poorly," the elf said after some hesitation. "If he survives thanks to you, he'll undoubtedly feel obliged to avenge you."

"You can be sure of that!" Dandelion burst out, pale as death. "You can be sure, you son of a bitch. Kill me too, because I promise otherwise I'll set the world against you. You'll see what lice from a fur coat can do! We'll finish you off even if we have to level those mountains of yours to the ground! You can be sure of that!"

"How stupid you are, Dandelion," sighed the witcher.

"Your mother gives birth to you only once and only once do you die," said the poet haughtily, the effect somewhat spoiled by his teeth rattling like castanets.

"That settles it." Filavandrel took his gloves from his belt and pulled them on. "It's time to end this."

At his command, the elves positioned themselves opposite Geralt and Dandelion with bows. They did it quickly; they'd obviously been waiting for this a long time. One of them, the witcher noticed, was still chewing a turnip. Toruviel, her mouth and nose bandaged with cloth and birch bark, stood next to the archers. Without a bow.

"Shall I bind your eyes?" asked Filavandrel.

"Go away." The witcher turned his head. "Go—"

"*A d'yeable aep arse,*" Dandelion finished for him, his teeth chattering.

"Oh, no!" the sylvan suddenly bleated, running up and sheltering the condemned men with his body. "Have you lost your mind? Filavandrel! This is not what we agreed! Not this! You were supposed to take them up to the mountains, hold them somewhere in some cave, until we'd finished—"

"Torque," said the elf, "I can't. I can't risk it. Did you see what he did to Toruviel while tied up? I can't risk it."

"I don't care what you can or can't! What do you imagine? You think I'll let you murder them? Here, on my land? Right next to my hamlet? You accursed idiots! Get out of here with your bows or I'll ram you down. Uk! Uk!"

"Torque." Filavandrel rested his hands on his belt. "This is necessary."

"Duvvelsheyss, not necessary!"

"Move aside, Torque."

The sylvan shook his ears, bleated even louder, stared and bent his elbow in an abusive gesture popular among dwarves.

"You're not going to murder anybody here! Get on your horses and out into the mountains, beyond the passes! Otherwise you'll have to kill me too!"

"Be reasonable," said the white-haired elf slowly. "If we let them live, people are going to learn what you're doing. They'll catch you and torture you. You know what they're like, after all."

"I do," bleated the sylvan still sheltering Geralt and Dandelion. "It turns out I know them better than I know you! And, verily, I don't know who to side with. I regret allying myself with you, Filavandrel!"

"You wanted to," said the elf coldly, giving a signal to the archers. "You wanted to, Torque. *L'sparellean! Evellienn!*"

The elves drew arrows from their quivers. "Go away, Torque," said Geralt, gritting his teeth. "It's senseless. Get aside." The sylvan, without budging from the spot, showed him the dwarves' gesture.

"I can hear...music..." Dandelion suddenly sobbed.

"It happens," said the witcher, looking at the arrowheads. "Don't worry. There's no shame in fear."

Filavandrel's face changed, screwed up in a strange grimace. The white-haired Seidhe suddenly turned round and gave a shout to the archers. They lowered their weapons.

Lille entered the glade.

She was no longer a skinny peasant girl in a sackcloth dress. Through the grasses covering the glade walked—no, not walked—floated a queen, radiant, golden-haired, fiery-eyed, ravishing. The Queen of the Fields, decorated with garlands of flowers, ears of corn, bunches of herbs. At her left-hand side, a young stag pattered on stiff legs, at her right rustled an enormous hedgehog.

"Dana Meadbh," said Filavandrel with veneration. And then bowed and knelt.

The remaining elves also knelt; slowly, reluctantly, they fell to their knees one after the other and bowed their heads low in veneration. Toruviel was the last to kneel.

"*Hael*, Dana Meadbh," repeated Filavandrel.

Lille didn't answer. She stopped several paces short of the elf and swept her blue eyes over Dandelion and Geralt. Torque, while bowing, started cutting through the knots. None of the Seidhe moved.

Lille stood in front of Filavandrel. She didn't say anything, didn't make the slightest sound, but the witcher saw the changes on the elf's face, sensed the aura surrounding them and was in no doubt they were communicating. The devil suddenly pulled at his sleeve.

ANDRZEJ SAPKOWSKI

"Your friend," he bleated quietly, "has decided to faint.
Right on time. What shall we do?"

"Slap him across the face a couple of times."

"With pleasure."

Filavandrel got up from his knees. At his command, the
elves fell to saddling the horses as quick as lightning.

"Come with us, Dana Meadbh," said the white-haired elf.
"We need you. Don't abandon us, Eternal One. Don't deprive
us of your love. We'll die without it."

Lille slowly shook her head and indicated east, the direction
of the mountains. The elf bowed, crumpling the ornate reins
of his white-maned mount in his hands.

Dandelion walked up, pale and dumbfounded, supported
by the sylvan. Lille looked at him and smiled. She looked into
the witcher's eyes. She looked long. She didn't say a word.
Words weren't necessary.

Most of the elves were already in their saddles when Filavandrel and Toruviel approached. Geralt looked into the elf's
black eyes, visible above the bandages.

"Toruviel..." he said. And didn't finish.

The elf nodded. From her saddlebow, she took a lute, a
marvelous instrument of light, tastefully inlaid wood with a
slender, engraved neck. Without a word, she handed the lute
to Dandelion. The poet accepted the instrument and smiled.
Also without a word, but his eyes said a great deal.

"Farewell, strange human," Filavandrel said quietly to Geralt. "You're right. Words aren't necessary. They won't change
anything."

Geralt remained silent.

"After some consideration," added the Seidhe, "I've come
to the conclusion that you were right. When you pitied us. So
goodbye. Goodbye until we meet again, on the day when we

descend into the valleys to die honorably. We'll look out for you then, Toruviel and I. Don't let us down."

For a long time, they looked at each other in silence. And then the witcher answered briefly and simply:

"I'll try."

VII

"By the gods, Geralt." Dandelion stopped playing, hugged the lute and touched it with his cheek. "This wood sings on its own! These strings are alive! What wonderful tonality! Bloody hell, a couple of kicks and a bit of fear is a pretty low price to pay for such a superb lute. I'd have let myself be kicked from dawn to dusk if I'd known what I was going to get. Geralt? Are you listening to me at all?"

"It's difficult not to hear you two." Geralt raised his head from the book and glanced at the sylvan, who was still stubbornly squeaking on a peculiar set of pipes made from reeds of various lengths. "I hear you; the whole neighborhood hears you."

"Duvvelsheyss, not neighborhood." Torque put his pipes aside. "A desert, that's what it is. A wilderness. A shit-hole. Eh, I miss my hemp!"

"He misses his hemp," laughed Dandelion, carefully turning the delicately engraved lute pegs. "You should have sat in the thicket quiet as a dormouse instead of scaring girls, destroying dykes and sullying the well. I think you're going to be more careful now and give up your tricks, eh, Torque?"

"I like tricks," declared the sylvan, baring his teeth. "And I can't imagine life without them. But have it your way. I promise to be more careful on new territory. I'll be more restrained."

The night was cloudy and windy. The gale beat down the

reeds and rustled in the branches of the bushes surrounding their camp. Dandelion threw some dry twigs into the fire. Torque wriggled around on his makeshift bed, swiping mosquitoes away with his tail. A fish leapt in the lake with a splash.

"I'll describe our whole expedition to the edge of the world in a ballad," declared Dandelion. "And I'll describe you in it, too, Torque."

"Don't think you'll get away with it," growled the sylvan. "I'll write a ballad too, then, and describe you, but in such a way as you won't be able to show your face in decent company for twelve years. So watch out! Geralt?"

"What?"

"Have you read anything interesting in that book which you so disgracefully wheedled out of those freemen?"

"I have."

"So read it to us, before the fire burns out."

"Yes, yes"—Dandelion strummed the melodious strings of Toruviel's lute—"read us something, Geralt."

The witcher leaned on his elbow, edging the volume closer to the fire.

"'Glimpsed she may be,'" he began, "'during the time of sumor, from the days of Mai and Juyn to the days of October, but most oft this haps on the Feste of the Scythe, which ancients would call Lammas. She revealeth herself as the Fairhaired Ladie, in flowers all, and all that liveth followeth her path and clingeth to her, as one, plant or beast. Hence her name is Lyfia. Ancients call her Danamebi and venerate her greatly. Even the Bearded, albeit in mountains not on fields they dwell, respect and call her Bloemenmagde.'"

"Danamebi," muttered Dandelion. "Dana Meadbh, the Lady of the Fields."

"'Whence Lyfia treads the earth blossometh and bringeth forth, and abundantly doth each creature breed, such is her might. All nations to her offer sacrifice of harvest in vain hope their field not another's will by Lyfia visited be. Because it is also said that there cometh a day at end when Lyfia will come to settle among that tribe which above all others will rise, but these be mere womenfolk tales. Because, forsooth, the wise do say that Lyfia loveth but one land and that which groweth on it and liveth alike, with no difference, be it the smallest of common apple trees or the most wretched of insects, and all nations are no more to her than that thinnest of trees because, forsooth, they too will be gone and new, different tribes will follow. But Lyfia eternal is, was and ever shall be until the end of time.'"

"Until the end of time!" sang the troubadour and strummed his lute. Torque joined in with a high trill on his reed pipes. "Hail, Lady of the Fields! For the harvest, for the flowers in Dol Blathanna, but also for the hide of the undersigned, which you saved from being riddled with arrows. Do you know what? I'm going to tell you something." He stopped playing, hugged the lute like a child and grew sad. "I don't think I'll mention the elves and the difficulties they've got to struggle with, in the ballad. There'd be no shortage of scum wanting to go into the mountains... Why hasten the—" The troubadour grew silent.

"Go on, finish," said Torque bitterly. "You wanted to say: hasten what can't be avoided. The inevitable."

"Let's not talk about it," interrupted Geralt. "Why talk about it? Words aren't necessary. Follow Lille's example."

"She spoke to the elf telepathically," muttered the bard. "I sensed it. I'm right, aren't I, Geralt? After all, you can sense communication like that. Did you understand what... what she was getting across to the elf?"

"What was she talking about?"

"Hope. That things renew themselves, and won't stop doing so."

"Is that all?"

"That was enough."

"Hmm... Geralt? Lille lives in the village, among people. Do you think that—"

"—that she'll stay with them? Here, in Dol Blathanna? Maybe. If..."

"If what?"

"If people prove worthy of it. If the edge of the world remains the edge of the world. If we respect the boundaries. But enough of this talk, boys. Time to sleep."

"True. It's nearly midnight; the fire's burning out. I'll sit up for a little while yet. I've always found it easiest to invent rhymes beside a dying fire. And I need a title for my ballad. A nice title."

"Maybe *The Edge of the World*?"

"Banal," snorted the poet. "Even if it really is the edge, it's got to be described differently. Metaphorically. I take it you know what a metaphor is, Geralt? Hmm... Let me think... 'Where...' Bloody hell. 'Where—'"

"Goodnight," said the devil.

CHAPTER SIX

THE VOICE OF REASON

The witcher unlaced his shirt and peeled the wet linen from his neck. It was very warm in the cave, hot, even, the air hung heavy and moist, the humidity condensing in droplets on the moss-covered boulders and basalt blocks of the walls.

Plants were everywhere. They grew out of beds hewn into the bedrock and filled with peat, in enormous chests, troughs and flowerpots. They climbed up rocks, up wooden trellises and stakes. Geralt examined them with interest, recognizing some rare specimens—those which made up the ingredients of a witcher's medicines and elixirs, magical philters and a sorcerer's decoctions, and others, even rarer, whose qualities he could only guess at. Some he didn't know at all, or hadn't even heard of. He saw stretches of star-leafed melilote, compact balls of puffheads pouring out of huge flowerpots, shoots of arenaria strewn with berries as red as blood. He recognized the meaty, thickly veined leaves of fastaim, the crimson-golden ovals of measure-me-nots and the dark arrows of sawcuts. He noticed pinnated pondblood moss huddled against stone blocks, the glistening tubers of raven's eye and the tiger-striped petals of the mousetail orchid.

In the shady part of the grotto bulged caps of the sewant mushroom, gray as stones in a field. Not far from them grew reachcluster, an antidote to every known toxin and venom. The modest yellow-gray brushes peering from chests deeply sunken into the ground revealed scarix, a root with powerful and universal medicinal qualities.

The center of the cave was taken up by aqueous plants. Geralt saw vats full of hornwort and turtle duckweed, and tanks covered in a compact skin of liverwort, fodder for the parasitic giant oyster. Glass reservoirs full of gnarled rhizomes of the hallucinogenic bitip, slender, dark-green cryptocorines and clusters of nematodes. Muddy, silted troughs were breeding grounds for innumerable phycomycetes, algae, molds and swamp lichen.

Nenneke, rolling up the sleeves of her priestess's robe, took a pair of scissors and a little bone rake from her basket and got to work. Geralt sat on a bench between shafts of light falling through huge crystal blocks in the cave's vault.

The priestess muttered and hummed under her breath, deftly plunging her hands into the thicket of leaves and shoots, snipping with her scissors and filling the basket with bunches of weeds. She adjusted the stakes and frames supporting the plants and, now and again, turned the soil with her small rake. Sometimes, muttering angrily, she pulled out dried or rotted stalks, threw them into the humus containers as food for mushrooms and other squamous and snake-like twisted plants which the witcher didn't recognize. He wasn't even sure they were plants at all—it seemed to him the glistening rhizomes moved a little, stretching their hair-like offshoots toward the priestess's hands.

It was warm. Very warm.

"Geralt?"

"Yes?" He fought off an overwhelming sleepiness. Nenneke, playing with her scissors, was looking at him from behind the huge pinnated leaves of sand-spurry flybush.

"Don't leave yet. Stay. A few more days."

"No, Nenneke. It's time for me to be on my way."

"Why the hurry? You don't have to worry about Hereward. And let that vagabond Dandelion go and break his neck on his own. Stay, Geralt."

"No, Nenneke."

The priestess snipped with scissors. "Are you in such haste to leave the temple because you're afraid that she'll find you here?"

"Yes," he admitted reluctantly. "You've guessed."

"It wasn't exactly difficult," she muttered. "But don't worry. Yennefer's already been here. Two months ago. She won't be back in a hurry, because we quarreled. No, not because of you. She didn't ask about you."

"She didn't ask?"

"That's where it hurts," the priestess laughed. "You're egocentric, like all men. There's nothing worse than a lack of interest, is there? Than indifference? No, but don't lose heart. I know Yennefer only too well. She didn't ask anything, but she did look around attentively, looking for signs of you. And she's mighty furious at you, that I did feel."

"What did you quarrel about?"

"Nothing that would interest you."

"I know anyway."

"I don't think so," said Nenneke calmly, adjusting the stakes. "You know her very superficially. As, incidentally, she knows you. It's quite typical of the relationship which binds you, or did bind you. Both parties aren't capable of anything other than a strongly emotional evaluation of the consequences, while ignoring the causes."

"She came looking for a cure," he remarked coldly. "That's what you quarreled about, admit it."

"I won't admit anything."

The witcher got up and stood in full light under one of the crystal sheets in the grotto's vault.

"Come here a minute, Nenneke. Take a look at this." He unknotted a secret pocket in his belt, dug out a tiny bundle, a miniature purse made of goat-leather, and poured the contents into his palm.

"Two diamonds, a ruby, three pretty nephrites, and an interesting agate." Nenneke was knowledgeable about everything. "How much did they cost you?"

"Two and a half thousand Temeria orens. Payment for the Wyzim striga."

"For a torn neck." The priestess grimaced. "Oh, well, it's a question of price. But you did well to turn cash into these trinkets. The oren is weak and the cost of stones in Wyzim isn't high; it's too near to the dwarves' mines in Mahakam. If you sell those in Novigrad, you'll get at least five hundred Novigrad crowns, and the crown, at present, stands at six and a half orens and is going up."

"I'd like you to take them."

"For safekeeping?"

"No. Keep the nephrites for the temple as, shall we say, my offering to the goddess Melitele. And the remaining stones... are for her. For Yennefer. Give them to her when she comes to visit you again, which will no doubt be soon."

Nenneke looked him straight in the eyes.

"I wouldn't do this if I were you. You'll make her even more furious, if that's possible, believe me. Leave everything as it is, because you're no longer in a position to mend anything or make anything better. Running away from her, you behaved... well, let's say, in a manner not particularly worthy of a mature man. By trying to wipe away your guilt with precious stones, you'll behave like a very, very over-mature man. I really don't know what sort of man I can stand less."

"She was too possessive," he muttered, turning away his face. "I couldn't stand it. She treated me like—"

"Stop it," she said sharply. "Don't cry on my shoulder. I'm not your mother, and I won't be your confidante either. I don't give a shit how she treated you and I care even less how you treated her. And I don't intend to be a go-between or give these stupid jewels to her. If you want to be a fool, do it without using me as an intermediary."

"You misunderstand. I'm not thinking of appeasing or bribing her. But I do owe her something, and the treatment she wants to undergo is apparently very costly. I want to help her, that's all."

"You're more of an idiot than I thought." Nenneke picked up the basket from the ground. "A costly treatment? Help? Geralt, these jewels of yours are, to her, knickknacks not worth spitting on. Do you know how much Yennefer can earn for getting rid of an unwanted pregnancy for a great lady?"

"I do happen to know. And that she earns even more for curing infertility. It's a shame she can't help herself in that respect. That's why she's seeking help from others—like you."

"No one can help her; it's impossible. She's a sorceress. Like most female magicians, her ovaries are atrophied and it's irreversible. She'll never be able to have children."

"Not all sorceresses are handicapped in this respect. I know something about that, and you do, too."

Nenneke closed her eyes. "Yes, I do."

"Something can't be a rule if there are exceptions to it. And please don't give me any banal untruths about exceptions proving the rule. Tell me something about exceptions as such."

"Only one thing," she said coldly, "can be said about exceptions. They exist. Nothing more. But Yennefer...Well, unfortunately, she isn't an exception. At least not as regards the handicap we're talking about. In other respects it's hard to find a greater exception than her."

"Sorcerers"—Geralt wasn't put off by Nenneke's coldness, or her allusion—"have raised the dead. I know of proven cases. And it seems to me that raising the dead is harder than reversing the atrophy of any organs."

"You're mistaken. Because I don't know of one single, proven, fully successful case of reversing atrophy or regenerating endocrine glands. Geralt, that's enough. This is beginning to sound like a consultation. You don't know anything about these things. I do. And if I tell you that Yennefer has paid for certain gifts by losing others, then that's how it is."

"If it's so clear, then I don't understand why she keeps on trying to—"

"You understand very little," interrupted the priestess. "Bloody little. Stop worrying about Yennefer's complaints and think about your own. Your body was also subjected to changes which are irreversible. She surprises you, but what about you? It ought to be clear to you too, that you're never going to be human, but you still keep trying to be one. Making human mistakes. Mistakes a witcher shouldn't be making."

He leaned against the wall of the cave and wiped the sweat from his brow.

"You're not answering," stated Nenneke, smiling faintly. "I'm not surprised. It's not easy to speak with the voice of reason. You're sick, Geralt. You're not fully fit. You react to elixirs badly. You've got a rapid pulse rate, the dilation of your eyes is slow, your reactions are delayed. You can't get the simplest Signs right. And you want to hit the trail? You have to be treated. You need therapy. And before that, a trance."

"Is that why you sent Iola to me? As part of the therapy? To make the trance easier?"

"You're a fool!"

"But not to such an extent."

Nenneke turned away and slipped her hands among the meaty stalks of creepers which the witcher didn't recognize. "Well, have it your way," she said easily. "Yes, I sent her to you. As part of the therapy. And let me tell you, it worked. Your reactions were much better the following day. You were calmer. And Iola needed some therapy, too. Don't be angry."

"I'm not angry because of the therapy, or because of Iola."

"But at the voice of reason you're hearing?"

He didn't answer.

"A trance is necessary," repeated Nenneke, glancing around at her cave garden. "Iola's ready. She's made both physical and psychic contact with you. If you want to leave, let's do it tonight."

"No. I don't want to. Look, Nenneke, Iola might start to prophesy during the trance. To predict, read the future."

"That's just it."

"Exactly. And I don't want to know the future. How could I do what I'm doing if I knew it? Besides, I know it anyway."

"Are you sure?" He didn't answer. "Oh, well, all right," she sighed. "Let's go. Oh, and, Geralt? I don't mean to pry but tell me... How did you meet? You and Yennefer? How did it all start?"

The witcher smiled. "It started with me and Dandelion not having anything for breakfast and deciding to catch some fish."

"Am I to understand that instead of fish you caught Yennefer?"

"I'll tell you what happened. But maybe after supper. I'm hungry."

"Let's go, then. I've got everything I need."

The witcher made a move toward the exit and once more looked around the cave hothouse.

"Nenneke?"

"Aha?"

"Half of the plants you've got here don't grow anywhere else anymore. Am I right?"

"Yes. More than half."

"How come?"

"If I said it was through the goddess Melitele's grace, I daresay that wouldn't be enough for you, would it?"

"I daresay it wouldn't."

"That's what I thought." Nenneke smiled. "You see, Geralt, this bright sun of ours is still shining, but not quite the way it used to. Read the great books if you like. But if you don't want to waste time on it, maybe you'll be happy with the explanation that the crystal roof acts like a filter. It eliminates the lethal rays which are increasingly found in sunlight. That's why plants which you can't see growing wild anywhere in the world grow here."

"I understand." The witcher nodded. "And us, Nenneke? What about us? The sun shines on us, too. Shouldn't we shelter under a roof like that?"

"In principle, yes," sighed the priestess. "But..."

"But what?"

"It's too late."

THE LAST WISH

I

The catfish stuck its barbelled head above the surface, tugged with force, splashed, stirred the water and flashed its white belly.

"Careful, Dandelion!" shouted the witcher, digging his heels into the wet sand. "Hold him, damn it!"

"I am holding him..." groaned the poet. "Heavens, what a monster! It's a leviathan, not a fish! There'll be some good eating on that, dear gods!"

"Loosen it. Loosen it or the line will snap!"

The catfish clung to the bed and threw itself against the current toward the bend in the river. The line hissed as Dandelion's and Geralt's gloves smoldered.

"Pull, Geralt, pull! Don't loosen it or it'll get tangled up in the roots!"

"The line will snap!"

"No, it won't. Pull!"

They hunched up and pulled. The line cut the water with a hiss, vibrated and scattered droplets which glistened like mercury in the rising sun. The catfish suddenly surfaced, set the water seething just below the surface, and the tension of the line eased. They quickly started to gather up the slack.

"We'll smoke it," panted Dandelion. "We'll take it to the village and get it smoked. And we'll use the head for soup!"

"Careful!"

Feeling the shallows under its belly, the catfish threw half of its twelve-foot-long body out of the water, tossed its head, whacked its flat tail and took a sharp dive into the depths. Their gloves smoldered anew.

"Pull, pull! To the bank, the son of a bitch!"

"The line is creaking! Loosen it, Dandelion!"

"It'll hold, don't worry! We'll cook the head . . . for soup . . ."

The catfish, dragged near to the bank again, surged and strained furiously against them as if to let them know he wasn't that easy to get into the pot. The spray flew six feet into the air.

"We'll sell the skin . . ." Dandelion, red with effort, pulled the line with both hands. "And the barbels . . . We'll use the barbels to make—"

Nobody ever found out what the poet was going to make from the catfish's barbels. The line snapped with a crack and both fishermen, losing their balance, fell onto the wet sand.

"Bloody hell!" Dandelion yelled so loud that the echo resounded through the osiers. "So much grub escaped! I hope you die, you son-of-a-catfish."

"I told you." Geralt shook his wet trousers. "I told you not to use force when you pull. You screwed up, my friend. You make as good a fisherman as a goat's arse makes a trumpet."

"That's not true." The troubadour was outraged. "It's my doing that the monster took the bait in the first place."

"Oh really? You didn't lift a finger to help me set the line. You played the lute and hollered so the whole neighborhood could hear you, nothing more."

"You're wrong." Dandelion bared his teeth. "When you fell asleep, you see, I took the grubs off the hook and attached a dead crow, which I'd found in the bushes. I wanted to see your face in the morning when you pulled the crow out. And the catfish took the crow. Your grubs would have caught shit-all."

"They would have, they would have." The witcher spat into the water, winding the line on to a little wooden rake. "But it snapped because you tugged like an idiot. Wind up the rest of the lines instead of gabbling. The sun's already up; it's time to go. I'm going to pack up."

"Geralt!"

"What?"

"There's something on the other line, too... No, dammit, it only got caught. Hell, it's holding like a stone. I can't do it! Ah, that's it... Ha, ha, look what I'm bringing in. It must be the wreck of a barge from King Dezmod's time! What great stuff! Look, Geralt!"

Dandelion was clearly exaggerating; the clump of rotted ropes, net and algae pulled out of the water was impressive but it was far from being the size of a barge dating from the days of the legendary king. The bard scattered the jumble over the bank and began to dig around in it with the tip of his shoe. The algae was alive with leeches, scuds and little crabs.

"Ha! Look what I've found!"

Geralt approached, curious. The find was a chipped stoneware jar, something like a two-handled amphora, tangled up in netting, black with rotten algae, colonies of caddis-larvae and snails, dripping with stinking slime.

"Ha!" Dandelion exclaimed again, proudly. "Do you know what this is?"

"It's an old pot."

"You're wrong," declared the troubadour, scraping away shells and hardened, shiny clay. "This is a charmed jar. There's a djinn inside who'll fulfill my three wishes."

The witcher snorted.

"You can laugh." Dandelion finished his scraping, bent over and rinsed the amphora. "But there's a seal on the spigot and a wizard's mark on the seal."

"What mark? Let's see."

"Oh, sure." The poet hid the jar behind his back. "And what more do you want? I'm the one who found it and I need all the wishes."

"Don't touch that seal! Leave it alone!"

"Let go, I tell you! It's mine!"

"Dandelion, be careful!"

"Sure!"

"Don't touch it! Oh, bloody hell!"

The jar fell to the sand during their scuffle, and luminous red smoke burst forth.

The witcher jumped back and rushed toward the camp for his sword. Dandelion, folding his arms across his chest, didn't move.

The smoke pulsated and collected in an irregular sphere level with Dandelion's eyes. The sphere formed a six-foot-wide distorted head with no nose, enormous eyes and a sort of beak.

"Djinn!" said Dandelion, stamping his foot. "I freed thee and as of this day, I am thy lord. My wishes—"

The head snapped its beak, which wasn't really a beak but something in the shape of drooping, deformed and ever-changing lips.

"Run!" yelled the witcher. "Run, Dandelion!"

"My wishes," continued the poet, "are as follows. Firstly, may Valdo Marx, the troubadour of Cidaris, die of apoplexy as soon as possible. Secondly, there's a count's daughter in Caelf called Virginia who refuses all advances. May she succumb to mine. Thirdly—"

No one ever found out Dandelion's third wish.

Two monstrous paws emerged from the horrible head and grabbed the bard by the throat. Dandelion screeched. Geralt reached the head in three leaps, swiped his silver sword and slashed it through the middle. The air howled, the head exhaled smoke and rapidly doubled in diameter. The monstrous jaw, now also much larger, flew open, snapped and whistled; the paws pulled the struggling Dandelion around and crushed him to the ground.

The witcher crossed his fingers in the Sign of Aard and threw as much energy as he could muster at the head. The energy materialized in a blinding beam, sliced through the glow surrounding the head and hit its mark. The boom was so loud that it stabbed Geralt's ears, and the air sucked in by the implosion made the willows rustle. The roar of the monster was deafening as it grew even larger, but it released the poet, soared up, circled and, waving its paws, flew away over the water.

The witcher rushed to pull Dandelion—who was lying motionless—away. At that moment, his fingers touched a round object buried in the sand.

It was a brass seal decorated with the sign of a broken cross and a nine-pointed star.

The head, suspended above the river, had become the size of a haystack, while the open, roaring jaws looked like the gates of an average-sized barn. Stretching out its paws, the monster attacked.

Geralt, not having the least idea of what to do, squeezed the seal in his fist and, extending his hand toward the assailant, screamed out the words of an exorcism a priestess had once taught him. He had never used those words until now because, in principle, he didn't believe in superstitions.

The effect surpassed his expectations.

The seal hissed and grew hot, burning his hand. The

gigantic head froze in the air, suspended, motionless above the river. It hung like that for a moment then, at last, it began to howl, roar, and dispersed into a pulsating bundle of smoke, into a huge, whirling cloud. The cloud whined shrilly and whisked upstream with incredible speed, leaving a trail of churned-up water on the surface. In a matter of seconds, it had disappeared into the distance; only a dwindling howl lingered across the water.

The witcher rushed to the poet, cowering on the sand.

"Dandelion? Are you dead? Dandelion, damn it! What's the matter with you?"

The poet jerked his head, shook his hands and opened his mouth to scream. Geralt grimaced and narrowed his eyes—Dandelion had a trained—loud—tenor voice and, when frightened, could reach extraordinary registers. But what emerged from the bard's throat was a barely audible, hoarse croak.

"Dandelion! What's the matter with you? Answer me!"

"Hhhh...eeee...kheeeee...theeee whhhhorrrrrrre..."

"Are you in pain? What's the matter? Dandelion!"

"Hhhh...Whhhooo..."

"Don't say anything. If everything's all right, nod."

Dandelion grimaced and, with great difficulty, nodded and then immediately turned on his side, curled up and—choking and coughing—vomited blood.

Geralt cursed.

II

"By all the gods!" The guard stepped back and lowered the lantern. "What's the matter with him?"

"Let us through, my good man," said the witcher quietly,

supporting Dandelion, who was huddled up in the saddle. "We're in great haste, as you see."

"I do." The guard swallowed, looking at the poet's pale face and chin covered in black, dried blood. "Wounded? It looks terrible, sir."

"I'm in haste," repeated Geralt. "We've been traveling since dawn. Let us through, please."

"We can't," said the other guard. "You're only allowed through between sunrise and sunset. None may pass at night. That's the order. There's no way through for anyone unless they've got a letter of safe-conduct from the king or the mayor. Or they're nobility with a coat of arms."

Dandelion croaked, huddled up even more, resting his forehead on the horse's mane, shuddered, shook and retched dryly. Another stream of blood trickled down the branched, dried pattern on his mount's neck.

"My good men," Geralt said as calmly as he could, "you can see for yourselves how badly he fares. I have to find someone who can treat him. Let us through. Please."

"Don't ask." The guard leaned on his halberd. "Orders are orders. I'll go to the pillory if I let you through. They'll chase me from service, and then how will I feed my children? No, sir, I can't. Take your friend down from the horse and put him in the room in the barbican. We'll dress him and he'll last out until dawn, if that's his fate. It's not long now."

"A dressing's not enough." The witcher ground his teeth. "We need a healer, a priest, a gifted doctor—"

"You wouldn't be waking up anyone like that at night anyway," said the second guard. "The most we can do is see that you don't have to camp out under the gate until dawn. It's warm in there and there's somewhere to put your friend; he'll fare better there than in the saddle. Come on, let us help you lower him from the horse."

It was warm, stuffy and cozy in the room within the barbican. A fire crackled merrily in the hearth, and behind it a cricket chirped fiercely.

Three men sat at the heavy square table laid with jugs and plates.

"Forgive us for disturbing you, squires…" said the guard, holding Dandelion up. "I trust you won't mind… This one here is a knight, hmm… And the other one is wounded, so I thought—"

"You thought well." One of the men turned his slender, sharp, expressive face toward them and got up. "Here, lay him down on the pallet."

The man was an elf, like the other one sitting at the table. Both, judging by their clothes, which were a typical mixture of human and elven fashion, were elves who had settled and integrated. The third man, who looked the eldest, was human, a knight, judging by the way he was dressed and by his salt-and-pepper hair, cut to fit beneath a helmet.

"I'm Chireadan," the taller of the elves, with an expressive face, introduced himself. As was usual with representatives of the Old People, it was difficult to guess his age; he could have been twenty or one hundred and twenty. "This is my cousin Errdil. And this nobleman is the knight Vratimir."

"A nobleman," muttered Geralt, but a closer look at the coat of arms embroidered on his tunic shattered his hopes: a shield divided per cross and bearing golden lilies was cut diagonally by a silver bar. Vratimir was not only illegitimate but came from a mixed, human-nonhuman union. As a result, although he was entitled to use a coat of arms, he couldn't consider himself a true nobleman, and the privilege of crossing the city gate after dusk most certainly wasn't extended to him.

"Unfortunately"—the witcher's scrutiny did not escape the elf's attention—"we, too, have to remain here until dawn. The law knows no exceptions, at least not for the likes of us. We invite you to join our company, sir knight."

"Geralt, of Rivia," the witcher introduced himself. "A witcher, not a knight."

"What's the matter with him?" Chireadan indicated Dandelion, whom the guards had laid on a pallet in the meantime. "It looks like poisoning. If it is poisoning, then I can help. I've got some good medicine with me."

Geralt sat down, then quickly gave a guarded account of events at the river. The elves looked at each other, and the knight spat through his teeth and frowned.

"Extraordinary," Chireadan remarked. "What could it have been?"

"A djinn in a bottle," muttered Vratimir. "Like a fairy tale—"

"Not quite." Geralt indicated Dandelion, curled up on the pallet. "I don't know of any fairy tale that ends like this."

"That poor fellow's injuries," said Chireadan, "are evidently of a magical nature. I fear that my medicine will not be of much use. But I can at least lessen his suffering. Have you already given him a remedy, Geralt?"

"A painkilling elixir."

"Come and help me. You can hold his head up."

Dandelion greedily drank the medicine, diluted with wine, choked on his last sip, wheezed and covered the leather pillow with spittle.

"I know him," Errdil said. "He's Dandelion, the troubadour and poet. I saw him singing at the court of King Ethain in Cidaris once."

"A troubadour," repeated Chireadan, looking at Geralt. "That's bad. Very bad. The muscles of his neck and throat are attacked. Changes in his vocal cords are starting to take place. The spell's action has to be halted as soon as possible otherwise... This might be irreversible."

"That means... Does that mean he won't be able to talk?"

"Talk, yes. Maybe. Not sing."

Geralt sat down at the table without saying a word and rested his forehead on his clenched fists.

"A wizard," said Vratimir. "A magical remedy or a curative spell is needed. You have to take him to some other town, witcher."

"What?" Geralt raised his head. "And here, in Rinde? Isn't there a wizard here?"

"Magicians are hard to come by in the whole of Redania," said the knight. "Isn't that true? Ever since King Heribert placed an exorbitant tax on spells, magicians have boycotted the capital and those towns which are rigorous in executing the king's edicts. And the councilors of Rinde are famous for their zeal in this respect. Chireadan, Errdil, am I right?"

"You are," confirmed Errdil. "But... Chireadan, may I?"

"You have to," said Chireadan, looking at the witcher. "There's no point in making a secret of it; everyone knows anyway. There's a sorceress staying in the town right now, Geralt."

"Incognito, no doubt?"

"Not very." The elf smiled. "The sorceress in question is something of an individualist. She's ignoring both the boycott imposed on Rinde by the Council of Wizards, and the disposition of the local councilors, and is doing rather splendidly out of it: the boycott means there's tremendous demand for magical services here and, of course, the sorceress isn't paying any levies."

"And the town council puts up with it?"

"The sorceress is staying with a merchant, a trade broker from Novigrad, who is also the honorary ambassador. Nobody can touch her there. She has asylum."

"It's more like house arrest than asylum," corrected Errdil. "She's just about imprisoned there. But she has no shortage of clients. Rich clients. She ostentatiously makes light of the councilors, holds balls and extravagant parties—"

"While the councilors are furious, turn whoever they can against her and tarnish her reputation as best they can," Chireadan cut in. "They spread foul rumors about her and hope, no doubt, that the Novigrad hierarchy will forbid the merchant to grant her asylum."

"I don't like meddling in things like that," muttered Geralt, "but I've got no choice. What's the merchant-ambassador's name?"

"Beau Berrant."

The witcher thought that Chireadan grimaced as he pronounced the name.

"Oh well, it really is your only hope. Or rather, the only hope for that poor fellow moaning on the bed. But whether the sorceress will want to help you . . . I don't know."

"Be careful when you go there," said Errdil. "The mayor's spies are watching the house. You know what to do if they stop you. Money opens all doors."

"I'll go as soon as they open the gates. What's the sorceress called?"

Geralt thought he detected a slight flush on Chireadan's expressive face. But it could have been the glow from the fire in the hearth.

"Yennefer of Vengerberg."

III

"My lord's asleep," repeated the doorman, looking down at Geralt. He was taller by a head and nearly twice as broad in the shoulders. "Are you deaf, you vagabond? The lord's asleep, I said."

"Then let him sleep," agreed the witcher. "I've not got business with your lord but with the lady who is staying here."

"Business, you say." The doorman, as it turned out, was surprisingly witty for someone of such stature and appearance. "Then go, you loiterer, to the whorehouse to satisfy your need. Scram."

Geralt unfastened the purse on his belt and, holding it by the straps, weighed it in his palm.

"You won't bribe me," the Cerberus said proudly.

"I don't intend to."

The porter was too huge to have the reflexes which would let him dodge or shield himself from a quick blow given by an ordinary man. He didn't even have time to blink before the witcher's blow landed. The heavy purse struck him in the temple with a metallic crash. He collapsed against the door, grabbing the frame with both hands. Geralt tore him away from it with a kick in the knee, shoved him with his shoulder and fetched him another blow with the purse. The doorman's eyes grew hazy and diverged in a comical squint, and his legs folded under him like two penknives. The witcher, seeing the strapping fellow moving, although almost unconscious, walloped him with force for the third time, right on the crown of his head.

"Money," he muttered, "opens all doors."

It was dark in the vestibule. A loud snoring came from the door on the left. The witcher peeped in carefully. A fat woman, her nightdress hitched up above her hips, was asleep on a tumbled pallet, snoring and snorting through her nose. It wasn't the most beautiful sight. Geralt dragged the porter into the little room and closed the door.

On the right was another door, half-opened, and behind

it stone steps led down. The witcher was about to pass them when an indistinct curse, a clatter and the dry crash of a vessel cracking reached him from below.

The room was a big kitchen, full of utensils, smelling of herbs and resinous wood. On the stone floor, among fragments of a clay jug, knelt a completely naked man with his head hanging low.

"Apple juice, bloody hell," he mumbled, shaking his head like a sheep which had rammed a wall by a mistake. "Apple... juice. Where... Where're the servants?"

"I beg your pardon?" the witcher asked politely.

The man raised his head and swallowed. His eyes were vague and very bloodshot.

"She wants juice from apples," he stated, then got up with evident difficulty, sat down on a chest covered with a sheep-skin coat, and leaned against the stove. "I have to...take it upstairs because—"

"Do I have the pleasure of speaking to the merchant Beau Berrant?"

"Quieter." The man grimaced painfully. "Don't yell. Listen, in that barrel there...Juice. Apple. Pour it into something... and help me get upstairs, all right?"

Geralt shrugged, then nodded sympathetically. He generally avoided overdoing the alcohol but the state in which the merchant found himself was not entirely unknown to him. He found a jug and a tin mug among the crockery and drew some juice from the barrel. He heard snoring and turned. Beau Berrant was fast asleep, his head hanging on his chest.

For a moment, the witcher considered pouring juice over him to wake him up, but he changed his mind. He left the kitchen, carrying the jug. The corridor ended in a heavy inlaid door. He entered carefully, opening it just enough to slip inside. It was dark, so he dilated his pupils. And wrinkled his nose.

A heavy smell of sour wine, candles and overripe fruit hung in the air. And something else, that brought to mind a mixture of the scents of lilac and gooseberries.

He looked around. The table in the middle of the chamber bore a battlefield of jugs, carafes, goblets, silver plates, dishes and ivory-handled cutlery. A creased tablecloth, which had been pushed aside, was soaked in wine, covered in purple stains and stiff with wax which had trickled down the candlesticks. Orange peel glowed like flowers among plum and peach stones, pear cores and grape stalks. A goblet had fallen over and smashed. The other was in one piece, half full, with a turkey bone sticking out of it. Next to the goblet stood a black, high-heeled slipper. It was made of basilisk skin. There wasn't a more expensive raw material which could be used in the making of shoes.

The other slipper lay under a chair on top of a carelessly discarded black dress with white frills and an embroidered flowery pattern.

For a moment Geralt stood undecided, struggling with embarrassment and the desire to turn on his heel and leave. But that would have meant his tussle with the Cerberus below had been unnecessary. And the witcher didn't like doing anything unnecessarily. He noticed winding stairs in the corner of the chamber.

On the steps, he found four withered white roses and a napkin stained with wine and crimson lipstick. The scent of lilac and gooseberries grew stronger. The stairs led to a bedroom, the floor of which was covered in an enormous, shaggy animal skin. A white shirt with lace cuffs, and umpteen white roses, lay on the skin. And a black stocking.

The other stocking hung from one of the four engraved posts which supported the domed canopy over the bed. The engravings on the posts depicted nymphs and fawns in various positions. Some of the positions were interesting. Others funny. Many repeated themselves.

Geralt cleared his throat loudly, looking at the abundant black locks visible from under the eiderdown. The eiderdown moved and moaned. Geralt cleared his throat even louder.

"Beau?" the abundance of black locks asked indistinctly. "Have you brought the juice?"

"Yes."

A pale triangular face, violet eyes and narrow, slightly contorted lips appeared beneath the black tresses.

"Ooooh…" The lips became even more contorted. "Ooooh… I'm dying of thirst…"

"Here you are."

The woman sat up, scrambling out of the bedclothes. She had pretty shoulders, a shapely neck and, around it, a black velvet choker with a star-shaped jewel sparkling with diamonds. Apart from the choker, she had nothing on.

"Thank you." She took the mug from his hand, drank greedily, then raised her arms and touched her temples. The eiderdown slipped down even further. Geralt averted his eyes—politely, but unwillingly.

"Who are you?" asked the black-haired woman, narrowing her eyes and covering herself with the eiderdown. "What are you doing here? And where, dammit, is Berrant?"

"Which question shall I answer first?"

He immediately regretted his sarcasm. The woman raised her hand and a golden streak shot out from her fingers. Geralt reacted instinctively, crossing both hands in the Sign of Heliotrope, and caught the spell just in front of his face, but the discharge was so strong that it threw him back against the wall. He sank to the floor.

"No need!" he shouted, seeing the woman raise her hand

again. "Lady Yennefer! I come in peace, with no evil intentions!"

A stamping came from the stairs and servants loomed in the bedroom doorway.

"Lady Yennefer!"

"Leave," the sorceress ordered calmly. "I don't need you. You're paid to keep an eye on the house. But since this individual has, nevertheless, managed to get in, I'll take care of him myself. Pass that on to Berrant. And prepare a bath for me."

The witcher got up with difficulty. Yennefer observed him in silence, narrowing her eyes.

"You parried my spell," she finally said. "You're not a sorcerer; that's obvious. But you reacted exceptionally fast. Tell me who you are, stranger who has come in peace. And I advise you to speak quickly."

"I'm Geralt of Rivia. A witcher."

Yennefer leaned out of the bed, grasping a faun—engraved on the pole—by a piece of anatomy well adapted to being grasped. Without taking her eyes off Geralt, she picked a coat with a fur collar up off the floor and wrapped herself up in it tightly before getting up. She poured herself another mug of juice without hurrying, drank it in one go, coughed and came closer. Geralt discreetly rubbed his lower back which, a moment ago, had collided painfully with the wall.

"Geralt of Rivia," repeated the sorceress, looking at him from behind black lashes. "How did you get in here? And for what reason? You didn't hurt Berrant, I hope?"

"No. I didn't. Lady Yennefer, I need your help."

"A witcher," she muttered, coming up even closer and wrapping the coat around her more tightly. "Not only is it the first one I've seen up close but it's none other than the famous White Wolf. I've heard about you."

"I can imagine."

"I don't know what you can imagine." She yawned, then came even closer. "May I?" She touched his cheek and looked him in the eyes. He clenched his jaw. "Do your pupils automatically adapt to light or can you narrow and dilate them according to your will?"

"Yennefer," he said calmly, "I rode nonstop all day from Rinde. I waited all night for the gates to open. I gave your doorman, who didn't want to let me in, a blow to the head. I disturbed your sleep and peace, discourteously and importunately. All because my friend needs help which only you can give him. Give it to him, please, and then, if you like, we can talk about mutations and aberrations."

She took a step back and contorted her lips unpleasantly. "What sort of help do you mean?"

"The regeneration of organs injured through magic. The throat, larynx and vocal cords. An injury caused by a scarlet mist. Or something very much like it."

"Very much like it," she repeated. "To put it in a nutshell, it wasn't a scarlet mist which has injured your friend. So what was it? Speak out. Being torn from my sleep at dawn, I have neither the strength nor the desire to probe your brain."

"Hmm... It's best I start from the beginning."

"Oh, no," she interrupted him. "If it's all that complicated, then wait. An aftertaste in my mouth, disheveled hair, sticky eyes and other morning inconveniences strongly affect my perceptive faculties. Go downstairs to the bath-chamber in the cellar. I'll be there in a minute and then you'll tell me everything."

"Yennefer, I don't want to be persistent but time is pressing. My friend—"

"Geralt," she interrupted sharply, "I climbed out of bed for you and I didn't intend to do that before the chime of midday. I'm prepared to do without breakfast. Do you know why?

Because you brought me the apple juice. You were in a hurry, your head was troubled with your friend's suffering, you forced your way in here, and yet you thought of a thirsty woman. You won me over, so my help is not out of the question. But I won't do anything without hot water and soap. Go. Please."

"Very well."

"Geralt."

"Yes." He stopped on the threshold.

"Make use of the opportunity to have a bath yourself. I can not only guess the age and breed of your horse, but also its color, by the smell."

IV

She entered the bath-chamber just as Geralt, sitting naked on a tiny stool, was pouring water over himself from a bucket. He cleared his throat and modestly turned his back to her.

"Don't be embarrassed," she said, throwing an armful of clothing on the hook. "I don't faint at the sight of a naked man. Triss Merigold, a friend, says if you've seen one, you've seen them all."

He got up, wrapping a towel round his hips.

"Beautiful scar." She smiled, looking at his chest. "What was it? Did you fall under the blade in a sawmill?"

He didn't answer. The sorceress continued to observe him, tilting her head coquettishly.

"The first witcher I can look at from close up, and completely naked at that. Aha!" She leaned over, listening. "I can hear your heart beat. It's very slow. Can you control how much adrenalin you secrete? Oh, forgive me my professional curiosity. Apparently, you're touchy about the qualities of your own body. You're wont to describe these qualities using words which I greatly dislike, lapsing into pompous sarcasm with it, something I dislike even more."

He didn't answer.

"Well, enough of that. My bath is getting cold." Yennefer moved as if she wanted to discard her coat, then hesitated. "I'll take my bath while you talk, to save time. But I don't want to embarrass you and, besides, we hardly know each other. So then, taking decency into account—"

"I'll turn around," he proposed hesitantly.

"No. I have to see the eyes of the person I'm talking to. I've got a better idea."

He heard an incantation being recited, felt his medallion quiver and saw the black coat softly slip to the floor. Then he heard the water splashing.

"Now I can't see your eyes, Yennefer," he said. "And that's a pity."

The invisible sorceress snorted and splashed in the tub. "Go on."

Geralt finished struggling with his trousers, pulling them on under his towel, and sat on the bench. Buckling up his boots, he related the adventure by the river, cutting out most of the skirmish with the catfish. Yennefer didn't seem the type to be interested in fishing.

When he got to the part where the cloud-creature escaped from the jar, the huge soapy sponge froze.

"Well, well," he heard, "that's interesting. A djinn in a bottle."

"No djinn," he contested. "It was some variant of scarlet mist. Some new, unknown type—"

"The new and unknown type deserves to be called something," said the invisible Yennefer. "The name djinn is no worse than any other. Continue, please."

He obeyed. The soap in the tub foamed relentlessly as he

continued his tale, and the water overflowed. Something caught his eye. Looking more carefully he discerned outlines and shapes revealed by the soap covering the invisible Yennefer. They fascinated him to the extent that he was struck dumb.

"Go on!" a voice coming from nothingness, from above the outlines which so absorbed him, urged. "What happened next?"

"That's all," he said. "I chased him away, that djinn, as you call him—"

"How?" The ladle rose and poured water. The soap vanished, as did the shapes.

Geralt sighed. "With an incantation," he said. "An exorcism."

"Which one?" The ladle poured water once more. The witcher started to observe the ladle's action more diligently because the water, albeit briefly, also revealed this and that. He repeated the incantation, substituting the vowel "e" with an intake of breath, according to the safety rule. He thought he'd impress the sorceress by knowing the rule so he was surprised when he heard laughter coming from the tub.

"What's so funny?"

"That exorcism of yours..." The towel flew off its peg and suddenly began to wipe the rest of the outlines. "Triss is going to kill herself laughing when I tell her. Who taught you that, witcher? That incantation?"

"A priestess from Huldra's sanctuary. It's a secret language of the temple—"

"Secret to some." The towel slapped against the brim of the tub, water sprayed on to the floor and wet footprints marked the sorceress's steps. "That wasn't an incantation, Geralt. Nor would I advise you to repeat those words in other temples."

"What was it, if not an incantation?" he asked, watching two black stockings outline shapely legs, one after the other.

"A witty saying." Frilly knickers clung to nothing in an unusually interesting manner. "If rather indecent."

A white shirt with an enormous flower-shaped ruffle fluttered upward and outlined Yennefer's body. She didn't, the witcher noticed, bother with the whalebone nonsense usually worn by women. She didn't have to.

"What saying?" he asked.

"Never mind."

The cork sprang from a rectangular crystal bottle standing on the stool. The bath-chamber started to smell of lilac and gooseberries. The cork traced several circles and jumped back into place. The sorceress fastened the cuffs of her shirt, pulled on a dress and materialized.

"Fasten me up." She turned her back to him while combing her hair with a tortoiseshell comb. He noticed that the comb had a long, sharp prong which could, if need be, easily take the place of a dagger.

He took a deliberately long time fastening her dress, one hook at a time, enjoying the scent of her hair, which fell halfway down her back in a black cascade.

"Going back to the bottle creature," said Yennefer, putting diamond earrings in her ears, "it's obvious that it wasn't your funny incantation that drove him away. The hypothesis that he discharged his fury on your friend and left seems closer to the truth."

"Probably," Geralt agreed, gloomily. "I don't think he flew off to Cidaris to do away with Valdo Marx."

"Who's Valdo Marx?"

"A troubadour who considers my companion, also a poet and musician, a talentless wastrel who panders to the taste of the masses."

The sorceress turned round with a strange glimmer in

her eyes. "Could it be that your friend managed to express a wish?"

"Two. Both stupid. Why do you ask? This fulfilling of wishes by genies is nonsense, after all, djinns, spirits of the lamp—"

"Clearly nonsense," repeated Yennefer with a smile. "Of course. It's an invention, a fairy tale devoid of any sense, like all the legends in which good spirits and fortune tellers fulfill wishes. Stories like that are made up by poor simpletons, who can't even dream of fulfilling their wishes and desires themselves. I'm pleased you're not one of them, Geralt of Rivia. It makes you closer in spirit to me. If I want something, I don't dream of it—I act. And I always get what I want."

"I don't doubt it. Are you ready?"

"I am." The sorceress finished fastening the straps of her slippers and stood up. Even in high heels, she wasn't impressively tall. She shook her hair which, he found, had retained its picturesque, disheveled and curling disarray despite the furious combing.

"I've got a question, Geralt. The seal which closed the bottle... Has your friend still got it?"

The witcher reflected. He had the seal, not Dandelion. But experience had taught him that sorcerers shouldn't be told too much.

"Hmm... I think so." He deceived her as to the reason for his delay in replying. "Yes, he probably does. Why? Is the seal important?"

"That's a strange question," she said sharply, "for a witcher and a specialist in supernatural monstrosities. Someone who ought to know that such a seal is important enough not to touch. And not to let their friend touch."

He clenched his jaw. The blow was well aimed.

"Oh, well." Yennefer changed her tone to a much gentler

one. "No one's infallible and no witcher's infallible, as we see. Everyone can make a mistake. Well, we can get it on our way. Where's your comrade?"

"Here, in Rinde. At Errdil's. The elf's."

She looked at him carefully.

"At Errdil's?" she repeated, contorting her lips in a smile. "I know where that is. And I gather his cousin Chireadan is there too?"

"That's right. But what—?"

"Nothing," she interrupted, raised her arms and closed her eyes.

The medallion around the witcher's neck pulsed, tugged at the chain.

On the damp bath-chamber wall shone the luminous outline of a door which framed a swirling phosphorescent milky nothingness. The witcher cursed. He didn't like magical portals, or traveling by them.

"Do we have to..." He cleared his throat. "It's not far—"

"I can't walk the streets of this town," she cut him short. "They're not too crazy about me here. They might insult me and throw stones—or do something worse. Several people are effectively ruining my reputation here, thinking they can get away with it. Don't worry, my portals are safe."

Geralt had once watched as only half a traveler using a safe portal flew through. The other half was never found. He knew of several cases where people had entered a portal and never been seen again.

The sorceress adjusted her hair again and pinned a pearl-embossed purse to her belt. The purse looked too small to hold anything other than a handful of coppers and a lipstick, but Geralt knew it was no ordinary purse.

"Hold me. Tighter. I'm not made of china. On our way!"

The medallion vibrated, something flashed and Geralt

suddenly found himself in black nothingness, in penetrating cold. He couldn't see, hear or feel anything. Cold was all that his senses could register.

He wanted to curse, but didn't have time.

V

"It's an hour since she went in." Chireadan turned over the hourglass standing on the table. "I'm starting to get worried. Was Dandelion's throat really so bad? Don't you think we ought to go and have a look?"

"She made it quite clear that she didn't want us to." Geralt finished his mug of herb tea, grimacing dreadfully. He valued and liked the settled elves for their intelligence, calm reserve and sense of humor, but he couldn't understand or share their taste in food or drink. "I don't intend to disturb her, Chireadan. Magic requires time. It can take all day and night, as long as Dandelion gets better."

"Oh well, you're right."

A sound of hammering came from the room next door. Errdil, as it turned out, lived in a deserted inn which he had bought intending to renovate and then open with his wife, a quiet, taciturn elf. Vratimir, who had taken to their company after a night spent with the elves in the guardroom, volunteered to help with the repairs. He got down to renovating the wood paneling, working alongside the married couple, as soon as the confusion created by the witcher and Yennefer leaping through the wall in the flash of a portal had subsided.

"I didn't think you'd find it so easy, if I'm to be honest," Chireadan went on. "Yennefer isn't the most spontaneous of people when it comes to help. Others' troubles don't particularly bother her, and don't disturb her sleep. In a word, I've never heard of her helping anyone if there wasn't something in it for her. I wonder what's in it for her to help you and Dandelion."

"Aren't you exaggerating?" The witcher smiled. "I didn't have such a bad impression of her. She likes to demonstrate her superiority, it's true, but compared with other wizards, with that whole arrogant bunch, she's walking charm and kindliness personified."

Chireadan also smiled. "It's almost as though you thought a scorpion were prettier than a spider," he said, "because it's got such a lovely tail. Be careful, Geralt. You're not the first to have judged her like that without knowing she's turned her charm and beauty into weapons. Weapons she uses skilfully and without scruple. Which, of course, doesn't change the fact that she's a fascinating and good-looking woman. You wouldn't disagree, would you?"

Geralt glanced keenly at the elf. For a second time, he thought he saw traces of a blush on his face. It surprised him no less than Chireadan's words. Pure-blooded elves were not wont to admire human women, even the very beautiful ones, and Yennefer, although attractive in her own way, couldn't pass as a great beauty.

Each to their own taste but, in actual fact, not many would describe sorceresses as good-looking. Indeed, all of them came from social circles where the only fate for daughters would be marriage. Who would have thought of condemning their daughter to years of tedious studies and the tortures of somatic mutations if she could be given away in marriage and advantageously allied? Who wished to have a sorceress in their family? Despite the respect enjoyed by magicians, a sorceress's family did not benefit from her in the least because by the time the girl had completed her education, nothing tied her to her family anymore—only brotherhood counted, to the exclusion of all else. So only daughters with no chance of finding a husband become sorceresses.

Unlike priestesses and druidesses, who only unwillingly took ugly or crippled girls, sorcerers took anyone who showed evidence of a predisposition. If the child passed the first years of training, magic entered into the equation—straightening and evening out legs, repairing bones which had badly knitted, patching harelips, removing scars, birthmarks and pox scars. The young sorceress would become attractive because the prestige of her profession demanded it. The result was pseudo-pretty women with the angry and cold eyes of ugly girls. Girls who couldn't forget their ugliness had been covered by the mask of magic only for the prestige of their profession.

No, Geralt couldn't understand Chireadan. His eyes, the eyes of a witcher, registered too many details.

"No, Chireadan," he answered. "I wouldn't disagree. Thank you for the warning. But this only concerns Dandelion. He suffered at my side, in my presence. I didn't manage to save him and I couldn't help him. I'd sit on a scorpion with my bare backside if I knew it would help him."

"That's precisely what you've got to beware of most." The elf smiled enigmatically. "Because Yennefer knows it and she likes to make the most of such knowledge. Don't trust her, Geralt. She's dangerous."

He didn't answer.

Upstairs, the door squeaked. Yennefer stood at the stairs, leaning on the gallery balustrade.

"Witcher, could you come here?"

"Of course."

The sorceress leaned her back against the door of one of the few rooms with furniture, where they had put the suffering troubadour.

The witcher approached, watchful and silent. He saw her

left shoulder, slightly higher than her right. Her nose, slightly too long. Her lips, a touch too narrow. Her chin, receding a little too much. Her brows a little too irregular. Her eyes...

He saw too many details. Quite unnecessarily.

"How's Dandelion?"

"Do you doubt my capabilities?"

He continued watching. She had the figure of a twenty-year-old, although he preferred not to guess at her real age. She moved with natural, unaffected grace. No, there was no way of guessing what she had been like before, what had been improved. He stopped thinking about it; there wasn't any sense.

"Your talented friend will be well," she said. "He'll recover his vocal talents."

"You have my gratitude, Yennefer."

She smiled. "You'll have an opportunity to prove it."

"Can I look in on him?"

She remained silent for a moment, watching him with a strange smile and drumming her fingers on the door-frame. "Of course. Go in."

The medallion on the witcher's neck started to quiver, sharply and rhythmically.

A glass sphere the size of a small watermelon, aflame with a milky light, lay in the center of the floor. The sphere marked the heart of a precisely traced nine-pointed star whose arms reached the corners and walls of the small chamber. A red pentagram was inscribed within the star. The tips of the pentagram were marked by black candles standing in weirdly shaped holders. Black candles had also been lit at the head of the bed where Dandelion, covered with sheepskins, rested. The poet was breathing peacefully; he didn't wheeze or rasp anymore and the rictus of pain had disappeared from his face, to be replaced by an idiotic smile of happiness.

"He's asleep," said Yennefer. "And dreaming."

Geralt examined the patterns traced on the floor. The magic hidden within them was palpable, but he knew it was a dormant magic. It brought to mind the purr of a sleeping lion, without suggesting how the roar might sound.

"What is this, Yennefer?"

"A trap."

"For what?"

"For you, for the time being." The sorceress turned the key in the lock, then turned it over in her hand. The key disappeared.

"And thus I'm trapped," he said coldly. "What now? Are you going to assault my virtue?"

"Don't flatter yourself." Yennefer sat on the edge of the bed. Dandelion, still smiling like a moron, groaned quietly. It was, without a doubt, a groan of bliss.

"What's this all about, Yennefer? If it's a game, I don't know the rules."

"I told you," she began, "that I always get what I want. As it happens, I desire something that Dandelion has. I'll get it from him and we can part ways. Don't worry, he won't come to any harm—"

"The things you've set on the floor," he interrupted, "are used to summon demons. Someone always comes to harm where demons are summoned. I won't allow it."

"—not a hair of his head will be harmed," continued the sorceress, without paying any attention to his words. "His voice will be even more beautiful and he'll be very pleased, even happy. We'll all be happy. And we'll part with no ill feelings or resentment."

"Oh, Virginia," moaned Dandelion without opening his eyes. "Your breasts are so beautiful, more delicate than a swan's down... Virginia..."

"Has he lost his mind? Is he raving?"

"He's dreaming." Yennefer smiled. "His dream wish is being satisfied in his sleep. I probed his mind to the very depths. There wasn't much there. A few obscenities, several dreams and masses of poetry. But be that as it may. The seal which plugged the bottle with the djinn, Geralt, I know he doesn't have it. You do. Please give it to me."

"What do you need the seal for?"

"How should I answer your question?" The sorceress smiled coquettishly. "Let's try this: it's none of your damned business, witcher. Does that satisfy you?"

"No." His smile was equally nasty. "It doesn't. But don't reproach yourself for it, Yennefer. I'm not easily satisfied. Only those who are above average have managed so far."

"Pity. So you'll remain unsatisfied. It's your loss. The seal, please. Don't pull that face; it doesn't suit either your good looks or your complexion. In case you hadn't noticed, let me tell you that you are now beginning to repay the gratitude you owe me. The seal is the first installment for the price to be paid for the singer's voice."

"I see you've divided the price into several installments," he said coldly. "Fine. I might have expected that. But let it be a fair trade, Yennefer. I bought your help. And I'll pay."

She contorted her lips in a smile, but her violet eyes remained wide open and cold.

"You shouldn't have any doubts as to that, witcher."

"Me," he repeated. "Not Dandelion. I'm taking him to a safe place. When I've done that, I'll come back and pay your second installment, and all the others. Because as to the first..."

He reached into a secret pocket of his belt and pulled out the brass seal with the sign of a star and broken cross.

"Here, take it. Not as an installment. Accept it from a

273

witcher as proof of his gratitude for having treated him more
kindly, albeit in a calculated manner, than the majority of your
brethren would have done. Accept it as evidence of goodwill,
which ought to convince you that, having seen to my friend's
safety, I'll return to repay you. I didn't see the scorpion amidst
the flowers, Yennefer. I'm prepared to pay for my inattention."

"A pretty speech." The sorceress folded her arms. "Touching and pompous. Pity it's in vain. I need Dandelion, so he's
staying here."

"He's already been close to the creature you intend to draw
here." Geralt indicated the patterns on the floor. "When you've
finished your handiwork and brought the djinn here, Dandelion is most certainly going to suffer despite all your promises,
maybe even more than before. Because it's the creature from
the bottle that you want, isn't it? Do you intend to master it,
force it to serve you? You don't have to answer. I know it's none
of my damned business. Do what you want, draw ten demons
in if you like. But without Dandelion. If you put him at risk,
this will no longer be an honest trade, Yennefer, and you don't
have the right to demand payment for that. I won't allow—"
He broke off.

"I wondered when you'd feel it," giggled the sorceress.

Geralt tensed his muscles and, clenching his jaw until it
hurt, strained his entire will. It didn't help. He was paralyzed,
like a stone statue, like a post which had been dug into the
ground. He couldn't even wiggle a toe.

"I knew you could deflect a spell thrown straight at you," said
Yennefer. "I also knew that before you tried anything, you'd
try to impress me with your eloquence. You were talking while
the spell hanging over you was working and slowly breaking
you. Now you can only talk. But you don't have to impress me
anymore. I know you're eloquent. Any further efforts in that
direction will only spoil the effect."

"Chireadan—" he said with an effort, still fighting the magical paralysis. "Chireadan will realize that you're up to something. He'll soon work it out, suspect something any minute now, because he doesn't trust you, Yennefer. He hasn't trusted you from the start—"

The sorceress swept her hand in a broad gesture. The walls of the chamber became blurred and took on a uniform dull gray appearance and color. The door disappeared, the windows disappeared, even the dusty curtains and pictures on the wall, splattered with flies, vanished.

"What if Chireadan does figure it out?" She grimaced maliciously. "Is he going to run for help? Nobody will get through my barrier. But Chireadan's not going to run anywhere. He won't do anything against me. Anything. He's under my spell. No, it's not a question of black sorcery. I didn't do anything in that way. It's a simple question of body chemistry. He's fallen in love with me, the blockhead. Didn't you know? Can you imagine, he even intended to challenge Beau to a duel. A jealous elf. That rarely happens. Geralt, it's not for nothing that I chose this house."

"Beau Berrant, Chireadan, Errdil, Dandelion. You really are heading for your goal as straight as you can. But me, Yennefer, you're not going to use me."

"Oh I am, I am." The sorceress got up from the bed and approached him, carefully avoiding the signs and symbols marked out on the floor. "After all, I did say that you owe me something for curing the poet. It's a matter of a trifle, a small favor. After what I've done, what I intend to do here in a moment, I'm leaving Rinde and I've still got unpaid accounts in this town. I've promised several people here something, and I always keep my promises. Since I won't have time to do so myself, you'll keep those promises for me."

He wrestled with all his might. In vain.

"Don't struggle, my little witcher." She smiled spitefully. "It's pointless. You've got a strong will and quite a bit of resistance to magic but you can't contend with me and my spell. And don't act out a farce for me; don't try to charm me with your hard and insolent masculinity. You are the only one to think you're insolent and hard. You'd do anything for me in order to save your friend, even without spells at that. You'd pay any price. You'd lick my boots. And maybe something else, too, if I unexpectedly wished to amuse myself."

He remained silent. Yennefer was standing in front of him, smiling and fiddling with the obsidian star sparkling with diamonds pinned to her velvet ribbon.

"I already knew what you were like," she continued, "after exchanging a few words with you in Beau's bedroom. And I knew what form of payment I'd demand from you. My accounts in Rinde could be settled by anyone, including Chireadan. But you're the one who's going to do it because you have to pay me. For your insolence, for the cold way you look at me, for the eyes which fish for every detail, for your stony face and sarcastic tone of voice. For thinking that you could stand face-to-face with Yennefer of Vengerberg and believe her to be full of self-admiration and arrogance, a calculating witch, while staring at her soapy tits. Pay up, Geralt of Rivia!"

She grabbed his hair with both hands and kissed him violently on the lips, sinking her teeth into them like a vampire. The medallion on his neck quivered and it felt to Geralt as if the chain was shrinking and strangling him. Something blazed in his head while a terrible humming filled his ears. He stopped seeing the sorceress's violet eyes and fell into darkness.

He was kneeling. Yennefer was talking to him in a gentle, soft voice.

"You remember?"

"Yes, my lady." It was his own voice.

"So go and carry out my instructions."

"At your command, my lady."

"You may kiss my hand."

"Thank you, my lady."

He felt himself approach her on his knees. Ten thousand bees buzzed in his head. Her hand smelt of lilac and gooseberries. Lilac and gooseberries... Lilac and gooseberries... A flash. Darkness.

A balustrade, stairs. Chireadan's face.

"Geralt! What's the matter with you? Geralt, where are you going?"

"I have to..." His own voice. "I have to go—"

"Oh, gods! Look at his eyes!"

Vratimir's face, contorted with horror. Errdil's face. And Chireadan's voice.

"No! Errdil! Don't touch him! Don't try to stop him! Out of his way—get out of his way!"

The scent of lilac and gooseberries. Lilac and gooseberries...

A door. The explosion of sunlight. It's hot. Humid. The scent of lilac and gooseberries. There's going to be a storm, he thought.

And that was his last thought.

VI

Darkness. The scent...

Scent? No, smell. Stench of urine, rotten straw and wet rags. The stink of a smoldering torch stuck into an iron grip set in a wall of uneven stone blocks. A shadow thrown by the light of the torch, a shadow on the dirt floor—the shadow of a grille.

The witcher cursed.

"At last." He felt someone lift him up, rest his back against the damp wall. "I was beginning to worry, you didn't regain consciousness for so long."

"Chireadan? Where—dammit, my head's splitting—where are we?"

"Where do you think?"

Geralt wiped his face and looked around. Three rogues were sitting by the opposite wall. He couldn't see them clearly; they were sitting as far from the torch light as possible, in near complete darkness. Something which looked like a heap of rags crouched under the grille which separated them from the lit corridor. It was, in fact, a thin old man with a nose like a stork's beak. The length of his matted stringy hair and the state of his clothes showed that he hadn't arrived yesterday.

"They've thrown us in the dungeon," he said gloomily.

"I'm glad you've regained your ability to draw logical conclusions," said the elf.

"Bloody hell... And Dandelion? How long have we been here? How much time has gone by since—?"

"I don't know. I was unconscious, just like you, when I was thrown in here." Chireadan raked up the straw to sit more comfortably. "Is it important?"

"And how, dammit! Yennefer—And Dandelion—Dandelion's there, with her, and she's planning—Hey, you! How long have we been in here?"

The other prisoners whispered among themselves. None replied.

"Have you gone deaf?" Geralt spat, still unable to get rid of the metallic taste in his mouth. "I'm asking you, what time of day is it? Or night? Surely you know what time they feed you?"

They muttered again, cleared their throats. "Sirs," said one of them at last. "Leave us in peace and don't talk to us. We be decent thieves, not some politicals. We didn't try to attack the authorities. We was only stealing."

"That be it," said another. "You've your corner, we've ours. And let each look after his own."

Chireadan snorted. The witcher spat.

"That's the way it goes," mumbled the hairy old man with a long nose. "Everyone in the clink guards his own corner and holds with his own."

"And you, old man," asked the elf sneeringly, "are you with them or with us? Which camp do you count yourself in?"

"None," he answered proudly, "because I'm innocent."

Geralt spat again. "Chireadan?" he asked, rubbing his temple. "This attempt on the authorities... Is it true?"

"Absolutely. You don't remember?"

"I walked out into the street... People were looking at me... Then... Then there was a shop—"

"A pawnbroker's." The elf lowered his voice. "You went into the pawnbroker's. As soon as you walked in, you punched the owner in the teeth. Hard. Very hard."

The witcher ground his teeth and cursed.

"The pawnbroker fell," Chireadan continued quietly. "And you kicked him several times in delicate places. The assistant ran to help his master and you threw him out of the window, into the street."

"I fear," muttered Geralt, "that wasn't the end of it."

"Your fears are well founded. You left the pawnbroker's and marched down the center of the street, jostling passersby and shouting some nonsense about a lady's honor. There was quite a crowd following you, Errdil, Vratimir and I among them. Then you stopped in front of Laurelnose the apothecary's house, went in, and were back in the street a moment later, dragging Laurelnose by the leg. And you made something of a speech to the crowd."

"What sort of a speech?"

"To put it simply, you stated that a self-respecting man

shouldn't ever call a professional harlot a whore because it's base and repugnant, while using the word *whore* to describe a woman one has never knocked off or paid any money for doing so, is childish and punishable. The punishment, you announced, would be dealt there and then, and it would be fitting for a spoilt child. You thrust the apothecary's head between his knees, pulled down his pants and thrashed his arse with a belt."

"Go on, Chireadan. Go on. Don't spare me."

"You beat Laurelnose on the backside and the apothecary howled and sobbed, called to gods and men alike for help, begged for mercy—he even promised to be better in the future, but you clearly didn't believe him. Then several armed bandits, who in Rinde go by the name of guards, came running up."

"And"—Geralt nodded—"that's when I made a hit at the authorities?"

"Not at all. You made a hit at them much earlier. Both the pawnbroker and Laurelnose are on the town council. Both had called for Yennefer to be thrown out of town. Not only did they vote for it at the council but they badmouthed her in taverns and spread vulgar gossip."

"I guessed that. Carry on. You stopped when the guards appeared. They threw me in here?"

"They wanted to. Oh, Geralt, what a sight it was. What you did to them, it's hard to describe. They had swords, whips, clubs, hatchets, and you only had an ash cane with a pommel, which you'd snatched from some dandy. And when they were all lying on the ground, you walked on. Most of us knew where you were going."

"I'd be happy to know too."

"You were going to the temple. Because the priest Krepp, who's also a member of the council, dedicated a lot of time to

Yennefer in his sermons. You promised him a lesson in respect for the fair sex. When you spoke of him, you omitted his title and threw in other descriptions, to the delight of the children trailing after you."

"Aha," muttered Geralt. "So blasphemy came into it, too. What else? Desecration of the temple?"

"No. You didn't manage to get in there. An entire unit of municipal guards, armed—it seemed to me—with absolutely everything they could lay their hands on in the armory apart from a catapult, was waiting in front of the temple. It looked as if they were going to slaughter you, but you didn't reach them. You suddenly grasped your head with both hands and fainted."

"You don't have to finish. So, Chireadan, how were you imprisoned?"

"Several guards ran to attack you when you fell. I got into a dispute with them. I got a blow over the head with a mace and came to here, in this hole. No doubt they'll accuse me of taking part in an anti-human conspiracy."

"Since we're talking about accusations"—the witcher ground his teeth again—"what's in store for us, do you think?"

"If Neville, the mayor, gets back from the capital on time," muttered Chireadan, "who knows...he's a friend. But if he doesn't, then sentence will be passed by the councilors, including Laurelnose and the pawnbroker, of course. And that means—"

The elf made a brief gesture across his neck. Despite the darkness, the gesture left little doubt as to Chireadan's meaning. The witcher didn't reply. The thieves mumbled to each other and the tiny old man, locked up for his innocence, seemed to be asleep.

"Great," said Geralt finally, and cursed vilely. "Not only will I hang, but I'll do so with the knowledge that I'm the cause of your death, Chireadan. And Dandelion's, too, no doubt. No, don't interrupt. I know it's Yennefer's prank, but I'm the guilty one. It's my foolishness. She deceived me, took the piss out of me, as the dwarves say."

"Hmm..." muttered the elf. "Nothing to add, nothing to take away. I warned you against her. Dammit, I warned you, and I turned out to be just as big an—pardon the word—idiot. You're worried that I'm here because of you, but it's quite the opposite. You're locked up because of me. I could have stopped you in the street, overpowered you, not allowed—But I didn't. Because I was afraid that when the spell she'd cast on you had dispelled, you'd go back and...harm her. Forgive me."

"I forgive you, because you've no idea how strong that spell was. My dear elf, I can break an ordinary spell within a few minutes and I don't faint while doing it. You wouldn't have managed to break Yennefer's spell and you would have had difficulty overpowering me. Remember the guards."

"I wasn't thinking about you. I repeat: I was thinking about her."

"Chireadan?"

"Yes?"

"Do you...Do you—"

"I don't like grand words," interrupted the elf, smiling sadly. "I'm greatly, shall we say, fascinated by her. No doubt you're surprised that anyone could be fascinated by her?"

Geralt closed his eyes to recall an image which, without using grand words, fascinated him inexplicably.

"No, Chireadan," he said. "I'm not surprised."

Heavy steps sounded in the corridor, and a clang of metal. The dungeon was filled with the shadows of four guards. A key grated. The innocent old man leapt away from the bars like a lynx and hid among the criminals.

"So soon?" the elf, surprised, half-whispered. "I thought it would take longer to build the scaffold..."

One of the guards, a tall, strapping fellow, bald as a knee, his mug covered with bristles like a boar, pointed at the witcher.

"That one," he said briefly.

Two others grabbed Geralt, hauled him up and pressed him against the wall. The thieves squeezed into their corner; the long-nosed granddad buried himself in the straw. Chireadan wanted to jump up, but he fell to the dirt floor, retreating from the short sword pointed at his chest.

The bald guard stood in front of the witcher, pulled his sleeves up and rubbed his fist.

"Councilor Laurelnose," he said, "told me to ask if you're enjoying our little dungeon. Perhaps there's something you need? Perhaps the chill is getting to you? Eh?"

Geralt did not answer. Nor could he kick the bald man, as the guards who restrained him were standing on his feet in their heavy boots.

The bald man took a short swing and punched the witcher in the stomach. It didn't help to tense his muscles in defense. Geralt, catching his breath with an effort, looked at the buckle of his own belt for a while; then the guards hauled him up again.

"Is there nothing you need?" the guard continued, stinking of onions and rotting teeth. "The councilor will be pleased that you have no complaints."

Another blow, in the same place. The witcher choked and would have puked, but he had nothing to throw up.

The bald guard turned sideways. He was changing hands.

Wham! Geralt looked at the buckle of his belt again. Although it seemed strange, there was no hole above it through which the wall could be seen.

"Well?" The guard backed away a little, no doubt planning

to take a wider swing. "Don't you have any wishes? Mr. Laurelnose asked whether you have any. But why aren't you saying anything? Tongue-tied? I'll get it straight for you!"

Wham!

Geralt didn't faint this time either. And he had to faint because he cared for his internal organs. In order to faint, he had to force the guard to—

The guard spat, bared his teeth and rubbed his fist again.

"Well? No wishes at all?"

"Just one..." moaned the witcher, raising his head with difficulty. "That you burst, you son-of-a-whore."

The bald guard ground his teeth, stepped back and took a swing—this time, according to Geralt's plan, aiming for his head. But the blow never came. The guard suddenly gobbled like a turkey, grew red, grabbed his stomach with both hands, howled, roared with pain...

And burst.

VII

"And what am I to do with you?"

A blindingly bright ribbon of lightning cut the darkened sky outside the window, followed by a sharp, drawn-out crash of thunder. The downpour was getting harder as the storm cloud passed over Rinde.

Geralt and Chireadan, seated on a bench under a huge tapestry depicting the Prophet Lebiodus pasturing his sheep, remained silent, modestly hanging their heads. Mayor Neville was pacing the chamber, snorting and panting with anger.

"You bloody, shitty sorcerers!" he yelled suddenly, standing still. "Are you persecuting my town, or what? Aren't there any other towns in the world?"

The elf and witcher remained silent.

"To do something like—" the mayor choked. "To turn the warder... Like a tomato! To pulp! To red pulp! It's inhuman!"

"Inhuman and godless," repeated the priest, also present. "So inhuman that even a fool could guess who's behind it. Yes, mayor. We both know Chireadan and the man here, who calls himself a witcher, wouldn't have enough Force to do this. It is all the work of Yennefer, that witch cursed by the gods!" There was a clap of thunder outside, as if confirming the priest's words. "It's her and no one else," continued Krepp. "There's no question about it. Who, if not Yennefer, would want revenge upon Laurelnose?"

"Hehehe," chuckled the mayor suddenly. "That's the thing I'm least angry about. Laurelnose has been scheming against me; he's been after my office. And now the people aren't going to respect him. When they remember how he got it in the arse—"

"That's all it needs, Mr. Neville, you to applaud the crime." Krepp frowned. "Let me remind you that had I not thrown an exorcism at the witcher, he would have raised his hand to strike me and the temple's majesty—"

"And that's because you spoke vilely about her in your sermons, Krepp. Even Berrant complained about you. But what's true is true. Do you hear that, you scoundrels?" The mayor turned to Geralt and Chireadan again. "Nothing justifies what you've done! I don't intend to tolerate such things here! That's enough, now get on with it, tell me everything, tell me what you have for your defense, because if you don't, I swear by all the relics that I'll lead you such a dance as you won't forget to your dying day! Tell me everything, right now, as you would in a confessional!"

Chireadan sighed deeply and looked meaningfully and pleadingly at the witcher.

Geralt also sighed, then cleared his throat. And he recounted everything. Well, almost everything.

"So that's it," said the priest after a moment's silence. "A fine kettle of fish. A genie released from captivity. And an enchantress who has her sights on the genie. Not a bad arrangement. This could end badly, very badly."

"What's a genie?" asked Neville. "And what does this Yennefer want?"

"Enchanters," explained Krepp, "draw their power from the forces of nature, or to put it more accurately, from the so-called Four Elements or Principles, commonly called the natural forces. Air, Water, Fire and Earth. Each of these elements has its own Dimension which is called a Plane in the jargon used by enchanters. There's a Water Plane, Fire Plane and so on. These Dimensions, which are beyond our reach, are inhabited by what are called genies—"

"That's what they're called in legends," interrupted the witcher. "Because as far as I know—"

"Don't interrupt," Krepp cut him short. "The fact that you don't know much was evident in your tale, witcher. So be quiet and listen to what those wiser than you have to say. Going back to the genies, there are four sorts, just as there are four Planes. Djinns are air creatures; marides are associated with the principle of water; afreet are Fire genies and d'ao, the genies of Earth—"

"You've run away with yourself, Krepp," Neville butted in. "This isn't a temple school; don't lecture us. Briefly, what does Yennefer want with this genie?"

"A genie like this, mayor, is a living reservoir of magical energy. A sorcerer who has a genie at their beck and call can direct that energy in the form of spells. They don't have to draw the Force from Nature; the genie does it for them. The power of such an enchanter is enormous, close to omnipotence—"

"Somehow I've never heard of a wizard who can do everything," contradicted Neville. "On the contrary, the power of most of them is clearly exaggerated. They can't do this, they can't—"

"The enchanter Stammelford," interrupted the priest, once more taking on the tone and poise of an academic lecturer, "once moved a mountain because it obstructed the view from his tower. Nobody has managed to do the like, before or since. Because Stammelford, so they say, had the services of a d'ao, an Earth genie. There are records of deeds accomplished by other magicians on a similar scale. Enormous waves and catastrophic rains are certainly the work of marides. Fiery columns, fires and explosions the work of afreets—"

"Whirlwinds, hurricanes, flights above the earth," muttered Geralt, "Geoffrey Monck."

"Exactly. I see you do know something after all." Krepp glanced at him more kindly. "Word has it old Monck had a way of forcing a djinn to serve him. There were rumors that he had more than one. He was said to keep them in bottles and make use of them when need arose. Three wishes from each genie, then it's free and escapes into its own dimension."

"The one at the river didn't fulfill anything," said Geralt emphatically. "He immediately threw himself at Dandelion's throat."

"Genies"—Krepp turned up his nose—"are spiteful and deceitful beings. They don't like being packed into bottles and ordered to move mountains. They do everything they possibly can to make it impossible for you to express your wishes and then they fulfill them in a way which is hard to control and foresee, sometimes literally, so you have to be careful what you say. To subjugate a genie, you need a will of iron, nerves of steel, a strong Force and considerable abilities. From what you say, it looks like your abilities, witcher, were too modest."

"Too modest to subjugate the cad," agreed Geralt. "But I did chase him away; he bolted so fast the air howled. And that's also something. Yennefer, it's true, ridiculed my exorcism—"

"What was the exorcism? Repeat it."

Geralt repeated it, word for word.

"What?!" The priest first turned pale, then red and finally blue. "How dare you! Are you making fun of me?"

"Forgive me," stuttered Geralt. "To be honest, I don't know...what the words mean."

"So don't repeat what you don't know! I've no idea where you could have heard such filth!"

"Enough of that." The mayor waved it all aside. "We're wasting time. Right. We now know what the sorceress wants the genie for. But you said, Krepp, that it's bad. What's bad? Let her catch him and go to hell, what do I care? I think—"

No one ever found out what Neville was thinking, even if it wasn't a boast. A luminous rectangle appeared on the wall next to the tapestry of Prophet Lebiodus, something flashed and Dandelion landed in the middle of the town hall.

"Innocent!" yelled the poet in a clear, melodious tenor, sitting on the floor and looking around, his eyes vague. "Innocent! The witcher is innocent! I wish you to believe it!"

"Dandelion!" Geralt shouted, holding Krepp back, who was clearly getting ready to perform an exorcism or a curse. "Where have you...here...Dandelion!"

"Geralt!" The bard jumped up.

"Dandelion!"

"Who's this?" Neville growled. "Dammit, if you don't put an end to your spells, there's no guarantee what I'll do. I've said that spells are forbidden in Rinde! First you have to put in a written application, then pay a tax and stamp duty...Eh? Isn't it that singer, the witch's hostage?"

"Dandelion," repeated Geralt, holding the poet by the shoulders. "How did you get here?"

"I don't know," admitted the bard with a foolish, worried expression. "To be honest, I'm rather unaware of what happened to me. I don't remember much and may the plague take me if I know what of that is real and what's a nightmare. But I do remember quite a pretty, black-haired female with fiery eyes—"

"What are you telling me about black-haired women for?" Neville interrupted angrily. "Get to the point, squire, to the point. You yelled that the witcher is innocent. How am I to understand that? That Laurelnose thrashed his own arse with his hands? Because if the witcher's innocent, it couldn't have been otherwise. Unless it was a mass hallucination."

"I don't know anything about any arses or hallucinations," said Dandelion proudly. "Or anything about laurel noses. I repeat, that the last thing I remember was an elegant woman dressed in tastefully coordinated black and white. She threw me into a shiny hole, a magic portal for sure. But first she gave me a clear and precise errand. As soon as I'd arrived, I was immediately to say, I quote: 'My wish is for you to believe the witcher is not guilty for what occurred. That, and no other, is my wish.' Word for word. Indeed, I tried to ask what all this was, what it was all about, and why. The black-haired woman didn't let me get a word in edgeways. She scolded me most inelegantly, grasped me by the neck and threw me into the portal. That's all. And now . . ." Dandelion pulled himself up, brushed his doublet, adjusted his collar and fancy—if dirty— ruffles. ". . . perhaps, gentlemen, you'd like to tell me the name of the best tavern in town and where it can be found."

"There are no bad taverns in my town," said Neville slowly. "But before you see them for yourself, you'll inspect the best dungeon in this town very thoroughly. You and your companions. Let me remind you that you're still not free, you scoundrels! Look at them! One tells incredible stories while the other leaps out of the wall and shouts about innocence. I wish, he yells, you to believe me. He has the audacity to wish—"

"My gods!" The priest suddenly grasped his bald crown. "Now I understand! The wish! The last wish!"

"What's happened to you, Krepp?" The mayor frowned. "Are you ill?"

"The last wish!" repeated the priest. "She made the bard express the last, the third wish. And Yennefer set a magical trap and, no doubt, captured the genie before he managed to escape into his own dimension! Mr. Neville, we must—"

It thundered outside. So strongly that the walls shook.

"Dammit," muttered the mayor, going up to the window. "That was close. As long as it doesn't hit a house. All I need now is a fire—Oh gods! Just look! Just look at this! Krepp! What is it?"

All of them, to a man, rushed to the window.

"Mother of mine!" yelled Dandelion, grabbing his throat. "It's him! It's that son of a bitch who strangled me!"

"The djinn!" shouted Krepp. "The Air genie!"

"Above Errdil's tavern!" shouted Chireadan, "above his roof!"

"She's caught him!" The priest leaned out so far he almost fell. "Can you see the magical light? The sorceress has caught the genie!"

Geralt watched in silence.

Once, years ago, when a little snot-faced brat following his studies in Kaer Morhen, the Witchers' Settlement, he and a friend, Eskel, had captured a huge forest bumblebee and tied it to a jug with a thread. They were in fits of laughter watching the antics of the tied bumblebee, until Vesemir, their tutor, caught them at it and tanned their hides with a leather strap.

The djinn, circling above the roof of Errdil's tavern, behaved exactly like that bumblebee. He flew up and fell, he sprang up and dived, he buzzed furiously in a circle. Because the djinn, exactly like the bumblebee in Kaer Morhen, was tied down. Twisted threads of blindingly bright light of various colors were tightly wrapped around him and ended at the roof. But the djinn had more options than the bumblebee, which couldn't knock down surrounding roofs, rip thatches to shreds, destroy chimneys, and shatter towers and garrets. The djinn could. And did.

"It's destroying the town," wailed Neville. "That monster's destroying my town!"

"Hehehe," laughed the priest. "She's found her match, it seems! It's an exceptionally strong djinn! I really don't know who's caught whom, the witch him or he the witch! Ha, it'll end with the djinn grinding her to dust. Very good! Justice will be done!"

"I shit on justice!" yelled the mayor, not caring if there were any voters under the window. "Look what's happening there, Krepp! Panic, ruin! You didn't tell me that, you bald idiot! You played the wise guy, gabbled on, but not a word about what's most important! Why didn't you tell me that that demon... Witcher! Do something! Do you hear, innocent sorcerer? Do something about that demon! I forgive you all your offences, but—"

"There's nothing can be done here, Mr. Neville," snorted Krepp. "You didn't listen to what I was saying, that's all. You never listen to me. This, I repeat, is an exceptionally strong djinn. If it wasn't for that, the sorceress would have hold of him already. Her spell is soon going to weaken, and then the djinn is going to crush her and escape. And we'll have some peace."

"And in the meantime, the town will go to ruins?"

"We've got to wait," repeated the priest, "but not idly.

Give out the orders, mayor. Tell the people to evacuate the surrounding houses and get ready to extinguish fires. What's happening there now is nothing compared to the hell that's going to break loose when the genie has finished with the witch."

Geralt raised his head, caught Chireadan's eye and looked away.

"Mr. Krepp," he suddenly decided, "I need your help. It's about the portal through which Dandelion appeared here. The portal still links the town hall to—"

"There's not even a trace of the portal anymore," the priest said coldly, pointing to the wall. "Can't you see?"

"A portal leaves a trace, even when invisible. A spell can stabilize such a trace. I'll follow it."

"You must be mad. Even if a passage like that doesn't tear you to pieces, what do you expect to gain by it? Do you want to find yourself in the middle of a cyclone?"

"I asked if you can cast a spell which could stabilize the trace."

"Spell?" The priest proudly raised his head. "I'm not a godless sorcerer! I don't cast spells! My power comes from faith and prayer!"

"Can you or can't you?"

"I can."

"Then get on with it, because time's pressing on."

"Geralt," said Dandelion, "you've gone stark raving mad! Keep away from that bloody strangler!"

"Silence, please," said Krepp, "and gravity. I'm praying."

"To hell with your prayers!" Neville hollered. "I'm off to gather the people. We've got to do something and not stand here gabbling! Gods, what a day! What a bloody day!"

The witcher felt Chireadan touch his shoulder. He turned. The elf looked him in the eyes, then lowered his own.

"You're going there because you have to, aren't you?"

Geralt hesitated. He thought he smelled the scent of lilac and gooseberries.

"I think so," he said reluctantly. "I do have to. I'm sorry, Chireadan—"

"Don't apologize. I know what you feel."

"I doubt it. Because I don't know myself."

The elf smiled. The smile had little to do with joy. "That's just it, Geralt. Precisely it."

Krepp pulled himself upright and took a deep breath. "Ready," he said, pointing with pride at the barely visible outline on the wall. "But the portal is unsteady and won't stay there for long. And there's no way to be sure it won't break. Before you step through, sir, examine your conscience. I can give you a blessing, but in order to forgive you your sins—"

"—there's no time," Geralt finished the sentence for him. "I know, Mr. Krepp. There's never enough time for it. Leave the chamber, all of you. If the portal explodes, it'll burst your eardrums."

"I'll stay," said Krepp, when the door had closed behind Dandelion and the elf. He waved his hands in the air, creating a pulsating aura around himself. "I'll spread some protection, just in case. And if the portal does burst...I'll try and pull you out, witcher. What are eardrums to me? They grow back."

Geralt looked at him more kindly.

The priest smiled. "You're a brave man," he said. "You want to save her, don't you? But bravery isn't going to be of much use to you. Djinns are vengeful beings. The sorceress is lost. And if you go there, you'll be lost, too. Examine your conscience."

"I have." Geralt stood in front of the faintly glowing portal. "Mr. Krepp, sir?"

"Yes."

"That exorcism which made you so angry... What do the words mean?"

"Indeed, what a moment for quips and jokes—"

"Please, Mr. Krepp, sir."

"Oh, well," said the priest, hiding behind the mayor's heavy oak table. "It's your last wish, so I'll tell you. It means... Hmm... Hmm... essentially... *get out of here and go fuck yourself!*"

Geralt entered the nothingness, where cold stifled the laughter which was shaking him.

VIII

The portal, roaring and whirling like a hurricane, spat him out with a force that bruised his lungs. The witcher collapsed on the floor, panting and catching his breath with difficulty.

The floor shook. At first he thought he was trembling after his journey through the splitting hell of the portal, but he rapidly realized his mistake. The whole house was vibrating, trembling and creaking.

He looked around. He was not in the small room where he had last seen Yennefer and Dandelion but in the large communal hall of Errdil's renovated tavern.

He saw her. She was kneeling between tables, bent over the magical sphere. The sphere was aflame with a strong, milky light, so bright, enough to shine red through her fingers. The light from the sphere illuminated a scene, flickering and swaying, but clear. Geralt saw the small room with a star and pentagram traced on the floor, blazing with white heat. He saw many-colored, creaking, fiery lines shooting from the pentagram and disappearing up over the roof toward the furious roar of the captured djinn.

Yennefer saw him, jumped up and raised her hand.

"No!" he shouted, "don't do this! I want to help you!"

"Help?" She snorted. "You?"

"Me."

"In spite of what I did to you?"

"In spite of it."

"Interesting. But not important. I don't need your help. Get out of here."

"No."

"Get out of here!" she yelled, grimacing ominously. "It's getting dangerous! The whole thing's getting out of control; do you understand? I can't master him. I don't get it, but the scoundrel isn't weakening at all! I caught him once he'd fulfilled the troubadour's third wish and I should have him in the sphere by now. But he's not getting any weaker! Dammit, it looks as if he's getting stronger! But I'm still going to get the better of him. I'll break—"

"You won't break him, Yennefer. He'll kill you."

"It's not so easy to kill me—"

She broke off. The whole roof of the tavern suddenly flared up. The vision projected by the sphere dissolved in the brightness. A huge fiery rectangle appeared on the ceiling. The sorceress cursed as she lifted her hands, and sparks gushed from her fingers.

"Run, Geralt!"

"What's happening, Yennefer?"

"He's located me..." She groaned, flushing red with effort. "He wants to get at me. He's creating his own portal to get in. He can't break loose but he'll get in by the portal. I can't—I can't stop him!"

"Yennefer—"

"Don't distract me! I've got to concentrate... Geralt, you've got to get out of here. I'll open my portal, a way for you to escape. Be careful; it'll be a random portal. I haven't got time or strength for any other...I don't know where you'll end up...but you'll be safe...Get ready—"

A huge portal on the ceiling suddenly flared blindingly, expanded and grew deformed. Out of the nothingness appeared the shapeless mouth already known to the witcher, snapping its drooping lips and howling loudly enough to pierce his ears. Yennefer jumped, waved her arms and shouted an incantation. A net of light shot from her palm and fell on the djinn. It gave a roar and sprouted long paws which shot toward the sorceress's throat like attacking cobras. Yennefer didn't back away.

Geralt threw himself toward her, pushed her aside and sheltered her. The djinn, tangled in the magical light, sprang from the portal like a cork from a bottle and threw himself at them, opening his jaws. The witcher clenched his teeth and hit him with the Sign without any apparent effect. But the genie didn't attack. He hung in the air just below the ceiling, swelled to an impressive size, goggled at Geralt with his pale eyes and roared. There was something in that roar, something like a command, an order. He didn't understand what it was.

"This way!" shouted Yennefer, indicating the portal which she had conjured up on the wall by the stairs. In comparison to the one created by the genie, the sorceress's portal looked feeble, extremely inferior. "This way, Geralt! Run for it!"

"Only with you!"

Yennefer, sweeping the air with her hands, was shouting incantations and the many-colored fetters showered sparks and creaked. The djinn whirled like the bumblebee, pulling the bonds tight, then loosening them. Slowly but surely he was drawing closer to the sorceress. Yennefer did not back away.

The witcher leapt to her, deftly tripped her up, grabbed her by the waist with one hand and dug the other into her hair at the nape. Yennefer cursed nastily and thumped him in the neck with her elbow. He didn't let go of her. The penetrating smell of ozone, created by the curses, didn't kill the smell of lilac and gooseberries. Geralt stilled the sorceress's kicking legs and jumped, raising her straight up to the opalescently flickering nothingness of the lesser portal.

The portal which led into the unknown.

They flew out in a tight embrace, fell onto a marble floor and slid across it, knocking over an enormous candlestick and a table from which crystal goblets, platters of fruit and a huge bowl of crushed ice, seaweed and oysters showered down with a crash. Screams and squeals came from around the room.

They were lying in the very center of a ballroom, bright with candelabra. Richly clad gentlemen and ladies, sparkling with jewels, had stopped dancing and were watching them in stunned silence. The musicians in the gallery finished their piece in a cacophony which grated on the ears.

"You moron!" Yennefer yelled, trying to scratch out his eyes. "You bloody idiot! You stopped me! I nearly had him!"

"You had shit-all!" he shouted back, furious. "I saved your life, you stupid witch!"

She hissed like a furious cat; her palms showered sparks.

Geralt, turning his face away, caught her by both wrists and they rolled among the oysters, seaweed and crushed ice.

"Do you have an invitation?" A portly man with the golden chain of a chamberlain on his chest was looking at them with a haughty expression.

"Screw yourself!" screamed Yennefer, still trying to scratch Geralt's eyes out.

"It's a scandal," the chamberlain said emphatically. "Verily, you're exaggerating with this teleportation. I'm going to complain to the Council of Wizards. I'll demand—"

No one ever heard what the chamberlain would demand.

Yennefer wrenched herself free, slapped the witcher in the ear with her open palm, kicked him forcefully in the shin and jumped into the fading portal in the wall.

Geralt threw himself after her, catching her hair and belt with a practiced move.

Yennefer, also having gained practice, landed him a blow with her elbow.

The sudden move split her dress at the armpit, revealing a shapely breast. An oyster flew from her torn dress.

They both fell into the nothingness of the portal. Geralt could still hear the chamberlain's voice.

"Music! Play on! Nothing has happened. Please take no notice of that pitiful incident!"

The witcher was convinced that with every successive journey through the portal, the risk of misfortune was multiplying and he wasn't mistaken. They hit the target, Errdil's tavern, but they materialized just under the ceiling. They fell, shattering the stair balustrade and, with a deafening crash, landed on the table. The table had the right not to withstand the blow, and it didn't.

Yennefer found herself under the table. He was sure she had lost consciousness. He was mistaken.

She punched him in the eye and fired a volley of insults straight at him which would do credit to a dwarven undertaker—and they were renowned for their foul language. The curses were accompanied by furious, chaotic blows dealt blindly, randomly.

Geralt grabbed her by the hands and, to avoid being hit by her forehead, thrust his face into the sorceress's cleavage which smelled of lilac, gooseberries and oysters.

"Let me go!" she screamed, kicking like a pony. "You idiot! Let go! The fetters are going to break any moment now. I've got to strengthen them or the djinn will escape!"

He didn't answer, although he wanted to. He grasped her even more tightly, trying to pin her down to the floor. Yennefer swore horribly, struggled, and with all her strength, kicked him in the crotch with her knee. Before he could catch his breath, she broke free and screamed an incantation. He felt a terrible force drag him from the ground and hurl him across the hall until, with a violence that near-stunned him, he slammed against a carved two-doored chest of drawers and shattered it completely.

IX

"What's happening there?!" Dandelion, clinging to the wall, strained his neck, trying to see through the downpour. "Tell me what's happening there, dammit!"

"They're fighting!" yelled an urchin, springing away from the tavern window as if he'd burned himself. His tattered friends also escaped, slapping the mud with their bare heels. "The sorcerer and the witch are fighting!"

"Fighting?" Neville was surprised. "They're fighting, and that shitty demon is ruining my town! Look, he's knocked another chimney down. And damaged the brick-kiln! Hey, you get over there, quick! Gods, we're lucky it's raining or there'd be a fire like nobody's business!"

"This won't last much longer," Krepp said gloomily. "The magical light is weakening, the bonds will break at any moment. Mr. Neville! Order the people to move back! All hell's going to break loose over there at any minute! There'll be only splinters left of that house! Mr. Errdil, what are you laughing at? It's your house. What makes you so amused?"

"I had that wreck insured for a massive sum!"

"Does the policy cover magical and supernatural events?"

"Of course."

"That's wise, Mr. Elf. Very wise. Congratulations. Hey, you people, get to some shelter! Don't get any closer, if you value your lives!"

A deafening crash came from within Errdil's house, and lightning flashed. The small crowd retreated, hiding behind the pillars.

"Why did Geralt go there?" groaned Dandelion. "What the hell for? Why did he insist on saving that witch? Why, dammit? Chireadan, do you understand?"

The elf smiled sadly. "Yes, I do, Dandelion," he said. "I do."

X

Geralt leapt away from another blazing orange shaft which shot from the sorceress's fingers. She was clearly tired, the shafts were weak and slow, and he avoided them with no great difficulty.

"Yennefer!" he shouted. "Calm down! Will you listen?! You won't be able—"

He didn't finish. Thin red bolts of lightning spurted from the sorceress's hands, reaching him in many places and wrapping him up thoroughly. His clothes hissed and started to smolder.

"I won't be able to?" she said through her teeth, standing over him. "You'll soon see what I'm capable of. It will suffice for you to lie there for a while and not get in my way."

"Get this off me!" he roared, struggling in the blazing spider's web. "I'm burning, dammit!"

"Lie there and don't move," she advised, panting heavily.

"It only burns when you move...I can't spare you any more time, witcher. We had a romp, but enough's enough. I've got to take care of the djinn; he's ready to run away—"

"Run away?" Geralt screamed. "It's you who should run away! That djinn...Yennefer, listen to me carefully. I've got to tell you the truth."

XI

The djinn gave a tug at the fetters, traced a circle, tightened the lines holding it, and swept the little tower off Beau Berrant's house.

"What a roar he's got!" Dandelion frowned, instinctively clasping his throat. "What a terrible roar! It looks as if he's bloody furious!"

"That's because he is," said Krepp. Chireadan glanced at him.

"What?"

"He's furious," repeated Krepp. "And I'm not surprised. I'd be furious too if I had to fulfill, to the letter, the first wish accidentally expressed by the witcher—"

"How's that?" shouted Dandelion. "Geralt? Wish?"

"He's the one who held the seal which imprisoned the djinn. The djinn's fulfilling his wishes. That's why the witch can't master it. But the witcher mustn't tell her, even if he's caught on to it by now. He shouldn't tell her."

"Dammit," muttered Chireadan. "I'm beginning to understand. The warder in the dungeon burst..."

"That was the witcher's second wish. He's still got one left. The last one. But, gods help us, he shouldn't reveal that to Yennefer!"

XII

She stood motionless, leaning over him, paying no attention to the djinn struggling at its bonds above the tavern roof. The building shook, lime and splinters poured from the ceiling, furniture crept along the floor, shuddering spasmodically.

"So that's how it is," she hissed. "Congratulations. You deceived me. Not Dandelion, but you. That's why the djinn's fighting so hard! But I haven't lost yet, Geralt. You underestimate me, and you underestimate my power. I've still got the djinn and you in my hand. You've still got one last wish, haven't you? So make it. You'll free the djinn and then I'll bottle it."

"You haven't got enough strength left, Yennefer."

"You underestimate my strength. The wish, Geralt!"

"No, Yennefer. I can't... The djinn might fulfill it, but it won't spare you. It'll kill you when it's free. It'll take its revenge on you ... You won't manage to catch it and you won't manage to defend yourself against it. You're weakened; you can barely stand. You'll die, Yennefer."

"That's my risk!" she shouted, enraged. "What's it to you what happens to me? Think rather what the djinn can give you! You've still got one wish! You can ask what you like! Make use of it! Use it, witcher! You can have anything! Anything!"

XIII

"Are they both going to die?" wailed Dandelion. "How come? Krepp, why? After all, the witcher—Why, by all perfidious and unexpected plagues, isn't he escaping? Why? What's keeping him? Why doesn't he leave that bloody witch to her fate and run away? It's senseless!"

"Absolutely senseless," repeated Chireadan bitterly. "Absolutely."

"It's suicide. And plain idiocy!"

"It's his job, after all," interrupted Neville. "The witcher's saving my town. May the gods be my witness—if he defeats the witch and chases the demon away, I'll reward him handsomely..."

Dandelion snatched the hat decorated with a heron's feather from his head, spat into it, threw it in the mud and trampled on it, spitting out words in various languages as he did.

"But he's..." he groaned suddenly, "still got one wish in reserve! He could save both her and himself! Mr. Krepp!"

"It's not that simple," the priest pondered. "But if... If he expressed the right wish... If he somehow tied his fate to the fate... No, I don't think it would occur to him. And it's probably better that it doesn't."

XIV

"The wish, Geralt! Hurry up! What do you desire? Immortality? Riches? Fame? Power? Might? Privileges? Hurry, we haven't any time!" He was silent. "Humanity," she said suddenly, smiling nastily. "I've guessed, haven't I? That's what you want; that's what you dream of! Of release, of the freedom to be who you want, not who you have to be. The djinn will fulfill that wish, Geralt. Just say it."

He stayed silent.

She stood over him in the flickering radiance of the wizard's sphere, in the glow of magic, amidst the flashes of rays restraining the djinn, streaming hair and eyes blazing violet, erect, slender, dark, terrible...

And beautiful.

All of a sudden she leaned over and looked him in the eyes. He caught the scent of lilac and gooseberries.

"You're not saying anything," she hissed. "So what is it you desire, witcher? What is your most hidden dream? Is it that you don't know or you can't decide? Look for it within yourself, look deeply and carefully because, I swear by the Force, you won't get another chance like this!"

But he suddenly knew the truth. He knew it. He knew what she used to be. What she remembered, what she couldn't forget, what she lived with. Who she really was before she had become a sorceress.

Her cold, penetrating, angry and wise eyes were those of a hunchback.

He was horrified. No, not of the truth. He was horrified that she would read his thoughts, find out what he had guessed. That she would never forgive him for it. He deadened that thought within himself, killed it, threw it from his memory forever, without trace, feeling, as he did so, enormous relief. Feeling that—

The ceiling cracked open. The djinn, entangled in the net of the now fading rays, tumbled right on top of them, roaring, and in that roar were triumph and murder lust. Yennefer leapt to meet him. Light beamed from her hands. Very feeble light.

The djinn opened his mouth and stretched his paws toward her.

The witcher suddenly understood what it was he wanted.

And he made his wish.

XV

The house exploded. Bricks, beams and planks flew up in a cloud of smoke and sparks. The djinn spurted from the dust-storm, as huge as a barn. Roaring and choking with triumphant laughter, the Air genie, free now, not tied to any-one's will, traced three circles above the town, tore the spire from the town hall, soared into the sky and vanished.

"It's escaped! It's escaped!" called Krepp. "The witcher's had his way! The genie has flown away! It won't be a threat to anyone anymore!"

"Ah," said Errdil with genuine rapture, "what a wonderful ruin!"

"Dammit, dammit!" hollered Dandelion, huddled behind the wall. "It's shattered the entire house! Nobody could survive that! Nobody, I tell you!"

"The witcher, Geralt of Rivia, has sacrificed himself for the town," mayor Neville said ceremoniously. "We won't forget him. We'll revere him. We'll think of a statue..."

Dandelion shook a piece of wicker matting bound with clay from his shoulder, brushed his jerkin free of lumps of rain-dampened plaster, looked at the mayor and, in a few well-chosen words, expressed his opinion about sacrifice, reverence, memory and all the statues in the world.

XVI

Geralt looked around. Water was slowly dripping from the hole in the ceiling. There were heaps of rubble and stacks of timber all around. By a strange coincidence, the place where they lay was completely clear. Not one plank or one brick had fallen on them. It was as if they were being protected by an invisible shield.

Yennefer, slightly flushed, knelt by him, resting her hands on her knees.

"Witcher." She cleared her throat. "Are you dead?"

"No." Geralt wiped the dust from his face and hissed.

Slowly, Yennefer touched his wrist and delicately ran her fingers along his palm. "I burnt you—"

"It's nothing. A few blisters—"

"I'm sorry. You know, the djinn's escaped. For good."

"Do you regret it?"

"Not much."

"Good. Help me up, please."

"Wait," she whispered. "That wish of yours . . . I heard what you wished for. I was astounded, simply astounded. I'd have expected anything but to . . . What made you do it, Geralt? Why . . . Why me?"

"Don't you know?"

She leaned over him, touched him. He felt her hair, smelling of lilac and gooseberries, brush his face and he suddenly knew that he'd never forget that scent, that soft touch, knew that he'd never be able to compare it to any other scent or touch. Yennefer kissed him and he understood that he'd never desire any lips other than hers, so soft and moist, sweet with lipstick. He knew that, from that moment, only she would exist, her neck, shoulders and breasts freed from her black dress, her delicate, cool skin, which couldn't be compared to any other he had ever touched. He gazed into her violet eyes, the most beautiful eyes in the world, eyes which he feared would become . . .

Everything. He knew.

"Your wish," she whispered, her lips very near his ear. "I don't know whether such a wish can ever be fulfilled. I don't know whether there's such a Force in Nature that could fulfill such a wish. But if there is, then you've condemned yourself. Condemned yourself to me."

He interrupted her with a kiss, an embrace, a touch, caresses and then with everything, his whole being, his every thought, his only thought, everything, everything, everything. They broke the silence with sighs and the rustle of clothing strewn on the floor. They broke the silence very gently, lazily, and they were considerate and very thorough. They were caring and tender and, although neither quite knew what caring and tenderness were, they succeeded because they very much wanted to. And they were in no hurry whatsoever. The whole world had ceased to exist for a brief moment, but to them, it seemed like a whole eternity.

And then the world started to exist again; but it existed very differently.

"Geralt?"

"Mmm?"

"What now?"

"I don't know."

"Nor do I. Because, you see, I . . . I don't know whether it was worth condemning yourself to me. I don't know how— Wait, what are you doing . . . ? I wanted to tell you—"

"Yennefer . . . Yen."

"Yen," she repeated, giving in to him completely. "Nobody's ever called me that. Say it again."

"Yen."

"Geralt."

XVII

It had stopped raining. A rainbow appeared over Rinde and cut the sky with a broken, colored arc. It looked as if it grew straight from the tavern's ruined roof.

"By all the gods," muttered Dandelion, "what silence . . . They're dead, I tell you. Either they've killed each other or my djinn's finished them off."

"We should go and see," said Vratimir, wiping his brow

307

with his crumpled hat. "They might be wounded. Should I call a doctor?"

"An undertaker, more like it," said Krepp. "I know that witch, and that witcher's got the devil in his eyes too. There's no two ways about it; we've got to start digging two pits in the cemetery. I'd advise sticking an aspen stake into that Yennefer before burying her."

"What silence," repeated Dandelion. "Beams were flying all over the place a moment ago and now it's as quiet as a grave."

They approached the tavern ruins very cautiously and slowly.

"Let the carpenter get the coffins ready," said Krepp. "Tell the carpenter—"

"Quiet," interrupted Errdil. "I heard something. What was it, Chireadan?"

The elf brushed the hair off his pointed ear and tilted his head.

"I'm not sure... Let's get closer."

"Yennefer's alive," said Dandelion suddenly, straining his musical ear. "I heard her moan. There, she moaned again!"

"Uhuh," confirmed Errdil. "I heard it, too. She moaned. She must really be suffering. Chireadan, where are you going? Careful!"

The elf backed away from the shattered window through which he had carefully peeped.

"Let's get out of here," he said quietly. "Let's not disturb them."

"They're both alive? Chireadan? What are they doing?"

"Let's get out of here," repeated the elf. "Let's leave them alone for a bit. Let them stay there, Yennefer, Geralt and his last wish. Let's wait in a tavern; they'll join us before long. Both of them."

"What are they doing?" Dandelion was curious. "Tell me, dammit!"

The elf smiled. Very, very sadly. "I don't like grand words," he said. "And it's impossible to give it a name without using grand words."

CHAPTER SEVEN

THE VOICE OF REASON

Falwick, in full armor, without a helmet and with the crimson coat of the Order flung over his shoulder, stood in the glade. Next to him, with his arms across his chest, was a stocky, bearded dwarf in an overcoat lined with fox fur over a chainmail shirt of iron rings. Tailles, wearing no armor but a short, quilted doublet, paced slowly, brandishing his unsheathed sword from time to time.

The witcher looked about, restraining his horse. All around glinted the cuirasses and flat helmets of soldiers armed with lances.

"Bloody hell," muttered Geralt. "I might have expected this."

Dandelion turned his horse and quietly cursed at the sight of the lances cutting off their retreat.

"What's this about, Geralt?"

"Nothing. Keep your mouth shut and don't butt in. I'll try to lie my way out of it somehow."

"What's it about, I ask you? More trouble?"

"Shut up."

"It was a stupid idea after all, to ride into town," groaned the troubadour, glancing toward the nearby towers of the temple visible above the forest. "We should have stayed at Nenneke's and not stirred beyond the walls—"

"Shut up. It'll all become clear, you'll see."

"Doesn't look like it."

Dandelion was right. It didn't. Tailles, brandishing his naked sword, continued pacing without looking in their direction. The soldiers, leaning on their spears, were watching gloomily and indifferently, with the expression of professionals for whom killing does not provoke much interest.

They dismounted. Falwick and the dwarf slowly approached.

"You've insulted Tailles, a man of good birth, witcher," said the count without preamble or the customary courtesies. "And Tailles, as you no doubt remember, threw down the gauntlet. It was not fit to press you within the grounds of the temple, so we waited until you emerged from behind the priestess's skirt. Tailles is waiting. You must fight."

"Must?"

"Must."

"But do you not think, Falwick"—Geralt smiled disapprovingly—"that Tailles, a man of good birth, does me too much honor? I never attained the honor of being knighted, and it's best not to mention the circumstances of my birth. I fear I'm not sufficiently worthy of... How does one say it, Dandelion?"

"Unfit to give satisfaction and joust in the lists," recited the poet, pouting. "The code of chivalry proclaims—"

"The Chapter of the Order is governed by its own code," interrupted Falwick. "If it were you who challenged a Knight of the Order, he could either refuse or grant you satisfaction, according to his will. But this is the reverse: it is the knight who challenges you and by this he raises you to his own level—but, of course, only for the time it takes to avenge the insult. You can't refuse. The refusal of accepting the dignity would render you unworthy."

"How logical," said Dandelion with an apelike expression. "I see you've studied the philosophers, sir Knight."

"Don't butt in." Geralt raised his head and looked into Falwick's eyes. "Go on, sir. I'd like to know where this is leading. What would happen if I turned out to be...unworthy?"

"What would happen?" Falwick gave a malicious smile. "I'd order you hung from a branch, you ratcatcher."

"Hold on," the dwarf said hoarsely. "Take it easy, sir. And no invective, all right?"

"Don't you teach me manners, Cranmer," hissed the knight. "And remember, the prince has given you orders which you're to execute to the letter."

"It's you who shouldn't be teaching me, Count." The dwarf rested his hand on the double-headed axe thrust into his belt. "I know how to carry out orders, and I can do without your advice. Allow me, Geralt sir. I'm Dennis Cranmer, captain of Prince Hereward's guards."

The witcher bowed stiffly, looking into the dwarf's eyes, light gray and steel-like beneath the bushy flaxen eyebrows.

"Stand your ground with Tailles, sir," Dennis Cranmer continued calmly. "It'll be better that way. It's not a fight to the death, only until one of you is rendered helpless. So fight in the field and let him render you helpless."

"I beg your pardon?"

"Sir Tailles is the prince's favorite," said Falwick, smiling spitefully. "If you touch him with your saber during the fight, you mutant, you will be punished. Captain Cranmer will arrest you and take you to face his Highness. To be punished. Those are his orders."

The dwarf didn't even glance at the knight; his cold, steel eyes did not leave Geralt.

The witcher smiled faintly but quite nastily. "If I understand correctly," he said, "I'm to fight the duel because, if I
refuse, I'll be hanged. If I fight, I'm to allow my opponent
to injure me because if I wound him, I'll be put to the rack.
What charming alternatives. Maybe I should save you the
bother? I'll thump my head against the pine tree and render
myself helpless. Will that grant you satisfaction?"

"Don't sneer," hissed Falwick. "Don't make your situation
any worse. You've insulted the Order, you vagabond, and you
have to be punished for it; do you understand? And young
Tailles needs the fame of defeating a witcher, so the Chapter
wants to give it to him. Otherwise you'd be hanging already.
You allow yourself to be defeated and you save your miserable
life. We don't care about your corpse; we want Tailles to nick
your skin. And your mutant skin heals quickly. So, go ahead.
Decide. You've got no choice."

"That's what you think, is it, sir?" Geralt smiled even more
nastily and looked around at the soldiers appraisingly. "But I
think I do."

"Yes, that's true," admitted Dennis Cranmer. "You do. But
then there'll be bloodshed, great bloodshed. Like at Blaviken.
Is that what you want? Do you want to burden your conscience
with blood and death? Because the alternative you're thinking
of, Geralt, is blood and death."

"Your argument is charming, Captain, fascinating even,"
mocked Dandelion. "You're trying to bait a man ambushed in
the forest with humanitarianism, calling on his nobler feelings.
You're asking him, as I understand, to deign not to spill the
blood of the brigands who attacked him. He's to take pity on
the thugs because the thugs are poor, have got wives, children
and, who knows, maybe even mothers. But don't you think,
Captain Cranmer, that your worrying is premature? Because I
look at your lancers and see that their knees are shaking at the

very thought of fighting with Geralt of Rivia, the witcher who dealt with a striga alone, with his bare hands. There won't be any bloodshed here; nobody will be harmed here—aside from those who might break their legs running away."

"I," said the dwarf calmly and pugnaciously, "have nothing to reproach my knees with. I've never run away from anyone and I'm not about to change my ways. I'm not married, don't know anything about any children and I'd prefer not to bring my mother, a woman with whom I'm not very well acquainted, into this. But I will carry out the orders I've been given. To the letter, as always. Without calling on any feelings, I ask Geralt of Rivia to make a decision. I will accept whatever he decides and will behave accordingly."

They looked each other in the eyes, the dwarf and the witcher.

"Very well," Geralt said finally. "Let's deal with it. It's a pity to waste the day."

"You agree, then." Falwick raised his head and his eyes glistened. "You'll fight a duel with the highborn Tailles of Dorndal?"

"Yes."

"Good. Prepare yourself."

"I'm ready." Geralt pulled on his gauntlets. "Let's not waste time. There'll be hell if Nenneke finds out about this. So let's sort it out quickly. Dandelion, keep calm. It's got nothing to do with you. Am I right, Cranmer, sir?"

"Absolutely," the dwarf stated firmly and looked at Falwick. "Absolutely, sir. Whatever happens, it only concerns you."

The witcher took the sword from his back.

"No," said Falwick, drawing his. "You're not going to fight with that razor of yours. Take my sword."

Geralt shrugged. He took the count's blade and swiped it to try it out.

"Heavy," he said coldly. "We could just as easily use spades."

"Tailles has the same. Equal chances."

"You're very funny, Falwick."

The soldiers surrounded the glade, forming a loose circle. Tailles and the witcher stood facing each other.

"Tailles? What do you say to an apology?"

The young knight screwed up his lips, folded his left arm behind his back and froze in a fencing position.

"No?" Geralt smiled. "You don't want to listen to the voice of reason? Pity."

Tailles squatted down, leapt and attacked without warning. The witcher didn't even make an effort to parry and avoided the flat point with a swift half-turn. The knight swiped broadly. The blade cut through the air once more. Geralt dodged beneath it in an agile pirouette, jumped softly aside and, with a short, light feint, threw Tailles off his rhythm. Tailles cursed, cut broadly from the right, lost his balance for a moment and tried to regain it while, instinctively, clumsily, holding his sword high to defend himself. The witcher struck with the speed and force of a lightning bolt, extending his arm to its full length and slashing straight ahead. The heavy sword thundered against Tailles' blade, deflecting it so hard it hit the knight in the face. Tailles howled, fell to his knees and touched the grass with his forehead.

Falwick ran up to him.

Geralt dug his sword into the ground and turned around.

"Hey, guards!" yelled Falwick, getting up. "Take him!"

"Stand still! To your places!" growled Dennis Cranmer, touching his axe. The soldiers froze.

"No, Count," the dwarf said slowly. "I always execute orders to the letter. The witcher did not touch Tailles. The kid hit himself with his own iron. His hard luck."

"His face is destroyed! He's disfigured for life!"

"Skin heals." Dennis Cranmer fixed his steel eyes on the witcher and bared his teeth. "And the scar? For a knight, a scar is a commendable reminder, a reason for fame and glory, which the Chapter so desired for him. A knight without a scar is a prick, not a knight. Ask him, Count, and you'll see that he's pleased."

Tailles was writhing on the ground, spitting blood, whimpering and wailing; he didn't look pleased in the least.

"Cranmer!" roared Falwick, tearing his sword from the ground, "you'll be sorry for this, I swear!"

The dwarf turned around, slowly pulled the axe from his belt, coughed and spat into his palm. "Oh, Count, sir," he rasped. "Don't perjure yourself. I can't stand perjurers and Prince Hereward has given me the right to punish them. I'll turn a deaf ear to your stupid words. But don't repeat them, if you please."

"Witcher." Falwick, puffing with rage, turned to Geralt. "Get yourself out of Ellander. Immediately. Without a moment's delay!"

"I rarely agree with him," muttered Dennis, approaching the witcher and returning his sword, "but in this case he's right. I'd ride out pretty quick."

"We'll do as you advise." Geralt slung the belt across his back. "But before that, I have words for the count. Falwick!"

The Knight of the White Rose blinked nervously and wiped his palms on his coat.

"Let's just go back to your Chapter's code for a minute," continued the witcher, trying not to smile. "One thing really interests me. If I, let us say, felt disgusted and insulted by your attitude in this whole affair, if I challenged you to the sword right now, what would you do? Would you consider me sufficiently worthy to cross blades with? Or would you refuse, even though you knew that by doing so I would take you to be unworthy even to be spat on, punched in the face and kicked in the arse under the eyes of the foot soldiers? Count Falwick, be so gracious as to satisfy my curiosity."

Falwick grew pale, took a step back, looked around. The soldiers avoided his eyes. Dennis Cranmer grimaced, stuck his tongue out and sent a jet of saliva a fair distance.

"Even though you're not saying anything," continued Geralt, "I can hear the voice of reason in your silence, Falwick, sir. You've satisfied my curiosity; now I'll satisfy yours. If the Order bothers Mother Nenneke or the priestesses in any way, or unduly intrudes upon Captain Cranmer, then may you know, Count, that I'll find you and, not caring about any code, will bleed you like a pig."

The knight grew even paler.

"Don't forget my promise, Count. Come on, Dandelion. It's time for us to leave. Take care, Dennis."

"Good luck, Geralt." The dwarf gave a broad smile. "Take care. I'm very pleased to have met you, and hope we'll meet again."

"The feeling's mutual, Dennis."

They rode away with ostensible slowness, not looking back. They began to canter only once they were hidden by the forest.

"Geralt," the poet said suddenly, "surely we won't head straight south? We'll have to make a detour to avoid Ellander and Hereward's lands, won't we? Or do you intend to continue with this show?"

"No, Dandelion, I don't. We'll go through the forests and then join the Traders' Trail. Remember, not a word in Nenneke's presence about this quarrel. Not a word."

"We are riding out without any delay, I hope?"

"Immediately."

II

Geralt leaned over, checked the repaired hoop of his stirrup and fitted the stirrup leather, still stiff, smelling of new skins and hard to buckle. He adjusted the saddle-girth, the travel bags, the horse blanket rolled up behind the saddle and the silver sword strapped to it. Nenneke was motionless next to him, her arms folded.

Dandelion approached, leading his bay gelding.

"Thank you for the hospitality, Venerable One," he said seriously. "And don't be angry with me anymore. I know that, deep down, you like me."

"Indeed," agreed Nenneke without smiling. "I do, you dolt, although I don't know why myself. Take care."

"So long, Nenneke."

"So long, Geralt. Look after yourself."

The witcher's smile was surly.

"I prefer to look after others. It turns out better in the long run."

From the temple, from between columns entwined with ivy, Iola emerged in the company of two younger pupils. She was carrying the witcher's small chest. She avoided his eyes awkwardly and her troubled smile combined with the blush on her freckled, chubby face made a charming picture. The pupils accompanying her didn't hide their meaningful glances and barely stopped themselves from giggling.

"For Great Melitele's sake," sighed Nenneke, "an entire parting procession. Take the chest, Geralt. I've replenished your elixirs. You've got everything that was in short supply. And that medicine, you know the one. Take it regularly for two weeks. Don't forget. It's important."

"I won't. Thanks, Iola."

The girl lowered her head and handed him the chest. She

so wanted to say something. She had no idea what ought to be said, what words ought to be used. She didn't know what she'd say, even if she could. She didn't know. And yet she so much wanted to.

Their hands touched.

Blood. Blood. Blood. Bones like broken white sticks. Tendons like whitish cords exploding from beneath cracking skin cut by enormous paws bristling with thorns, and sharp teeth. The hideous sound of torn flesh, and shouting—shameless and horrifying in its shamelessness. The shamelessness of the end. Of death. Blood and shouting. Shouting. Blood. Shouting—

"Iola!"

Nenneke, with extraordinary speed considering her girth, rushed to the girl lying on the ground, shaken by convulsions, and held her down by her shoulders and hair. One of the pupils stood as if paralyzed, the other, more clearheaded, knelt on Iola's legs. Iola arched her back, opened her mouth in a soundless, mute cry.

"Iola!" Nenneke shouted. "Iola! Speak! Speak, child! Speak!"

The girl stiffened even more, clenched her jaws, and a thin trickle of blood ran down her cheek. Nenneke, growing red with the effort, shouted something which the witcher didn't understand, but his medallion tugged at his neck so hard that he was forced to bend under the pressure of its invisible weight.

Iola stilled.

Dandelion, pale as a sheet, sighed deeply. Nenneke raised herself to her knees and stood with an effort.

"Take her away," she said to the pupils. There were more of them now; they'd gathered, grave and silent.

"Take her," repeated the priestess, "carefully. And don't leave her alone. I'll be there in a minute."

She turned to Geralt. The witcher was standing motionless, fiddling with the reins in his sweaty hands.

"Geralt . . . Iola—"

"Don't say anything, Nenneke."

"I saw it, too . . . for a moment. Geralt, don't go."

"I've got to."

"Did you see . . . did you see that?"

"Yes. And not for the first time."

"And?"

"There's no point in looking over your shoulder."

"Don't go, please."

"I've got to. See to Iola. So long, Nenneke."

The priestess slowly shook her head, sniffed and, in an abrupt move, wiped a tear away with her wrist.

"Farewell," she whispered, not looking him in the eye.

extras

orbit

meet the author

ANDRZEJ SAPKOWSKI was born in 1948 in Poland. He studied economy and business, but the success of his fantasy cycle about the sorcerer Geralt of Rivia turned him into a bestselling writer and a winner of a World Fantasy Award for Lifetime Achievement. He is now one of Poland's most famous and successful authors.

if you enjoyed
THE LAST WISH

look out for

SWORD OF DESTINY
Tales of the Witcher

by

Andrzej Sapkowski

A collection of unmissable tales set in the epic fantasy universe that inspired the Netflix show and the hit video games, Sword of Destiny *follows Geralt the Witcher as he battles monsters, demons, and prejudices alike...*

Geralt is a witcher, a man whose magic powers, enhanced by long training and a mysterious elixir, have made him a brilliant fighter and a merciless assassin. Yet he is no ordinary murderer. His targets are the monsters and vile fiends that ravage the land and attack the innocent.

THE BOUNDS OF REASON

I

'He won't get out of there, I'm telling you,' the pockmarked man said, shaking his head with conviction. 'It's been an hour and a quarter since he went down. That's the end of 'im.'

The townspeople, crammed among the ruins, stared in silence at the black hole gaping in the debris, at the rubble-strewn opening. A fat man in a yellow jerkin shifted from one foot to the other, cleared his throat and took off his crumpled biretta.

'Let's wait a little longer,' he said, wiping the sweat from his thinning eyebrows.

'For what?' the spotty-faced man snarled. 'Have you forgotten, Alderman, that a basilisk is lurking in that there dungeon? No one who goes in there comes out. Haven't enough people perished? Why wait?'

'But we struck a deal,' the fat man muttered hesitantly. 'This just isn't right.'

'We made a deal with a living man, Alderman,' said the spotty-faced man's companion, a giant in a leather butcher's apron. 'And now he's dead, sure as eggs is eggs. It was plain from the start he was heading to his doom, just like the others. Why, he even went in without a looking glass, taking only a sword. And you can't kill a basilisk without a looking glass, everyone knows that.'

'You've saved yourself a shilling, Alderman,' the spotty-faced man added. 'For there's no one to pay for the basilisk. So get off home nice and easy. And we'll take the sorcerer's horse and chattels. Shame to let goods go to waste.'

'Aye,' the butcher said. 'A sturdy mare, and saddlebags nicely stuffed. Let's take a peek at what's inside.'

'This isn't right. What are you doing?'

'Quiet, Alderman, and stay out of this, or you're in for a hiding,' the spotty-faced man warned.

'Sturdy mare,' the butcher repeated.

'Leave that horse alone, comrade.'

The butcher turned slowly towards the newcomer, who had appeared from a recess in the wall, and the people gathered around the entrance to the dungeon.

The stranger had thick, curly, chestnut hair. He was wearing a dark brown tunic over a padded coat and high riding boots. And he was not carrying a weapon.

'Move away from the horse,' he repeated, smiling venomously. 'What is this? Another man's horse, saddlebags and property, and you can't take your watery little eyes off them, can't wait to get your scabby mitts on them? Is that fitting behaviour?'

The spotty-faced man, slowly sliding a hand under his coat, glanced at the butcher. The butcher nodded, and beckoned towards a part of the crowd, from which stepped two stocky men with close-cropped hair. They were holding clubs of the kind used to stun animals in a slaughterhouse.

'Who are you,' the spotty-faced man asked, still holding his hand inside his coat, 'to tell us what is right and what is not?'

'That is not your concern, comrade.'

'You carry no weapon.'

''Tis true.' The stranger smiled even more venomously. 'I do not.'

'That's too bad.' The spotty-faced man removed his hand – and with it a long knife – from inside his coat. 'It is very unfortunate that you do not.'

The butcher also drew a knife, as long as a cutlass. The other two men stepped forward, raising their clubs.

'I have no need,' the stranger said, remaining where he stood. 'My weapons follow me.'

Two young women came out from behind the ruins, treading with soft, sure steps. The crowd immediately parted, then stepped back and thinned out.

The two women grinned, flashing their teeth and narrowing their eyes, from whose corners broad, tattooed stripes ran towards their ears. The muscles of their powerful thighs were visible beneath lynx skins wrapped around their hips, and on their sinuous arms, naked above their mail gloves. Sabre hilts stuck up behind their shoulders, which were also protected by chainmail.

Slowly, very slowly, the spotty-faced man bent his knees and dropped his knife on the ground.

A rattle of stones and a scraping sound echoed from the hole in the rubble, and then two hands, clinging to the jagged edge of the wall, emerged from the darkness. After the hands then appeared, in turn, a head of white hair streaked with brick dust, a pale face, and a sword hilt projecting above the shoulders. The crowd murmured.

The white-haired man reached down to haul a grotesque shape from the hole; a bizarre bulk smeared in blood-soaked dust. Holding the creature by its long, reptilian tail, he threw it without a word at the fat Alderman's feet. He sprang back, tripping against a collapsed fragment of wall, and looked at the curved, birdlike beak, webbed wings and the hooked talons on the scaly feet. At the swollen dewlap, once crimson, now a dirty russet. And at the glazed, sunken eyes.

'There's your basilisk,' the white-haired man said, brushing the dust from his trousers, 'as agreed. Now my two hundred lintars, if you please. Honest lintars, not too clipped. I'll check them, you can count on it.'

The Alderman drew out a pouch with trembling hands. The white-haired man looked around, and then fixed his gaze for a moment on the spotty-faced man and the knife lying by his foot. He looked at the man in the dark brown tunic and at the young women in the lynx skins.

'As usual,' he said, taking the pouch from the Alderman's trembling hands, 'I risk my neck for you for a paltry sum, and in the meantime you go after my things. You never change; a pox on the lot of you.'

'Haven't been touched,' the butcher muttered, moving back. The men with the clubs had melted into the crowd long before. 'Your things haven't been touched, sir.'

'That pleases me greatly,' the white-haired man smiled. At the sight of the smile burgeoning on his pale face, like a wound bursting, the small crowd began to quickly disperse. 'And for that reason, friend, you shall also remain untouched. Go in peace. But make haste.'

The spotty-faced man was also retreating. The spots on his white face were unpleasantly conspicuous.

'Hey, stop there,' the man in the dark brown tunic said to him. 'You've forgotten something.'

'What is that... sir?'

'You drew a knife on me.'

The taller of the women suddenly swayed, legs planted widely apart, and twisted her hips. Her sabre, which no one saw her draw, hissed sharply through the air. The spotty-faced man's head flew upwards in an arc and fell into the gaping opening to the dungeon. His body toppled stiffly and heavily, like a tree being felled, among the crushed bricks. The crowd let out a scream. The second woman, hand on her sword hilt, whirled around nimbly, protecting her partner's back. Needlessly. The crowd, stumbling and falling over on the rubble, fled towards the town as fast as they could. The Alderman loped at the front with impressive strides, outdistancing the huge butcher by only a few yards.

'An excellent stroke,' the white-haired man commented coldly, shielding his eyes from the sun with a black-gloved hand. 'An excellent stroke from a Zerrikanian sabre. I bow before the skill and beauty of the free warriors. I'm Geralt of Rivia.'

'And I,' the stranger in the dark brown tunic pointed at the faded coat of arms on the front of his garment, depicting three black birds sitting in a row in the centre of a uniformly gold field, 'am Borch, also known as Three Jackdaws. And these are my girls, Téa and Véa. That's what I call them, because you'll twist your tongue on their right names. They are both, as you correctly surmised, Zerrikanian.'

'Thanks to them, it appears, I still have my horse and belongings. I thank you, warriors. My thanks to you too, sir.'

'Three Jackdaws. And you can drop the "sir". Does anything detain you in this little town, Geralt of Rivia?'

'Quite the opposite.'

'Excellent. I have a proposal. Not far from here, at the crossroads on the road to the river port, is an inn. It's called the Pensive Dragon. The vittles there have no equal in these parts. I'm heading there with food and lodging in mind. It would be my honour should you choose to keep me company.'

'Borch.' The white-haired man turned around from his horse and looked into the stranger's bright eyes. 'I wouldn't want anything left unclear between us. I'm a witcher.'

'I guessed as much. But you said it as you might have said "I'm a leper".'

extras

'There are those,' Geralt said slowly, 'who prefer the company of lepers to that of a witcher.'

'There are also those,' Three Jackdaws laughed, 'who prefer sheep to girls. Ah, well, one can only sympathise with the former and the latter. I repeat my proposal.'

Geralt took off his glove and shook the hand being proffered.

'I accept, glad to have made your acquaintance.'

'Then let us go, for I hunger.'

if you enjoyed
THE LAST WISH

look out for

THE TOWER OF FOOLS

Book One of the Hussite Trilogy

by

Andrzej Sapkowski

Andrzej Sapkowski, winner of the World Fantasy Award for Lifetime Achievement, created an international phenomenon with his New York Times bestselling Witcher series. Now he introduces readers to a new hero: Reynevan, a young alchemist and healer journeying across a war-torn land.

When a thoughtless indiscretion finds Reinmar of Bielau caught in the crosshairs of a powerful noble family, he is forced to flee his home.

extras

But once he passes beyond the city walls, he finds that there are dangers ahead as well as behind. Pursued by dark forces both human and mystic, Reynevan finds himself in the Narrenturm, *the Tower of Fools, a medieval asylum for the mad—or for those who dare to think differently and challenge the prevailing order.*

Gloria Patri, et Filio et Spiritui sancto.
Sicut erat in principio, et nunc, et semper
et in saecula saeculorum, Amen.
Alleluia!

As the monks concluded the Gloria, Reynevan, kissing the back of Adèle of Stercza's neck, placed his hand beneath her orchard of pomegranates, engrossed, mad, like a young hart skipping upon the mountains to his beloved...

A mailed fist struck the door, which thudded open with such force that the lock was torn off the frame and shot through the window like a meteor. Adèle screamed shrilly as the Stercza brothers burst into the chamber.

Reynevan tumbled out of bed, positioning it between himself and the intruders, grabbed his clothes and began to hurriedly put them on. He largely succeeded, but only because the brothers Stercza had directed their frontal attack at their sister-in-law.

"You vile harlot!" bellowed Morold of Stercza, dragging a naked Adèle from the bedclothes.

"Wanton whore!" chimed in Wittich, his older brother, while Wolfher—next oldest after Adèle's husband Gelfrad—did not even open his mouth, for pale fury had deprived him of speech. He struck Adèle hard in the face. The Burgundian screamed. Wolfher struck her again, this time backhanded.

"Don't you dare hit her, Stercza!" yelled Reynevan, but his voice broke and trembled with fear and a paralysing feeling of impotence, caused by his trousers being round his knees. "Don't you dare!"

His cry achieved its effect, although not the way he had intended. Wolfher and Wittich, momentarily forgetting their adulterous sister-in-law, pounced on Reynevan, raining down a hail of punches and kicks on the boy. He cowered under the blows, but rather than defend or protect himself, he stubbornly pulled on his trousers as though they were some kind of magical armour. Out of the corner of one eye, he saw Wittich drawing a knife. Adèle screamed.

"Don't," Wolfher snapped at his brother. "Not here!"

Reynevan managed to get onto his knees. Wittich, face white with fury, jumped at him and punched him, throwing him to the floor again. Adèle let out a piercing scream, which broke off as Morold struck her in the face and pulled her hair.

"Don't you dare..." Reynevan groaned "...hit her, you scoundrels!"

"Bastard!" yelled Wittich. "Just you wait!"

Wittich leaped forward, punched and kicked once and twice. Wolfher stopped him at the third.

"Not here," Wolfher repeated calmly, but it was a baleful calm. "Into the courtyard with him. We'll take him to Bierutów. That slut, too."

"I'm innocent!" wailed Adèle of Stercza. "He bewitched me! Enchanted me! He's a sorcerer! *Sorcier! Diab*—"

Morold silenced her with another punch. "Hold your tongue, trollop," he growled. "You'll get the chance to scream. Just wait awhile."

"Don't you *dare* hit her!" yelled Reynevan.

"We'll give you a chance to scream, too, little rooster," Wolfher added, still menacingly calm. "Come on, out with him."

The Stercza brothers threw Reynevan down the garret's steep stairs and the boy tumbled onto the landing, splintering part of the wooden balustrade. Before he could get up, they seized him again and threw him out into the courtyard, onto sand strewn with steaming piles of horse shit.

"Well, well, well," said Nicolaus of Stercza, the youngest of the brothers, barely a stripling, who was holding the horses. "Look who's stopped by. Could it be Reinmar of Bielawa?"

"The scholarly braggart Bielawa," snorted Jentsch of Knobelsdorf, known as Eagle Owl, a comrade and relative of the Sterczas. "The arrogant know-all Bielawa!"

"Shitty poet," added Dieter Haxt, another friend of the family. "Bloody Abélard!"

"And to prove to him we're well read, too," said Wolfher as he descended the stairs, "we'll do to him what they did to Abélard when he was caught with Héloïse. Well, Bielawa? How do you fancy being a capon?"

"Go fuck yourself, Stercza."

"What? What?" Although it seemed impossible, Wolfher Stercza had turned even paler. "The rooster still has the audacity to open his beak? To crow? The bullwhip, Jentsch!"

"Don't you dare beat him!" Adèle called impotently as she was led down the stairs, now clothed, albeit incompletely. "Don't you dare! Or I'll tell everyone what you are like! That you courted me yourself, pawed me and tried to debauch me behind your brother's back! That you swore vengeance on me if I spurned you! Which is why you are so...so..."

She couldn't find the German word and the entire tirade fell apart. Wolfher just laughed.

"Verily!" he mocked. "People will listen to the Frenchwoman, the lewd strumpet. The bullwhip, Eagle Owl!"

The courtyard was suddenly awash with black Augustinian habits.

"What is happening here?" shouted the venerable Prior Erasmus Steinkeller, a bony and sallow old man. "Christians, what are you doing?"

"Begone!" bellowed Wolfher, cracking the bullwhip. "Begone, shaven-heads, hurry off to your prayer books! Don't interfere in knightly affairs, or woe betide you, blackbacks!"

"Good Lord." The prior put his liver-spotted hands together. "Forgive them, for they know not what they do. *In nomine Patris, et Filii—*"

"Morold, Wittich!" roared Wolfher. "Bring the harlot here! Jentsch, Dieter, bind her paramour!"

"Or perhaps," snarled Stefan Rotkirch, another friend of the family who had been silent until then, "we'll drag him behind a horse a little?"

"We could. But first, we'll give him a flogging!"

Wolfher aimed a blow with the horsewhip at the still-prone Reynevan but did not connect, as his wrist was seized by Brother Innocent, nicknamed "Brother Insolent" by his fellow friars, whose impressive height and build were apparent despite his humble monkish stoop. His vicelike grip held Wolfher's arm motionless.

Stercza swore coarsely, jerked himself away and gave the monk a hard shove. But he might as well have shoved the tower in Oleśnica Castle for all the effect it had. Brother Innocent didn't budge an inch. He shoved Wolfher back, propelling him halfway across the courtyard and dumping him in a pile of muck.

For a moment, there was silence. And then they all rushed the huge monk. Eagle Owl, the first to attack, was punched in the teeth and tumbled across the sand. Morold of Stercza took a thump to the ear and staggered off to one side, staring vacantly. The others swarmed over the Augustinian like ants, raining blows on the monk's huge form. Brother Insolent retaliated just as savagely and in a distinctly unchristian way, quite at odds with Saint Augustine's rule of humility.

The sight enraged the old prior. He flushed like a beetroot, roared like a lion and rushed into the fray, striking left and right with heavy blows of his rosewood crucifix.

"*Pax!*" he bellowed as he struck. "*Pax! Vobiscum!* Love thy neighbour! *Proximum tuum! Sicut te ipsum!* Whoresons!"

Dieter Haxt punched him hard. The old man was flung over backwards and his sandals flew up, describing pretty trajectories in the air. The Augustinians cried out and several of them charged into battle, unable to restrain themselves. The courtyard was seething in earnest.

Wolfher of Stercza, who had been shoved out of the confusion, drew a short sword and brandished it—bloodshed looked inevitable. But Reynevan, who had finally managed to stand up, whacked him in the back of the head with the handle of the bullwhip he had picked up. Stercza held his head and turned around, only for Reynevan to lash him across the face. As Wolfher fell to the ground, Reynevan rushed towards the horses.

"Adèle! Here! To me!"

Adèle didn't even budge, and the indifference painted on her face was alarming. Reynevan leaped into the saddle. The horse neighed and fidgeted.

"Adèèèèèèle!"

Morold, Wittich, Haxt and Eagle Owl were now running towards him. Reynevan reined the horse around, whistled piercingly and spurred it hard, making for the gate.

"After him!" yelled Wolfher. "To your horses and get after him!"

Reynevan's first thought was to head towards Saint Mary's Gate and out of the town into the woods, but the stretch of Cattle Street leading to the gate was totally crammed with wagons. Furthermore, the horse, urged on and frightened by the cries of an unfamiliar rider, was showing great individual initiative, so before he knew it, Reynevan was hurtling along at a gallop towards the town square, splashing mud and scattering passers-by. He didn't have to look back to know the others were hot on his heels given the thudding of hooves, the neighing of horses, the angry roaring of the Sterczas and the furious yelling of people being jostled.

He jabbed the horse to a full gallop with his heels, hitting and knocking over a baker carrying a basket. A shower of loaves and pastries flew into the mud, soon to be trodden beneath the hooves of the Sterczas' horses. Reynevan didn't even look back, more concerned with what was ahead of him than behind. A cart piled high with faggots of brushwood loomed up before his eyes. The cart was blocking almost the entire street, the rest of which was occupied by a group of half-clothed urchins, kneeling down and busily digging something extremely engrossing out of the muck.

"We have you, Bielawa!" thundered Wolfher from behind, also seeing the obstruction.

Reynevan's horse was racing so swiftly there was no chance of stopping it. He pressed himself against its mane and closed his eyes. As a result, he didn't see the half-naked children scatter with the speed and grace of rats. He didn't look back, so nor did he see a peasant in a sheepskin jerkin turn around, somewhat stupefied, as he hauled a cart into the road. Nor did he see the Sterczas riding broadside into the cart. Nor Jentsch of Knobelsdorf soaring from the saddle and sweeping half of the faggots from the cart with his body.

Reynevan galloped down Saint John's Street, between the town hall and the burgermeister's house, hurtling at full speed into Oleśnica's huge and crowded town square. Pandemonium erupted. Aiming for the southern frontage and the squat, square tower of the Oława Gate visible above it, Reynevan galloped through the crowds, leaving havoc behind him. Townsfolk yelled and pigs squealed, as overturned stalls and benches showered a hail of household goods and foodstuffs of every kind in all directions. Clouds of feathers flew everywhere as the Sterczas—hot on Reynevan's heels—added to the destruction.

Reynevan's horse, frightened by a goose flying past its nose, recoiled and hurtled into a fish stall, shattering crates and bursting open barrels. The enraged fishmonger made a great swipe with a keep net, missing Reynevan but striking the horse's rump. The horse whinnied and slewed sideways, upending a stall selling thread and ribbons, and only a miracle prevented Reynevan from falling. Out of the corner of one eye, he saw the stallholder running after him brandishing a huge cleaver (serving God only knew what purpose in the haberdashery trade). Spitting out some goose feathers stuck to his lips, he brought the horse under control and galloped through the shambles, knowing that the Oława Gate was very close.

"I'll tear your balls off, Bielawa!" Wolfher of Stercza roared from behind. "I'll tear them off and stuff them down your throat!"

"Kiss my arse!"

Only four men were chasing him now—Rotkirch had been pulled from his horse and was being roughed up by some infuriated market traders.

Reynevan darted like an arrow down an avenue of animal carcasses suspended by their legs. Most of the butchers leaped back in alarm, but one carrying a large haunch of beef on one shoulder tumbled under the hooves of Wittich's horse, which took fright, reared up and was ploughed into by Wolfher's horse. Wittich flew from the saddle straight onto the meat stall, nose-first into livers, lights and kidneys, and was then landed on by Wolfher. His foot was caught in the stirrup and before he could free himself, he had destroyed a large number of stalls and covered himself in mud and blood.

At the last moment, Reynevan quickly lowered his head over the horse's neck to duck under a wooden sign with a piglet's head painted on it. Dieter Haxt, who was bearing down on him, wasn't quick enough and the cheerfully grinning piglet slammed into his forehead. Dieter flew from the saddle and crashed into a pile of refuse, frightening some cats. Reynevan turned around. Now only Nicolaus of Stercza was keeping up with him.

Reynevan shot out of the chaos at a full gallop and into a small square where some tanners were working. As a frame hung with wet hides loomed up before him, he urged his horse to jump. It did. And Reynevan didn't fall off. Another miracle.

Nicolaus wasn't as lucky. His horse skidded to a halt in front of the frame and collided with it, slipping on the mud and scraps of meat and fat. The youngest Stercza shot over his horse's head, with very unfortunate results. He flew belly-first right onto a scythe used for scraping leather which the tanners had left propped up against the frame.

At first, Nicolaus had no idea what had happened. He got up from the ground, caught hold of his horse, and only when it snorted and stepped back did his knees sag and buckle beneath him. Still not really knowing what was happening, the youngest Stercza slid across the mud after the panicked horse, which was still moving back and snorting. Finally, as he released the reins and tried to get to his feet again, he realised something was wrong and looked down at his midriff.

And screamed.

He dropped to his knees in the middle of a rapidly spreading pool of blood.

Dieter Haxt rode up, reined in his horse and dismounted. A moment later, Wolfher and Wittich followed suit.

Nicolaus sat down heavily. Looked at his belly again. Screamed and then burst into tears. His eyes began to glaze over as the blood gushing from him mingled with the blood of the oxen and hogs butchered that morning.

"Nicolaaaaus!" yelled Wolfher.

Nicolaus of Stercza coughed and choked. And died.

"You are dead, Reinmar of Bielawa!" Wolfher of Stercza, pale with fury, bellowed towards the gate. "I'll catch you, kill you, destroy you. Exterminate you and your entire viperous family. Your entire viperous family, do you hear?"

Reynevan didn't. Amid the thud of horseshoes on the bridge planks, he was leaving Oleśnica and dashing south, straight for the Wrocław highway.

orbit

Follow us:

f **/orbitbooksUS**

🐦 **/orbitbooks**

▶ **/orbitbooks**

Join our mailing list
to receive alerts on our
latest releases and deals.

orbitbooks.net

Enter our monthly
giveaway for the chance
to win some epic prizes.

orbitloot.com

SWORD OF DESTINY

By Andrzej Sapkowski

The Last Wish
Sword of Destiny
Blood of Elves
The Time of Contempt
Baptism of Fire
The Tower of Swallows
The Lady of the Lake
Season of Storms

The Malady and Other Stories:
An Andrzej Sapkowski Sampler (e-only)

SWORD OF DESTINY

ANDRZEJ SAPKOWSKI

Translated by David French

www.orbitbooks.net

Originally published in Polish as *Miecz Przeznaczenia*

Orbit
Hachette Book Group
1290 Avenue of the Americas
New York, NY 10104
www.orbitbooks.net

Printed in the United States of America

LSC-C

First U.S. ebook edition: May 2015
First U.S. paperback edition: December 2015
Originally published in Great Britain by Gollancz

Printing 21, 2021

Orbit is an imprint of Hachette Book Group.
The Orbit name and logo are trademarks of Little, Brown Book Group Limited.

The Hachette Speakers Bureau provides a wide range of authors for speaking events. To find out more, go to www.hachettespeakersbureau.com or call (866) 376-6591.

The publisher is not responsible for websites (or their content) that are not owned by the publisher.

Library of Congress Control Number: 2015916031

ISBN: 978-0-316-38970-9

CONTENTS

THE BOUNDS OF REASON

I

'He won't get out of there, I'm telling you,' the pockmarked man said, shaking his head with conviction. 'It's been an hour and a quarter since he went down. That's the end of 'im.'

The townspeople, crammed among the ruins, stared in silence at the black hole gaping in the debris, at the rubble-strewn opening. A fat man in a yellow jerkin shifted from one foot to the other, cleared his throat and took off his crumpled biretta.

'Let's wait a little longer,' he said, wiping the sweat from his thinning eyebrows.

'For what?' the spotty-faced man snarled. 'Have you forgotten, Alderman, that a basilisk is lurking in that there dungeon? No one who goes in there comes out. Haven't enough people perished? Why wait?'

'But we struck a deal,' the fat man muttered hesitantly. 'This just isn't right.'

'We made a deal with a living man, Alderman,' said the spotty-faced man's companion, a giant in a leather butcher's apron. 'And now he's dead, sure as eggs is eggs. It was plain from the start he was heading to his doom, just like the others. Why, he even went in without a looking glass, taking only a sword. And you can't kill a basilisk without a looking glass, everyone knows that.'

'You've saved yourself a shilling, Alderman,' the spotty-faced man added. 'For there's no one to pay for the basilisk. So get off home nice and easy. And we'll take the sorcerer's horse and chattels. Shame to let goods go to waste.'

'Aye,' the butcher said. 'A sturdy mare, and saddlebags nicely stuffed. Let's take a peek at what's inside.'

'This isn't right. What are you doing?'

'Quiet, Alderman, and stay out of this, or you're in for a hiding,' the spotty-faced man warned.

'Sturdy mare,' the butcher repeated.

'Leave that horse alone, comrade.'

The butcher turned slowly towards the newcomer, who had appeared from a recess in the wall, and the people gathered around the entrance to the dungeon.

The stranger had thick, curly, chestnut hair. He was wearing a dark brown tunic over a padded coat and high riding boots. And he was not carrying a weapon.

'Move away from the horse,' he repeated, smiling venomously. 'What is this? Another man's horse, saddlebags and property, and you can't take your watery little eyes off them, can't wait to get your scabby mitts on them? Is that fitting behaviour?'

The spotty-faced man, slowly sliding a hand under his coat, glanced at the butcher. The butcher nodded, and beckoned towards a part of the crowd, from which stepped two stocky men with close-cropped hair. They were holding clubs of the kind used to stun animals in a slaughterhouse.

'Who are you,' the spotty-faced man asked, still holding his hand inside his coat, 'to tell us what is right and what is not?'

'That is not your concern, comrade.'

'You carry no weapon.'

''Tis true.' The stranger smiled even more venomously. 'I do not.'

'That's too bad.' The spotty-faced man removed his hand – and with it a long knife – from inside his coat. 'It is very unfortunate that you do not.'

The butcher also drew a knife, as long as a cutlass. The other two men stepped forward, raising their clubs.

'I have no need,' the stranger said, remaining where he stood. 'My weapons follow me.'

Two young women came out from behind the ruins, treading

with soft, sure steps. The crowd immediately parted, then stepped back and thinned out.

The two women grinned, flashing their teeth and narrowing their eyes, from whose corners broad, tattooed stripes ran towards their ears. The muscles of their powerful thighs were visible beneath lynx skins wrapped around their hips, and on their sinuous arms, naked above their mail gloves. Sabre hilts stuck up behind their shoulders, which were also protected by chainmail.

Slowly, very slowly, the spotty-faced man bent his knees and dropped his knife on the ground.

A rattle of stones and a scraping sound echoed from the hole in the rubble, and then two hands, clinging to the jagged edge of the wall, emerged from the darkness. After the hands then appeared, in turn, a head of white hair streaked with brick dust, a pale face, and a sword hilt projecting above the shoulders. The crowd murmured.

The white-haired man reached down to haul a grotesque shape from the hole; a bizarre bulk smeared in blood-soaked dust. Holding the creature by its long, reptilian tail, he threw it without a word at the fat Alderman's feet. He sprang back, tripping against a collapsed fragment of wall, and looked at the curved, birdlike beak, webbed wings and the hooked talons on the scaly feet. At the swollen dewlap, once crimson, now a dirty russet. And at the glazed, sunken eyes.

'There's your basilisk,' the white-haired man said, brushing the dust from his trousers, 'as agreed. Now my two hundred lintars, if you please. Honest lintars, not too clipped. I'll check them, you can count on it.'

The Alderman drew out a pouch with trembling hands. The white-haired man looked around, and then fixed his gaze for a moment on the spotty-faced man and the knife lying by his foot. He looked at the man in the dark brown tunic and at the young women in the lynx skins.

'As usual,' he said, taking the pouch from the Alderman's trembling hands, 'I risk my neck for you for a paltry sum, and in the meantime you go after my things. You never change; a pox on the lot of you.'

'Haven't been touched,' the butcher muttered, moving back. The

3

men with the clubs had melted into the crowd long before. 'Your things haven't been touched, sir.'

'That pleases me greatly,' the white-haired man smiled. At the sight of the smile burgeoning on his pale face, like a wound bursting, the small crowd began to quickly disperse. 'And for that reason, friend, you shall also remain untouched. Go in peace. But make haste.'

The spotty-faced man was also retreating. The spots on his white face were unpleasantly conspicuous.

'Hey, stop there,' the man in the dark brown tunic said to him. 'You've forgotten something.'

'What is that . . . sir?'

'You drew a knife on me.'

The taller of the women suddenly swayed, legs planted widely apart, and twisted her hips. Her sabre, which no one saw her draw, hissed sharply through the air. The spotty-faced man's head flew upwards in an arc and fell into the gaping opening to the dungeon. His body toppled stiffly and heavily, like a tree being felled, among the crushed bricks. The crowd let out a scream. The second woman, hand on her sword hilt, whirled around nimbly, protecting her partner's back. Needlessly. The crowd, stumbling and falling over on the rubble, fled towards the town as fast as they could. The Alderman loped at the front with impressive strides, outdistancing the huge butcher by only a few yards.

'An excellent stroke,' the white-haired man commented coldly, shielding his eyes from the sun with a black-gloved hand. 'An excellent stroke from a Zerrikanian sabre. I bow before the skill and beauty of the free warriors. I'm Geralt of Rivia.'

'And I,' the stranger in the dark brown tunic pointed at the faded coat of arms on the front of his garment, depicting three black birds sitting in a row in the centre of a uniformly gold field, 'am Borch, also known as Three Jackdaws. And these are my girls, Téa and Véa. That's what I call them, because you'll twist your tongue on their right names. They are both, as you correctly surmised, Zerrikanian.'

'Thanks to them, it appears, I still have my horse and belongings. I thank you, warriors. My thanks to you too, sir.'

'Three Jackdaws. And you can drop the "sir". Does anything detain you in this little town, Geralt of Rivia?'

'Quite the opposite.'

'Excellent. I have a proposal. Not far from here, at the crossroads on the road to the river port, is an inn. It's called the Pensive Dragon. The vittals there have no equal in these parts. I'm heading there with food and lodging in mind. It would be my honour should you choose to keep me company.'

'Borch.' The white-haired man turned around from his horse and looked into the stranger's bright eyes. 'I wouldn't want anything left unclear between us. I'm a witcher.'

'I guessed as much. But you said it as you might have said "I'm a leper".'

'There are those,' Geralt said slowly, 'who prefer the company of lepers to that of a witcher.'

'There are also those,' Three Jackdaws laughed, 'who prefer sheep to girls. Ah, well, one can only sympathise with the former and the latter. I repeat my proposal.'

Geralt took off his glove and shook the hand being proffered.

'I accept, glad to have made your acquaintance.'

'Then let us go, for I hunger.'

II

The innkeeper wiped the rough table top with a cloth, bowed and smiled. Two of his front teeth were missing.

'Right, then . . . ' Three Jackdaws looked up for a while at the blackened ceiling and the spiders dancing about beneath it.

'First . . . First, beer. To save your legs, an entire keg. And to go with the beer . . . What do you propose with the beer, comrade?'

'Cheese?' risked the innkeeper.

'No,' Borch grimaced. 'We'll have cheese for dessert. We want something sour and spicy with the beer.'

'At your service,' the innkeeper smiled even more broadly. His two front teeth were not the only ones he lacked. 'Elvers with garlic in olive oil and green pepper pods in vinegar or marinated . . . '

'Very well. We'll take both. And then that soup I once ate here, with diverse molluscs, little fish and other tasty morsels floating in it.'

'Log drivers' soup?'

'The very same. And then roast lamb with onions. And then three-score crayfish. Throw as much dill into the pot as you can. After that, sheep's cheese and lettuce. And then we'll see.'

'At your service. Is that for everyone? I mean, four times?'

The taller Zerrikanian shook her head, patting herself knowingly on her waist, which was now hugged by a tight, linen blouse.

'I forgot.' Three Jackdaws winked at Geralt. 'The girls are watching their figures. Lamb just for the two of us, innkeeper. Serve the beer right now, with those elvers. No, wait a while, so they don't go cold. We didn't come here to stuff ourselves, but simply to spend some time in conversation.'

'Very good.' The innkeeper bowed once more.

'Prudence is a matter of import in your profession. Give me your hand, comrade.'

Gold coins jingled. The innkeeper opened his gap-toothed mouth to the limit.

'That is not an advance,' Three Jackdaws announced, 'it is a bonus. And now hurry off to the kitchen, good fellow.'

It was warm in the snug. Geralt unbuckled his belt, took off his tunic and rolled up his shirtsleeves.

'I see,' he said, 'that you aren't troubled by a shortage of funds. Do you live on the privileges of a knightly estate?'

'Partially,' Three Jackdaws smiled, without offering further details.

They dealt quickly with the elvers and a quarter of the keg. Neither of the two Zerrikanians stinted on the beer, and soon were both in visible good humour. They were whispering something to each other. Véa, the taller one, suddenly burst out in throaty laughter.

'Are the warriors versed in the Common Speech?' Geralt asked quietly, sneaking a sideways glance at them.

'Poorly. And they are not garrulous. For which they deserve credit. How do you find the soup, Geralt?'

'Mmm.'

'Let us drink.'

'Mmm.'

'Geralt,' Three Jackdaws began, putting aside his spoon and hiccoughing in a dignified manner, 'I wish to return, for a moment, to the conversation we had on the road. I understand that you, a witcher, wander from one end of the world to the other, and should you come across a monster along the way, you kill it. And you earn money doing that. Does that describe the witcher's trade?'

'More or less.'

'And does it ever happen that someone specifically summons you somewhere? On a special commission, let's say. Then what? You go and carry it out?'

'That depends on who asks me and why.'

'And for how much?'

'That too,' the Witcher shrugged. 'Prices are going up, and one has to live, as a sorceress acquaintance of mine used to say.'

'Quite a selective approach; very practical, I'd say. But at the root of it lies some idea, Geralt. The conflict between the forces of Order and the forces of Chaos, as a sorcerer acquaintance of mine used to say. I imagine that you carry out your mission, defending people from Evil, always and everywhere. Without distinction. You stand on a clearly defined side of the palisade.'

'The forces of Order, the forces of Chaos. Awfully high-flown words, Borch. You desperately want to position me on one side of the palisade in a conflict, which is generally thought to be perennial, began long before us and will endure long after we've gone. On which side does the farrier, shoeing horses, stand? Or our innkeeper, hurrying here with a cauldron of lamb? What, in your opinion, defines the border between Chaos and Order?'

'A very simple thing,' said Three Jackdaws, and looked him straight in the eye. 'That which represents Chaos is menace, is the aggressive side. While Order is the side being threatened, in need of protection. In need of a defender. But let us drink. And make a start on the lamb.'

'Rightly said.'

The Zerrikanians, watching their figures, were taking a break from eating, time they spent drinking more quickly. Véa, leaning over on her companion's shoulder, whispered something again, brushing the table top with her plait. Téa, the shorter of the two, laughed loudly, cheerfully narrowing her tattooed eyelids.

'Yes,' Borch said, picking a bone clean. 'Let us continue our talk, if you will. I understand you aren't keen on being placed on either side. You do your job.'

'That's correct.'

'But you cannot escape the conflict between Chaos and Order. Although it was your comparison, you are not a farrier. I've seen you work. You go down into a dungeon among some ruins and come out with a slaughtered basilisk. There is, comrade, a difference between shoeing horses and killing basilisks. You said that if the payment is fair, you'll hurry to the end of the world and dispatch the monster you're asked to. Let's say a fierce dragon is wreaking havoc on a—'

'Bad example,' Geralt interrupted. 'You see, right away you've mixed up Chaos and Order. Because I do not kill dragons; and they, without doubt, represent Chaos.'

'How so?' Three Jackdaws licked his fingers. 'Well, I never! After all, among all monsters, dragons are probably the most bestial, the cruellest and fiercest. The most revolting of reptiles. They attack people, breathe fire and carry off, you know, virgins. There's no shortage of tales like that. It can't be that you, a witcher, don't have a few dragons on your trophy list.'

'I don't hunt dragons,' Geralt said dryly. 'I hunt forktails, for sure. And dracolizards. And flying drakes. But not true dragons; the green, the black or the red. Take note, please.'

'You astonish me,' Three Jackdaws said. 'Very well, I've taken note. In any case, that's enough about dragons for the moment, I see something red on the horizon and it is surely our crayfish. Let us drink!'

Their teeth crunched through the red shells, and they sucked out the white flesh. The salt water, stinging painfully, trickled down over their wrists. Borch poured the beer, by now scraping the ladle across the bottom of the keg. The Zerrikanians were even more cheerful, the two of them looking around the inn and smiling ominously. The Witcher was convinced they were searching out an opportunity for a brawl. Three Jackdaws must also have noticed, because he suddenly shook a crayfish he was holding by the tail at them. The women giggled and Téa pouted her lips for a kiss and winked. Combined with her tattooed face, this made for a gruesome sight.

'They are as savage as wildcats,' Three Jackdaws murmured to Geralt. 'They need watching. With them, comrade, suddenly – before you know it – the floor's covered in guts. But they're worth every penny. If you knew what they're capable of . . . '

'I know,' Geralt nodded. 'You couldn't find a better escort. Zerrikanians are born warriors, trained to fight from childhood.'

'I didn't mean that.' Borch spat a crayfish claw onto the table. 'I meant what they're like in bed.'

Geralt glanced anxiously at the women. They both smiled. Véa reached for the dish with a swift, almost imperceptible movement.

Looking at the Witcher through narrowed eyes, she bit open a shell with a crack. Her lips glistened with the salt water. Three Jackdaws belched loudly.

'And so, Geralt,' he said. 'You don't hunt dragons; neither green nor any other colour. I've made a note of it. And why, may I ask, only those three colours?'

'Four, to be precise.'

'You mentioned three.'

'Dragons interest you, Borch. For any particular reason?'

'No. Pure curiosity.'

'Aha. Well, about those colours: it's customary to define true dragons like that, although they are not precise terms. Green dragons, the most common, are actually greyish, like ordinary dracolizards. Red dragons are in fact reddish or brick-red. It's customary to call the large dark brown ones "black". White dragons are the rarest. I've never seen one. They occur in the distant North. Reputedly.'

'Interesting. And do you know what other dragons I've also heard about?'

'I do,' Geralt sipped his beer. 'The same ones I've heard about. Golden dragons. There are no such creatures.'

'On what grounds do you claim that? Because you've never seen one? Apparently, you haven't seen a white one either.'

'That's not the point. Beyond the seas, in Ofir and Zangvebar, there are white horses with black stripes. I haven't seen them, but I know they exist. But golden dragons are mythical creatures. Fabled. Like the phoenix, let's say. There are no phoenixes or golden dragons.'

Véa, leaning on her elbows, looked at him curiously.

'You must know what you're talking about, you're a witcher,' Borch ladled beer from the keg, 'but I think that every myth, every fable, must have some roots. Something lies among those roots.'

'It does,' Geralt confirmed. 'Most often a dream, a wish, a desire, a yearning. Faith that there are no limits to possibility. And occasionally chance.'

'Precisely, chance. Perhaps there once was a golden dragon, an accidental, unique mutation?'

'If there were, it met the fate of all mutants.' The Witcher turned his head away. 'It differed too much to endure.'

'Ha,' Three Jackdaws said, 'now you are denying the laws of nature, Geralt. My sorcerer acquaintance was wont to say that every being has its own continuation in nature and survives in some way or another. The end of one is the beginning of another, there are no limits to possibility; or at least nature doesn't know any.'

'Your sorcerer acquaintance was a great optimist. But he failed to take one thing into consideration: a mistake committed by nature. Or by those who trifle with it. Golden dragons and other similar mutants, were they to exist, couldn't survive. For a very natural limit of possibilities prevents it.'

'What limit is that?'

'Mutants,' the muscles in Geralt's jaw twitched violently, 'mutants are sterile, Borch. Only in fables survives what cannot survive in nature. Only myths and fables do not know the limits of possibility.'

Three Jackdaws said nothing. Geralt looked at the Zerrikanians, at their faces, suddenly grown serious. Véa unexpectedly leant over towards him and put a hard, muscular arm around his neck. He felt her lips, wet from beer, on his cheek.

'They like you,' Three Jackdaws said slowly. 'Well, I'll be damned, they like you.'

'What's strange about that?' the Witcher smiled sadly.

'Nothing. But we must drink to it. Innkeeper. Another keg!'

'Take it easy. A pitcher at most.'

'Two pitchers!' Three Jackdaws yelled. 'Téa, I have to go out for a while.'

The Zerrikanian stood up, took her sabre from the bench and swept the room with a wistful gaze. Although previously, as the Witcher had observed, several pairs of eyes had lit up greedily at the sight of Borch's bulging purse, no one seemed in a hurry to go after him as he staggered slightly towards the door to the courtyard. Téa shrugged, following her employer.

'What is your real name?' Geralt asked the one who had remained at the table. Véa flashed her white teeth. Her blouse was very loosely

laced, almost to the limits of possibility. The Witcher had no doubt
it was intentionally provocative.

'Alvéaenerle.'

'Pretty.' The Witcher was sure the Zerrikanian would purse her
lips and wink at him. He was not mistaken.

'Véa?'

'Mm?'

'Why do you ride with Borch? You, free warriors? Would you
mind telling me?'

'Mm.'

'Mm, what?'

'He is . . .' the Zerrikanian, frowning, searched for the words. 'He
is . . . the most . . . beautiful.'

The Witcher nodded. Not for the first time, the criteria by which
women judged the attractiveness of men remained a mystery to him.

Three Jackdaws lurched back into the snug fastening his trousers, and issued loud instructions to the innkeeper. Téa, walking two
steps behind him, feigning boredom, looked around the inn, and the
merchants and log drivers carefully avoided her gaze. Véa was sucking the contents from another crayfish, and continually throwing the
Witcher meaningful glances.

'I've ordered us an eel each, baked this time,' Three Jackdaws sat
down heavily, his unfastened belt clinking. 'I struggled with those
crayfish and seem to have worked up an appetite. And I've organised a bed for you, Geralt. There's no sense in you roaming around
tonight. We can still amuse ourselves. Here's to you, girls!'

'Vessekheal,' Véa said, saluting him with her beaker. Téa winked
and stretched; and her bosom, contrary to Geralt's expectations, did
not split the front of her blouse.

'Let's make merry!' Three Jackdaws leant across the table and
slapped Téa on the backside. 'Let's make merry, Witcher. Hey,
landlord! Over here!'

The innkeeper scuttled briskly over, wiping his hands on his
apron.

'Could you lay your hands on a tub? The kind you launder clothes
in, sturdy and large?'

'How large, sir?'

'For four people.'

'For . . . four . . . ' the innkeeper opened his mouth.

'For four,' Three Jackdaws confirmed, drawing a full purse from his pocket.

'I could.' The innkeeper licked his lips.

'Splendid,' Borch laughed. 'Have it carried upstairs to my room and filled with hot water. With all speed, comrade. And have beer brought there too. Three pitchers.'

The Zerrikanians giggled and winked at the same time.

'Which one do you prefer?' Three Jackdaws asked. 'Eh? Geralt?'

The Witcher scratched the back of his head.

'I know it's difficult to choose,' said Three Jackdaws, understandingly. 'I occasionally have difficulty myself. Never mind, we'll give it some thought in the tub. Hey, girls. Help me up the stairs!'

III

There was a barrier on the bridge. The way was barred by a long, solid beam set on wooden trestles. In front and behind it stood halberdiers in studded leather coats and mail hoods. A purple banner bearing the emblem of a silver gryphon fluttered lazily above the barrier.

'What the devil?' Three Jackdaws said in surprise, approaching at a walk. 'Is there no way through?'

'Got a safe-conduct?' the nearest halberdier asked, without taking the stick he was chewing, either from hunger or to kill time, from his mouth.

'Safe-conduct? What is it, the plague? Or war, perhaps? On whose orders do you obstruct the way?'

'Those of King Niedamir, Lord of Caingorn,' the guardsman replied, shifting the stick to the other side of his mouth and pointing at the banner. 'Without a safe-conduct you can't go up.'

'Some sort of idiocy,' Geralt said in a tired voice. 'This isn't Caingorn, but Barefield's territory. Barefield, not Caingorn, levies tolls from the bridges on the Braa. What has Niedamir to do with it?'

'Don't ask me,' the guard said, spitting out his stick. 'Not my business. I'm here to check safe-conducts. If you want, talk to our decurion.'

'And where might he be?'

'He's basking in the sun over there, behind the toll collector's lodgings,' the halberdier said, looking not at Geralt but at the naked thighs of the Zerrikanians, who were stretching languidly in their saddles.

Behind the toll collector's cottage sat a guard on a pile of dry logs, drawing a woman in the sand with the end of his halberd. It was

14

actually a certain part of a woman, seen from an unusual perspective. Beside him, a slim man with a fanciful plum bonnet pulled down over his eyes, adorned with a silver buckle and a long, twitching heron's feather, was reclining, gently plucking the strings of a lute.

Geralt knew that bonnet and that feather, which were famed from the Buina to the Yaruga, known in manor houses, fortresses, inns, taverns and whorehouses. Particularly whorehouses.

'Dandelion!'

'Geralt the Witcher!' A pair of cheerful cornflower-blue eyes shone from under the bonnet, now shoved back on his head. 'Well, I never! You're here too? You don't have a safe-conduct by any chance?'

'What's everyone's problem with this safe-conduct?' The Witcher dismounted. 'What's happening here, Dandelion? We wanted to cross the Braa, myself and this knight, Borch Three Jackdaws, and our escort. And we cannot, it appears.'

'I can't either,' Dandelion stood up, took off his bonnet and bowed to the Zerrikanians with exaggerated courtesy. 'They don't want to let me cross either. This decurion here won't let me, Dandelion, the most celebrated minstrel and poet within a thousand miles, through, although he's also an artist, as you can see.'

'I won't let anyone cross without a safe-conduct,' the decurion said resolutely, at which he completed his drawing with a final detail, prodding the end of his halberd shaft in the sand.

'No matter,' the Witcher said. 'We'll ride along the left bank. The road to Hengfors is longer that way, but needs must.'

'To Hengfors?' the bard said, surprised. 'Aren't you following Niedamir, Geralt? And the dragon?'

'What dragon?' Three Jackdaws asked with interest.

'You don't know? You really don't know? Oh, I shall have to tell you everything, gentlemen. I'm waiting here, in any case; perhaps someone who knows me will come with a safe-conduct and let me join them. Please be seated.'

'Just a moment,' Three Jackdaws said. 'The sun is almost a quarter to the noontide and I have an awful thirst. We cannot talk on an empty stomach. Téa, Véa, head back to the town at a trot and buy a keg.'

'I like the cut of your jib, sire . . . '

'Borch, also known as Three Jackdaws.'

'Dandelion, also known as the Unparalleled. By certain girls.'

'Talk, Dandelion,' the Witcher said impatiently. 'We aren't going to loiter around here till evening.'

The bard seized the fingerboard of his lute and plucked the strings vigorously.

'How would you prefer it, in verse or in normal speech?'

'Normal speech.'

'As you please,' Dandelion said, not putting his lute down. 'Listen then, noble gentlemen, to what occurred a week ago near the free town of Barefield. 'Twas thus, that at the crack of dawn, when the rising sun had barely tinged pink the shrouds of mist hanging pendent above the meadows—'

'It was supposed to be normal speech,' Geralt reminded him.

'Isn't it? Very well, very well. I understand. Concise, without metaphors. A dragon alighted on the pastures outside Barefield.'

'Oh, come on,' the Witcher said. 'It doesn't seem very likely to me. No one has seen a dragon in these parts for years. Wasn't it just a common or garden dracolizard? Dracolizard specimens can occasionally be as large as—'

'Don't insult me, Witcher. I know what I'm talking about. I saw it. As luck would have it I was at the market in Barefield and saw it all with my own eyes. The ballad's composed, but you didn't want—'

'Go on. Was it big?'

'The length of three horses. No taller than a horse at the withers, but much fatter. Sand grey.'

'In other words, green.'

'Yes. It swooped down unexpectedly, flew right into a flock of sheep, scattered the shepherds, did for about a dozen beasts, devoured four of them and flew away.'

'Flew away . . . ' Geralt shook his head. 'And that was all?'

'No. Because it came again the next day, this time nearer to the town. It swooped down on a knot of women washing their linen on the banks of the Braa. And how they bolted, old friend! I've never laughed so much. Then the dragon circled Barefield a couple of times and flew towards the pastures, where it fell on the sheep again. Only then did the chaos and confusion begin, because few had believed the herdsmen before. The mayor called out the town constabulary and the guilds, but before they could form up, the plebs took matters into their own hands and did for it.'

'How?'

'In a forceful peasant manner. The local master cobbler, a certain Sheepbagger, came up with a way of dealing with the brute. They killed a sheep, stuffed it full of hellebore, deadly nightshade, poison parsley, brimstone and cobbler's tar. Just to be sure, the local apothecary poured in two quarts of his concoction for carbuncles, and the priest from the temple of Kreve said prayers over the carcass. Then they stood the poisoned sheep among the flock, held up by a stake. If truth be told, no one believed the dragon would be lured by that shit, which stank to high heaven, but reality surpassed our expectations. Ignoring the living and bleating baa-lambs, the reptile swallowed the bait and the stake.'

'And what then? Go on, Dandelion.'

'What do you think I'm doing? I am telling you. Listen to what happened next. In less time than a skilled man needs to unlace a woman's corset, the dragon suddenly began to roar and vent smoke from its front and rear ends. It turned somersaults, tried to take off, and then collapsed and lay still. Two volunteers set off to check whether the poisoned reptile was still breathing. It was the local gravedigger and the town halfwit, the fruit of the union between the retarded daughter of a woodcutter and a squad of hired pikemen who marched through Barefield at the time of Warlord Nelumbo's rebellion.'

'Now you're lying, Dandelion.'

'Not lying, just embellishing, and there's a difference.'

'Not much of one. Speak on, we're wasting time.'

'Well then, as I was saying, the gravedigger and the doughty idiot set off as scouts. Afterwards, we built them a small, but pleasing, burial mound.'

'Aha,' Borch said, 'that means the dragon was still alive.'

'And how,' Dandelion said cheerfully. 'It was alive. But it was so weak it didn't devour either the gravedigger or the halfwit, it just lapped up their blood. And then, to general consternation, it flew away, taking flight with some difficulty. Every furlong it fell with a clatter and then rose again. It walked occasionally, dragging its back legs. Some courageous individuals followed it, keeping it in view. And do you know what?'

'Speak, Dandelion.'

'The dragon disappeared among the ravines of the Kestrel Mountains, near the source of the Braa, and hid in the caves there.'

'Now everything's clear,' Geralt said. 'The dragon has probably lived in those caves for centuries, in a state of torpor. I've heard of cases like that. And his treasure hoard must be there too. Now I know why they're blocking the bridge. Someone wants to get his greedy hands on the treasure. And that someone is Niedamir of Caingorn.'

'Exactly,' the troubadour confirmed. 'The whole of Barefield is fair seething for that reason, because they claim that the dragon and its hoard belongs to them. But they hesitate to cross Niedamir. Niedamir's a young whelp, who hasn't started shaving, but he's already proved it doesn't pay to fall foul of him. And he wants that dragon, like the very devil, which is why he's reacted so fast.'

'Wants the treasure, you mean.'

'Actually, more the dragon than the treasure. For you see, Niedamir has his eye on the kingdom of Malleore. A princess, of a – so to speak – beddable age was left there after the sudden and odd death of the prince. The noblemen of Malleore look on Niedamir and the other suitors with reluctance, for they know that the new ruler will keep them on a short leash – unlike the callow princess. So they dug up some dusty old prophecy saying that the mitre and the lass's hand belong to the man who vanquishes the dragon. Because no one had seen a dragon there for ages, they thought they were safe. Niedamir, of course, laughed at the legend, took Malleore by force, and that was that, but when the news of the Barefield dragon got out, he realised he could hoist the Malleore nobility by their own petard. If he showed up there clutching the dragon's head, the people would greet him like a monarch sent by the gods, and the noblemen wouldn't dare breathe a word. Does it surprise you, then, that he rushed after the dragon like a scalded cat? Particularly since it's dead on its feet? For him it's a real godsend, a stroke of luck, by thunder.'

'And he's shut the competition out.'

'So it would appear. And the people of Barefield. Except that he sent riders with safe-conducts throughout the countryside. They're for the ones who are supposed to actually kill the dragon, because Niedamir himself is in no hurry to walk into a cave wielding a sword. In a flash he drafted in the most renowned dragon slayers. You probably know most of them, Geralt.'

'Possibly. Who has turned up?'

'Eyck of Denesle, to begin with.'

'Damn . . . ' the Witcher whistled softly. 'The pious and virtuous Eyck, a knight without flaw or blemish, in person.'

'Do you know him, Geralt?' Borch asked. 'Is he really the scourge of dragons?'

'Not just dragons. Eyck is a match for any monster. He's even killed manticores and gryphons. He's dispatched a few dragons, so I've heard. He's good. But he spoils my business, the swine, because he doesn't take any money for it. Who else, Dandelion?'

'The Crinfrid Reavers.'

'Well, that's the dragon done for. Even if it has recovered. That trio are a good team. They fight pretty dirty, but they're effective. They've wiped out all the dracolizards and forktails in Redania, not to mention three red and one black dragon which they also dispatched, and that's no mean feat. Is that everybody?'

'No. Six dwarves under the command of Yarpen Zigrin have joined in.'

'I don't know him.'

'But you *have* heard of the dragon Ocvist from Quartz Mountain?'

'Yes. And I saw some gemstones from its hoard. There were sapphires of remarkable colour and diamonds as large as cherries.'

'Well, know you that because Yarpen Zigrin and his dwarves did for Ocvist. A ballad was composed about it, but it was lousy because it wasn't one of mine. You've missed nothing if you haven't heard it.'

'Is that everybody?'

'Yes. Not counting you. You claim not to know about the dragon. Who knows, perhaps that's true? But now you do. Well?'

'Nothing. That dragon doesn't interest me.'

'Hah! Very crafty, Geralt. Because you don't have a safe-conduct anyway.'

'The dragon doesn't interest me, I told you. But what about you, Dandelion? What draws you here?'

'The usual,' the troubadour shrugged. 'I need to be near the action and the excitement. Everyone will be talking about the fight with the dragon. Of course, I could compose a ballad based on reports, but it'll sound different sung by someone who saw the fight with his own eyes.'

'Fight?' Three Jackdaws laughed. 'More like some kind of pig-sticking or a carcass being quartered. I'm listening and I'm astounded. Celebrated warriors rushing here as fast as they can to finish off a half-dead dragon, poisoned by a peasant. It makes me want to laugh and vomit.'

'You're wrong,' Geralt said. 'If the dragon hasn't expired from the poison, its constitution has probably already fought it off and it's back at full strength. It actually doesn't make much difference. The Crinfrid Reavers will kill it anyway, but it'll put up a fight, if you want to know.'

'So you're betting on the Reavers, Geralt?'

'Naturally.'

'Don't be so sure.' The artistic guard, who had been silent up to then, spoke up. 'A dragon is a magical creature and you can't kill it any other way than with spells. If anybody can deal with it then it's that sorceress who rode through yesterday.'

'Who was that?' Geralt cocked his head.

'A sorceress,' the guard repeated, 'I told you.'

'Did she give her name?'

'She did, but I've forgotten it. She had a safe-conduct. She was young, comely, in her own way, but those eyes . . . You know how it is, sire. You come over all cold when they look at you.'

'Know anything about this, Dandelion? Who could it be?'

'No,' the bard grimaced. 'Young, comely and "those eyes". Some help that is. They're all like that. Not one of them that I know – and I know plenty – looks older than twenty-five, thirty; though some of them, I've heard, can recall the times when the forest soughed as far as where Novigrad stands today. Anyway, what are elixirs and mandrake for? And they also sprinkle mandrake in their eyes to make them shine. As women will.'

'Was her hair red?' the Witcher asked.

'No, sire,' the decurion said. 'Coal-black.'

'And her horse, what colour was it? Chestnut with a white star?'

'No. Black, like her hair. Well, gentlemen, I'm telling you, she'll kill the dragon. A dragon's a job for a sorcerer. Human strength isn't enough against it.'

'I wonder what the cobbler Sheepbagger would have to say about that,' Dandelion laughed. 'If he'd had something stronger to hand than hellebore and deadly nightshade the dragon's skin would be drying on the Barefield stockade, the ballad would be ready, and I wouldn't be fading in this sun . . . '

'Why exactly didn't Niedamir take you with him?' Geralt asked, looking askance at the poet. 'You were in Barefield when he set off, after all. Could it be that the king doesn't like artists? How come you're fading here, instead of strumming an air by the royal stirrups?'

'The cause was a certain young widow,' Dandelion said dejectedly. 'The hell with it. I tarried, and the next day Niedamir and the others were already over the river. They even took that Sheepbagger with them and some scouts from the Barefield constabulary; they just forgot about me. I've explained it to the decurion, but he keeps repeating—'

'If there's a safe-conduct, I let you through,' the halberdier said dispassionately, relieving himself on the wall of the toll collector's cottage. 'If there isn't, I don't let you through. I've got me orders—'

'Oh,' Three Jackdaws interrupted him, 'the girls are returning with the beer.'

'And they aren't alone,' Dandelion added, standing up. 'Look at that horse. Big as a dragon.'

The Zerrikanians galloped up from the birch wood, flanking a rider sitting on a large, restless warhorse.

The Witcher also stood up.

The rider was wearing a long, purple, velvet kaftan with silver braid and a short coat trimmed with sable fur. Sitting erect in the saddle, he looked imperiously down at them. Geralt knew that kind of look. And was not fond of it.

'Greetings, gentlemen. I am Dorregaray,' the rider introduced himself, dismounting slowly and with dignity. 'Master Dorregaray. Sorcerer.'

'Master Geralt. Witcher.'

'Master Dandelion. Poet.'

'Borch, also known as Three Jackdaws. And my girls, who are removing the bung from that keg, you have already met, Master Dorregaray.'

'That is so, indeed,' the sorcerer said without a smile. 'We exchanged bows, I and the beautiful warriors from Zerrikania.'

'Well then, cheers,' Dandelion distributed the leather cups brought by Véa. 'Drink with us, Master Sorcerer. My Lord Borch, shall I also serve the decurion?'

'Of course. Join us, soldier.'

'I presume,' the sorcerer said, after taking a small, distinguished sip, 'that the same purpose has brought you gentlemen to the barrier on the bridge, as it has me?'

'If you have the dragon in mind, Master Dorregaray,' Dandelion said, 'that is so, indeed. I want to be there and compose a ballad. Unfortunately, that decurion there, clearly a fellow without refinement, doesn't want to let me through. He demands a safe-conduct.'

'I beg your pardon,' the halberdier said, draining his cup and smacking his lips. 'I've been ordered on pain of death not to let anyone through without a safe-conduct. And I'm told the whole of Barefield has already gathered with wagons, and plans to head up after the dragon. I have my orders—'

'Your orders, soldier,' Dorregaray frowned, 'apply to the rabble, who might hinder; trollops, who might spread debauchery and foul sicknesses; thieves, scum and rabble. But not to me.'

'I won't let anyone through without a safe-conduct,' the decurion glowered, 'I swear—'

'Don't swear,' Three Jackdaws interrupted him. 'Better to have another drink. Téa, pour this stout-hearted soldier a beer. And let us be seated, gentlemen. Drinking standing up, in a rush and without due reverence, does not become the nobility.'

They sat down on logs around the keg. The halberdier, newly raised to nobility, blushed with pleasure.

'Drink, brave centurion,' Three Jackdaws urged.

'But I am a decurion, not a centurion,' the halberdier said, blushing even more intensely.

'But you will be a centurion, for certain,' Borch grinned. 'You're an astute fellow, you'll be promoted in no time.'

Dorregaray, declining a refill, turned towards Geralt.

'People are still talking about the basilisk in town, Witcher, sir, and you now have your eye on the dragon, I see,' he said softly. 'I wonder whether you're so short of money, or whether you murder endangered creatures for the simple pleasure of it.'

'Curious interest,' Geralt answered, 'coming from someone who is rushing not to be late for the butchering of a dragon, in order to knock out its teeth, so crucial, after all, in the making of magical cures and elixirs. Is it true, sorcerer, sir, that the best ones are those removed from a living dragon?'

'Are you certain that is why I am going there?'

'I am. But someone has already beaten you to it, Dorregaray. A female companion of yours has already gone through with a safe-conduct, which you don't have. She is black-haired, if that's of any interest to you.'

'On a black horse?'

'Apparently.'

'Yennefer,' Dorregaray said, glumly. Unnoticed by anybody, the Witcher twitched.

A silence fell, broken only by the belching of the future centurion.

'Nobody . . . without a safe-conduct . . . '

'Will two hundred lintars suffice?' Geralt calmly took from his pocket the purse received from the fat Alderman.

'Ah, Geralt,' Three Jackdaws smiled mysteriously, 'so you—'

'My apologies, Borch. I'm sorry, but I won't ride with you to Hengfors. Another time perhaps. Perhaps we'll meet again.'

'I have no interest in going to Hengfors,' Three Jackdaws said slowly. 'Not at all, Geralt.'

'Put away that purse, sire,' the future centurion said menacingly, 'that's sheer bribery. I won't even let you through for three hundred.'

'And for five hundred?' Borch took out his pouch. 'Put away that purse, Geralt. I'll pay the toll. This has begun to amuse me. Five hundred, soldier, sir. One hundred a piece, counting my girls as one gorgeous item. What?'

'Oh dear, oh dear,' the future centurion said, distressed, stowing Borch's pouch away under his jacket. 'What will I tell the king?'

'Tell him,' Dorregaray said, straightening up and removing an ornate ivory wand from his belt, 'that you were overcome by fear when you saw it.'

'Saw what, sire?'

The sorcerer flourished his wand and shouted an incantation. A pine tree on the riverbank burst into flames. In one moment the entire tree was engulfed from top to bottom in a blaze of fire.

'To horse!' cried Dandelion, springing up and slinging his lute across his back. 'To horse, gentlemen! And ladies!'

'Raise the barrier!' the rich decurion with a good chance of becoming a centurion shouted to the halberdiers.

On the bridge, beyond the barrier, Véa reined in her horse. It skittered, hooves thudding on the planking. The woman, tossing her plaits, screamed piercingly.

'That's right, Véa!' Three Jackdaws shouted back. 'Onwards, my lords. To horse! We'll ride in the Zerrikanian fashion, with a thundering and a yelling!'

IV

'Well, just look,' said the oldest of the Reavers, Boholt, massive and burly, like the trunk of an old oak tree. 'So Niedamir didn't chase you away, my good sirs, though I was certain he would. But it's not for us paupers to question royal commands. Join us by the campfire. Make yourselves a pallet, boys. And between you and me, Witcher, what did you talk to the king about?'

'About nothing,' Geralt said, making himself comfortable by leaning back against his saddle, which he had dragged over beside the fire. 'He didn't even come out of his tent to talk to us. He just sent that flunky of his, what's his name . . .'

'Gyllenstiern,' said Yarpen Zigrin, a stocky, bearded dwarf, who was rolling a huge resinous tree stump he had dragged from the undergrowth into the fire. 'Pompous upstart. Fat hog. When we joined the hunt he came over, nose stuck up towards the heavens, pooh-pooh, "remember, you dwarves", he says, "who's in command, who you have to obey, King Niedamir gives the orders here and his word is law" and so on. I stood and listened and I thought to myself, I'll have my lads knock him to the ground and I'll piss all over his cape. But I dropped the idea, you know, because word would get around again that dwarves are nasty, that they're aggressive, that they're whoresons and it's impossible to live with them in . . . what the hell was it? . . . harmonium, or whatever it is. And right away there'd be another pogrom somewhere, in some little town or other. So I just listened politely and nodded.'

'It looks like that's all Lord Gyllenstiern knows,' Geralt said, 'because he said the same to us and all we did was nod too.'

'And I reckon,' the second Reaver said, spreading a blanket over a pile of brushwood, 'it was a bad thing Niedamir didn't chase you away. Doesn't bear thinking how many people are after this dragon.

26

Swarms of them. It's not a hunting expedition no more, it's a funeral procession. I need elbow room when I'm fighting.'

'Come off it, Gar,' Boholt said, 'the more the merrier. What, never hunted a dragon before? There's always a swarm of people behind a dragon, a noisy rabble, a veritable bordello on wheels. But when the reptile shows up, guess who's left standing in the field. Us, that's who.'

Boholt was silent for a moment, took a long draw from a large, wicker-bound demijohn, blew his nose loudly and coughed.

'Another thing,' he continued. 'In practice it's often only after the dragon's been killed that the merrymaking and bloodletting begins and the heads start rolling. It's only when the treasure's being shared out that the hunters go for each others' throats. Right, Geralt? Oi? Am I right? Witcher, I'm talking to you.'

'I'm aware of cases like that,' Geralt concurred dryly.

'Aware, you say. No doubt from hearsay, because I can't say I've ever heard of you stalking a dragon. Never in all my born days have I heard of a witcher hunting dragons. Which makes it all the stranger you're here.'

'True,' drawled Kennet, also known as Beanpole, the youngest Reaver. 'That's strange. And we—'

'Wait, Beanpole, I'm talking,' Boholt cut in, 'and besides, I don't plan to talk for too long. Anyway, the Witcher knows what I'm on about. I know him and he knows me, and up to now we haven't got in each other's way and we probably never will. See, lads, if I wanted to disrupt the Witcher's work or snatch the loot from under his nose, the Witcher would waste no time slashing me with that witcher razor of his, and he'd be within his rights. Agreed?'

No one seconded or challenged this. There was nothing to suggest that Boholt cared either way.

'Aye,' he continued, 'the more the merrier, as I said. And the Witcher may prove useful to the company. It's wild and deserted round here, and should a frightener, or ilyocoris, or a striga, jump out at us, there might be trouble. But if Geralt's standing by there won't be any trouble, because that's his speciality. But dragons aren't his speciality. Right?'

Once more no one seconded or challenged this.

'Lord Three Jackdaws is with Geralt,' continued Boholt, handing the demijohn to Yarpen, 'and that's enough of a guarantee for me. So who's bothering you, Gar, Beanpole? Can't be Dandelion, can it?'

'Dandelion,' Yarpen Zigrin said, passing the demijohn to the bard, 'always tags along whenever something interesting's happening and everybody knows he doesn't interfere, doesn't help and won't slow the march down. Bit like a burr on a dog's tail. Right, boys?'

The 'boys' – stocky, bearded dwarves – cackled, shaking their beards. Dandelion pushed his bonnet back and drank from the demijohn.

'Oooh, bloody hell,' he groaned, gasping for air. 'It takes your voice away. What was it distilled from, scorpions?'

'There's one thing irking me, Geralt,' Beanpole said, taking the demijohn from the minstrel, 'and that's you bringing that sorcerer along. We can hardly move for sorcerers.'

'That's true,' the dwarf butted in. 'Beanpole's right. We need that Dorregaray like a pig needs a saddle. For some time now we've had our very own witch, the noble Yennefer. Ugh.' He spat her name.

'Yes indeed,' Boholt said, scratching himself on his bull neck, from which a moment earlier he had unfastened a leather collar, bristling with steel studs. 'There are too many sorcerers here, gentlemen. Two too many, to be precise. And they're a sight too thick with our Niedamir. Just look, we're under the stars around a fire, and they, gentlemen, are in the warm, plotting in the royal tent, the cunning foxes. Niedamir, the witch, the wizard and Gyllenstiern. And Yennefer's the worst. And do you want to know what they're plotting? How to cheat us, that's what.'

'And stuffing themselves with venison,' Beanpole interjected gloomily. 'And what did we eat? Marmot! And what's a marmot, I ask you? A rat, nothing else. So what have we eaten? Rat!'

'Never mind,' Gar said, 'We'll soon be sampling dragon's tail. There's nothing like dragon's tail, roasted over charcoal.'

'Yennefer,' Boholt went on, 'is a foul, nasty, mouthy bint. Not like your lasses, Lord Borch. They are quiet and agreeable, just look,

28

they've sat down by the horses, they're sharpening their sabres. I walked past, said something witty, they smiled and showed their little teeth. Yes, I'm glad they're here, not like Yennefer, all she does is scheme and scheme. And I tell you, we have to watch out, because we'll end up with shit all from our agreement.'

'What agreement, Boholt?'

'Well, Yarpen, do we tell the Witcher?'

'Ain't got nothing against it,' the dwarf answered.

'There's no more booze,' Beanpole interjected, turning the demijohn upside down.

'Get some then. You're the youngest, m'lord. The agreement was our idea, Geralt, because we aren't hirelings or paid servants, and we won't be having Niedamir send us after that dragon and then toss a few pieces of gold in our direction. The truth is we'll cope with that dragon without Niedamir, but Niedamir won't cope without us. So it's clear from that who's worth more and whose share should be bigger. And we put the case fairly – whoever takes on the dragon in mortal combat and bests it takes half of the treasure hoard. Niedamir, by virtue of his birthright and title, takes a quarter, in any event. And the rest, provided they help, will share the remaining quarter between themselves, equally. What do you think about that?'

'And what does Niedamir think about it?'

'He said neither yes nor no. But he'd better not put up a fight, the whippersnapper. I told you, he won't take on the dragon himself, he has to count on experts, which means us, the Reavers, and Yarpen and his lads. We, and no one else, will meet the dragon at a sword's length. The rest, including the sorcerers, if they give honest assistance, will share a quarter of the treasure among themselves.'

'Who do you include in the rest, apart from the sorcerers?' Dandelion asked with interest.

'Certainly not buskers and poetasters,' Yarpen Zigrin cackled. 'We include those who put in some work with a battle-axe, not a lute.'

'Aha,' Three Jackdaws said, looking up at the starry sky. 'And how will the cobbler Sheepbagger and his rabble be contributing?'

Yarpen Zigrin spat into the campfire, muttering something in dwarven.

'The constabulary from Barefield know these bloody mountains and will act as guides,' Boholt said softly, 'hence it will be fair to allow them a share of the spoils. It's a slightly different matter with the cobbler. You see, it will go ill if the peasantry become convinced that when a dragon shows up in the land, instead of sending for professionals, they can casually poison it and go back to humping wenches in the long grass. If such a practice became widespread, we'd probably have to start begging. Yes?'

'That's right,' Yarpen added. 'For which reason, I tell you, something bad ought to befall that cobbler, before the bastard passes into legend.'

'If it's meant to befall him, it'll befall him,' Gar said with conviction. 'Leave it to me.'

'And Dandelion,' the dwarf took up, 'will blacken his name in a ballad, make him look a fool. So that he'll suffer shame and dishonour, for generations to come.'

'You've forgotten about one thing,' Geralt said. 'There's one person here who could throw a spoke in the wheel. Who won't assent to any divisions or agreements. I mean Eyck of Denesle. Have you talked to him?'

'What about?' Boholt said, grinding his teeth, using a stout stick to move the logs around in the campfire. 'You won't get anywhere with Eyck, Geralt. He knows nothing about business.'

'As we rode up to your camp,' Three Jackdaws said, 'we met him. He was kneeling on the rocks, in full armour, staring at the sky.'

'He's always doing that,' Beanpole said. 'He's meditating, or saying his prayers. He says he must, because he has orders from the gods to protect people from evil.'

'Back home in Crinfrid,' Boholt muttered, 'we keep people like that on a chain in the cowshed, and give them a piece of coal so they can draw outlandish pictures on the walls. But that's enough gossip about my neighbours, we're talking business.'

A petite, young woman with black hair held tightly by a gold hairnet, wrapped in a woollen cloak, noiselessly entered the circle of light.

'What reeks so much round here?' Yarpen Zigrin asked, pretending not to see her. 'Not brimstone, is it?'

'No,' Boholt, glancing to the side and sniffing pointedly, 'it's musk or some other scent.'

'No, it has to be . . . ' the dwarf grimaced. 'Oh! Why it's the noble Madam Yennefer! Welcome, welcome.'

The sorceress's eyes slowly swept over the company, her shining eyes coming to rest for a while on the Witcher. Geralt smiled faintly.

'May I join you?'

'But of course, good lady,' Boholt said and hiccoughed. 'Sit down here, on the saddle. Move your arse, Kennet, and give the noble sorceress the saddle.'

'From what I hear, you're talking business, gentlemen.' Yennefer sat down, stretching out her shapely, black-stockinged legs in front of her. 'Without me?'

'We didn't dare,' Yarpen Zigrin said, 'trouble such an important personage.'

'It would be better, Yarpen' – Yennefer narrowed her eyes, turning her head towards the dwarf – 'if you kept quiet. From the very first day you've been treating me as if I were nothing but air, so please continue, don't let me bother you. Because it doesn't bother me either.'

'Really, m'lady,' Yarpen's smile revealed uneven teeth. 'May I be infested by ticks, if I haven't been treating you better than the air. I've been known, for example, to spoil the air, which there's no way I'd dare to do in your presence.'

The bearded 'boys' roared with thunderous laughter, but fell silent immediately at the sight of the blue glow which suddenly enveloped the sorceress.

'One more word and you'll end as spoiled air, Yarpen,' Yennefer said in a voice with a metallic edge, 'and a black stain on the grass.'

'Indeed,' Boholt cleared his throat, relieving the silence that had fallen. 'Quiet, Zigrin. Let's hear what Madam Yennefer has to say to us. She just complained that we're talking about business without her. From which I conclude she has some kind of offer for us. Let's hear, my lords, what kind of offer it is. As long as she doesn't suggest killing the dragon by herself, using spells.'

'And what if I do?' Yennefer raised her head. 'Don't think it's possible, Boholt?'

'It might be possible. But it's not profitable, because you'd be certain to demand half the dragon's hoard.'

'At least half,' the sorceress said coldly.

'Well, you see for yourself there's no profit in it for us. We, my lady, are poor warriors, and if the loot passes us by, hunger will come beckoning. We live on sorrel and pigweed . . . '

'Only once in a blue moon do we manage to catch a marmot,' Yarpen Zigrin interrupted in a sombre voice.

' . . . we drink spring water,' Boholt took a swig from the demijohn and shuddered slightly. 'There's no choice for us, Madam Yennefer. It's either loot, or freeze to death in the winter huddled against a fence. For inns cost money.'

'Beer does too,' Gar added.

'And dirty strumpets,' Beanpole said, daydreaming.

'Which is why,' Boholt said, looking up at the sky, 'we will kill the dragon, by ourselves, without spells and without your help.'

'Are you certain about that? Just remember there are limits to what is possible, Boholt.'

'Perhaps there are, but I've never come across them. No, m'lady. I repeat, we'll kill the dragon ourselves, without any spells.'

'Particularly,' Yarpen Zigrin added, 'since spells surely have their own limits, which, unlike our own, we don't know.'

'Did you come up with that yourself?' Yennefer asked slowly. 'Or did someone put you up to it? Does the presence of the Witcher in this select company give you the right to such brazenness?'

'No,' Boholt replied, looking at Geralt, who seemed to be dozing, stretched out lazily on a blanket with his saddle beneath his head, 'the Witcher has nothing to do with it. Listen, noble Yennefer. We put forward a proposition to the king, but he hasn't honoured us with an answer. We're patient, we'll wait till the morning. Should the king agree to a settlement, we ride on together. If not, we go back.'

'Us too,' the dwarf snarled.

'There won't be any bargaining,' Boholt continued. 'Take it or leave it. Repeat our words to Niedamir, Madam Yennefer. And I'll tell you; a deal's also good for you and for Dorregaray, if you come to an agreement with him. We don't need the dragon's carcass, mark you, we'll take but the tail. And the rest is yours, you can have whatever you want. We won't stint you with the teeth or the brain; we'll keep nothing that you need for sorcery.'

'Of course,' Yarpen Zigrin added, chuckling, 'the carrion will be for you, sorcerers, no one will take it from you. Unless some other vultures do.'

Yennefer stood up, throwing her cloak over her shoulder.

'Niedamir won't wait until morning,' she said sharply. 'He has agreed to your conditions already. Against mine and Dorregaray's advice, mark you.'

'Niedamir,' Boholt slowly drawled, 'is displaying astonishing wisdom for one so young. To me, Madam Yennefer, wisdom includes the ability to turn a deaf ear to foolish or insincere advice.'

Yarpen Zigrin snorted into his beard.

'You'll be singing a different tune,' the sorceress put her hands on her hips, 'when the dragon lacerates and perforates you and shatters your shinbones. You'll be licking my shoes and begging for help. As usual. How well, oh, how very well do I know your sort. I know you so well it makes me sick.'

She turned away and disappeared into the gloom, without saying goodbye.

'In my day,' Yarpen Zigrin said, 'sorceresses stayed in their towers, read learned books and stirred cauldrons. They didn't get under warriors' feet, didn't interfere in our business. And didn't wiggle their bottoms in front of a fellow.'

'Frankly speaking, she can wiggle all she likes,' Dandelion said, tuning his lute. 'Right, Geralt? Geralt? Hey, where's the Witcher?'

'What do we care?' Boholt muttered, throwing another log on the fire. 'He went somewhere. Perhaps he had to relieve himself, my lord. It's his business.'

'That's right,' the bard agreed and strummed the strings. 'Shall I sing you something?'

'Sing, dammit,' Yarpen Zigrin said and spat. 'But don't be thinking, Dandelion, that I'll give you as much as a shilling for your bleating. It's not the royal court, son.'

'I can see that,' the troubadour nodded.

V

'Yennefer.'

She turned around, as though surprised, though the Witcher was in doubt she had heard his steps well before. She placed a small wooden pail on the floor, straightened up and brushed aside some hair which had freed itself from her golden hairnet and fell in curls onto her shoulders.

'Geralt.'

She was wearing just two colours, as usual: black and white. Black hair, long, black eyelashes forcing one to guess the colour of the eyes concealed beneath them. A black skirt and a short, black tunic with a white fur collar. A white blouse of the sheerest linen. On her neck a black velvet ribbon adorned with an obsidian star bestrewn with tiny diamonds.

'You haven't changed at all.'

'Neither have you,' she sneered. 'And in both cases it is equally normal. Or, if you prefer, equally abnormal. In any case, the mention of it, though it may not be a bad way to begin the conversation, is meaningless. Am I right?'

'You are,' he nodded, looking to one side, towards Niedamir's tent and the fires of the royal bowmen obscured by the dark shapes of wagons. From the more distant campfire floated Dandelion's sonorous voice singing *The Stars above the Path*, one of his most popular romantic ballads.

'Well, now that we have the preliminaries out of the way,' the sorceress said, 'I wonder what's coming next'.

'You see, Yennefer—'

'I see,' she interrupted sharply, 'But I don't understand. Why did you come here, Geralt? Surely not because of the dragon? I presume nothing has changed in that regard?'

'No. Nothing's changed.'

'Why, then, I pray, have you joined the party?'

'If I said that it was because of you, would you believe me?'

She looked at him in silence, and there was something in her flashing eyes which Geralt did not like.

'I believe you, why not?' she finally said. 'Men like to meet their former lovers, like to relive memories. They like to imagine that erstwhile erotic ecstasies give them some kind of perpetual ownership of their partner. It enhances their self-importance. You are no exception. In spite of everything.'

'Nevertheless,' he smiled, 'you're right, Yennefer. The sight of you makes me feel wonderful. In other words, I'm glad to see you.'

'And is that all? Well, let's say I'm also glad. Having said that, I wish you goodnight. I am retiring for the night, as you can see. Before that I intend to bathe and I usually get undressed to perform that activity. Withdraw, then, in order graciously to assure me a minimum of discretion.'

'Yen,' he held his hands out to her.

'Don't call me that!' she hissed furiously, springing back, blue and red sparks streaming from her extended fingers. 'And if you touch me I'll scorch your eyes out, you bastard.'

The Witcher moved back. The sorceress, somewhat calmer, brushed her hair aside once again and stood before him with her fists resting on her hips.

'What did you think, Geralt? That we'd have a nice, cheerful gossip, that we'd reminisce about the old days? That perhaps at the end of our chat we'd get onto a wagon and make love on the sheepskins, just like that, for old times' sake? Did you?'

Geralt, not certain if the sorceress was magically reading his mind or had only guessed right, kept silent, smiling wryly.

'Those four years left their mark, Geralt. I'm over it now, which is the only reason why I didn't spit in your eyes during today's encounter. But don't let my civility deceive you.'

'Yennefer . . .'

'Be quiet! I gave you more than I've ever given any other man, you scoundrel. I don't know, myself, why I gave it to you. And you

. . . Oh, no, my dear. I'm not a slut or an elf-woman met by chance in the forest, who can be discarded in the morning, walked out on without being woken, with a posy of violets left on the table. Who can be made a mockery of. Beware! Utter a single word and you will regret it!'

Geralt did not utter a single word, correctly sensing the anger seething in Yennefer.

The sorceress once again brushed aside some unruly locks and looked him in the eyes, from close up.

'We've met, that's too bad,' she said softly. 'But we shall not make a spectacle of ourselves for everybody. We shall save face. We'll pretend to be good friends. But don't be mistaken, Geralt. There is nothing between us now. Nothing, understood? And be glad of it, because it means I have now abandoned the plans which, until recently I still harboured regarding you. But that in no way means I've forgiven you. I shall never forgive you, Witcher. Never.'

She turned around suddenly, seized the pail, spraying water around, and disappeared behind a wagon.

Geralt chased away a mosquito whining above his ear and slowly walked back towards the campfire, where Dandelion's performance was being rewarded with half-hearted applause. He looked up at the dark blue sky above the black, serrated saw blade of the mountain peaks. He felt like bursting out laughing. He did not know why.

VI

'Careful up there! Take heed!' Boholt called, turning around on the coachman's seat to look back towards the column. 'Closer to the rocks! Take heed!'

The wagons trundled along, bouncing on stones. The wagoners swore, lashing the horses with their reins and leaning out. They glanced anxiously to see if the wheels were sufficiently far from the edge of the ravine, along which ran a narrow, uneven road. Below, at the bottom of the chasm, the waters of the River Braa foamed white among the boulders.

Geralt reined back his horse, pressing himself against the rock wall, which was covered with sparse brown moss and white lichen. He let the Reavers' wagon overtake him. Beanpole galloped up from the head of the column where he had been leading the cavalcade with the Barefield scouts.

'Right!' he shouted, 'With a will! It widens out up ahead!'

King Niedamir and Gyllenstiern, both on horseback, accompanied by several mounted bowmen, came alongside Geralt. Behind them rattled the wagons of the royal caravan. Even further back trundled the dwarves' wagon, driven by Yarpen Zigrin, who was yelling relentlessly.

Niedamir, a very thin, freckled youngster in a white sheepskin jacket, passed the Witcher, casting him a haughty, though distinctly bored, look. Gyllenstiern straightened up and reined in his horse.

'Over here, Witcher, sir,' he said overbearingly.

'Yes?' Geralt jabbed his mare with his heels, and rode slowly over to the chancellor, behind the caravan. He was astonished that, in spite of having such an impressive paunch, Gyllenstiern preferred horseback to a comfortable ride in a wagon.

'Yesterday,' Gyllenstiern said, gently tugging his gold-studded reins, and throwing a turquoise cape off his shoulder, 'yesterday you said the dragon does not interest you. What does interest you then, Witcher, sir? Why do you ride with us?'

'It's a free country, chancellor.'

'For the moment. But in this cortege, my dear Geralt, everyone should know his place. And the role he is to fulfil, according to the will of King Niedamir. Do you comprehend that?'

'What are you driving at, my dear Gyllenstiern?'

'I shall tell you. I've heard that it has recently become tiresome to negotiate with you witchers. The thing is that, whenever a witcher is shown a monster to be killed, the witcher, rather than take his sword and slaughter it, begins to ponder whether it is right, whether it is transgressing the limits of what is possible, whether it is not contrary to the code and whether the monster really *is* a monster, as though it wasn't clear at first glance. It seems to me that you are simply doing too well. In my day, witchers didn't have two pennies to rub together, just two stinking boots. They didn't question, they slaughtered what they were ordered to, whether it was a werewolf, a dragon or a tax collector. All that counted was a clean cut. So, Geralt?'

'Do you have a job for me, Gyllenstiern?' the Witcher asked coldly. 'If so, tell me what. I'll think it over. But if you don't, there's no sense wasting our breath, is there?'

'Job?' the chancellor sighed. 'No, I don't. This all concerns a dragon, and that clearly transgresses your limits, Witcher. So I prefer the Reavers. I merely wanted to alert you. Warn you. King Niedamir and I may tolerate the whims of witchers and their classification of monsters into good and bad, but we do not wish to hear about them, much less see them effected in our presence. Don't meddle in royal matters, Witcher. And don't consort with Dorregaray.'

'I am not accustomed to consorting with sorcerers. Why such an inference?'

'Dorregaray,' Gyllenstiern said, 'surpasses even witchers with his whims. He does not stop at categorising monsters into good and bad. He considers them all good.'

'That's overstating the case somewhat.'

'Clearly. But he defends his views with astonishing obstinacy. I truly would not be surprised if something befell him. And the fact he joined us keeping such curious company—'

'I am not Dorregaray's companion. And neither is he mine.'

'Don't interrupt. The company is strange. A witcher crawling with scruples like a fox's pelt with fleas. A sorcerer spouting druidic humbug about equilibrium in nature. The silent knight Borch Three Jackdaws and his escort from Zerrikania, where – as is generally known – sacrifices are made before the image of a dragon. And suddenly they all join in the hunt. Strange, isn't it?'

'If you insist, then yes it is.'

'Know then,' the chancellor said, 'that the most mysterious problems find – as experience proves – the simplest solutions. Don't compel me, Witcher, to use them.'

'I don't understand.'

'Oh, but you do. Thank you for the conversation, Geralt.'

Geralt stopped. Gyllenstiern urged his horse on and joined the king, catching up with the caravan. Eyck of Denesle rode alongside wearing a quilted kaftan of light-coloured leather marked with the impressions of a breastplate, pulling a packhorse laden with a suit of armour, a uniformly silver shield and a powerful lance. Geralt greeted him by raising his hand, but the knight errant turned his head to the side, tightening his thin lips, and spurred his horse on.

'He isn't keen on you,' Dorregaray said, riding over. 'Eh, Geralt?'

'Clearly.'

'Competition, isn't it? The two of you have similar occupations. Except that Eyck is an idealist, and you are a professional. A minor difference, particularly for the ones you kill.'

'Don't compare me to Eyck, Dorregaray. The devil knows who you wrong with that comparison, him or me, but don't compare us.'

'As you wish. To me, frankly speaking, you are equally loathsome.'

'Thank you.'

'Don't mention it,' the sorcerer patted the neck of his horse, which had been scared by all the yelling from Yarpen and his dwarves. 'To me, Witcher, calling killing a vocation is loathsome, low and nonsensical. Our world is in equilibrium. The annihilation, the killing, of any creatures that inhabit this world upsets that equilibrium. And a lack of equilibrium brings closer extinction; extinction and the end of the world as we know it.'

'A druidic theory,' Geralt pronounced. 'I know it. An old hierophant expounded it to me once, back in Rivia. Two days after our conversation he was torn apart by wererats. It was impossible to prove any upset in equilibrium.'

'The world, I repeat,' Dorregaray glanced at him indifferently, 'is in equilibrium. Natural equilibrium. Every species has its own natural enemies, every one is the natural enemy of other species. That also includes humans. The extermination of the natural enemies of humans, which you dedicate yourself to, and which one can begin to observe, threatens the degeneration of the race.'

'Do you know what, sorcerer?' Geralt said, annoyed. 'One day, take yourself to a mother whose child has been devoured by a basilisk, and tell her she ought to be glad, because thanks to that the human race has escaped degeneration. See what she says to you.'

'A good argument, Witcher,' Yennefer said, riding up to them on her large, black horse. 'And you, Dorregaray, be careful what you say.'

'I'm not accustomed to concealing my views.'

Yennefer rode between them. The Witcher noticed that the golden hairnet had been replaced by a rolled up white kerchief.

'Start concealing them as quickly as possible, Dorregaray,' she said, 'especially before Niedamir and the Reavers, who already suspect you plan to interfere in the killing of the dragon. As long as you only talk, they treat you like a harmless maniac. If, however, you try to start anything they'll break your neck before you manage to let out a sigh.'

The sorcerer smiled contemptuously and condescendingly.

'And besides,' Yennefer continued, 'by expressing those views you damage the solemnity of our profession and vocation.'

'How so?'

'You can apply your theory to all sorts of creatures and vermin,

Dorregaray. But not to dragons. For dragons are the natural, greatest enemies of man. And I do not refer to the degeneration of the human race, but to its survival. In order to survive, one has to crush one's enemies, enemies which might prevent that survival.'

'Dragons aren't man's enemies,' Geralt broke in. The sorceress looked at him and smiled. But only with her lips.

'In that matter,' she said, 'leave the judging to us *humans*. Your role, Witcher, is not to judge. It's to get a job done.'

'Like a programmed, servile golem?'

'That was your comparison, not mine,' Yennefer replied coldly. 'But, well, it's apt.'

'Yennefer,' Dorregaray said, 'for a woman of your education and age you are coming out with some astonishing tripe. Why is it that dragons have been promoted in your eyes to become the foremost enemies of man? Why not other – a hundredfold more dangerous – creatures, those that have a hundredfold more victims on their consciences than dragons? Why not hirikkas, forktails, manticores, amphisbaenas or gryphons? Why not wolves?'

'I'll tell you why not. The advantage of men over other races and species, the fight for their due place in nature, for living space, can only be won when nomadism, wandering from place to place in search of sustenance in accordance with nature's calendar, is finally eliminated. Otherwise the proper rhythm of reproduction will not be achieved, since human children are dependent for too long. Only a woman safe and secure behind town walls or in a stronghold can bear children according to the proper rhythm, which means once a year. Fecundity, Dorregaray, is growth, is the condition for survival and domination. And now we come to dragons. Only a dragon, and no other monster, can threaten a town or stronghold. Were dragons not to be wiped out, people would – for their own safety – disperse, instead of cleaving together, because dragon's fire in a densely populated settlement is a nightmare, means hundreds of victims, and terrible destruction. That is why dragons must be utterly wiped out, Dorregaray.'

Dorregaray looked at her with a strange smile on his face.

'Do you know what, Yennefer, I wouldn't like to see the day your idea of the dominance of man comes about, when people like you will occupy their due place in nature. Fortunately, it will never come to that. You would rather poison or slaughter each other, expire from typhoid fever and typhus, because it is filth and lice – and not dragons – which threaten your splendid cities, where women are delivered of children once a year, but where only one new-born baby in ten lives longer than ten days. Yes, Yennefer, fecundity, fecundity and once again fecundity. So take up bearing children, my dear; it's the most natural pursuit for you. It will occupy the time you are currently fruitlessly wasting on dreaming up nonsense. Farewell.'

Urging on his horse, the sorcerer galloped off towards the head of the column. Geralt, having glanced at Yennefer's pale, furiously twisted face, began to feel sorry for him in advance. He knew what this was about. Yennefer, like most sorceresses, was barren. But unlike most sorceresses she bemoaned the fact and reacted with genuine rage at the mention of it. Dorregaray certainly knew that. But he probably did not know how vengeful she was.

'He's in trouble,' she hissed. 'Oh, yes. Beware, Geralt. Don't think that when the time comes and you don't show good sense, I'll protect you.'

'Never fear,' he smiled. 'We – and I mean witchers and servile golems – always act sensibly. Since the limits within which we operate are clearly and explicitly demarcated.'

'Well, I never,' Yennefer said, looking at him, still pale. 'You're taking umbrage like a tart whose lack of chastity has been pointed out to her. You're a witcher, you can't change that. Your vocation . . . '

'That's enough about vocations, Yen, because it's beginning to make me queasy.'

'I told you not to call me that. And I'm not especially bothered about your queasiness. Nor any other reactions in your limited witcher's range of reactions.'

'Nevertheless, you'll see some of them if you don't stop plying me with tales about lofty missions and the fight between good and evil. And about dragons; the dreadful enemies of the human tribe. I know better.'

'Oh, yes?' The sorceress narrowed her eyes. 'And what do you know, Witcher?'

'Only,' Geralt said, ignoring the sudden warning vibration of the medallion around his neck, 'that if dragons didn't have treasure hoards, not a soul would be interested in them; and certainly not sorcerers. Isn't it interesting that whenever a dragon is being hunted, some sorcerer closely linked to the Goldsmiths' Guild is always hanging around. Just like you. And later, although a deal of gemstones ought to end up on the market, it never happens and their price doesn't go down. So don't talk to me about vocation and the fight for the survival of the race. I know you too well, have known you too long.'

'Too long,' she repeated, sneering malevolently. 'Unfortunately. But don't think you know me well, you whore's son. Dammit, how stupid I've been . . . Oh, go to hell! I can't stand the sight of you!'

She screamed, yanked her horse's reins and galloped fiercely ahead. The Witcher reined back his mount, and let through the wagon of dwarves, yelling, cursing and whistling through bone pipes. Among them, sprawled on some sacks of oats, lay Dandelion, plucking his lute.

'Hey!' roared Yarpen Zigrin, who was sitting on the box, pointing at Yennefer. 'There's something black on the trail! I wonder what it is? It looks like a nag!'

'Without doubt!' Dandelion shouted, shoving his plum bonnet back, 'It's a nag! Riding a gelding! Astounding!'

The beards of Yarpen's boys shook in general laughter. Yennefer pretended not to hear.

Geralt reined back his horse again and let Niedamir's mounted bowmen through. Borch was riding slowly some distance beyond them, and the Zerrikanians brought up the rear just behind him. Geralt waited for them to catch up and led his mare alongside Borch's horse. They rode on in silence.

'Witcher,' Three Jackdaws suddenly said, 'I want to ask you a question.'

'Ask it.'

'Why don't you turn back?'

The Witcher looked at him in silence for a moment.

'Do you really want to know?'

'Yes, I do,' Three Jackdaws said, turning his face towards Geralt.

'I'm riding with them because I'm a servile golem. Because I'm a wisp of oakum blown by the wind along the highway. Tell me, where should I go? And for what? At least here some people have gathered with whom I have something to talk about. People who don't break off their conversations when I approach. People who, though they may not like me, say it to my face, and don't throw stones from behind a fence. I'm riding with them for the same reason I rode with you to the log drivers' inn. Because it's all the same to me. I don't have a goal to head towards. I don't have a destination at the end of the road.'

Three Jackdaws cleared his throat.

'There's a destination at the end of every road. Everybody has one. Even you, although you like to think you're somehow different.'

'Now I'll ask you a question.'

'Ask it.'

'Do you have a destination at the end of the road?'

'I do.'

'Lucky for you.'

'It is not a matter of luck, Geralt. It is a matter of what you believe in and what you serve. No one ought to know that better than . . . than a witcher.'

'I keep hearing about goals today,' Geralt sighed. 'Niedamir's aim is to seize Malleore. Eyck of Denesle's calling is to protect people from dragons. Dorregaray feels obligated to something quite the opposite. Yennefer, by virtue of certain changes which her body was subjected to, cannot fulfil her wishes and is terribly undecided. Dammit, only the Reavers and the dwarves don't feel a calling, and simply want to line their pockets. Perhaps that's why I'm so drawn to them?'

'You aren't drawn to them, Geralt of Rivia. I'm neither blind nor deaf. It wasn't at the sound of their name you pulled out that pouch. But I surmise . . . '

'There's no need to surmise,' the Witcher said, without anger.

'I apologise.'

'There's no need to apologise.'

They reined back their horses just in time, in order not to ride into the column of bowmen from Caingorn which had suddenly been called to a halt.

'What has happened?' Geralt stood up in his stirrups. 'Why have we stopped?'

'I don't know.' Borch turned his head away. Véa, her face strangely contorted, uttered a few quick words.

'I'll ride up to the front,' the Witcher said, 'to see what's going on.'

'Stay here.'

'Why?'

Three Jackdaws was silent for a moment, eyes fixed on the ground.

'Why?' Geralt repeated.

'Go,' Borch said. 'Perhaps it'll be better that way.'

'What'll be better?'

'Go.'

The bridge connecting the two edges of the chasm looked sound. It was built from thick, pine timbers and supported on a quadrangular pier, against which the current crashed and roared in long strands of foam.

'Hey, Beanpole!' yelled Boholt, who was driving the wagon. 'Why've you stopped?'

'I don't know if the bridge will hold.'

'Why are we taking this road?' Gyllenstiern asked, riding over. 'It's not to my liking to take the wagons across the bridge. Hey, cobbler! Why are you leading us this way, and not by the trail? The trail continues on towards the west, doesn't it?'

The heroic poisoner of Barefield approached, removing his sheep-skin cap. He looked ridiculous, dressed up in an old-fashioned half-armour probably hammered out during the reign of King Sambuk, pulled down tightly over a shepherd's smock.

'The road's shorter this way, Your Majesty,' he said, not to the chancellor, but directly to Niedamir, whose face still expressed thoroughly excruciated boredom.

'How is that?' Gyllenstiern asked, frowning. Niedamir did not even grace the cobbler with a more attentive glance.

'Them's,' Sheepbagger said, indicating the three notched peaks towering over the surrounding area, 'is Chiava, Great Kestrel and Harbinger's Fang. The trail leads toward the ruins of the old stronghold, and skirts around Chiava from the north, beyond the river's source. But we can shorten the way by takin' the bridge. We'll pass through the gorge and onto the plain 'tween the mountains. And if we don't find no sign of the dragon there, we'll continue on eastwards, we'll search the ravines. And even further eastward there are flat pastures, where there's a straight road to Caingorn, towards your lands, sire.'

'And where, Sheepbagger, did you acquire such knowledge about these mountains?' Boholt asked. 'At your cobbler's last?'

'No, sir. I herded sheep here as a young 'un.'

'And that bridge won't give way?' Boholt stood up on the box, and looked downwards at the foaming river. 'That must be a drop of forty fathoms.'

'It'll 'old, sir.'

'What's a bridge doing in this wilderness anyhow?'

'That there bridge,' Sheepbagger said, 'was built by trolls in the olden days, and whoever came this way had to pay them a pretty penny. But since folk seldom came this way the trolls were reduced to beggary. But the bridge remains.'

'I repeat,' Gyllenstiern said irately. 'We have wagons with tackle and provender, and we may become bogged down in the wilderness. Is it not better to take the trail?'

'We could take the trail,' the cobbler shrugged, 'but it's longer that way. And the king said 'e'd give 'is earteeth to get to that dragon soon.'

'Eyeteeth,' the chancellor corrected him.

'Have it your way, eyeteeth,' Sheepbagger agreed. 'But it's still quicker by the bridge.'

'Right, let's go, Sheepbagger,' Boholt decided. 'Forge ahead, you and your men. We have a custom of letting the most valiant through first.'

'No more than one wagon at a time,' Gyllenstiern warned.

'Right,' Boholt lashed his horses and the wagon rumbled onto the bridge's timbers. 'Follow us, Beanpole! Make sure the wheels are rolling smoothly!'

Geralt reined back his horse, his way barred by Niedamir's bowmen in their purple and gold tunics, crowded on the stone bridgehead.

The Witcher's mare snorted.

The earth shuddered. The mountains trembled, the jagged edge of the rock wall beside them became blurred against the sky, and the wall itself suddenly spoke with a dull, but audible rumbling.

'Look out!' Boholt yelled, now on the other side of the bridge. 'Look out, there!'

The first, small stones pattered and rattled down the spasmodically shuddering rock wall. Geralt watched as part of the road they had followed, very rapidly widening into a yawning, black crack, broke off and plunged into the chasm with a thunderous clatter.

'To horse!' Gyllenstiern yelled. 'Your Majesty! To the other side!'

Niedamir, head buried in his horse's mane, charged onto the bridge, and Gyllenstiern and several bowmen leapt after him. Behind them, the royal wagon with its flapping gryphon banner rumbled onto the creaking timbers.

'It's a landslide! Get out of the way!' Yarpen Zigrin bellowed from behind, lashing his horses' rumps, overtaking Niedamir's second wagon and jostling the bowmen. 'Out of the way, Witcher! Out of the way!'

Eyck of Denesle, stiff and erect, galloped beside the dwarves' wagon. Were it not for his deathly pale face and mouth contorted in a quivering grimace, one might have thought the knight errant had not noticed the stones and boulders falling onto the trail. Further back, someone in the group of bowmen screamed wildly and horses whinnied.

Geralt tugged at the reins and spurred his horse, as right in front of him the earth boiled from the boulders cascading down. The dwarves' wagon rattled over the stones. Just before the bridge it jumped up and landed with a crack on its side, onto a broken axle. A wheel bounced off the railing and plunged downwards into the spume.

The Witcher's mare, lacerated by sharp shards of stone, reared up. Geralt tried to dismount, but caught his boot buckle in the stirrup and fell to the side, onto the trail. His mare neighed and dashed ahead, straight towards the bridge, dancing over the chasm. The dwarves ran across the bridge yelling and cursing.

'Hurry, Geralt!' Dandelion yelled, running behind him and looking back.

'Jump on, Witcher!' Dorregaray called, threshing about in the saddle, struggling to control his terrified horse.

Further back, behind them, the entire road was engulfed in a cloud of dust stirred up by falling rocks, shattering Niedamir's wagons. The Witcher seized the straps of the sorcerer's saddle bags. He heard a cry.

Yennefer had fallen with her horse, rolled to the side, away from the wildly kicking hooves, and flattened herself to the ground, shielding her head with her arms. The Witcher let go of the saddle, ran towards her, diving into the deluge of stones and leaping across the rift opening under his feet. Yennefer, yanked by the arm, got up onto her knees. Her eyes were wide open and the trickle of blood running down from her cut brow had already reached her ear.

'Stand up, Yen!'

'Geralt! Look out!'

An enormous, flat block of stone, scraping against the side of the rock wall with a grinding, clattering sound, slid down and plummeted towards them. Geralt dropped, shielding the sorceress with his body. At the very same moment the block exploded, bursting into a billion fragments, which rained down on them, stinging like wasps.

'Quick!' Dorregaray cried. Brandishing his wand atop the skittering horse, he blasted more boulders which were tumbling down from the cliff into dust. 'Onto the bridge, Witcher!'

Yennefer waved a hand, bending her fingers and shrieking incomprehensibly. As the stones came into contact with the bluish hemisphere which had suddenly materialised above their heads they vaporised like drops of water falling on red-hot metal.

'Onto the bridge, Geralt!' the sorceress yelled. 'Stay close to me!'

They ran, following Dorregaray and several fleeing bowmen. The bridge rocked and creaked, the timbers bending in all directions as it flung them from railing to railing.

'Quick!'

The bridge suddenly slumped with a piercing, penetrating crack, and the half they had just crossed broke off, tumbling with a clatter into the gulf, taking the dwarves' wagon with it, which shattered against the rocky teeth to the sound of the horses' frantic whinnying. The part they were now standing on was still intact, but Geralt suddenly realised they were now running upwards across a rapidly tilting slope. Yennefer panted a curse.

'Get down, Yen! Hang on!'

The rest of the bridge grated, cracked and sagged into a ramp. They fell with it, digging their fingers into the cracks between the timbers. Yennefer could not hold on. She squealed like a little girl and dropped. Geralt, hanging on with one hand, drew a dagger, plunged the blade between the timbers and seized the haft in both hands. His elbow joints creaked as Yennefer tugged him down, suspended by the belt and scabbard slung across his back. The bridge made a cracking noise again and tilted even more, almost vertically.

'Yen,' the Witcher grunted. 'Do something . . . Cast a bloody spell!'

'How can I?' he heard a furious, muffled snarl. 'I'm hanging on!'

'Free one of your hands!'

'I can't . . . '

'Hey!' Dandelion yelled from above. 'Can you hold on? Hey!'

Geralt did not deign to reply.

'Throw down a rope!' Dandelion bellowed. 'Quickly, dammit!'

The Reavers, the dwarves and Gyllenstiern appeared beside the troubadour. Geralt heard Boholt's quiet words.

'Wait, busker. She'll soon fall. Then we'll pull the Witcher up.'

Yennefer hissed like a viper, writhing and suspended from Geralt's back. His belt dug painfully into his chest.

'Yen? Can you find a hold? Using your legs? Can you do anything with your legs?'

'Yes,' she groaned. 'Swing them around.'

Geralt looked down at the river seething and swirling among the sharp rocks, against which some bridge timbers, a horse and a body in the bright colours of Caingorn were bumping. Beyond the rocks, in the emerald, transparent maelstrom, he saw the tapered bodies of large trout, languidly moving in the current.

'Can you hold on, Yen?'

'Just about . . . yes . . . '

'Heave yourself up. You have to get a foothold . . . '

'I . . . can't . . . '

'Throw down a rope!' Dandelion yelled. 'Have you all gone mad? They'll both fall!'

'Perhaps that's not so bad?' Gyllenstiern wondered, out of sight.

The bridge creaked and sagged even more. Geralt's fingers, gripping the hilt of his dagger, began to go numb.

'Yen . . . '

'Shut up . . . and stop wriggling about . . . '

'Yen?'

'Don't call me that . . . '

'Can you hold on?'

'No,' she said coldly. She was no longer struggling, but simply hanging from his back; a lifeless, inert weight.

'Yen?'

'Shut up.'

'Yen. Forgive me.'

'No. Never.'

Something crept downwards over the timbers. Swiftly. Like a snake. A rope, emanating with a cold glow, twisting and curling, as though alive, searched for and found Geralt's neck with its moving tip, slid under his armpits, and ravelled itself into a loose knot. The sorceress beneath him moaned, sucking in air. He was certain she would start sobbing. He was mistaken.

'Careful!' Dandelion shouted from above. 'We're pulling you up! Gar! Kennet! Pull them up! Heave!'

A tug, the painful, constricting tension of the taut rope. Yennefer sighed heavily. They quickly travelled upwards, bellies scraping against the coarse timbers.

At the top, Yennefer was the first to stand up.

VII

'We saved but one wagon from the entire caravan, Your Majesty,' Gyllenstiern said, 'not counting the Reavers' wagon. Seven bowmen remain from the troop. There's no longer a road on the far side of the chasm, just scree and a smooth wall, as far as the breach permits one to look. We know not if anyone survived of those who remained when the bridge collapsed.'

Niedamir did not answer. Eyck of Denesle, standing erect, stood before the king, staring at him with shining, feverish eyes.

'The ire of the gods is hounding us,' he said, raising his arms. 'We have sinned, King Niedamir. It was a sacred expedition, an expedition against evil. For the dragon is evil, yes, each dragon is evil incarnate. I do not pass by evil indifferently, I crush it beneath my foot . . . Annihilate it. Just as the gods and the Holy Book demand.'

'What is he drivelling on about?' Boholt asked, frowning.

'I don't know,' Geralt said, adjusting his mare's harness. 'I didn't understand a single word.'

'Be quiet,' Dandelion said, 'I'm trying to remember it, perhaps I'll be able to use it if I can get it to rhyme.'

'The Holy Book says,' Eyck said, now yelling loudly, 'that the serpent, the foul dragon, with seven heads and ten horns, will come forth from the abyss! And on his back will sit a woman in purple and scarlet, and a golden goblet will be in her hand, and on her forehead will be written the sign of all and ultimate whoredom!'

'I know her!' Dandelion said, delighted. 'It's Cilia, the wife of the Alderman of Sommerhalder!'

'Quieten down, poet, sir,' Gyllenstiern said. 'And you, O knight from Denesle, speak more plainly, if you would.'

'One should act against evil, O King,' Eyck called, 'with a pure heart and conscience, with head raised! But who do we see here? Dwarves, who are pagans, are born in the darkness and bow down before dark forces! Blasphemous sorcerers, usurping divine laws, powers and privileges! A witcher, who is an odious aberration, an accursed, unnatural creature. Are you surprised that a punishment has befallen us? King Niedamir! We have reached the limits of possibility! Divine grace is being sorely tested. I call you, king, to purge the filth from our ranks, before—'

'Not a word about me,' Dandelion interjected woefully. 'Not a mention of poets. And I try so hard.'

Geralt smiled at Yarpen Zigrin, who with slow movements was stroking the blade of his battle-axe, which was stuck into his belt. The dwarf, amused, grinned. Yennefer turned away ostentatiously, pretending that her skirt, torn up to her hip, distressed her more than Eyck's words.

'I think you were exaggerating a little, Sir Eyck,' Dorregaray said sharply, 'although no doubt for noble reasons. I regard the making known of your views about sorcerers, dwarves and witchers as quite unnecessary. Although, I think, we have all become accustomed to such opinions, it is neither polite, nor chivalrous, Sir Eyck. And it is utterly incomprehensible after you, and no one else, ran and used a magical, elven rope to save a witcher and a sorceress whose lives were in danger. I conclude from what you say that you should rather have been praying for them to fall.'

'Dammit,' Geralt whispered to Dandelion. 'Did he throw us that rope? Eyck? Not Dorregaray?'

'No,' the bard muttered. 'Eyck it was, indeed.'

Geralt shook his head in disbelief. Yennefer cursed under her breath and straightened up.

'Sir Eyck,' she said with a smile that anyone other than Geralt might have taken as pleasant and friendly. 'Why was that? I'm blasphemous, but you save my life?'

'You are a lady, Madam Yennefer,' the knight bowed stiffly. 'And your comely and honest face permits me to believe that you will one day renounce this accursed sorcery.'

Boholt snorted.

'I thank you, sir knight,' Yennefer said dryly, 'and the Witcher Geralt also thanks you. Thank him, Geralt.'

'I'd rather drop dead,' the Witcher sighed, disarmingly frank. 'What exactly should I thank him for? I'm an odious aberration, and my uncomely face does not augur any hope for an improvement. Sir Eyck hauled me out of the chasm by accident, simply because I was tightly clutching the comely damsel. Had I been hanging there alone, Eyck would not have lifted a finger. I'm not mistaken, am I, sir knight?'

'You are mistaken, Geralt, sir,' the knight errant replied calmly. 'I never refuse anybody in need of help. Even a witcher.'

'Thank him, Geralt. And apologise,' the sorceress said sharply, 'otherwise you will be confirming that, at least with regard to you, Eyck was quite right. You are unable to coexist with people. Because you are different. Your participation in this expedition is a mistake. A nonsensical purpose brought you here. Thus it would be sensible to leave the party. I think you understand that now. And if not, it's time you did.'

'What purpose are you talking about, madam?' Gyllenstiern cut in. The sorceress looked at him, but did not answer. Dandelion and Yarpen Zigrin smiled meaningfully at each other, but so that the sorceress would not notice.

The Witcher looked into Yennefer's eyes. They were cold.

'I apologise and thank you, O knight of Denesle,' he bowed. 'I thank everybody here present. For the swift rescue offered at once. I heard, as I hung there, how you were all raring to help. I ask everybody here present for forgiveness. With the exception of the noble Yennefer, whom I thank, but ask for nothing. Farewell. The dregs leave the company of their own free will. Because these dregs have had enough of you. Goodbye, Dandelion.'

'Hey, Geralt,' Boholt called, 'don't pout like a maiden, don't make a mountain out of a molehill. To hell with—'

'Look out everyoooone!'

Sheepbagger and several members of the Barefield constabulary, who had been sent ahead to reconnoitre, were running back from the narrow opening to the gorge.

'What is it? Why's he bellowing like that?' Gar lifted his head up.

'Good people . . . Your . . . Excellencies . . . ' the cobbler panted.

'Get it out, man,' Gyllenstiern said, hooking his thumbs into his golden belt.

'A dragon! There's a dragon there!'

'Where?'

'Beyond the gorge . . . On level ground . . . Sire, he . . . '

'To horse!' Gyllenstiern ordered.

'Gar!' Boholt yelled, 'onto the wagon! Beanpole, get mounted and follow me!'

'Look lively, lads!' Yarpen Zigrin roared. 'Look lively, by thunder!'

'Hey, wait for me!' Dandelion slung his lute over his shoulder. 'Geralt! Take me with you!'

'Jump on!'

The gorge ended in a mound of light-coloured rocks, which gradually thinned out, creating an irregular ring. Beyond them the ground descended gently into a grassy, undulating mountain pasture, enclosed on all sides by limestone walls, gaping with thousands of openings. Three narrow canyons, the mouths of dried-up streams, opened out onto the pasture.

Boholt, the first to gallop to the barrier of rocks, suddenly reined in his horse and stood up in his stirrups.

'Oh, hell,' he said. 'Oh, bloody hell. It . . . it can't be!'

'What?' Dorregaray asked, riding up. Beside him Yennefer, dismounting from the Reavers' wagon, pressed her chest against the rocky block, peeped out, moved back and rubbed her eyes.

'What? What is it?' Dandelion shouted, leaning out from behind Geralt's back. 'What is it, Boholt?'

'That dragon . . . is golden.'

No further than a hundred paces from the gorge's rocky entrance from which they had emerged, on the road to the northward-leading canyon, on a gently curving, low hill, sat the creature. It was sitting, arching its long, slender neck in a smooth curve, inclining its narrow head onto its domed chest, wrapping its tail around its extended front feet.

There was something inexpressibly graceful in the creature and the way it was sitting; something feline, something that contradicted its clearly reptilian origins. But it was also undeniably reptilian. For the creature was covered in distinctly outlined scales, which shone with a glaring blaze of bright, yellow gold. For the creature sitting on the hillock was golden; golden from the tips of its talons, dug into the ground, to the end of its long tail, which was moving very gently among the thistles growing on the hill. Looking at them with its large, golden eyes, the creature unfurled its broad, golden, bat-like wings and remained motionless, demanding to be admired.

'A golden dragon,' Dorregaray whispered. 'It's impossible . . . A living fable!'

'There's no such thing as a bloody golden dragon,' Gar pronounced and spat. 'I know what I'm talking about.'

'Then what's sitting on that hillock?' Dandelion asked pointedly.

'It's some kind of trickery.'

'An illusion.'

'It is not an illusion,' Yennefer said.

'It's a golden dragon,' Gyllenstiern said. 'An absolutely genuine, golden dragon.'

'Golden dragons only exist in fables!'

'Stop that, all of you,' Boholt suddenly broke in. 'There's no point getting worked up. Any blockhead can see it's a golden dragon. And what difference does it make, my lords, if it's golden, lapis lazuli, shit-coloured or chequered? It's not that big, we'll sort it out in no time. Beanpole, Gar, clear the debris off the wagon and get the gear out. What's the difference if it's golden or not?'

'There is a difference, Boholt,' Beanpole said. 'And a vital one. That isn't the dragon we're stalking. Not the one that was poisoned outside Barefield, which is now sitting in its cave on a pile of ore and jewels. That one's just sitting on its arse. What bloody use is it to us?'

'That dragon is golden, Kennet,' Yarpen Zigrin snarled. 'Have you ever seen anything like it? Don't you understand? We'll get more for its hide than we would for a normal treasure hoard.'

'And without flooding the market with precious stones,' Yennefer added, smiling unpleasantly. 'Yarpen's right. The agreement is still binding. Quite something to divide up, isn't it?'

'Hey, Boholt?' Gar shouted from the wagon, where he was clattering amongst the tackle. 'What shall we equip ourselves and the horses with? What could that golden reptile belch, hey? Fire? Acid? Steam?'

'Haven't got an effing clue,' Boholt said, sounding worried. 'Hey, sorcerers! Anything in the fables about golden dragons, about how to kill them?'

'How do you kill them? The usual way!' Sheepbagger suddenly shouted. 'No point pondering, give us an animal. We'll stuff it full of something poisonous and feed it to the reptile, and good riddance.'

Dorregaray looked askance at the cobbler, Boholt spat, and Dandelion turned his head away with a grimace of disgust. Yarpen Zigrin smiled repulsively, hands on hips.

'Wha' you looking at?' Sheepbagger asked. 'Let's get to work, we have to decide what to stuff the carcass with so the reptile quickly perishes. It 'as to be something which is extremely toxic, poisonous or rotten.'

'Aha,' the dwarf spoke, still smiling. 'Well, what's poisonous, foul and stinks? Do you know what, Sheepbagger? Looks like it's you.'

'What?'

'You bloody heard. Get lost, bodger, out of my sight.'

'Lord Dorregaray,' Boholt said, walking over to the sorcerer. 'Make yourself useful. Call to mind some fables and tales. What do you know about golden dragons?'

The sorcerer smiled, straightening up self-importantly.

'What do I know about golden dragons, you ask? Not much, but enough.'

'We're listening.'

'Then listen and listen attentively. Over there, before us, sits a golden dragon. A living legend, possibly the last and only creature of its kind to have survived your murderous frenzy. One doesn't kill legends. I, Dorregaray, will not allow you to touch that dragon. Is that understood? You can get packed, fasten your saddlebags and go home.'

Geralt was convinced an uproar would ensue. He was mistaken.

'Noble sorcerer, sir,' Gyllenstiern's voice interrupted the silence. 'Heed what and to whom you speak. King Niedamir may order you, Dorregaray, to fasten your saddlebags and go to hell. But not the other way around. Is that clear?'

'No,' the sorcerer said proudly, 'it is not. For I am Master Dorregaray, and will not be ordered around by someone whose kingdom encompasses an area visible from the height of the palisade on a mangy, filthy, stinking stronghold. Do you know, Lord Gyllenstiern, that were I to speak a charm and wave my hand, you would change into a cowpat, and your underage king into something ineffably worse? Is *that* clear?'

Gyllenstiern did not manage to answer, for Boholt walked up to Dorregaray, caught him by the shoulder and pulled him around to face him. Gar and Beanpole, silent and grim, appeared from behind Boholt.

'Just listen, magician, sir,' the enormous Reaver said. 'Before you wave that hand, listen to me. I could spend a long time explaining what I would do with your prohibitions, your fables and your foolish chatter. But I have no wish to. Let this suffice as my answer.'

Boholt placed a finger against his nose and from a short distance ejected the contents onto the toes of the sorcerer's boots.

Dorregaray blanched, but did not move. He saw – as everyone did – the morning star mace on a cubit-long shaft hanging low at Gar's side. He knew – as everyone did – that the time he needed to cast a spell was incomparably longer than the time Gar needed to smash his head to pieces.

'Very well,' Boholt said. 'And now move nicely out of the way, your lordship. And should the desire to open your gob occur to you, quickly shove a bunch of grass into it. Because if I hear you whining again, I'll give you something to remember me by.'

Boholt turned away and rubbed his hands.

'Right, Gar, Beanpole, let's get to work, because that reptile won't hang around forever.'

'Doesn't seem to be planning on going anywhere,' Dandelion said, looking at the foreground. 'Look at it.'

The golden dragon on the hill yawned, lifted its head, waved its wings and lashed the ground with its tail.

'King Niedamir and you, knights!' it yelled with a roar like a brass trumpet. 'I am the dragon Villentretenmerth! As I see, the landslide which I – though I say it, as shouldn't – sent down on your heads did not completely stop you. You have come this far. As you know, there are only three ways out of this valley. East, towards Barefield, and west, towards Caingorn. And you may use those roads. You will not take the northern gorge, gentlemen, because I, Villentretenmerth, forbid you. However, if anyone does not wish to respect my injunction, I challenge him to fight an honourable, knightly duel. With conventional weapons, without spells, without breathing fire. A fight to the utter capitulation of one of the sides. I await an answer through your herald, as custom dictates!'

Everyone stood with their mouths open wide.

'It can talk!' Boholt panted. 'Remarkable!'

'Not only that, but very intelligently,' Yarpen Zigrin said. 'Anyone know what a conventional weapon is?'

'An ordinary, non-magical one,' Yennefer said frowning. 'But something else puzzles me. With a forked tongue it's not capable of articulated speech. The rogue is using telepathy! Be careful, it works in both directions. It can read your thoughts.'

'Has it gone completely barmy, or what?' Kennet Beanpole said, annoyed. 'An honourable duel? With a stupid reptile? Not a chance! We'll attack him together! There's strength in numbers!'

'No.'

They looked around.

Eyck of Denesle, already mounted in full armour, with his lance set by his stirrup, looked much better than he had on foot. His feverish eyes blazed from beneath his raised visor and his face was pale.

'No, Kennet, sir,' the knight repeated. 'Unless it is over my dead body. I will not permit knightly honour to be insulted in my presence. Whomsoever dares to violate the principles of this honourable duel . . .'

60

Eyck was talking louder and louder. His exalted voice was cracking and he was trembling with excitement.

'... whomsoever affronts honour, also affronts me, and his or my blood will be shed on this tired earth. The beast calls for a duel? Very well! Let the herald trumpet my name! May divine judgement decide! On the dragon's side is the power of fang and talon and infernal fury, and on my side ...'

'What a moron,' Yarpen Zigrin muttered.

'... on my side righteousness, faith, the tears of virgins, whom this reptile—'

'That's enough, Eyck, you make me want to puke!' Boholt yelled. 'Go on, to the lists! Don't talk, set about that dragon!'

'Hey, Boholt, wait,' one of the dwarves, tugging on his beard, suddenly said. 'Forgotten about the agreement? If Eyck lays low the serpent, he'll take half ...'

'Eyck won't take anything,' Boholt grinned. 'I know him. He'll be happy if Dandelion writes a song about him.'

'Silence!' Gyllenstiern declared. 'Let it be. Against the dragon will ride out the virtuous knight errant, Eyck of Denesle, fighting in the colours of Caingorn as the lance and sword of King Niedamir. That is the kingly will!'

'There you have it,' Yarpen Zigrin gnashed his teeth. 'The lance and sword of Niedamir. The Caingorn kinglet has fixed us. What now?'

'Nothing,' Boholt spat. 'I reckon you don't want to cross Eyck, Yarpen? He talks nonsense, but if he's already mounted his horse and roused himself, better get out of his way. Let him go, dammit, and sort the dragon out. And then we'll see.'

'Who shall be the herald?' Dandelion asked. 'The dragon wanted a herald. Maybe me?'

'No. We don't need a song, Dandelion,' Boholt frowned. 'Yarpen Zigrin can be the herald. He's got a voice like a bull.'

'Very well, no bother,' Yarpen said. 'Bring me a flag-bearer with a banner so that everything is as it should be.'

'Just talk politely, dwarf, sir. And courteously,' Gyllenstiern cautioned.

'Don't learn me how to talk,' the dwarf proudly stuck out his belly. 'I was sent on diplomatic missions when you lot were still knee-high to a grasshopper.'

The dragon continued to sit patiently on the hillock, waving its tail cheerfully. The dwarf clambered up onto the largest boulder, hawked and spat.

'Hey, you there!' he yelled, putting his hands on his hips. 'You fucking dragon, you! Listen to what the herald has to say! That means me! The first one to take you on honourably will be the meandering knight, Eyck of Denesle! And he will stick his lance in your paunch, according to the holy custom, to your confusion, and to the joy of poor virgins and King Niedamir! It will be a fair fight and honourable, breathing fire is not allowed, and you may only lambast the other confessionally, until the other gives up the ghost or expires! Which we sincerely wish on you! Understood, dragon?'

The dragon yawned, flapped its wings, and then, flattening itself to the ground, quickly descended from the hillock to level ground.

'I have understood, noble herald!' it yelled back. 'Then may the virtuous Eyck of Denesle enter the fray. I am ready!'

'What a pantomime,' Boholt spat, following Eyck with a grim expression, as he walked his horse over the barrier of boulders. 'A ruddy barrel of laughs . . . '

'Shut your yap, Boholt,' Dandelion shouted, rubbing his hands. 'Look, Eyck is preparing to charge! It'll be a bloody beautiful ballad!'

'Hurrah! Long live Eyck!' someone shouted from Niedamir's troop of bowmen.

'And I,' Sheepbagger said gloomily, 'would still have stuffed him full of brimstone, just to be certain.'

Eyck, already in the field, saluted the dragon with his upraised lance, slammed down his visor and struck his horse with his spurs.

'Well, well,' the dwarf said. 'He may be stupid, but he knows how to charge. Look at him go!'

Eyck, lent forward, braced in the saddle, lowered his lance at full gallop. The dragon, contrary to Geralt's expectations, did not leap aside, did not move in a semicircle, but, flattened to the ground, rushed straight at the attacking knight.

'Hit him! Hit him, Eyck!' Yarpen yelled.

Eyck, although in full gallop, did not strike headlong, straight ahead. At the last moment he nimbly changed direction, shifting the lance over his horse's head. Flashing past the dragon, he thrust with all his might, standing up in the stirrups. Everybody shouted in unison. Geralt did not join in with the choir.

The dragon evaded the blow with a delicate, agile, graceful turn and, coiling like a living, golden ribbon, as quick as lightning, but softly, catlike, reached a foot beneath the horse's belly. The horse squealed, jerking its croup high up, and the knight rocked in the saddle, but did not release his lance. Just as the horse was about to hit the ground snout first, the dragon swept Eyck from the saddle with a fierce swipe of his clawed foot. Everybody saw his breastplate spinning upwards and everybody heard the clanking and thudding with which the knight fell onto the ground.

The dragon, sitting on its haunches, pinned the horse with a foot, and lowered its toothy jaws. The horse squealed shrilly, struggled and then was quiet.

In the silence that fell everybody heard the deep voice of the dragon Villentretenmerth.

'The doughty Eyck of Denesle may now be taken from the battle-field, for he is incapable of fighting any longer. Next, please.'

'Oh, fuck,' Yarpen Zigrin said in the silence that followed.

VIII

'Both legs,' Yennefer said wiping her hands on a linen cloth, 'and probably something with his spine. The armour on his back is dented as though he'd been hit by a pile driver. He injured his legs with his own lance. He won't be mounting a horse for some time. If he ever mounts one again.'

'Professional hazard,' Geralt muttered. The sorceress frowned.

'Is that all you have to say?'

'And what else would you like to hear, Yennefer?'

'That dragon is unbelievably fast, Geralt. Too fast for a *man* to fight it.'

'I understand. No, Yen. Not me.'

'Principles,' the sorceress smiled spitefully, 'or ordinary, commonplace fear? The only human feeling that wasn't eradicated in you?'

'One and the other,' the Witcher agreed dispassionately. 'What difference does it make?'

'Precisely,' Yennefer came closer. 'None. Principles may be broken, fear can be overcome. Kill that dragon, Geralt. For me.'

'For you?'

'For me. I want that dragon, Geralt. In one piece. I want to have him all for myself.'

'So cast a spell and kill it.'

'No. You kill it. And I'll use my spells to hold back the Reavers and the others so they don't interfere.'

'You'll kill them, Yennefer.'

'Since when has that ever bothered you? You take care of the dragon, I'll deal with the people.'

'Yennefer,' the Witcher said coldly, 'I don't understand. What do you want with that dragon? Does the yellowness of its scales dazzle you to that degree? You don't suffer from poverty, after all. You have numerous sources of income; you're famous. What are you about? Just don't talk about a calling, I beg you.'

Yennefer was silent, then finally, twisting her lips, aimed a powerful kick at a stone lying in the grass.

'There's someone who can help me, Geralt. Apparently, it's . . . you know what I'm talking about . . . Apparently it isn't irreversible. There's a chance. I could still have . . . Do you understand?'

'I do.'

'It's a complex operation, costly. But in exchange for a golden dragon . . . Geralt?'

The Witcher remained silent.

'When we were hanging on the bridge,' the sorceress said, 'you asked me for something. I'll meet your request. In spite of everything.'

The Witcher smiled sadly and touched the obsidian star on Yennefer's neck with his index finger.

'It's too late, Yen. We aren't hanging now. It's stopped mattering to me. In spite of everything.'

He expected the worst: a cascade of fire, lightning, a smack in the face, abuse, curses. He was surprised just to see the suppressed trembling of her lips. Yennefer slowly turned away. Geralt regretted his words. He regretted the emotion which had engendered them. The limit of possibility overstepped, now snapped like a lute string. He looked at Dandelion and saw the troubadour quickly turn his head away and avoid his gaze.

'Well, we've got the issue of knightly honour out of the way, my lords,' Boholt called, now dressed in armour and standing before Niedamir, who was still sitting on a stone with an unvarying expression of boredom on his face. 'Knightly honour is lying there, groaning softly. It was a lousy idea, Lord Gyllenstiern, to send out Eyck as your knight and vassal. I wouldn't dream of pointing the finger, but I know whom Eyck can thank for his broken pins. Yes, I swear, we've killed two birds with one stone. One was a lunatic, insanely reviving the legends of how a bold knight defeats a dragon in a duel. And the other a swindler, who wanted to make money from it. Do you know who I'm talking about, Gyllenstiern, what? Good. And now our move. Now the dragon is ours. Now we, the Reavers, will sort out that dragon. But by ourselves.'

'And the agreement, Boholt?' the chancellor drawled. 'What about the agreement?'

'I don't give a shit about the agreement.'

'This is outrageous! This is lese-majesty!' Gyllenstiern stamped his foot. 'King Niedamir—'

'What about the king?' Boholt yelled, resting on an enormous, two-handed sword. 'Perhaps the king will personally decide to take on the dragon by himself? Or perhaps you, his faithful chancellor, will squeeze your belly into a suit of armour and go into battle? Why not, please do, we'll wait, my lord. You had your chance, Gyllenstiern. Had Eyck mortally lanced the dragon, you would have taken it in its entirety, nothing would have been left to us because we hadn't helped, not one golden scale on its back. But it's too late now. Open your eyes. There's no one to fight under Caingorn's colours. You won't find another chump like Eyck.'

'That's not true!' the cobbler Sheepbagger said, hurrying to the king, who was still busy watching a point on the horizon of interest only to him. 'O King! Just wait a little, and our men from Barefield will be arriving, they'll be 'ere any moment! To hell with the cock-sure nobility, chase them away! You'll see who is really brave, who is strong in deed, and not just in word!'

'Shut your trap,' Boholt said calmly, wiping a spot of rust from his breastplate. 'Shut your trap, peasant, because if you don't I'll shut it so hard I'll shove your teeth down your throat.'

Sheepbagger, seeing Kennet and Gar approaching, quickly backed away and hid among the Barefield constables.

'King!' Gyllenstiern called. 'O King, what do you command?'

The expression of boredom suddenly vanished from Niedamir's face. The underage monarch wrinkled his freckly nose and stood up.

'What do I command?' he said in a shrill voice. 'You've finally asked, Gyllenstiern, rather than decide for me and speak for me and on my behalf? I'm very pleased. And may it thus remain,

Gyllenstiern. From this moment you will be silent and listen to my orders. Here is the first of them. Muster the men and order Eyck of Denesle be placed on a wagon. We're going back to Caingorn.'

'But sire—'

'Not a word, Gyllenstiern. Madam Yennefer, noble lords, I bid you farewell. I've lost some time on this expedition, but have gained much. I have learned a great deal. Thank you for your words, Madam Yennefer, Master Dorregaray, Sir Boholt. And thank you for your silence, Sir Geralt.'

'O King,' Gyllenstiern said. 'What do you mean? The dragon is in our grasp. It's there for the taking. King, your dream . . .'

'My dream,' Niedamir repeated pensively. 'I do not have it yet. And should I stay here . . . Then I might never have it.'

'But Malleore? And the hand of the princess?' The chancellor waved his arms, not giving up. 'And the throne? King, the people there will acknowledge you as . . .'

'I don't give a shit about the people there, as Sir Boholt would say,' Niedamir laughed. 'The throne of Malleore is mine anyway, because in Caingorn I have three hundred armoured troops and fifteen hundred foot soldiers against their thousand crappy spearmen. Do they acknowledge me? They will have to. I'll keep hanging, beheading and dismembering until they do. And their princess is a fat goose and to hell with her hand, I only need her womb. Let her bear me an heir, and then I'll poison her anyway. Using Master Sheepbagger's method. That's enough chatter, Gyllenstiern. Set about carrying out my orders.'

'Indeed,' Dandelion whispered to Geralt, 'he has learned a great deal.'

'A great deal,' Geralt confirmed, looking at the hillock where the golden dragon, with its triangular head lowered, was licking something grey-green sitting in the grass beside it with its forked, scarlet tongue. 'But I wouldn't like to be his subject, Dandelion.'

'And what do you think will happen now?'

The Witcher looked calmly at the tiny, grey-green creature, fluttering its bat-like wings beside the golden talons of the stooping dragon.

'And what's your opinion about all this, Dandelion? What do you think?'

'What does it matter what I think? I'm a poet, Geralt. Does my opinion matter at all?'

'Yes it does.'

'Well I'll tell you then. When I see a reptile, Geralt, a viper, let's say, or some other serpent, it gives me the creeps, the vileness disgusts and terrifies me. But that dragon . . . '

'Yeah?'

'It . . . it's pretty, Geralt.'

'Thank you, Dandelion.'

'What for?'

Geralt turned his head away, and with a slow movement reached for the buckle of his belt, which crossed his chest diagonally, and shortened it by two holes. He lifted his right hand to check if his sword hilt was positioned correctly. Dandelion looked on with eyes wide open.

'Geralt! Do you plan to . . . ?'

'Yes,' the Witcher said calmly, 'there is a limit to what I can accept as possible. I've had enough of all this. Are you going with Niedamir or staying, Dandelion?'

The troubadour leaned over, placed his lute beneath a stone cautiously and with great care and then straightened up.

'I'm staying. What did you say? The limits of possibility? I'm bagging that as the title of a ballad.'

'It could be your last one, Dandelion.'

'Geralt?'

'Mm?'

'Don't kill it . . . Can you not?'

'A sword is a sword, Dandelion. Once drawn . . . '

'Please try.'

'I will.'

Dorregaray chuckled, turned towards Yennefer and the Reavers, and pointed at the receding royal caravan.

'Over there,' he said, 'King Niedamir is leaving. He no longer gives orders through Gyllenstiern's mouth. He is departing, having demonstrated good sense. I'm glad you're here, Dandelion. I suggest you begin composing a ballad.'

'What about?'

'About,' the sorcerer drew his wand from his coat, 'Master Dorregaray, sorcerer, chasing back home the rabble who wanted to use vulgar methods to kill the last golden dragon left in the world. Don't move, Boholt! Yarpen, hands off your battle-axe! Don't move a muscle, Yennefer! Off you go, good-for-nothings, follow the king, like good little boys. Be off, mount your horses or wagons. I warn you that if anybody makes a false move all that will remain of him will be a burning smell and a bit of fused sand. I am serious.'

'Dorregaray!' Yennefer hissed.

'My lord sorcerer,' Boholt said conciliatorily. 'Is this any way to act—'

'Be quiet, Boholt. I told you not to touch that dragon. Fables are not to be killed. About-turn and scram.'

Yennefer's hand suddenly shot forward, and the ground around Dorregaray exploded in blue flame, seething in a dust cloud of torn turf and grit.

The sorcerer staggered, encircled by fire. Gar leaped forward and struck him in the face with the heel of his hand. Dorregaray fell to the ground, a bolt of red lightning shooting from his wand and harmlessly zapping out among the rocks. Beanpole sprang at him from the other side, kicked the sorcerer to the ground, and took a backswing to repeat the blow. Geralt fell among them, pushed Beanpole away, drew his sword and thrust flat, aiming between the breastplate and the spaulder. He was thwarted by Boholt, who parried the blow with the broad blade of his two-handed sword. Dandelion tried to trip Gar, but ineffectively; Gar clung to the bard's rainbow-hued jerkin and thumped him between the eyes with his fist. Yarpen Zigrin, leaping from behind, tripped Dandelion, hitting him behind his knees with the haft of a hatchet.

Geralt spun into a pirouette, evading Boholt's sword, and jabbed at the onrushing Beanpole, tearing off his iron bracer. Beanpole leaped back, tripped and fell over. Boholt grunted and whirled his sword like a scythe. Geralt jumped over the whistling blade, slammed the hilt of his sword into Boholt's breastplate, fended him off, and thrust, aiming for his cheek. Boholt, realising he could not parry with his heavy sword, threw himself backwards, falling on his back. The Witcher leaped at him and at that moment felt the earth fall away from under his rapidly numbing feet. He saw the horizon going from horizontal to vertical. Vainly trying to form a protective Sign with his fingers, he fell heavily onto the ground on his side, his sword slipping from his numb hand. There was a pounding and a buzzing in his ears.

'Tie them up before the spell stops working,' Yennefer said, somewhere above and very far away. 'All three of them.'

Dorregaray and Geralt, befuddled and paralysed, allowed themselves to be bound and tethered to a wagon, silently and without resisting. Dandelion fought and cursed, so he received a punch in the face before he was tied to the wagon.

'Why tie 'em up, traitors, sons of dogs?' Sheepbagger said, walking over. 'They should be clubbed to death at once and be done with it.'

'You're a son yourself, and not a dog's,' Yarpen Zigrin said, 'Don't insult dogs here. Scram, you heel.'

'You're awfully brave,' Sheepbagger snapped. 'We'll see if you're brave enough when my comrades arrive from Barefield. They'll be here any moment. You'll . . . '

Yarpen, twisting with surprising agility considering his build, whacked Sheepbagger over the head with his hatchet. Gar, standing alongside, gave him a kick for good measure. Sheepbagger flew a few feet through the air and fell nose-first in the grass.

'You'll be sorry!' he yelled, crawling on all fours. 'I'll fix . . . '

'Lads!' Yarpen Zigrin roared. 'Kick the cobbler in the cobblers! Grab 'im, Gar!'

Sheepbagger did not wait. He sprang up and dashed towards the eastern canyon. The Barefield trackers followed him, cringing. The dwarves, cackling, sent a hail of stones after them.

'The air's freshened up already,' Yarpen laughed. 'Right, Boholt, let's get down to the dragon.'

'Hold on,' Yennefer raised a hand. 'The only thing you're getting down to is the bottom of the valley. Be gone, all of you.'

'Excuse me?' Boholt bent over, his eyes blazing ominously. 'What did you say, Most Honourable Madam Witch?'

'Follow that cobbler,' Yennefer repeated. 'All of you. I'll deal with the dragon myself. Using unconventional weapons. And you can thank me as you leave. Had it not been for me you would have tasted the Witcher's sword. Come now, quickly, Boholt, before I lose my temper. I warn you that I know a spell which can make you all geldings. I just have to raise my hand.'

'Is that so?' Boholt drawled. 'My patience has reached its limits. I won't be made a fool of. Beanpole, unhook the shaft from the cart. I feel I'll also be needing unconventional weapons. Someone is soon going to get a damn good thrashing, my lords. I won't point the finger, but a certain hideous witch is going to get a bloody sound hiding.'

'Just try, Boholt. You'll brighten up my day.'

'Why, Yennefer?' the dwarf asked reproachfully.

'Perhaps I simply don't like sharing, Yarpen?'

'Well now,' Yarpen Zigrin smiled. 'That's profoundly human. So human it's almost dwarven. It's nice to see familiar qualities in a sorceress. Because I don't like sharing, either, Yennefer.'

He hunched into a short, very rapid backswing. A steel ball, appearing out of his pocket as if from nowhere, whirred through the air and smacked Yennefer right in the forehead. Before the sorceress had time to come to her senses, she was suspended in the air, being held up by Beanpole and Gar, and Yarpen was binding her ankles with twine. Yennefer screamed furiously, but one of Yarpen's boys threw the wagon's reins over her head from behind and pulled them tight, the leather strap digging into her open mouth, stifling her cries.

'Well, Yennefer,' Boholt said as he walked over, 'how do you plan to turn me into a gelding now? When you can't move a hand?'

He tore the collar of her coat and then ripped and wrenched open her blouse. Yennefer shrieked, choked by the reins.

'I don't have the time now,' Boholt said, groping her shamelessly to the cackling of the dwarves, 'but wait a little while, witch. Once we've sorted out the dragon, we'll make merry. Tie her firmly to the wheel, boys. Both little hands to the rim, so she won't be able to lift a finger. And no one's to bloody touch her yet, my lords. We'll sort the order out depending on who does a good job on the dragon.'

'Beware, Boholt,' Geralt, arms tied, said, softly, calmly and ominously. 'I'll follow you to the ends of the world.'

'You surprise me,' the Reaver replied, just as calmly. 'In your place I'd keep mum. I know you, and I know I have to take your threat seriously. I won't have a choice. You might not come out of this alive, Witcher. We'll return to this matter. Gar, Beanpole, to horse.'

'What bad luck,' Dandelion snapped. 'Why the hell did I get mixed up in this?'

Dorregaray, lowering his head, watched the thick drops of blood slowly dripping from his nose onto his belly.

'Would you stop staring!' the sorceress screamed at Geralt. She was writhing like a snake in her bonds, vainly trying to conceal her exposed charms. The Witcher obediently turned his head away. Dandelion did not.

'You must have used an entire barrel of mandrake elixir on what I can see, Yennefer,' the bard laughed. 'Your skin's like a sixteen-year-old's, dammit.'

'Shut your trap, whore's son!' the sorceress bellowed.

'How old are you, actually, Yennefer?' Dandelion asked, not giving up. 'Two hundred? Well, a hundred and fifty, let's say. And you're behaving like . . . '

Yennefer twisted her neck and spat at him, but was wide of the mark.

'Yen,' the Witcher said reproachfully, wiping his spit-covered ear on his shoulder.

'I wish he would stop staring!'

'Not on your life,' Dandelion said, without taking his eyes off the bedraggled sorceress. 'I'm here because of her. They may slit our throats, but at least I'll die happy.'

'Shut up, Dandelion,' the Witcher said.

'I have no intention of so doing. In fact I plan to compose the Ballad of the Two Tits. Please don't interfere.'

'Dandelion,' Dorregaray sniffed through his bloody nose. 'Be serious.'

'I am being bloody serious.'

The dwarves heaved Boholt up into the saddle. He was heavy and squat from the armour and the leather pads he was wearing. Gar and Beanpole were already mounted, holding huge, two-handed swords across their saddles.

'Right,' Boholt rasped, 'let's have at him.'

'Oh, no,' said a deep voice, sounding like a brass trumpet. 'I have come to you!'

From beyond the ring of boulders emerged a long snout shimmering with gold, a slender neck armed with a row of triangular, serrated projections and, behind, taloned feet. The evil, reptilian eyes, with their vertical pupils, peered from beneath horned eyelids.

'I was tired of waiting in the open,' the dragon Villentretenmerth said, looking around, 'so I came myself. Fewer and fewer challengers, I see.'

Boholt held the reins in his teeth and a longsword two-handed.

'Thas nuff,' he said indistinctly, holding the strap in his teeth. 'Stah an fight, heptile!'

'I am,' the dragon said, arching its back and lifting its tail insultingly.

Boholt looked around. Gar and Beanpole slowly, almost ostentatiously, calmly, flanked the dragon. Yarpen Zigrin and his boys waited behind, holding battle-axes.

'Aaaargh!' Boholt roared, striking his horse hard with his heels and lifting his sword.

The dragon curled up, flattened itself to the ground and struck with its tail from above and behind, like a scorpion, hitting not Boholt, but Gar, who was attacking from the side. Gar fell over with his horse amid a clanking, screaming and neighing tumult. Boholt, charging at a gallop, struck with a terrible blow, but the dragon nimbly dodged the wide blade. The momentum of the gallop carried Boholt alongside the dragon's body. The dragon twisted, standing on its hind legs, and clawed Beanpole, tearing open his horse's belly and the rider's thigh with a single slash. Boholt, leaning far out from the saddle, managed to steer his horse around, pulling the reins with his teeth, and attacked once more.

The dragon lashed its tail over the dwarves rushing towards it, knocking them all over, and then lunged at Boholt, en route – seemingly in passing – stamping vigorously on Beanpole, who was trying to get up. Boholt, jerking his head around, tried to steer his galloping horse, but the dragon was infinitely quicker and more agile. Cunningly stealing up on Boholt from the left in order to obstruct his swing, it struck with a taloned foot. The horse reared up and lurched over to one side. Boholt flew from the saddle, losing his sword and helmet, tumbling backwards onto the ground, banging his head against a rock.

'Run for it, lads! Up the hill!' Yarpen Zigrin bellowed, outshouting the screams of Gar, who was pinned down by his horse. Beards fluttering, the dwarves dashed towards the rocks at a speed that belied their short legs. The dragon did not give chase. It sat calmly and looked around. Gar was thrashing and screaming beneath the horse. Boholt lay motionless. Beanpole was crawling towards the rocks, sideways, like a huge, iron crab.

'Staggering,' Dorregaray whispered. 'Staggering . . . '

'Hey!' Dandelion struggled in his bonds, making the wagon shake. 'What is it? Over there! Look!'

A great cloud of dust could be seen on the eastern side of the gorge, and shouting, rattling and the tramping of hooves quickly reached them. The dragon extended its neck to look.

Three large wagons full of armed men rolled onto the plain. Splitting up, they began to surround the dragon.

'It's . . . Dammit, it's the constabulary and guilds from Barefield!' Dandelion called. 'They came around by the source of the Braa! Yes, it's them! Look, it's Sheepbagger, there, at the front!'

The dragon lowered its head and gently pushed a small, green-greyish, mewling creature towards the wagon. Then it struck the ground with its tail, roared loudly and shot like an arrow towards the encounter with the men of Barefield.

'What is it?' Yennefer asked, 'That little thing? Crawling around in the grass? Geralt?'

'It's what the dragon was protecting from us,' the Witcher said. 'That's what hatched some time ago in the cave, over there in the northern canyon. It's the dragonling from the egg of the dragon that Sheepbagger poisoned.'

The dragonling, stumbling and dragging its bulging belly across the ground, scurried unsteadily over to the wagon, squealed, stood on its hind legs, stretched out its little wings, and then without a second's thought clung to the sorceress's side. Yennefer, with an extremely queer look on her face, sighed loudly.

'It likes you,' Geralt murmured.

'He's young, but he ain't stupid,' Dandelion twisting in his fetters, grinned. 'Look where he's stuck his snout. I'd like to be in his shoes, dammit. Hey, little one, run away! That's Yennefer! Terror of dragons! And witchers. Well, at least one witcher—'

'Quiet, Dandelion,' Dorregaray shouted. 'Look over there, on the battlefield! They've got him, a pox on them!'

The Barefield wagons, rumbling like war chariots, raced towards the attacking dragon.

'Smack 'im!' Sheepbagger yelled, hanging on to the wagoner's back. 'Smack 'im, kinsmen, anywhere and anyhow! Don't hold back!'

The dragon nimbly eluded the first advancing wagon, flashing with scythe blades, forks and spears, but ended up between the next two, from which a huge double fishing net pulled by straps dropped onto it. The dragon, fully enmeshed, fell down, rolled over, curled up in a ball, and spread its legs. The net tore to shreds with a sharp rending noise. More nets were thrown onto it from the first wagon, which had managed to turn around, this time utterly entangling the dragon. The two other wagons also turned back, dashed towards the dragon, rattling and bouncing over bumps.

'You're caught in the net, you carp!' Sheepbagger bawled. 'And we'll soon scale you!'

The dragon roared and belched a cloud of steam into the sky. The Barefield constables rushed towards him, spilling out of the wagons. The dragon bellowed again, desperately, with a thundering roar.

From the northern canyon came a reply, a high-pitched, battle cry.

Out from the gorge, straining forward in a frenzied gallop, blonde plaits streaming, whistling piercingly, surrounded by the flickering flashes of sabres, charged . . .

'The Zerrikanians!' the Witcher shouted, helplessly tugging at the ropes.

'Oh, shit!' Dandelion chimed in. 'Geralt! Do you understand?'

The Zerrikanians rode through the throng like hot knives through a barrel of butter, scattering their path with massacred corpses, and then leaped from their horses in full flight, to stand beside the dragon struggling in the net. The first of the onrushing constables immediately lost his head. The second aimed a blow with his pitchfork at Véa, but the Zerrikanian, holding her sabre in both hands, upside down, with the tip pointing towards the ground, slashed him open from crotch to sternum. The others beat a hurried retreat.

'To the wagons!' Sheepbagger yelled. 'To the wagons, kinsmen! We'll crush them under the wagons!'

'Geralt!' Yennefer suddenly shouted, pulling up her bound legs and pushing them with a sudden thrust under the wagon, beneath the arms of the Witcher, which were bound and twisted behind him. 'The Igni Sign! Make it! Can you feel the rope? Cast the bloody thing!'

'Without looking?' Geralt groaned. 'I'll burn you, Yen!'

'Make the Sign! I can take it!'

He obeyed, and felt a tingling in his fingers, which were forming the Igni Sign just above the sorceress's bound ankles. Yennefer turned her head away, biting down on her coat collar and stifling a moan. The dragonling, squealing, beat its wings beside her.

'Yen!'

'Make it!' she bellowed.

Her bonds gave way in an instant, as the disgusting, nauseating odour of charred skin became unbearable. Dorregaray uttered a strange noise and fainted, suspended by his fetters from the wagon wheel.

The sorceress, wincing with the pain, straightened up, lifting her now free leg. She screamed in a furious voice, full of pain and rage. The medallion on Geralt's neck jerked as though it were alive. Yennefer straightened her thigh, waved her foot towards the charging wagons of the Barefield constabulary, and shouted out a spell. The air crackled and gave off the smell of ozone.

'O, ye Gods,' Dandelion wailed in admiration. 'What a ballad this will be, Yennefer!'

The spell, cast by her shapely little foot, was not totally effective. The first wagon – and everything on it – took on the yellow colour of a kingcup, which the Barefield soldiers in the frenzy of battle did not even notice. It did better with the second wagon, whose entire crew were transformed into huge, rough-skinned frogs, which hopped around in all directions, croaking comically. The wagon, now bereft of a driver, tipped over and fell apart. The horses, neighing hysterically, fled into the distance, dragging the broken shaft behind them.

Yennefer bit her lip and waved her leg in the air again. The king-cup-yellow wagon suddenly dissolved into kingcup-yellow smoke to the sound of lively musical tones drifting down from above, and its entire crew flopped onto the grass, stupefied, forming a picturesque heap. The wheels of the third wagon went from round to square and the result was instant. The horses reared up, the wagon crashed over, and the Barefield constabulary were tipped out and thrown onto the ground. Yennefer, now driven by pure vindictiveness, flourished a leg ferociously and yelled out a spell, transforming the Barefielders randomly into turtles, geese, woodlice, flamingos and stripy piglets. The Zerrikanians expertly and methodically finished off the rest.

The dragon, having finally torn the nets to shreds, leaped up, flapped its wings, roared and hurtled, as straight as a ramrod, after the unharmed and fleeing Sheepbagger. Sheepbagger was dashing like a stag, but the dragon was faster. Geralt, seeing the gaping jaws and razor-sharp flashing teeth, turned his head away. He heard a gruesome scream and a revolting crunching sound. Dandelion gave a stifled shout. Yennefer, her face as white as a sheet, bent over double, turned to one side and vomited under the wagon.

A silence fell, interrupted only by the occasional gaggling, croaking and squealing of the remains of the Barefield constabulary.

Véa, smiling unpleasantly, stood over Yennefer, legs wide apart. The Zerrikanian raised her sabre. Yennefer, pale, raised a leg.

'No,' said Borch, also known as Three Jackdaws, who was sitting on a stone. In his lap he was holding the dragonling, peaceful and content.

'We aren't going to kill Madam Yennefer,' the dragon Villentretenmerth repeated. 'It is over. What is more, we are grateful to Madam Yennefer for her invaluable assistance. Release them, Véa.'

'Do you understand, Geralt?' Dandelion whispered, chafing feeling into his numb arms. 'Do you understand? There's an ancient ballad about a golden dragon. A golden dragon can . . . '

'Can assume any form it wishes,' Geralt muttered, 'even that of a human. I've heard that too. But I didn't believe it.'

'Yarpen Zigrin, sir!' Villentretenmerth called to the dwarf, who was hanging onto a vertical rock twenty ells above the ground. 'What are you looking for there? Marmots? Not your favourite dish, if memory serves me. Climb down and busy yourself with the Reavers. They need help. There won't be any more killing. Of anybody.'

Dandelion, casting anxious glances at the Zerrikanians, who were vigilantly patrolling the battlefield, was still trying to revive the unconscious Dorregaray. Geralt was dressing Yennefer's scorched ankles and rubbing ointment into them. The sorceress was hissing with pain and mumbling spells.

Having completed his task, the Witcher stood up.

'Stay here,' he said. 'I have to talk to him.'

Yennefer stood up, wincing.

'I'm going with you, Geralt,' she said, linking her arm in his. 'May I? Please, Geralt.'

'With me, Yen? I thought . . . '

'Don't think,' she pressed herself against his arm.

'Yen?'

'It's alright, Geralt.'

He looked into her eyes, which were warm. As they used to be. He lowered his head and kissed her lips; hot, soft and willing. As they used to be.

They walked over. Yennefer, held up by Geralt, curtsied low, as though before a king, holding her dress in her fingertips.

'Three Jack . . . Villentretenmerth . . . ' the Witcher said.

'My name, when freely translated into your language, means Three Black Birds,' the dragon said. The dragonling, little claws digging into his forearm, arched its back to be stroked.

'Chaos and Order,' Villentretenmerth smiled. 'Do you remember, Geralt? Chaos is aggression, Order is protection against it. It's worth rushing to the ends of the world, to oppose aggression and evil, isn't it, Witcher? Particularly, as you said, when the pay is fair. And this time it was. It was the treasure hoard of the she-dragon Myrgtabrakke, the one poisoned outside Barefield. She summoned me to help her, to stop the evil threatening her. Myrgtabrakke flew away soon after Eyck of Denesle was removed from the battlefield. She had sufficient time, while you were talking and quarrelling. But she left me her treasure as my payment.'

The dragonling squealed and flapped its little wings.

'So you . . . '

'That is right,' the dragon interrupted. 'Well, it's the times we live in. For some time, creatures, which you usually call monsters, have been feeling more and more under threat from people. They can no longer cope by themselves. They need a Defender. Some kind of . . . witcher.'

'And the destination . . . The goal at the end of the road?'

'This is it,' Villentretenmerth lifted his forearm. The dragonling squealed in alarm. 'I've just attained it. Owing to him I shall survive, Geralt of Rivia, I shall prove there are no limits of possibility. One day, you will also find such a purpose, Witcher. Even those who are different can survive. Farewell, Geralt. Farewell, Yennefer.'

The sorceress, grasping the Witcher's arm more firmly, curtsied again.

Villentretenmerth stood up and looked at her, and his expression was very serious.

'Forgive me my frankness and forthrightness, Yennefer. It is written all over your faces, I don't even have to try to read your thoughts. You were made for each other, you and the Witcher. But nothing will come of it. Nothing. I'm sorry.'

'I know,' Yennefer blanched slightly. 'I know, Villentretenmerth. But I would also like to believe there are no limits of possibility. Or at least I would like to believe that they are still very far away.'

Véa walked over, touched Geralt's shoulder, and quickly uttered a few words. The dragon laughed.

'Geralt, Véa says she will long remember the tub at the Pensive Dragon. She hopes we'll meet again some day.'

'What?' Yennefer answered, narrowing her eyes.

'Nothing,' the Witcher said quickly, 'Villentretenmerth . . . '

'Yes, Geralt of Rivia?'

'You can assume any form. Any that you wish.'

'Indeed.'

'Why then, a man? Why Borch with three black birds on his coat of arms?'

The dragon smiled cheerfully.

'I don't know, Geralt, in what circumstances the distant ancestors of our races encountered one another for the first time. But the fact is that for dragons, there is nothing more repugnant than man. Man arouses instinctive, irrational disgust in a dragon. With me it's different. To me you're . . . likeable. Farewell.'

It was not a gradual, blurred transformation, or a hazy, pulsating trembling as with an illusion. It was as sudden as the blink of an eye. Where a second before had stood a curly-haired knight in a tunic decorated with three black birds, now sat a golden dragon, gracefully extending its long, slender neck. Inclining its head, the dragon spread its wings, dazzlingly gold in the sunshine. Yennefer sighed loudly.

Véa, already mounted beside Téa, waved.

'Véa,' the Witcher said, 'you were right.'

'Hm?'

'He is the most beautiful.'

A SHARD OF ICE

I

The dead sheep, swollen and bloated, its stiff legs pointing towards the sky, moved. Geralt, crouching by the wall, slowly drew his sword, careful not to let the blade grate against the scabbard. Ten paces from him, a pile of refuse suddenly arched up and heaved. The Witcher straightened and jumped before the wave of stench emanating from the disturbed midden reached him.

A tentacle ending in a rounded, tapering protuberance, bristling with spikes, suddenly shot out from under the rubbish, hurtling out towards him at incredible speed. The Witcher landed surely on the remains of a broken piece of furniture tottering on a pile of rotten vegetables, swayed, regained his balance, and slashed the tentacle with a short blow of his sword, cutting off the tentacular club. He sprang back at once, but this time slipped from the boards and sank up to his thighs in the boggy midden.

The rubbish heap erupted, throwing up viscous, foul-smelling slime, fragments of pots, rotten rags and pale threads of sauerkraut, and from beneath it all burst an enormous, bulbous body, as deformed as a grotesque potato, lashing the air with three tentacles and the stump of a fourth.

Geralt, trapped and immobilised, struck with a broad twist of his hips, smoothly hacking off another tentacle. The remaining two, as thick as tree boughs, fell on him with force, plunging him more deeply into the waste. The body glided towards him, ploughing into the midden like a barrel being dragged along. He saw the hideous,

83

bulbous shape snap open, gaping with a wide maw full of large, lumpish teeth.

He let the tentacles encircle his waist, pull him with a squelch from the stinking slime and drag him towards the body, now boring into the refuse heap with circular movements. The toothed maw snapped savagely and ferociously. Having been dragged close to the dreadful jaws, the Witcher struck with his sword, two-handed, the blade biting smoothly and easily. The obnoxious, sweetish odour took his breath away. The monster hissed and shuddered, and the tentacles released their grip, flapping convulsively in the air. Geralt, bogged down in the refuse, slashed again, backhanded, the blade repulsively crunching and grating on the bared teeth. The creature gurgled and drooped, but immediately swelled, hissing, vomiting putrid slime over the Witcher. Keeping his balance with strenuous movements of his legs, still stuck in the muck, Geralt broke free and lunged forward, cleaving the refuse with his chest like a swimmer moving through water, and struck with all his strength from above, powerfully bearing down on the blade as it cut into the body, between the weakly glowing eyes. The monster groaned, flapped around, unfolding onto the pile of muck like a punctured bladder, emitting palpable, warm gusts of stench. The tentacles twitched and writhed among the rubbish.

The Witcher clambered out of the treacly slime and stood on slippery but hard ground. He felt something sticky and revolting which had got into his boot crawling over his calf. To the well, he thought, wash it off, wash off all the repulsiveness as soon as possible. Wash myself. The creature's tentacles flapped on the refuse one last time, sloppy and wet, and then stopped moving.

A star fell, a brief flash of lightning illuminating the black firmament, flecked with unmoving dots of light. The Witcher made no wish.

He was breathing heavily, wheezing, and feeling the effects of the elixirs he had drunk before the fight wearing off. The gigantic heap of rubbish and waste piled up against the town walls, descending steeply towards the glistening ribbon of the river, looked pretty and alluring in the starlight. The Witcher spat.

The monster was dead, now part of the midden where it had dwelled.

Another star fell.

'A garbage heap,' the Witcher said with effort. 'Muck, filth and shit.'

II

'You reek, Geralt,' Yennefer grimaced, not turning from the mirror, where she was cleaning off the colouring from her eyelids and eyelashes. 'Take a bath.'

'There's no water,' he said, looking into the tub.

'We shall remedy that,' the sorceress stood up and threw the window open. 'Do you prefer sea water or fresh water?'

'Sea water, for a change.'

Yennefer spread her arms vigorously and shouted a spell, making a brief, intricate movement with her hands. Suddenly a sharp, wet coldness blew in through the open window, the shutters juddered, and a green cloud gushed into the room with a hiss, billowing in an irregular sphere. The tub foamed with water, rippling turbulently, banging against the edges and splashing onto the floor. The sorceress sat down and resumed her previously interrupted activity.

'How did it go?' she asked. 'What was it, on the midden?'

'A zeugl, as I suspected,' Geralt said, pulling off his boots, discarding his clothes and lowering a foot into the tub. 'Bloody hell, Yen, that's cold. Can't you heat the water?'

'No,' the sorceress, moving her face towards the looking glass and instilling something into her eye using a thin glass rod. 'That spell is bloody wearying and makes me feel sick. And the cold will do you good after the elixirs.'

Geralt did not argue. There was absolutely no point arguing with Yennefer.

'Did the zeugl cause you any problems?' The sorceress dipped the rod into a vial and dropped something into her other eye, twisting her lips comically.

'Not particularly.'

From outside the open window there was a thud, the sharp crack of wood breaking and an inarticulate voice, tunelessly and incoherently repeating the chorus of a popular, obscene song.

'A zeugl,' said the sorceress as she reached for another vial from the impressive collection on the table, and removed the cork from it. The fragrance of lilac and gooseberries filled the room. 'Well, well. Even in a town it's easy for a witcher to find work, you don't have to roam through the wilds at all. You know, Istredd maintains it's becoming a general rule. The place of every creature from the forests and swamps that becomes extinct is occupied by something else, some new mutation, adapted to the artificial environment created by people.'

As usual, Geralt winced at the mention of Istredd. He was beginning to be sick of Yennefer's admiration for Istredd's brilliance. Even if Istredd was right.

'Istredd is right,' Yennefer continued, applying the lilac-and-gooseberry perfumed something to her cheeks and eyelids. 'Look for yourself; pseudorats in sewers and cellars, zeugls in rubbish dumps, neocorises in polluted moats and sewers, taggirs in millponds. It's virtually symbiosis, don't you think?'

And ghouls in cemeteries, devouring corpses the day after the funeral, he thought, rinsing off the soap. Total symbiosis.

'Yes,' the sorceress put aside the vials and jars, 'witchers can be kept busy in towns, too. I think one day you'll settle in a city for good, Geralt.'

I'd rather drop dead, he thought. But he did not say it aloud. Contradicting Yennefer, as he knew, inevitably led to a fight, and a fight with Yennefer was not the safest thing.

'Have you finished, Geralt?'

'Yes.'

'Get out of the tub.'

Without getting up, Yennefer carelessly waved a hand and uttered a spell. The water from the tub – including everything which had spilled onto the floor or was dripping from Geralt – gathered itself with a swoosh into a translucent sphere and whistled through the window. He heard a loud splash.

'A pox on you, whoresons!' an infuriated yell rang out from below. 'Have you nowhere to pour away your piss? I bloody hope you're eaten alive by lice, catch the ruddy pox and croak!'

The sorceress closed the window.

'Dammit, Yen,' the Witcher chuckled. 'You could have chucked the water somewhere else.'

'I could have,' she purred, 'but I didn't feel like it.'

She took the oil lamp from the table and walked over to him. The white nightdress clinging to her body as she moved made her tremendously appealing. More so than if she were naked, he thought.

'I want to look you over,' she said, 'the zeugl might have injured you.'

'It didn't. I would have felt it.'

'After the elixirs? Don't be ridiculous. After the elixirs you wouldn't even have felt an open fracture, until the protruding bones started snagging on hedges. And there might have been anything on the zeugl, including tetanus and cadaveric poison. If anything happens there's still time for counter-measures. Turn around.'

He felt the soft warmth of the lamp's flame on his body and the occasional brushing of her hair.

'Everything seems to be in order,' she said. 'Lie down before the elixirs knock you off your feet. Those mixtures are devilishly dangerous. They'll destroy you in the end.'

'I have to take them before I fight.'

Yennefer did not answer. She sat down at the looking glass once more and slowly combed her black, curly, shimmering locks. She always combed her hair before going to bed. Geralt found it peculiar, but he adored watching her doing it. He suspected Yennefer was aware of it.

He suddenly felt very cold, and the elixirs indeed jolted him, numbed the nape of his neck and swirled around the bottom of his stomach in vortices of nausea. He cursed under his breath and fell heavily onto the bed, without taking his eyes off Yennefer.

A movement in the corner of the chamber caught his attention. A smallish, pitch-black bird sat on a set of antlers nailed crookedly to the wall and festooned in cobwebs.

Glancing sideways, it looked at the Witcher with a yellow, fixed eye.

'What's that, Yen? How did it get here?'

'What?' Yennefer turned her head. 'Oh, that. It's a kestrel.'

'A kestrel? Kestrels are rufous and speckled, and that one's black.'

'It's an enchanted kestrel. I made it.'

'What for?'

'I need it,' she cut him off. Geralt did not ask any more questions, knowing that Yennefer would not answer.

'Are you seeing Istredd tomorrow?'

The sorceress moved the vials to the edge of the table, put her comb into a small box and closed the side panels of the looking glass.

'Yes. First thing. Why?'

'Nothing.'

She lay down beside him, without snuffing out the lamp. She never doused lights; she could not bear to fall asleep in the dark. Whether an oil lamp, a lantern, or a candle, it had to burn right down. Always. One more foible. Yennefer had a remarkable number of foibles.

'Yen?'

'Uh-huh?'

'When are we leaving?'

'Don't be tedious,' she tugged the eiderdown sharply. 'We've only been here three days, and you've asked that question at least thirty times. I've told you, I have things to deal with.'

'With Istredd?'

'Yes.'

He sighed and embraced her, not concealing his intentions.

'Hey,' she whispered. 'You've taken elixirs . . .'

'What of it?'

'Nothing,' she giggled like a schoolgirl, cuddling up to him, arching her body and lifting herself to allow her nightdress to slip off. As usual, the delight in her nakedness coursed in a shudder down his back and tingled in his fingers as they touched her skin. His lips touched her breasts, rounded and delicate, with nipples so pale they were visible only by their contours. He entwined his fingers in her hair, her lilac-and-gooseberry perfumed hair.

She succumbed to his caresses, purring like a cat, rubbing her bent knee against his hip.

It rapidly turned out – as usual – that he had overestimated his stamina regarding the witcher elixirs, had forgotten about their disagreeable effects on his body. But perhaps it's not the elixirs, he thought, perhaps it's exhaustion brought on by fighting, risks, danger and death? Exhaustion, which has simply become routine? But my body, even though artificially enhanced, doesn't succumb to routine. It reacts naturally. Just not when it's supposed to. Dammit.

But Yennefer, as usual, was not discouraged by a mere trifle. He felt her touch him, heard her purr right by his ear. As usual, he involuntarily pondered over the colossal number of occasions she must have used that most practical of spells. And then he stopped pondering.

As usual it was anything but ordinary.

He looked at her mouth, at its corners, twitching in an unwitting smile. He knew that smile well, it always seemed to him more one of triumph than of happiness. He had never asked her about it. He knew she would not answer.

The black kestrel sitting on the antlers beat its wings and snapped its curved beak. Yennefer turned her head away and sighed. Very sadly.

'Yen?'

'It's nothing, Geralt,' she said, kissing him. 'It's nothing.'

The oil lamp glimmered and flickered. A mouse was scratching in the wall, and a deathwatch beetle in the dresser clicked softly, rhythmically and monotonously.

'Yen?'

'Mhm?'

'Let's get away. I feel bad here. This town has an awful effect on me.'

She turned over on her side, ran a hand across his cheek, brushing some strands of hair away. Her fingers travelled downwards, touching the coarse scars marking the side of his neck.

'Do you know what the name of this town means? Aedd Gynvael?'

'No. Is it in the elven speech?'

'Yes. It means a shard of ice.'

'Somehow, it doesn't suit this lousy dump.'

'Among the elves,' the sorceress whispered pensively, 'there is a legend about a Winter Queen who travels the land during snow-storms in a sleigh drawn by white horses. As she rides, she casts hard, sharp, tiny shards of ice around her, and woe betide anyone whose eye or heart is pierced by one of them. That person is then lost. No longer will anything gladden them; they find anything that doesn't have the whiteness of snow ugly, obnoxious, repugnant. They will not find peace, will abandon everything, and will set off after the Queen, in pursuit of their dream and love. Naturally, they will never find it and will die of longing. Apparently here, in this town, something like that happened in times long gone. It's a beautiful legend, isn't it?'

'Elves can couch everything in pretty words,' he muttered drowsily, running his lips over her shoulder. 'It's not a legend at all, Yen. It's a pretty description of the hideous phenomenon that is the Wild Hunt, the curse of several regions. An inexplicable, collective madness, compelling people to join a spectral cavalcade rushing across the sky. I've seen it. Indeed, it often occurs during the winter. I was offered rather good money to put an end to that blight, but I didn't take it. There's no way of dealing with the Wild Hunt . . .'

'Witcher,' she whispered, kissing his cheek, 'there's no romance in you. And I . . . I like elven legends, they are so captivating. What a pity humans don't have any legends like that. Perhaps one day they will? Perhaps they'll create some? But what would human legends deal with? All around, wherever one looks, there's greyness and dullness. Even things which begin beautifully lead swiftly to boredom and dreariness, to that human ritual, that wearisome rhythm called life. Oh, Geralt, it's not easy being a sorceress, but comparing it to mundane, human existence . . . Geralt?' She laid her head on his chest, which was rising and falling with slow breathing.

'Sleep,' she whispered. 'Sleep, Witcher.'

III

The town was having a bad effect on him.

Since first thing that morning everything was spoiling his mood, making him dejected and angry. Everything. It annoyed him that he had overslept, so the morning had become to all intents and purposes the afternoon. He was irritated by the absence of Yennefer, who had left before he woke up.

She must have been in a hurry, because the paraphernalia she usually neatly put away in boxes was lying on the table, randomly strewn like dice cast by a soothsayer performing a prophecy ritual. Brushes made from delicate horsehair: the large ones used for powdering her face, the smaller ones which she used to apply lipstick to her mouth, and the utterly tiny ones for the henna she used to dye her eyelashes. Pencils and sticks for her eyelids and eyebrows. Delicate silver tweezers and spoons. Small jars and bottles made of porcelain and milky glass, containing, as he knew, elixirs and balms with ingredients as banal as soot, goose grease and carrot juice, and as menacingly mysterious as mandrake, antimony, belladonna, cannabis, dragon's blood and the concentrated venom of the giant scorpion. And above all of that, all around, in the air, the fragrance of lilac and gooseberry, the scent she always used.

She was present in those objects. She was present in the fragrance.

But she was not there.

He went downstairs, feeling anxiety and anger welling up in him. About everything.

He was annoyed by the cold, congealed scrambled egg he was served for breakfast by the innkeeper, who tore himself away for a moment from groping a girl in the kitchen. He was annoyed that the girl was no more than twelve years old. And had tears in her eyes.

The warm, spring weather and cheerful chatter of the vibrant streets did not improve Geralt's mood. He still did not enjoy being in Aedd Gynvael, a small town which he deemed to be a nasty parody of all the small towns he knew; it was grotesquely noisier, dirtier, more oppressive and more irritating.

He could still smell the faint stench of the midden on his clothes and in his hair. He decided to go to the bathhouse.

In the bathhouse, he was annoyed by the expression of the attendant, looking at his witcher medallion and his sword lying on the edge of the tub. He was annoyed by the fact that the attendant did not offer him a whore. He had no intention of availing himself of one, but in bathhouses everybody was offered them, so he was annoyed by the exception being made for him.

When he left, smelling strongly of lye ash soap, his mood had not improved, and Aedd Gynvael was no more attractive. There was still nothing there that he could find to like. The Witcher did not like the piles of sloppy manure filling the narrow streets. He did not like the beggars squatting against the wall of the temple. He did not like the crooked writing on the wall reading: 'ELVES TO THE RESERVATION!'.

He was not allowed to enter the castle; instead they sent him to speak to the mayor in the merchants' guild. That annoyed him. He was also annoyed when the dean of the guild, an elf, ordered him to search for the mayor in the market place, looking at him with a curious contempt and superiority for someone who was about to be sent to a reservation.

The market place was teeming with people; it was full of stalls, carts, wagons, horses, oxen and flies. On a platform stood a pillory with a criminal being showered by the throng in mud and dung. The criminal, with admirable composure, showered his tormentors with vile abuse, making little effort to raise his voice.

For Geralt, who possessed considerable refinement, the mayor's reason for being among this clamour was absolutely clear. The visiting merchants from caravans included bribes in their prices, and thus had to give someone the bribes. The mayor, well aware of this custom, would appear, to ensure that the merchants would not have to go to any trouble.

The place from which he officiated was marked by a dirty-blue canopy supported on poles. Beneath it stood a table besieged by vociferous applicants. Mayor Herbolth sat behind the table, displaying on his faded face scorn and disdain to all and sundry.

'Hey! Where might you be going?'

Geralt slowly turned his head. He instantly suppressed the anger he felt inside, overcame his annoyance and froze into a cold, hard shard of ice. He could not allow himself to become emotional. The man who stopped him had hair as yellow as oriole feathers and the same colour eyebrows over pale, empty eyes. His slim, long-fingered hands were resting on a belt made from chunky brass plates, weighed down by a sword, mace and two daggers.

'Aha,' the man said. 'I know you. The Witcher, isn't it? To see Herbolth?'

Geralt nodded, watching the man's hands the whole time. He knew it would be dangerous to take his eyes off them.

'I've heard of you, the bane of monsters,' said the yellow-haired man, also vigilantly observing Geralt's hands. 'Although I don't think we've ever met, you must also have heard of me. I'm Ivo Mirce. But everyone calls me Cicada.'

The Witcher nodded to indicate he had heard of him. He also knew the price that had been offered for Cicada's head in Vizima, Caelf and Vattweir. Had he been asked his opinion he would have said it was a low price. But he had not been asked.

'Very well,' Cicada said. 'The mayor, from what I know, is waiting for you. You may go on. But you leave your sword, friend. I'm paid here, mark you, to make sure etiquette is observed. No one is allowed to approach Herbolth with a weapon. Understood?'

Geralt shrugged indifferently, unfastened his belt, wrapped it around the scabbard and handed the sword to Cicada. Cicada raised the corners of his mouth in a smile.

'Well, well,' he said. 'How meek, not a word of protest. I knew the rumours about you were exaggerated. I'd like you to ask for my sword one day; then you'd see my answer.'

'Hi, Cicada!' the mayor called, getting up. 'Let him through! Come here, Lord Geralt, look lively, greetings to you. Step aside, my dear merchants, leave us for a moment. Your business dealings must yield to issues of greater note for the town. Submit your entreaties to my secretary!'

The sham geniality of the greeting did not deceive Geralt. He knew it served exclusively as a bargaining ploy. The merchants were being given time to worry whether their bribes were sufficiently high.

'I'll wager Cicada tried to provoke you,' Herbolth said, raising his hand nonchalantly in response to the Witcher's equally nonchalant nod. 'Don't fret about it. Cicada only draws his weapon when ordered to. True, it's not especially to his liking, but while I pay him he has to obey, or he'll be out on his ear, back on the highway. Don't fret about it.'

'Why the hell do you need someone like Cicada, mayor? Is it so dangerous here?'

'It's not dangerous, because I'm paying Cicada,' Herbolth laughed. 'His fame goes before him and that suits me well. You see, Aedd Gynvael and the other towns in the Dogbane valley fall under the authority of the viceroys of Rakverelin. And in recent times the viceroys have changed with every season. No one knows why they keep changing, because anyway every second one is a half-elf or quarter-elf; accursed blood and race. Everything bad is the fault of the elves.'

Geralt did not add that it was also the fault of the carters, because the joke, although well-known, did not amuse everybody.

'Every new viceroy,' Herbolth continued in a huff, 'begins by removing the castellans and mayors of the old regime, in order to give his friends and relations jobs. But after what Cicada once did to the emissaries of a certain viceroy, no one tries to unseat me from my position any more and I'm the oldest mayor of the oldest regime. Which one, I can't even remember. Well, but we're sitting here chin-wagging, and we need to get on, as my late first wife was wont to say. Let's get to the point. What kind of creature had infested our muck heap?'

'A zeugl.'

'First time I've ever heard of anything like that. I trust it's dead?'

'It is.'

'How much will it cost the town treasury? Seventy?'

'A hundred.'

'Oh, really, Witcher, sir! You must have been drinking hemlock! A hundred marks for killing a lousy worm that burrowed into a pile of shit?'

'Worm or no worm, mayor, it devoured eight people, as you said yourself.'

'People? I like that! The brute, so I am informed, ate old Zakorek, who was famous for never being sober, one old bag from up near the castle and several children of the ferryman Sulirad, which wasn't discovered very quickly, because Sulirad himself doesn't know how many children he has. He produces them too quickly to count them. People, my hat! Eighty.'

'Had I not killed the zeugl, it would soon have devoured somebody more important. The apothecary, let us say. And then where would you get your chancre ointment from? One hundred.'

'A hundred marks is a good deal of money. I don't know if I'd give that much for a nine-headed hydra. Eighty-five.'

'A hundred, Mayor Herbolth. Mark that although it wasn't a nine-headed hydra, no local man, including the celebrated Cicada, was capable of dealing with the zeugl.'

'Because no local man is accustomed to slopping around in dung and refuse. This is my last word: ninety.'

'A hundred.'

'Ninety-five, by all the demons and devils!'

'Agreed.'

'Well, now,' Herbolth said, smiling broadly, 'that's settled. Do you always bargain so famously, Witcher?'

'No,' Geralt did not smile. 'Seldom, actually. But I wanted to give you the pleasure, mayor.'

'And you did, a pox on you,' Herbolth cackled. 'Hey, Peregrib! Over here! Give me the ledger and a purse and count me out ninety marks at once.'

'It was supposed to be ninety-five.'

'What about the tax?'

The Witcher swore softly. The mayor applied his sprawling mark to the receipt and then poked around in his ear with the clean end of the quill.

'I trust things'll be quiet on the muck heap now? Hey, Witcher?'

'Ought to be. There was only one zeugl. Though there is a chance it managed to reproduce. Zeugls are hermaphroditic, like snails.'

'What poppycock is that?' Herbolth asked, looking askance at him. 'You need two to reproduce, I mean a male and a female. What, do those zeugls hatch like fleas or mice, from the rotten straw in a palliasse? Every dimwit knows there aren't he-mice and she-mice, that they're all identical and hatch out of themselves from rotten straw.'

'And snails hatch from wet leaves,' secretary Peregrib interjected, still busy piling up coins.

'Everyone knows,' Geralt concurred, smiling cheerfully. 'There aren't he-snails and she-snails. There are only leaves. And anyone who thinks differently is mistaken.'

'Enough,' the mayor interrupted, looking at him suspiciously. 'I've heard enough about vermin. I asked whether anything might hatch from the muck heap, so be so gracious as to answer, clearly and concisely.'

'In a month or so the midden ought to be inspected, ideally using dogs. Young zeugls aren't dangerous.'

'Couldn't you do it, Witcher? We can come to agreement about payment.'

'No,' Geralt said, taking the money from Peregrib's hands. 'I have no intention of being stuck in your charming town for even a week, quite less a month.'

'Fascinating, what you're telling me.' Herbolth smiled wryly, looking him straight in the eye. 'Fascinating, indeed. Because I think you'll be staying here longer.'

'You think wrong, mayor.'

'Really? You came here with that black-haired witch, what was it again, I forget . . . Guinevere, wasn't it? You've taken lodgings with her at The Sturgeon. In a single chamber, they say.'

'And what of it?'

'Well, whenever she comes to Aedd Gynvael, she does not leave so quickly. It's not the first time she's been here.'

Peregrib smiled broadly, gap-toothed and meaningfully. Herbolth continued to look Geralt in the eye, without smiling. Geralt also smiled, as hideously as he could.

'Actually, I don't know anything,' the mayor looked away and bored his heel into the ground. 'And it interests me as much as dog's filth. But the wizard Istredd is an important figure here, mark you. Indispensable to this municipality. Invaluable, I'd say. People hold him in high regard, locals and outsiders, too. We don't stick our noses in his sorcery and especially not in his other matters.'

'Wisely, perhaps,' the Witcher agreed. 'And where does he live, if I may ask?'

'You don't know? Oh, it's right there, do you see that house? That tall, white one stuck between the storehouse and the armoury like, if you'll pardon the expression, a candle between two arsecheeks. But you won't find him there now. Not long ago, Istredd dug something up by the southern embankment and is now burrowing around there like a mole. And he's put some men to work on the excavation. I went over there and asked politely, why, master, are you digging holes like a child, folk are beginning to laugh. What is in that ground there? And he looks at me like I'm some sort of pillock and says: "History". What do you mean, history? I asks. And he goes: "The history of humanity. Answers to questions. To the question of what there was, and the question of what there will be". There was fuck-all here, I says to that, except green fields, bushes and werewolves, before they built the town. And what there will be depends on who they appoint viceroy in Rakverelin; some lousy half-elf again. And there's no history in the ground, there's nothing there, except possibly worms, if someone's fond of angling. Do you think he listened? Fat chance. He's still digging. So if you want to see him, go to the southern embankment.'

'Oh, come on, mayor,' Peregrib snorted. ''E's at 'ome now. Why would 'e want to be at the diggings, when he's . . .'

Herbolth glanced at him menacingly. Peregrib bent over and

cleared his throat, shuffling his feet. The Witcher, still smiling unpleasantly, crossed his arms on his chest.

'Yes, hem, hem,' the mayor coughed. 'Who knows, perhaps Istredd really is at home. After all, what does it . . .'

'Farewell, mayor,' Geralt said, not even bothering with an imitation of a bow. 'I wish you a good day.'

He went over to Cicada, who was coming out to meet him, his weapons clinking. Without a word he held out his hand for his sword, which Cicada was holding in the crook of his elbow. Cicada stepped back.

'In a hurry, Witcher?'

'Yes.'

'I've examined your sword.'

Geralt shot a look at him which, with the best will in the world, could not have been described as warm.

'That's quite something,' he nodded. 'Not many have. And even fewer could boast about it.'

'Ho, ho.' Cicada flashed his teeth. 'That sounded so menacing it's given me the shivers. It's always interested me, Witcher, why people are so afraid of you. And now I think I know.'

'I'm in a hurry, Cicada. Hand over the sword, if you don't mind.'

'Smoke in the eyes, Witcher, nothing but smoke. You witchers frighten people like a beekeeper frightens his bees with smoke and stench, with your stony faces, with all your talk and those rumours, which you probably spread about yourselves. And the bees run from the smoke, foolish things, instead of shoving their stings in the witcher's arse, which will swell up like any other. They say you can't feel like people can. That's lies. If one of you was properly stabbed, you'd feel it.'

'Have you finished?'

'Yes,' Cicada said, handing him back his sword. 'Know what interests me, Witcher?'

'Yes. Bees.'

'No. I was wondering if you was to enter an alley with a sword from one side and me from the other, who would come out the other side? I reckon it's worth a wager.'

'Why are you goading me, Cicada? Looking for a fight? What's it about?'

'Nothing. It just intrigues me how much truth there is in what folk say. That you're so good in a fight, you witchers, because there's no heart, soul, mercy or conscience in you. And that suffices? Because they say the same about me, for example. And not without reason. So I'm terribly interested which of us, after going into that alley, would come out of it alive. What? Worth a wager? What do you think?'

'I said I'm in a hurry. I'm not going to waste time on your nonsense. And I'm not accustomed to betting. But if you ever decide to hinder me walking down an alley, take my advice, Cicada, think about it first.'

'Smoke,' Cicada smiled. 'Smoke in the eyes, Witcher. Nothing more. To the next time. Who knows, maybe in some alley?'

'Who knows.'

IV

'We'll be able to talk freely here. Sit down, Geralt.'

What was most conspicuous about the workshop was the impressive number of books; they took up most of the space in the large chamber. Bulky tomes filled the bookcases on the walls, weighed down shelves, and were piled high on chests and cabinets. The Witcher judged that they must have cost a fortune. Of course, neither was there any shortage of other typical elements of décor: a stuffed crocodile, dried porcupine fish hanging from the ceiling, a dusty skeleton, and a huge collection of jars full of alcohol containing, it seemed, every conceivable abomination: centipedes, spiders, serpents, toads, and also countless human and non-human parts, mainly entrails. There was even a homunculus, or something that resembled a homunculus, but might just as likely have been a smoked new-born baby.

The collection made no impression on Geralt, who had lived with Yennefer in Vengerberg for six months, and Yennefer had a yet more fascinating collection, even including a phallus of exceptional proportions, allegedly that of a mountain troll. She also possessed a very expertly stuffed unicorn, on whose back she liked to make love. Geralt was of the opinion that if there existed a place less suitable for having sex it was probably only the back of a live unicorn. Unlike him, who considered his bed a luxury and valued all the possible uses of that marvellous piece of furniture, Yennefer was capable of being extremely extravagant. Geralt recalled some pleasant moments spent with the sorceress on a sloping roof, in a tree hollow full of rotten wood, on a balcony (someone else's, to boot), on the railing of a bridge, in a wobbly boat on a rushing river and levitating thirty fathoms above the earth. But the unicorn was the worst. One happy day, however, the dummy broke beneath him, split and fell apart, supplying much amusement.

'What amuses you so much, Witcher?' Istredd asked, sitting down behind a long table overlaid with a considerable quantity of mouldy skulls, bones and rusty ironware.

'Whenever I see things like that,' the Witcher said, sitting down opposite the sorcerer, pointing at the array of jars, 'I wonder whether you really can't make magic without all that stomach-turning ghastliness.'

'It's a matter of taste,' the sorcerer said, 'and also of habit. What disgusts one person, somehow doesn't bother another. And what, Geralt, repels you? I wonder what might disgust someone, who, as I've heard, is capable of standing up to his neck in dung and filth? Please do not treat that question as insulting or provocative. I am genuinely fascinated to learn what might trigger a feeling of repugnance in a witcher.'

'Does this jar, by any chance, contain the menstrual blood of an undefiled virgin, Istredd? Well it disgusts me when I picture you, a serious sorcerer, with a phial in your hand, trying to obtain that precious liquid, drop by drop, kneeling, so to speak, at the very source.'

'Touché,' Istredd said, smiling. 'I refer, naturally, to your cutting wit, because as regards the jar's contents, you were wide of the mark.'

'But you do use blood occasionally, don't you? You can't even contemplate some spells, I've heard, without the blood of a virgin, ideally one killed by a lightning bolt from a clear sky during a full moon. In what way, one wonders, is that blood better than that of an old strumpet, who fell, drunk, from a palisade?'

'In no way,' the sorcerer agreed, a pleasant smile playing on his lips. 'But if it became common knowledge that that role could actually be played just as easily by hog's blood, which is much easier to obtain, then the rabble would begin experimenting with spells. But if it means the rabble having to gather and use virgin's blood, dragon's tears, white tarantula's venom, decoction of severed babies' hands or a corpse exhumed at midnight, many would think again.'

They were silent. Istredd, apparently deep in thought, tapped his fingernails on a cracked, browned skull, which lacked its lower jaw, and ran his index finger over the serrated edge of a hole gaping in the temporal bone. Geralt observed him unobtrusively. He wondered how old the sorcerer might be. He knew that the more talented among them were capable of curbing the ageing process permanently and at any age they chose. Men preferred a mature age, suggesting knowledge and experience, for reasons of reputation and prestige. Women, like Yennefer, were concerned less with prestige and more with attractiveness. Istredd looked no older than a well-earned, robust forty. He had straight, slightly grizzled, shoulder-length hair and numerous wrinkles on his forehead, around his mouth and at the corners of his eyelids. Geralt did not know whether the profundity and wisdom in his benign, grey eyes were natural or brought on by charms. A moment later he concluded that it made no difference.

'Istredd,' he interrupted the awkward silence, 'I came here because I wanted to see Yennefer. Even though she isn't here, you invited me inside. To talk. About what? About the rabble trying to break your monopoly on the use of magic? I know you include me among that rabble. That's nothing new to me. For a while I had the impression you would turn out to be different to your confreres, who have often entered into serious conversations with me, in order just to inform me that they don't like me.'

'I have no intention of apologising to you for my – as you call them – confreres,' the sorcerer answered calmly. 'I understand them for, just like them, in order to gain any level of proficiency at sorcery, I had to apply myself seriously. While still a mere stripling, when my peers were running around fields with bows, fishing or playing odds and evens, I was poring over manuscripts. My bones and joints ached from the stone floor in the tower – in the summer, of course, because in the winter the enamel on my teeth cracked. I would cough from the dust on old scrolls and books until my eyes bulged from their sockets, and my master, old Roedskilde, never passed up an opportunity to flog me with a knout, clearly believing that without it I would not achieve satisfactory progress in my studies. I didn't enjoy soldiering or wenching or drinking during the years when all those pleasures taste the best.'

'Poor thing,' the Witcher grimaced. 'Indeed, it brings a tear to my eye.'

'Why the sarcasm? I'm trying to explain why sorcerers aren't fond of village quacks, charmers, healers, wise women and witchers. Call it what you will, even simple envy, but here lies the cause of the animosity. It annoys us when we see magic – a craft we were taught to treat as an elite art, a privilege of the few and a sacred mystery – in the hands of laymen and dilettantes. Even if it is shoddy, pitiable, derisory magic. That is why my confreres don't like you. Incidentally, I don't like you either.'

Geralt had had enough of the discussion, of pussyfooting around, of the feeling of anxiety which was crawling over the nape of his neck and his back like a snail. He looked straight into Istredd's eyes and gripped the edge of the table.

'It's about Yennefer, isn't it?'

The sorcerer lifted his head, but continued to tap the skull on the table with his fingernails.

'I commend your perspicacity,' he said, steadily returning the Witcher's gaze. 'My congratulations. Yes, it's about Yennefer.'

Geralt was silent. Once, years ago, many, many years ago, as a young witcher, he had been waiting to ambush a manticore. And he sensed the manticore approaching. He did not see or hear it. He sensed it. He had never forgotten that feeling. And now he felt exactly the same.

'Your perspicacity,' the sorcerer went on, 'will save us a great deal of the time we would have wasted on further fudging. And this way the issue is out in the open.'

Geralt did not comment.

'My close acquaintance with Yennefer,' Istredd continued, 'goes back a long way, Witcher. For a long time it was an acquaintance without commitment, based on longer or shorter, more or less regular periods of time together. This kind of noncommittal partnership is widely practised among members of our profession. It's just that it suddenly stopped suiting me. I determined to propose to her that she remain with me permanently.'

'How did she respond?'

'That she would think it over. I gave her time to do so. I know it is not an easy decision for her.'

'Why are you telling me this, Istredd? What drives you, apart from this admirable – but astonishing – candour, so rarely seen among members of your profession? What lies behind it?'

'Prosaicness,' the sorcerer sighed. 'For, you see, your presence hinders Yennefer in making a decision. I thus request you to remove yourself. To vanish from her life, to stop interfering. In short: that you get the hell out of here. Ideally quietly and without saying good-bye, which, as she confided in me, you are wont to do.'

'Indeed,' Geralt smiled affectedly, 'your blunt sincerity astonishes me more and more. I might have expected anything, but not such a request. Don't you think that instead of asking me, you ought rather to leap out and blast me with ball lightning? You'd be rid of the obstacle and there'd just be a little soot to scrape off the wall. An easier – and more reliable – method. Because, you see, a request can be declined, but ball lightning can't be.'

'I do not countenance the possibility of your refusing.'

'Why not? Would this strange request be nothing but a warning preceding the lightning bolt or some other cheerful spell? Or is this request to be supported by some weighty arguments? Or a sum which would stupefy an avaricious witcher? How much do you intend to pay me to get out of the path leading to your happiness?'

The sorcerer stopped tapping the skull, placed his hand on it and clenched his fingers around it. Geralt noticed his knuckles whitening.

'I did not mean to insult you with an offer of that kind,' he said. 'I had no intention of doing so. But . . . if . . . Geralt, I *am* a sorcerer, and not the worst. I wouldn't dream of feigning omnipotence here, but I could grant many of your wishes, should you wish to voice them. Some of them as easily as this.'

He waved a hand, carelessly, as though chasing away a mosquito. The space above the table suddenly teemed with fabulously coloured Apollo butterflies.

'My wish, Istredd,' the Witcher drawled, shooing away the insects fluttering in front of his face, 'is for you to stop pushing in between me and Yennefer. I don't care much about the propositions you're offering her. You could have proposed to her when she was with you. Long ago. Because then was then, and now is now. Now she's with me. You want me to get out of the way, make things easy for you? I decline. Not only will I not help you, but I'll hinder you, as well as my modest abilities allow. As you see, I'm your equal in candour.'

'You have no right to refuse me. Not you.'

'What do you take me for, Istredd?'

The sorcerer looked him in the eye and leaned across the table.

'A fleeting romance. A passing fascination, at best a whim, an adventure, of which Yenna has had hundreds, because Yenna loves to play with emotions; she's impulsive and unpredictable in her whims. That's what I take you for, since having exchanged a few words with you I've rejected the theory that she treats you entirely as an object. And, believe me, that happens with her quite often.'

'You misunderstood the question.'

'You're mistaken; I didn't. But I'm intentionally talking solely about Yenna's emotions. For you are a witcher and you cannot experience any emotions. You do not want to agree to my request, because you think she matters to you, you think she . . . Geralt, you're only with her because she wants it, and you'll only be with her as long as she wants it. And what you feel is a projection of her emotions, the interest she shows in you. By all the demons of the Netherworld, Geralt, you aren't a child; you know what you are. You're a mutant. Don't understand me wrongly. I don't say it to insult you or show you contempt. I merely state a fact. You're a mutant, and one of the basic traits of your mutation is utter insensitivity to emotions. You were created like that, in order to do your job. Do you understand? You cannot feel anything. What you take for emotion is cellular, somatic memory, if you know what those words mean.'

'It so happens I do.'

'All the better. Then listen. I'm asking you for something which I can ask of a witcher, but which I couldn't ask of a man. I am being frank with a witcher; with a man I couldn't afford to be frank. Geralt, I want to give Yenna understanding and stability, affection and happiness. Could you, hand on heart, pledge the same? No,

you couldn't. Those are meaningless words to you. You trail after
Yenna like a child, enjoying the momentary affection she shows you.
Like a stray cat that everyone throws stones at, you purr, contented,
because here is someone who's not afraid to stroke you. Do you
understand what I mean? Oh, I know you understand. You aren't a
fool, that's plain. You see yourself that you have no right to refuse
me if I ask politely.'

'I have the same right to refuse as you have to ask,' Geralt drawled,
'and in the process they cancel each other out. So we return to the
starting point, and that point is this: Yen, clearly not caring about
my mutation and its consequences, is with me right now. You proposed to her, that's your right. She said she'd think it over? That's
her right. Do you have the impression I'm hindering her in taking
a decision? That she's hesitating? That I'm the cause of her hesitation? Well, that's my right. If she's hesitating, she clearly has reason
for doing so. I must be giving her something, though perhaps the
word is absent from the witcher dictionary.'

'Listen—'

'No. You listen to me. She used to be with you, you say? Who
knows, perhaps it wasn't me but you who was the fleeting romance,
a caprice, a victim of those uncontrolled emotions so typical of her.
Istredd, I cannot even rule out her treatment of you as completely
objectionable. That, my dear sorcerer, cannot be ruled out just on
the basis of a conversation. In this case, it seems to me, the object
may be more relevant than eloquence.'

Istredd did not even flinch, he did not even clench his jaw. Geralt
admired his self-control. Nonetheless the lengthening silence seemed
to indicate that the blow had struck home.

'You're playing with words,' the sorcerer said finally. 'You're
becoming intoxicated with them. You try to substitute words for
normal, human feelings, which you do not have. Your words don't
express feelings, they are only sounds, like those that skull emits
when you tap it. For you are just as empty as this skull. You have
no right—'

'Enough,' Geralt interrupted harshly, perhaps even a little too
harshly. 'Stop stubbornly denying me rights. I've had enough of it,

do you hear? I told you our rights are equal. No, dammit, mine are greater.'

'Really?' the sorcerer said, paling somewhat, which caused Geralt unspeakable pleasure. 'For what reason?'

The Witcher wondered for a moment and decided to finish him off.

'For the reason,' he shot back, 'that last night she made love with me, and not with you.'

Istredd pulled the skull closer to himself and stroked it. His hand, to Geralt's dismay, did not even twitch.

'Does that, in your opinion, give you any rights?'

'Only one. The right to draw a few conclusions.'

'Ah,' the sorcerer said slowly. 'Very well. As you wish. She made love with *me* this morning. Draw your own conclusions, you have the right. I already have.'

The silence lasted a long time. Geralt desperately searched for words. He found none. None at all.

'This conversation is pointless,' he finally said, getting up, angry at himself, because it sounded blunt and stupid. 'I'm going.'

'Go to hell,' Istredd said, equally bluntly, not looking at him.

V

When she entered he was lying on the bed fully dressed, with his hands under his head.

He pretended to be looking at the ceiling. He looked at her.

Yennefer slowly closed the door behind her. She was ravishing.

How ravishing she is, he thought. Everything about her is ravishing. And menacing. Those colours of hers; that contrast of black and white. Beauty and menace. Her raven-black, natural curls. Her cheekbones, pronounced, emphasising a wrinkle, which her smile – if she deigned to smile – created beside her mouth, wonderfully narrow and pale beneath her lipstick. Her eyebrows, wonderfully irregular, when she washed off the kohl that outlined them during the day. Her nose, exquisitely too long. Her delicate hands, wonderfully nervous, restless and adroit. Her waist, willowy and slender, emphasised by an excessively tightened belt. Slim legs, setting in motion the flowing shapes of her black skirt. Ravishing.

She sat down at the table without a word, resting her chin on clasped hands.

'Very well, let's begin,' she said. 'This growing, dramatic silence is too banal for me. Let's sort this out. Get out of bed and stop staring at the ceiling looking upset. The situation is idiotic enough and there's no point making it any more idiotic. Get up, I said.'

He got up obediently, without hesitation, and sat astride the stool opposite her. She did not avoid his gaze. He might have expected that.

'As I said, let's sort it out and sort it out quickly. In order not to put you in an awkward situation, I'll answer any questions at once. You don't even have to ask them. Yes, it's true that when I came with you to Aedd Gynvael I was coming to meet Istredd and I knew

110

I would go to bed with him. I didn't expect it to come out, that you'd boast about it to each other. I know how you feel now and I'm sorry about that. But no, I don't feel guilty.'

He said nothing.

Yennefer shook her head, her shining, black locks cascading from her shoulders.

'Geralt, say something.'

'He . . .' The Witcher cleared his throat, 'he calls you Yenna.'

'Yes,' she said, not lowering her eyes, 'and I call him Val. It's his first name. Istredd is a nickname. I've known him for years. He's very dear to me. Don't look at me like that. You're also dear to me. And that's the whole problem.'

'Are you considering accepting his proposal?'

'For your information, I am. I told you, we've known each other for years. For . . . many years. We share common interests, goals and ambitions. We understand each other wordlessly. He can give me support, and – who knows – perhaps there'll come a day when I'll need it. And above all . . . he . . . he loves me. I think.'

'I won't stand in your way, Yen.'

She tossed her head and her violet eyes flashed with blue fire.

'In my way? Don't you understand anything, you idiot? If you'd been in my way, if you were bothering me, I'd have got rid of the obstacle in the blink of an eye, I'd have teleported you to the end of Cape Bremervoord or transported you to the land of Hann in a whirlwind. With a bit of effort I'd have embedded you in a piece of quartz and put you in the garden in a bed of peonies. I could have purged your brain such that you would have forgotten who I was and what my name was. I could have done all that had I felt like it. But I could also have simply said: "It was agreeable, farewell". I could have quietly taken flight, as you once did when you fled my house in Vengerberg.'

'Don't shout, Yen, don't be aggressive. And don't drag up that story from Vengerberg, we swore not to go back to it, after all. I don't bear a grudge against you, Yen, I'm not reproaching you, am I? I know you can't be judged by ordinary standards. And the fact that I'm saddened . . . the fact that I know I'm losing you . . . is cellular memory. The atavistic remnants of feelings in a mutant purged of emotion—'

'I can't stand it when you talk like that!' she exploded. 'I can't bear it when you use that word. Don't ever use it again in my presence. Never!'

'Does it change the fact? After all, I *am* a mutant.'

'There is no fact. Don't utter that word in front of me.'

The black kestrel sitting on the stag's antlers flapped its wings and scratched the perch with its talons. Geralt glanced at the bird, at its motionless, yellow eye. Once again, Yennefer rested her chin on clasped hands.

'Yen.'

'Yes, Geralt.'

'You promised to answer my questions. Questions I don't even have to ask. One remains; the most important. The one I've never asked you. Which I've been afraid to ask. Answer it.'

'I'm incapable of it, Geralt,' she said firmly.

'I don't believe you, Yen. I know you too well.'

'No one can know a sorceress well.'

'Answer my question, Yen.'

'My answer is: I don't know. But what kind of answer is that?'

They were silent. The din from the street had diminished, calmed down.

The sun setting in the west blazed through the slits of the shutters and pierced the chamber with slanting beams of light.

'Aedd Gynvael,' the Witcher muttered. 'A shard of ice . . . I felt it. I knew this town . . . was hostile to me. Evil.'

'Aedd Gynvael,' she repeated slowly. 'The sleigh of the Elf Queen. Why? Why, Geralt?'

'I'm travelling with you, Yen, because the harness of my sleigh got entangled, caught up in your runners. And a blizzard is all around me. And a frost. It's cold.'

'Warmth would melt the shard of ice in you, the shard I stabbed you with,' she whispered. 'Then the spell would be broken and you would see me as I really am.'

'Then lash your white horses, Yen. May they race north, where a thaw never sets in. I hope it never sets in. I want to get to your ice castle as quickly as I can.'

'That castle doesn't exist,' Yennefer said, her mouth twitching. She grimaced. 'It's a symbol. And our sleigh ride is the pursuit of a dream which is unattainable. For I, the Elf Queen, desire warmth. That is my secret. Which is why, every year, my sleigh carries me amidst a blizzard through some little town and every year someone dazzled by my spell gets their harness caught in my runners. Every year. Every year someone new. Endlessly. Because the warmth I so desire at the same time blights the spell, blights the magic and the charm. My sweetheart, stabbed with that little icy star, suddenly becomes an ordinary nobody. And I become, in his thawed out eyes, no better than all the other . . . mortal women . . .'

'And from under the unblemished whiteness emerges spring,' he said. 'Emerges Aedd Gynvael, an ugly little town with a beautiful name. Aedd Gynvael and its muck heap, that enormous, stinking pile of garbage which I have to enter, because they pay me to, because I was created to enter filth which fills other people with disgust and revulsion. I was deprived of the ability to feel so I wouldn't be able to feel how dreadfully vile is that vileness, so I wouldn't retreat from it, wouldn't run horror-stricken from it. Yes, I was stripped of feelings. But not utterly. Whoever did it made a botch of it, Yen.'

They were silent. The black kestrel rustled its feathers, unfurling and folding its wings.

'Geralt . . .'

'Yes, Yen.'

'Now you answer my question. The question I've never asked you. The one I've always feared. I won't ask you it this time, either, but answer it. Because . . . because I greatly desire to hear your answer. It's the one word, the only word you've never told me. Utter it, Geralt. Please.'

'I cannot, Yen.'

'Why not?'

'You don't know?' he smiled sadly. 'My answer would just be a word. A word which doesn't express a feeling, doesn't express an emotion, because I'm bereft of them. A word which would be nothing but the sound made when you strike a cold, empty skull.'

She looked at him in silence. Her eyes, wide open, assumed an ardent violet colour. 'No, Geralt,' she said, 'that's not the truth. Or perhaps it is, but not the whole truth. You aren't bereft of feeling. Now I see it. Now I know you . . .'

She was silent.

'Complete the sentence, Yen. You've decided. Don't lie. I know you. I can see it in your eyes.'

She did not lower her eyes. He knew.

'Yen,' he whispered.

'Give me your hand,' she said.

She took his hand between hers and at once he felt a tingling and the pulsing of blood in the veins of his forearm. Yennefer whispered a spell in a serene, measured voice, but he saw the beads of sweat which the effort caused to stipple her pale forehead, saw her pupils dilate in pain.

Releasing his arm, she extended her hands, and moved them, smoothing an invisible shape with tender strokes, slowly, from top to bottom. The air between her fingers began to congeal and become turbid, swell and pulsate like smoke.

He watched in fascination. Creational magic – considered the most elevated accomplishment among sorcerers – always fascinated him, much more than illusions or transformational magic. Yes, Istredd was right, he thought. In comparison with this kind of magic my Signs just look ridiculous.

The form of a bird, as black as coal, slowly materialised between Yennefer's hands, which were trembling with effort. The sorceress' fingers gently stroked the ruffled feathers, the small, flattened head and curved beak. One more hypnotically fluid, delicate movement and a black kestrel, turning its head, cried loudly. Its twin, still sitting motionless on the antlers, gave an answering cry.

'Two kestrels,' Geralt said softly. 'Two black kestrels, created by magic. I presume you need them both.'

'You presume right,' she said with effort. 'I need them both. I was wrong to believe one would suffice. How wrong I was, Geralt. To what an error the vanity of the Ice Queen, convinced of her omnipotence, has brought me. For there are some . . . things . . . which there is no way of obtaining, even by magic. And there are gifts which may not be accepted, if one is unable to . . . reciprocate them . . . with something equally precious. Otherwise such a gift will slip through the fingers, melt like a shard of ice gripped in the hand. Then only regret, the sense of loss and hurt will remain . . .'

'Yen—'

'I am a sorceress, Geralt . . . The power over matter which I possess is a gift. A reciprocated gift. For it I paid . . . with everything I possessed. Nothing remained.'

He said nothing. The sorceress wiped her forehead with a trembling hand.

'I was mistaken,' she repeated. 'But I shall correct my mistake. Emotions and feelings . . .'

She touched the black kestrel's head. The bird fluffed up its feathers and silently opened its curved beak.

'Emotions, whims and lies, fascinations and games. Feelings and their absence. Gifts, which may not be accepted. Lies and truth. What is truth? The negation of lies? Or the statement of a fact? And if the fact is a lie, what then is the truth? Who is full of feelings which torment him, and who is the empty carapace of a cold skull? Who? What is truth, Geralt? What is the essence of truth?'

'I don't know, Yen. Tell me.'

'No,' she said and lowered her eyes. For the first time. He had never seen her do that before. Never.

'No,' she repeated. 'I cannot, Geralt. I cannot tell you that. That bird, begotten from the touch of your hand, will tell you. Bird? What is the essence of truth?'

'Truth,' the kestrel said, 'is a shard of ice.'

VI

Although it seemed to him he was roaming the streets aimlessly and purposelessly, he suddenly found himself at the southern wall, by the excavations, among the network of trenches criss-crossing the ruins by the stone wall and wandering in zigzags among the exposed squares of ancient foundations.

Istredd was there. Dressed in a smock with rolled-up sleeves and high boots, he was shouting instructions to his servants, who were digging with hoes into the coloured stripes of earth, clay and charcoal which made up the walls of the excavation. Alongside, on planks, lay blackened bones, shards of pots and other objects; unidentifiable, corroded and gnarled into rusty lumps.

The sorcerer noticed him immediately. After giving the workers some loud instructions, he jumped out of the trench, and walked over, wiping his hands on his britches.

'Yes? What is it?' he asked bluntly.

The Witcher, standing in front of him without moving, did not answer. The servants, pretending to work, watched them attentively, whispering among themselves.

'You're almost bursting with hatred.' Istredd grimaced. 'What is it, I asked? Have you decided? Where's Yenna? I hope she—'

'Don't hope too much, Istredd.'

'Oho,' the sorcerer said. 'What do I hear in your voice? Is it what I sense it is?'

'And what is it you sense?'

Istredd placed his fists on his hips and looked at the Witcher provocatively.

'Let's not deceive ourselves, Geralt,' he said. 'I hate you and you

116

hate me. You insulted me by saying that Yennefer . . . you know what. I came back with a similar insult. You're in my way and I'm in your way. Let's solve this like men. I don't see any other solution. That's why you've come here, isn't it?'

'Yes,' Geralt said, rubbing his forehead. 'That's right, Istredd. That's why I came here. Undeniably.'

'Indeed. It cannot go on like this. Only today did I learn that for several years Yenna has been circulating between us like a rag ball. First she's with me, then she's with you. She runs from me to look for you, then the other way around. The others she's with during the breaks don't count. Only we two count. This can't go on. There are two of us, but only one can remain.'

'Yes,' Geralt repeated, without removing his hand from his forehead. 'Yes . . . You're right.'

'In our conceit,' the sorcerer continued, 'we thought that Yenna would, without hesitation, choose the better man. Neither of us was in any doubt as to who that was. In the end, we started to argue over her favours like whipsters, and like foolish whipsters understood what those favours were and what they meant. I suppose that, like me, you've thought it through and know how mistaken the two of us were. Yenna, Geralt, hasn't the slightest intention of choosing between us, were we even to assume she's capable of choosing. Well, we'll have to decide for her. For I wouldn't dream of sharing Yenna with anyone, and the fact that you're here says the same about you. We, Geralt, simply know her too well. While there are two of us neither of us can be certain. There can only be one. That's the truth, isn't it?'

'It is,' the Witcher said, moving his numb lips with difficulty. 'The truth is a shard of ice . . .'

'What?'

'Nothing.'

'What's the matter with you? Are you infirm or in your cups? Or perhaps stuffed full of witcher herbs?'

'There's nothing wrong with me. I've . . . I've got something in my eye. Istredd, there can only be one. Yes, that's why I came here. Undeniably.'

'I knew,' the sorcerer said. 'I knew you'd come. As a matter of fact, I'm going to be frank with you. You anticipated my plans.'

'Ball lightning?' the Witcher asked, smiling wanly. Istredd frowned.

'Perhaps,' he said. 'Perhaps there'll be ball lightning. But definitely not shot from around the corner. Honourably, face to face. You're a witcher; that evens things out. Very well, decide when and where.'

Geralt pondered. And decided.

'That little square . . .' He pointed. 'I passed through it . . .'

'I know. There's a well there called the Green Key.'

'By the well then. Yes indeed. By the well . . . Tomorrow, two hours after sunup.'

'Very well. I shall be on time.'

They stood still for a moment, not looking at each other. The sorcerer finally muttered something to himself, kicked a lump of clay and crushed it under his heel.

'Geralt?'

'What?'

'Do you feel foolish, by any chance?'

'Yes, I do,' the Witcher reluctantly admitted.

'That's a relief,' Istredd muttered. 'Because I feel like an utter dolt. I never expected I'd ever have to fight a witcher to the death over a woman.'

'I know how you feel, Istredd.'

'Well . . .' the sorcerer smiled affectedly. 'The fact that it's come to this, that I've decided to do something so utterly against my nature, proves that . . . that it has to be done.'

'I know, Istredd.'

'Needless to say, you know that whichever of us survives will have to flee at once and hide from Yenna at the end of the world?'

'I do.'

'And needless to say you count on being able to go back to her when she simmers down?'

'Of course.'

'It's all settled then,' the sorcerer said, and made to turn away, but after a moment's hesitation held out his hand to him. 'Till tomorrow, Geralt.'

'Till tomorrow,' the Witcher said, shaking his hand. 'Till tomorrow, Istredd.'

VII

'Hey, Witcher!'

Geralt looked up from the table, on which he had been absent-mindedly sketching fanciful squiggles in the spilled beer.

'It was hard to find you,' Mayor Herbolth said, sitting down and moving aside the jugs and beer mugs. 'They said in the inn that you'd moved out to the stables, but I only found a horse and some bundles of clothes there. And you're here . . . This is probably the most disreputable inn in the entire town. Only the worst scum comes here. What are you doing?'

'Drinking.'

'I can see that. I wanted to converse with you. Are you sober?'

'As a child.'

'I'm pleased.'

'What is it you want, Herbolth? As you can see, I'm busy,' Geralt smiled at the wench who was putting another jug on the table.

'There's a rumour doing the rounds,' the mayor said, frowning, 'that you and our sorcerer plan to kill each other.'

'That's our business. His and mine. Don't interfere.'

'No, it isn't your business,' Herbolth countered. 'We need Istredd, we can't afford another sorcerer.'

'Go to the temple and pray for his victory, then.'

'Don't scoff,' the mayor snapped, 'and don't be a smart-arse, you vagrant. By the Gods, if I didn't know that the sorcerer would never forgive me, I would have thrown you into the dungeons, right at the very bottom, or dragged you beyond the town behind two horses, or ordered Cicada to stick you like a pig. But, alas, Istredd has a thing about honour and wouldn't have excused me it. I know you wouldn't forgive me, either.'

'It's turned out marvellously,' the Witcher said, draining another mug and spitting out a straw which had fallen into it. 'I'm a lucky fellow, amn't I. Is that all?'

'No,' Herbolth said, taking a full purse out from under his coat. 'Here is a hundred marks, Witcher. Take it and get out of Aedd Gynvael. Get out of here, at once if possible, but in any case before sunrise. I told you we can't afford another sorcerer, and I won't let ours risk his neck in a duel with someone like you, for a stupid reason, because of some—'

He broke off, without finishing, although the Witcher did not even flinch.

'Take your hideous face away, Herbolth,' Geralt said. 'And stick your hundred marks up your arse. Go away, because the sight of you makes me sick. A little longer and I'll cover you in puke from your cap to your toes.'

The mayor put away the purse and put both hands on the table.

'If that's how you want it,' he said. 'I tried to let you leave of your own free will, but it's up to you. Fight, cut each other up, burn each other, tear each other to pieces for that slut, who spreads her legs for anyone who wants her. I think Istredd will give you such a thrashing, you thug, that only your boots will be left, and if not, I'll catch you before his body cools off and break all your bones on the wheel. I won't leave a single part of you intact, you—'

He did not manage to remove his hands from the table, the Witcher's movement was so swift. The arm which shot out from under the table was a blur in front of the mayor's eyes and a dagger lodged with a thud between his fingers.

'Perhaps,' the Witcher whispered, clenching his fist on the dagger's haft, and staring into Herbolth's face, from which the blood had drained, 'perhaps Istredd will kill me. But if not . . . Then I'll leave, and don't try to stop me, you vile scum, if you don't want the streets of your filthy town to foam with blood. Now get out of here.'

'Mayor. What's going on here? Hey, you—'

'Calm down, Cicada,' Herbolth said, slowly withdrawing his hand, cautiously sliding it across the table, as far as possible from the dagger's blade. 'It's nothing. Nothing.'

Cicada returned his half-drawn sword to its scabbard. Geralt did not look at him. He did not look at the mayor as he left the inn, shielded by Cicada from the staggering log drivers and carters. A small man with a ratty face and piercing, black eyes sitting a few tables away was watching him.

I'm annoyed, he realised in amazement. My hands are trembling. Really, my hands are trembling. It's astonishing what's happening to me. Could it mean that . . .?

Yes, he thought, looking at the little man with the ratty face. I think so.

I'll have to, he thought.

How cold it is . . .

He got up.

He smiled as he looked at the small man. Then he drew aside the front of his jacket, took two coins from the full purse and threw them on the table. The coins clinked. One of them rolled across the table and struck the dagger's blade, still stuck into the polished wood.

VIII

The blow fell unexpectedly, the club swished softly in the darkness, so fast that the Witcher only just managed to protect his head by instinctively raising an arm, and only just managed to cushion the blow by lithely twisting his body. He sprang aside, dropping on one knee, somersaulted, landed on his feet, felt a movement of the air yielding before another swing of the club, evaded the blow with a nimble pirouette, spinning between the two shapes closing in on him in the dark, and reached above his right shoulder. For his sword.

His sword was not there.

Nothing can take these reactions from me, he thought, leaping smoothly aside. Routine? Cellular memory? I'm a mutant, I react like a mutant, he thought, dropping to one knee again, dodging a blow, and reaching into his boot for his dagger. There was no dagger.

He smiled wryly and was hit on the head with a club. A light blazed in his eyes and the pain shot down to his fingertips. He fell, relaxing, still smiling.

Somebody flopped onto him, pressing him against the ground. Somebody else ripped the purse from his belt. His eye caught sight of a knife flashing. The one kneeling on his chest tore open his jerkin at the neck, seized the chain and pulled out his medallion. And immediately let go of it.

'By Baal-Zebuth,' Geralt heard somebody pant. 'It's a witcher . . . A real bruiser . . .'

The other swore, breathing heavily.

'He didn't have a sword . . . O Gods, save us from the Evil . . . Let's scarper, Radgast! Don't touch him.'

For a moment the moon shone through a wispy cloud. Geralt saw just above him a gaunt, ratty face and small, black, shining eyes. He

123

heard the other man's loud footsteps fading away, vanishing into an alleyway reeking of cats and burnt fat.

The small man with the ratty face slowly removed his knee from Geralt's chest.

'Next time . . .' Geralt heard the clear whisper, 'next time you feel like killing yourself, Witcher, don't drag other people into it. Just hang yourself in the stable from your reins.'

IX

It must have rained during the night.

Geralt walked out in front of the stable, wiping his eyes, combing the straw from his hair with his fingers. The rising sun glistened on the wet roofs, gleamed gold in the puddles. The Witcher spat. He still had a nasty taste in his mouth and the lump on his head throbbed with a dull ache.

A scrawny black cat sat on a rail in front of the stable, licking a paw intently.

'Here, kitty, kitty,' the Witcher said. The cat stopped what it was doing and looked at him malevolently, flattened its ears and hissed, baring its little fangs.

'I know,' Geralt nodded. 'I don't like you either. I'm only joking.'

He pulled tight the loosened buckles and clasps of his jerkin with unhurried movements, smoothed down the creases in his clothing, and made sure it did not hinder his freedom of movement at any point. He slung his sword across his back and adjusted the position of the hilt above his right shoulder. He tied a leather band around his forehead, pulling his hair back behind his ears. He pulled on long combat gloves, bristling with short, conical silver spikes.

He glanced up at the sun once more, his pupils narrowing into vertical slits. A glorious day, he thought. A glorious day for a fight.

He sighed, spat and walked slowly down the narrow road, beside walls giving off the pungent, penetrating aroma of wet plaster and lime mortar.

'Hey, freak!'

He looked around. Cicada, flanked by three suspicious-looking, armed individuals, sat on a heap of timbers piled up beside the embankment. He rose, stretched and walked into the middle of the alley, carefully avoiding the puddles.

'Where you going?' he asked, placing his slender hands on his belt, weighed down with weapons.

'None of your business.'

'Just to be clear, I don't give a tinker's cuss about the mayor, the sorcerer or this whole shitty town,' Cicada said, slowly emphasising the words. 'This is about you, Witcher. You won't make it to the end of this alley. Hear me? I want to find out how good a fighter you are. The matter's tormenting me. Stop, I said.'

'Get out of my way.'

'Stop!' Cicada yelled, placing a hand on his sword hilt. 'Didn't you hear what I said? We're going to fight! I'm challenging you! We'll soon see who's the better man!'

Geralt shrugged without slowing down.

'I'm challenging you to fight! Do you hear me, mutant?' Cicada shouted, barring his way again. 'What are you waiting for? Draw your weapon! What, got cold feet? Or perhaps you're nothing more than one of those other fools who's humped that witch of yours, like Istredd?'

Geralt walked on, forcing Cicada to retreat, to walk clumsily backwards. The individuals with Cicada got up from the pile of timbers and followed them, although they hung back a little way off. Geralt heard the mud squelching beneath their boots.

'I challenge you!' Cicada repeated, blanching and flushing by turns. 'Do you hear me, you witcher pox? What else do I have to do to you? Spit in your ugly face?'

'Go ahead and spit.'

Cicada stopped and indeed took a breath, pursing his lips to spit. He was watching the Witcher's eyes, not his hands, and that was a mistake. Geralt, still not slowing down, struck him very fast, without a backswing, just flexing from the knees, his fist encased in the spiked glove. He punched Cicada right in the mouth, straight in his twisted lips. They split, exploding like mashed cherries. The Witcher crouched and struck once again, in the same place, this time from a short backswing, feeling the fury spilling from him with the force and the momentum. Cicada, whirling around with one foot in the mud and the other in the air, spat blood and splashed onto his back into a puddle. The Witcher, hearing behind him the hiss of a sword blade in the scabbard, stopped and turned sinuously around, his hand on his sword hilt.

'Well,' he said in a voice trembling with anger, 'be my guests.'

The one who had drawn the sword looked him in the eyes. Briefly. Then he averted his gaze. The others began to fall back. First slowly, then more and more quickly. Hearing it, the man with the sword also stepped back, noiselessly moving his lips. The furthest away of them turned and ran, splattering mud. The others froze to the spot, not attempting to come closer.

Cicada turned over in the mud and dragged himself up on his elbows. He mumbled, hawked and spat out something white amid a lot of red. As Geralt passed he casually kicked him in the face, shattering his cheekbone, and sending him splashing into the puddle again.

He walked on without looking back.

Istredd was already by the well and stood leaning against it, against the wooden cover, green with moss. He had a sword in his belt. A magnificent, light, Terganian sword with a half-basket hilt, the metal-fitted end of the scabbard resting against the shining leg of a riding boot. A black bird with ruffled feathers sat on the sorcerer's shoulder.

It was a kestrel.

'You're here, Witcher,' Istredd said, proffering the kestrel a gloved hand and gently and cautiously setting the bird down on the canopy of the well.

'Yes, I am, Istredd.'

'I hadn't expected you to come. I thought you'd leave town.'

'I didn't.'

The sorcerer laughed loudly and freely, throwing his head back.

'She wanted . . . she wanted to save us,' he said. 'Both of us. Never mind, Geralt. Let's cross swords. Only one of us can remain.'

'Do you mean to fight with a sword?'

'Does that surprise you? After all, you do. Come on, have at you.'

'Why, Istredd? Why with swords and not with magic?'

The sorcerer blanched and his mouth twitched anxiously.

'Have at you, I said!' he shouted. 'This is not the time for questions; that time has passed! Now is the time for deeds!'

'I want to know,' Geralt said slowly. 'I want to know why with swords. I want to know why you have a black kestrel and where it came from. I have the right to know. I have the right to know the truth, Istredd.'

'The truth?' the sorcerer repeated bitterly. 'Yes, perhaps you have. Perhaps you have. Our rights are equal. The kestrel, you ask? It came at dawn, wet from the rain. It brought a letter. A very short one, I know it by heart. "Farewell, Val. Forgive me. There are gifts which one may not accept, and there is nothing in me I could repay you with. And that is the truth, Val. Truth is a shard of ice". Well, Geralt? Are you satisfied? Have you availed yourself of your right?'

The Witcher slowly nodded.

'Good,' Istredd said. 'Now I shall avail myself of mine. Because I don't acknowledge that letter. Without her, I cannot . . . I prefer to . . . Have at you, dammit!'

He crouched over and drew his sword with a swift, lithe movement, demonstrating his expertise. The kestrel cried.

The Witcher stood motionless, his arms hanging at his sides.

'What are you waiting for?' the sorcerer barked.

Geralt slowly raised his head, looked at him for a moment and then turned on his heel.

'No, Istredd,' he said quietly. 'Farewell.'

'What do you bloody mean?'

Geralt stopped.

'Istredd,' he said over his shoulder. 'Don't drag other people into your suicide. If you must, hang yourself in the stable from your reins.'

'Geralt!' the sorcerer screamed, and his voice suddenly cracked, jarring the ear with a false, wrong note. 'I'm not giving up! She won't run away from me! I'll follow her to Vengerberg, I'll follow her to the end of the world. I'll find her! I'll never give her up! Know that!'

'Farewell, Istredd.'

He walked off into the alley, without turning back at all. He walked, paying no attention to the people quickly getting out of his way, or to the hurried slamming of doors and shutters. He did not notice anybody or anything.

He was thinking about the letter waiting for him in the inn.

He speeded up. He knew that a black kestrel, wet from the rain, holding a letter in its curved beak, was waiting for him on the bedhead. He wanted to read the letter as soon as possible.

Even though he knew what was in it.

ETERNAL FLAME

I

'You pig! You plague-stricken warbler! You trickster!'

Geralt, his interest piqued, led his mare around the corner of the alleyway. Before he located the source of the screams, a deep, stickily glassy clink joined them. A large jar of cherry preserve, thought the Witcher. A jar of cherry preserve makes that noise when you throw it at somebody from a great height or with great force. He remembered it well. When he lived with Yennefer she would occasionally throw jars of preserve at him in anger. Jars she had received from clients. Yennefer had no idea how to make preserve – her magic was fallible in that respect.

A large group of onlookers had formed around the corner, outside a narrow, pink-painted cottage. A young, fair-haired woman in a nightdress was standing on a tiny balcony decorated with flowers, just beneath the steep eaves of the roof. Bending a plump, fleshy arm, visible beneath the frills of her nightdress, the woman hurled down a chipped flowerpot.

A slim man in a plum bonnet with a white feather jumped aside like a scalded cat, and the flowerpot crashed onto the ground just in front of him, shattering into pieces.

'Please, Vespula!' the man in the bonnet shouted, 'Don't lend credence to the gossip! I was faithful to you, may I perish if it is not true!'

'You bastard! You son of the Devil! You wretch!' the plump blonde yelled and went back into the house, no doubt in search of further missiles.

131

'Hey, Dandelion,' called the Witcher, leading his resisting and snorting mare onto the battlefield. 'How are you? What's going on?'

'Nothing special,' said the troubadour, grinning. 'The usual. Greetings, Geralt. What are you doing here? Bloody hell, look out!'

A tin cup whistled through the air and bounced off the cobbles with a clang. Dandelion picked it up, looked at it and threw it in the gutter.

'Take those rags,' the blonde woman screamed, the frills on her plump breasts swaying gracefully, 'and get out of my sight! Don't set foot here again, you bastard!'

'These aren't mine,' Dandelion said in astonishment, taking a pair of men's trousers with odd-coloured legs from the ground. 'I've never had trousers like these in my life.'

'Get out! I don't want to see you anymore! You . . . you . . . Do you know what you're like in bed? Pathetic! Pathetic, do you hear! Do you hear, everybody?'

Another flowerpot whistled down, a dried stalk that had grown out of it flapping. Dandelion barely managed to dodge. Following the flowerpot, a copper cauldron of at least two and a half gallons came spinning down. The crowd of onlookers standing a safe distance away from the cannonade reeled with laughter. The more active and unprincipled jokers among them applauded and incited the blonde to further action.

'She doesn't have a crossbow in the house, does she?' the Witcher asked anxiously.

'It can't be ruled out,' said the poet, lifting his head up towards the balcony. 'She has a load of junk in there. Did you see those trousers?'

'Perhaps we ought to get out of here? You can come back when she calms down.'

'Hell no,' Dandelion grimaced. 'I shall never go back to a house from which calumny and copper pots are showered on me. I consider this fickle relationship over. Let's just wait till she throws my . . . Oh, mother, no! Vespula! My lute!'

He lunged forward, arms outstretched, stumbled, fell and caught the instrument at the last moment, just above the cobbles. The lute spoke plaintively and melodiously.

'Phew,' sighed the bard, springing up, 'I've got it. It's fine, Geralt, we can go now. Admittedly my cloak with the marten collar is still there, but too bad, let it be my grievance. Knowing her she won't throw the cloak down.

'You lying sloven!' the blonde screamed and spat copiously from the balcony. 'You vagrant! You croaking pheasant!'

'What's the matter with her? What have you been up to, Dandelion?'

'Nothing unusual,' the troubadour shrugged. 'She demands monogamy, like they all do, and then throws another man's trousers at a fellow. Did you hear what she was screaming about me? By the Gods, I also know some women who decline their favours more prettily than she gives hers, but I don't shout about it from the rooftops. Let's go.'

'Where do you suggest we go?'

'Are you serious? The temple of the Eternal Fire? Let's drop into the Spear Blade. I have to calm my nerves.'

Without protest, the Witcher led his mare after Dandelion, who had headed off briskly into a narrow lane. The troubadour tightened the pegs of his lute as he strode, strummed the strings to test them, and played a deep, resounding chord.

The air bears autumn's cool scent
Our words seized by an icy gust
Your tears have my heart rent
But all is gone and part we must.

He broke off, waving cheerfully at two maids who were passing, carrying baskets of vegetables. The girls giggled.

'What brings you to Novigrad, Geralt?'

'Fitting out. A harness, some tackle. And a new jacket.' The Witcher pulled down the creaking, fresh-smelling leather. 'How do you like it, Dandelion?'

'You don't keep up with the fashion,' the bard grimaced, brushing a chicken feather from his gleaming, cornflower-blue kaftan with puffed sleeves and a serrated collar. 'Oh, I'm glad we've met. Here in Novigrad, the capital of the world, the centre and cradle of culture. *Here* a cultured man can live life to the full.'

'Let's live it one lane further on,' suggested Geralt, glancing at a tramp who had squatted down and was defecating, eyes bulging, in an alleyway.

'Your constant sarcasm is becoming annoying,' Dandelion said, grimacing again. 'Novigrad, I tell you, is the capital of the world. Almost thirty thousand dwellers, Geralt, not counting travellers; just imagine! Brick houses, cobbled main streets, a seaport, stores, shops, four watermills, slaughterhouses, sawmills, a large manufactory making beautiful slippers, and every conceivable guild and trade. A mint, eight banks and nineteen pawnbrokers. A castle and guardhouse to take the breath away. And diversions: a scaffold, a gallows with a drop, thirty-five taverns, a theatre, a menagerie, a market and a dozen whorehouses. And I can't remember how many temples, but plenty. Oh, and the women, Geralt; bathed, coiffured and fragrant; those satins, velvets and silks, those whalebones and ribbons . . . Oh, Geralt! The rhymes pour out by themselves:

Around your house, now white from frost
Sparkles ice on the pond and marsh
Your longing eyes grieve what is lost
But naught can change this parting harsh . . .

'A new ballad?'

'Aye. I'll call it *Winter*. But it's not ready yet, I can't finish it. Vespula's made me completely jittery and the rhymes won't come together. Ah, Geralt, I forgot to ask, how is it with you and Yennefer?'

'It isn't.'

'I understand.'

'No you bloody don't. Is it far to this tavern?'

'Just round the corner. Ah, here we are. Can you see the sign?'

'Yes, I can.'

'My sincere and humble greetings!' Dandelion flashed a smile at the wench sweeping the steps. 'Has anyone ever told you, my lady, that you are gorgeous?'

The wench flushed and gripped her broom tightly. For a moment Geralt thought she would whack the troubadour with the handle. He was mistaken. The wench smiled engagingly and fluttered her eyelashes. Dandelion, as usual, paid absolutely no attention.

'Greetings to one and all! Good day!' he bellowed, entering the tavern and plucking the lute strings hard with his thumb. 'Master Dandelion, the most renowned poet in this land, has visited your tawdry establishment, landlord! For he has a will to drink beer! Do you mark the honour I do you, swindler?'

'I do,' said the innkeeper morosely, leaning forward over the bar. 'I'm content to see you, minstrel, sir. I see that your word is indeed your bond. After all, you promised to stop by first thing to pay for yesterday's exploits. And I – just imagine – presumed you were lying, as usual. I swear I am ashamed.'

'There is no need to feel shame, my good man,' the troubadour said light-heartedly, 'for I have no money. We shall converse about that later.'

'No,' the innkeeper said coldly. 'We shall converse about it right away. Your credit has finished, my lord poet. No one befools me twice in a row.'

Dandelion hung up his lute on a hook protruding from the wall, sat down at a table, took off his bonnet and pensively stroked the egret's feather pinned to it.

'Do you have any funds, Geralt?' he asked with hope in his voice.

'No, I don't. Everything I had went on the jacket.'

'That is ill, that is ill,' Dandelion sighed. 'There's not a bloody soul to stand a round. Innkeeper, why is it so empty here today?'

'It's too early for ordinary drinkers. And the journeymen masons who are repairing the temple have already been and returned to the scaffolding, taking their master with them.'

'And there's no one, no one at all?'

'No one aside from the honourable merchant Biberveldt, who is breaking his fast in the large snug.'

'Dainty's here?' Dandelion said, pleased. 'You should have said at once. Come to the snug, Geralt. Do you know the halfling, Dainty Biberveldt?'

135

'No.'

'Never mind. You can make his acquaintance. Ah!' the troubadour called, heading towards the snug. 'I smell from the east a whiff
and hint of onion soup, pleasing to my nostrils. Peekaboo! It's us!
Surprise!'

A chubby-cheeked, curly-haired halfling in a pistachio-green
waistcoat was sitting at the table in the centre of the chamber, beside
a post decorated with garlands of garlic and bunches of herbs. In his
left hand he held a wooden spoon and in his right an earthenware
bowl. At the sight of Dandelion and Geralt, the halfling froze and
opened his mouth, and his large nut-brown eyes widened in fear.

'What cheer, Dainty?' Dandelion said, blithely waving his
bonnet. The halfling did not move or close his mouth. His hand,
Geralt noticed, was trembling a little, and the long strips of boiled
onion hanging from the spoon were swinging like a pendulum.

'Gggreetings . . . gggreetings, Dandelion,' he stammered and
swallowed loudly.

'Do you have the hiccoughs? Would you like me to frighten you?
Look out: your wife's been seen on the turnpike! She'll be here soon.
Gardenia Biberveldt in person! Ha, ha, ha!'

'You really are an ass, Dandelion,' the halfling said reproachfully.

Dandelion laughed brightly again, simultaneously playing two
complicated chords on his lute.

'Well you have an exceptionally stupid expression on your face,
and you're goggling at us as though we had horns and tails. Perhaps
you're afraid of the Witcher? What? Perhaps you think halfling
season has begun? Perhaps—'

'Stop it,' Geralt snapped, unable to stay quiet, and walked over to
the table. 'Forgive us, friend. Dandelion has experienced a serious
personal tragedy, and he still hasn't got over it. He's trying to mask
his sorrow, dejection and disgrace by being witty.'

'Don't tell me,' the halfling said, finally slurping up the contents
of the spoon. 'Let me guess. Vespula has finally thrown you out on
your ear? What, Dandelion?'

'I don't engage in conversations on sensitive subjects with individuals who drink and gorge themselves while their friends stand,'

the troubadour said, and then sat down without waiting. The halfling scooped up a spoon of soup and licked off the threads of cheese
hanging from it.

'Right you are,' he said glumly. 'So, be my guests. Sit you down,
and help yourselves. Would you like some onion potage?'

'In principle I don't dine at such an early hour,' Dandelion said,
putting on airs, 'but very well. Just not on an empty stomach. I say,
landlord! Beer, if you please! And swiftly!'

A lass with an impressive, thick plait reaching her hips brought
them mugs and bowls of soup. Geralt, observing her round, downy
face, thought that she would have a pretty mouth if she remembered
to keep it closed.

'Forest dryad!' Dandelion cried, seizing the girl's arm and kissing
her on her open palm. 'Sylph! Fairy! O, Divine creature, with eyes
like azure lakes! Thou art as exquisite as the morn, and the shape of
thy parted lips are enticingly . . .'

'Give him some beer, quick,' Dainty groaned. 'Or it'll end in
disaster.'

'No, it won't, no, it won't,' the bard assured him. 'Right, Geralt?
You'd be hard pressed to find more composed men than we two. I,
dear sir, am a poet and a musician, and music soothes the savage
breast. And the Witcher here present is menacing only to monsters. I present Geralt of Rivia, the terror of strigas, werewolves and
sundry vileness. You've surely heard of Geralt, Dainty?'

'Yes, I have,' the halfling said, glowering suspiciously at the
Witcher. 'What . . . What brings you to Novigrad, sir? Have some
dreadful monsters been sighted here? Have you been . . . hem, hem
. . . commissioned?'

'No,' smiled the Witcher, 'I'm here for my own amusement.'

'Oh,' Dainty said, nervously wriggling his hirsute feet, which
were dangling half a cubit above the floor, 'that's good . . .'

'What's good?' Dandelion asked, swallowing a spoonful of soup
and sipping some beer. 'Do you plan to support us, Biberveldt? In
our amusements, I mean? Excellent. We intend to get tipsy, here, in
the Spear Blade. And then we plan to repair to the Passiflora, a very
dear and high-class den of iniquity, where we may treat ourselves to

a half-blood she-elf, and who knows, maybe even a pure-blood she-elf. Nonetheless, we need a sponsor.'

'What do you mean?'

'Someone to pay the bills.'

'As I thought,' Dainty muttered. 'I'm sorry. Firstly, I've arranged several business meetings. Secondly, I don't have the funds to sponsor such diversions. Thirdly, they only admit humans to the Passiflora.'

'What are we, then, short-eared owls? Oh, I understand? They don't admit halflings. That's true. You're right, Dainty. This is Novigrad. The capital of the world.'

'Right then . . .' the halfling said, still looking at the Witcher and twisting his mouth strangely. 'I'll be off. I'm due to be—'

The door to the chamber opened with a bang and in rushed . . . Dainty Biberveldt.

'O, ye Gods!' Dandelion yelled.

The halfling standing in the doorway in no way differed from the halfling sitting at the table, if one were to disregard the fact that the one at the table was clean and the one in the doorway was dirty, dishevelled and haggard.

'Got you, you bitch's tail!' the dirty halfling roared, lunging at the table. 'You thief!'

His clean twin leaped to his feet, overturning his stool and knocking the dishes from the table. Geralt reacted instinctively and very quickly. Seizing his scabbarded sword from the table, he lashed Biberveldt on the nape of his neck with the heavy belt. The halfling tumbled onto the floor, rolled over, dived between Dandelion's legs and scrambled towards the door on all fours, his arms and legs suddenly lengthening like a spider's. Seeing this the dirty Dainty Biberveldt swore, howled and jumped out of the way, slamming his back into the wooden wall. Geralt threw aside the scabbard and kicked the stool out of the way, darting after him. The clean Dainty Biberveldt – now utterly dissimilar apart from the colour of his waistcoat – cleared the threshold like a grasshopper and hurtled into the common bar, colliding with the lass with the half-open mouth. Seeing his long limbs and melted, grotesque physiognomy, the lass opened her mouth to its full extent and uttered an ear-splitting scream. Geralt, taking advantage of the loss of momentum caused by the collision, caught up with the creature in the centre of the chamber and knocked it to the ground with a deft kick behind the knee.

'Don't move a muscle, chum,' he hissed through clenched teeth, holding the point of his sword to the oddity's throat. 'Don't budge.'

'What's going on here?' the innkeeper yelled, running over clutching a spade handle. 'What's this all about? Guard! Detchka, run and get the guard!'

'No!' the creature wailed, flattening itself against the floor and deforming itself even more. 'Have mercy, nooooo!'

'Don't call them!' the dirty halfling echoed, rushing out of the snug. 'Grab that girl, Dandelion!'

The troubadour caught the screaming Detchka, carefully choosing the places to seize her by. Detchka squealed and crouched on the floor by his legs.

'Calm down, innkeeper,' Dainty Biberveldt panted. 'It's a private matter, we won't call out the guard. I'll pay for any damage.'

'There isn't any damage,' the innkeeper said level-headedly, looking around.

'But there will be,' the plump halfling said, gnashing his teeth, 'because I'm going to thrash him. And properly. I'm going to thrash him cruelly, at length and frenziedly, and then everything here will be broken.'

The long-limbed and spread-out caricature of Dainty Biberveldt flattened on the floor snivelled pathetically.

'Nothing doing,' the innkeeper said coldly, squinting and raising the spade handle a little. 'Thrash it in the street or in the yard, sir, not here. And I'm calling the guard. Needs must, it is my duty. Forsooth . . . it's some kind of monster!'

'Innkeeper, sir,' Geralt said calmly, not relieving the pressure on the freak's neck, 'keep your head. No one is going to destroy anything, there won't be any damage. The situation is under control. I'm a witcher, and as you can see, I have the monster in my grasp. And because, indeed, it does look like a private matter, we'll calmly sort it out here in the snug. Release the girl, Dandelion, and come here. I have a silver chain in my bag. Take it out and tie the arms of this gentleman securely, around the elbows behind its back. Don't move, chum.'

The creature whimpered softly.

'Very well, Geralt,' Dandelion said, 'I've tied it up. Let's go to the snug. And you, landlord, what are you standing there for? I ordered beer. And when I order beer, you're to keep serving me until I shout "Water".'

Geralt pushed the tied-up creature towards the snug and roughly sat him down by the post. Dainty Biberveldt also sat down and looked at him in disgust.

'It's monstrous, the way it looks,' he said. 'Just like a pile of fermenting dough. Look at its nose, Dandelion, it'll fall off any second, gorblimey. And its ears are like my mother-in-law's just before her funeral. Ugh!'

'Hold hard, hold hard,' Dandelion muttered. 'Are you Biberveldt? Yes, you are, without doubt. But whatever's sitting by that post was you a moment ago. If I'm not mistaken. Geralt! Everybody's watching you. You're a witcher. What the bloody hell is going on here? What is it?'

'It's a mimic.'

'You're a mimic yourself,' the creature said in a guttural voice, swinging its nose. 'I am not a mimic, I'm a doppler, and my name is Tellico Lunngrevink Letorte. Penstock for short. My close friends call me Dudu.'

'I'll give you Dudu, you whoreson!' Dainty yelled, aiming a punch at him. 'Where are my horses? You thief!'

'Gentlemen,' the innkeeper cautioned them, entering with a jug and a handful of beer mugs, 'you promised things would be peaceful.'

'Ah, beer,' the halfling sighed. 'Oh, but I'm damned thirsty. And hungry!'

'I could do with a drink, too,' Tellico Lunngrevink Letorte declared gurglingly. He was totally ignored.

'What is it?' the innkeeper asked, contemplating the creature, who at the sight of the beer stuck its long tongue out beyond sagging, doughy lips. 'What is it, gentlemen?'

'A mimic,' the Witcher repeated, heedless of the faces the monster was making. 'It actually has many names. A changeling, shapeshifter, vexling, or fetch. Or a doppler, as it called itself.'

'A vexling!' the innkeeper yelled. 'Here, in Novigrad? In my inn? Swiftly, we must call the guard! And the priests! Or it will be on my head . . .'

'Easy does it,' Dainty Biberveldt rasped, hurriedly finishing off Dandelion's soup from a bowl which by some miracle had not been spilled. 'There'll be time to call anyone we need. But later. This scoundrel robbed me and I have no intention of handing it over to the local law before recovering my property. I know you Novigradians – and your judges. I might get a tenth, nothing more.'

'Have mercy,' the doppler whimpered plaintively. 'Don't hand me over to humans! Do you know what they do to the likes of me?'

'Naturally we do,' the innkeeper nodded. 'The priests perform exorcisms on any vexling they catch. Then they tie it up with a stick between its knees and cover it thickly with clay mixed with iron filings, roll it into a ball, and bake it in a fire until the clay hardens into brick. At least that's what used to be done years ago, when these monsters occurred more often.'

'A barbaric custom. Human indeed,' Dainty, said, grimacing and pushing the now empty bowl away, 'but perhaps it is a just penalty for banditry and thievery. Well, talk, you good-for-nothing, where are my horses? Quickly, before I stretch that nose of yours between your legs and shove it up your backside! Where are my horses, I said.'

'I've . . . I've sold them,' Tellico Lunngrevink Letorte stammered, and his sagging ears suddenly curled up into balls resembling tiny cauliflowers.

'Sold them! Did you hear that?' the halfling cried, frothing at the mouth. 'It sold my horses!'

'Of course,' Dandelion said. 'It had time to. It's been here for three days. For the last three days you've . . . I mean, it's . . . Dammit, Dainty, does that mean—'

'Of course that's what it means!' the merchant yelled, stamping his hairy feet. 'It robbed me on the road, a day's ride from the city! It came here as me, get it? And sold my horses! I'll kill it! I'll strangle it with my bare hands!'

'Tell us how it happened, Mr Biberveldt.'

'Geralt of Rivia, if I'm not mistaken? The Witcher?'

Geralt nodded in reply.

'That's a stroke of luck,' the halfling said. 'I'm Dainty Biberveldt of Knotgrass Meadow. Farmer, stock breeder and merchant. Call me Dainty, Geralt.'

'Say on, Dainty.'

'Very well, it was like this. Me and my ostlers were driving my horses to be sold at the market in Devil's Ford. We had our last stop a day's ride from the city. We overnighted, having first dealt with a small cask of burnt caramel vodka. I woke up in the middle of the night feeling like my bladder was about to burst, got off the wagon, and I thought to myself I'll take a look at what the nags are doing in the meadow. I walk out, fog thick as buggery, I look and sud-denly someone's coming. Who goes there? I ask. He says nothing. I walk up closer and see . . . myself. Like in a looking glass. I think I oughtn't to have drunk that bloody moonshine, accursed spirit. And this one here – for that's what it was – ups and conks me on the noggin! I saw stars and went arse over tit. The next day I woke up in a bloody thicket, with a lump like a cucumber on my head, and not a soul in sight, not a sign of our camp, either. I wandered the whole day before I finally found the trail. Two days I trudged, eating roots and raw mushrooms. And in the meantime that . . . that lousy Dudulico, or whatever it was, has ridden to Novigrad as me and flogged my horses! I'll get the bloody . . . And I'll thrash my ostlers! I'll give each one a hundred lashes on his bare arse, the cretins! Not to recognise their own guvnor, to let themselves be outwitted like that! Numbskulls, imbeciles, sots . . .'

'Don't be too hard on them, Dainty,' Geralt said. 'They didn't have a chance. A mimic copies so exactly there's no way of distin-guishing it from the original – I mean, from its chosen victim. Have you never heard of mimics?'

'Some. But I thought it was all fiction.'

'Well it isn't. All a doppler has to do is observe its victim closely in order to quickly and unerringly adapt to the necessary material structure. I would point out that it's not an illusion, but a complete, precise transformation. To the minutest detail. How a mimic does it, no one knows. Sorcerers suspect the same component of the blood is at work here as with lycanthropy, but I think it's either something totally different or a thousandfold more powerful. After all, a were-wolf has only two – at most three – different forms, while a doppler can transform into anything it wants to, as long as the body mass more or less tallies.'

'Body mass?'

'Well, he won't turn into a mastodon. Or a mouse.'

'I understand. And the chain you've bound him up in, what's that about?'

'It's silver. It's lethal to a lycanthrope, but as you see, for a mimic it merely stops the transmutations. That's why it's sitting here in its own form.'

The doppler pursed its glutinous lips and glowered at the Witcher with an evil expression in its dull eyes, which had already lost the hazel colour of the halfling's irises and were now yellow.

'I'm glad it's sitting, cheeky bastard,' Dainty snarled. 'Just to think it even stopped here, at the Blade, where I customarily lodge! It already thinks it's me!'

Dandelion nodded.

'Dainty,' he said, 'It *was* you. I've been meeting it here for three days now. It looked like you and spoke like you. And when it came to standing a round, it was as tight as you. Possibly even tighter.'

'That last point doesn't worry me,' the halfling said, 'because per-haps I'll recover some of my money. It disgusts me to touch it. Take the purse off it, Dandelion, and check what's inside. There ought to be plenty, if that horse thief really did sell my nags.'

'How many horses did you have, Dainty?'

'A dozen.'

'Calculating according to world prices,' the troubadour said, look-ing into the purse, 'what's here would just about buy a single horse, if you chanced upon an old, foundered one. Calculating according to Novigradian prices, there's enough for two goats, three at most.'

The merchant said nothing, but looked as though he were about to cry. Tellico Lunngrevink Letorte hung his nose down low, and his lower lip even lower, after which he began to softly gurgle.

'In a word,' the halfling finally sighed, 'I've been robbed and ruined by a creature whose existence I previously didn't believe in. That's what you call bad luck.'

'That about sums it up,' the Witcher said, casting a glance at the doppler huddled on the stool. 'I was also convinced that mimics had been wiped out long ago. In the past, so I've heard, plenty of them used to live in the nearby forests and on the plateau. But their ability to mimic seriously worried the first settlers and they began to hunt them. Quite effectively. Almost all of them were quickly exterminated.'

'And lucky for us,' the innkeeper said, spitting onto the floor. 'I swear on the Eternal Fire, I prefer a dragon or a demon, which is always a dragon or a demon. You know where you are with them. But werewolfery, all those transmutations and metamorphoses, that hideous, demonic practice, trickery and the treacherous deceit conjured up by those hideous creatures, will be the detriment and undoing of people! I tell you, let's call the guard and into the fire with this repugnance!'

'Geralt?' Dandelion asked curiously. 'I'd be glad to hear an expert's opinion. Are these mimics really so dangerous and aggressive?'

'Their ability to mimic,' the Witcher said, 'is an attribute which serves as defence rather than aggression. I haven't heard of—'

'A pox on it,' Dainty interrupted angrily, slamming his fist down on the table. 'If thumping a fellow in the head and plundering him isn't aggression, I don't know what it is. Stop being clever. The matter is simple; I was waylaid and robbed, not just of my hard-earned property, but also of my own form. I demand compensation, and I shall not rest—'

'The guard, we must call the guard,' the innkeeper said. 'And we should summon the priests! And burn that monster, that non-human!'

144

'Give over, landlord,' the halfling said, raising his head. 'You're becoming a bore with that guard of yours. I would like to point out that that non-human hasn't harmed anybody else, only me. And incidentally, I'm also a non-human.'

'Don't be ridiculous, Mr Biberveldt,' the innkeeper laughed nervously. 'What are you and what is that? You're not far off being a man, and that's a monster. It astonishes me that you're sitting there so calmly, Witcher, sir. What's your trade, if you'll pardon me? It's your job to kill monsters, isn't it?'

'Monsters,' Geralt said coldly, 'but not the members of intelligent races.'

'Come, come, sir,' the innkeeper said. 'That's a bit of an exaggeration.'

'Indeed,' Dandelion cut in, 'you've overstepped the mark, Geralt, with that "intelligent race". Just take a look at it.'

Tellico Lunngrevink Letorte, indeed, did not resemble a member of an intelligent race at that moment. He resembled a puppet made of mud and flour, looking at the Witcher with a beseeching look in its dull, yellow eyes. Neither were the snuffling sounds being emitted from its nose – which now reached the table – consistent with a member of an intelligent race.

'Enough of this empty bullshit!' Dainty Biberveldt suddenly roared. 'There's nothing to argue about! The only thing that counts is my horses and my loss! Do you hear, you bloody slippery jack, you? Who did you sell my nags to? What did you do with the money? Tell me now, before I kick you black and blue and flay you alive!'

Detchka, opening the door slightly, stuck her flaxen-haired head into the chamber.

'We have visitors, father,' she whispered. 'Journeymen masons from the scaffolding and others. I'm serving them, but don't shout so loudly in here, because they're beginning to look funny at the snug.'

'By the Eternal Fire!' the innkeeper said in horror, looking at the molten doppler. 'If someone looks in and sees it . . . Oh, it'll look bad. If we aren't to call the guard, then . . . Witcher, sir! If it really is a vexling, tell it to change into something decent, as a disguise, like. Just for now.'

'That's right,' Dainty said. 'Have him change into something, Geralt.'

'Into whom?' the doppler suddenly gurgled. 'I can only take on a form I've had a good look at. Which of you shall I turn into?'

'Not me,' the innkeeper said hurriedly.

'Nor me,' Dandelion snorted. 'Anyway, it wouldn't be any disguise. Everybody knows me, so the sight of two Dandelions at one table would cause a bigger sensation than the one here in person.'

'It would be the same with me,' Geralt smiled. 'That leaves you, Dainty. And it's turned out well. Don't be offended, but you know yourself that people have difficulty distinguishing one halfling from another.'

The merchant did not ponder this for long.

'Very well,' he said. 'Let it be. Take the chain off him, Witcher. Right then, turn yourself into me, O intelligent race.'

After the chain had been removed the doppler rubbed its doughy hands together, felt its nose and stared goggle-eyed at the halfling. The sagging skin on its face tightened up and acquired colour. Its nose shrank and drew in with a dull, squelching sound, and curly hair sprouted on its bald pate. Now it was Dainty's turn to goggle, the innkeeper opened his mouth in mute astonishment and Dandelion heaved a sigh and groaned.

The last thing to change was the colour of its eyes.

The second Dainty Biberveldt cleared its throat, reached across the table, seized the first Dainty Biberveldt's beer mug and greedily pressed its mouth to it.

'It can't be, it can't be,' Dandelion said softly. 'Just look, he's been copied exactly. They're indistinguishable. Down to the last detail. This time even the mosquito bites and stains on its britches . . . Yes, on its britches! Geralt, not even sorcerers can manage that! Feel it, it's real wool, that's no illusion! Extraordinary! How does it do it?'

'No one knows,' the Witcher muttered. 'It doesn't, either. I said it has the complete ability for the free transformation of material structure, but it is an organic, instinctive ability . . .'

'But the britches . . . What has it made the britches out of? And the waistcoat?'

'That's its own adapted skin. I don't think it'd be happy to give up those trousers. Anyway, they'd immediately lose the properties of wool—'

'Pity,' Dainty said, showing cunning, 'because I was just wondering whether to make it change a bucket of matter into a bucket of gold.'

The doppler, now a faithful copy of the halfling, lounged comfortably and grinned broadly, clearly glad to be the centre of interest. It was sitting in an identical pose to Dainty, swinging its hairy feet the same way.

'You know plenty about dopplers, Geralt,' it said, then took a swig from the mug, smacked its lips and belched. 'Plenty, indeed.'

'Ye Gods, its voice and mannerisms are also Biberveldt's,' Dandelion said. 'Haven't any of you got a bit of red silk thread? We ought to mark it, dammit, because there might be trouble.'

'Come on, Dandelion,' the first Dainty Biberveldt said indignantly. 'Surely you won't mistake it for me? The differences are clear at . . .'

'. . . first glance,' the second Dainty Biberveldt completed the sentence and belched again gracefully. 'Indeed, in order to be mistaken you'd have to be more stupid than a mare's arse.'

'Didn't I say?' Dandelion whispered in amazement. 'It thinks and talks like Biberveldt. They're indistinguishable . . .'

'An exaggeration,' the halfling said, pouting. 'A gross exaggeration.'

'No,' Geralt rebutted. 'It's not an exaggeration. Believe it or not, but at this moment it *is* you, Dainty. In some unknown way the doppler also precisely copies its victim's mentality.'

'Mental what?'

'The mind's properties, the character, feelings, thoughts. The soul. Which would confirm what most sorcerers and all priests would deny. That the soul is also matter.'

'Blasphemy!' The innkeeper gasped.

'And poppycock,' Dainty Biberveldt said firmly. 'Don't tell

stories, Witcher. The mind's properties, I like that. Copying some-one's nose and britches is one thing, but someone's mind is no bloody mean feat. I'll prove it to you now. If that lousy doppler had copied my merchant's mind he wouldn't have sold the horses in Novigrad, where there's no market for them; he would have ridden to the horse fair in Devil's Ford where they're sold to the highest bidder. You don't lose money there—'

'Well actually, you do.' The doppler imitated the halfling's offended expression and snorted characteristically. 'First of all, the prices at the auctions in Devil's Ford are coming down, because the merchants are fixing the bidding. And in addition you have to pay the auctioneer's commission.'

'Don't teach me how to trade, you prat,' Biberveldt said indig-nantly. 'I would have taken ninety or a hundred a piece in Devil's Ford. And how much did you get off those Novigradian chancers?'

'A hundred and thirty,' the doppler replied.

'You're lying, you rascal.'

'I am not. I drove the horses straight to the port, sir, and found a foreign fur trader. Furriers don't use oxen when they assemble their caravans, because oxen are too slow. Furs are light, but costly, so one needs to travel swiftly. There's no market for horses in Novigrad, so neither are there any horses. I had the only available ones, so I could name my price. Simple—'

'Don't teach me, I said!' Dainty yelled, flushing red. 'Very well, you made a killing. So where's the money?'

'I reinvested it,' Tellico said proudly, imitating the halfling's typ-ical raking of his fingers through his thick mop of hair. 'Money, Mr Dainty, has to circulate, and business has to be kept moving.'

'Be careful I don't wring your neck! Tell me what you did with the cash you made on the horses.'

'I told you. I sank it into goods.'

'What goods? What did you buy, you freak?'

'Co . . . cochineal,' the doppler stuttered, and then enumerated quickly: 'A thousand bushels of cochineal, sixty-two hundredweight of mimosa bark, fifty-five gallons of rose oil, twenty-three barrels of cod liver oil, six hundred earthenware bowls and eighty pounds of beeswax. I bought the cod liver oil very cheaply, incidentally, because it was a little rancid. Oh, yes, I almost forgot. I also bought a hundred cubits of cotton string.'

A long – very long – silence fell.

'Cod liver oil,' Dainty finally said, enunciating each word very slowly. 'Cotton string. Rose oil. I must be dreaming. Yes, it's a nightmare. You can buy anything in Novigrad, every precious and everyday thing, and this moron here spends my money on shit. Pretending to be me. I'm finished, my money's lost, my merchant's reputation is lost. No, I've had enough of this. Lend me your sword, Geralt. I'll cut him to shreds here and now.'

The door to the chamber creaked open.

'The merchant Biberveldt!' crowed an individual in a purple toga which hung on his emaciated frame as though on a stick. He had a hat on his head shaped like an upturned chamber pot. 'Is the merchant Biberveldt here?'

'Yes,' the two halflings answered in unison.

The next moment, one of the Dainty Biberveldts flung the contents of the mug in the Witcher's face, deftly kicked the stool from under Dandelion and slipped under the table towards the door, knocking over the individual in the ridiculous hat on the way.

'Fire! Help!' it yelled, rushing out towards the common chamber. 'Murder! Calamity!'

Geralt, shaking off the beer froth, rushed after him, but the second Biberveldt, who was also tearing towards the door, slipped on the sawdust and fell in front of him. The two of them fell over, right on the threshold. Dandelion, clambering out from under the table, cursed hideously.

'Assaaault!' yelled the skinny individual, entangled in his purple toga, from the floor. 'Rooobberrrryyyy! Criminals!

Geralt rolled over the halfling and rushed into the main chamber, to see the doppler – jostling the drinkers – running out into the street. He rushed after him, only to run into a resilient but hard wall of men barring his way. He managed to knock one of them over, smeared with clay and stinking of beer, but others held him fast in the iron grip of powerful hands. He fought furiously, but heard the dry report of snapping thread and rending leather, and the sleeve become loose under his right armpit. The Witcher swore and stopped struggling.

'We 'ave 'im!' the masons yelled. 'We've got the robber! What do we do now, master?'

'Lime!' the master bellowed, raising his head from the table and looking around with unseeing eyes.

'Guaaard!' the purple one yelled, crawling from the chamber on all fours. 'An official has been assaulted! Guard! It will be the gallows for you, villain!'

'We 'ave 'im!' the masons shouted. 'We 'ave 'im, sir!'

'That's not him!' the individual in the toga bellowed, 'Catch the scoundrel! After him!'

'Who?'

'Biberveldt, the halfling! After him, give chase! To the dungeons with him!'

'Hold on a moment,' Dainty said, emerging from the snug. 'What's it all about, Mr Schwann? Don't drag my name through the mud. And don't sound the alarm, there's no need.'

Schwann was silent and looked at the halfling in astonishment. Dandelion emerged from the chamber, bonnet at an angle, examining his lute. The masons, whispering among themselves, finally released Geralt. The Witcher, although absolutely furious, limited himself to spitting copiously on the floor.

'Merchant Biberveldt!' Schwann crowed, narrowing his myopic eyes. 'What is the meaning of this? An assault on a municipal official may cost you dearly . . . Who was that? That halfling, who bolted?'

'My cousin,' Dainty said quickly. 'A distant cousin . . .'

'Yes, yes,' Dandelion agreed, swiftly backing him up and feeling in his element. 'Biberveldt's distant cousin. Known as Nutcase-Biberveldt. The black sheep of the family. When he was a child he fell into a well. A dried-up well. But unfortunately the pail hit him directly on his head. He's usually peaceful, it's just that the colour purple infuriates him. But there's nothing to worry about, because he's calmed by the sight of red hairs on a lady's loins. That's why he rushed straight to Passiflora. I tell you, Mr Schwann—'

'That's enough, Dandelion,' the Witcher hissed. 'Shut up, dammit.'

Schwann pulled his toga down, brushed the sawdust off it and straightened up, assuming a haughty air.

'Now, then,' he said. 'Heed your relatives more attentively, merchant Biberveldt, because as you well know, you are responsible. Were I to lodge a complaint . . . But I cannot afford the time. I am here, Biberveldt, on official business. On behalf of the municipal authorities I summon you to pay tax.'

'Eh?'

'Tax,' the official repeated, and pouted his lips in a grimace probably copied from someone much more important. 'What are you doing? Been infected by your cousin? If you make a profit, you have to pay taxes. Or you'll have to do time in the dungeon.'

'Me?' Dainty roared. 'Me, make a profit? All I have is losses, for fuck's sake! I—'

'Careful, Biberveldt,' the Witcher hissed, while Dandelion kicked the halfling furtively in his hairy shin. The halfling coughed.

'Of course,' he said, struggling to put a smile on his chubby face, 'of course, Mr Schwann. If you make a profit, you have to pay taxes. High profits, high taxes. And the other way around, I'd say.'

'It is not for me to judge your business, sir,' the official said, making a sour face. He sat down at the table, removing from the fathomless depths of his toga an abacus and a scroll of parchment, which he unrolled on the table, first wiping it with a sleeve. 'It is my job to count up and collect. Now, then . . . Let us reckon this up . . . That will be . . . hmmm . . . Two down, carry the one . . . Now, then . . . one thousand five hundred and fifty-three crowns and twenty pennies.

A hushed wheeze escaped Dainty Biberveldt's lips. The masons muttered in astonishment. The innkeeper dropped a bowl. Dandelion gasped.

'Very well. Goodbye, lads,' the halfling said bitterly. 'If anybody asks; I'm in the dungeon.'

II

'By tomorrow at noon,' Dainty groaned. 'And that whoreson, that Schwann, damn him, the repulsive creep, could have extended it. Over fifteen hundred crowns. How am I to come by that kind of coin by tomorrow? I'm finished, ruined, I'll rot in the dungeons! Don't let's sit here, dammit, let's catch that bastard doppler, I tell you! We have to catch it!'

The three of them were sitting on the marble sill of a disused fountain, occupying the centre of a small square among sumptuous, but extremely tasteless, merchants' townhouses. The water in the fountain was green and dreadfully dirty, and the golden ides swimming among the refuse worked their gills hard and gulped in air from the surface through open mouths. Dandelion and the halfling were chewing some fritters which the troubadour had swiped from a stall they had just passed.

'In your shoes,' the bard said, 'I'd forget about catching it and start looking around for somebody to borrow the money off. What will you get from catching the doppler? Perhaps you think Schwann will accept it as an equivalent?'

'You're a fool, Dandelion. When I catch the doppler, I'll get my money back.'

'What money? Everything he had in that purse went on covering the damage and a bribe for Schwann. It didn't have any more.'

'Dandelion,' the halfling grimaced. 'You may know something about poetry, but in business matters, forgive me, you're a total blockhead. Did you hear how much tax Schwann is charging me? And what do you pay tax on? Hey? On what?'

'On everything,' the poet stated. 'I even pay tax on singing. And they don't give a monkey's about my explanations that I was only singing from an inner need.'

'You're a fool, I said. In business you pay taxes on profits. On profits. Dandelion! Do you comprehend? That rascal of a doppler impersonated me and made some business transactions – fraudulent ones, no doubt. And made money on them! It made a profit! And I'll have to pay tax, and probably cover the debts of that scoundrel, if it has run up any debts! And if I don't pay it off, I'm going to the dungeons, they'll brand me with a red-hot iron in public and send me to the mines! A pox on it!'

'Ha,' Dandelion said cheerfully. 'So you don't have a choice, Dainty. You'll have to flee the city in secret. Know what? I have an idea. We'll wrap you up in a sheepskin. You can pass through the gate calling: "I'm a little baa-lamb, baa, baa". No one will recognise you.'

'Dandelion,' the halfling said glumly. 'Shut up or I'll kick you. Geralt?'

'What, Dainty?'

'Will *you* help me catch the doppler?'

'Listen,' the Witcher said, still trying in vain to sew up his torn jacket sleeve, 'this is Novigrad. A population of thirty thousand: humans, dwarves, half-elves, halflings and gnomes, and probably as many out-of-towners again. How do you mean to find someone in this rabbit warren?'

Dainty swallowed a fritter and licked his fingers.

'And magic, Geralt? Those witcher spells of yours, about which so many tales circulate?'

'A doppler is only magically detectable in its own form, and it doesn't walk down the street in it. And even if it did, magic would be no use, because there are plenty of weak sorcerers' signals all around. Every second house has a magical lock on the door and three quarters of the people wear amulets, of all kinds: against thieves, fleas and food poisoning. Too many to count.'

Dandelion ran his fingers over the lute's fingerboard and strummed the strings.

'Spring will return, with warm rain perfumed!' he sang. 'No, that's no good. Spring will return, the sun— No, dammit. It's just not coming. Not at all . . .'

'Stop squawking,' the halfling snapped. 'You're getting on my nerves.'

Dandelion threw the ides the rest of his fritter and spat into the fountain.

'Look,' he said. 'Golden fish. It's said that they grant wishes.'

'Those ones are red,' Dainty observed.

'Never mind, it's a trifle. Dammit, there are three of us, and they grant three wishes. That works out at one each. What, Dainty? Wouldn't you wish for the fish to pay the tax for you?'

'Of course. And apart from that for something to fall from the sky and whack the doppler on the noggin. And also—'

'Stop, stop. We also have our wishes. I'd like the fish to supply me with an ending for my ballad. And you, Geralt?'

'Get off my back, Dandelion.'

'Don't spoil the game, Witcher. Tell us what you'd wish for.'

The Witcher got up.

'I would wish,' he murmured, 'that the fact we're being surrounded would turn out to be a misunderstanding.'

From an alleyway opposite the fountain emerged four individuals dressed in black, wearing round, leather caps, heading slowly towards them. Dainty swore softly and looked around.

Another four men came out of a street behind their backs. They did not come any closer and, having positioned themselves, stood blocking the street. They were holding strange looking discs resembling coiled ropes. The Witcher looked around and moved his shoulders, adjusting the sword slung across his back. Dandelion groaned.

From behind the backs of the individuals in black emerged a small man in a white kaftan and a short, grey cape. The gold chain on his neck sparkled to the rhythm of his steps, flashing yellow.

'Chappelle . . .' Dandelion groaned. 'It's Chappelle . . .'

The individuals in black behind them moved slowly towards the fountain. The Witcher reached for his sword.

'No, Geralt,' Dandelion whispered, moving closer to him. 'For the Gods' sake, don't draw your weapon. It's the temple guard. If we resist we won't leave Novigrad alive. Don't touch your sword.'

The man in the white kaftan walked swiftly towards them. The individuals in black followed him, surrounding the fountain at a march, and occupied strategic, carefully chosen positions. Geralt observed them vigilantly, crouching slightly. The strange discs they were holding were not – as he had first thought – ordinary whips. They were lamias.

The man in the white kaftan approached them.

'Geralt,' the bard whispered. 'By all the Gods, keep calm—'

'I won't let them touch me,' the Witcher muttered. 'I won't let them touch me, whoever they are. Be careful, Dandelion . . . When it starts, you two flee, as fast as you can. I'll keep them busy . . . for some time . . .'

Dandelion did not answer. Slinging the lute over one shoulder, he bowed low before the man in the white kaftan, which was ornately embroidered with gold and silver threads in an intricate, mosaic pattern.

'Venerable Chappelle . . .'

The man addressed as Chappelle stopped and swept them with his gaze. His eyes, Geralt noticed, were frost-cold and the colour of steel. His forehead was pale, beaded unhealthily with sweat and his cheeks were flushed with irregular, red blotches.

'Mr Dainty Biberveldt, merchant,' he said. 'The talented Dandelion. And Geralt of Rivia, a representative of the oh-so rare witcher's profession. A reunion of old friends? Here, in Novigrad?'

None of them answered.

'I consider it highly regrettable,' Chappelle continued, 'that a report has been submitted about you.'

Dandelion blanched slightly and the halfling's teeth chattered. The Witcher was not looking at Chappelle. He did not take his eyes off the weapons of the men in leather caps surrounding the fountain. In most of the countries known to Geralt the production and possession of spiked lamias, also called Mayhenian scourges, were strictly prohibited. Novigrad was no exception. Geralt had seen people struck in the face by a lamia. He would never forget those faces.

'The keeper of the Spear Blade inn,' Chappelle continued, 'had

155

the audacity to accuse you gentlemen of collusion with a demon, a monster, known as a changeling or a vexling.'

None of them answered. Chappelle folded his arms on his chest and looked at them coldly.

'I felt obliged to forewarn you of that report. I shall also inform you that the above-mentioned innkeeper has been imprisoned in the dungeons. There is a suspicion that he was raving under the influence of beer or vodka. Astonishing what people will concoct. Firstly, there are no such things as vexlings. It is a fabrication of superstitious peasants.'

No one commented on this.

'Secondly, what vexling would dare to approach a witcher,' Chappelle smiled, 'and not be killed at once? Am I right? The innkeeper's accusation would thus be ludicrous, were it not for one vital detail.'

Chappelle nodded, pausing dramatically. The Witcher heard Dainty slowly exhaling a large lungful of air.

'Yes, a certain, vital detail,' Chappelle repeated. 'Namely, we are facing heresy and sacrilegious blasphemy here. For it is a well-known fact that no vexling, absolutely no vexling, nor any other monster, could even approach the walls of Novigrad, because here, in nineteen temples, burns the Eternal Fire, whose sacred power protects the city. Whoever says that he saw a vexling at the Spear Blade, a stone's throw from the chief altar of the Eternal Fire, is a blasphemous heretic and will have to retract his claim. Should he not want to, he shall be assisted by the power and means, which, trust me, I keep close at hand in the dungeons. Thus, as you can see, there is nothing to be concerned about.'

The expressions on the faces of Dandelion and the halfling showed emphatically that they both thought differently.

'There is absolutely nothing to be concerned about,' Chappelle repeated. 'You may leave Novigrad without let or hindrance. I will not detain you. I do have to insist, gentlemen, however, that you do not broadcast the lamentable fabrications of the innkeeper, that you do not discuss this incident openly. Statements calling into question the divine power of the Eternal Fire, irrespective of the intention, we, the humble servants of the temple, would have to treat as heresy, with all due consequences. Your personal religious convictions, whatever they might be, and however I respect them, are of no significance. Believe in what you will. I am tolerant while somebody venerates the Eternal Fire and does not blaspheme against it. But should they blaspheme, I shall order them burnt at the stake, and that is that. Everybody in Novigrad is equal before the law. And the law applies equally to everybody; anyone who blasphemes against the Eternal Fire perishes at the stake, and their property is confiscated. But enough of that. I repeat; you may pass through the gates of Novigrad without hindrance. Ideally . . .'

Chappelle smiled slightly, sucked in his cheeks in a cunning grimace, and his eyes swept the square. The few passers-by observing the incident quickened their step and rapidly turned their heads away.

'. . . ideally,' Chappelle finished, 'ideally with immediate effect. Forthwith. Obviously, with regard to the honourable merchant Biberveldt, that "forthwith" means "forthwith, having settled all fiscal affairs". Thank you for the time you have given me.'

Dainty turned away, mouth moving noiselessly. The Witcher had no doubt that the noiseless word had been 'whoreson'. Dandelion lowered his head, smiling foolishly.

'My dear Witcher,' Chappelle suddenly said, 'a word in private, if you would.'

Geralt approached and Chappelle gently extended an arm. If he touches my elbow, I'll strike him, the Witcher thought. I'll strike him, whatever happens.

Chappelle did not touch Geralt's elbow.

'My dear Witcher,' he said quietly, turning his back on the others, 'I am aware that some cities, unlike Novigrad, are deprived of the divine protection of the Eternal Fire. Let us then suppose that a creature similar to a vexling was prowling in one of those cities. I wonder how much you would charge in that case for undertaking to catch a vexling alive?'

'I don't hire myself out to hunt monsters in crowded cities,' the Witcher shrugged. 'An innocent bystander might suffer harm.'

'Are you so concerned about the fate of innocent bystanders?'

'Yes, I am. Because I am usually held responsible for their fate. And have to cope with the consequences.'

'I understand. And would not your concern for the fate of innocent bystanders be in inverse proportion to the fee?'

'It would not.'

'I do not greatly like your tone, Witcher. But no matter, I understand what you hint at by it. You are hinting that you do not want to do . . . what I would ask you to do, making the size of the fee meaningless. And the form of the fee?'

'I do not understand.'

'Come, come.'

'I mean it.'

'Purely theoretically,' Chappelle said, quietly, calmly, without any anger or menace in his voice, 'it might be possible that the fee for your services would be a guarantee that you and your friends would leave this— leave the theoretical city alive. What then?'

'It is impossible,' the Witcher said, smiling hideously, 'to answer that question theoretically. The situation you are discussing, Reverend Chappelle, would have to be dealt with in practice. I am in no hurry to do so, but if the necessity arises . . . If there proves to be no other choice . . . I am prepared to go through with it.'

'Ha, perhaps you are right,' Chappelle answered dispassionately. 'Too much theory. As concerns practice, I see that there will be no collaboration. A good thing, perhaps? In any case, I cherish the hope that it will not be a cause for conflict between us.'

'I also cherish that hope.'

'Then may that hope burn in us, Geralt of Rivia. Do you know what the Eternal Fire is? A flame that never goes out, a symbol of permanence, a way leading through the gloom, a harbinger of progress, of a better tomorrow. The Eternal Fire, Geralt, is hope. For everybody, everybody without exception. For if something exists that embraces us all . . . you, me . . . others . . . then that something is precisely hope. Remember that. It was a pleasure to meet you, Witcher.'

Geralt bowed stiffly, saying nothing. Chappelle looked at him for a moment, then turned about energetically and marched through the small square, without looking around at his escort. The men armed with the lamias fell in behind him, forming up into a well-ordered column.

'Oh, mother of mine,' Dandelion whimpered, timidly watching the departing men, 'but we were lucky. If that is the end of it. If they don't collar us right away—'

'Calm down,' the Witcher said, 'and stop whining. Nothing happened, after all.'

'Do you know who that was, Geralt?'

'No.'

'That was Chappelle, minister for security affairs. The Novigrad secret service is subordinate to the temple. Chappelle is not a priest but the eminence grise to the hierarch, the most powerful and most dangerous man in the city. Everybody, even the Council and the guilds, shake in their shoes before him, because he's a first-rate bastard, Geralt, drunk on power, like a spider drunk on fly's blood. It's common knowledge – though not discussed openly in the city – what he's capable of. People vanishing without trace. Falsified accusations, torture, assassinations, terror, blackmail and plain plunder. Extortion, swindles and fraud. By the Gods, you've landed us in a pretty mess, Biberveldt.'

'Give it a rest, Dandelion,' Dainty snapped. 'It's not that you have to be afraid of anything. No one ever touches a troubadour. For unfathomable reasons you are inviolable.'

'In Novigrad,' Dandelion whined, still pale, 'an inviolable poet may still fall beneath a speeding wagon, be fatally poisoned by a fish, or accidentally drown in a moat. Chappelle specialises in mishaps of that nature. I consider the fact that he talked to us at all something exceptional. One thing is certain, he didn't do it without a reason. He's up to something. You'll see, they'll soon embroil us in something, clap us in irons and drag us off to be tortured with the sanction of the law. That's how things are done here!'

'There is quite some truth,' the halfling said to Geralt, 'in what he says. We must watch out. It's astonishing that that scoundrel Chappelle hasn't keeled over yet. For years they've been saying he's sick, that his heart will give out, and everybody's waiting for him to croak . . .'

'Be quiet, Biberveldt,' the troubadour hissed apprehensively, looking around, 'because somebody's bound to be listening. Look how everybody's staring at us. Let's get out of here, I'm telling you. And I suggest we treat seriously what Chappelle told us about the doppler. I, for example, have never seen a doppler in my life, and if it comes to it I'll swear as much before the Eternal Fire.'

'Look,' the halfling suddenly said. 'Somebody is running towards us.'

'Let's flee!' Dandelion howled.

'Calm yourself, calm yourself,' Dainty grinned and combed his mop of hair with his fingers. 'I know him. It's Muskrat, a local merchant, the Guild's treasurer. We've done business together. Hey, look at the expression on his face! As though he's shat his britches. Hey, Muskrat, are you looking for me?'

'I swear by the Eternal Fire,' Muskrat panted, pushing back a fox fur cap and wiping his forehead with his sleeve, 'I was certain they'd drag you off to the barbican. It's truly a miracle. I'm astonished—'

'It's nice of you,' the halfling sneeringly interrupted, 'to be astonished. You'll delight us even more if you tell us why.'

'Don't play dumb, Biberveldt,' Muskrat frowned. 'The whole city already knows the profit you made on the cochineal. Everybody's talking about it already and it has clearly reached the hierarch and Chappelle. How cunning you are, how craftily you benefited from what happened in Poviss.'

'What are you blathering about, Muskrat?'

'Ye Gods, would you stop trying to play the innocent, Dainty? Did you buy that cochineal? For a song, at ten-forty a bushel? Yes, you did. Taking advantage of the meagre demand you paid with a backed bill, without paying out a penny of cash. And what happened? In the course of a day you palmed off the entire cargo at four times the price, for cash on the table. Perhaps you'll have the cheek to say it was an accident, a stroke of luck? That when buying the cochineal you knew nothing about the coup in Poviss?'

'The what? What are you talking about?'

'There was a coup in Poviss!' Muskrat yelled. 'And one of those, you know . . . levorutions! King Rhyd was overthrown and now the Thyssenid clan is in power! Rhyd's court, the nobility and the army wore blue, and the weaving mills there only bought indigo. But the colour of the Thyssenids is scarlet, so the price of indigo went down, and cochineal's gone up, and then it came out that you, Biberveldt, had the only available cargo in your grasp! Ha!'

Dainty fell silent and looked distressed.

'Crafty, Biberveldt, must be said,' Muskrat continued. 'And you didn't tell anybody anything, not even your friends. If you'd let on, we might both have made a profit, might even have set up a joint factory. But you preferred to act alone, softly-softly. Your choice; but don't count on me any longer either. On the Eternal Fire, it's true that every halfling is a selfish bastard and a whoreson. Vimme Vivaldi never gives me a backed bill; and you? On the spot. Because you're one tribe, you damned inhumans, you poxy halflings and dwarves. Damn the lot of you!'

Muskrat spat, turned on his heel and walked off. Dainty, lost in thought, scratched his head until his mop of hair crunched.

'Something's dawning on me, boys,' he said at last. 'Now I know what needs to be done. Let's go to the bank. If anyone can make head or tail of all this, that someone is the banker friend of mine, Vimme Vivaldi.'

III

'I imagined the bank differently,' Dandelion whispered, looking around the room. 'Where do they keep the money, Geralt?'

'The Devil only knows,' the Witcher answered quietly, hiding his torn jacket sleeve. 'In the cellars, perhaps?'

'Not a chance. I've had a look around. There aren't any cellars here.'

'They must keep it in the loft then.'

'Would you come to my office, gentlemen?' Vimme Vivaldi asked.

Young men and dwarves of indiscernible age sitting at long tables were busy covering sheets of parchment with columns of figures and letters. All of them – without exception – were hunched over, with the tips of their tongues sticking out. The work, the Witcher judged, was fiendishly monotonous, but seemed to preoccupy the staff utterly. In the corner, on a low stool, sat an elderly, beggarly-looking man busy sharpening quills. He was making hard work of it.

The banker carefully closed the door to the office, stroked his long, white, well-groomed beard, spotted here and there with ink, and straightened a claret-coloured velvet jerkin stretched over a prominent belly.

'You know, Dandelion, sir,' he said, sitting down at an enormous, mahogany table, piled with parchments, 'I imagined you quite differently. And I know your songs, I know them, I've heard them. About Princess Vanda, who drowned in the River Duppie, because no one wanted her. And about the kingfisher that fell into a privy—'

'They aren't mine,' Dandelion flushed in fury. 'I've never written anything like that!'

'Ah. I'm sorry then.'

'Perhaps we could get to the point?' Dainty cut in. 'Time is short, and you're talking nonsense. I'm in grave difficulties, Vimme.'

'I was afraid of that,' the dwarf nodded. 'As you recall, I warned you, Biberveldt. I told you three days ago not to sink any resources into that rancid cod liver oil. What if it was cheap? It is not the nominal price that is important, but the size of the profit on resale. The same applies to the rose oil and the wax, and those earthenware bowls. What possessed you, Dainty, to buy that shit, and in hard cash to boot, rather than judiciously pay with a letter of credit or by draft? I told you that storage costs in Novigrad are devilishly high; in the course of two weeks they will surpass the value of those goods threefold. But you—'

'Yes,' the halfling quietly groaned. 'Tell me, Vivaldi. What did I do?'

'But you told me not to worry, that you would sell everything in the course of twenty-four hours. And now you come and declare that you are in trouble, smiling foolishly and disarmingly all the while. But it's not selling, is it? And costs are rising, what? Ha, that's not good, not good. How am I to get you out of it, Dainty? Had you at least insured that junk, I would have sent one of the clerks at once to quietly torch the store. No, my dear, the only thing to be done is to approach the matter philosophically, and say to oneself: "Fuck this for a game of soldiers". This is business; you win some, you lose some. What kind of profit was it anyway, that cod liver oil, wax and rose oil? Risible. Let us talk about serious business. Tell me if I should sell the mimosa bark yet, because the offers have begun to stabilise at five and five-sixths.'

'Hey?'

'Are you deaf?' the banker frowned. 'The last offer was exactly five and five-sixths. You came back, I hope, to close the deal? You won't get seven, anyhow, Dainty.'

'I came back?'

Vivaldi stroked his beard and picked some crumbs of fruit cake from it.

'You were here an hour since,' he said calmly, 'with instructions to hold out for seven. A sevenfold increase on the price you paid is two crowns five-and-forty pennies a pound. That is too high, Dainty, even for such a perfectly timed market. The tanneries will already have reached agreement and they will solidly stick to the price. I'm absolutely certain—'

The door to the office opened and something in a green felt cap and a coat of dappled coney fur girded with hempen twine rushed in.

'Merchant Sulimir is offering two crowns fifteen!' it squealed.

'Six and one-sixth,' Vivaldi swiftly calculated. 'What do we do, Dainty?'

'Sell!' the halfling yelled. 'A six-fold profit, and you're still bloody wondering?'

Another something in a yellow cap and a mantle resembling an old sack dashed into the office. Like the first something, it was about two cubits tall.

'Merchant Biberveldt instructs not to sell for below seven!' it shouted, wiped its nose on its sleeve and ran out.

'Aha,' the dwarf said after a long silence. 'One Biberveldt orders us to sell, and another Biberveldt orders us to wait. An interesting situation. What do we do, Dainty? Do you set about explaining at once, or do we wait until a third Biberveldt orders us to load the bark onto galleys and ship it to the Land of the Cynocephali? Hey?'

'What is that?' Dandelion stammered, pointing at the something in a green cap still standing in the doorway. 'What the bloody hell is it?'

'A young gnome,' Geralt said.

'Undoubtedly,' Vivaldi confirmed coldly. 'It is not an old troll. Anyway, it's not important what it is. Very well, Dainty, if you please.'

'Vimme,' the halfling said. 'If you don't mind. Don't ask questions. Something awful has happened. Just accept that I, Dainty Biberveldt of Knotgrass Meadow, an honest merchant, do not have a clue what's happening. Tell me everything, in detail. The events of the last three days. Please, Vimme.'

'Curious,' the dwarf said. 'Well, for the commission I take I have to grant the wishes of the client, whatever they might be. So listen. You came rushing in here three days ago, out of breath, gave me a deposit of a thousand crowns and demanded an endorsement on a bill amounting to two thousand five hundred and twenty, to the bearer. I gave you that endorsement.'

'Without a guaranty?'

'Correct. I like you, Dainty.'

'Go on, Vimme.'

'The next day you rushed in with a bang and a clatter, demanding that I issue a letter of credit on a bank in Vizima. For the considerable sum of three thousand five hundred crowns. The beneficiary was to be, if I remember rightly, a certain Ther Lukokian, alias Truffle. Well, I issued that letter of credit.'

'Without a guaranty,' the halfling said hopefully.

'My affection for you, Biberveldt,' the banker said, 'ceases at around three thousand crowns. This time I took from you a written obligation that in the event of insolvency the mill would be mine.'

'What mill?'

'That of your father-in-law, Arno Hardbottom, in Knotgrass Meadow.'

'I'm not going home,' Dainty declared glumly, but determinedly. 'I'll sign on to a ship and become a pirate.'

Vimme Vivaldi scratched an ear and looked at him suspiciously.

'Oh, come on,' he said, 'you took that obligation and tore it up almost right away. You are solvent. No small wonder, with profits like that—'

'Profits?'

'That's right, I forgot,' muttered the dwarf. 'I was meant not to be surprised by anything. You made a good profit on the cochineal, Biberveldt. Because, you see, there was a coup in Poviss—'

'I already know,' the halfling interrupted. 'Indigo's gone down and cochineal's gone up. And I made a profit. Is that true, Vimme?'

'Yes, it is. You have in my safe keeping six thousand three hundred and forty-six crowns and eighty pennies. Net, after deducting my commission and tax.'

'You paid the tax for me?'

'What else would I do?' Vivaldi said in astonishment. 'After all, you were here an hour ago and told me to pay it. The clerk has already delivered the entire sum to city hall. Something around fifteen hundred, because the sale of the horses was, of course, included in it.'

The door opened with a bang and something in a very dirty cap came running in.

'Two crowns thirty!' it shouted. 'Merchant Hazelquist!'

'Don't sell!' Dainty called. 'We'll wait for a better price! Be gone, back to the market with the both of you!'

The two gnomes caught some coppers thrown to them by the dwarf, and disappeared.

'Right . . . Where was I?' Vivaldi wondered, playing with a huge, strangely-formed amethyst crystal serving as a paperweight. 'Aha, with the cochineal bought with a bill of exchange. And you needed the letter of credit I mentioned to purchase a large cargo of mimosa bark. You bought a deal of it, but quite cheaply, for thirty-five pennies a pound, from a Zangwebarian factor, that Truffle, or perhaps Morel. The galley sailed into port yesterday. And then it all began.'

'I can imagine,' Dainty groaned.

'What is mimosa bark needed for?' Dandelion blurted out.

'Nothing,' the halfling muttered dismally. 'Unfortunately.'

'Mimosa bark, poet, sir,' the dwarf explained, 'is an agent used for tanning hides.'

'If somebody was so stupid,' Dainty interrupted, 'as to buy mimosa bark from beyond the seas, when oak bark can be bought in Temeria for next to nothing . . .'

'And here is the nub of the matter,' Vivaldi said, 'because in Temeria the druids have just announced that if the destruction of oaks is not stopped immediately they will afflict the land with a plague of hornets and rats. The druids are being supported by the dryads, and the king there is fond of dryads. In short: since yesterday there has been a total embargo on Temerian oak, for which reason mimosa is going up. Your information was accurate, Dainty.'

A stamping was heard from the chambers beyond the room, and then the something in a green cap came running into the office, out of breath.

'The honourable merchant Sulimir . . .' the gnome panted, 'has instructed me to repeat that merchant Biberveldt, the halfling, is a reckless, bristly swine, a profiteer and charlatan, and that he, Sulimir, hopes that Biberveldt gets the mange. He'll give two crowns forty-four and that is his last word.'

'Sell,' the halfling blurted out. 'Go on, shorty, run off and accept it. Count it up, Vimme.'

Vivaldi reached beneath some scrolls of parchment and took out a dwarven abacus, a veritable marvel. Unlike abacuses used by humans, the dwarven one was shaped like a small openwork pyramid. Vivaldi's abacus, though, was made of gold wires, over which slid angular beads of ruby, emerald, onyx and black agate, which fitted into each other. The dwarf slid the gemstones upwards, downwards and sideways for some time, with quick, deft movements of his plump finger.

'That will be . . . hmm, hmm . . . Minus the costs and my commission . . . Minus tax . . . Yes. Fifteen thousand six hundred and twenty-two crowns and five-and-twenty pennies. Not bad.'

'If I've reckoned correctly,' Dainty Biberveldt said slowly, 'all together, net, then I ought to have in my account . . .'

'Precisely twenty-one thousand nine hundred and sixty-nine crowns and five pennies. Not bad.'

'Not bad?' Dandelion roared. 'Not bad? You could buy a large village or a small castle for that! I've never, ever, seen that much money at one time!'

'I haven't either,' the halfling said. 'But simmer down, Dandelion. It so happens that no one has seen that money yet, and it isn't certain if anyone ever will.'

'Hey, Biberveldt,' the dwarf snorted. 'Why such gloomy thoughts? Sulimir will pay in cash or by a bill of exchange, and Sulimir's bills are reliable. What then, is the matter? Are you afraid of losing on that stinking cod liver oil and wax? With profits like that you'll cover the losses with ease . . .'

'That's not the point.'

'So what *is* the point?'

Dainty coughed, and lowered his curly mop.

'Vimme,' he said, eyes fixed on the floor. 'Chappelle is snooping around me.'

The banker clicked his tongue.

'Very bad,' he drawled. 'But it was to be expected. You see, Biberveldt, the information you used when carrying out the transactions does not just have commercial significance, but also political. No one knew what was happening in Poviss and Temeria – Chappelle included – and Chappelle likes to be the first to know. So now, as you can imagine, he is wracking his brains about how you knew. And I think he has guessed. Because I think I've also worked it out.'

'That's fascinating.'

Vivaldi swept his eyes over Dandelion and Geralt, and wrinkled his snub nose.

'Fascinating? I'll tell you what's fascinating; your party, Dainty,' he said. 'A troubadour, a witcher and a merchant. Congratulations. Master Dandelion shows up here and there, even at royal courts, and no doubt keeps his ears open. And the Witcher? A bodyguard? Someone to frighten debtors?'

'Hasty conclusions, Mr Vivaldi,' Geralt said coldly. 'We are not partners.'

'And I,' Dandelion said, flushing, 'do not eavesdrop anywhere. I'm a poet, not a spy!'

'People say all sorts of things,' the dwarf grimaced. 'All sorts of things, Master Dandelion.'

'Lies!' the troubadour yelled. 'Damned lies!'

'Very well, I believe you, I believe you. I just don't know if Chappelle will believe it. But who knows, perhaps it will all blow over. I tell you, Biberveldt, that Chappelle has changed a lot since his last attack of apoplexy. Perhaps the fear of death looked him in the arse and forced him to think things over? I swear, he is not the same Chappelle. He seems to have become courteous, rational, composed and . . . and somehow honest.'

'Get away,' the halfling said. 'Chappelle, honest? Courteous? Impossible.'

'I'm telling you how it is,' Vivaldi replied. 'And how it is, is what I'm telling you. What is more, now the temple is facing another problem: namely the Eternal Fire.'

'What do you mean?'

'The Eternal Fire, as it's known, is supposed to burn everywhere. Altars dedicated to that fire are going to be built everywhere, all over the city. A huge number of altars. Don't ask me for details, Dainty, I am not very familiar with human superstitions. But I know that all the priests, and Chappelle also, are concerned about almost nothing else but those altars and that fire. Great preparations are being made. Taxes will be going up, that is certain.'

'Yes,' Dainty said. 'Cold comfort, but—'

The door to the office opened again and the Witcher recognised the something in a green cap and coney fur coat.

'Merchant Biberveldt,' it announced, 'instructs to buy more pots, should they run out. Price no object.'

'Excellent,' the halfling smiled, and his smile called to mind the twisted face of a furious wildcat. 'We will buy huge quantities of pots; Mr Biberveldt's wish is our command. What else shall we buy more of? Cabbage? Wood tar? Iron rakes?'

'Furthermore,' the something in the fur coat croaked, 'merchant Biberveldt requests thirty crowns in cash, because he has to pay a bribe, eat something and drink some beer, and three miscreants stole his purse in the Spear Blade.'

'Oh. Three miscreants,' Dainty said in a slow, drawling voice. 'Yes, this city seems to be full of miscreants. And where, if one may ask, is the Honourable Merchant Biberveldt at this very moment?'

'Where else would he be,' the something said, sniffing, 'than at the Western Market?'

'Vimme,' Dainty said malevolently, 'don't ask questions, but find me a stout, robust stick from somewhere. I'm going to the Western Market, but I can't go without a stick. There are too many miscreants and thieves there.'

'A stick, you say? Of course. But, Dainty, I'd like to know something, because it is preying on me. I was supposed not to ask any questions, but I shall make a guess, and you can either confirm or deny it. All right?'

'Guess away.'

'That rancid cod liver oil, that oil, that wax and those bowls, that bloody twine, it was all a tactical gambit, wasn't it? You wanted to distract the competition's attention from the cochineal and the mimosa, didn't you? To stir up confusion on the market? Hey, Dainty?'

The door opened suddenly and something without a cap ran in.

'Sorrel reports that everything is ready!' it yelled shrilly. 'And asks if he should start pouring.'

'Yes, he should!' the halfling bellowed. 'At once!'

'By the red beard of old Rhundurin!' Vimme Vivaldi bellowed, as soon as the gnome had shut the door. 'I don't understand anything! What is happening here? Pour what? Into what?'

'I have no idea,' Dainty admitted. 'But, Vimme, the wheels of business must be oiled.'

IV

Pushing through the crowd with difficulty, Geralt emerged right in front of a stall laden with copper skillets, pots and frying pans, sparkling in the rays of the twilight sun. Behind the stall stood a red-bearded dwarf in an olive-green hood and heavy sealskin boots. The dwarf's face bore an expression of visible dislike; to be precise he looked as though any moment he intended to spit on the female customer sifting through the goods. The customer's breast was heaving, she was shaking her golden curls and was besetting the dwarf with a ceaseless and chaotic flow of words.

The customer was none other than Vespula, known to Geralt as the thrower of missiles. Without waiting for her to recognise him, he melted swiftly back into the crowd.

The Western Market was bustling with life and getting through the crowd was like forcing one's way through a hawthorn bush. Every now and then something caught on his sleeves and trouser legs; at times it was children who had lost their mothers while they were dragging their fathers away from the beer tent, at others it was spies from the guardhouse, at others shady vendors of caps of invisibility, aphrodisiacs and bawdy scenes carved in cedar wood. Geralt stopped smiling and began to swear, making judicious use of his elbows.

He heard the sound of a lute and a familiar peal of laughter. The sounds drifted from a fabulously coloured stall, decorated with the sign: 'Buy your wonders, amulets and fish bait here'.

'Has anyone ever told you, madam, that you are gorgeous?' Dandelion yelled, sitting on the stall and waving his legs cheerfully. 'No? It cannot be possible! This is a city of blind men, nothing but a city of blind men. Come, good folk! Who would hear a ballad of love? Whoever would be moved and enriched spiritually, let him

171

toss a coin into the hat. What are you shoving your way in for, you bastard? Keep your pennies for beggars, and don't insult an artist like me with copper. Perhaps *I* could forgive you, but art never could!'

'Dandelion,' Geralt said, approaching. 'I thought we had split up to search for the doppler. And you're giving concerts. Aren't you ashamed to sing at markets like an old beggar?'

'Ashamed?' the bard said, astonished. 'What matters is *what* and *how* one sings, and not *where*. Besides, I'm hungry, and the stall-holder promised me lunch. As far as the doppler is concerned, look for it yourselves. I'm not cut out for chases, brawls or mob law. I'm a poet.'

'You would do better not to attract attention, O poet. Your fiancée is here. There could be trouble.'

'Fiancée?' Dandelion blinked nervously. 'Which one do you mean? I have several.'

Vespula, clutching a copper frying pan, had forced her way through the audience with the momentum of a charging aurochs. Dandelion jumped up from the stall and darted away, nimbly leaping over some baskets of carrots. Vespula turned towards the Witcher, dilating her nostrils. Geralt stepped backwards, his back coming up against the hard resistance of the stall's wall.

'Geralt!' Dainty Biberveldt shouted, jumping from the crowd and bumping into Vespula. 'Quickly, quickly! I've seen him! Look, there, he's getting away!'

'I'll get you yet, you lechers!' Vespula screamed, trying to regain her balance. 'I'll catch up with the whole of your debauched gang! A fine company! A pheasant, a scruff and a midget with hairy heels! You'll be sorry!'

'This way, Geralt!' Dainty yelled as he ran, jostling a small group of schoolboys intently playing the shell game. 'There, there, he's scarpered between those wagons! Steal up on him from the left! Quick!'

They rushed off in pursuit, the curses of the stallholders and cus-tomers they had knocked over ringing in their ears. By a miracle Geralt avoided tripping over a snot-nosed tot caught up in his legs. He jumped over it, but knocked over two barrels of herrings, for which an enraged fisherman lashed him across the back with a live eel, which he was showing to some customers at that moment.

They saw the doppler trying to flee past a sheep pen.

'From the other side!' Dainty yelled. 'Cut him off from the other side, Geralt!'

The doppler shot like an arrow along the fence, green waistcoat flashing. It was becoming clear why he was not changing into anybody else. No one could rival a halfling's agility. No one. Apart from another halfling. Or a witcher.

Geralt saw the doppler suddenly changing direction, kicking up a cloud of dust, and nimbly ducking into a hole in the fence surrounding a large tent serving as a slaughterhouse and a shambles. Dainty also saw it. The doppler jumped between the palings and began to force his way between the flock of bleating sheep crowded into the enclosure. It was clear he would not make it. Geralt turned and rushed after him between the palings. He felt a sudden tug, heard the crack of leather tearing, and the leather suddenly became very loose under his other arm.

The Witcher stopped. Swore. Spat. And swore again.

Dainty rushed into the tent after the doppler. From inside came screaming, the noise of blows, cursing and an awful banging noise.

The Witcher swore a third time, extremely obscenely, then gnashed his teeth, raised his hand and formed his fingers into the Aard Sign, aiming it straight at the tent. The tent billowed up like a sail during a gale, and from the inside reverberated a hellish howling, clattering and lowing of oxen. The tent collapsed.

The doppler, crawling on its belly, darted out from beneath the canvas and dashed towards another, smaller tent, probably the cold store. Right away, Geralt pointed his hand towards him and jabbed him in the back with the Sign. The doppler tumbled to the ground as though struck by lightning, turned a somersault, but immediately sprang up and rushed into the tent. The Witcher was hot on his heels.

It stank of meat inside the tent. And it was dark.

Tellico Lunngrevink Letorte was standing there, breathing heavily, clinging with both hands onto a side of pork hanging on a pole.

There was no other way out of the tent, the canvas firmly fastened to the ground with numerous pegs.

'It's a pleasure to meet you again, mimic,' Geralt said coldly.

The doppler was breathing heavily and hoarsely.

'Leave me alone,' it finally grunted. 'Why are you tormenting me, Witcher?'

'Tellico,' Geralt said, 'You're asking foolish questions. In order to come into possession of Biberveldt's horses and identity, you cut his head open and abandoned him in the wilds. You're still making use of his personality and ignoring the problems you are causing him. The Devil only knows what else you're planning, but I shall confuse those plans, in any event. I don't want to kill you or turn you over to the authorities, but you must leave the city. I'll see to it that you do.'

'And if I don't want to?'

'I'll carry you out in a sack on a handcart.'

The doppler swelled up abruptly, and then suddenly became thinner and began to grow, his curly, chestnut hair turning white and straightening, reaching his shoulders. The halfling's green waistcoat shone like oil, becoming black leather, and silver studs sparkled on the shoulders and sleeves. The chubby, ruddy face elongated and paled.

The hilt of a sword extended above its right shoulder.

'Don't come any closer,' the second Witcher said huskily and smiled. 'Don't come any nearer, Geralt. I won't let you lay hands on me.'

What a hideous smile I have, Geralt thought, reaching for his sword. What a hideous face I have. And how hideously I squint. So is that what I look like? Damn.

The hands of the doppler and the Witcher simultaneously touched their sword hilts, and both swords simultaneously sprang from their scabbards. Both witchers simultaneously took two quick, soft steps; one to the front, the other to the side. Both of them simultaneously raised their swords and swung them in a short, hissing moulinet.

Simultaneously, they both stopped dead, frozen in position.

'You cannot defeat me,' the doppler snarled. 'Because I am you, Geralt.'

'You are mistaken, Tellico,' the Witcher said softly. 'Drop your sword and resume Biberveldt's form. Otherwise you'll regret it, I warn you.'

'I am you,' the doppler repeated. 'You will not gain an advantage over me. You cannot defeat me, because I am you!'

'You cannot have any idea what it means to be me, mimic.'

Tellico lowered the hand gripping the sword.

'I am you,' he repeated.

'No,' the Witcher countered, 'you are not. And do you know why? Because you're a poor, little, good-natured doppler. A doppler who, after all, could have killed Biberveldt and buried his body in the undergrowth, by so doing gaining total safety and utter certainty that he would not be unmasked, ever, by anybody, including the halfling's spouse, the famous Gardenia Biberveldt. But you didn't kill him, Tellico, because you didn't have the courage. Because you're a poor, little, good-natured doppler, whose close friends call him Dudu. And whoever you might change into you'll always be the same. You only know how to copy what is good in us, because you don't understand the bad in us. That's what you are, doppler.'

Tellico moved backwards, pressing his back against the tent's canvas.

'Which is why,' Geralt continued, 'you will now turn back into Biberveldt and hold your hands out nicely to be tied up. You aren't capable of defying me, because I am what you are unable of copying. You are absolutely aware of this, Dudu. Because you took over my thoughts for a moment.'

Tellico straightened up abruptly. His face's features, still those of the Witcher, blurred and spread out, and his white hair curled and began to darken.

'You're right, Geralt,' he said indistinctly, because his lips had begun to change shape. 'I took over your thoughts. Only briefly, but it was sufficient. Do you know what I'm going to do now?'

The leather witcher jacket took on a glossy, cornflower blue colour. The doppler smiled, straightened his plum bonnet with its egret's feather, and tightened the strap of the lute slung over his shoulder. The lute which had been a sword a moment ago.

'I'll tell you what I'm going to do, Witcher,' he said, with the rippling laughter characteristic of Dandelion. 'I'll go on my way, squeeze my way into the crowd and change quietly into any-old-body, even a beggar. Because I prefer being a beggar in Novigrad to being a doppler in the wilds. Novigrad owes me something, Geralt. The building of a city here tainted a land we could have lived in; lived in in our natural form. We have been exterminated, hunted down like rabid dogs. I'm one of the few to survive. I want to survive and I will survive. Long ago, when wolves pursued me in the winter, I turned into a wolf and ran with the pack for several weeks. And survived. Now I'll do that again, because I don't want to roam about through wildernesses and be forced to winter beneath fallen trees. I don't want to be forever hungry, I don't want to serve as target practice all the time. Here, in Novigrad, it's warm, there's grub, I can make money and very seldom do people shoot arrows at each other. Novigrad is a pack of wolves. I'll join that pack and survive. Understand?'

Geralt nodded reluctantly.

'You gave dwarves, halflings, gnomes and even elves,' the doppler continued, twisting his mouth in an insolent, Dandelion smile, 'the modest possibility of assimilation. Why should I be any worse off? Why am I denied that right? What do I have to do to be able to live in this city? Turn into a she-elf with doe eyes, silky hair and long legs? Well? In what way is a she-elf better than me? Only that at the sight of the she-elf you pick up speed, and at the sight of me you want to puke? You know where you can stuff an argument like that. I'll survive anyway. I know how to. As a wolf I ran, I howled and I fought without others over a she-wolf. As a resident of Novigrad I'll trade, weave wicker baskets, beg or steal; as one of you I'll do what one of you usually does. Who knows, perhaps I'll even take a wife.'

The Witcher said nothing.

'Yes, as I said,' Tellico continued calmly. 'I'm going. And you, Geralt, will not even try to stop me. Because I, Geralt, knew your thoughts for a moment. Including the ones you don't want to admit to, the ones you even hide from yourself. Because to stop me you'd have to kill me. And the thought of killing me in cold blood fills you with disgust. Doesn't it?'

The Witcher said nothing.

Tellico adjusted the strap of the lute again, turned away and walked towards the exit. He walked confidently, but Geralt saw him hunch his neck and shoulders in expectation of the whistle of a sword blade. He put his sword in its scabbard. The doppler stopped in mid-step, and looked around.

'Farewell, Geralt,' he said. 'Thank you.'

'Farewell, Dudu,' the Witcher replied. 'Good luck.'

The doppler turned away and headed towards the crowded bazaar, with Dandelion's sprightly, cheerful, swinging gait. Like Dandelion, he swung his left arm vigorously and just like Dandelion he grinned at the wenches as he passed them. Geralt set off slowly after him. Slowly.

Tellico seized his lute in full stride; after slowing his pace he played two chords, and then dextrously played a tune Geralt knew. Turning away slightly, he sang.

Exactly like Dandelion.

Spring will return, on the road the rain will fall
Hearts will be warmed by the heat of the sun
It must be thus, for fire still smoulders in us all
An eternal fire, hope for each one.

'Pass that on to Dandelion, if you remember,' he called, 'and tell him that *Winter* is a lousy title. The ballad should be called *The Eternal Fire*. Farewell, Witcher!'

'Hey!' suddenly resounded. 'You, pheasant!'

Tellico turned around in astonishment. From behind a stall emerged Vespula, her breast heaving violently, raking him up with a foreboding gaze.

'Eyeing up tarts, you cad?' she hissed, breast heaving more and more enticingly. 'Singing your little songs, are you, you knave?'

Tellico took off his bonnet and bowed, broadly smiling Dandelion's characteristic smile.

'Vespula, my dear,' he said ingratiatingly, 'how glad I am to see you. Forgive me, my sweet. I owe you—'

'Oh, you do, you do,' Vespula interrupted loudly. 'And what you owe me you will now pay me! Take that!'

An enormous copper frying pan flashed in the sun and with a deep, loud clang smacked into the doppler's head. Tellico staggered and fell with an indescribably stupid expression frozen on his face, arms spread out, and his physiognomy suddenly began to change, melt and lose its similarity to anything at all. Seeing it, the Witcher leaped towards him, in full flight snatching a large kilim from a stall. Having unfurled the kilim on the ground, he sent the doppler onto it with two kicks and rolled it up in it quickly but tightly.

Sitting down on the bundle, he wiped his forehead with a sleeve. Vespula, gripping the frying pan, looked at him malevolently, and the crowd closed in all around.

'He's sick,' the Witcher said and smiled affectedly. 'It's for his own good. Don't crowd, good people, the poor thing needs air.'

'Did you hear?' Chappelle asked calmly but resonantly, suddenly pushing his way through the throng. 'Please do not form a public gathering here! Please disperse! Public gatherings are forbidden. Punishable by a fine!'

In the blink of an eye the crowd scattered to the sides, only to reveal Dandelion, approaching swiftly, to the sounds of his lute. On seeing him, Vespula let out an ear-splitting scream, dropped the frying pan and fled across the square.

'What happened?' Dandelion asked. 'Did she see the Devil?'

Geralt stood up, holding the bundle, which had begun to move weakly. Chappelle slowly approached. He was alone and his personal guard was nowhere to be seen.

'I wouldn't come any closer,' Geralt said quietly. 'If I were you, Lord Chappelle, sir, I wouldn't come any closer.'

'You wouldn't?' Chappelle tightened his thin lips, looking at him coldly.

'If I were you, Lord Chappelle, I would pretend I never saw anything.'

'Yes, no doubt,' Chappelle said. 'But you are not me.'

Dainty Biberveldt ran up from behind the tent, out of breath and sweaty. On seeing Chappelle he stopped, began to whistle, held his hands behind his back and pretended to be admiring the roof of the granary.

Chappelle went over and stood by Geralt, very close. The Witcher did not move, but only narrowed his eyes. For a moment they looked at each other and then Chappelle leaned over the bundle.

'Dudu,' he said to Dandelion's strangely deformed cordovan boots sticking out of the rolled-up kilim. 'Copy Biberveldt, and quickly.'

'What?' Dainty yelled, stopping staring at the granary. 'What's that?'

'Be quiet,' Chappelle said. 'Well, Dudu, are things coming along?'

'I'm just,' a muffled grunting issued from the kilim. 'I'm . . . Just a moment . . .'

The cordovan boots sticking out of the kilim stretched, became blurred and changed into the halfling's bare, hairy feet.

'Get out, Dudu,' Chappelle said. 'And you, Dainty, be quiet. All halflings look the same, don't they?'

Dainty mumbled something indistinctly. Geralt, eyes still narrowed, looked at Chappelle suspiciously. The minister, however, straightened up and looked all around, and all that remained of any gawkers who were still in the vicinity was the clacking of wooden clogs dying away in the distance.

The second Dainty Biberveldt scrambled and rolled out of the bundle, sneezed, sat up and rubbed his eyes and nose. Dandelion perched himself on a trunk lying alongside, and strummed away on his lute with an expression of moderate interest on his face.

'Who do you think that is, Dainty?' Chappelle asked mildly. 'Very similar to you, don't you think?'

'He's my cousin,' the halfling shot back and grinned. 'A close relative. Dudu Biberveldt of Knotgrass Meadow, an astute business-man. I've actually just decided . . .'

'Yes, Dainty?'

'I've decided to appoint him my factor in Novigrad. What do you say to that, cousin?'

'Oh, thank you, cousin,' his close relative, the pride of the

Biberveldt clan, and an astute businessman, smiled broadly. Chappelle also smiled.

'Has your dream about life in the city come true?' Geralt muttered. 'What do you see in this city, Dudu . . . and you, Chappelle?'

'Had you lived on the moors,' Chappelle muttered back, 'and eaten roots, got soaked and frozen, you'd know. We also deserve something from life, Geralt. We aren't inferior to you.'

'Very true,' Geralt nodded. 'You aren't. Perhaps it even happens that you're better. What happened to the real Chappelle?'

'Popped his clogs,' the second Chappelle whispered. 'Two months ago now. Apoplexy. May the earth lie lightly on him, and may the Eternal Fire light his way. I happened to be in the vicinity . . . No one noticed . . . Geralt? You aren't going to—'

'What didn't anyone notice?' the Witcher asked, with an inscrutable expression.

'Thank you,' Chappelle muttered.

'Are there more of you?'

'Is it important?'

'No,' agreed the Witcher, 'it isn't.'

A two-cubit-tall figure in a green cap and spotted coney fur coat dashed out from behind the wagons and stalls and trotted over.

'Mr Biberveldt,' the gnome panted and stammered, looking around and sweeping his eyes from one halfling to the other.

'I presume, shorty,' Dainty said, 'that you have a matter for my cousin, Dudu Biberveldt, to deal with. Speak. Speak. That is him.'

'Sorrel reports that everything has gone,' the gnome said and smiled broadly, showing small, pointed teeth, 'for four crowns apiece.'

'I think I know what it's about,' Dainty said. 'Pity Vivaldi's not here, he would have calculated the profit in no time.'

'If I may, cousin,' Tellico Lunngrevink Letorte, Penstock for short, Dudu to his close friends, and for the whole of Novigrad a member of the large Biberveldt family, spoke up. 'If I may, I'll calculate it. I have an infallible memory for figures. As well as for other things.'

'By all means,' Dainty gave a bow. 'By all means, cousin.'

'The costs,' the doppler frowned, 'were low. Eighteen for the oil, eight-fifty for the cod liver oil, hmm . . . Altogether, including the string, forty-five crowns. Takings: six hundred at four crowns, makes two thousand four hundred. No commission, because there weren't any middlemen . . .'

'Please do not forget about the tax,' the second Chappelle reminded him. 'Please do not forget that standing before you is a representative of the city authorities and the temple, who treats his duties gravely and conscientiously.'

'It's exempt from tax,' Dudu Biberveldt declared. 'Because it was sold in a sacred cause.'

'Hey?'

'The cod liver oil, wax and oil dyed with a little cochineal,' the doppler explained, 'need only be poured into earthenware bowls with a piece of string dipped into it. The string, when lit, gives a beautiful, red flame, which burns for a long time and doesn't smell. The Eternal Fire. The priests needed vigil lights for the altars of the Eternal Fire. Now they don't need them.'

'Bloody hell . . .' Chappelle muttered. 'You're right. They needed vigil lights . . . Dudu, you're brilliant.'

'I take after my mother,' Tellico said modestly.

'Yes, indeed, the spitting image of his mother,' Dainty agreed. 'Just look into those intelligent eyes. Begonia Biberveldt, my darling aunt, as I live and breathe.'

'Geralt,' Dandelion groaned. 'He's earned more in three days than I've earned in my whole life by singing!'

'In your place,' the Witcher said gravely, 'I'd quit singing and take up commerce. Ask him, he may take you on as an apprentice.'

'Witcher,' Tellico said, tugging him by the sleeve. 'Tell me how I could . . . repay you . . . ?'

'Twenty-two crowns.'

'What?'

'For a new jacket. Look what's left of mine.'

'Do you know what?' Dandelion suddenly yelled. 'Let's all go to the house of ill repute! To Passiflora! The Biberveldts are paying!'

'Do they admit halflings?' Dainty asked with concern.

'Just let them try not to,' Chappelle put on a menacing expression. 'Just let them try and I'll accuse their entire bordello of heresy.'

'Right,' Dandelion called. 'Very satisfactory. Geralt? Are you coming?'

The Witcher laughed softly.

'Do you know what, Dandelion?' he said. 'I'll come with pleasure.'

A LITTLE SACRIFICE

I

The mermaid emerged to waist-height from the water and splashed her hands violently and hard against the surface. Geralt saw that she had gorgeous, utterly perfect breasts. Only the colour spoiled the effect; the nipples were dark green and the areolae around them were only a little lighter. Nimbly aligning herself with an approaching wave, the mermaid arched gracefully, shook her wet, willow-green hair and sang melodiously.

'What?' The duke leaned over the side of the cog. 'What is she saying?'

'She's declining,' Geralt said. 'She says she doesn't want to.'

'Have you explained that I love her? That I can't imagine life without her? That I want to wed her? Only her, no other?'

'Yes, I have.'

'And?'

'And nothing.'

'Say it again.'

The Witcher touched his lips and produced a quavering warble. Struggling to find the words and the intonation, he began to translate the duke's avowal.

The mermaid, lying back on the water, interrupted.

'Don't translate, don't tire yourself,' she sang. 'I understand. When he says he loves me he always puts on such a foolish expression. Did he say anything definite?'

'Not really.'

'Pity,' the mermaid said, before she flapped in the water and dived under, flexing her tail powerfully and making the sea foam with her notched flukes, which resembled the tail of a mullet.

'What? What did she say?' the duke asked.

'That it's a shame.'

'What's a shame? What does she mean, "shame"?'

'I'd say she turned you down.'

'Nobody refuses me!' the duke roared, denying the obvious facts.

'My Lord,' the skipper of the cog muttered, walking over to them. 'The nets are ready, all we need do is cast them and she will be yours . . .'

'I wouldn't advise it,' Geralt said softly. 'She's not alone. There are more of them beneath the waves, and there may be a kraken deeper down there.'

The skipper quaked, blanched and seized his backside with both hands, in a nonsensical gesture.

'A kra— kraken?'

'Yes, a kraken,' the Witcher repeated. 'I don't advise fooling around with nets. All she need do is scream, and all that'll be left of this tub will be a few floating planks. They'd drown us like kittens. Besides, Agloval, you should decide whether you want to wed her or catch her in a net and keep her in a barrel.'

'I love her,' Agloval said firmly. 'I want her for my wife. But for that she must have legs and not a scaly tail. And it's feasible, since I bought a magical elixir with a full guarantee, for two pounds of exquisite pearls. After drinking it she'll grow legs. She'll just suffer a little, for three days, no more. Call her, Witcher, tell her again.'

'I've already told her twice. She said absolutely no, she doesn't consent. But she added that she knows a witch, a sea witch, who is prepared to cast a spell to turn your legs into a handsome tail. Painlessly.'

'She must be insane! She thinks I would have a fishy tail? Not a chance! Call her, Geralt!'

The Witcher leaned far out over the side. The water in the boat's shadow was green and seemed as thick as jelly. He did not have to call. The mermaid suddenly shot out above the surface in a fountain of water. For a moment she literally stood on her tail, then dived down into the waves and turned on her back, revealing her attributes in all their glory. Geralt swallowed.

'Hey!' she sang. 'Will this take much longer? My skin's getting chapped from the sun! White Hair, ask him if he consents.'

'He does not,' the Witcher sang back. 'Sh'eenaz, understand, he cannot have a tail, cannot live beneath the water. You can breathe air, but he cannot breathe underwater!'

'I knew it!' the mermaid screamed shrilly. 'I knew it! Excuses, foolish, naive excuses, not a bit of sacrifice! Whoever loves makes sacrifices! I made sacrifices for him, every day I hauled myself out onto the rocks for him, I wore out the scales on my bottom, frayed my fins; I caught colds for him! And he will not sacrifice those two hideous pegs for me? Love doesn't just mean taking, one also has to be able to give up things, to make sacrifices! Tell him that!'

'Sh'eenaz!' Geralt called. 'Don't you understand? He cannot survive in the water!'

'I don't accept stupid excuses! I . . . I like him too and want to have his fry, but how can I, if he doesn't want to be a spawner? Where should I deposit my eggs, hey? In his cap?'

'What is she saying?' the duke yelled. 'Geralt! I didn't bring you here to chat with her—'

'She's digging her heels in. She's angry.'

'Cast those nets!' Agloval roared. 'I'll keep her in a pool for a month and then she'll—'

'Shove it!' the skipper yelled back, demonstrating what he was to shove with his middle finger. 'There might be a kraken beneath us! Ever seen a kraken, My Lord? Hop into the water, if that is your will, and catch her with your hands! I'm not getting involved. I make my living by fishing from this cog!'

'You make your living by my goodwill, you scoundrel! Cast your net or I'll order you strung up!'

'Kiss a dog's arse! I'm in charge on this cog!'

'Be quiet, both of you!' Geralt shouted irately. 'She's saying something, it's a difficult dialect, I need to concentrate!'

'I've had enough!' Sh'eenaz yelled melodiously. 'I'm hungry! Well, White Hair, he must decide, decide at once. Tell him just one thing: I will not be made a laughing stock of any longer or associate with him if he's going to look like a four-armed starfish. Tell him I have girlfriends who are much better at those frolics he was suggesting on the rocks! But I consider them immature games, fit for children before they shed their scales. I'm a normal, healthy mermaid—'

'Sh'eenaz—'

'Don't interrupt! I haven't finished yet! I'm healthy, normal and ripe for spawning, and if he really desires me, he must have a tail, fins and everything a normal merman has. Otherwise I don't want to know him!'

Geralt translated quickly, trying not to be vulgar. He was not very successful. The duke flushed and swore foully.

'The brazen hussy!' he yelled. 'The frigid mackerel! Let her find herself a cod!'

'What did he say?' Sh'eenaz asked curiously, swimming over.

'That he doesn't want a tail!'

'Then tell him . . . Tell him to dry up!'

'What did she say?'

'She told you,' the Witcher translated, 'to go drown yourself.'

II

'Ah well,' Dandelion said. 'Pity I couldn't sail with you, but what could I do? Sailing makes me puke like nobody's business. But you know what, I've never spoken to a mermaid. It's a shame, dammit.'

'I know you,' Geralt said, fastening his saddle bags. 'You'll write a ballad anyway.'

'Never fear. I already have the first stanzas. In my ballad the mermaid will sacrifice herself for the duke, she'll exchange her fishtail for slender legs, but will pay for it by losing her voice. The duke will betray her, abandon her, and then she'll perish from grief, and turn into foam, when the first rays of sunshine . . .'

'Who'd believe such rot?'

'It doesn't matter,' Dandelion snorted. 'Ballads aren't written to be believed. They are written to move their audience. But why am I talking to you about this, when you know bugger all about it? You'd better tell me how much Agloval paid you.'

'He didn't pay me anything. He claimed I had failed to carry out the task. That he had expected something else, and he pays for results, not good intentions.'

Dandelion shook his head, took off his bonnet and looked at the Witcher with a forlorn grimace on his mouth.

'You mean we still don't have any money?'

'So it would seem.'

Dandelion made an even more forlorn face.

'It's all my fault,' he moaned. 'I'm to blame for it all. Geralt, are you angry at me?'

No, the Witcher wasn't angry at Dandelion. Not at all.

There was no doubt Dandelion was to blame for what had befallen them. He had insisted they went to the fair at Four Maples. Organising festivities, the poet argued, satisfied people's profound and natural needs. From time to time, the bard maintained, a chap has to meet other people in a place where he can have a laugh and a singsong, gorge himself on kebabs and pierogis, drink beer, listen to music and squeeze a girl as he swung her around in the dance. If every chap wanted to satisfy those needs, Dandelion argued, individually, periodically and randomly, an indescribable mess would arise. For that reason holidays and festivities were invented. And since holidays and festivities exist, a chap ought to frequent them.

Geralt did not challenge this, although taking part in festivities occupied a very low position on the list of his own profound and natural needs. Nonetheless, he agreed to accompany Dandelion, for he was counting on obtaining information from the gathered concentration of people about a possible mission or job; he'd had no work for a long time and his cash reserves had shrunk alarmingly.

The Witcher did not bear Dandelion a grudge for provoking the Rangers of the Forest. He was not innocent either; for he could have intervened and held the bard back. He did not, however, for he could not stand the infamous Guardians of the Forest, known as the Rangers, a volunteer force whose mission was to eradicate non-humans. It had annoyed him to hear their boasts about elves, spriggans and eerie wives bristling with arrows, butchered or hanged. Dandelion, though, who after travelling for some time with the Witcher had become convinced of his impunity from retaliation, had surpassed himself. Initially, the Rangers had not reacted to his mockery, taunts or filthy suggestions, which aroused the thunderous laughter of the watching villagers. When, however, Dandelion sang a hastily-composed obscene and abusive couplet, ending with the words: 'If you want to be a nothing, be a Ranger,' an argument and then a fierce, mass punch-up broke out. The shed serving as the dancehall went up in smoke. Intervention came in the form of a squad of men belonging to Castellan Budibog, also known as the Emptyheaded, on whose estates lay Four Maples. The Rangers, Dandelion and Geralt were found jointly guilty of all the damage and offences, which included the seduction of a red-headed and mute girl, who was found in the bushes behind the barn following the incident, blushing and grinning foolishly, with her shift torn up to her armpits. Fortunately, Castellan Budibog knew Dandelion, so it ended with a fine being paid, which nonetheless ate up all the money they had. They also had to flee from Four Maples as fast as they could ride, because the Rangers, who had been chased out of the village, were threatening revenge, and an entire squad of them, numbering over forty men, was hunting rusalkas in the neighbouring forests. Geralt did not have the slightest desire to be hit by one of the Rangers' arrows, whose heads were barbed like harpoons and inflicted dreadful injuries.

So they had to abandon their original plan, which had involved doing the rounds of the villages on the edge of the forest, where the Witcher had reasonable prospects of work. Instead they rode to Bremervoord, on the coast. Unfortunately, apart from the love affair between Duke Agloval and the mermaid Sh'eenaz, which offered small chances of success, the Witcher had failed to find a job. They had already sold Geralt's gold signet for food, and an alexandrite brooch the troubadour had once been given as a souvenir by one of his numerous paramours. Things were tight. But no, the Witcher was not angry with Dandelion.

'No, Dandelion,' he said. 'I'm not angry with you.'

Dandelion did not believe him, which was quite apparent by the fact that he kept quiet. Dandelion was seldom quiet. He patted his horse's neck, and fished around in his saddlebags for the umpteenth time. Geralt knew he would not find anything there they could sell. The smell of food, borne on a breeze from a nearby tavern, was becoming unbearable.

'Master?' somebody shouted. 'Hey, master!'

'Yes?' Geralt said, turning around. A big-bellied, well-built man in felt boots and a heavy fur-lined, wolf-skin coat clambered out of a cart pulled by a pair of onagers which had just stopped alongside.

'Erm . . . that is,' the paunchy man said, embarrassed, walking over, 'I didn't mean you, sir, I meant . . . I meant Master Dandelion . . .'

'It is I.' The poet proudly sat up straight, adjusting his bonnet bearing an egret feather. 'What is your need, my good man?'

'Begging your pardon,' the paunchy man said. 'I am Teleri

Drouhard, spice merchant and dean of our local Guild. My son, Gaspard, has just plighted his troth to Dalia, the daughter of Mestvin, the cog skipper.'

'Ha,' Dandelion said, maintaining a haughty air. 'I offer my congratulations and extend my wishes of happiness to the betrothed couple. How may I be of help? Does it concern *jus primae noctis*? I never decline that.'

'Hey? No . . . that is . . . You see, the betrothal banquet and ball are this evening. Since it got out that you, master, have come to Bremervoord, my wife won't let up – just like a woman. Listen, she says, Teleri, we'll show everybody we aren't churls like them, that we stand for culture and art. That when we have a feast, it's refined, and not an excuse to get pissed and throw up. I says to her, silly moo, but we've already hired one bard, won't that suffice? And she says one is too few, ho-ho, Master Dandelion, well, I never, such a celebrity, that'll be one in the eye for our neighbours. Master? Do us the honour . . . I'm prepared to give five-and-twenty talars, as a gesture, naturally – to show my support for the arts—'

'Do my ears deceive me?' Dandelion drawled. 'I, I am to be the second bard? An appendix to some other musician? I? I have not sunk so low, my dear sir, as to *accompany* somebody!'

Drouhard blushed.

'Forgive me, master,' he gibbered. 'That isn't what I meant . . . It was my wife . . . Forgive me . . . Do us the honour . . .'

'Dandelion,' Geralt hissed softly, 'don't put on airs. We need those few pennies.'

'Don't try to teach me!' the poet yelled. 'Me, putting on airs? Me? Look at him! What should I say about you, who rejects a lucrative proposition every other day? You won't kill hirikkas, because they're an endangered species, or mecopterans, because they're harmless, or night spirits, because they're sweet, or dragons, because your code forbids it. I, just imagine it, also have my self-respect! I also have a code!'

'Dandelion, please, do it for me. A little sacrifice, friend, nothing more. I swear, I won't turn my nose up at the next job that comes along. Come on, Dandelion . . .'

The troubadour looked down at the ground and scratched his chin, which was covered in soft, fair bristles. Drouhard, mouth gaping, moved closer.

'Master . . . Do us this honour. My wife won't forgive me if I don't invite you. Now then . . . I'll make it thirty.'

'Thirty-five,' Dandelion said firmly.

Geralt smiled and hopefully breathed in the scent of food wafting from the tavern.

'Agreed, master, agreed,' Teleri Drouhard said quickly, so quickly it was evident he would have given forty, had the need arisen. 'And now . . . My home, if you desire to groom yourself and rest, is your home. And you, sir . . . What do they call you?'

'Geralt of Rivia.'

'And I invite you too, sir, of course. For a bite to eat and something to drink . . .'

'Certainly, with pleasure,' Dandelion said. 'Show us the way, my dear sir. And just between us, who is the other bard?'

'The honourable Miss Essi Daven.'

III

Geralt rubbed a sleeve over the silver studs of his jacket and his belt buckle one more time, smoothed down his hair, which was held down with a clean headband, and polished his boots by rubbing one leg against the other.

'Dandelion?'

'Mm?' The bard smoothed the egret feather pinned to his bonnet, and straightened and pulled down his jerkin. The two of them had spent half the day cleaning their garments and tidying them up. 'What, Geralt?'

'Behave in such a way as they throw us out after supper and not before.'

'You must be joking,' the poet said indignantly. 'Watch your manners yourself. Shall we go in?'

'We shall. Do you hear? Somebody's singing. A woman.'

'Have you only just noticed? That's Essi Daven, known as Little Eye. What, have you never met a female troubadour? True, I forgot you steer clear of places where art flourishes. Little Eye is a gifted poet and singer, though not without her flaws, among which impertinence, so I hear, is not the least. What she is singing now happens to be one of my ballads. She will soon hear a piece of my mind which will make that little eye of hers water.'

'Dandelion, have mercy. They'll throw us out.'

'Don't interfere. These are professional issues. Let's go in.'

'Dandelion?'

'Hey?'

'Why Little Eye?'

'You'll see.'

The banquet was being held in a huge storeroom, emptied of barrels of herrings and cod liver oil. The smell had been killed – though

not entirely – by hanging up bunches of mistletoe and heather decorated with coloured ribbons wherever possible. Here and there, as
is customary, were also hung plaits of garlic meant to frighten off
vampires.

The tables and benches, which had been pushed towards the
walls, had been covered with white linen, and in a corner there was
a large makeshift hearth and spit. It was crowded but not noisy.
More than four dozen people of various estates and professions, not
to mention the pimply youth and his snub-nosed fiancée, with her
eyes fixed on her husband-to-be, were listening reverentially to a
sonorous and melodious ballad sung by a young woman in a demure
blue frock, sitting on a platform with a lute resting on her knee. The
woman could not have been older than eighteen, and was very slim.
Her long, luxuriant hair was the colour of dark gold. They entered
as the girl finished the song and thanked the audience for the thunderous applause with a nod of her head, which shook her hair gently.

'Greetings, master, greetings,' Drouhard, dressed in his best
clothes, leapt briskly over to them and pulled them towards the
centre of the storeroom. 'Greetings to you, too, Gerard, sir . . . I am
honoured . . . Yes . . . Come here . . . Noble ladies, noble gentlemen!
Here is our honoured guest, who gave us this honour and honoured
us . . . Master Dandelion, the celebrated singer and poetast . . . poet,
I mean, has honoured us with this great honour . . . Thus honoured,
we . . .'

Cheers and applause resounded, and just in time, for it was looking as though Drouhard would honour and stammer himself to
death. Dandelion, blushing with pride, assumed a superior air and
bowed carelessly, then waved a hand at a row of girls sitting on a
long bench, like hens on a roost, being chaperoned by older matrons.
The girls were sitting stiffly, giving the impression they had been
stuck to the bench with carpenter's glue or some other powerful
adhesive. Without exception they were holding their hands on
tightly-clenched knees and their mouths were half-open.

'And presently,' Drouhard called. 'Come forth, help yourself
to beer, fellows, and to the vittles! Prithee, prithee! Avail
yourselves . . .'

The girl in the blue dress forced her way through the crowd, which had crashed onto the food-laden tables like a sea wave.

'Greetings, Dandelion,' she said.

Geralt considered the expression 'eyes like stars' banal and hackneyed, particularly since he had begun travelling with Dandelion, as the troubadour was inclined to throw that compliment about freely, usually, indeed, undeservedly. However, with regard to Essi Daven, even somebody as little susceptible to poetry as the Witcher had to concede the aptness of her nickname. For in her agreeable and pretty, but otherwise unremarkable, little face shone a huge, beautiful, shining, dark blue eye, which riveted the gaze. Essi Daven's other eye was largely covered and obscured by a golden curl, which fell onto her cheek. From time to time Essi flung the curl away with a toss of her head or a puff, at which point it turned out that Little Eye's other little eye was in every way the equal of the first.

'Greetings, Little Eye,' Dandelion said, grimacing. 'That was a pretty ballad you just sang. You've improved your repertoire considerably. I've always maintained that if one is incapable of writing poetry oneself one should borrow other people's. Have you borrowed many of them?'

'A few,' Essi Daven retorted at once and smiled, revealing little white teeth. 'Two or three. I wanted to use more, but it wasn't possible. Dreadful gibberish, and the tunes, though pleasant and unpretentious in their simplicity – not to say primitivism – are not what my audiences expect. Have you written anything new, Dandelion? I don't seem to be aware of it.'

'Small wonder,' the bard sighed. 'I sing my ballads in places to which only the gifted and renowned are invited, and you don't frequent such locations, after all.'

Essi blushed slightly and blew the lock of hair aside.

'Very true,' she said. 'I don't frequent bordellos, as the atmosphere depresses me. I sympathise with you that you have to sing in places like that. But well, that's the way it is. If one has no talent, one can't choose one's audiences.'

Now Dandelion visibly blushed. Little Eye, however, laughed

joyously, flung an arm around his neck all of a sudden and kissed him on the cheek. The Witcher was taken aback, but not too greatly. A professional colleague of Dandelion's could not, indeed, differ much from him in terms of predictability.

'Dandelion, you old bugger,' Essi said, still hugging the bard's neck. 'I'm glad to see you again, in good health and in full possession of your mental faculties.'

'Pshaw, Poppet.' Dandelion seized the girl around the waist, picked her up and spun her around so that her dress billowed around her. 'You were magnificent, by the Gods, I haven't heard such marvellous spitefulness for ages. You bicker even more captivatingly than you sing! And you look simply stunning!'

'I've asked you so many times,' Essi said, blowing her lock of hair away and glancing at Geralt, 'not to call me Poppet, Dandelion. Besides, I think it's high time you introduced me to your companion. I see he doesn't belong to our guild.'

'Save us, O Gods,' the troubadour laughed. 'He, Poppet, has no voice or ear, and can only rhyme "rear" with "beer". This is Geralt of Rivia, a member of the guild of witchers. Come closer, Geralt, and kiss Little Eye's hand.'

The Witcher approached, not really knowing what to do. One usually only kissed ladies of the rank of duchess and higher on the hand, or the ring, and one was supposed to kneel. Regarding women of lower standing that gesture, here, in the South, was considered erotically unambiguous and as such tended to be reserved only for close couples.

Little Eye dispelled his doubts, however, by willingly holding her hand out high with the fingers facing downwards. He grasped it clumsily and feigned a kiss. Essi, her beautiful eye still popping out of her head, blushed.

'Geralt of Rivia,' she said. 'What company you keep, Dandelion.'

'It is an honour for me,' the Witcher muttered, aware he was rivalling Drouhard in eloquence. 'Madam—'

'Damn it,' Dandelion snorted. 'Don't abash Little Eye with all that stammering and titling. She's Essi, he's Geralt. End of introductions. Let's get to the point, Poppet.'

'If you call me Poppet once more you'll get a slap. What point do we have to get to?'

'We have to agree on how we're going to sing. I suggest one after the other, a few ballads each. For the effect. Of course, singing our own ballads.'

'Suits me.'

'How much is Drouhard paying you?'

'None of your business. Who goes first?'

'You.'

'Agreed. Hey, look who's joined us. The Most Noble Duke of Agloval. He's just coming in, look.'

'Well, well,' Dandelion said gleefully. 'The audience is going up-market. Although, on the other hand, we oughtn't to count on him. He's a skinflint. Geralt can confirm it. The local duke bloody hates paying. He hires, admittedly. But he's not so good at paying.'

'I've heard a few things about him.' Essi, looking at Geralt, tossed the lock of hair back from her cheek. 'They were talking about it in the harbour and by the jetty. The famous Sh'eenaz, right?'

Agloval responded to the deep bows of the two rows by the door with a brief nod, and then almost immediately went over to Drouhard and drew him away into a corner, giving a sign that he was not expecting deference or ceremony in the centre of the storehouse. Geralt watched them out of the corner of his eye. They spoke softly, but it was apparent that they were both agitated. Drouhard kept wiping his forehead with a sleeve, shaking his head, and scratching his neck. He was asking questions which the duke, surly and dour, was responding to by shrugging.

'His Grace,' Essi said quietly, moving closer to Geralt, 'looks pre-occupied. Affairs of the heart again? The misunderstanding from earlier today with his famous mermaid? Hey, Witcher?'

'Perhaps,' Geralt answered, looking askance at the poet, aston-ished and strangely annoyed by her question. 'Well, everybody has some personal problems. However, not everybody likes them to be sung about from the rooftops.'

Little Eye blanched slightly, blew away her lock of hair and looked at him defiantly.

'By saying that did you mean to offend or only tease me?'

'Neither one nor the other. I merely wanted to forestall further questions about the problems between Agloval and the mermaid. Questions I do not feel entitled to answer.'

'I understand.' Essi Daven's gorgeous eye narrowed slightly. 'I won't burden you with a similar dilemma. I shall not ask you any of the questions I meant to ask, and which, if I'm to be frank, I treated only as a prelude and invitation to a pleasant conversation. Very well, that conversation will not come to pass, then, and you need fear not that the content will be sung from some rooftop. It has been my pleasure.'

She turned on her heel and walked off towards the tables, where she was immediately greeted with respect. Dandelion shifted his weight from foot to foot and coughed tellingly.

'I won't say that was exquisitely courteous of you, Geralt.'

'It came out wrongly,' the Witcher agreed. 'I hurt her, quite unintentionally. Perhaps I should follow her and apologise?'

'Drop it,' the bard said and added aphoristically, 'There is never a second opportunity to make a first impression. Come on, let's have a beer instead.'

They did not make it to the beer. Drouhard pushed his way through a garrulous group of merchants.

'Gerard, sir,' he said. 'Please step this way. His Grace would like to talk to you.'

'Very well.'

'Geralt,' Dandelion seized him by the sleeve. 'Don't forget.'

'Forget what?'

'You promised to agree to any task, without complaint. I shall hold you to it. What was it you said? A little sacrifice?'

'Very well, Dandelion.'

He went off with Drouhard into the corner of the storeroom, away from the guests. Agloval was sitting at a low table. He was accompanied by a colourfully dressed, weather-beaten man with a short, black beard whom Geralt had not noticed earlier.

'We meet again, Witcher,' the duke said. 'Although this morning I swore I didn't want to see you again. But I do not have another witcher to hand, so you will have to do. Meet Zelest, my bailiff and pearl diving steward. Speak, Zelest.'

'This morning,' said the weather-beaten individual in a low voice, 'we planned to go diving outside the usual grounds. One boat went further westwards, beyond the headland, towards the Dragons Fangs.'

'The Dragons Fangs,' Agloval cut in, 'are two volcanic reefs at the end of the headland. They can be seen from our coast.'

'Aye,' Zelest confirmed. 'People don't usually sail there, for there are whirlpools and rocks, it's dangerous to dive there. But there's fewer and fewer pearls by the coast. Aye, one boat went there. A crew of seven souls, two sailors and five divers, including one woman. When they hadn't returned by the eventide we began to fret, although the sea was calm, as if oil had been poured on it. I sent a few swift skiffs there and we soon found the boat drifting on the sea. There was no one in it, not a living soul. Vanished into thin air. We know not what happened. But there must have been fighting there, a veritable massacre. There were signs . . .'

'What signs?' the Witcher squinted.

'Well, the whole deck was spattered in blood.'

Drouhard hissed and looked around anxiously. Zelest lowered his voice.

'It was as I said,' he repeated, clenching his jaw. 'The boat was spattered in gore, length and breadth. No question but a veritable massacre took place on board. Something killed those people. They say it was a sea monster. No doubt, a sea monster.'

'Not pirates?' asked Geralt softly. 'Or pearl diving competition? Do you rule out a normal knife fight?'

'We do,' said the duke. 'There are no pirates here, no competition. And knife fights don't result in everybody – to the last man – disappearing. No, Geralt. Zelest is right. It was a sea monster, and nothing else. Listen, now no one dares go to sea, not even to the nearby and familiar fishing grounds. The people are scared stiff and the harbour is paralysed. Even the cogs and galleys aren't setting out. Do you see, Witcher?'

'I see,' Geralt nodded. 'Who will show me this place?'

'Ha,' Agloval placed a hand on the table and drummed his fingers. 'I like that. That's witcher talk. Getting to the point at once, without unnecessary chatter. Yes, I like that. Do you see, Drouhard? I told you, a hungry witcher is a good witcher. Well, Geralt? After all, were it not for your musical companion you would have gone to bed without your supper again. My information is correct, is it not?'

Drouhard lowered his head. Zelest stared vacantly ahead.

'Who'll show me the place?' Geralt repeated, looking coldly at Agloval.

'Zelest,' said the duke, his smile fading. 'Zelest will show you the Dragons Fangs and the route to them. When will you start work?'

'First thing tomorrow morning. Be at the harbour, Mr Zelest.'

'Very well, Master Witcher.'

'Excellent.' The duke rubbed his hands and smiled mockingly again. 'Geralt, I'm relying on you to do better with this monster than you did with the Sh'eenaz situation. I really am. Aha, one more thing. I forbid any gossiping about this incident; I don't want any more panic than we already have on our hands. Do you understand, Drouhard? I'll order your tongue torn out if you breathe a word.'

'I understand, Your Grace.'

'Good,' Agloval said, getting up. 'Then I shall go, I shall not interfere with the ball, nor provoke any rumours. Farewell, Drouhard. Wish the betrothed couple happiness on my behalf.'

'My thanks, Duke.'

Essi Daven, who was sitting on a low stool surrounded by a dense crowd of listeners, was singing a melodious and wistful ballad about the woeful fate of a betrayed lover. Dandelion, leaning against a post, was muttering something under his breath and counting bars and syllables on his fingers.

'Well?' he asked. 'Do you have a job, Geralt?'

'Yes,' the Witcher answered, not going into details, which in any case did not concern the bard.

'I told you I smelt a rat – and money. Good, very good. I'll make some money, you will too, we'll be able to afford to revel. We'll go to Cidaris, in time for the grape harvest festival. And now, if you'll excuse me, I've spotted something interesting on the bench over there.'

Geralt followed the poet's gaze, but aside from about a dozen girls with half-open mouths he saw nothing interesting. Dandelion pulled down his jerkin, set his bonnet over his right ear and approached the bench in long swinging strides. Having passed the matrons guarding the maidens with a deft flanking manoeuvre, he began his customary ritual of flashing a broad smile.

Essi Daven finished her ballad, and was rewarded with applause, a small purse and a large bouquet of pretty – though somewhat withered – chrysanthemums.

The Witcher circulated among the guests, looking for an opportunity to finally occupy a seat at the table, which was laden with vittles. He gazed longingly at the rapidly vanishing pickled herrings, stuffed cabbage leaves, boiled cod heads and mutton chops, at the rings of sausage and capons being torn into pieces, and the smoked salmon and hams being chopped up with knives. The problem was that there were no vacant seats at the table.

The maidens and matrons, somewhat livened up, surrounded Dandelion, calling squeakily for a performance. Dandelion smiled falsely and made excuses, ineffectually feigning modesty.

Geralt, overcoming his embarrassment, virtually forced his way to the table. An elderly gentleman, smelling strongly of vinegar, moved aside surprisingly courteously and willingly, almost knocking off several guests sitting alongside him. Geralt got down to eating without delay and in a flash had cleared the only dish he could reach. The gentleman smelling of vinegar passed him another. In gratitude, the Witcher listened attentively to the elderly gentleman's long tirade concerning the present times and the youth of today. The elderly gentleman stubbornly described sexual freedom as 'laxity', so Geralt had some difficulty keeping a straight face.

Essi stood by the wall, beneath bunches of mistletoe, alone, tuning her lute. The Witcher saw a young man in a brocaded waisted kaftan approaching and saying something to the poet, smiling wanly the while. Essi looked at the young man, her pretty mouth sneering slightly, and said several quick words. The young man cowered and walked hurriedly away, and his ears, as red as beetroots, glowed in the semi-darkness for a long time afterwards.

'. . . abomination, shame and disgrace,' the elderly gentleman smelling of vinegar continued. 'One enormous laxity, sir.'

'Indeed,' Geralt nodded tentatively, wiping his plate with a hunk of bread.

'May I request silence, noble ladies, noble lords,' Drouhard called, walking into the middle of the room. 'The celebrated Master Dandelion, in spite of being a little bodily indisposed and weary, shall now sing for us his celebrated ballad about Queen Marienn and the Black Raven! He shall do it at the urgent plea of Miss Veverka, the miller's daughter, whom, he said, he may not refuse.'

Miss Veverka, one of the less comely girls on the bench, became beautified in the blink of an eye. Uproar and applause erupted, drowning out further laxity from the elderly gentleman smelling of vinegar. Dandelion waited for total silence, played a striking prelude on his lute, after which he began to sing, without taking his eyes off Miss Veverka, who was growing more beautiful with each verse. Indeed, Geralt thought, that whoreson is more effective than all the magical oils and creams Yennefer sells in her little shop in Vengerberg.

He saw Essi steal behind the crowded semicircle of Dandelion's audience and cautiously vanish through the door to the terrace. Driven by a strange impulse, he slipped nimbly out from behind the table and followed her.

She stood, leaning forward, resting her elbows on the railing of the jetty, head drawn into her delicate, upraised shoulders. She was gazing at the rippling sea, glistening from the light of the moon and the fires burning in the harbour. A board creaked beneath Geralt's foot. Essi straightened up.

'I'm sorry, I didn't mean to disturb you,' he said, stiffly, searching for that sudden grimace on her lips to which she had treated the young man in brocade a moment earlier.

'You aren't disturbing me,' she replied, smiling and tossing back her lock of hair. 'I'm not seeking solitude here, but fresh air. Was all that smoke and airlessness bothering you too?'

'A little. But I'm more bothered by knowing that I offended you. I came here to apologise, Essi, to try to regain the chance of a pleasant conversation.'

'You deserve my apology,' she said, pressing her hands down on the railing. 'I reacted too impetuously. I always react too impetuously, I don't know how to control myself. Excuse me and give me another chance. For a conversation.'

He approached and leaned on the railing beside her. He felt the warmth emanating from her, and the faint scent of verbena. He liked the scent of verbena, although the scent of verbena was not the scent of lilac and gooseberry.

'What do you connect with the sea, Geralt?' she asked suddenly.

'Unease,' he answered, almost without thinking.

'Interesting. And you seem so calm and composed.'

'I didn't say I feel unease. You asked for associations.'

'Associations are the image of the soul. I know what I'm talking about, I'm a poet.'

'And what do you associate with the sea, Essi?' he asked quickly, to put an end to discussions about the unease he was feeling.

'With constant movement,' she answered after a pause. 'With change. And with riddles, with mystery, with something I cannot grasp, which I might be able to describe in a thousand different ways, in a thousand poems, never actually reaching the core, the heart of the matter. Yes, that's it.'

'And so,' he said, feeling the verbena affecting him more and more strongly. 'What you feel is also unease. And you seem so calm and composed.'

She turned towards him, tossing back her golden curl and fixing her gorgeous eyes on him.

'I'm not calm or composed, Geralt.'

It happened suddenly, utterly unexpectedly. The movement he made, which was supposed to have been just a touch, a gentle touch of her arms, turned into a powerful grasp of both hands around her very slender waist, into a rapid, though not rough, pulling of her closer, and into a sudden, passionate contact of their bodies. Essi stiffened suddenly, straightened, bent her torso powerfully backwards, pressed her hands down on his, firmly, as though she wanted to pull away and push his hands from her waist, but instead of that she seized them tightly, tipped her head forward, parted her lips and hesitated.

'Why . . . Why this?' she whispered. Her eye was wide open, her golden curl had fallen onto her cheek.

Calmly and slowly he tipped his head forward, brought his face closer and suddenly and quickly pursed his lips into a kiss. Essi, however, even then, did not release his hands grasping her waist and still powerfully arched her back, avoiding bodily contact. Remaining like that they turned around slowly, as though in a dance. She kissed him eagerly, expertly. For a long time.

Then she nimbly and effortlessly freed herself from his embrace, turned away, once again leaned on the railing, and drew her head into her shoulders. Geralt suddenly felt dreadfully, indescribably stupid. The feeling stopped him from approaching her, from putting an arm around her hunched back.

'Why?' she asked coolly, without turning around. 'Why did you do that?'

She glanced at him out of the corner of her eye and the Witcher suddenly understood he had made a mistake. He suddenly knew that insincerity, lies, pretence and bravado would lead him straight into a swamp, where only a springy, matted layer of grass and moss, liable to yield, tear or break at any moment, separated him from the abyss below.

'Why?' she repeated.

He did not answer.

'Are you looking for a woman for the night?'

He did not reply. Essi turned slowly and touched his arm.

'Let's go back in,' she said easily, but he was not deceived by her manner, sensing how tense she was. 'Don't make that face. It was nothing. And the fact that I'm not looking for a man for tonight isn't your fault. Is it?'

'Essi . . .'

'Let's go back, Geralt. Dandelion has played three encores. It's my turn. Come on, I'll sing . . .'

She glanced at him strangely and blew her lock of hair away from her eye.

'I'll sing for you.'

IV

'Oho,' the Witcher said, feigning surprise. 'So you're here? I thought you wouldn't be back tonight.'

Dandelion locked the door with the hasp, hung up his lute and his bonnet with the egret's feather on a peg, took off his jerkin, brushed it down and laid it on some sacks lying in the corner of the small room. Apart from the sacks, a wooden pail and a huge palliasse stuffed with dried bean stalks there was no furniture in the attic room – even the candle stood on the floor in a hardened pool of wax. Drouhard admired Dandelion, but clearly not enough to give him the run of a chamber or even a boxroom.

'And why,' asked Dandelion, removing his boots, 'did you think I wouldn't be back tonight?'

'I thought,' the Witcher lifted himself up on an elbow, crunching bean straw, 'you'd go and sing serenades beneath the window of Miss Veverka, at whom your tongue has been hanging out the whole evening like a pointer at the sight of a bitch.'

'Ha, ha,' the bard laughed. 'But you're so oafishly stupid. You didn't understand anything. Veverka? I don't care about Veverka. I simply wanted to stab Miss Akeretta with jealousy, as I shall make a pass at her tomorrow. Move over.'

Dandelion collapsed on the palliasse and pulled the blanket off Geralt. Geralt, feeling a strange anger, turned his head towards the tiny window, through which, had it not been for some industrious spiders, he would have seen the starry sky.

'Why so huffy?' the poet asked. 'Does it bother you that I make advances to girls? Since when? Perhaps you've become a druid and taken a vow of chastity? Or perhaps . . .'

'Don't go on. I'm tired. Have you not noticed that for the first time in two weeks we have a palliasse and a roof over our heads?

Doesn't it gladden you that the rain won't be dripping on us in the wee small hours?'

'For me,' Dandelion fantasised, 'a palliasse without a girl isn't a palliasse. It's incomplete happiness, and what is incomplete happiness?'

Geralt groaned softly, as usual when Dandelion was assailed by nocturnal talkativeness.

'Incomplete happiness,' the bard continued, engrossed in his own voice, 'is like . . . a kiss interrupted . . . Why are you grinding your teeth, if I may ask?'

'You're incredibly boring, Dandelion. Nothing but palliasses, girls, bums, tits, incomplete happiness and kisses interrupted by dogs set on you by your lovers' parents. Why, you clearly can't behave any differently. Clearly only easy lewdness, not to say uncritical promiscuity, allows you musicians to compose ballads, write poems and sing. That is clearly – write it down – the dark side of your talent.'

He had said too much and had not cooled his voiced sufficiently. And Dandelion saw through him effortlessly and unerringly.

'Aha,' he said calmly. 'Essi Daven, also known as Little Eye. The alluring little eye of Little Eye fixed its gaze on the Witcher and caused confusion in the Witcher. The Witcher behaved like a little schoolboy before a queen. And rather than blame himself he is blaming her and searching for her dark side.'

'You're talking rubbish, Dandelion.'

'No, my dear. Essi made an impression on you, you can't hide it. I don't see anything wrong with that, actually. But beware, and don't make a mistake. She is not what you think. If her talent has its dark sides, they certainly aren't what you imagine.'

'I conjecture,' said the Witcher, trying to control his voice, 'that you know her very well.'

'Quite well. But not in the way you think. Not like that.'

'Quite original for you, you'll admit.'

'You're stupid,' the bard said, stretching and placing both hands under his neck. 'I've known Poppet almost since she was a child. To me she's like . . . well . . . like a younger sister. So I repeat, don't make any silly mistakes about her. You'd be harming her greatly, because you also made an impression on her. Admit it, you desire her?'

'Even if I did, unlike you I'm not accustomed to talking about it,' Geralt said sharply. 'Or writing songs about it. I thank you for your words about her, because perhaps you have indeed saved me from a stupid mistake. But let that be an end to it. I regard the subject as exhausted.'

Dandelion lay motionless for a moment, saying nothing, but Geralt knew him too well.

'I know,' the poet said at last. 'Now I know everything.'

'You know fuck all, Dandelion.'

'Do you know what your problem is, Geralt? You think you're different. You flaunt your otherness, what you consider abnormal. You aggressively impose that abnormality on others, not understanding that for people who think clear-headedly you're the most normal man under the sun, and they all wish that everybody was so normal. What of it that you have quicker reflexes than most and vertical pupils in sunlight? That you can see in the dark like a cat? That you know a few spells? Big deal. I, my dear, once knew an innkeeper who could fart for ten minutes without stopping, playing the tune to the psalm *Greet us, greet us, O, Morning Star*. Heedless of his – let's face it – unusual talent, that innkeeper was the most normal among the normal; he had a wife, children and a grandmother afflicted by palsy—'

'What does that have to do with Essi Daven? Could you explain?'

'Of course. You wrongfully thought, Geralt, that Little Eye was interested in you out of morbid, downright perverted curiosity, that she looks at you as though you were a queer fish, a two-headed calf or a salamander in a menagerie. And you immediately became annoyed, gave her a rude, undeserved reprimand at the first opportunity, struck back at a blow she hadn't dealt. I witnessed it, after all. I didn't witness the further course of events, of course, but I noticed your flight from the room and saw her glowing cheeks when you returned. Yes, Geralt. I'm alerting you to a mistake, and you have already made it. You wanted to take revenge on her for – in your opinion – her morbid curiosity. You decided to exploit that curiosity.'

'You're talking rubbish.'

'You tried,' the bard continued, unmoved, 'to learn if it was possible to bed her in the hay, if she was curious to find out what it's like to make love with a misfit, with a witcher. Fortunately, Essi turned out to be smarter than you and generously took pity on your stupidity, having understood its cause. I conclude this from the fact you did not return from the jetty with a fat lip.'

'Have you finished?'

'Yes, I have.'

'Goodnight, then.'

'I know why you're furious and gnashing your teeth.'

'No doubt. You know everything.'

'I know who warped you like that, who left you unable to understand a normal woman. Oh, but that Yennefer of yours was a troublemaker; I'm damned if I know what you see in her.'

'Drop it, Dandelion.'

'Do you really not prefer normal girls like Essi? What do sorceresses have that Essi doesn't? Age, perhaps? Little Eye may not be the youngest, but she's as old as she looks. And do you know what Yennefer once confessed to me after a few stiff drinks? Ha, ha . . . she told me that the first time she did it with a man it was exactly a year after the invention of the two-furrow plough.'

'You're lying. Yennefer loathes you like the plague and would never confide in you.'

'All right, I was lying, I confess.'

'You don't have to. I know you.'

'You only think you know me. Don't forget: I'm complicated by nature.'

'Dandelion,' the Witcher sighed, now genuinely tired. 'You're a cynic, a lecher, a womaniser and a liar. And there's nothing, believe me, nothing complicated about that. Goodnight.'

'Goodnight, Geralt.'

V

'You rise early, Essi.'

The poet smiled, holding down her hair, which was being blown around by the wind. She stepped gingerly onto the jetty, avoiding the holes and rotten planks.

'I couldn't miss the chance of watching the Witcher at work. Will you think me nosey again, Geralt? Why, I don't deny it, I really am nosey. How goes it?'

'How goes what?'

'Oh, Geralt,' she said. 'You underestimate my curiosity, and my talent for gathering and interpreting information. I know everything about the case of the pearl divers, I know the details of your agreement with Agloval. I know you're looking for a sailor willing to sail there, towards the Dragons Fangs. Did you find one?'

He looked at her searchingly for a moment, and then suddenly decided.

'No,' he replied, 'I didn't. Not one.'

'Are they afraid?'

'Yes, they are.'

'How, then, do you intend to carry out an exploration if you can't go to sea? How, without sailing, do you plan to get at the monster that killed the pearl divers?'

He took her by the hand and led her from the jetty. They walked slowly along the edge of the sea, across the pebbly beach, beside the launches pulled up on the shore, among the rows of nets hung up on stilts, among the curtains of split, drying fish being blown by the wind. Geralt unexpectedly found that the poet's company did not bother him at all, that it was not wearisome or intrusive. Apart from that, he hoped that a calm and matter-of-fact conversation would

209

erase the results of that stupid kiss on the terrace. The fact that Essi had come to the jetty filled him with the hope that she did not bear him a grudge. He was content.

'"Get at the monster",' he muttered, repeating her words. 'If only I knew how. I know very little about sea monsters.'

'Interesting. From what I know, there are many more monsters in the sea than there are on land, both in terms of number and variety of species. It would seem, thus, that the sea ought to be a great opportunity for witchers to show what they can do.'

'Well, it isn't.'

'Why?'

'The expansion of people onto the sea,' he said, clearing his throat and turning his face away, 'hasn't lasted very long. Witchers were needed long ago, on the land, during the first phase of colonisation. We aren't cut out to fight sea-dwelling creatures, although you are right, the sea is full of all sorts of aggressive filth. But our witcher abilities are insufficient against sea monsters. Those creatures are either too big for us, or are too well armoured, or are too sure in their element. Or all three.'

'And the monster that killed the pearl divers? You have no idea what it was?'

'A kraken, perhaps?'

'No. A kraken would have wrecked the boat, but it was intact. And, as they said, totally full of blood,' Little Eye swallowed and visibly paled. 'Don't think I'm being a know-all. I grew up by the sea, and I've seen a few things.'

'In that case what could it have been? A giant squid? It might have dragged those people from the deck . . .'

'There wouldn't have been any blood. It wasn't a squid, Geralt, or a killer whale, or a dracoturtle, because whatever it was didn't destroy or capsize the boat. Whatever it was went on board and carried out the slaughter there. Perhaps you're making a mistake looking for it in the sea?'

The Witcher pondered.

'I'm beginning to admire you, Essi,' he said. The poet blushed. 'You're right. It may have attacked from the air. It may have been an ornithodracon, a gryphon, a wyvern, a flying drake or a forktail. Possibly even a roc—'

'Excuse me,' Essi said, 'Look who's coming.'

Agloval was approaching along the shore, alone, his clothes sopping wet. He was visibly angry, and flushed with rage on seeing them.

Essi curtseyed slightly, Geralt bent his head, pressing his fist to his chest. Agloval spat.

'I sat on the rocks for three hours, almost from daybreak,' he snarled. 'She didn't even make an appearance. Three hours, like an ass, on rocks swept by the waves.'

'I'm sorry . . .' the Witcher muttered.

'You're sorry?' the duke exploded. 'Sorry? It's your fault. You fouled everything up. You spoiled everything.'

'What did I spoil? I was only working as an interpreter—'

'To hell with work like that,' Agloval interrupted angrily, showing off his profile. His profile was indeed kingly, worthy of being struck on coinage. 'Verily, it would have been better not to hire you. It sounds paradoxical, but while we didn't have an interpreter we understood each other better, Sh'eenaz and I, if you know what I mean. But now – do you know what they're saying in town? Rumours are spreading that the pearl divers perished because I enraged the mermaid. That it's her revenge.'

'Nonsense,' the Witcher commented coldly.

'How am I to know that it's nonsense?' the duke growled. 'How do I know you didn't tell her something? Do I really know what she's capable of? What monsters she chums around with down in the depths? By all means prove to me that it's nonsense. Bring me the head of the beast that killed the pearl divers. Get to work, instead of flirting on the beach—'

'To work?' Geralt reacted angrily. 'How? Am I to go out to sea straddling a barrel? Your Zelest threatened the sailors with torture and the noose, but in spite of that no one wants to sail out with me. Zelest himself isn't too keen either. So how—?'

'What does it bother me how?' Agloval yelled, interrupting. 'That's your problem! What are witchers for if not so that decent folk don't have to wrack their brains about how to rid themselves of monsters? I've hired you to do the job and I demand you carry it out. If not, get out of here before I drive you to the borders of my realm with my whip!'

'Calm down, Your Grace,' Little Eye said softly, but her paleness and trembling hands betrayed her irritation. 'And please don't threaten Geralt. It so happens that Dandelion and I have several friends. King Ethain of Cidaris, to mention but one, likes us and our ballads very much. King Ethain is an enlightened monarch and always says that our ballads aren't just lively music and rhymes, but a way of spreading news, that they are a chronicle of humankind. Do you wish, Your Grace, to be written into the chronicle of humankind? I can have it arranged.'

Agloval looked at her for a while with a cold, contemptuous gaze.

'The pearl divers who died had wives and children,' he finally said, much more quietly and calmly. 'When hunger afflicts the remaining ones they will put to sea again. Pearl, sponge and oyster divers, lobster fishers, fishermen; all of them. Now they are afraid, but hunger will overcome their fear. They will go to sea. But will they return? What do you say to that, Geralt? Miss Daven? I'd be interested to hear the ballad which will sing of that. A ballad about a witcher standing idly on the shore looking at the blood-spattered decks of boats and weeping children.'

Essi blanched even more, but raised her head proudly, blew away the lock of hair and was just preparing a riposte, when Geralt seized her hand and squeezed it, stopping her words.

'That is enough,' he said. 'In this entire flood of words only one has true significance. You hired me, Agloval. I accepted the task and shall accomplish it, if it is feasible.'

'I'm relying on it,' the duke said curtly. 'Then goodbye. My respects, Miss Daven.'

Essi did not curtsey, she only tilted her head. Agloval hauled up his wet trousers and headed off towards the harbour, walking unsteadily over the pebbles. Only then did Geralt notice he was still holding the poet's hand, but she was not trying to free herself at all.

He released her hand. Essi, slowly returning to her normal colours, turned her face towards his.

'It's easy to make you take a risk,' she said. 'All it takes is a few words about women and children. And so much is said about how unfeeling you witchers are. Geralt, Agloval doesn't give a hoot about women, children or the elderly. He wants the pearl fishing to begin again because he's losing money every day they don't come back with a catch. He's taking you for a ride with those starving children, and you're ready to risk your life—'

'Essi,' he interrupted. 'I'm a witcher. It's my trade to risk my life. Children have nothing to do with it.'

'You can't fool me.'

'Why the assumption that I mean to?'

'Perhaps because if you were the heartless professional you pretend to be, you would have tried to push up the price. But you didn't say a word about your fee. Oh, never mind, enough of all that. Are we going back?'

'Let's walk on a little.'

'Gladly. Geralt?'

'Yes.'

'I told you I grew up by the sea. I know how to steer a boat and—'

'Put that out of your head.'

'Why?'

'Put that out of your head,' he repeated sharply.

'You might,' she said, 'have phrased that more politely.'

'I might have. But you would have taken it as . . . the Devil only knows what. And I *am* an unfeeling witcher and heartless professional. I risk my life. Not other people's.'

Essi fell silent. He saw her purse her lips and toss her head. A gust of wind ruffled her hair again, and her face was covered for a moment by a confusion of golden curls.

'I only wanted to help you,' she said.

'I know. Thank you.'

'Geralt?'

'Yes.'

'What if there is something behind the rumours Agloval was talking about? You know well that mermaids aren't always friendly. There have been cases—'

'I don't believe them.'

'Sea witches,' Little Eye continued, pensively. 'Nereids, mermen, sea nymphs. Who knows what they're capable of. And Sh'eenaz . . . she had reason—'

'I don't believe it,' he interrupted.

'You don't believe or you don't want to believe?'

He did not reply.

'And you want to appear the cold professional?' she asked with a strange smile. 'Someone who thinks with his sword hilt? If you want, I'll tell you what you really are.'

'I know what I really am.'

'You're sensitive,' she said softly. 'Deep in your angst-filled soul. Your stony face and cold voice don't deceive me. You are sensitive, and your sensitivity makes you fear that whatever you are going to face with sword in hand may have its own arguments, may have the moral advantage over you . . .'

'No, Essi,' he said slowly. 'Don't try to make me the subject of a moving ballad, a ballad about a witcher with inner conflicts. Perhaps I'd like it to be the case, but it isn't. My moral dilemmas are resolved for me by my code and education. By my training.'

'Don't talk like that,' she said in annoyance. 'I don't understand why you try to—'

'Essi,' he interrupted her again. 'I don't want you to pick up false notions about me. I'm not a knight errant.'

'You aren't a cold and unthinking killer either.'

'No,' he agreed calmly. 'I'm not, although there are some who think differently. For it isn't my sensitivity and personal qualities that place me higher, but the vain and arrogant pride of a professional convinced of his value. A specialist, in whom it was instilled that the code of his profession and cold routine is more legitimate than emotion, that they protect him against making a mistake, which could be made should he become entangled in the dilemmas of Good and Evil, of Order and Chaos. No, Essi. It's not *I* that am sensitive, but you. After all, your profession demands that, doesn't it? It's you who became alarmed by the thought that an apparently pleasant mermaid attacked the pearl divers in an act of desperate revenge after being insulted. You immediately look for an excuse for the mermaid, extenuating circumstances; you balk at the thought that a witcher, hired by the duke, will murder an exquisite mermaid just because she dared to yield to emotion. But the Witcher, Essi, is free of such dilemmas. And of emotion. Even if it turns out that it *was* the mermaid, the Witcher won't kill the mermaid, because the code forbids him. The code solves the dilemma for the Witcher.'

Little Eye looked at him, abruptly lifting up her head.

'All dilemmas?' she asked quickly.

She knows about Yennefer, he thought. She knows. Dandelion, you bloody gossip . . .

They looked at one another.

What is concealed in your deep blue eyes, Essi? Curiosity? Fascination with otherness? What are the dark sides of your talent, Little Eye?

'I apologise,' she said. 'The question was foolish. And naive. It hinted that I believed what you were saying. Let's go back. That wind chills to the marrow. Look how rough the sea is.'

'It is. Do you know what's fascinating, Essi?'

'What?'

'I was certain the rock where Agloval met his mermaid was nearer the shore and bigger. And now it's not visible.'

'It's the tide,' Essi said shortly. 'The water will soon reach all the way to the cliff.'

'All that way?'

'Yes. The water rises and falls here considerably, well over ten cubits, because here in the strait and the mouth of the river there are so-called tidal echoes, as the sailors call them.'

Geralt looked towards the headland, at the Dragons Fangs, biting into a roaring, foaming breaker.

'Essi,' he asked. 'And when the tide starts going out?'

'What?'

'How far back does the sea go?'

'But what . . . ? Ah, I get it. Yes, you're right. It goes back to the line of the shelf.'

'The line of the what?'

'Well, it's like a shelf – flat shallows – forming the seabed, which ends with a lip at the edge of the deep waters.'

'And the Dragons Fangs . . .'

'Are right on that lip.'

'And they are reachable by wading? How long would I have?'

'I don't know,' Little Eye frowned. 'You'd have to ask the locals. But I don't think it would be a good idea. Look, there are rocks between the land and the Fangs, the entire shore is scored with bays and fjords. When the tide starts going out, gorges and basins full of water are formed there. I don't know if—'

From the direction of the sea and the barely visible rocks came a splash. And a loud, melodic cry.

'White Hair!' the mermaid called, gracefully leaping over the crest of a wave, threshing the water with short, elegant strokes of her tail.

'Sh'eenaz!' he called back, waving a hand.

The mermaid swam over to the rocks, stood erect in the foaming, green water and used both hands to fling back her hair, at the same time revealing her torso with all its charms. Geralt glanced at Essi. The girl blushed slightly and with an expression of regret and embarrassment on her face looked for a moment at her own charms, which barely protruded beneath her dress.

'Where is my man?' Sh'eenaz sang, swimming closer. 'He was meant to have come.'

'He did. He waited for three hours and then left.'

'He left?' the mermaid said in a high trill of astonishment. 'He didn't wait? He could not endure three meagre hours? Just as I thought. Not a scrap of sacrifice! Not a scrap! Despicable, despicable, despicable! And what are you doing here, White Hair? Did you come here for a walk with your beloved? You'd make a pretty couple, were you not marred by your legs.'

'She is not my beloved. We barely know each other.'

'Yes?' Sh'eenaz said in astonishment. 'Pity. You suit each other, you look lovely together. Who is it?'

'I'm Essi Daven, poet,' Little Eye sang with an accent and melody beside which the Witcher's voice sounded like the cawing of a crow.

'Nice to meet you, Sh'eenaz.'

The mermaid slapped her hands on the water and laughed brightly.

'How gorgeous!' she cried. 'You know our tongue! Upon my word, you astonish me, you humans. Verily, not nearly as much divides us as people say.'

The Witcher was no less astonished than the mermaid, although he might have guessed that the educated and well-read Essi would know the Elder Speech better than him. It was the language of the elves, a euphonious version of which was used by mermaids, sea witches and nereids. It also ought to have been clear to him that the melodiousness and complicated intonation pattern of the mermaids' speech, which for him was a handicap, made it easier for Little Eye.

'Sh'eenaz!' he called. 'A few things divide us, nevertheless, and what occasionally divides us is spilled blood! Who . . . who killed the pearl divers, over there, by the two rocks? Tell me!'

The mermaid dived down, churning the water. A moment later she spurted back out onto the surface again, and her pretty little face was contracted and drawn into an ugly grimace.

'Don't you dare!' she screamed, piercingly shrilly. 'Don't you dare go near the steps! It is not for you! Don't fall foul of them! It is not for you!'

'What? What isn't for us?'

'Not for you!' Sh'eenaz yelled, falling onto her back on the waves. Splashes of water shot high up. For just a moment longer they saw her forked, finned tail flapping over the waves. Then she vanished under the water.

Little Eye tidied her hair, which had been ruffled by the wind. She stood motionless with her head bowed.

'I didn't know,' Geralt said, clearing his throat, 'that you knew the Elder Speech so well, Essi.'

'You couldn't have known,' she said with a distinct bitterness in her voice. 'After all . . . after all, you barely know me.'

VI

'Geralt,' Dandelion said, looking around and sniffing like a hound. 'It stinks terribly here, don't you think?'

'Does it?' the Witcher sniffed. 'I've been in places where it smelled worse. It's only the smell of the sea.'

The bard turned his head away and spat between two rocks. The water bubbled in the rocky clefts, foaming and soughing, exposing gorges full of sea-worn pebbles.

'Look how nicely it's dried out, Geralt. Where has the water gone? What is it with those bloody tides? Where do they come from? Haven't you ever thought about it?'

'No. I've had other concerns.'

'I think,' Dandelion said, trembling slightly, 'that down there in the depths, at the very bottom of this bloody ocean, crouches a huge monster, a fat, scaly beast, a toad with horns on its vile head. And from time to time it draws water into its belly, and with the water everything that lives and can be eaten: fish, seals, turtles – everything. And then, having devoured its prey, it pukes up the water and we have the tide. What do you think about that?'

'I think you're a fool. Yennefer once told me that the moon causes the tides.'

Dandelion cackled.

'What bloody rubbish! What does the moon have to do with the sea? Only dogs howl at the moon. She was having you on, Geralt, that little liar of yours, she put one over on you. Not for the first time either, I'd say.'

The Witcher did not comment. He looked at the boulders glistening with water in the ravines exposed by the tide. The water was still exploding and foaming in them, but it looked as though they would get through.

'Very well, let's get to work,' he said, standing and adjusting his sword on his back. 'We can't wait any longer, or we won't make it back before the tide comes in. Do you still insist on coming with me?'

'Yes. Subjects for ballads aren't fir cones, you don't find them under a tree. Aside from that, it's Poppet's birthday tomorrow.'

'I don't see the link.'

'Pity. There exists the custom among we – normal – people of giving one another presents on birthdays. I can't afford to buy her anything. So I shall find something for her on the seabed.'

'A herring? Or a cuttlefish?'

'Dolt. I'll find some amber, perhaps a seahorse, or maybe a pretty conch. The point is it's a symbol, a sign of concern and affection. I like Little Eye and I want to please her. Don't you understand? I thought not. Let's go. You first, because there might be a monster down there.'

'Right.' The Witcher slid down from the cliff onto the slippery rocks, covered with algae. 'I'll go first, in order to protect you if needs be. As a sign of my concern and affection. Just remember, if I shout, run like hell and don't get tangled up in my sword. We aren't going to gather seahorses. We're going to deal with a monster that murders people.'

They set off downwards, into the rifts of the exposed seabed, in some places wading through the water still swirling in the rocky vents. They splashed around in hollows lined with sand and bladder wrack. To make matters worse it began to rain, so they were soon soaked from head to foot. Dandelion kept stopping and digging around in the pebbles and tangles of seaweed.

'Oh, look, Geralt, a little fish. It's all red, by the Devil. And here, look, a little eel. And this? What is it? It looks like a great big, transparent flea. And this . . . Oh, mother! Geraaalt!'

The Witcher turned around at once, with his hand on his sword.

It was a human skull, white, worn smooth by the rocks, jammed into a rocky crevice, full of sand. But not only sand. Dandelion, seeing a lugworm writhing in the eye socket, shuddered and made an unpleasant noise. The Witcher shrugged and headed towards the rocky plain exposed by the sea, in the direction of the two jagged reefs, known as the Dragons Fangs, which now looked like mountains. He moved cautiously. The seabed was strewn with sea cucumbers, shells and piles of bladder wrack. Large jellyfish swayed and brittle stars whirled in the rock pools and hollows. Small crabs, as colourful as hummingbirds, fled from them, creeping sideways, their legs scurrying busily.

Geralt noticed a corpse some way off, wedged between the rocks. The drowned man's chest could be seen moving beneath his shirt and the seaweed, though in principle there was no longer anything to move it. It was teeming with crabs, outside and inside. The body could not have been in the water longer than a day, but the crabs had picked it so clean it was pointless examining it closer. The Witcher changed direction without a word, giving the corpse a wide berth. Dandelion did not notice anything.

'Why, but it stinks of rot here,' he swore, trying to catch up with Geralt. He spat and shook water from his bonnet. 'And it's tipping down and I'm cold. I'll catch a chill and lose my bloody voice . . .'

'Stop moaning. If you want to go back you know the way.'

Right beyond the base of the Dragons Fangs stretched out a flat, rocky shelf, and beyond it was deep water, the calmly rippling sea. The limit of the tide.

'Ha, Geralt,' Dandelion said, looking around. 'I think that monster of yours had enough sense to withdraw to the high sea with the tide. And I guess you thought it'd be lazing about here somewhere, waiting for you to hack it to pieces?'

'Be quiet.'

The Witcher approached the edge of the shelf and knelt down, cautiously resting his hands on the sharp shells clinging to the rocks. He could not see anything. The water was dark, and the surface was cloudy, dulled by the drizzle.

Dandelion searched the recesses of the reefs, kicking the more aggressive crabs from his legs, examining and feeling the dripping rocks bearded with sagging seaweed and specked with coarse colonies of crustaceans and molluscs.

'Hey, Geralt!'

'What?'

'Look at those shells. They're pearl oysters, aren't they?'

'No.'

'Know anything about them?'

'No.'

'So keep your opinions to yourself until you do know something. They are pearl oysters, I'm certain. I'll start collecting pearls, at least there'll be some profit from this expedition, not just a cold. Shall I begin, Geralt?'

'Go ahead. The monster attacks pearl divers. Pearl collectors probably fall into the same category.'

'Am I to be bait?'

'Start collecting. Take the bigger ones, because if you don't find any pearls we can make soup out of them.'

'Forget it. I'll just collect pearls; fuck the shells. Dammit . . . Bitch . . . How do you . . . bloody . . . open it? Do you have a knife, Geralt?'

'Haven't you even brought a knife?'

'I'm a poet, not some knifer. Oh, to hell with it, I'll put them in a bag and we'll get the pearls out later. Hey, you! Scram!'

He kicked off a crab, which flew over Geralt's head and splashed into the water. The Witcher walked slowly along the edge of the shelf, eyes fixed on the black, impenetrable water. He heard the rhythmic tapping of the stone Dandelion was using to dislodge the shells from the rock.

'Dandelion! Come and look!'

The jagged, cracked shelf suddenly ended in a level, sharp edge, which fell downwards at an acute angle. Immense, angular, regular blocks of white marble, overgrown with seaweed, molluscs and sea anemones swaying in the water like flowers in the breeze, could clearly be seen beneath the surface of the water.

'What is it? They look like – like steps.'

'Because they *are* steps,' Dandelion whispered in awe. 'Ooo, they're steps leading to an underwater city. To the legendary Ys, which was swallowed up by the sea. Have you heard the legend of the city of the chasm, about Ys-Beneath-The-Waves? I shall write such a ballad the competition won't know what's hit them. I have to see it up close . . . Look, there's some kind of mosaic, something is engraved or carved there . . . Some kind of writing? Move away, Geralt.'

'Dandelion! That's a trench! You'll slip off . . .'

'Never mind. I'm wet anyway. See, it's shallow here, barely waist-deep on this first step. And as wide as a ballroom. Oh, bloody hell . . .'

Geralt jumped very quickly into the water and grabbed the bard, who had fallen in up to his neck.

'I tripped on that shit,' Dandelion said, gasping for air, recovering himself and lifting a large, flat mollusc dripping water from its cobalt blue shell, overgrown with threads of algae. 'There's loads of these on the steps. It's a pretty colour, don't you think? Grab it and shove it into your bag, mine's already full.'

'Get out of there,' the Witcher snapped, annoyed. 'Get back on the shelf this minute, Dandelion. This isn't a game.'

'Quiet. Did you hear that? What was it?'

Geralt heard it. The sound was coming from below, from under the water. Dull and deep, although simultaneously faint, soft, brief, broken off. The sound of a bell.

'It's a bloody bell,' Dandelion whispered, clambering out onto the shelf. 'I was right, Geralt. It's the bell of the sunken Ys, the bell of the city of monsters muffled by the weight of the depths. It's the damned reminding us . . .'

'Will you shut up?'

The sound repeated. Considerably closer.

'. . . reminding us,' the bard continued, squeezing out the soaking tail of his jerkin, 'of its dreadful fate. That bell is a warning . . .'

The Witcher stopped paying attention to Dandelion's voice and concentrated on his other senses. He sensed. He sensed something.

'It's a warning,' Dandelion said, sticking the tip of his tongue out, as was his custom when he was concentrating. 'A warning, because . . . hmm . . . So we would not forget . . . hmm . . . hmmm . . . I've got it!

'*The heart of the bell sounds softly, it sings a song of death*

222

Of death, which can be born more easily than oblivion . . .'

The water right next to the Witcher exploded. Dandelion screamed. The goggle-eyed monster emerging from the foam aimed a broad, serrated, scythe-like blade at Geralt. Geralt's sword was already in his hand, from the moment the water had begun to swell, so now he merely twisted confidently at the hips and slashed the monster across its drooping, scaly dewlap. He immediately turned the other way, where another creature was churning up the water. It was wearing a bizarre helmet and something resembling a suit of armour made of tarnished copper. The Witcher parried the blade of the short spear being thrust towards him with a broad sweep of his sword and with the momentum the parry gave him struck across the ichthyoid-reptilian toothy muzzle. He leapt aside towards the edge of the shelf, splashing water.

'Fly, Dandelion!'

'Give me your hand!'

'Fly, dammit!'

Another creature emerged from the water, the curved sword whistling in its rough green hands. The Witcher thrust his back against the edge of the shellfish-covered rock, assumed a fighting position, but the fish-eyed creature did not approach. It was the same height as Geralt. The water also reached to its waist, but the impressively puffed-up comb on its head and its dilated gills gave the impression of greater size. The grimace distorting the broad maw armed with teeth was deceptively similar to a cruel smile.

The creature, paying no attention to the two twitching bodies floating in the red water, raised its sword, gripping the long hilt without a cross guard in both hands. Puffing up its comb and gills even more, it deftly spun the blade in the air. Geralt heard the light blade hiss and whirr.

The creature took a pace forward, sending a wave towards the Witcher. Geralt took a swing and whirled his sword in response. And also took a step, taking up the challenge.

The fish-eyed creature deftly twisted its long clawed fingers on the hilt and slowly lowered its arms, which were protected by tortoiseshell and copper, and plunged them up to its elbows, concealing the weapon beneath the water. The Witcher grasped his sword in both hands; his right hand just below the cross guard, his left by the pommel, and lifted the weapon up and a little to the side, above his right shoulder. He looked into the monster's eyes, but they were the iridescent eyes of a fish, eyes with spherical irises, glistening coldly and metallically. Eyes which neither expressed nor betrayed anything. Nothing that might warn of an attack.

From the depths at the bottom of the steps, disappearing into the black chasm, came the sound of a bell. Closer and closer, more and more distinct.

The fish-eyed creature lunged forward, pulling its blade from under the water, attacking as swiftly as a thought, with a montante thrust. Geralt was simply lucky; he had expected the blow to be dealt from the right. He parried with his blade directed downwards, powerfully twisting his body, and rotated his sword, meeting the monster's sword flat. Now everything depended on which of them would twist their fingers more quickly on the hilt, who would be first to move from the flat, static impasse of the blades to a blow, a blow whose force was now being generated by both of them, by shifting their bodyweight to the appropriate leg. Geralt already knew they were as fast as each other.

But the fish-eyed creature had longer fingers.

The Witcher struck it in the side, above the hips, twisted into a half-turn, smote, pressing down on the blade, and easily dodged a wide, chaotic, desperate and clumsy blow. The monster, noiselessly opening its ichthyoid mouth, disappeared beneath the water, which was pulsating with crimson clouds.

'Give me your hand! Quickly!' Dandelion yelled. 'They're coming, a whole gang of them! I can see them!'

The Witcher seized the bard's right hand and hauled him out of the water onto the rocky shelf. A broad wave splashed behind him.

The tide had turned.

They fled swiftly, pursued by the swelling wave. Geralt looked back and saw numerous other fish-like creatures bursting from the water, saw them giving chase, leaping nimbly on their muscular legs. Without a word he speeded up.

Dandelion was panting, running heavily and splashing around the now knee-high water. He suddenly stumbled and fell, sloshing among the bladder wrack, supporting himself on trembling arms. Geralt caught him by the belt and hauled him out of the foam, now seething all around them.

'Run!' he cried. 'I'll hold them back!'

'Geralt—'

'Run, Dandelion! The water's about to fill the rift and then we won't get out of here! Run for your life!'

Dandelion groaned and ran. The Witcher ran after him, hoping the monsters would become strung out in the chase. He knew he had no chance taking on the entire group.

They chased him just beside the rift, because the water there was deep enough for them to swim, while he was clambering the slippery rocks with difficulty, wallowing in the foam. In the rift, however, it was too tight for them to assail him from all sides. He stopped in the basin where Dandelion had found the skull.

He stopped and turned around. And calmed down.

He struck the first with the very tip of his sword, where the temple would have been on a man. He split open the belly of the next one, which was armed with something resembling a short battle-axe. A third fled.

The Witcher rushed up the gorge, but at the same time a surging wave boomed, erupting in foam, seethed in an eddy in the vent, tore him off the rocks and dragged him downwards, into the boiling water. He collided with a fishy creature flapping about in the eddy, and thrust it away with a kick. Something caught him by his legs and pulled him down, towards the seafloor. He hit the rock on his back, opened his eyes just in time to see the dark shapes of the creatures, two swift blurs. He parried the first blur with his sword, and instinctively protected himself from the second by raising his left arm. He felt a blow, pain, and immediately afterwards the sharp sting of salt. He pushed off from the bottom with his feet, splashed upwards towards the surface, formed his fingers together and released a Sign. The explosion was dull and stabbed his ears with a brief paroxysm of pain. If I get out of this, he thought, beating the water with his arms and legs, if I get out of this, I'll ride to Yen in Vengerberg and I'll try again . . . If I get out of this . . .

He thought he could hear the booming of a trumpet. Or a horn.

The tidal wave, exploding again in the chimney, lifted him up and tossed him out on his belly onto a large rock. Now he could clearly hear a booming horn and Dandelion's cries, seemingly coming from all sides at once. He snorted the saltwater from his nose and looked around, tossing his wet hair from his face.

He was on the shore, right where they had set out from. He was lying belly-down on the rocks, and a breaker was seething white foam around him.

Behind him, in the gorge – now a narrow bay – a large grey dolphin danced on the waves. On its back, tossing her wet, willow-green hair, sat the mermaid. She still had beautiful breasts.

'White Hair!' she sang, waving a hand which was holding a large, conical, spirally twisting conch. 'Are you in one piece?'

'Yes,' the Witcher said in amazement. The foam around him had become pink. His left arm had stiffened and was stinging from the salt. His jacket sleeve was cut, straight and evenly, and blood was gushing from the cut. I got out of it, he thought, I pulled it off again. But no, I'm not going anywhere.

He saw Dandelion, who was running towards him, stumbling over the wet pebbles.

'I've held them back!' the mermaid sang, and sounded the conch again. 'But not for long! Flee and return here no more, White Hair! The sea . . . is not for you!'

'I know!' he shouted back. 'I know. Thank you, Sh'eenaz!'

VII

'Dandelion,' Little Eye said, tearing the end of the bandage with her teeth and tying a knot on Geralt's wrist. 'Explain to me how a pile of snail shells ended up at the bottom of the stairs? Drouhard's wife is clearing them up right now and is making it clear what she thinks of you two.'

'Shells?' Dandelion asked. 'What shells? I have no idea. Perhaps some passing ducks dropped them?'

Geralt smiled, turning his head toward the shadow. He smiled at the memory of Dandelion's curses; he had spent the entire afternoon opening shells and rummaging around in the slippery flesh, during which process he had nicked himself and soiled his shirt, but hadn't found a single pearl. And no small wonder, as they weren't pearl oysters at all, but ordinary scallops and mussels. They abandoned the idea of making soup from the shellfish when Dandelion opened the first shell; the mollusc looked unappealing and stank to high heaven.

Little Eye finished bandaging him and sat down on an upturned tub. The Witcher thanked her, examining his neatly bandaged arm. The wound was deep and quite long, extending as far as the elbow, and intensely painful when he moved it. He had put on a makeshift dressing by the seashore, but before they had got back it had begun to bleed again. Just before the girl arrived, Geralt had poured a coagulating elixir onto his mutilated forearm, and boosted it with an anaesthetic elixir, and Essi had caught them just as he and Dandelion were suturing the wound using a fishing line tied to a hook. Little Eye swore at them and got down to making a dressing herself, while Dandelion regaled her with a colourful tale of the fight, several times reserving himself the exclusive right to compose a ballad about the whole incident. Essi, naturally, flooded Geralt with an avalanche of questions, which he was unable to answer. She took that badly, and evidently had the impression he was concealing something from her. She became sullen and ceased her questioning.

'Agloval already knows,' she said. 'You were seen returning, and Mrs Drouhard ran off to spread the word when she saw the blood on the stairs. The people dashed towards the rocks, hoping the sea would toss something out. They're still hanging around there, but haven't found anything, from what I know.'

'Nor will they,' the Witcher said. 'I shall visit Agloval tomorrow, but ask him, if you would, to forbid people from hanging around the Dragons Fangs. Just not a word, please, about those steps or Dandelion's fantasies about the city of Ys. Treasure and sensation hunters would immediately go, and there'll be further deaths—'

'I'm not a gossip,' Essi said sulkily, sharply tossing her lock from her forehead. 'If I ask you something it isn't in order to dash off to the well at once and blab it to the washerwomen.'

'I'm sorry.'

'I must go,' Dandelion suddenly said. 'I've got a rendezvous with Akeretta. Geralt, I'm taking your jerkin, because mine is incredibly filthy and wet.'

'Everything here is wet,' Little Eye said sneeringly, nudging the articles of clothing strewn around with the tip of her shoe in disgust. 'How can you? They need to be hung up and properly dried . . . You're dreadful.'

'It'll dry off by itself,' Dandelion pulled on Geralt's damp jacket and examined the silver studs on the sleeves with delight.

'Don't talk rubbish. And what's this? Oh, no, that bag is still full of sludge and seaweed! And this – what's this? Yuck!'

Geralt and Dandelion silently observed the cobalt blue shell Essi was holding between two fingers. They had forgotten. The mollusc was slightly open and clearly reeked.

'It's a present,' the troubadour said, moving back towards the door. 'It's your birthday tomorrow, isn't it, Poppet? Well, that's a present for you.'

'This?'

'Pretty, isn't it?' Dandelion sniffed it and added quickly. 'It's from Geralt. He chose it for you. Oh, is that the time? Farewell . . .'

Little Eye was quiet for a moment after he had gone. The Witcher looked at the stinking shellfish and felt ashamed. Of Dandelion and of himself.

'Did you remember my birthday?' Essi asked slowly, holding the shell at arm's length. 'Really?'

'Give it to me,' he said sharply. He got up from the palliasse, protecting his bandaged arm. 'I apologise for that idiot . . .'

'No,' she protested, removing a small knife from a sheath at her belt. 'It really is a pretty shell, I'll keep it as a memento. It only needs cleaning, after I've got rid of the . . . contents. I'll throw them out of the window, the cats can eat them.'

Something clattered on the floor and rolled away. Geralt widened his pupils and saw what it was long before Essi.

It was a pearl. An exquisitely iridescent and shimmering pearl of faintly blue colour, as big as a swollen pea.

'By the Gods.' Little Eye had also caught sight of it. 'Geralt . . . A pearl!'

'A pearl,' he laughed. 'And so you did get a present, Essi. I'm glad.'

'Geralt, I can't accept it. That pearl is worth . . .'

'It's yours,' he interrupted. 'Dandelion, though he plays the fool, really did remember your birthday. He really wanted to please you. He talked about it, talked aloud about it. Well, fate heard him and did what had to be done.'

'And you, Geralt?'

'Me?'

'Did you . . . also want to please me? That pearl is so beautiful . . . It must be hugely valuable – don't you regret it?'

'I'm pleased you like it. And if I regret anything, it's that there was only one. And that . . .'

'Yes?'

'That I haven't known you as long as Dandelion, long enough to be able to know and remember your birthday. To be able to give you presents and please you. To be able to call you Poppet.'

She moved closer and suddenly threw her arms around his neck. He nimbly and swiftly anticipated her movement, dodged her lips and kissed her coldly on the cheek, embracing her with his unin-jured arm, clumsily, with reserve, gently. He felt the girl stiffen and slowly move back, but only to the length of her arms, which were still resting on his shoulders. He knew what she was waiting for, but did not do it. He did not draw her towards him.

Essi let him go and turned towards the open, dirty little window.

'Of course,' she said suddenly. 'You barely know me. I forgot that you barely know me.'

'Essi,' he said after a moment's silence. 'I—'

'I barely know you either,' she blurted, interrupting him. 'What of it? I love you. I can't help it. Not at all.'

'Essi!'

'Yes. I love you, Geralt. I don't care what you think. I've loved you from the moment I saw you at that engagement party . . .'

She broke off, lowering her head.

She stood before him and Geralt regretted it was her and not the fish-eyed creature with a sword who had been hidden beneath the water. He had stood a chance against that creature. But against her he had none.

'You aren't saying anything,' she said. 'Nothing, not a word.'

I'm tired, he thought, and bloody weak. I need to sit down, I'm feeling dizzy, I've lost some blood and haven't eaten anything . . . I have to sit down. Damned little attic, he thought, I hope it gets struck by lightning and burns down during the next storm. And there's no bloody furniture, not even two stupid chairs and a table, which divides you, across which you can so easily and safely talk; you can even hold hands. But I have to sit down on the palliasse, have to ask her to sit down beside me. And the palliasse stuffed with bean stalks is dangerous, you can't escape from it, take evasive action.

'Sit beside me, Essi.'

She sat down. Reluctantly. Tactfully. Far away. Too close.

'When I found out,' she whispered, interrupting the long silence, 'when I heard that Dandelion had dragged you onto the beach, bleeding, I ran out of the house like a mad thing, rushed blindly, paying no attention to anything. And then . . . Do you know what

I thought? That it was magic, that you had cast a spell on me, that you had secretly, treacherously bewitched me, spellbound me, with your wolfish medallion, with the evil eye. That's what I thought, but I didn't stop, kept running, because I understood that I desire . . . I desire to fall under your spell. And the reality turned out to be more awful. You didn't cast any spell on me, you didn't use any charms. Why, Geralt? Why didn't you bewitch me?'

He was silent.

'If it had been magic,' she said, 'it would all be so simple and easy. I would have succumbed to your power and I'd be happy. But this . . . I must . . . I don't know what's happening to me . . .'

Dammit, he thought, if Yennefer feels like I do now when she's with me, I feel sorry for her. And I shall never be astonished again. I will never hate her again . . . Never again.

Because perhaps Yennefer feels what I'm feeling now, feels a profound certainty that I ought to fulfil what it is impossible to fulfil, even more impossible to fulfil than the relationship between Agloval and Sh'eenaz. Certainty that a little sacrifice isn't enough here; you'd have to sacrifice everything, and there'd still be no way of knowing if that would be enough. No, I won't continue to hate Yennefer for not being able and not wanting to give me more than a little sacrifice. Now I know that a little sacrifice is a hell of a lot.

'Geralt,' Little Eye moaned, drawing her head into her shoulders. 'I'm so ashamed. I'm ashamed of what I'm feeling, it's like an accursed infirmity, like malaria, like being unable to breathe . . .'

He was silent.

'I always thought it was a beautiful and noble state of mind, noble and dignified, even if it makes one unhappy. After all, I've composed so many ballads about it. And it is organic, Geralt, meanly and heartbreakingly organic. Someone who is ill or who has drunk poison might feel like this. Because like someone who has drunk poison, one is prepared to do anything in exchange for an antidote. Anything. Even be humiliated.'

'Essi. Please . . .'

'Yes. I feel humiliated, humiliated by having confessed everything to you, disregarding the dignity that demands one suffers in silence.

By the fact that my confession caused you embarrassment. I feel humiliated by the fact that you're embarrassed. But I couldn't have behaved any differently. I'm powerless. At your mercy, like someone who's bedridden. I've always been afraid of illness, of being weak, helpless, hopeless and alone. I've always been afraid of sickness, always believing it the worst thing that could befall me . . .'

He was silent.

'I know,' she groaned again. 'I know I ought to be grateful to you for . . . for not taking advantage of the situation. But I'm not grateful to you. And I'm ashamed of it. For I hate your silence, your terrified eyes. I hate you. For staying silent. For not lying, for not . . . And I hate her, that sorceress of yours, I'd happily stab her for . . . I hate her. Make me go, Geralt. Order me to leave here. For of my own free will I cannot, but I want to get out of here, go to the city, to a tavern . . . I want to have my revenge on you for my shame, for the humiliation, I'll go to the first man I find . . .'

Dammit, he thought, hearing her voice dropping like a rag ball rolling down the stairs. She'll burst into tears, he thought, there's no doubt, she'll burst into tears. What to do, what to bloody do?

Essi's hunched up shoulders were trembling hard. The girl turned her head away and began to weep, crying softly, dreadfully calmly and unrelentingly.

I don't feel anything, he noticed with horror, nothing, not the smallest emotion. That fact that I will embrace her is a deliberate, measured response, not a spontaneous one. I'll hug her, for I feel as though I ought to, not because I want to. I feel nothing.

When he embraced her, she stopped crying immediately, wiped away her tears, shaking her head forcefully and turning away so that he could not see her face. And then she pressed herself to him firmly, burying her head in his chest.

A little sacrifice, he thought, just a little sacrifice. For this will calm her, a hug, a kiss, calm caresses. She doesn't want anything more. And even if she did, what of it? For a little sacrifice, a very little sacrifice, is beautiful and worth . . . Were she to want more . . . It would calm her. A quiet, calm, gentle act of love. And I . . .

Why, it doesn't matter, because Essi smells of verbena, not lilac and gooseberry, doesn't have cool, electrifying skin. Essi's hair is not a black tornado of gleaming curls, Essi's eyes are gorgeous, soft, warm and cornflower blue; they don't blaze with a cold, unemotional, deep violet. Essi will fall asleep afterwards, turn her head away, open her mouth slightly, Essi will not smile in triumph. For Essi . . .

Essi is not Yennefer.

And that is why I cannot. I cannot find that little sacrifice inside myself.

'Please, Essi, don't cry.'

'I won't,' she said, moving very slowly away from him. 'I won't. I understand. It cannot be any other way.'

They said nothing, sitting beside each other on the palliasse stuffed with bean stalks. Evening was approaching.

'Geralt,' she suddenly said, and her voice trembled. 'But perhaps . . . Perhaps it would be like it was with that shell, with that curious gift? Perhaps we could find a pearl? Later? When some time has passed?'

'I can see that pearl,' he said with effort, 'set in silver, in a little silver flower with intricate petals. I see it around your neck, on a delicate silver chain, worn like I wear my medallion. That will be your talisman, Essi. A talisman, which will protect you from all evil.'

'My talisman,' she repeated, lowering her head. 'My pearl, which I shall set in silver, and from which I shall never part. My jewel, which I was given instead of . . . Can a talisman like that bring me luck?'

'Yes, Essi. Be sure of it.'

'Can I stay here a little longer? With you?'

'You may.'

Twilight was approaching and dusk falling, and they were sitting on a palliasse stuffed with bean stalks, in the garret, where there was no furniture, where there was only a wooden tub and an unlit candle on the floor, in a puddle of hardened wax.

They sat in utter silence for a very long time. And then Dandelion came. They heard him approaching, strumming his lute and humming to himself. Dandelion entered, saw them and did not say anything, not a word. Essi also said nothing, stood up and went out without looking at them.

Dandelion did not say a word. But the Witcher saw in his eyes the words that remained unsaid.

VIII

'An intelligent race,' Agloval repeated pensively, resting an elbow on the armrest, and his fist on his chin. 'An underwater civilisation. Fishlike people living on the seabed. Steps leading to the depths. Geralt, you take me for a bloody gullible duke.'

Little Eye, standing beside Dandelion, snarled angrily. Dandelion shook his head in disbelief. Geralt was not in the least bothered.

'It makes no difference to me,' he said quietly, 'if you believe me or not. It is, however, my duty to warn you. Any boat that sails towards the Dragons Fangs, or people who appear there when the tide is out, are in danger. Mortal danger. If you want to find out if it's true, if you want to risk it, that's your business. I'm simply warning you.'

'Ha,' the steward Zelest, who was sitting in a window seat behind Agloval, suddenly said. 'If they are monsters the like of elves or other goblins, we don't need to worry. We feared it was something worse, or, God save us, something magical. From what the Witcher says, they are some kind of sea drowners or other sea monsters. There are ways of dealing with drowners. I heard tell that one sorcerer gave some drowners short shrift in Lake Mokva. He poured a small barrel of magical philtre into the water and did for the fuckers. Didn't leave a trace.'

'That's true,' Drouhard said, who up to then had been silent. 'There wasn't a trace. Nor a trace of bream, pike, crayfish or mussels. Even the waterweed on the lake floor rotted away and the alders on the bank withered.'

'Capital,' Agloval said derisively. 'Thank you for that excellent suggestion, Zelest. Do you have any more?'

'Aye, fair enough,' the steward said, blushing. 'The wizard over-did it a mite with his wand, waved it about a jot too much. But we

235

ought to manage without wizards too, Your Grace. The Witcher says that one can fight those monsters and also kill 'em. That's war, sire. Like the old days. Nothing new there, eh? Werelynxes lived in the mountains, and where are they now? Wild elves and eerie wives still roam the forests, but there'll soon be an end to that. We'll secure what is ours. As our granddaddies . . .'

'And only my grandchildren will see the pearls?' The duke grimaced. 'It is too long to wait, Zelest.'

'Well, it won't be that bad. Seems to me it's like this: two boats of archers to each boat of divers. We'll soon learn those monsters some sense. Learn them some fear. Am I right, Witcher, sir?'

Geralt looked coldly at him, but did not respond.

Agloval turned his head away, showing his noble profile, and bit his lip. Then he looked at the Witcher, narrowing his eyes and frowning.

'You didn't complete your task, Geralt,' he said. 'You fouled things up again. You had good intentions, I can't deny that. But I don't pay for good intentions. I pay for results. For the effect. And the effect, excuse the expression, is shitty. So you earn shit.'

'Marvellous, Your Grace,' Dandelion jibed. 'Pity you weren't with us at the Dragons Fangs. The Witcher and I might have given you the opportunity for an encounter with one of those from the sea, sword in hand. Perhaps then you would understand what this is about, and stop bickering about payment—'

'Like a fishwife,' Little Eye interjected.

'I am not accustomed to bickering, bargaining or discussing,' Agloval said calmly. 'I said I shall not pay you a penny, Geralt. The agreement ran: remove the danger, remove the threat, enable the fishing of pearls without any risk to people. But you? You come and tell me about an intelligent race from the seabed. You advise me to stay away from the place which brings me profit. What did you do? You reputedly killed . . . How many?'

'It matters not how many,' Geralt said, blanching slightly. 'At least, not to you, Agloval.'

'Precisely. Particularly since there is no proof. If you had at least brought the right hands of those fish-toads, who knows, perhaps I would have splashed out on the normal fee my forester takes for a pair of wolf's ears.'

'Well,' the Witcher said coldly. 'I'm left with no choice but to say farewell.'

'You are mistaken,' the duke said. 'Something does remain. Permanent work for quite decent coin and lodgings. The position and ticket of skipper of my armed guard, which from now on will accompany the divers. It does not have to be forever, but only until your reputed intelligent race gains enough good sense to keep well away from my boats, to avoid them like the plague. What do you say?'

'No thank you, I decline,' the Witcher grimaced. 'A job like that doesn't suit me. I consider waging war against other races idiocy. Perhaps it's excellent sport for bored and jaded dukes. But not for me.'

'Oh, how proud,' Agloval smiled. 'How haughty. You reject offers in a way some kings wouldn't be ashamed of. You give up decent money with the air of a wealthy man after a lavish dinner. Geralt? Did you have lunch today? No? And tomorrow? And the day after? I see little chance, Witcher, very little. It's difficult for you to find work normally and now, with your arm in a sling—'

'How dare you!' Little Eye cried shrilly. 'How dare you speak like that to him, Agloval! The arm he now carries in a sling was cut carrying out your mission! How can you be so base—'

'Stop it,' Geralt said. 'Stop, Essi. There's no point.'

'Not true,' she said angrily. 'There *is* a point. Someone has to tell it straight to this self-appointed duke, who took advantage of the fact that no one was challenging him for the title deed to rule this scrap of rocky coastline, and who now thinks he has the right to insult other people.'

Agloval flushed and tightened his lips, but said nothing and did not move.

'Yes, Agloval,' Essi continued, clenching her shaking hands into fists. 'The opportunity to insult other people amuses and pleases you. You delight in the contempt you can show the Witcher, who is prepared to risk his neck for your money. You should know the

Witcher mocks your contempt and slights, that they do not make the faintest impression on him. He doesn't even notice them. No, the Witcher does not even feel what your servants and subjects, Zelest and Drouhard, feel, and they feel shame, deep, burning shame. The Witcher doesn't feel what Dandelion and I feel, and we feel revulsion. Do you know why that is, Agloval? I'll tell you. The Witcher knows he is superior. He is worthier than you. And that gives him his strength.'

Essi fell silent and lowered her head, but not quickly enough for Geralt not to see the tear which sparkled in the corner of her gorgeous eye. The girl touched the little flower with silver petals hanging around her neck, the flower in the centre of which nestled a large, sky blue pearl. The little flower had intricate, plaited petals, executed in masterly fashion. Drouhard, the Witcher thought, had come up trumps. The craftsman he had recommended did a good job. And had not taken a penny from them. Drouhard had paid for everything.

'So, Your Grace,' Little Eye continued, raising her head, 'don't make a fool of yourself by offering the Witcher the role of a mercenary in an army you plan to field against the ocean. Don't expose yourself to ridicule, for your suggestion could only prompt mirth. Don't you understand yet? You can pay the Witcher for carrying out a task, you can hire him to protect people from evil, to remove the danger that threatens them. But you cannot buy the Witcher, you cannot use him to your own ends. Because the Witcher – even wounded and hungry – is better than you. Has more worth. That is why he scorns your meagre offer. Do you understand?'

'No, Miss Daven,' Agloval said coldly. 'I do not understand. On the contrary, I understand less and less. And the fundamental thing I indeed do not understand is why I have not yet ordered your entire trio hanged, after having you thrashed with a scourge and scorched with red-hot irons. You, Miss Daven, are endeavouring to give the impression of somebody who knows everything. Tell me, then, why I do not do that.'

'As you please,' the poet shot back at once. 'You do not do that, Agloval, because somewhere, deep inside, glimmers in you a little spark of decency, a scrap of honour, not yet stifled by the vainglory of a nouveau riche and petty trader. Inside, Agloval. At the bottom of your heart. A heart which, after all, is capable of loving a mermaid.'

Agloval went as white as a sheet and gripped the armrests of his chair. Bravo, the Witcher thought, bravo, Essi, wonderful. He was proud of her. But at the same time he felt sorrow, tremendous sorrow.

'Go away,' Agloval said softly. 'Go away. Wherever you wish. Leave me in peace.'

'Farewell, duke,' Essi said. 'And on parting accept some good advice. Advice which the Witcher ought to be giving you; but I don't want him to stoop to giving you advice. So I'll do it for him.'

'Very well.'

'The ocean is immense, Agloval. No one has explored what lies beyond the horizon, if anything is there at all. The ocean is bigger than any wilderness, deep into which you have driven the elves. It is less accessible than any mountains or ravines where you have massacred werelynxes. And on the floor of the ocean dwells a race which uses weapons and knows the arcana of metalworking. Beware, Agloval. If archers begin to sail with the pearl divers, you will begin a war with something you don't understand. What you mean to disturb may turn out to be a hornets' nest. I advise you, leave them the sea, for the sea is not for you. You don't know and will never know whither lead those steps, which go down to the bottom of the Dragons Fangs.'

'You are mistaken, Miss Daven,' Agloval said calmly. 'We shall learn whither lead those steps. Further, we shall descend those steps. We shall find out what is on that side of the ocean, if there is anything there at all. And we shall draw from the ocean everything we can. And if not we, then our grandsons will do it, or our grandsons' grandsons. It is just a matter of time. Yes, we shall do it, though the ocean will run red with blood. And you know it, Essi, O wise Essi, who writes the chronicles of humanity in your ballads. Life is not a ballad, O poor, little gorgeous-eyed poet, lost among her fine words. Life is a battle. And we were taught that struggle by these witchers, whose worth is greater than ours. It was they who showed us the way, who paved the way for us. They strewed the path with the corpses of those who stood in the way of humans, and defended that world from us. We, Essi, are only continuing that battle. It is we, not your ballads, who create the chronicles of humanity. And we no longer need witchers, and now nothing will stop us. Nothing.'

Essi blanched, blew her lock away and tossed her head.

'Nothing, Agloval?'

'Nothing, Essi.'

The poet smiled.

A sudden noise, shouts and stamping, came from the anterooms. Pages and guards rushed into the chamber. They knelt or bowed by the door in two rows. Sh'eenaz stood in the doorway.

Her willow-green hair was elaborately coiffured, pinned up with a marvellous circlet encrusted with coral and pearls. She was in a gown the colour of seawater, with frills as white as foam. The gown had a plunging neckline, so that the mermaid's charms, though partly concealed and decorated with a necklace of nephrite and lapis lazuli, still earned the highest admiration.

'Sh'eenaz . . .' Agloval groaned, dropping to his knees. 'My . . . Sh'eenaz . . .'

The mermaid slowly came closer and her gait was soft and graceful, as fluid as an approaching wave.

She stopped in front of the duke, flashed her delicate, white, little teeth in a smile, then quickly gathered her gown in her small hands and lifted it, quite high, high enough for everyone to be able to judge the quality of the marine sorceress, the sea witch. Geralt swallowed. There was no doubt: the sea witch knew what shapely legs were and how to make them.

'Ha!' Dandelion cried. 'My ballad . . . It is just like in my ballad . . . She has gained legs for him, but has lost her voice!'

'I have lost nothing,' Sh'eenaz said melodiously in the purest Common Speech. 'For the moment. I am as good as new after the operation.'

'You speak our tongue?'

'What, mayn't I? How are you, White Hair? Oh, and your

beloved one, Essi Daven, if I recall, is here. Do you know her better or still barely?'

'Sh'eenaz . . .' Agloval groaned heartrendingly, moving towards her on his knees. 'My love! My beloved . . . my only . . . And so, at last. At last, Sh'eenaz!'

With a graceful movement the mermaid proffered her hand to be kissed.

'Indeed. Because I love you too, you loon. And what kind of love would it be if the one who loves were not capable of a little sacrifice?'

IX

They left Bremervoord early on a cool morning, among fog which dulled the intensity of the red sun rolling out from below the horizon. They rode as a threesome, as they had agreed. They did not talk about it, they were making no plans – they simply wanted to be together. For some time.

They left the rocky headland, bade farewell to the precipitous, jagged cliffs above the beaches, the fantastic limestone formations carved out by the sea and gales. But as they rode into the green, flower-strewn valley of Dol Adalatte, they still had the scent of the sea in their nostrils, and in their ears the roar of breakers and the piercing, urgent cries of seagulls.

Dandelion talked ceaselessly, hopping from one subject to another and virtually not finishing any. He talked about the Land of Barsa, where a stupid custom required girls to guard their chastity until marriage; about the iron birds of the island of Inis Porhoet; about living water and dead water; about the taste and curious properties of the sapphire wine called 'cill'; and about the royal quadruplets of Ebbing – dreadful, exasperating brats called Putzi, Gritzi, Mitzi and Juan Pablo Vassermiller. He talked about new trends in poetry promoted by his rivals, which were, in Dandelion's opinion, phantoms simulating the movements of the living.

Geralt remained silent. Essi also said nothing or replied in monosyllables. The Witcher felt her gaze on him. He avoided her eyes.

They crossed the River Adalatte on the ferry, having to pull the ropes themselves, since the ferryman happened to be in a pathetic drunken state of deathly white, rigid-trembling, gazing-into-the-abyss pallor, unable to let go of the pillar in his porch, which he was clinging to with both hands, and answering every question they asked him with a single word, which sounded like 'voorg'.

242

The Witcher had taken a liking to the country on the far side of the Adalatte; the riverside villages were mainly surrounded by palisades, which portended a certain likelihood of finding work.

Little Eye walked over to him while they were watering the horses in the early afternoon, taking advantage of the fact that Dandelion had wandered off. The Witcher was not quick enough. She surprised him.

'Geralt,' she said softly. 'I can't . . . I can't bear this. I don't have the strength.'

He tried to avoid the necessity of looking her in the eye, but she would not let him. She stood in front of him, toying with the sky blue pearl set in a small, silver flower hanging around her neck. She stood like that and he wished again that it was the fish-eyed creature with its sword hidden beneath the water in front of him.

'Geralt . . . We have to do something about this, don't we?'

She waited for his answer. For some words. For a little sacrifice. But the Witcher had nothing he could sacrifice and he knew it. He did not want to lie. And he truly did not have it in him, because he could not find the courage to cause her pain.

The situation was saved by the sudden appearance of Dandelion, dependable Dandelion. Dandelion with his dependable tact.

'Of course!' he yelled and heaved into the water the stick he had been using to part the rushes and the huge, riverside nettles. 'And of course you have to do something about it, it's high time! I have no wish to watch what is going on between you any longer! What do you expect from him, Poppet? The impossible? And you, Geralt, what are you hoping for? That Little Eye will read your thoughts like . . . like the other one? And she will settle for that, and you will conveniently stay quiet, not having to explain, declare or deny anything? And not have to reveal yourself? How much time, how many facts do you both need, to understand? And when you'll want to recall it in a few years, in your memories? I mean we have to part tomorrow, dammit!

'I've had enough, by the Gods, I'm up to here with you, up to here! Very well, listen: I'm going to break myself off a hazel rod and go fishing, and you will have some time to yourselves, you'll be able to tell each other everything. Tell each other everything, try to understand each other. It is not as difficult as you think. And after that, by the Gods, do it. Do it with him, Poppet. Do it with her, Geralt, and be good to her. And then, you'll either bloody get over it, or . . .'

Dandelion turned around rapidly and walked away, breaking reeds and cursing. He made a rod from a hazel branch and horsehair and fished until dusk fell.

After he had walked off, Geralt and Essi stood for a long time, leaning against a misshapen willow tree bent over the water. They stood, holding hands. Then the Witcher spoke, spoke softly for a long time, and Little Eye's little eye was full of tears.

And then, by the Gods, they did it, she and he.

And everything was all right.

X

The next day they organised something of a ceremonial supper. Essi and Geralt bought a dressed lamb in a village they passed through. While they were haggling, Dandelion surreptitiously stole some garlic, onions and carrots from the vegetable patch behind the cottage. As they were riding away they also swiped a pot from the fence behind the smithy. The pot was a little leaky, but the Witcher soldered it using the Igni Sign.

The supper took place in a clearing deep in the forest. The fire crackled merrily and the pot bubbled. Geralt carefully stirred the stew with a star-shaped stirrer made from the top of a spruce tree stripped of bark. Dandelion peeled the onions and carrots. Little Eye, who had no idea about cooking, made the time more pleasant by playing the lute and singing racy couplets.

It was a ceremonial supper. For they were going to part in the morning. In the morning each of them was going to go their own way; in search of something they already had. But they did not know they had it, they could not even imagine it. They could not imagine where the roads they were meant to set off on the next morning would lead. Each of them travelling separately.

After they had eaten, and drunk the beer Drouhard had given them, they gossiped and laughed, and Dandelion and Essi held a singing contest. Geralt lay on a makeshift bed of spruce branches with his hands under his head and thought he had never heard such beautiful voices or such beautiful ballads. He thought about Yennefer. He thought about Essi, too. He had a presentiment that . . .

At the end, Little Eye and Dandelion sang the celebrated duet of Cynthia and Vertvern, a wonderful song of love, beginning with the words: '*Many tears have I shed . . .*' It seemed to Geralt that even the trees bent down to listen to the two of them.

Then Little Eye, smelling of verbena, lay down beside him, squeezed in under his arm, wriggled her head onto his chest, sighed maybe once or twice and fell peacefully asleep. The Witcher fell asleep, much, much later.

Dandelion, staring into the dying embers, sat much longer, alone, quietly strumming his lute.

It began with a few bars, from which an elegant, soothing melody emerged. The lyric suited the melody, and came into being simultaneously with it, the words blending into the music, becoming set in it like insects in translucent, golden lumps of amber.

The ballad told of a certain witcher and a certain poet. About how the witcher and the poet met on the seashore, among the crying of seagulls, and how they fell in love at first sight. About how beautiful and powerful was their love. About how nothing – not even death – was able to destroy that love and part them.

Dandelion knew that few would believe the story told by the ballad, but he was not concerned. He knew ballads were not written to be believed, but to move their audience.

Several years later, Dandelion could have changed the contents of the ballad and written about what had really occurred. He did not. For the true story would not have moved anyone. Who would have wanted to hear that the Witcher and Little Eye parted and never, ever, saw each other again? About how four years later Little Eye died of the smallpox during an epidemic raging in Vizima? About how he, Dandelion, had carried her out in his arms between corpses being cremated on funeral pyres and had buried her far from the city, in the forest, alone and peaceful, and, as she had asked, buried two things with her: her lute and her sky blue pearl. The pearl from which she was never parted.

No, Dandelion stuck with his first version. And he never sang it. Never. To no one.

Right before the dawn, while it was still dark, a hungry, vicious werewolf crept up to their camp, but saw that it was Dandelion, so he listened for a moment and then went on his way.

THE SWORD OF DESTINY

I

He found the first body around noon.

The sight of victims of violent death seldom shocked the Witcher; much more often he looked at corpses with total indifference. This time he was not indifferent.

The boy was around fifteen. He was lying on his back, legs sprawled, his face frozen in a grimace of terror. In spite of that Geralt knew the boy had died at once, had not suffered, and probably had not even known he was dying. The arrow had struck him in the eye and was driven deep into the skull, through the occipital bone. The arrow was fletched with striped, pheasant flight feathers dyed yellow. The shaft stuck up above the tufts of grass.

Geralt looked around, and quickly and easily found what he was hunting for. A second, identical arrow, lodged in the trunk of a pine tree, around six paces behind the corpse. He knew what had happened. The boy had not understood the warning, and hearing the whistle and thud of the arrow had panicked and begun to run the wrong way. Towards the one who had ordered him to stop and withdraw at once. The hissing, venomous, feathered whistle and the short thud of the arrowhead cutting into the wood. *Not a step further, man,* said that whistle and that thud. *Begone, man, get out of Brokilon at once. You have captured the whole world, man, you are everywhere. Everywhere you introduce what you call modernity, the era of change, what you call progress. But we want neither you nor your progress here. We do not desire the changes you bring. We do not desire anything you bring. A whistle and a thud. Get out of Brokilon!*

Get out of Brokilon, thought Geralt. *Man*. No matter that you are fifteen and struggling through the forest, insane with fear, unable to find your way home. No matter that you are seventy and have to gather brushwood, because otherwise they will drive you from the cottage for being useless, they will stop giving you food. No matter that you are six and you were lured by a carpet of little blue flowers in a sunny clearing. *Get out of Brokilon!* A whistle and a thud.

Long ago, thought Geralt, before they shot to kill, they gave two warnings. Even three.

Long ago, he thought, continuing on his way. Long ago.

Well, that's progress.

The forest did not seem to deserve the dreadful notoriety it enjoyed. It was terribly wild and arduous to march through, but it was the commonplace arduousness of a dense forest, where every gap, every patch of sunlight filtered by the boughs and leafy branches of huge trees, was immediately exploited by dozens of young birches, alders and hornbeams, by brambles, junipers and ferns, their tangle of shoots covering the crumbly mire of rotten wood, dry branches and decayed trunks of the oldest trees, the ones that had lost the fight, the ones that had lived out their lifespan. The thicket, however, did not generate the ominous, weighty silence which would have suited the place more. No, Brokilon was alive. Insects buzzed, lizards rustled the grass underfoot, iridescent beetles scuttled, thousands of spiders tugged webs glistening with drops of water, woodpeckers thumped tree trunks with sharp series of raps and jays screeched.

Brokilon was alive.

But the Witcher did not let himself be deceived. He knew where he was. He remembered the boy with the arrow in his eye. He had occasionally seen white bones with red ants crawling over them among the moss and pine needles.

He walked on, cautiously but swiftly. The trail was fresh. He hoped to reach and send back the men walking in front of him. He deluded himself that it was not too late.

But it was.

He would not have noticed the next corpse had it not been for the sunlight reflecting on the blade of the short sword it was gripping.

It was a grown man. His simple clothing, coloured a practical dun, indicated his lowly status. His garments – not counting the blood stains surrounding the two feathers sticking into his chest – were clean and new, so he could not have been a common servant.

Geralt looked around and saw a third body, dressed in a leather jacket and short, green cape. The ground around the dead man's legs was churned up, the moss and pine needles were furrowed right down to the sand. There was no doubt; this man had taken a long time to die.

He heard a groan.

He quickly parted the juniper bushes and saw the deep tree throw they were concealing. A powerfully built man, with black, curly hair and beard contrasting with the dreadful, downright deathly pallor of his face, was lying in the hollow on the exposed roots of the pine. His pale, deerskin kaftan was red with blood.

The Witcher jumped into the hollow. The wounded man opened his eyes.

'Geralt . . .' he groaned. 'O, ye Gods . . . I must be dreaming . . .'

'Frexinet?' the Witcher asked in astonishment. 'You, here?'

'Yes, me . . . Ooooow . . .'

'Don't move,' Geralt said, kneeling beside him. 'Where were you hit? I can't see the arrow . . .'

'It passed . . . right through. I broke off the arrowhead and pulled it out . . . Listen Geralt—'

'Be quiet, Frexinet, or you'll choke on your blood. You have a punctured lung. A pox on it, I have to get you out of here. What the bloody hell were you doing in Brokilon? It's dryad territory, their sanctuary, no one gets out of here alive. I can't believe you didn't know that.'

'Later . . .' Frexinet groaned and spat blood. 'I'll tell you later . . . Now get me out. Oh, a pox on it. Have a care . . . Oooooow . . .'

'I can't do it,' Geralt said, straightening up and looking around. 'You're too heavy.'

'Leave me,' the wounded man grunted. 'Leave me, too bad . . . But save her . . . by the Gods, save her . . .'

'Who?'

'The princess . . . Oh . . . Find her, Geralt.'

'Lie still, dammit! I'll knock something up and haul you out.'

Frexinet coughed hard and spat again; a viscous, stretching thread of blood hung from his chin. The Witcher cursed, vaulted out of the hollow and looked around. He needed two young saplings. He moved quickly towards the edge of the clearing, where he had seen a clump of alders.

A whistle and thud.

Geralt froze to the spot. The arrow, buried in a tree trunk at head height, had hawk feather fletchings. He looked at the angle of the ashen shaft and knew where it had been shot from. About four dozen paces away there was another hollow, a fallen tree, and a tangle of roots sticking up in the air, still tightly gripping a huge lump of sandy earth. There was a dark mass of blackthorn there amid the lighter stripes of birches. He could not see anyone. He knew he would not.

He raised both hands, very slowly.

'Ceádmil! Vá an Eithné meáth e Duén Canell! Esseá Gwynbleidd!'

This time he heard the soft twang of the bowstring and saw the arrow, for it had been shot for him to see. Powerfully. He watched it soar upwards, saw it reach its apex and then fall in a curve. He did not move. The arrow plunged into the moss almost vertically, two paces from him. Almost immediately a second lodged next to the first, at exactly the same angle. He was afraid he might not see the next one.

'Meáth Eithné!' he called again. 'Esseá Gwynbleidd!'

'Gláeddyv vort!' A voice like a breath of wind. A voice, not an arrow. He was alive. He slowly unfastened his belt buckle, drew his sword well away from himself and threw it down. A second dryad emerged noiselessly from behind a fir trunk wrapped around with juniper bushes, no more than ten paces from him. Although she was small and very slim, the trunk seemed thinner. He had no idea how he had not seen her as he approached. Perhaps her outfit had disguised her; a patchwork which accentuated her shapely form, sewn weirdly from scraps of fabric in numerous shades of green and brown, strewn with leaves and pieces of bark. Her hair, tied with a black scarf around her forehead, was olive green and her face was criss-crossed with stripes painted using walnut-shell dye.

Naturally, her bowstring was taut and she was aiming an arrow at him.

'Eithné . . .' he began.

'Tháess aep!'

He obediently fell silent, standing motionless, holding his arms away from his trunk. The dryad did not lower her bow.

'Dunca!' she cried. 'Braenn! Caemm vort!'

The one who had shot the arrows earlier darted out from the blackthorn and slipped over the upturned trunk, nimbly clearing the depression. Although there was a pile of dry branches in it Geralt did not hear even one snap beneath her feet. He heard a faint murmur close behind, something like the rustling of leaves in the wind. He knew there was a third.

It was that one, dashing out from behind him, who picked up his sword. Her hair was the colour of honey and was tied up with a band of bulrush fibres. A quiver full of arrows swung on her back.

The furthest one approached the tree throw swiftly. Her outfit was identical to that of her companions. She wore a garland woven from clover and heather on her dull, brick-red hair. She was holding a bow, not bent, but with an arrow nocked.

'T'en thesse in meáth aep Eithné llev?' she asked, coming over. Her voice was extremely melodious and her eyes huge and black. 'Ess' Gwynbleidd?'

'Aé . . . aesseá . . .' he began, but the words in the Brokilon dialect, which sounded like singing in the dryad's mouth, stuck in his throat and made his lips itchy. 'Do none of you know the Common Speech? I don't speak your—'

'An' váill. Vort llinge,' she cut him off.

'I am Gwynbleidd. White Wolf. Lady Eithné knows me. I am travelling to her as an envoy. I have been in Brokilon before. In Duén Canell.'

'Gwynbleidd.' The redhead narrowed her eyes. 'Vatt'ghern?'

'Yes,' he confirmed. 'The Witcher.'

The olive-haired one snorted angrily, but lowered her bow. The red-haired one looked at him with eyes wide open, but her face – smeared with green stripes – was quite motionless, expressionless, like that of a statue. The immobility meant her face could not be categorised as pretty or ugly. Instead of such classification, a thought came to him about indifference and heartlessness, not to say cruelty. Geralt reproached himself for that judgement, catching himself mistakenly humanising the dryad. He ought to have known, after all, that she was older than the other two. In spite of appearances she was much, much older than them.

They stood in indecisive silence. Geralt heard Frexinet moaning, groaning and coughing. The red-haired one must also have heard, but her face did not even twitch. The Witcher rested his hands on his hips.

'There's a wounded man over there in the tree hole,' he said calmly. 'He will die if he doesn't receive aid.'

'Tháess aep!' the olive-haired one snapped, bending her bow and aiming the arrowhead straight at his face.

'Will you let him die like a dog?' he said, not raising his voice. 'Will you leave him to drown slowly in his own blood? In that case better to put him out of his misery.'

'Be silent!' the dryad barked, switching to the Common Speech. But she lowered her bow and released the tension on the bowstring. She looked at the other questioningly. The red-haired one nodded, indicating the tree hollow. The olive-haired one ran over, quickly and silently.

'I want to see Lady Eithné,' Geralt repeated. 'I'm on a diplomatic mission . . .'

'She,' the red-haired one pointed to the honey-haired one, 'will lead you to Duén Canell. Go.'

'Frex . . . And the wounded man?'

The dryad looked at him, squinting. She was still fiddling with the nocked arrow.

'Do not worry,' she said. 'Go. She will lead you there.'

'But . . .'

'Va'en vort!' She cut him off, her lips tightening.

He shrugged and turned towards the one with the hair the colour of honey. She seemed the youngest of the three, but he might have been mistaken. He noticed she had blue eyes.

'Then let us go.'

'Yes,' the honey-coloured haired one said softly. After a short moment of hesitation she handed him his sword. 'Let us go.'

'What is your name?' he asked.

'Be silent.'

She moved very swiftly through the dense forest, not looking back. Geralt had to exert himself to keep up with her. He knew the dryad was doing it deliberately, knew that she wanted the man following her to get stuck, groaning, in the undergrowth, or to fall to the ground exhausted, incapable of going on. She did not know, of course, that she was dealing with a witcher, not a man. She was too young to know what a witcher was.

The young woman – Geralt now knew she was not a pure-blood dryad – suddenly stopped and turned around. He saw her chest heaving powerfully beneath her short, dappled jacket, saw that she was having difficulty stopping herself from breathing through her mouth.

'Shall we slow down?' he suggested with a smile.

'Yeá.' She looked at him with hostility. 'Aeén esseáth Sidh?'

'No, I'm not an elf. What is your name?'

'Braenn,' she answered, marching on, but now at a slower pace, not trying to outdistance him. They walked alongside each other, close. He smelled the scent of her sweat, the ordinary sweat of a young woman. The sweat of dryads carried the scent of delicate willow leaves crushed in the hands.

'And what were you called before?'

She glanced at him and suddenly grimaced; he thought she would become annoyed or order him to be silent. She did not.

'I don't remember,' she said reluctantly. He did not think it was true.

She did not look older than sixteen and she could not have been in Brokilon for more than six or seven years. Had she come earlier, as a very young child or simply a baby, he would not now be able to see the human in her. Blue eyes and naturally fair hair did occur among dryads. Dryad children, conceived in ritual mating with elves or humans, inherited organic traits exclusively from their mothers, and were always girls. Extremely infrequently, as a rule, in a subsequent generation a child would nonetheless occasionally be born with the eyes or hair of its anonymous male progenitor. But Geralt was certain that Braenn did not have a single drop of dryad blood. And anyway, it was not especially important. Blood or not, she was now a dryad.

'And what,' she looked askance at him, 'do they call you?'

'Gwynbleidd.'

She nodded.

'Then we shall go . . . Gwynbleidd.'

They walked more slowly than before, but still briskly. Braenn, of course, knew Brokilon; had he been alone, Geralt would have been unable to maintain the pace or the right direction. Braenn stole through the barricade of dense forest using winding, concealed paths, clearing gorges, running nimbly across fallen trees as though they were bridges, confidently splashing through glistening stretches of swamp, green from duckweed, which the Witcher would not have dared to tread on. He would have lost hours, if not days, skirting around.

Braenn's presence did not only protect him from the savagery of the forest; there were places where the dryad slowed down, walking extremely cautiously, feeling the path with her foot and holding him by the hand. He knew the reason. Brokilon's traps were legendary; people talked about pits full of sharpened stakes, about booby-trapped bows, about falling trees, about the terrible urchin – a spiked ball on a rope, which, falling suddenly, swept the path clear. There were also places where Braenn would stop and whistle melodiously, and answering whistles would come from the undergrowth. There were other places where she would stop with her hand on the arrows in her quiver, signalling for him to be silent, and wait, tense, until whatever was rustling in the thicket moved away.

In spite of their fast pace, they had to stop for the night. Braenn chose an excellent spot; a hill onto which thermal updrafts carried gusts of warm air. They slept on dried bracken, very close to one another, in dryad custom. In the middle of the night Braenn hugged him close. And nothing more. He hugged her back. And nothing more. She was a dryad. The point was to keep warm.

They set off again at daybreak, while it was still almost dark.

II

They passed through a belt of sparsely forested hills, creeping cautiously across small valleys full of mist, moving through broad, grassy glades, and across clearings of wind-felled trees.

Braenn stopped once again and looked around. She had apparently lost her way, but Geralt knew that was impossible. Taking advantage of a break in the march, however, he sat down on a fallen tree.

And then he heard a scream. Shrill. High-pitched. Desperate.

Braenn knelt down in a flash, at once drawing two arrows from her quiver. She seized one in her teeth and nocked the other, bent her bow, taking aim blindly through the bushes towards the sound of the voice.

'Don't shoot!' he cried.

He leaped over the tree trunk and forced his way through the brush.

A small creature in a short grey jacket was standing in a small clearing, at the foot of a rocky cliff, with its back pressed against the trunk of a withered hornbeam. Something was moving slowly about five paces in front of it, parting the grass. That thing was about twelve feet long and was dark brown. At first Geralt thought it was a snake. But then he noticed the wriggling, yellow, hooked limbs and flat segments of the long thorax and realised it was not a snake. It was something much more sinister.

The creature hugging the tree cried out shrilly. The immense myriapod raised above the grass long, twitching feelers with which it sensed odours and warmth.

'Don't move!' The Witcher yelled and stamped to attract the scolopendromorph's attention. But the myriapod did not react, for its feelers had already caught the scent of the nearer victim. The monster wriggled its limbs, coiled itself up like an 'S' and moved forward. Its bright yellow limbs rippled through grass, evenly, like the oars of a galley.

'Yghern!' Braenn yelled.

Geralt hurtled into the clearing in two bounds, jerking his sword from its scabbard on his back as he ran, and in full flight struck the petrified creature beneath the tree with his hip, shoving it aside into some brambles. The scolopendromorph rustled the grass, wriggled its legs and attacked, raising its anterior segments, its venom-dripping pincers chattering. Geralt danced, leaped over the flat body and slashed it with his sword from a half-turn, aiming at a vulnerable spot between the armoured plates on its body.

The monster was too swift, however, and the sword struck the chitinous shell, without cutting through it; the thick carpet of moss absorbed the blow. Geralt dodged, but not deftly enough. The scolopendromorph wound the posterior part of its body around his legs with enormous strength. The Witcher fell, rolled over and tried to pull himself free. In vain.

The myriapod flexed and turned around to reach him with its pincers, and at the same time fiercely dug its claws into the tree and wrapped itself around it. Right then an arrow hissed above Geralt's head, penetrating the armour with a crack, pinning the creature to the trunk. The scolopendromorph writhed, broke the arrow and freed itself, but was struck at once by two more. The Witcher kicked the thrashing abdomen off and rolled away to the side.

Braenn, kneeling, was shooting at an astonishing rate, sending arrow after arrow into the scolopendromorph. The myriapod was breaking the shafts to free itself, but each successive arrow would pin it to the trunk again. The creature snapped its flat, shiny, dark-red maw and clanged its pincers by the places which had been pierced by the arrows, instinctively trying to reach the enemy which was wounding it.

Geralt leaped at it from the side, took a big swing and hacked with his sword, ending the fight with one blow. The tree acted like an executioner's block.

Braenn approached slowly, an arrow nocked, kicked the body

writing in the grass, its limbs thrashing around, and spat on it.

'Thanks,' the Witcher said, crushing the beast's severed head with blows of his heel.

'Eh?'

'You saved my life.'

The dryad looked at him. There was neither understanding nor emotion in her expression.

'Yghern,' she said, nudging the writhing body with a boot. 'It broke my arrows.'

'You saved my life and that little dryad's,' Geralt repeated. 'Where the bloody hell is she?'

Braenn deftly brushed aside the bramble thicket and plunged an arm among the thorny shoots.

'As I thought,' she said, pulling the little creature in the grey jacket from the thicket. 'See for yourself, Gwynbleidd.'

It was not a dryad. Neither was it an elf, sylph, puck or halfling. It was a quite ordinary little human girl. In the centre of Brokilon, it was the most extraordinary place to come across an ordinary, human little girl.

She had fair, mousy hair and huge, glaringly green eyes. She could not have been more than ten years old.

'Who are you?' he asked. 'How did you get here?'

She did not reply. Where have I seen her before? he wondered. I've seen her before somewhere. Either her or someone very similar to her.

'Don't be afraid,' he said, hesitantly.

'I'm not afraid,' she mumbled indistinctly. She clearly had a cold.

'Let us get out of here,' Braenn suddenly said, looking all around. 'Where there is one yghern, you can usually expect another. And I have few arrows now.'

The girl looked at her, opened her mouth and wiped it with the back of her hand, smearing dust over her face.

'Who the hell are you?' Geralt asked again, leaning forward. 'What are you doing . . . in this forest? How did you get here?'

The girl lowered her head and sniffed loudly.

'Cat got your tongue? Who are you, I said? What's your name?'

'Ciri,' she said, sniffing.

Geralt turned around. Braenn, examining her bow, glanced at him.

'Listen, Braenn . . .'

'What?'

'Is it possible . . . Is it possible she . . . has escaped from Duén Canell?'

'Eh?'

'Don't play dumb,' he said, annoyed. 'I know you abduct little girls. And you? What, did you fall from the sky into Brokilon? I'm asking if it's possible . . .'

'No,' the dryad cut him off. 'I have never seen her before.'

Geralt looked at the little girl. Her ashen-grey hair was dishevelled, full of pine needles and small leaves, but smelled of cleanliness, not smoke, nor the cowshed, nor tallow. Her hands, although incredibly dirty, were small and delicate, without scars or calluses. The boy's clothes, the jacket with a red hood she had on, did not indicate anything, but her high boots were made of soft, expensive calfskin. No, she was certainly not a village child. Frexinet, the Witcher suddenly thought. This was the one that Frexinet was looking for. He'd followed her into Brokilon.

'Where are you from? I'm asking you, you scamp.'

'How dare you talk to me like that!' The little girl lifted her head haughtily and stamped her foot. The soft moss completely spoiled the effect.

'Ha,' the Witcher said, and smiled. 'A princess, indeed. At least in speech, for your appearance is wretched. You're from Verden, aren't you? Do you know you're being looked for? Don't worry, I'll deliver you home. Listen, Braenn . . .'

The moment he looked away the girl turned very quickly on her heel and ran off through the forest, across the gentle hillside.

'Bloede dungh!' the dryad yelled, reaching for her quiver. 'Caemm aere!'

The little girl, stumbling, rushed blindly through the forest, crunching over dry branches.

'Stop!' shouted Geralt. 'Where are you bloody going!?'

Braenn bent her bow in a flash. The arrow hissed venomously, describing a flat parabola, and the arrowhead thudded into the tree trunk, almost brushing the little girl's hair. The girl cringed and flattened herself to the ground.

'You bloody fool,' the Witcher hissed, hurrying over to the dryad. Braenn deftly drew another arrow from her quiver. 'You might have killed her!'

'This is Brokilon,' she said proudly.

'But she's only a child!'

'What of it?'

He looked at the arrow's shaft. It had striped fletchings made from a pheasant's flight feathers dyed yellow in a decoction of tree bark. He did not say a word. He turned around and went quickly into the forest. The little girl was lying beneath the tree, cowering, cautiously raising her head and looking at the arrow stuck into the tree. She heard his steps and leaped to her feet, but he reached her with a single bound and seized her by the red hood of her jacket. She turned her head and looked at him, then at his hand, holding her hood. He released her.

'Why did you run away?'

'None of your business,' she sniffed. 'Leave me alone, you, you—'

'Foolish brat,' he hissed furiously. 'This is Brokilon. Wasn't the myriapod enough? You wouldn't last till morning in this forest. Haven't you got it yet?'

'Don't touch me!' she yelled. 'You peasant! I am a princess, so you'd better be careful!'

'You're a foolish imp.'

'I'm a princess!'

'Princesses don't roam through forests alone. Princesses have clean noses.'

'I'll have you beheaded! And her too!' The girl wiped her nose with her hand and glared at the approaching dryad. Braenn snorted with laughter.

'Alright, enough of this,' the Witcher cut her off. 'Why were you running away, Your Highness? And where to? What were you afraid of?'

She said nothing, and sniffed.

'Very well, as you wish,' he winked at the dryad. '*We're* going. If you want to stay alone in the forest, that's your choice. But the next time a yghern attacks you, don't yell. It doesn't befit a princess. A princess dies without even a squeal, having first wiped her snotty nose. Let's go, Braenn. Farewell, Your Highness.'

'W . . . wait.'

'Aha?'

'I'm coming with you.'

'We are greatly honoured. Aren't we, Braenn?'

'But you won't take me to Kistrin again? Do you swear?'

'Who is—?' he began. 'Oh, dammit. Kistrin. Prince Kistrin? The son of King Ervyll of Verden?'

The little girl pouted her little lips, sniffed and turned away.

'Enough of these trifles,' said Braenn grimly. 'Let us march on.'

'Hold on, hold on.' The Witcher straightened up and looked down at the dryad. 'Our plans are changing somewhat, my comely archer.'

'Eh?' Braenn said, raising her eyebrows.

'Lady Eithné can wait. I have to take the little one home. To Verden.'

The dryad squinted and reached for her quiver.

'You're not going anywhere. Nor is she.'

The Witcher smiled hideously.

'Be careful, Braenn,' he said. 'I'm not that pup whose eye you speared with an arrow from the undergrowth. I can look after myself.'

'Bloede arss!' she hissed, raising her bow. 'You're going to Duén Canell, and so is she! Not to Verden!'

'No. Not to Verden!' the mousy-haired girl said, throwing herself at the dryad and pressing herself against her slim thigh. 'I'm going with you! And he can go to Verden by himself, to silly old Kistrin, if he wants!'

Braenn did not even look at her, did not take her eyes off Geralt. But she lowered her bow.

'Ess dungh!' she said, spitting at his feet. 'Very well! Then go on your way! We'll see how you fare. You'll kiss an arrow before you leave Brokilon.'

She's right, thought Geralt. I don't have a chance. Without her I won't get out of Brokilon nor reach Duén Canell. Too bad, we shall see. Perhaps I'll manage to persuade Eithné . . .

'Very well, Braenn,' he said placatingly, and smiled. 'Don't be furious, fair one. Very well, have it your way. We shall all go to Duén Canell. To Lady Eithné.'

The dryad muttered something under her breath and unnocked the arrow.

'To the road, then,' she said, straightening her hairband. 'We have tarried too long.'

'Ooow . . .' the little girl yelped as she took a step.

'What's the matter?'

'I've done something . . . To my leg.'

'Wait, Braenn! Come here, scamp, I'll carry you pick-a-back.'

She was warm and smelt like a wet sparrow.

'What's your name, princess? I've forgotten.'

'Ciri.'

'And your estates, where do they lie, if I may ask?'

'I won't tell,' she grunted. 'I won't tell, and that's that.'

'I'll get by. Don't wriggle or sniff right by my ear. What were you doing in Brokilon? Did you get lost? Did you lose your way?'

'Not a chance! I never get lost.'

'Don't wriggle. Did you run away from Kistrin? From Nastrog Castle? Before or after the wedding?'

'How did you know?' She sniffed, intent.

'I'm staggeringly intelligent. Why did you run away to Brokilon, of all places? Weren't there any safer directions?'

'I couldn't control my stupid horse.'

'You're lying, princess. Looking at your size, the most you could ride is a cat. And a gentle one at that.'

'I was riding with Marck. Sir Voymir's esquire. But the horse fell in the forest and broke its leg. And we lost our way.'

'You said that never happens to you.'

'He got lost, not me. It was foggy. And we lost our way.'

You got lost, thought Geralt. Sir Voymir's poor esquire, who had the misfortune to happen upon Braenn and her companions. A young stripling, who had probably never known a woman, helped the green-eyed scamp escape, because he'd heard a lot of knightly stories about virgins being forced to marry. He helped her escape, to fall to a dryad's dyed arrow – one who probably hasn't known a man herself. But already knows how to kill.

'I asked you if you bolted from Nastrog Castle before or after the wedding?'

'I just scarpered and it's none of your business,' she grunted. 'Grandmamma told me I had to go there and meet him. That Kistrin. Just meet him. But that father of his, that big-bellied king . . .'

'Ervyll.'

' . . . kept on: "the wedding, the wedding". But I don't want him. That Kistrin. Grandmamma said—'

'Is Prince Kistrin so revolting?'

'I don't want him,' Ciri proudly declared, sniffing loudly. 'He's fat, stupid and his breath smells. Before I went there they showed me a painting, but he wasn't fat in the painting. I don't want a husband like that. I don't want a husband at all.'

'Ciri,' the Witcher said hesitantly. 'Kistrin is still a child, like you. In a few years he might turn into a handsome young man.'

'Then they can send me another painting, in a few years,' she snorted. 'And him too. Because he told me that I was much prettier in the painting they showed him. And he confessed that he loves Alvina, a lady-in-waiting and he wants to be a knight. See? He doesn't want me and I don't want him. So what use is a wedding?'

'Ciri,' the Witcher muttered, 'he's a prince and you're a princess. Princes and princesses marry like that, that's how it is. That's the custom.'

'You sound like all the rest. You think that just because I'm small you can lie to me.'

'I'm not lying.'

'Yes you are.'

Geralt said nothing. Braenn, walking in front of them, turned around, probably surprised by the silence. She shrugged and set off.

'Which way are we going?' Ciri asked glumly. 'I want to know!'
Geralt said nothing.

'Answer, when I ask a question!' she said menacingly, backing up
the order with a loud sniff. 'Do you know . . . who's sitting on you?'
He didn't react.

'I'll bite you in the ear!' she yelled.

The Witcher had had enough. He pulled the girl off his back and
put her on the ground.

'Now listen, you brat,' he said harshly, struggling with his belt
buckle. 'In a minute I'll put you across my knee, pull down your
britches and tan your backside. No one will stop me doing it, because
this isn't the royal court, and I'm not your flunkey or servant. You'll
soon regret you didn't stay in Nastrog. You'll soon see it's better
being a princess than a snot-nosed kid who got lost in the forest.
Because, it's true, a princess is allowed to act obnoxiously. And no
one thrashes a princess's backside with a belt. At most her husband,
the prince, might with his own hand.'

Ciri cowered and sniffed a few times. Braenn watched dispassionately, leaning against a tree.

'Well?' the Witcher asked, wrapping his belt around his wrist.
'Are we going to behave with dignity and temperance? If not,
we shall set about tanning Her Majesty's hide. Well? What's it
to be?'

The little girl snivelled and sniffed, then eagerly nodded.

'Are you going to be good, princess?'

'Yes,' she mumbled.

'Gloaming will soon fall,' the dryad said. 'Let us make haste,
Gwynbleidd.'

The forest thinned out. They walked through a sandy young
forest, across moors, and through fog-cloaked meadows with herds
of red deer grazing. It was growing cooler.

'Noble lord . . .' Ciri began after a long, long silence.

'My name is Geralt. What's the matter?'

'I'm awffy, awffy hungry.'

'We'll stop in a moment. It'll be dark soon.'

'I can't go on,' she snivelled. 'I haven't eaten since—'

'Stop whining.' He reached into a saddlebag and took out a piece of fatback, a small round of white cheese and two apples. 'Have that.'

'What's that yellow stuff?'

'Fatback.'

'I won't eat that,' she grunted.

'That's fine,' he said indistinctly, stuffing the fatback into his mouth. 'Eat the cheese. And an apple. Just one.'

'Why only one.'

'Don't wriggle. Have both.'

'Geralt?'

'Mhm?'

'Thank you.'

'Don't mention it. Food'll do you good.'

'I didn't . . . Not for that. That too, but . . . You saved me from that centipede . . . Ugh . . . I almost died of fright.'

'You almost died,' he confirmed seriously. You almost died in an extremely painful and hideous way, he thought. 'But you ought to thank Braenn.'

'What is she?'

'A dryad.'

'An eerie wife?'

'Yes.'

'So she's . . . They kidnap children! She's kidnapped us? Hey, but you aren't small. But why does she speak so strangely?'

'That's just her way, it's not important. What's important is how she shoots. Don't forget to thank her when we stop.'

'I won't forget,' she sniffed.

'Don't wriggle, future Princess of Verden, ma'am.'

'I'm not going to be a princess,' she muttered.

'Very well, very well. You won't be a princess. You'll become a hamster and live in a burrow.'

'No I won't! You don't know anything!'

'Don't squeak in my ear. And don't forget about the strap!'

'I'm not going to be a princess. I'm going to be . . .'

'Yes? What?'

'It's a secret.'

'Oh, yes, a secret. Splendid.' He raised his head. 'What is it, Braenn?'

The dryad had stopped. She shrugged and looked at the sky.

'I cannot go on,' she said softly. 'Neither can you, I warrant, with her on your back, Gwynbleidd. We shall stop here. It will darken soon.'

III

'Ciri?'

'Mhm?' the little girl sniffed and rustled the branches she was lying on.

'Aren't you cold?'

'No,' she sighed. 'It's warm today. Yesterday . . . Yesterday I froze awffy, oh my, how I did.'

'It is a marvel,' Braenn said, loosening the straps of her long, soft boots. 'A tiny little moppet, but she has covered a long stride of forest. And she got past the lookouts, through the bog and the thicket. She is robust, healthy and stout. Truly, she would come in useful. To us.'

Geralt glanced quickly at the dryad, at her eyes shining in the semi-darkness. Braenn leaned back against a tree, removed her hairband and let her hair down with a shake of her head.

'She entered Brokilon,' she muttered, forestalling his comment. 'She is ours, Gwynbleidd. We are marching to Duén Canell.'

'Lady Eithné will decide,' he responded tartly. But he knew Braenn was right.

Pity, he thought, looking at the little girl wriggling on the green bed. She's such a determined rascal! Where have I seen her before? Never mind. But it's a pity. The world is so big and so beautiful. And Brokilon will now be her world, until the end of her days. And there may not be many. Perhaps only until the day she falls in the bracken, amidst cries and the whistles of arrows, fighting in this senseless battle for the forest. On the side of those who will lose. Who have to lose. Sooner or later.

'Ciri?'

'Yes?'

'Where do your parents live?'

267

'I don't have any parents,' she sniffed. 'They drowned at sea when I was tiny.'

Yes, he thought, that explains a lot. A princess, the child of a deceased royal couple. Who knows if she isn't the third daughter following four sons? A title which in practice means less than that of chamberlain or equerry. A mousy-haired, green-eyed thing hanging around the court, who ought to be shoved out as quickly as possible and married off. As quickly as possible, before she matures and becomes a young woman and brings the threat of scandal, misalliance or incest, which would not be difficult in a shared castle bedchamber.

Her escape did not surprise the Witcher. He had frequently met princesses – and even queens – roaming around with troupes of wandering players, happy to have escaped some decrepit king still desirous of an heir. He had seen princes, preferring the uncertain fate of a soldier of fortune to marriage to a lame or pockmarked princess – chosen by their father – whose withered or doubtful virginity was to be the price of an alliance or dynastic coalition.

He lay down beside the little girl and covered her with his jacket.

'Sleep,' he said. 'Sleep, little orphan.'

'Orphan? Humph!' she growled. 'I'm a princess, not an orphan. And I have a grandmamma. And my grandmamma is a queen, so you'd better be careful. When I tell her you wanted to give me the strap, my grandmamma will order your head chopped off, you'll see.'

'Ghastly! Ciri, have mercy!'

'Not a chance!'

'But you're a good little girl. And beheading hurts awfully. You won't say anything, will you?'

'I will.'

'Ciri.'

'I will, I will, I will! Afraid, are you?'

'Dreadfully. You know, Ciri, you can die from having your head cut off.'

'Are you mocking me?'

'I wouldn't dream of it.'

'She'll put you in your place, you'll see. No one takes liberties with my grandmamma. When she stamps her foot the greatest knights and warriors kneel before her; I've seen it myself. And if one of them is disobedient, then it's "chop" and off with his head.'

'Dreadful. Ciri?'

'Uh-huh?'

'I think they'll cut off your head.'

'*My* head?'

'Naturally. After all, your grandmamma, the queen, arranged a marriage with Kistrin and sent you to Nastrog Castle in Verden. You were disobedient. As soon as you return . . . it'll be "chop!" and off with *your* head.'

The little girl fell silent. She even stopped fidgeting. He heard her smacking her lips, biting her lower lip and sniffing.

'You're wrong,' she said. 'Grandmamma won't let anyone chop off my head, because . . . Because she's my grandmamma, isn't she? Oh, at most I'll get . . .'

'Aha,' Geralt laughed. 'There's no taking liberties with grandmamma, is there? The switch has come out, hasn't it?'

Ciri snorted angrily.

'Do you know what?' he said. 'We'll tell your grandmamma that I've already whipped you, and you can't be punished twice for the same crime. Is it a deal?'

'You must be silly!' Ciri raised herself on her elbows, making the branches rustle. 'When grandmamma hears that you thrashed me, they'll chop your head off just like that!'

'So you are worried for my head then?'

The little girl fell silent and sniffed again.

'Geralt . . .'

'What, Ciri?'

'Grandmamma knows I have to go home. I can't be a princess or the wife of that stupid Kistrin. I have to go home, and that's that.'

You do, he thought. Regrettably, it doesn't depend on you or on your grandmamma. It depends on the mood of old Eithné. And on my persuasive abilities.

'Grandmamma knows,' Ciri continued. 'Because I . . . Geralt, promise you won't tell anybody. It's a terrible secret. Dreadful, I'm serious. Swear.'

'I swear.'

'Very well, I'll tell you. My mama was a witch, so you'd better watch your step. And my papa was enchanted, too. It was all told to me by one of my nannies, and when grandmamma found out about it, there was a dreadful to-do. Because I'm destined, you know?'

'To do what?'

'I don't know,' Ciri said intently. 'But I'm destined. That's what my nanny said. And grandmamma said she won't let anyone . . . that the whole ruddy castle will collapse first. Do you understand? And nanny said that nothing, nothing at all, can help with destiny. Ha! And then nanny wept and grandmamma yelled. Do you see? I'm destined. I won't be the wife of that silly Kistrin. Geralt?'

'Go to sleep,' he yawned, so that his jaw creaked. 'Go to sleep, Ciri.'

'Tell me a story.'

'What?'

'Tell me a story,' she snorted. 'How am I supposed to sleep without a story? I mean, really!'

'I don't know any damned stories. Go to sleep.'

'You're lying. You do. What, no one told you stories when you were little? What are you laughing about?'

'Nothing. I just recalled something.'

'Aha! You see. Go on.'

'What?'

'Tell me a story.'

He laughed again, put his hands under his head and looked up at the stars twinkling beyond the branches above their heads.

'There was once . . . a cat,' he began. 'An ordinary, tabby mouser. And one day that cat went off, all by itself, on a long journey to a terrible, dark forest. He walked . . . And he walked . . . And he walked . . .'

'Don't think,' Ciri mumbled, cuddling up to him, 'that I'll fall asleep before he gets there.'

'Keep quiet, rascal. So . . . he walked and he walked until he came across a fox. A red fox.'

Braenn sighed and lay down beside the Witcher, on the other side, and also snuggled up a little.

'Very well,' Ciri sniffed. 'Say what happened next.'

'The fox looked at the cat. "Who are you?" he asked. "I'm a cat," said the cat. "Ha," said the fox. "But aren't you afraid, cat, to be roaming the forest alone? What will you do if the king comes a-hunting? With hounds and mounted hunters and beaters? I tell you, cat," said the fox, "the chase is a dreadful hardship to creatures like you and I. You have a pelt, I have a pelt, and hunters never spare creatures like us, because hunters have sweethearts and lovers, and their little hands and necks get cold, so they make muffs and collars for those strumpets to wear".'

'What are muffs?' Ciri asked.

'Don't interrupt. And the fox went on. "I, cat, know how to outwit them; I have one thousand, two hundred and eighty-six ways to outfox those hunters, so cunning am I. And you, cat, how many ways do you have?"'

'Oh, what a fine tale,' Ciri said, cuddling more tightly to the Witcher. 'What did the cat say?'

'Aye,' whispered Braenn from the other side. 'What did the cat say?'

The Witcher turned his head. The dryad's eyes were sparkling, her mouth was half-open and she was running her tongue over her lips. He could understand. Little dryads were hungry for tales. Just like little witchers. Because both of them were seldom told bedtime stories. Little dryads fell asleep listening raptly to the wind blowing in the trees. Little witchers fell asleep listening raptly to their aching arms and legs. Our eyes also shone like Braenn's when we listened to the tales of Vesemir in Kaer Morhen. But that was long ago . . . So long ago . . .

'Well,' Ciri said impatiently. 'What then?'

'The cat said: "I, fox, don't have any ways. I only know one thing; up a tree as quick as can be. That ought to be enough, oughtn't it?" The fox burst out laughing. "Hah," he said. "What a goose you are!

Flourish your stripy tail and flee, for you'll perish if the hunters trap you." And suddenly, from nowhere, the horns began to sound! And the hunters leaped out from the bushes. And they saw the cat and the fox. And they were upon them!'

'Oh!' Ciri sniffed, and the dryad shifted suddenly.

'Quiet. And they were upon them, yelling: "Have them, skin them! We'll make muffs out of them, muffs!" And they set the hounds on the fox and the cat. And the cat darted up a tree, like every cat does. Right to the very top. But the hounds seized the fox! And before Reynard had time to use any of his cunning ways, he'd been made into a collar. And the cat meowed from the top of the tree and hissed at the hunters, but they couldn't do anything to him, because the tree was as high as hell. They stood at the foot of the tree, swearing like troopers, but they had to go away empty-handed. And then the cat climbed down from the tree and slunk calmly home.'

'What happened then?'

'Nothing. That's the end.'

'What about the moral?' Ciri asked. 'Tales always have a moral, don't they?'

'Hey?' Braenn said, hugging Geralt even harder. 'What's a moral?'

'A good story has a moral and a bad one doesn't,' Ciri sniffed with conviction.

'That was a good one,' the dryad yawned. 'So it has what it ought to have. You, moppet, should have scurried up a tree from that yghern, like that canny tomcat. Not pondered, but scurried up the tree without a thought. And that is all the wisdom in it. To survive. Not to be caught.'

The Witcher laughed softly.

'Weren't there any trees in the castle grounds, Ciri? In Nastrog? Instead of coming to Brokilon you could have skinned up a tree and stayed there, at the very top, until Kistrin's desire to wed had waned.'

'Are you mocking me?'

'Uh-huh.'

'Know what? I can't stand you.'

'That's dreadful. Ciri, you've stabbed me in the very heart.'

'I know,' she nodded gravely, sniffing, and then clung tightly to him.

'Sleep well, Ciri,' he muttered, breathing in her pleasant, sparrow scent. 'Sleep well. Goodnight, Braenn.'

'Deárme, Gwynbleidd.'

Above their heads a billion Brokilon branches soughed and hundreds of billions of Brokilon leaves rustled.

IV

The next day they reached the Trees. Braenn knelt down and bent her head. Geralt felt the need to do the same. Ciri heaved a sigh of awe.

The Trees – chiefly oaks, yews and hickories – had girths of over a hundred feet, some much more. It was impossible to say how high their crowns were. The places where the mighty, twisted roots joined the vertical trunks were high above their heads, however. They could have walked more quickly, as the giants grew slowly and no other vegetation could survive in their shadows; there was only a carpet of decaying leaves.

They could have walked more quickly. But they walked slowly. In silence. With bowed heads. Among the Trees they were small, insignificant, irrelevant. Unimportant. Even Ciri kept quiet – she did not speak for almost half an hour.

And after an hour's walk they passed the belt of Trees and once again plunged deep into ravines and wet beechwood forests.

Ciri's cold was troubling her more and more. Geralt did not have a handkerchief, and having had enough of her incessant sniffing, taught her to clear her nose directly onto the ground. The little girl was delighted by it. Looking at her smirk and shining eyes, the Witcher was deeply convinced that she was savouring the thought of showing off her new trick at court, during a ceremonial banquet or an audience with a foreign ambassador.

Braenn suddenly stopped and turned around.

'Gwynbleidd,' she said, unwinding a green scarf wrapped around her elbow. 'Come here. I will blindfold you. I must.'

'I know.'

'I will lead you. Give me your hand.'

'No,' protested Ciri. 'I'll lead him. May I, Braenn?'

'Very well, moppet.'

'Geralt?'

'Uh-huh?'

'What does "Gwyn . . . bleidd" mean?'

'White Wolf. The dryads call me that.'

'Beware, there's a root. Don't trip! Do they call you that because you have white hair?'

'Yes . . . Blast!'

'I said there was a root.'

They walked on. Slowly. It was slippery under their feet from fallen leaves. He felt warmth on his face, the sunlight shining through the blindfold.

'Oh, Geralt,' he heard Ciri's voice. 'How delightful it is here . . . Pity you can't see. There are so many flowers. And birds. Can you hear them singing? Oh, there's so many of them. Heaps. Oh, and squirrels. Careful, we're going to cross a stream, over a stone bridge. Don't fall in. Oh, so many little fishes! Hundreds. They're swimming in the water, you know. So many little animals, oh my. There can't be so many anywhere else.'

'There can't,' he muttered. 'Nowhere else. This is Brokilon.'

'What?'

'Brokilon. The Last Place.'

'I don't understand.'

'No one understands. No one wants to understand.'

V

'You can take off the blindfold now, Gwynbleidd. We have arrived.'

Braenn stood up to her knees in a dense carpet of fog.

'Duén Canell,' she said, pointing.

Duén Canell, the Place of the Oak. The Heart of Brokilon.

Geralt had already been there. Twice. But he had never told anyone about it. No one would have believed him.

A basin enclosed by the crowns of mighty green trees. Bathed in fog and mist rising from the earth, the rocks and the hot springs. A basin . . .

The medallion around his neck vibrated slightly.

A basin bathed in magic. Duén Canell. The Heart of Brokilon.

Braenn lifted her head and adjusted the quiver on her back.

'We must go. Give me your little hand, moppet.'

At first, the valley seemed to be lifeless. Deserted. But not for long. A loud, modulated whistling rang out, and a slender, dark-haired dryad, dressed, like all of them, in dappled, camouflaged attire slid nimbly down barely perceptible steps of bracket mushrooms winding around the nearest trunk.

'Ceád, Braenn.'

'Ceád, Sirssa. Va'n vort meáth Eithné á?'

'Neén, aefder,' the dark-haired dryad answered, sweeping her gaze up and down the Witcher. 'Ess' ae'n Sidh?'

She smiled, flashing white teeth. She was incredibly comely, even according to human standards. Geralt felt uncertain and foolish, aware that the dryad was inspecting him uninhibitedly.

'Neén,' Braenn shook her head. 'Ess' vatt'ghern, Gwynbleidd, á váen meáth Eithné va, a'ss.'

'Gwynbleidd?' the beautiful dryad said, grimacing. 'Bloede caérme! Aen'ne caen n'wedd vort! T'ess foile!'

276

Braenn sniggered.

'What is it?' the Witcher asked, growing angry.

'Nothing,' Braenn sniggered again. 'Nothing. Let us be moving.'

'Oh,' Ciri said in delight. 'Look at those funny cottages, Geralt!'

Duén Canell really began deep in the valley; the 'funny cottages', resembling huge bunches of mistletoe in shape, clung to the trunks and bows at various heights, both low, just above the ground, and high, occasionally very high, right beneath the very crowns. Geralt also saw several larger constructions on the ground, shelters made of woven branches, still covered in leaves. He saw movements in the openings to the shelters, but the dryads themselves could barely be made out. There were far fewer than there had been the last time he was there.

'Geralt,' Ciri whispered. 'Those cottages are living. They've got little leaves!'

'They're made of living wood,' the Witcher nodded. 'That's how dryads live, that's how they build their houses. No dryad will ever harm a tree by chopping or sawing it. They love trees. However, they can make the branches grow to form those dwellings.'

'How sweet. I'd like to have a little house like that on our estate.'

Braenn stopped in front of one of the larger shelters.

'Enter, Gwynbleidd,' she said. 'You will wait here for Lady Eithné. Vá fáill, moppet.'

'What?'

'That was a farewell, Ciri. She said "goodbye".'

'Oh. Goodbye, Braenn.'

They went inside. The interior of the 'cottage' twinkled like a kaleidoscope, from the patches of sunlight filtered and diffused through the roof structure.

'Geralt!'

'Frexinet!'

'You're alive, by the Devil!' the wounded man said, flashing his teeth, raising himself up on a makeshift bed of spruce. He saw Ciri clinging to the Witcher's thigh and his eyes widened, a flush rushing to his face.

'You little beast!' he yelled. 'I almost lost my life thanks to you! Oh, you're fortunate I cannot stand, for I'd tan your hide!'

Ciri pouted.

'You're the second person,' she said, wrinkling her nose comically, 'to want to thrash me. I'm a little girl and little girls can't be beaten!'

'I'd soon show you . . . what's allowed and what isn't,' Frexinet coughed. 'You little wretch! Ervyll is beside himself . . . He's sending out word, terrified that your grandmother's army is marching on him. Who will believe that you bolted? Everyone knows what Ervyll's like and what his pleasures are. Everyone thinks he . . . did something to you in his cups, and then had you drowned in the fishpond! War with Nilfgaard is looming, and because of you the treaty and the alliance with your grandmother have gone up in smoke! See what you've done?'

'Don't excite yourself,' the Witcher warned, 'for you might open your wounds. How did you get here so swiftly?'

'The Devil only knows, I've been lying half-dead most of the time. They poured something revolting down my throat. By force. They held my nose and . . . What a damned disgrace . . .'

'You're alive thanks to what they poured down your throat. Did they bring you here?'

'They dragged me here on a sledge. I asked after you but they said nothing. I was certain you'd caught an arrow. You vanished so suddenly . . . But you're hale and hearty, not even in fetters, and not only that, prithee, you rescued Princess Cirilla . . . A pox on it, you get by everywhere, Geralt, and you always fall on your feet.'

The Witcher smiled but did not respond. Frexinet hacked, turned his head away and spat out saliva tinged pink.

'Well,' he added. 'And you're sure to be the reason they didn't finish me off. They know you, bloody eerie wives. That's the second time you've got me out of trouble.'

'Oh, come on, baron.'

Frexinet, moaning, tried to sit up, but abandoned the attempt.

'Bollocks to my barony,' he panted. 'I was a baron back in Hamm. Now I'm something like a governor at Ervyll's court in Verden. I mean I was. Even if I get out of this forest somehow, there's no place for me in Verden now, apart from on the scaffold. This little weasel, Cirilla, slipped out of my hands and my protection. Do you think the three of us went to Brokilon for the hell of it? No, Geralt, I was fleeing too, and could only count on Ervyll's mercy if I brought her back. And then I happened on those accursed eerie wives . . . If not for you I'd have expired in that hollow. You've rescued me again. It's destiny, that's as clear as day.'

'You're exaggerating.'

Frexinet shook his head.

'It's destiny,' he repeated. 'It must have been written up there that we'd meet again, Witcher. That you'd save my skin again. Remember, people talked about it in Hamm after you lifted that bird curse from me.'

'Chance,' Geralt said coldly. 'Pure chance, Frexinet.'

'What chance? Dammit, if it hadn't been for you, I'd probably still be a cormorant—'

'You were a cormorant?' Ciri cried in excitement. 'A real cormorant? A bird?'

'I was,' the baron grinned. 'I was cursed by . . . by a bitch . . . Damn her . . . for revenge.'

'I bet you didn't give her a fur,' Ciri said, wrinkling up her nose. 'For a, you know . . . muff.'

'There was another reason,' Frexinet blushed slightly, then glowered angrily at the little girl. 'But what business is it of yours, you tyke!'

Ciri looked offended and turned her head away.

'Yes,' Frexinet coughed. 'Where was I . . . Aha, when I was cursed in Hamm. Were it not for you, Geralt, I would have remained a cormorant till the end of my days, I would be flying around the lake, shitting on tree branches, deluding myself that the shirt made of nettle fibres stubbornly woven by my dear sister would save me. Dammit, when I recall that shirt of hers, I feel like kicking somebody. That idiot—'

'Don't say that,' the Witcher smiled. 'She had the best of intentions. She was badly informed, that's all. Lots of nonsensical myths circulate about undoing curses. You were lucky, anyway, Frexinet. She might have ordered you to dive into a barrel of boiling milk. I've heard of a case like that. Donning a nettle shirt, if you think about it, isn't very harmful to the health, even if it doesn't help much.'

'Ha, perhaps you're right. Perhaps I expect too much of her. Eliza was always stupid, from a child she was stupid and lovely, as a matter of fact; splendid material for a king's wife.'

'What is lovely material?' Ciri asked. 'And why for a wife?'

'Don't interfere, you tyke, I said. Yes, Geralt, I was lucky you turned up in Hamm then. And that my brother-in-law king was ready to spend the few ducats you demanded for lifting the spell.'

'You know, Frexinet,' Geralt said, smiling even more broadly, 'that news of the incident spread far and wide?'

'The true version?'

'I wouldn't say that. To begin with, they gave you ten more brothers.'

'Oh no!' The baron raised himself on an elbow and coughed. 'And so, counting Eliza, there were said to be twelve of us? What bloody idiocy! My mama wasn't a rabbit!'

'That's not all. It was agreed that cormorants aren't romantic enough.'

'Because they aren't! There's nothing romantic about them!' The baron grimaced, feeling his chest, wrapped in bast and sheets of birch bark. 'What was I turned into, according to the tale?'

'A swan. I mean swans. There were eleven of you, don't forget.'

'And how is a swan more romantic than a cormorant?'

'I don't know.'

'I don't either. But I'll bet that in the story Eliza lifted the curse from me with the help of her gruesome nettle blouse?'

'You win. How is Eliza?'

'She has consumption, poor thing. She won't last long.'

'That's sad.'

'It is,' Frexinet agreed dispassionately, looking away.

'Coming back to the curse . . .' Geralt leaned back against a wall made of woven, springy switches. 'You don't have any recurrences? You don't sprout feathers?'

'No, may the Gods be praised,' the baron sighed. 'Everything is in good order. The one thing that I was left with from those times is a taste for fish. There are no better vittles for me, Geralt, than fish. Occasionally I go down to the fishermen on the jetty early in the morning, and before they find me something more refined, I gobble down a handful or two of bleak straight from the holding cage, a few minnows, dace or chub . . . It's pure bliss, not food.'

'He was a cormorant,' Ciri said slowly, looking at Geralt. 'And you lifted the curse from him. You can do magic!'

'I think it's obvious,' Frexinet said, 'that he can. Every witcher can.'

'Wi . . . witcher?'

'Didn't you know he was a witcher? The famous Geralt Riv? True enough, how is a little tyke like you to know what a witcher is? Things aren't what they used to be. Now there are very few witchers. You'd have a job finding one. You've probably never seen a witcher before?'

Ciri shook her head slowly, not taking her eyes off Geralt.

'A witcher, little tyke, is a . . .' Frexinet broke off and paled, seeing Braenn entering the cottage. 'No, I don't want it! I won't let you pour any more of it down my throat, never, never again! Geralt! Tell her—'

'Calm down.'

Braenn did not grace Frexinet with anything more than a fleeting glance. She walked over to Ciri, who was squatting beside the Witcher.

'Come,' she said. 'Come, moppet.'

'Where to?' Ciri grimaced. 'I'm not going. I want to be with Geralt.'

'Go,' the Witcher managed a smile. 'You can play with Braenn and the young dryads. They'll show you Duén Canell . . .'

'She didn't blindfold me,' Ciri said very slowly. 'She didn't blindfold me while we were walking here. She blindfolded you. So you couldn't find your way back here when you leave. That means . . .'

Geralt looked at Braenn. The dryad shrugged and then hugged the little girl tightly.

'That means . . .' Ciri's voice suddenly cracked. 'That means I'm not leaving here. Doesn't it?'

'No one can escape their destiny.'

All heads turned at the sound of that voice. Quiet, but sonorous, hard and decisive. A voice demanding obedience, which brooked no argument. Braenn bowed. Geralt went down on one knee.

'Lady Eithné.'

The ruler of Brokilon was wearing a flowing, gauzy, light-green gown. Like most dryads she was small and slender, but her proudly raised head, grave, sharp-featured face and resolute mouth made her seem taller and more powerful. Her hair and eyes were the colour of molten silver.

She entered the shelter escorted by two younger dryads armed with bows. Without a word she nodded towards Braenn, who immediately took Ciri by the hand and pulled her towards the door, bowing her head low. Ciri trod stiffly and clumsily, pale and speechless. When they passed Eithné, the silver-haired dryad seized her swiftly beneath the chin, lifted it and looked long in the girl's eyes. Geralt could see that Ciri was trembling.

'Go,' Eithné finally said. 'Go, my child. Fear naught. Nothing is capable of changing your destiny. You are in Brokilon.'

Ciri followed Braenn obediently. In the doorway she turned around. The Witcher noticed that her mouth was quivering, and her green eyes were misty with tears. He didn't say a word.

He continued to kneel, head bowed.

'Get up, Gwynbleidd. Welcome.'

'Greetings, Eithné, Lady of Brokilon.'

'I have the pleasure to host you in my Forest once again. Although you come here without my knowledge or permission. Entering Brokilon without my knowledge or permission is perilous, White Wolf. Even for you.'

'I come on a mission.'

'Ah . . .' the dryad smiled slightly. 'That explains your boldness, which I shall not describe using other, more blunt words. Geralt, the inviolability of envoys is a custom observed by humans. I do not recognise it. I recognise nothing human. This is Brokilon.'

'Eithné—'

'Be silent,' she interrupted, without raising her voice. 'I ordered you to be spared. You will leave Brokilon alive. Not because you are an envoy. For other reasons.'

'Are you not curious whose envoy I am? Where I come from, on whose behalf?'

'Frankly speaking, no. This is Brokilon. You come here from the outside, from a world that concerns me not. Why then would I waste time listening to supplications? What could some kind of proposal, some kind of ultimatum, devised by someone who thinks and feels differently to me, mean to me? What could I care what King Venzlav thinks?'

Geralt shook his head in astonishment.

'How do you know I come from Venzlav?'

'For it is obvious,' the dryad said with a smile. 'Ekkehard is too stupid. Ervyll and Viraxas detest me too much. No other realms border Brokilon.'

'You know a great deal about what happens beyond Brokilon, Eithné.'

'I know much, White Wolf. It is a privilege of my age. Now, though, if you permit, I would like to deal with a confidential matter. That man with the appearance of a bear,' the dryad stopped smiling and looked at Frexinet. 'Is he your friend?'

'We are acquainted. I once removed a curse from him.'

'The problem is,' Eithné said coldly, 'that I don't know what to do with him. I cannot, after all, order him put to death. I have permitted him to recover his health, but he represents a threat. He does not look like a fanatic. Thus he must be a scalp-hunter. I know that Ervyll pays for every dryad scalp. I do not recall how much. In any case, the price rises as the value of money falls.'

'You are in error. He is not a scalp-hunter.'

'Why then did he enter Brokilon?'

'To seek the girl-child whose care he was entrusted with. He risked his life to find her.'

'Most foolish,' Eithné said coldly. 'Difficult to call it even a risk. He was heading for certain death. The fact that he lives at all he owes

283

entirely to his iron constitution and endurance. As far as the child is concerned, it also survived by chance. My girls did not shoot, for they thought it was a puck or a leprechaun.'

She looked once again at Frexinet, and Geralt saw that her mouth had lost its unpleasant hardness.

'Very well. Let us celebrate this day in some way.'

She walked over to the bed of branches. The two dryads accompanying her also approached. Frexinet blanched and cowered, without becoming any smaller.

Eithné looked at him for a while, narrowing her eyes a little.

'Have you children?' she finally asked. 'I am talking to you, blockhead.'

'Eh?'

'I trust I express myself clearly.'

'I'm not . . .' Frexinet hemmed and coughed. 'I'm not married.'

'Your marital status is of little concern to me. What interests me is whether you are capable of mustering anything from your suety loins. By the Great Tree! Have you ever made a woman with child?'

'Errr . . . Yes . . . Yes, my lady, but—'

Eithné waved a hand carelessly and turned towards Geralt.

'He shall stay in Brokilon,' she said, 'until he is fully healed and then a little longer. Afterwards . . . He may go whither he so wish.'

'Thank you, Eithné,' the Witcher bowed.' And . . . the little girl? What about her?'

'Why do you ask?' The dryad looked at him with a cold glint in her silver eyes. 'You know.'

'She is not an ordinary, village child. She is a princess.'

'That makes no impression on me. Nor makes any difference.'

'Listen . . .'

'Not another word, Gwynbleidd.'

He fell silent and bit his lip.

'What about my petition?'

'I shall listen to it,' the dryad sighed. 'No, not out of curiosity. I shall do it for you, that you might distinguish yourself before Venzlav and collect the fee he probably promised you for reaching me. But not now, now I shall be busy. Come to my Tree this evening.'

When she had gone, Frexinet raised himself on an elbow, groaned, coughed and spat on his hand.

'What is it all about, Geralt? Why am I to stay here? And what did she mean about those children? What have you got me mixed up in, eh?'

The Witcher sat down.

'You'll save your hide, Frexinet,' he said in a weary voice. 'You'll become one of the few to get out of here alive, at least recently. And you'll become the father of a little dryad. Several, perhaps.'

'What the . . . ? Am I to be . . . a stud?'

'Call it what you will. You have limited choices.'

'I get it,' the baron winked and grinned lewdly. 'Why, I've seen captives working in mines and digging canals. It could be worse . . . Just as long as my strength suffices. There's quite a few of them here . . .'

'Stop smiling foolishly,' Geralt grimaced, 'and daydreaming. Don't imagine adoration, music, wine, fans and swarms of adoring dryads. There'll be one, perhaps two. And there won't be any adoration. They will treat the entire matter very practically. And you even more so.'

'Doesn't it give them pleasure? It can't cause them any harm?'

'Don't be a child. In this respect they don't differ in any way from women. Physically, at least.'

'What do you mean?'

'It depends on you whether it'll be agreeable or disagreeable. But that doesn't change the fact that the only thing that interests her is the result. You are of minor importance. Don't expect any gratitude. Aha, and under no circumstances try anything on your own initiative.'

'My own what?'

'Should you meet her in the morning,' the Witcher explained patiently, 'bow, but without any damned smirks or winks. For a dryad it is a deadly serious matter. Should she smile or approach you, you can talk to her. About trees, ideally. If you don't know much about trees, then about the weather. But should she pretend not to see you, stay well away from her. And stay well away from other dryads, and watch your hands. Those matters do not exist to a dryad who is not ready. If you touch her she'll stab you, because she won't understand your intentions.'

'You're familiar,' Frexinet smiled, 'with their mating habits. Has it ever befallen you?'

The Witcher did not reply. Before his eyes was the beautiful, slender dryad and her impudent smile. *Vatt'ghern, bloede caérme.* A witcher, dammit. Why did you bring him here, Braenn? What use is he to us? No benefit from a witcher . . .

'Geralt?'

'What?'

'And Princess Cirilla?'

'Forget about her. They'll turn her into a dryad. In two or three years she'd shoot an arrow in her own brother's eye, were he to try to enter Brokilon.'

'Dammit,' Frexinet swore, scowling. 'Ervyll will be furious. Geralt? Couldn't I—?'

'No,' the Witcher cut him off. 'Don't even try. You wouldn't get out of Duén Canell alive.'

'That means the lass is lost.'

'To you, yes.'

VI

Eithné's Tree was, naturally, an oak, but it was actually three oaks fused together, still green, not betraying any signs of age, although Geralt reckoned they were at least three hundred years old. The trees were hollow inside and the cavity had the dimensions of a large chamber with a high ceiling narrowing into a cone. The interior was lit by a cresset which did not smoke, and it had been modestly – but not crudely – transformed into comfortable living quarters.

Eithné was kneeling inside on something like a fibrous mat. Ciri sat cross-legged before her, erect and motionless, as though petrified. She had been bathed and cured of her cold, and her huge, emerald eyes were wide open. The Witcher noticed that her little face, now that the dirt and the grimace of a spiteful little devil had vanished from it, was quite pretty.

Eithné was combing the little girl's long hair, slowly and tenderly.

'Enter, Gwynbleidd. Be seated.'

He sat down, after first ceremonially going down on one knee.

'Are you rested?' the dryad asked, not looking at him, and continuing to comb. 'When can you embark on your return journey? What would you say to tomorrow morn?'

'When you give the order,' he said coldly. 'O Lady of Brokilon. One word from you will suffice for me to stop vexing you with my presence in Duén Canell.'

'Geralt,' Eithné slowly turned her head. 'Do not misunderstand me. I know and respect you. I know you have never harmed a dryad, rusalka, sylph or nymph; quite the opposite, you have been known to act in their defence, to save their lives. But that changes nothing. Too much divides us. We belong to different worlds. I neither want nor am able to make exceptions. For anybody. I shall not ask if you understand, for I know it is thus. I ask whether you accept it.'

'What does it change?'

'Nothing. But I want to know.'

'I do,' he confirmed. 'But what about her? What about Ciri? She also belongs to another world.'

Ciri glanced at him timidly and then upwards at the dryad. Eithné smiled.

'But not for long,' she said.

'Eithné, please. First think it over.'

'What for?'

'Give her to me. Let her return with me. To the world she belongs to.'

'No, White Wolf,' the dryad plunged the comb into the little girl's mousy hair again. 'I shall not. You of all people ought to understand.'

'Me?'

'Yes, you. Certain tidings from the world even reach Brokilon. Tidings about a certain witcher, who for services rendered occasionally demanded curious vows. "You will give me what you do not expect to find at home." "You will give me what you already have, but about which you do not know." Does that sound familiar? After all, for some time you witchers have been trying in this way to direct fate, you have been seeking boys designated by fate to be your successors, wishing to protect yourself from extinction and oblivion. From nihilism. Why, then, are you surprised at me? I care for the fate of the dryads. Surely that is just? A young human girl for each dryad killed by humans.'

'By keeping her here, you will arouse hostility and the desire for vengeance, Eithné. You will arouse a consuming hatred.'

'Human hatred is nothing new to me. No, Geralt. I shall not give her up. Particularly since she is hale. That has been uncommon recently.'

'Uncommon?'

The dryad fixed her huge, silver eyes on him.

'They abandon sick little girls with me. Diphtheria, scarlet fever, croup, recently even smallpox. They think we are not immune, that the epidemic will annihilate or at least decimate us. We disappoint

them, Geralt. We have something more than immunity. Brokilon
cares for its children.'

She fell silent, leaning over, carefully combing out a lock of Ciri's
tangled hair, using her other hand to help.

'May I,' the Witcher cleared his throat, 'turn to the petition, with
which King Venzlav has sent me?'

'Is it not a waste of time?' Eithné lifted her head. 'Why bother?
I know perfectly well what King Venzlav wants. For that, I do not
need prophetic gifts at all. He wants me to give him Brokilon, probably as far as the River Vda, which, I gather, he considers – or would
like to consider – the natural border between Brugge and Verden. In
exchange, I presume, he is offering me a small and untamed corner
of the forest. And probably gives his kingly word and offers kingly
protection that that small, untamed corner, that scrap of forest, will
belong to me forever and ever and that no one will dare to disturb
the dryads there. That the dryads there will be able to live in peace.
So what, Geralt? Venzlav would like to put an end to the war over
Brokilon, which has lasted two centuries. And in order to end it,
the dryads would have to give up what they have been dying in the
defence of for two hundred years? Simply hand it over? Give up
Brokilon?'

Geralt was silent. He had nothing to add. The dryad smiled.

'Did the royal proposal run thus, Gwynbleidd? Or perhaps it was
more blunt, saying: "Don't put on airs, you sylvan monster, beast of
the wilderness, relict of the past, but listen to what I, King Venzlav,
want. I want cedar, oak and hickory, mahogany and golden birch,
yew for bows and pine for masts, because Brokilon is close at hand,
and otherwise I have to bring wood from beyond the mountains. I
want the iron and copper that are beneath the earth. I want the gold
that lies on Craag An. I want to fell and saw, and dig in the earth,
without having to listen to the whistling of arrows. And most impor-
tantly; I want at last to be a king, one to whom everything bows
down in his kingdom. I do not wish for some Brokilon in our kingdom, for a forest I cannot enter. Such a forest affronts me, rouses
me to wrath and affords me sleepless nights, for I am a man, we rule
over the world. We may, if we wish, tolerate a few elves, dryads or

rusalkas in this world. If they are not too insolent. Submit to my will, O Witch of Brokilon. Or perish."'

'Eithné, you admitted yourself that Venzlav is not a fool or a fanatic. You know, I am certain, that he is a just and peace-loving king. The blood shed here pains and troubles him . . .'

'If he stays away from Brokilon not a single drop of blood shall be shed.'

'You well know . . .' Geralt raised his head.' You well know it is not thus. People have been killed in Burnt Stump, in Eight-Mile, in the Owl Hills. People have been killed in Brugge and on the left bank of the Ribbon. Beyond Brokilon.'

'The places you have mentioned,' the dryad responded calmly, 'are Brokilon. I do not recognise human maps or borders.'

'But the forest was cleared there a hundred summers ago!'

'What is a hundred summers to Brokilon? Or a hundred winters?' Geralt fell silent.

The dryad put down the comb and stroked Ciri's mousy hair.

'Agree to Venzlav's proposal, Eithné.'

The dryad looked at him coldly.

'How shall we profit by that? We, the children of Brokilon?'

'With the chance of survival. No, Eithné, do not interrupt. I know what you would say. I understand your pride in Brokilon's sovereignty. Nonetheless, the world is changing. Something is ending. Whether you like it or not, man's dominion over this world is a fact. Only those who assimilate with humans will survive. The rest will perish. Eithné, there are forests where dryads, rusalkas and elves live peacefully, having come to agreement with humans. We are so close to each other, after all. Men can be the fathers of your children. What will you gain through this war you are waging? The potential fathers of your children are perishing from your arrows. And what is the result? How many of Brokilon's dryads are pure-blood? How many of them are abducted human girls you have modified? You even have to make use of Frexinet, because you have no choice. I seem to see few tiny dryads, Eithné. I see only her; a little human girl, terrified, dulled by narcotics, paralysed by fear—'

'I'm not afraid at all!' Ciri suddenly cried, assuming her little devil face for a moment. 'And I'm not parrotised! So you'd better watch your step! Nothing can happen to me here. Be sure! I'm not afraid. My grandmamma says that dryads aren't evil, and my grandmamma is the wisest woman in the world! My grandmamma . . . My grandmamma says there should be more forests like this one . . .'

She fell silent and lowered her head. Eithné laughed.

'A Child of the Elder Blood,' she said. 'Yes, Geralt. There are still being born Children of the Elder Blood, of whom the prophesies speak. And you tell me that something is ending . . . You worry whether we shall survive—'

'The scamp was supposed to marry Kistrin of Verden,' Geralt interrupted. 'It's a pity it will not be. Kistrin will one day succeed Ervyll, and were he influenced by a wife with such views, perhaps he would cease raids on Brokilon?'

'I don't want that Kistrin!' the little girl screamed shrilly, and something flashed in her green eyes. 'Kistrin can go and find some gorgeous, stupid material! I'm not material! I won't be a princess!'

'Soft, Child of the Elder Blood,' the dryad said, hugging Ciri. 'Don't shout. Of course you will not be a princess—'

'Of course,' the Witcher interjected caustically. 'You, Eithné, and I well know what she will be. I see it has already been decided. So it goes. What answer should I take to King Venzlav, O Lady of Brokilon?'

'None.'

'What do you mean, "none"?'

'None. He will understand. Long ago, long, long ago, before Venzlav was in the world, heralds rode up to Brokilon's borders. Horns and trumpets blared, armour glinted, and pennants and standards fluttered. "Humble yourself, Brokilon!" they cried. "King Goat Tooth, king of Bald Hillock and Marshy Meadow, orders you to humble yourself, Brokilon!" And Brokilon's answer was always the same. As you are leaving my Forest, Gwynbleidd, turn around and listen. In the rustle of the leaves you will hear Brokilon's answer. Pass it on to Venzlav and add that he will never hear another while the oaks still stand in Duén Canell. Not while a single tree still grows or a single dryad still lives here.'

Geralt was silent.

'You say something is ending,' Eithné slowly went on. 'Not true. There are things that never end. You talk of survival? I am fighting to survive. Brokilon endures thanks to my fight, for trees live longer than men, as long as they are protected from your axes. You talk to me of kings and princes. Who are they? Those whom I know are white skeletons lying in the necropolises of Craag An, deep in the forest. In marble tombs, on piles of yellow metal and shining gems. But Brokilon endures, the trees sough above the ruins of palaces, their roots break up the marble. Does your Venzlav recall those kings? Do you, Gwynbleidd? And if not, how can you claim that something is ending? How do you know whose destiny is destruction and whose eternity? What entitles you to speak of destiny? Do you actually know what it is?'

'No,' the Witcher agreed, 'I do not. But—'

'If you know not,' she interrupted, 'there is no place for any "but". You know not. You simply know not.'

She was silent, touched her forehead with her hand and turned her face away.

'When you came here the first time, years ago,' she said, 'you did not know either. And Morénn . . . My daughter . . . Geralt, Morénn is dead. She fell by the Ribbon, defending Brokilon. I did not recognise her when they brought her to me. Her face had been crushed by the hooves of your horses. Destiny? And today, you, Witcher, who could not give Morénn a child, bring her – the Child of the Elder Blood – to me. A little girl who knows what destiny is. No, it is not knowledge which would suit you, knowledge which you could accept. She simply believes. Say it again, Ciri, repeat what you told me before the Witcher, Geralt of Rivia, White Wolf, entered. That witcher who does not know. Say it again, Child of the Elder Blood.'

'Your Maj . . . Venerable lady,' Ciri said in a voice that cracked. 'Do not keep me here. I cannot . . . I want to go . . . home. I want to return home with Geralt. I must go . . . With him . . .'

'Why with him?'

'For he . . . is my fate.'

Eithné turned away. She was very pale.

'What do you say to that, Geralt?'

He did not reply. Eithné clapped her hands. Braenn entered the oak tree, emerging like a ghost from the night outside, holding a large, silver goblet in both hands. The medallion around the Witcher's neck began vibrating rapidly and rhythmically.

'What do you say to that?' repeated the silver-haired dryad, standing up. 'She does not want to remain in Brokilon! She does not wish to be a dryad! She does not want to replace Morénn, she wants to leave, walk away from her fate! Is that right, Child of the Elder Blood? Is that what you actually want?'

Ciri nodded her bowed head. Her shoulders were trembling. The Witcher had had enough.

'Why are you bullying the child, Eithné? We both know you will soon give her the Water of Brokilon and what she wants will cease to mean anything. Why are you doing this? Why are you doing it in my presence?'

'I want to show you what destiny is. I want to prove to you that nothing is ending. That everything is only beginning.'

'No, Eithné,' he said, standing up. 'I'm sorry if I'm spoiling this display for you, but I have no intention of watching it. You have gone too far, Lady of Brokilon, desirous to stress the chasm dividing us. You, the Elder Folk, like to say that hatred is alien to you, that it is a feeling known only to humans. But it is not true. You know what hatred is and are capable of hating, you merely evince it a little differently, more wisely and less savagely. But because of that it may be more cruel. I accept your hatred, Eithné, on behalf of all humankind. I deserve it. I am sorry about Morénn.'

The dryad did not respond.

'And that is precisely Brokilon's answer, which I am to communicate to Venzlav of Brugge, isn't it? A warning and a challenge? Clear proof of the hatred and Power slumbering among these trees, by whose will a human child will soon drink poison which will destroy its memory, taking it from the arms of another human child whose psyche and memory have already been annihilated? And that answer is to be carried to Venzlav by a witcher who knows and feels affection for both children? The witcher who is guilty of your daughter's death? Very well, Eithné, let it be in accordance with your will. Venzlav will hear your answer, will hear my voice, will see my eyes and read everything in them. But I do not have to look on what is to occur here. And I do not want to.'

Eithné still said nothing.

'Farewell, Ciri,' Geralt knelt down and hugged the little girl. Ciri's shoulders were trembling powerfully.

'Don't cry. Nothing evil can happen to you here.'

Ciri sniffed. The Witcher stood up.

'Farewell, Braenn,' he said to the younger dryad. 'Good health and take care. Survive, Braenn; live as long as your tree. Like Brokilon. And one more thing . . .'

'Yes, Gwynbleidd?' Braenn lifted her head and something wet glistened in her eyes.

'It is easy to kill with a bow, girl. How easy it is to release the bow-string and think, it is not I, not I, it is the arrow. The blood of that boy is not on my hands. The arrow killed him, not I. But the arrow does not dream anything in the night. May you dream nothing in the night either, blue-eyed dryad. Farewell, Braenn.'

'Mona . . .' Braenn said indistinctly. The goblet she was holding shuddered and the transparent liquid filling it rippled.

'What?'

'Mona!' she wailed. 'I am Mona! Lady Eithné! I—'

'Enough of this,' Eithné said sharply. 'Enough. Control yourself, Braenn.'

Geralt laughed drily.

'There you have your destiny, Lady of the Forest. I respect your doggedness and your fight. But I know that soon you will be fighting alone. The last dryad of Brokilon sending dryads – who nonetheless still remember their real names – to their deaths. In spite of everything I wish you fortune, Eithné. Farewell.'

'Geralt . . .' Ciri whispered, still sitting motionless, with her head lowered. 'Don't leave me . . . all by myself . . .'

'White Wolf,' Eithné said, embracing the little girl's hunched back. 'Did you have to wait until she asked you? Not to abandon her? To remain with her until the end? Why do you wish to abandon her at this moment? To leave her all alone? Where do you wish to flee to, Gwynbleidd? And from what?'

Ciri's head slumped further down. But she did not cry.

'Until the end,' the Witcher said, nodding. 'Very well, Ciri. You will not be alone. I will be with you. Do not fear anything.'

Eithné took the goblet from Braenn's trembling hands and raised it up.

'Can you read Old Runes, White Wolf?'

'Yes, I can.'

'Read what is engraved on the goblet. It is from Craag An. It was drunk from by kings whom no one now remembers.'

'Duettaeánn aef cirrán Cáerme Gláeddyv. Yn á esseáth.'

'Do you know what that means?'

'The Sword of Destiny has two blades ... You are one of them.'

'Stand up, Child of the Elder Blood.' The dryad's voice clanged like steel in an order which could not be defied, a will which had to be yielded to. 'Drink. It is the Water of Brokilon.'

Geralt bit his lips and stared at Eithné's silver eyes. He did not look at Ciri, who was slowly bringing her lips to the edge of the goblet. He had seen it before, once, long ago. The convulsions, the tremors; the incredible, horrifying, slowly dwindling cry. And the emptiness, torpor and apathy in the slowly opening eyes. He had seen it before.

Ciri drank. A tear rolled slowly down Braenn's unmoving face.

'That will do,' Eithné took the goblet away, placed it on the ground, and stroked the little girl's hair, which fell onto her shoulders in mousy waves.

'O Child of the Elder Blood,' she said. 'Choose. Do you wish to remain in Brokilon, or do you follow your destiny?'

The Witcher shook his head in disbelief. Ciri was flushed and breathing a little more quickly. And nothing else. Nothing.

'I wish to follow my destiny,' she said brightly, looking the dryad in the eyes.

'Then let it be,' Eithné said, coldly and tersely. Braenn sighed aloud.

'I wish to be alone,' Eithné said, turning her back on them. 'Please leave.'

Braenn took hold of Ciri and touched Geralt's arm, but the Witcher pushed her arm away.

'Thank you, Eithné,' he said. The dryad slowly turned to face him.

'What are you thanking me for?'

'For destiny,' he smiled. 'For your decision. For that was not the Water of Brokilon, was it? It was Ciri's destiny to return home. But you, Eithné, played the role of destiny. And for that I thank you.'

'How little you know of destiny,' the dryad said bitterly. 'How little you know, Witcher. How little you see. How little you understand. You thank me? You thank me for the role I have played? For a vulgar spectacle? For a trick, a deception, a hoax? For the sword of destiny being made, as you judge, of wood dipped in gold paint? Then go further; do not thank, but expose me. Have it your own way. Prove that the arguments are in your favour. Fling your truth in my face, show me the triumph of sober, human truth, thanks to which, in your opinion, you gain mastery of the world. This is the Water of Brokilon. A little still remains. Dare you? O conqueror of the world?'

Geralt, although annoyed by her words, hesitated, but only for a moment. The Water of Brokilon, even if it were authentic, would have no effect on him. He was completely immune to the toxic, hallucinogenic tannins. But there was no way it could have been the Water of Brokilon; Ciri had drunk it and nothing had happened. He reached for the goblet with both hands and looked into the dryad's silver eyes.

The ground rushed from under his feet all at once and hurled him on his back. The powerful oak tree whirled around and shook. He fumbled all around himself with his numb arms and opened his eyes with difficulty; it was as though he were throwing off a marble tombstone. He saw above him Braenn's tiny face, and beyond her Eithné's eyes, shining like quicksilver. And other eyes; as green as emeralds. No; brighter. Like spring grass. The medallion around his neck was quivering, vibrating.

'Gwynbleidd,' he heard. 'Watch carefully. No, closing your eyes will not help you at all. Look, look at your destiny.'

'Do you remember?'

A sudden explosion of light rending a curtain of smoke, huge candelabras heavy with candles, dripping garlands of wax. Stone walls, a steep staircase. Descending the staircase, a green-eyed, mousy-haired girl in a small circlet with an intricately carved gemstone, in a silver-blue gown with a train held up by a page in a short, scarlet jacket.

'Do you remember?'

His own voice speaking . . . speaking . . .

I shall return in six years . . .

A bower, warmth, the scent of flowers, the intense, monotonous hum of bees. He, alone, on his knees, giving a rose to a woman with mousy locks spilling from beneath a narrow, gold band. Rings set with emeralds – large, green cabochons – on the fingers taking the rose from his hand.

'Return here,' the woman said. 'Return here, should you change your mind. Your destiny will be waiting.'

I shall never return here, he thought. I never . . . went back there. I never returned to . . .

Whither?

Mousy hair. Green eyes.

His voice again in the darkness, in a gloom in which everything was engulfed. There are only fires, fires all the way to the horizon. A cloud of sparks in the purple smoke. Beltane! May Day Eve! Dark, violet eyes, shining in a pale, triangular face veiled by a black, rippling shock of curls, look out from the clouds of smoke.

Yennefer!

'Too little,' the apparition's thin lips suddenly twist, a tear rolls down the pale cheek, quickly, quicker and quicker, like a drop of wax down a candle.

'Too little. Something more is needed.'

'Yennefer!'

'Nothingness for nothingness,' the apparition says in Eithné's voice.

'The nothingness and void in you, conqueror of the world, who is unable even to win the woman he loves. Who walks away and flees, when his destiny is within reach. The sword of destiny has two blades. You are one of them. But what is the other, White Wolf?'

'There is no destiny,' his own voice. 'There is none. None. It does not exist. The only thing that everyone is destined for is death.'

'That is the truth,' says the woman with the mousy hair and the mysterious smile. 'That is the truth, Geralt.'

The woman is wearing a silvery suit of armour, bloody, dented and punctured by the points of pikes or halberds. Blood drips in a thin stream from the corner of her mysteriously and hideously smiling mouth.

'You sneer at destiny,' she says, still smiling. 'You sneer at it, trifle with it. The sword of destiny has two blades. You are one of them. Is the second . . . death? But it is we who die, die because of you. Death cannot catch up with you, so it must settle for us. Death dogs your footsteps, White Wolf. But others die. Because of you. Do you remember me?'

'Ca . . . Calanthe!'

'You can save him,' the voice of Eithné, from behind the curtain of smoke. 'You can save him, Child of the Elder Blood. Before he plunges into the nothingness which he has come to love. Into the black forest which has no end.'

Eyes, as green as spring grass. A touch. Voices, crying in chorus, incomprehensibly. Faces.

He could no longer see anything. He was plummeting into the chasm, into the void, into darkness. The last thing he heard was Eithné's voice.

'Let it be so.'

VII

'Geralt! Wake up! Please wake up!'

He opened his eyes and saw the sun, a golden ducat with distinct edges, high up above the treetops, beyond the turbid veil of the morning mist. He was lying on damp, spongy moss and a hard root was digging into his back.

Ciri was kneeling beside him, tugging at his jacket.

'Curses . . .' He cleared his throat and looked around. 'Where am I? How did I end up here?'

'I don't know,' she answered. 'I woke up a moment ago, here, beside you, awffy frozen. I can't remember how . . . Do you know what? It's magic!'

'You're probably right,' he said, sitting up and pulling pine needles from his collar. 'You're probably right, Ciri. Bloody Water of Brokilon . . . Looks like the dryads were enjoying themselves at our expense.'

He stood up, picked up his sword, which was lying alongside him and slung the strap across his back.

'Ciri?'

'Uh-huh?'

'You were also enjoying yourself at my expense.'

'Me?'

'You're the daughter of Pavetta and the granddaughter of Calanthe of Cintra. You knew who I was from the very beginning, didn't you?'

'No,' she blushed. 'Not from the beginning. You lifted the curse from my daddy, didn't you?'

'That's not true,' he said, shaking his head. 'Your mama did. And your grandmamma. I only helped.'

'But my nanny said . . . She said that I'm destined. Because I'm a Surprise. A Child of Surprise. Geralt?'

'Ciri,' he looked at her, shaking his head and smiling. 'Believe me, you're the greatest surprise I could have come across.'

'Ha!' The little girl's face brightened up. 'It's true! I'm destined. My nanny said a witcher would come who would have white hair and would take me away. But grandmamma yelled . . . Oh, never mind! Tell me where you're taking me.'

'Back home. To Cintra.'

'Ah . . . But I thought you . . . ?'

'You'll have time to think on the way. Let's go, Ciri, we must leave Brokilon. It isn't a safe place.'

'I'm not afraid!'

'But I am.'

'Grandmamma said that witchers aren't afraid of anything.'

'Grandmamma overstated the facts. Let's go, Ciri. If I only knew where we . . .'

He looked up at the sun.

'Right, let's risk it . . . We'll go this way.'

'No.' Ciri wrinkled her nose and pointed in the opposite direction. 'That way. Over there.'

'And how do you know, may I ask?'

'I just know,' she shrugged and gave him a helpless, surprised, emerald look. 'Somehow . . . Somewhere, over there . . . I don't know . . .'

Pavetta's daughter, he thought. A Child . . . A Child of the Elder Blood? She might have inherited something from her mother.

'Ciri.' He tugged open his shirt and drew out his medallion. 'Touch this.'

'Oh,' she said, opening her mouth. 'What a dreadful wolf. What fangs he has . . .'

'Touch it.'

'Oh, my!'

The Witcher smiled. He had also felt the sudden vibration of the medallion, the sharp wave running through the silver chain.

'It moved!' Ciri sighed. 'It moved!'

'I know. Let's go, Ciri. You lead.'

'It's magic, isn't it!'

'Naturally.'

It was as he had expected. The little girl could sense the direction. How, he did not know. But soon – sooner than he had expected – they came out onto a track, onto a forked, three-way junction. It was the border of Brokilon – according to humans, at least. Eithné did not recognise it, he remembered.

Ciri bit her lip, wrinkled her nose and hesitated, looking at the junction, at the sandy, rutted track, furrowed by hooves and cart-wheels. But Geralt now knew where he was and did not want to depend on her uncertain abilities. He set off along the road heading eastwards, towards Brugge. Ciri, still frowning, was looking back towards the west.

'That leads to Nastrog Castle,' he jibed. 'Are you missing Kistrin?'

The little girl grunted and followed him obediently, but looked back several times.

'What is it, Ciri?'

'I don't know,' she whispered. 'But we're going the wrong way, Geralt.'

'Why? We're going to Brugge, to King Venzlav, who lives in a splendid castle. We shall take baths and sleep on a feather bed . . .'

'It's a bad road,' she said. 'A bad road.'

'That's true, I've seen better. Don't be sniffy, Ciri. Let's go. With a will.'

They went around an overgrown bend. And it turned out Ciri had been right.

They were suddenly, quickly, surrounded, from all sides. Men in conical helmets, chainmail and dark-blue tunics with the gold and black chequered pattern of Verden on their chests. They encircled the pair, but none of the men approached or reached for a weapon.

'Whence and whither?' barked a thickset individual in worn-out, green apparel, standing before Geralt with bandy legs set wide apart. His face was as swarthy and wrinkled as a prune. A bow and white-fletched arrows protruded behind him, high above his head.

'We've come from Burnt Stump,' the Witcher lied effortlessly, squeezing Ciri's little hand knowingly. 'And we're going home to Brugge. What's happening?'

'Royal service,' the dark-faced individual said courteously, as though he had only then noticed the sword on Geralt's back. 'We . . .'

'Bring 'im 'ere, Junghans!' yelled someone standing further down the road. The mercenaries parted.

'Don't look, Ciri,' Geralt said quickly. 'Avert your eyes. Don't look.'

A fallen tree lay on the road, blocking the way with a tangle of boughs. Long white splinters radiated from the partly-hacked and broken trunk standing in the roadside thicket. A loaded wagon covered with a tarpaulin stood before the tree. Two small, shaggy horses, stuck with arrows and exposing yellow teeth, were lying on the ground caught up in the shafts and halters. One was still alive and was snorting heavily and kicking.

There were also people lying in dark patches of blood soaked into the sand, hanging over the side of the wagon and hunched over the wheels.

Two men slowly emerged from among the armed men gathered around the wagon, to be joined by a third. The others – there were around ten of them – stood motionless, holding their horses.

'What happened?' the Witcher asked, standing so as to block out Ciri's view of the massacre.

A beady-eyed man in a short coat of mail and high boots gave him a searching look and audibly rubbed his bristly chin. He had a worn, shiny leather bracer of the kind archers use on his left forearm.

'Ambush,' he said curtly. 'Eerie wives did for these merchants. We're looking into it.'

'Eerie wives? Ambushing merchants?'

'You can see for yourself,' the beady-eyed man pointed. 'Stuck with arrows like urchins. On the highway! They're becoming more and more impudent, those forest hags. You can't just not venture into the forest now, you can't even travel the road by the forest.'

'And you,' the Witcher asked, squinting. 'Who are you?'

'Ervyll's men. From the Nastrog squads. We were serving under Baron Frexinet. But the baron was lost in Brokilon.'

Ciri opened her mouth, but Geralt squeezed her hand hard, ordering her to stay quiet.

'Blood for blood, I say!' roared the beady-eyed man's companion, a giant in a brass-studded kaftan. 'Blood for blood! You can't let that go. First Frexinet and the kidnapped princess from Cintra, and now merchants. By the Gods, vengeance, vengeance, I say! For if not, you'll see, tomorrow or the next day they'll start killing people on their own thresholds!'

'Brick's right,' the beady-eyed one said. 'Isn't he? And you, fellow, where are you from?'

'From Brugge,' the Witcher lied.

'And the girl? Your daughter?'

'Aye,' Geralt squeezed Ciri's hand again.

'From Brugge,' Brick frowned. 'So I'll tell you, fellow, that your king, Venzlav, is emboldening the monstrosities right now. He doesn't want to join forces with Ervyll, nor with Viraxas of Kerack. But if we marched on Brokilon from three sides, we'd finally destroy that scum . . .'

'How did the slaughter happen?' Geralt asked slowly. 'Does anybody know? Did any of the merchants survive?'

'There aren't any witnesses,' the beady-eyed one said. 'But we know what happened. Junghans, a forester, can read spoors like a book. Tell him, Junghans.'

'Well,' said the one with the wrinkled face, 'it were like this: the merchants were travelling along the highway. And their way were blocked. You see, sir, that fallen pine lying across the road, freshly felled. There are tracks in the thicket, want to see? Well, when the merchants stopped to clear away the tree, they were shot, just like that. Over there, from the bushes by that crooked birch. There are tracks there too. And the arrows, mark you, all dryad work, fletchings stuck on with resin, shafts bound with bast . . .'

'I see,' the Witcher interrupted, looking at the bodies. 'Some of them, I think, survived the arrows and had their throats cut. With knives.'

One more man emerged from behind the group of mercenaries standing in front of him. He was skinny and short, in an elk-hide kaftan. He had black, short hair, and his cheeks were blue from closely-shaved, black beard growth. One glance at the small, narrow hands in short, black, fingerless gloves, at the pale, fish-like eyes, at his sword and at the hafts of the daggers stuck into his belt and down his left boot was all the Witcher needed. Geralt had seen too many murderers not to recognise one more instantly.

'You've a keen eye,' said the black-haired man, extremely slowly. 'Indeed, you see much.'

'And well he does,' said the beady-eyed man. 'Let him tell his king what he saw. Venzlav still swears eerie wives shouldn't be killed, because they are agreeable and good. I'll bet he visits them on May Day and ruts them. Perhaps they're good for that. We'll find out for ourselves if we take one alive.'

'Or even half-dead,' Brick cackled. 'Hi, where's that bloody druid? Almost noon, but no sign of him. We must off.'

'What do you mean to do?' Geralt asked, without releasing Ciri's hand.

'What business is it of yours?' the black-haired man hissed.

'Oh, why so sharp right away, Levecque?' the beady-eyed one asked, smiling foully. 'We're honest men, we have no secrets. Ervyll is sending us a druid, a great magician, who can even talk with trees. Him'll guide us into the forest to avenge Frexinet and try and rescue the princess. We aren't out for a picnic, fellow, but on a punitive ex— ex—'

'Expedition,' the black-haired man, Levecque, prompted.

'Aye. Took the words out of me mouth. So then go on your way, fellow, for it may get hot here anon.'

'Aaaye,' Levecque drawled, looking at Ciri. ''Twill be dangerous here, particularly with a young 'un. Eerie wives are just desperate for girls like that. Hey, little maid? Is your mama at home waiting?'

Ciri, trembling, nodded.

''Twould be disastrous,' the black-haired one continued, not taking his eye off her, 'were you not to make it home. She would surely race to King Venzlav and say: "You were lax with the dryads,

king, and now you have my daughter and husband on your conscience." Who knows, perhaps Venzlav would weigh up an alliance
with Ervyll once more?'

'Leave them, Mr Levecque,' Junghans snarled, and his wrinkled
face wrinkled up even more. 'Let them go.'

'Farewell, little maid,' Levecque said and held out his hand to
stroke Ciri on the head. Ciri shuddered and withdrew.

'What is it? Are you afraid?'

'You have blood on your hand,' the Witcher said softly.

'Ah,' Levecque said, raising his hand. 'Indeed. It's their blood.
The merchants. I checked to see if any of them had survived. But
alas, the eerie wives shoot accurately.'

'Eerie wives?' said Ciri in a trembling voice, not reacting to the
Witcher's squeeze of her hand. 'Oh, noble knights, you are mistaken. It could not be dryads!'

'What are you squeaking about, little maid?' The pale eyes of
the black-haired man narrowed. Geralt glanced to the right and left,
estimating the distances.

'It wasn't dryads, sir knight,' Ciri repeated. 'It's obvious!'

'Ay?'

'I mean, that tree . . . That tree was chopped down! With an axe!
But no dryad would ever chop a tree down, would they?'

'Indeed,' Levecque said and glanced at the beady-eyed man. 'Oh,
what a clever little girl, you are. Too clever.'

The Witcher had already seen his thin, gloved hands creeping like
a black spider towards the haft of his dagger. Although Levecque
had not taken his eyes off Ciri, Geralt knew the blow would be
aimed at him. He waited for the moment when Levecque touched
his weapon, while the beady-eyed man held his breath.

Three movements. Just three. His silver-studded forearm
slammed into the side of the black-haired man's head. Before he
fell, the Witcher was standing between Junghans and the beady-
eyed man, and his sword, hissing out of the scabbard, whined in the
air, slashing open the temple of Brick, the giant in the brass-studded
kaftan.

'Run, Ciri!'

305

The beady-eyed man, who was drawing his sword, leaped, but was not fast enough. The Witcher slashed him across his chest, diagonally, downwards, and immediately, taking advantage of the blow's momentum, upwards, from a kneeling position, cutting the mercenary open in a bloody 'X'.

'Men!' Junghans yelled at the rest, who were frozen in astonishment. 'Over here!'

Ciri leaped into a crooked beech tree and scampered like a squirrel up the branches, disappearing among the foliage. The forester sent an arrow after her but missed. The remaining men ran over, breaking up into a semi-circle, pulling out bows and arrows from quivers. Geralt, still kneeling, put his fingers together and struck with the Aard Sign, not at the bowmen, for they were too far away, but at the sandy road in front of them, spraying them in a cloud of sand.

Junghans, leaping aside, nimbly drew another arrow from his quiver.

'No!' Levecque yelled, springing up from the ground with his sword in his right hand and a dagger in his left. 'Leave him, Junghans!'

The Witcher spun around smoothly, turning to face him.

'He's mine,' Levecque said, shaking his head and wiping his cheek and mouth with his forearm. 'Leave him to me!'

Geralt, crouching, started to circle, but Levecque did not, instead attacking at once, leaping forward in two strides.

He's good, the Witcher thought, working hard to connect with the killer's blade with a short moulinet, avoiding the dagger's jab with a half-turn. He intentionally did not reply, but leaped back, counting on Levecque trying to reach him with a long, extended thrust and losing his balance. But the killer was no novice. He dropped into a crouch and also moved around in a semi-circle with soft, feline steps. He unexpectedly bounded forward, swung his sword and whirled, shortening the distance. The Witcher did not meet him halfway, but restricted himself to a swift, high feint which forced the killer to dodge. Levecque stooped over, offered a quarte, hiding the hand with the dagger behind his back. The Witcher did not attack this time either, did not move in, but described a semi-circle again, skirting around him.

'Aha,' Levecque drawled, straightening up. 'Shall we prolong the game? Why not? You can never have too much amusement!'

He leaped, spun, struck, once, twice, thrice, in a rapid rhythm; a cut from above with his sword and immediately from the left with a flat, scything blow of his dagger. The Witcher did not disturb the rhythm; parried, leaped back and once again circled, forcing the killer to move around. Levecque suddenly drew back, circling in the opposite direction.

'Every game,' he hissed through clenched teeth, 'must have its end. What would you say to a single blow, trickster? A single blow and then we'll shoot your little brat down from the tree. How about that?'

Geralt saw that Levecque was watching his shadow, waiting for it to reach his opponent, indicating that he had the sun in his eyes. Geralt stopped circling to make the killer's job easier.

And narrowed his pupils into vertical slits, two narrow lines.

In order to maintain the illusion, he screwed his eyes up a little, pretending to be blinded.

Levecque leaped, spun, keeping his balance by extending his dagger hand out sideways, and struck with a simply impossible bend of his wrist, upwards, aiming at the Witcher's crotch. Geralt shot forward, spun, deflected the blow, bending his arm and wrist equally impossibly, throwing the killer backwards with the momentum of the parry and slashing him across his left cheek with the tip of his blade. Levecque staggered, grabbing his face. The Witcher twisted into a half-turn, shifted his bodyweight onto his left leg and cleaved open his opponent's carotid artery with a short blow. Levecque curled up, bleeding profusely, dropped to his knees, bent over and fell headfirst onto the sand.

Geralt slowly turned towards Junghans. Junghans, contorting his wrinkled face in a furious grimace, took aim with his bow. The Witcher crouched, gripping his sword in both hands. The remaining mercenaries also raised their bows, in dead silence.

'What are you waiting for?' the forester roared. 'Shoot! Shoot hi—' He stumbled, staggered, tottered forwards and fell on his face with an arrow sticking out of his back. The arrow's shaft had striped fletchings made from a pheasant's flight feathers, dyed yellow in a concoction of tree bark.

The arrows flew with a whistle and hiss in long, flat parabolas from the black wall of the forest. They flew apparently slowly and calmly, their fletchings sighing, and it seemed as though they picked up speed and force as they struck their targets. And they struck unerringly, scything down the Nastrog mercenaries, knocking them over into the sand, inert and mown down, like sunflowers hit with a stick.

The ones who survived rushed towards the horses, jostling one another. The arrows continued to whistle, catching up with them as they ran, hitting them as they sat in the saddle. Only three managed to rouse their horses to a gallop and ride off, yelling, their spurs bloodying their mounts' flanks. But not even they got far.

The forest closed up, blocking the way. Suddenly the sandy highway, bathed in sunlight, disappeared. It was now a dense, impenetrable wall of black tree trunks.

The mercenaries, terrified and stupefied, spurred their horses, but the arrows flew unceasingly. And hit them, knocking them from their saddles among the hoof-falls and neighing of the horses, and screams.

And afterwards a silence fell.

The wall of trees blocking the highway shimmered, became blurred, shone brightly and vanished. The road could be seen again and on it stood a grey horse and on the grey horse sat a rider – mighty, with a flaxen, fan-shaped beard, in a jerkin of sealskin with a tartan, woollen sash.

The grey horse, turning its head away and champing at the bit, moved forward, lifting its fore hooves high, snorting and becoming agitated by the corpses and the smell of blood. The rider, upright in the saddle, raised a hand and a sudden gust of wind struck the trees' branches.

From the undergrowth on the distant edge of the forest emerged small shapes in tight-fitting garments patched green and brown, with faces streaked with walnut-shell dye.

'Ceádmil, Wedd Brokiloéne!' the rider called. 'Fáill, Aná Woedwedd!'

'Fáill!' replied a voice from the forest like a gust of wind.

The green and brown shapes began to disappear, one after the other, melting into the thicket of the forest. Only one remained, with flowing hair the colour of honey. She took several steps and approached.

'Vá fáill, Gwynbleidd!' she called, coming even closer.

'Farewell, Mona,' the Witcher said. 'I will not forget you.'

'Forget me,' she responded firmly, adjusting her quiver on her back. 'There is no Mona. Mona was a dream. I am Braenn. Braenn of Brokilon!'

She waved at him once more. And disappeared.

The Witcher turned around.

'Mousesack,' he said, looking at the rider on the grey horse.

'Geralt,' the rider nodded, eyeing him up and down coldly. 'An interesting encounter. But let us begin with the most important things. Where is Ciri?'

'Here!' the girl yelled from the foliage. 'Can I come down yet?'

'Yes, you may,' the Witcher said.

'But I don't know how!'

'The same way as you climbed up, just the other way around.'

'I'm afraid! I'm right at the very top!'

'Get down, I said! We need to have a serious conversation, young lady!'

'What about?'

'About why the bloody hell you climbed up there instead of running into the forest? I would have followed you instead of . . . Oh, blow it. Get down!'

'I did what the cat in the story did! Whatever I do it's always wrong! Why, I'd like to know.'

'I would too,' the druid said, dismounting. 'I would also like to know. And your grandmamma, Queen Calanthe, would like to know, too. Come on, climb down, princess.'

Leaves and dry branches fell from the tree. Then there was a sharp crack of tearing material, and finally Ciri appeared, sliding astride the trunk. She had picturesque shreds instead of a hood on her jacket.

'Uncle Mousesack!'

'In person.' The druid embraced and cuddled the little girl.

'Did grandmamma send you? Uncle? Is she very worried?'

'Not very,' Mousesack smiled. 'She is too busy soaking her switch. The way to Cintra, Ciri, will take us some time. Devote it to thinking up an explanation for your deeds. It ought to be, if you want to benefit from my counsel, a very short and matter-of-fact explanation. One which can be given very, very quickly. For in any case I judge you will be screaming at the end of it, princess. Very, very loudly.'

Ciri grimaced painfully, wrinkled up her nose, snorted softly, and her hands involuntarily went towards the endangered place.

'Let's go,' Geralt said, looking around. 'Let's go, Mousesack.'

VIII

'No,' the druid said. 'Calanthe has changed her plans, she does not want the marriage of Ciri and Kistrin to go ahead now. She has her reasons. Additionally, I presume I don't have to explain that following that dreadful scandal with the sham ambush on the merchants, King Ervyll has gone down a long way in my estimation, and my estimation matters in the kingdom. No, we won't even stop off at Nastrog. I'll take the lass straight to Cintra. Ride with us, Geralt.'

'What for?' The Witcher glanced at Ciri, who was now slumbering beneath a tree, wrapped in Mousesack's jerkin.

'You well know what for. That child, Geralt, is linked to you by destiny. For the third time, yes, the third, your paths have crossed. Metaphorically, of course, particularly as regards the previous two occasions. You surely can't call it coincidence?'

'What does it matter what I call it?' The Witcher smiled wryly. 'The essence is not in the name, Mousesack. Why ought I to ride to Cintra? I have already been to Cintra; I have already, as you described it, crossed paths. What of it?'

'Geralt, you demanded a vow from Calanthe, then from Pavetta and her husband. The vow has been kept. Ciri is the Child of Destiny. Destiny demands . . .'

'That I take the child and turn her into a witcher? A little girl? Take a good look at me, Mousesack. Can you imagine me as a comely lass?'

'To hell with witchering,' the druid said, annoyed. 'What are you talking about? What has the one to do with the other? No, Geralt, I see that you understand nothing, I shall have to use simple words. Listen, any fool, including you, may demand a vow, may exact a promise, and will not become remarkable because of it. It is the child who is extraordinary. And the bond which comes into being when

311

the child is born is extraordinary. Need I be more clear? Very well, Geralt. From the moment Ciri was born, what you wanted and what you planned to do ceased to matter, and what you don't want and what you mean to give up doesn't make any difference either. You don't bloody matter! Don't you understand?'

'Don't shout, you'll wake her up. Our destiny is asleep. And when she awakes . . . Mousesack, one must occasionally give up . . . Even the most extraordinary things.'

'But you know,' the druid looked at him coldly, 'you will never have a child of your own.'

'Yes.'

'And you're still giving her up?'

'Yes, I am. I'm surely permitted to, aren't I?'

'You are,' Mousesack said. 'Indeed. But it is risky. There is an old prophecy saying that the sword of destiny . . .'

'. . . has two blades,' Geralt completed the sentence. 'I've heard it.'

'Oh, do as you think fit,' the druid turned his head away and spat. 'Just think, I was prepared to stick my neck out for you . . .'

'You?'

'Me. Unlike you, I believe in destiny. And I knew that it is hazardous to trifle with a two-edged sword. Don't trifle with it, Geralt. Take advantage of the chance which is presenting itself. Turn what connects you to Ciri into the normal, healthy bond of a child with its guardian. For if you do not . . . Then that bond may manifest itself differently. More terribly. In a negative and destructive way. I want to protect you both from that. If you wanted to take her, I would not protest. I would take upon myself the risk of explaining why to Calanthe.'

'How do you know Ciri would want to go with me? Because of some old prophecies?'

'No,' Mousesack said gravely. 'Because she only fell asleep after you cuddled her. Because she mutters your name and searches for your hand in her sleep.'

'Enough,' Geralt got up, 'because I'm liable to get emotional. Farewell, bearded one. My compliments to Calanthe. And think something up . . . For Ciri's sake.'

'You will not escape, Geralt.'

'From destiny?' The Witcher tightened the girth of the captured horse.

'No,' the druid said, looking at the sleeping child. 'From her.'

The Witcher nodded and jumped into the saddle. Mousesack sat motionless, poking a stick into the dying campfire.

He rode slowly away, through heather as high as his stirrups, across the hillside leading into the valley, towards the black forest.

'Geraaalt!'

He turned around. Ciri was standing on the brow of the hill, a tiny, grey figure with windblown, mousy hair.

'Don't go!'

She waved.

'Don't go!'

She yelled shrilly.

'Don't goooo!'

I have to, he thought. I have to, Ciri. Because . . . I always do.

'You won't get away!' she cried. 'Don't go thinking that! You can't run away! I'm your destiny, do you hear?'

There is no destiny, he thought. It does not exist. The only thing that everyone is destined for is death. Death is the other blade of the two-edged sword. I am the first blade. And the second is death, which dogs my footsteps. I cannot, I may not expose you to that, Ciri.

'I am your destiny!'

The words reached his ears from the hilltop, more softly, more despairingly.

He nudged the horse with his heel and rode straight ahead, heading deep into the black, cold and boggy forest, as though into an abyss, into the pleasant, familiar shade, into the gloom which seemed to have no end.

SOMETHING MORE

I

When hooves suddenly rapped on the timbers of the bridge, Yurga did not even raise his head; he just howled softly, released the wheel rim he was grappling with and crawled under the cart as quickly as he could. Flattened, scraping his back against the rough manure and mud caked onto the underside of the vehicle, he whined and trembled with fear.

The horse moved slowly towards the cart. Yurga saw it place its hooves cautiously on the rotted, moss-covered timbers.

'Get out,' the unseen horseman said. Yurga's teeth chattered and he pulled his head into his shoulders. The horse snorted and stamped.

'Easy, Roach,' the horseman said. Yurga heard him pat his mount on the neck. 'Get out from under there, fellow. I won't do you any harm.'

The merchant did not believe the stranger's declaration in the slightest. There was something calming and at the same time intriguing in his voice, however, though it was by no means a voice which could be described as pleasant. Yurga, mumbling prayers to a dozen deities all at once, timidly stuck his head out from under the cart.

The horseman had hair as white as milk, tied back from his forehead with a leather band, and a black, woollen cloak falling over the rump of the chestnut mare. He did not look at Yurga. Leaning from his saddle, he was examining the cartwheel, sunk up to the hub between the bridge's broken beams. He suddenly raised his head,

315

flicked a gaze over the merchant and observed the undergrowth above the banks of the ravine.

Yurga scrambled out, blinked and rubbed his nose with a hand, smearing wood tar from the wheel hub over his face. The horseman fixed dark, narrowed, piercing eyes, as sharp as a spear tip, on him. Yurga was silent.

'The two of us won't be able to pull it out,' said the stranger finally, pointing at the stuck wheel. 'Were you travelling alone?'

'There were three of us,' Yurga stammered. 'Servants, sir. But they fled, the scoundrels . . .'

'I'm not surprised,' said the horseman, looking under the bridge towards the bottom of the ravine. 'I'm not surprised at all. I think you ought to do the same. Time is short.'

Yurga did not follow the stranger's gaze. He did not want to look at the mass of skulls, ribs and shinbones scattered among the rocks, peeping out from the burdock and nettles covering the bottom of the dried-up stream. He was afraid that with just one more glance, one more glimpse of the black eye sockets, grinning teeth and cracked bones, something would snap in him, the remains of his desperate courage would escape like air from a fish's bladder, and he would dash back up the highway, stifling a scream, just as the carter and his lad had less than an hour before.

'What are you waiting for?' the horseman asked softly, reining his horse around. 'For nightfall? It'll be too late then. They'll come for you as soon as it begins to get dark. Or maybe even sooner. Let's go, jump up behind me. Let's both get out of here as quick as we can.'

'But the cart, sir?' Yurga howled at the top of his voice, not knowing if from fear, despair or rage. 'And my goods? That's a whole year's work! I'd rather drop dead! I'm not leaving it!'

'I think you still don't know where the bloody hell you are, friend,' the stranger said calmly, extending a hand towards the ghastly graveyard beneath the bridge. 'Won't leave your cart, you say? I tell you, when darkness falls not even King Dezmod's treasury will save you, never mind your lousy cart. What the hell came over you to take a shortcut through this wilderness? Don't you know what has infested this place since the war?'

Yurga shook his head.

'You don't know,' nodded the stranger. 'But you've seen what's down there? It'd be difficult not to notice. That's all the other men who took a shortcut through here. And you say you won't leave your cart. And what, I wonder, do you have in your cart?'

Yurga did not reply, but glowered at the horseman, trying to choose between 'oakum' and 'old rags'.

The horseman did not seem particularly interested in the answer. He reassured his chestnut, who was chewing its bit and tossing its head.

'Please, sir . . .' the merchant finally muttered. 'Help me. Save me. My eternal gratitude . . . Don't leave . . . I'll give you whatever you want, whatever you ask . . . Save me, sir!'

The stranger, resting both hands on the pommel of his saddle, suddenly turned his head towards him.

'What did you say?'

Yurga opened his mouth but said nothing.

'You'll give me whatever I ask for? Say it again.'

Yurga smacked his lips, closed his mouth and wished he was agile enough to kick himself in the arse. His head was spinning with fantastic theories as to the reward that this weird stranger might demand. Most of them, including the privilege of weekly use of his rosy-cheeked young wife, did not seem as awful as the prospect of losing the cart, and certainly not as macabre as the possibility of ending up at the bottom of the canyon as one more bleached skeleton. His merchant's experience forced him into some rapid calculations. The horseman, although he did not resemble a typical ruffian, tramp or marauder – of which there were plenty on the roads after the war – surely wasn't a magnate or governor either, nor one of those proud little knights with a high opinion of themselves who derive pleasure from robbing the shirt off their neighbours' backs. Yurga reckoned him at no more than twenty pieces of gold. However, his commercial instincts stopped him from naming a price. So he limited himself to mumbling something about 'lifelong gratitude'.

'I asked you,' the stranger calmly reminded him, after waiting for the merchant to be quiet, 'if you'll give me whatever I ask for?'

There was no way out. Yurga swallowed, bowed his head and nodded his agreement. The stranger, in spite of Yurga's expectations, did not laugh portentously; quite the opposite, he did not show any sign of being delighted by his victory in the negotiations. Leaning over in the saddle, he spat into the ravine.

'What am I doing?' he said grimly. 'What the fuck am I doing? Well, so be it. I'll try to get you out of this, though I don't know that it won't finish disastrously for us both. But if I succeed, in exchange you will . . .'

Yurga curled up, close to tears.

'You will give me,' the horseman in the black cloak suddenly and quickly recited, 'whatever you come across at home on your return, but did not expect. Do you swear?'

Yurga groaned and nodded quickly.

'Good,' the stranger grimaced. 'And now stand aside. It would be best if you got back under the cart. The sun is about to set.'

He dismounted and took his cloak from his shoulders. Yurga saw that the stranger was carrying a sword on his back, on a belt slung diagonally across his chest. He had a vague sense he had once heard of people with a similar way of carrying a weapon. The black, leather, hip-length jacket with long sleeves sparkling with silver studs might have indicated that the stranger came from Novigrad or the surroundings, but the fashion for such dress had recently become widespread, particularly among youngsters. Although this stranger was no youngster.

After removing his saddlebags from his mount the horseman turned around. A round medallion hung on a silver chain around his neck. He was holding a small, metal-bound chest and an oblong parcel wrapped in skins and fastened with a strap under one arm.

'Aren't you under the cart yet?' he asked, approaching. Yurga saw that a wolf's head with open jaws and armed with fangs was depicted on the medallion. He suddenly recalled.

'Would you be . . . a witcher? Sir?'

The stranger shrugged.

'You guess right. A witcher. Now move away. To the other side of the cart. Don't come out from there and be silent. I must be alone for a while.'

Yurga obeyed. He hunkered down by the wheel, wrapped in a mantle. He didn't want to look at what the stranger was doing on the other side of the cart, even less at the bones at the bottom of the ravine. So he looked at his boots and at the green, star-shaped shoots of moss growing on the bridge's rotten timbers.

A witcher.

The sun was setting.

He heard footsteps.

Slowly, very slowly, the stranger moved out from behind the cart, into the centre of the bridge. He had his back to Yurga, who saw that the sword on his back was not the sword he had seen earlier. Now it was a splendid weapon; the hilt, crossguard and fittings of the scabbard shone like stars. Even in the gathering darkness they reflected light, although there was almost none; not even the golden-purple glow which a short while earlier had been hanging over the forest.

'Sir—'

The stranger turned his head. Yurga barely stifled a scream.

The stranger's face was white – white and porous, like cheese drained and unwrapped from a cloth. And his eyes . . . Ye Gods, something howled inside Yurga. His eyes . . .

'Behind the cart. Now,' the stranger rasped. It was not the voice Yurga had heard before. The merchant suddenly felt his full bladder troubling him terribly. The stranger turned and walked further along the bridge.

A witcher.

The horse tied to the cart's rack snorted, neighed, and stamped its hooves dully on the beams.

A mosquito buzzed above Yurga's ear. The merchant did not even move a hand to shoo it away. A second one joined it. Whole clouds of mosquitoes were buzzing in the thicket on the far side of the ravine. Buzzing.

And howling.

Yurga, clenching his teeth till they hurt, realised they were not mosquitoes.

From the thickening darkness on the overgrown side of the ravine emerged some small, misshapen forms – less than four feet tall, horribly gaunt, like skeletons. They stepped onto the bridge with a peculiar, heron-like gait, feet high, making staccato, jerky movements as they lifted their bony knees. Their eyes, beneath flat, dirty foreheads, shone yellow, and pointed little fangs gleamed white in wide, frog-like maws. They came closer, hissing.

The stranger, as still as a statue in the centre of the bridge, suddenly raised his right hand, making a bizarre shape with his fingers. The monstrous little beasts retreated, hissing loudly, before once again moving forwards, quickly, quicker and quicker, on their long, spindly, taloned forefeet.

Claws scraped on the timbers to the left, as another monster jumped out from under the bridge, and the remaining ones on the bank rushed forwards in bewildering leaps. The stranger spun around on the spot and the sword, which had suddenly appeared in his hand, flashed. The head of the creature scrambling onto the bridge flew two yards up into the air, trailing a ribbon of blood behind it. Then the white-haired man fell on a group of them and whirled, slashing swiftly all around him. The monsters, flailing their arms and wailing, attacked him from all sides, ignoring the luminous blade cutting them like a razor. Yurga cowered, hugging the cart.

Something fell right at his feet, bespattering him with gore. It was a long, bony hand, four-clawed and scaly, like a chicken's foot.

The merchant screamed.

He sensed something flitting past him. He cowered, intending to dive under the cart, just as something landed on his neck, and a scaly hand seized him by the temple and cheek. He covered his eyes, howling and jerking his head, leaped to his feet and staggered into the middle of the bridge, stumbling over the corpses sprawled across the timbers. A battle was raging there – but Yurga could not see anything apart from a furious swarm, a mass, within which the silver blade kept flashing.

'Help meeeee!' he howled, feeling the sharp fangs penetrating the felt of his hood and digging into the back of his head.

'Duck!'

He pressed his chin down onto his chest, looking out for the flash of the blade. It whined in the air and grazed his hood. Yurga heard a hideous, wet crunching sound and then a hot liquid gushed down his back. He fell to his knees, dragged down by the now inert weight hanging from his neck.

He watched as three more monsters scuttled out from under the bridge. Leaping like bizarre grasshoppers, they latched onto the stranger's thighs. One of them, slashed with a short blow across its toadlike muzzle, took a few steps upright and fell onto the timbers. Another, struck with the very tip of the sword, collapsed in squirming convulsions. The remaining ones swarmed like ants over the white-haired man, pushing him towards the edge of the bridge. One flew out of the swarm bent backwards, spurting blood, quivering and howling, and right then the entire seething mass staggered over the edge and plummeted into the ravine. Yurga fell to the ground, covering his head with his hands.

From below the bridge he heard the monsters' triumphant squeals, suddenly transforming into howls of pain, those howls silenced by the whistling of the blade. Then from the darkness came the rattle of stones and the crunch of skeletons being trodden on and crushed, and then once again came the whistle of a falling sword and a despairing, bloodcurdling shriek which suddenly broke off.

And then there was only silence, interrupted by the sudden cry of a terrified bird, deep in the forest among the towering trees. And then the bird fell silent too.

Yurga swallowed, raised his head and stood up with difficulty. It was still quiet; not even the leaves rustled, the entire forest seemed to be dumbstruck with terror. Ragged clouds obscured the sky.

'Hey . . .'

He turned around, involuntarily protecting himself with raised arms. The Witcher stood before him, motionless, black, with the shining sword in his lowered hand. Yurga noticed he was standing somehow crookedly, leaning over to one side.

'What's the matter, sir?'

The Witcher did not reply. He took a step, clumsily and heavily, limping on his left leg. He held out a hand and grasped the cart. Yurga saw blood, black and shining, dripping onto the timbers.

'You're wounded, sir!'

The Witcher did not reply. Looking straight into the merchant's eyes, he fell against the cart's box and slowly collapsed onto the bridge.

II

'Careful, easy does it . . . Under his head . . . One of you support his head!'

'Here, here, onto the cart!'

'Ye Gods, he'll bleed to death . . . Mr Yurga, the blood's seeping through the dressing—'

'Quiet! Drive on, Pokvit, make haste! Wrap him in a sheepskin, Vell, can't you see how he shivers?'

'Shall I pour some vodka down his throat?'

'Can't you see he's unconscious? You astonish me, Vell. But give me that vodka, I need a drink . . . You dogs, you scoundrels, you rotten cowards! Scarpering like that and leaving me all alone!'

'Mr Yurga! He said something!'

'What? What's he saying?'

'Err, can't make it out . . . seems to be a name . . .'

'What name?'

'Yennefer . . .'

III

'Where am I?'

'Lie still, sir, don't move, or everything will tear open again. Those vile creatures bit your thigh down to the bone, you've lost a deal of blood . . . Don't you know me? It's Yurga! You saved me on the bridge, do you recall?'

'Aha . . .'

'Do you have a thirst?'

'A hell of one . . .'

'Drink, sir, drink. You're burning with fever.'

'Yurga . . . Where are we?'

'We're riding in my cart. Don't say anything, sir, don't move. We had to venture out of the forest towards human settlements. We must find someone with healing powers. What we've wrapped round your leg may be insufficient. The blood won't stop coming—'

'Yurga . . .'

'Yes, sir?'

'In my chest . . . A flacon . . . With green sealing wax. Strip off the seal and give it to me . . . In a bowl. Wash the bowl well, don't let a soul touch the flacon . . . If you value your life . . . Swiftly, Yurga. Dammit, how this cart shakes . . . The flacon, Yurga . . .'

'I have it . . . Drink, sir.'

'Thanks . . . Now pay attention. I'll soon fall asleep. I'll thrash around and rave, then lie as though dead. It's nothing, don't be afeared . . .'

'Lie still, sir, or the wound will open and you'll lose blood.'

He fell back onto the skins, turned his head and felt the merchant drape him in a sheepskin and a blanket stinking of horse sweat. The

324

cart shook and with each jolt pangs of fierce pain shot through his thigh and hip. Geralt clenched his teeth. He saw above him billions of stars. So close it seemed he could reach out and touch them. Right above his head, just above the treetops.

As he walked he picked his way in order to stay away from the light, away from the glow of bonfires, in order to remain within the compass of rippling shadow. It was not easy – pyres of fir logs were burning all around, sending into the sky a red glow shot with the flashes of sparks, marking the darkness with brighter pennants of smoke, crackling, exploding in a blaze among the figures dancing all around.

Geralt stopped to let through a frenzied procession, boisterous and wild, which was barring his way and lurching towards him. Someone tugged him by the arm, trying to shove into his hand a wooden beer mug, dripping with foam. He declined and gently but firmly pushed away the man, who was staggering and splashing beer all around from the small cask he was carrying under one arm. Geralt did not want to drink.

Not on a night like this.

Close by – on a frame of birch poles towering above a huge fire – the fair-haired May King, dressed in a wreath and coarse britches, was kissing the red-haired May Queen, groping her breasts through her thin, sweat-soaked blouse. The monarch was more than a little drunk and tottered, trying to keep his balance, as he hugged the queen, pressing a fist clamped onto a mug of beer against her back. The queen, also far from sober, wearing a wreath which had slipped down over her eyes, hung on the king's neck and leaned close against him in anticipation. The throng was dancing beneath the frame, singing, yelling and shaking poles festooned with garlands of foliage and blossom.

'Beltane!' screamed a short, young woman right in Geralt's ear. Pulling him by the sleeve, she forced him to turn around among the procession encircling them. She cavorted by him, fluttering her skirt and shaking her hair, which was full of flowers. He let her spin him in the dance and whirled around, nimbly avoiding the other couples.

'Beltane! May Day Eve!'

Besides them there was a struggle, a squealing and the nervous laugh of another young woman, feigning a fight and resistance, being carried off by a young man into the darkness, beyond the circle of light. The procession, hooting, snaked between the burning pyres. Someone stumbled and fell, breaking the chain of hands, rending the procession apart into smaller groups.

The young woman, looking at Geralt from under the leaves decorating her brow, came closer and pressed herself urgently against him, encircling him with her arms and panting. He grabbed her more roughly than he had intended and felt the hot dampness of her body, perceptible on his hands through the thin linen pressing against her back. She raised her head. Her eyes were closed and her teeth flashed from beneath her raised, twisted upper lip. She smelled of sweat and sweet grass, smoke and lust.

Why not? he thought, crumpling her dress and kneading her back with his hands, enjoying the damp, steaming warmth on his fingers. The woman was not his type. She was too small and too plump – under his hand he felt the line where the too-tight bodice of her dress was cutting into her body, dividing her back into two distinctly perceptible curves, where he should not have been able to feel them. Why not? he thought, on a night like this, after all . . . It means nothing.

Beltane . . . Fires as far as the horizon. Beltane, May Day Eve.

The nearest pyre devoured the dry, outstretched pine branches being thrown onto it with a crack, erupted in a golden flash, lighting everything up. The young woman's eyes opened wide, looking up into his face. He heard her suck air in, felt her tense up and violently push her hands against his chest. He released her at once. She hesitated. Tilted her trunk away to the length of her almost straightened arms, but she did not peel her hips away from his thighs. She lowered her head, then withdrew her hands and drew away, looking to the side.

They stood motionless for a moment until the returning procession barged into them, shook and jostled them again. The young woman quickly turned and fled, clumsily trying to join the dancers. She looked back. Just once.

Beltane . . .

What am I doing here?

A star shone in the dark, sparkling, drawing his gaze. The medallion around the Witcher's neck vibrated. Geralt involuntarily dilated his pupils, his vision effortlessly penetrating the obscurity.

She was not a peasant woman. Peasant women did not wear black velvet cloaks. Peasant women – carried or dragged into the bushes by men – screamed, giggled, squirmed and tensed their bodies like trout being pulled out of the water. None of them gave the impression that it was *they* who were leading their tall, fair-haired swains with gaping shirts into the gloom.

Peasant women never wore velvet ribbons or diamond-encrusted stars of obsidian around their necks.

'Yennefer.'

Wide-open, violet eyes blazing in a pale, triangular face.

'Geralt . . .'

She released the hand of the fair-haired cherub whose breast was shiny as a sheet of copper with sweat. The lad staggered, tottered, fell to his knees, rolled his head, looked around and blinked. He stood up slowly, glanced at them uncomprehending and embarrassed, and then lurched off towards the bonfires. The sorceress did not even glance at him. She looked intently at the Witcher, and her hand tightly clenched the edge of her cloak.

'Nice to see you,' he said easily. He immediately sensed the tension which had formed between them falling away.

'Indeed,' she smiled. He seemed to detect something affected in the smile, but he could not be certain. 'Quite a pleasant surprise, I don't deny. What are you doing here, Geralt? Oh . . . Excuse me, forgive my indiscretion. Of course, we're doing the same thing. It's Beltane, after all. Only you caught me, so to speak, in flagrante delicto.'

'I interrupted you.'

'I'll survive,' she laughed. 'The night is young. I'll enchant another if the fancy takes me.'

'Pity I'm unable to do that,' he said trying hard to affect indifference. 'A moment ago a girl saw my eyes in the light and fled.'

'At dawn,' she said, smiling more and more falsely, 'when they really let themselves go, they won't pay any attention. You'll find another, just you wait . . .'

'Yen—' The rest of the words stuck in his throat. They looked at one another for a long, long time, and the red reflection of fire flickered on their faces. Yennefer suddenly sighed, veiling her eyes with her eyelashes.

'Geralt, no. Don't let's start—'

'It's Beltane,' he interrupted. 'Have you forgotten?'

She moved slowly closer, placed her hands on his arms, and slowly and cautiously snuggled against him, touching his chest with her forehead. He stroked her raven-black hair, strewn in locks coiled like snakes.

'Believe me,' she whispered, lifting her head. 'I wouldn't think twice, if it were only to be . . . But it's senseless. Everything will start again and finish like last time. It would be senseless if we were to—'

'Does everything have to make sense? It's Beltane.'

'Beltane,' she turned her head. 'What of it? Something drew us to these bonfires, to these people enjoying themselves. We meant to dance, abandon ourselves, get a little intoxicated and take advantage of the annual loosening of morals which is inextricably linked to the celebration of the endless natural cycle. And, prithee, we run right into each other after . . . How long has passed since . . . A year?'

'One year, two months and eighteen days.'

'How touching. Was that deliberate?'

'It was. Yen—'

'Geralt,' she interrupted, suddenly moving away and tossing her head. 'Let me make things perfectly clear. I don't want to.'

He nodded to indicate that was sufficiently clear.

Yennefer threw her cloak back over one shoulder. Beneath her cloak she had on a very thin, white blouse and a black skirt girdled with a belt of silver links.

'I don't want,' she repeated, 'to start again. And the thought of doing with you . . . what I meant to do with that young blond boy . . .

According to the same rules . . . The thought, Geralt, seems to me somewhat improper. An affront to both of us. Do you understand?'

He nodded once more. She looked at him from beneath lowered eyelashes.

'Will you go?'

'No.'

She was silent for a moment, fidgeting nervously.

'Are you angry?'

'No.'

'Right, come on, let's sit down somewhere, away from this hubbub, let's talk for a while. Because, as you can see, I'm glad we've met. Truly. Let's sit together for a while. Alright?'

'Let us, Yen.'

They headed off into the gloom, far onto the moors, towards the black wall of trees, avoiding couples locked in embraces. They had to go a long way in order to find a secluded spot. A dry hilltop marked by a juniper bush, as slender as a cypress.

The sorceress unfastened the brooch from her cloak, shook it out and spread it on the ground. He sat down beside her. He wanted to embrace her very much, but contrariness stopped him. Yennefer tidied up her deeply unbuttoned blouse, looked at him penetratingly, sighed and embraced him. He might have expected it. She had to make an effort to read his mind, but sensed his intentions involuntarily.

They said nothing.

'Oh, dammit,' she suddenly said, pulling away. She raised her hand and cried out a spell. Red and green spheres flew above their heads, breaking up high in the air, forming colourful, fluffy flowers. Laughter and joyous cries drifted up from the bonfires.

'Beltane . . . ' she said bitterly. 'May Day Eve . . . The cycle repeats. Let them enjoy themselves . . . if they can.'

There were other sorcerers in the vicinity. In the distance, three orange lightning bolts shot into the sky and away over by the forest a veritable geyser of rainbow-coloured, whirling meteors exploded. The people by the bonfires gave awe-struck gasps and cried out. Geralt, tense, stroked Yennefer's curls and breathed in the scent of

329

lilac and gooseberry they gave off. If I desire her too intensely, he thought, she'll sense it and she'll be put off. Her hackles will rise, she'll bristle and spurn me. I'll ask her calmly how she's doing . . .

'Nothing to report,' she said, and something in her voice quavered. 'Nothing worth mentioning.'

'Don't do that to me, Yen. Don't read me. It unsettles me.'

'Forgive me. It's automatic. And what's new with you, Geralt?'

'Nothing. Nothing worth mentioning.'

They said nothing.

'Beltane!' she suddenly snapped, and he felt the arm she was pressing against his chest stiffen and tauten. 'They're enjoying themselves. They're celebrating the eternal cycle of nature regenerating itself. And us? What are we doing here? We, relicts, doomed to obliteration, to extinction and oblivion? Nature is born again, the cycle repeats itself. But not for us, Geralt. We cannot reproduce ourselves. We were deprived of that potential. We were given the ability to do extraordinary things with nature, occasionally literally against her. And at the same time what is most natural and simple in nature was taken from us. What if we live longer than them? After our winter will come the spring, and we shall not be reborn; what finishes will finish along with us. But both you and I are drawn to those bonfires, though our presence here is a wicked, blasphemous mockery of this world.'

He was silent. He didn't like it when she fell into a mood like this, the origin of which he knew only too well. Once again, he thought, once again it's beginning to torment her. There was a time when it seemed she had forgotten, that she had become reconciled to it like the others. He embraced her, hugged her, rocked her very gently like a child. She let him. It didn't surprise him. He knew she needed it.

'You know, Geralt,' she suddenly said, now composed. 'I miss your silence the most.'

He touched her hair and ear with his mouth. I desire you, Yen, he thought, I desire you, but you know that. You know that, don't you, Yen?

'Yes, I do,' she whispered.

'Yen . . .'

She sighed again.

'Just today,' she said, looking at him with eyes wide open. 'Just this night, which will soon slip away. Let it be our Beltane. We shall part in the morning. Don't expect any more; I cannot, I could not . . . Forgive me. If I have hurt you, kiss me and go away.'

'If I kiss you I won't go away.'

'I was counting on that.'

She tilted her head. He touched her parted lips with his own. Tentatively. First the upper, then the lower. He entwined his fingers in her winding locks, touched her ear, her diamond earring, her neck. Yennefer, returning the kiss, clung to him, and her nimble fingers quickly and surely unfastened the buckles of his jacket.

She fell back onto her cloak, spread out on the soft moss. He pressed his mouth to her breast and felt the nipple harden and press against the very fine stuff of her blouse. She was breathing shallowly.

'Yen . . .'

'Don't say anything . . . Please . . .'

The touch of her naked, smooth, cool skin electrified his fingers and his palms. A shiver down his back being pricked by her fingernails. From the bonfires screams, singing, a whistle; a far, distant cloud of sparks in purple smoke. Caresses and touches. He touching her. She touching him. A shiver. And impatience. The gliding skin of her slim thighs gripping his hips, drawing closed like a clasp.

Beltane!

Breathing, riven into gasps. Flashes beneath their eyelids, the scent of lilac and gooseberry. The May Queen and May King? A blasphemous mockery? Oblivion?

Beltane! May Day Eve!

A moan. Hers? His? Black curls on his eyes, on his mouth. Intertwined fingers, quivering hands. A cry. Hers? Black eyelashes. A moan. His?

Silence. All eternity in the silence.

Beltane . . . Fires all the way to the horizon . . .

'Yen?'

'Oh, Geralt . . .'

'Yen . . . Are you weeping?'

'No!'

'Yen . . .'

'I promised myself . . . I promised . . .'

'Don't say anything. There's no need. Aren't you cold?'

'Yes, I am.'

'And now?'

'Now I'm warmer.'

The sky grew lighter at an alarming rate, the contours of the black wall of trees becoming more prominent, the distinct, serrated line of the treetops emerging from the shapeless gloom. The blue foretoken of dawn creeping up from behind it spread along the horizon, extinguishing the lamps of the stars. It had grown cooler. He hugged her more tightly and covered her with his cloak.

'Geralt?'

'Mhm?'

'It'll soon be dawn.'

'I know.'

'Have I hurt you?'

'A little.'

'Will it begin again?'

'It never ended.'

'Please . . . You make me feel . . .'

'Don't say anything. Everything is all right.'

The smell of smoke creeping among the heather. The scent of lilac and gooseberry.

'Geralt?'

'Yes?'

'Do you remember when we met in the Owl Mountains? And that golden dragon . . . What was he called?'

'Three Jackdaws. Yes, I do.'

'He told us . . .'

'I remember, Yen.'

She kissed him where the neck becomes the collarbone and then nuzzled her head in, tickling him with her hair.

'We're made for each other,' she whispered. 'Perhaps we're destined for each other? But nothing will come of it. It's a pity, but when dawn breaks, we shall part. It cannot be any other way. We have to part so as not to hurt one another. We two, destined for each other. Created for each other. Pity. The one or ones who created us for each other ought to have made more of an effort. Destiny alone is insufficient, it's too little. Something more is needed. Forgive me. I had to tell you.'

'I know.'

'I knew it was senseless for us to make love.'

'You're wrong. It wasn't. In spite of everything.'

'Ride to Cintra, Geralt.'

'What?'

'Ride to Cintra. Ride there and this time don't give up. Don't do what you did then . . . When you were there . . .'

'How did you know?'

'I know everything about you. Have you forgotten? Ride to Cintra, go there as fast as you can. Fell times are approaching, Geralt. Very fell. You cannot be late . . .'

'Yen . . .'

'Please don't say anything.'

It was cooler. Cooler and cooler. And lighter and lighter.

'Don't go yet. Let's wait until the dawn . . .'

'Yes, let's.'

IV

'Don't move, sir. I must change your dressing. The wound is getting messy and your leg is swelling something terrible. Ye Gods, it looks hideous . . . We must find a doctor as fast as we can . . .'

'Fuck the doctor,' the Witcher groaned. 'Hand me the chest, Yurga. Yes, that flacon there . . . Pour it straight onto the wound. Oh, bloody hell! It's nothing, nothing, keep pouring . . . Ooooow! Right. Bandage it up well and cover me . . .'

'It's swollen, sir, the whole thigh. And you're burning with fever—'

'Fuck the fever. Yurga?'

'Yes, sir?'

'I forgot to thank you . . .'

'It's not you who should be doing the thanking, sir, but me. You saved my life, you suffered an injury in my defence. And me? What did I do? I bandaged a wounded man, who'd fainted away, and put him on my cart and didn't leave him to expire. It's an ordinary matter, Witcher, sir.'

'It's not so ordinary, Yurga. I've been left . . . in similar situations . . . Like a dog . . .'

The merchant, lowering his head, said nothing.

'Well, what can I say, it's a base world,' he finally muttered. 'But that's no reason for us all to become despicable. What we need is kindness. My father taught me that and I teach it to my sons.'

The Witcher was silent, and observed the branches of the trees above the road, sliding past as the cart went on. His thigh throbbed. He felt no pain.

'Where are we?'

'We've forded the River Trava, now we're in the Groundcherry

Forests. It's no longer Temeria, but Sodden. You were asleep when we crossed the border, when the customs officers were rummaging in the cart. I'll tell you, though, they were astonished by you. But their senior officer knew you and ordered us through without delay.'

'He knew me?'

'Aye, there's no doubt. He called you Geralt. That's what he said; Geralt of Rivia. Is that your name?'

'It is...'

'And he promised to send a man ahead with the tidings that a doctor is needed. And I gave him a little something so as he wouldn't forget.'

'Thank you, Yurga.'

'No, Witcher, sir. I've already said, it's me as thanks you. And not just that. I'm also in your debt. We have an agreement... What is it, sir? Are you feeling faint?'

'Yurga... The flacon with the green seal...'

'Sir... You'll start... You were calling out dreadfully in your sleep...'

'I must, Yurga...'

'As you wish. Wait, I'll pour it into a bowl right away... By the Gods, we need a doctor as quickly as possible, otherwise...'

The Witcher turned his head away. He heard the cries of children playing in a dried-up, inner moat surrounding the castle grounds. There were around ten of them. The youngsters were making an ear-splitting din, outshouting each other in shrill, excited voices which kept breaking into falsetto. They were running to and fro along the bottom of the moat, like a shoal of swift little fishes, unexpectedly and very quickly changing direction, but always staying together. As usual, behind the screeching older boys, as skinny as scarecrows, ran a little child, panting and quite incapable of catching up.

'There are plenty of them,' the Witcher observed.

Mousesack smiled sourly, tugging at his beard, and shrugged.

'Aye, plenty.'

'And which of them . . . Which of these boys is the celebrated Child of Destiny?'

The druid looked away.

'I am forbidden, Geralt . . .'

'Calanthe?'

'Of course. You cannot have deluded yourself that she would give the child up so easily? You have met her, after all. She is a woman of iron. I shall tell you something, something I ought not to say, in the hope that you'll understand. I hope too, that you will not betray me before her.'

'Speak.'

'When the child was born six years ago she summoned me and ordered me to cheat you. And kill it.'

'You refused.'

'No one refuses Calanthe,' Mousesack said, looking him straight in the eyes. 'I was prepared to take to the road when she summoned me once again. She retracted the order, without a word of explanation. Be cautious when you talk to her.'

'I shall. Mousesack, tell me, what happened to Duny and Pavetta?'

'They were sailing from Skellige to Cintra. They were surprised by a storm. Not a single splinter was found of the ship. Geralt . . . That the child was not with them then is an incredibly queer matter. Inexplicable. They were meant to take it with them but at the last moment did not. No one knows why, Pavetta could never be parted from—'

'How did Calanthe bear it?'

'What do you think?'

'Of course.'

Shrieking like a band of goblins, the boys hurtled upwards and flashed beside them. Geralt noticed that not far behind the head of the rushing herd hurried a little girl, as thin and clamorous as the boys, only with a fair plait waving behind her. Howling wildly, the band spilled down the moat's steep slope again. At least half of them, including the girl, slid down on their behinds. The smallest one, still unable to keep up, fell over, rolled down to the bottom and began crying loudly, clutching a grazed knee. The other boys surrounded him, jeering and mocking, and then ran on. The little girl knelt by the little boy, hugged him and wiped away his tears, smudging dust and dirt over his face.

'Let us go, Geralt. The queen awaits.'

'Let's go, Mousesack.'

Calanthe was sitting on a large bench suspended on chains from the bough of a huge linden tree. She appeared to be dozing, but that was belied by an occasional push of her foot to swing the bench every now and again. There were three young women with her. One of them was sitting on the grass beside the swing, her spread-out dress shining bright white against the green like a patch of snow. The other two were not far away, chatting as they cautiously pulled apart the branches on some raspberry bushes.

'Ma'am,' Mousesack bowed.

The queen raised her head. Geralt went down on one knee.

'Witcher,' she said drily.

As in the past she was decorated with emeralds, which matched her green dress. And the colour of her eyes. As in the past, she was wearing a narrow, gold band on her mousy hair. But her hands, which he remembered as white and slender, were less slender now. She had gained weight.

'Greetings, Calanthe of Cintra.'

'Welcome, Geralt of Rivia. Rise. I've been waiting for you. Mousesack, my friend, escort the young ladies back to the castle.'

'At your behest, Your Majesty.'

They were left alone.

'Six years,' began Calanthe unsmilingly. 'You are horrifyingly punctual, Witcher.'

He did not comment.

'There were moments – what am I saying – years, when I convinced myself that you would forget. Or that other reasons would prevent you from coming. No, I did not in principle wish misfortune on you, but I had to take into consideration the none-too-safe nature of your profession. They say that death dogs your footsteps, Geralt of Rivia, but that you never look back. And later . . . When Pavetta . . . Do you know?'

'I do,' Geralt bowed his head. 'I sympathise with all my heart—'

'No,' she interrupted. 'It was long ago. I no longer wear mourning, as you see. I did, for long enough. Pavetta and Duny . . . Destined for each other. Until the very end. How can one not believe in the power of destiny?'

They were both silent. Calanthe moved her foot and set the swing in motion again.

'And so the Witcher has returned after six years, as agreed,' she said slowly, and a strange smile bloomed on her face. 'He has returned and demands the fulfilment of the oath. Do you think, Geralt, that storytellers will tell of our meeting in this way, when a hundred years have passed? I think so. Except they will probably colour the tale, tug on heart strings, play on the emotions. Yes, they know how. I can imagine it. Please listen. And the cruel Witcher spake thus: "Fulfil your vow, O Queen, or my curse shall fall on you". And the queen, weeping fulsomely, fell on her knees before the Witcher, crying: "Have mercy! Do not take the child from me! It is all I have left!".'

'Calanthe—'

'Don't interrupt,' she said sharply. 'I am telling a story, haven't you noticed? Listen on. The evil, cruel Witcher stamped his foot, waved his arms and cried: "Beware, faithless one, beware of fate's vengeance. If you do not keep your vow you will never escape punishment". And the queen replied: "Very well, Witcher. Let it be as fate wishes it. Look over there, where ten children are frolicking. Choose the one destined to you, and you shall take it as your own and leave me with a broken heart".'

The Witcher said nothing.

'In the story,' Calanthe's smile became more and more ugly, 'the queen, I presume, would let the Witcher guess thrice. But we aren't in a story, Geralt. We are here in reality, you and I, and our problem. And our destiny. It isn't a fairy story, it's real life. Lousy, evil, onerous, not sparing of errors, harm, sorrow, disappointments or misfortunes; not sparing of anyone, neither witchers, nor queens. Which is why, Geralt of Rivia, you will only have one guess.'

The Witcher still said nothing.

'Just one, single attempt,' Calanthe repeated. 'But as I said, this is not a fairy tale but life, which we must fill with moments of happiness for ourselves, for, as you know, we cannot count on fate to smile on us. Which is why, irrespective of the result of your choice, you will not leave here with nothing. You will take one child. The one you choose. A child you will turn into a witcher. Assuming the child survives the Trial of the Grasses, naturally.'

Geralt jerked up his head. The queen smiled. He knew that smile, hideous and evil, contemptuous because it did not conceal its artificiality.

'You are astonished,' she stated. 'Well, I've studied a little. Since Pavetta's child has the chance of becoming a witcher, I went to great pains. My sources, Geralt, reveal nothing, however, regarding how many children in ten withstand the Trial of the Grasses. Would you like to satisfy my curiosity in this regard?'

'O Queen,' Geralt said, clearing his throat. 'You certainly went to sufficient pains in your studies to know that the code and my oath forbid me from even uttering that name, much less discussing it.'

Calanthe stopped the swing abruptly by jabbing a heel into the ground.

'Three, at most four in ten,' she said, nodding her head in feigned pensiveness. 'A stringent selection, very stringent, I'd say, and at every stage. First the Choice and then the Trials. And then the Changes. How many youngsters ultimately receive medallions and silver swords? One in ten? One in twenty?'

The Witcher said nothing.

'I've pondered long over this,' Calanthe continued, now without a smile. 'And I've come to the conclusion that the selection of the children at the stage of the Choice has scant significance. What difference does it make, in the end, Geralt, which child dies or goes insane, stuffed full of narcotics? What difference does it make whose brain bursts from hallucinations, whose eyes rupture and gush forth, instead of becoming cats' eyes? What difference does it make whether the child destiny chose or an utterly chance one dies in its own blood and puke? Answer me.'

The Witcher folded his arms on his chest, in order to control their trembling.

'What's the point of this?' he asked. 'Are you expecting an answer?'

'You're right, I'm not,' the queen smiled again. 'As usual you are quite correct in your deductions. Who knows, perhaps even though I'm not expecting an answer I would like benignly to devote a little attention to your frank words, freely volunteered? Words, which, who knows, perhaps you would like to unburden yourself of, and along with them whatever is oppressing your soul? But if not, too bad. Come on, let's get down to business, we must supply the story-tellers with material. Let's go and choose a child, Witcher.'

'Calanthe,' he said, looking her in the eyes. 'It's not worth wor-rying about storytellers. If they don't have enough material they'll make things up anyway. And if they do have authentic material at their disposal, they'll distort it. As you correctly observed, this isn't a fairy tale, it's life. Lousy and evil. And so, damn it all, let's live it decently and well. Let's keep the amount of harm done to others to the absolute minimum. In a fairy tale, I grant you, the queen has to beg the witcher and the witcher can demand what's his and stamp his foot. In real life the queen can simply say: "Please don't take the child". And the Witcher can reply: "Since you ask – I shall not". And go off into the setting sun. Such is life. But the storyteller wouldn't get a penny from his listeners for an ending to a fairy tale like that. At most they'd get a kick up the arse. Because it's dull.'

Calanthe stopped smiling and something he had seen once before flashed in her eyes.

'What?' she hissed.

'Let's not beat about the bush, Calanthe. You know what I mean. As I came here, so I shall leave. Should I choose a child? Why would I need one? Do you think it matters so much to me? That I came here to Cintra, driven by an obsession to take your grandchild away from you? No, Calanthe. I wanted, perhaps, to see this child, look destiny in the eyes ... For I don't know myself ... But don't be afraid. I shan't take it, all you have to do is ask—'

340

Calanthe sprang up from the bench and a green flame blazed in her eyes.

'Ask?' she hissed furiously. 'Me, afraid? Of you? I should be afraid of you, you accursed sorcerer? How dare you fling your scornful pity in my face? Revile me with your compassion? Accuse me of cowardice, challenge my will? My overfamiliarity has emboldened you! Beware!'

The Witcher decided not to shrug, concluding it would be safer to genuflect and bow his head. He was not mistaken.

'Well,' Calanthe hissed, standing over him. Her hands were lowered, clenched into fists bristling with rings. 'Well, at last. That is the right response. One answers a queen from such a position, when a queen asks one a question. And if it is not a question, but an order, one bows one's head even lower and goes off to carry it out, without a moment's delay. Is that clear?'

'Yes, O Queen.'

'Splendid. Now stand up.'

He stood up. She gazed at him and bit her lip.

'Did my outburst offend you very much? I refer to the form, not the content.'

'Not especially.'

'Good. I shall try not to flare up again. And so, as I was saying, ten children are playing in the moat. You will choose the one you regard as the most suitable, you will take it, and by the Gods, make a witcher of it, because that is what destiny expects. And if not destiny, then know that I expect it.'

He looked her in the eyes and bowed low.

'O Queen,' he said. 'Six years ago I proved to you that some things are more powerful than a queen's will. By the Gods – if such exist – I shall prove that to you one more time. You will not compel me to make a choice I do not wish to make. I apologise for the form, but not the content.'

'I have deep dungeons beneath the castle. I warn you, one second more, one word more and you will rot in them.'

'None of the children playing in the moat is fit to be a witcher,' he said slowly. 'And Pavetta's son is not among them.'

Calanthe squinted her eyes. He did not even shudder.

'Come,' she finally said, turning on her heel.

He followed her among rows of flowering shrubs, among flower-beds and hedges. The queen entered an openwork summerhouse. Four large wicker chairs stood around a malachite table. A pitcher and two silver goblets stood on the veined table top supported by four legs in the shape of gryphons.

'Be seated. And pour.'

She drank to him, vigorously, lustily. Like a man. He responded in kind, remaining standing.

'Be seated,' she repeated. 'I wish to talk.'

'Yes, ma'am.'

'How did you know Pavetta's son is not among the children in the moat?'

'I didn't,' Geralt decided to be frank. 'It was a shot in the dark.'

'Aha. I might have guessed. And that none of them is fit to be a witcher? Is that true? And how were you able to tell that? Were you aided by magic?'

'Calanthe,' he said softly. 'I did not have to state it or find it out. What you said earlier contained the whole truth. Every child is fit. Selection decides. Later.'

'By the Gods of the Sea, as my permanently absent husband would say!' she laughed. 'So nothing is true? The whole Law of Surprise? Those legends about children that somebody was not expecting and about the ones who were first encountered? I suspected as much! It's a game! A game with chance, a game with destiny! But it's an awfully dangerous game, Geralt.'

'I know.'

'A game based on somebody's suffering. Why then, answer me, are parents or guardians forced to make such difficult and burdensome vows? Why are children taken from them? After all, there are plenty of children around who don't need to be taken away from anybody. Entire packs of homeless children and orphans roam the roads. One can buy a child cheaply enough in any village; every peasant is happy to sell one during the hungry gap, for why worry when he can easily sire another? Why then? Why did you force an oath on Duny, on Pavetta and on me? Why have you turned up here exactly six years after the birth of the child? And why, dammit, don't you want one, why do you say it's of no use?'

He was silent. Calanthe nodded.

'You do not reply,' she said, leaning back in her chair. 'Let's ponder on the reason for your silence. Logic is the mother of all knowledge. And what does she hint at? What do we have here? A witcher searching for destiny concealed in the strange and doubtful Law of Surprise. The witcher finds his destiny. And suddenly gives it up. He claims not to want the Child of Destiny. His face is stony; ice and metal in his voice. He judges that a queen – a woman when all's said and done – may be tricked, deceived by the appearances of hard maleness. No, Geralt, I shall not spare you. I know why you are declining the choice of a child. You are quitting because you do not believe in destiny. Because you are not certain. And you, when you are not certain . . . you begin to fear. Yes, Geralt. What leads you is fear. You are afraid. Deny that.'

He slowly put the goblet down on the table. Slowly, so that the clink of silver against malachite would not betray the uncontrollable shaking of his hand.

'You do not deny it?'

'No.'

She quickly leaned forward and seized his arm. Tightly.

'You have gained in my eyes,' she said. And smiled. It was a pretty smile. Against his will, almost certainly against his will, he responded with a smile.

'How did you arrive at that, Calanthe?'

'I arrived at nothing,' she said, without releasing his arm. 'It was a shot in the dark.'

They both burst out laughing. And then sat in silence among the greenery and the scent of wild cherry blossom, among the warmth and the buzzing of bees.

'Geralt?'

'Yes, Calanthe?'

'Don't you believe in destiny?'

'I don't know if I believe in anything. And as regards . . . I fear it isn't enough. Something more is necessary.'

'I must ask you something. What happened to you? I mean you were reputedly a Child of Destiny yourself. Mousesack claims—'

'No, Calanthe. Mousesack was thinking about something completely different. Mousesack . . . He probably knows. But he uses those convenient myths when it suits him. It's not true that I was an unexpected encounter at home, as a child. That's not how I became a witcher. I'm a commonplace foundling, Calanthe. The unwanted bastard of a woman I don't remember. But I know who she is.'

The queen looked at him penetratingly, but the Witcher did not continue.

'Are all stories about the Law of Surprise myths?'

'Yes. It's hard to call an accident destiny.'

'But you witchers do not stop searching?'

'No, we don't. But it's senseless. Nothing has any point.'

'Do you believe a Child of Destiny would pass through the Trials without danger?'

'We believe such a child would not require the Trials.'

'One question, Geralt. Quite a personal one. May I?'

He nodded.

'There is no better way to pass on hereditary traits than the natural way, as we know. You went through the Trials and survived. So if you need a child with special qualities and endurance . . . Why don't you find a woman who . . . I'm tactless, aren't I? But I think I've guessed, haven't I?'

'As usual,' he said, smiling sadly, 'you are correct in your deductions, Calanthe. You guessed right, of course. What you're suggesting is impossible for me.'

'Forgive me,' she said, and the smile vanished from her face. 'Oh, well, it's a human thing.'

'It isn't human.'

'Ah . . . So, no witcher can—'

'No, none. The Trial of the Grasses, Calanthe, is dreadful. And what is done to boys during the time of the Changes is even worse. And irreversible.'

'Don't start feeling sorry for yourself,' she muttered. 'Because it ill behooves you. It doesn't matter what was done to you. I can see the results. Quite satisfactory, if you ask me. If I could assume that Pavetta's child would one day be similar to you I wouldn't hesitate for a moment.'

'The risks are too great,' he said quickly. 'As you said. At most, four out of ten survive.'

'Dammit, is only the Trial of the Grasses hazardous? Do only potential witchers take risks? Life is full of hazards, selection also occurs in life, Geralt. Misfortune, sicknesses and wars also select. Defying destiny may be just as hazardous as succumbing to it. Geralt . . . I would give you the child. But . . . I'm afraid, too.'

'I wouldn't take the child. I couldn't assume the responsibility. I wouldn't agree to burden you with it. I wouldn't want the child to tell you one day . . . As I'm telling you—'

'Do you hate that woman, Geralt?'

'My mother? No, Calanthe. I presume she had a choice . . . Or perhaps she didn't? No, but she did; a suitable spell or elixir would have been sufficient . . . A choice. A choice which should be respected, for it is the holy and irrefutable right of every woman. Emotions are unimportant here. She had the irrefutable right to her decision and she took it. But I think that an encounter with her, the face she would make then . . . Would give me something of a perverse pleasure, if you know what I mean.'

'I know perfectly well what you mean,' she smiled. 'But you have slim chances of enjoying such a pleasure. I cannot judge your age, Witcher, but I suppose you're much, much older than your appearance would indicate. So, that woman—'

'That woman,' he interrupted coldly, 'probably looks much, much younger than I do now.'

'A sorceress?'

'Yes.'

'Interesting. I thought sorceresses couldn't . . . ?'

'She probably thought so too.'

'Yes. But you're right, let's not discuss a woman's right to this decision, because it is a matter beyond debate. Let us return to our problem. You will not take the child? Definitely?'

'Definitely.'

'And if . . . If destiny is not merely a myth? If it really exists, doesn't a fear arise that it may backfire?'

'If it backfires, it'll backfire on me,' he answered placidly. 'For I am the one acting against it. You, after all, have carried out your side of the bargain. For if destiny isn't a myth, I would have to choose the appropriate child among the ones you have shown me. But is Pavetta's child among those children?'

'Yes,' Calanthe slowly nodded her head. 'Would you like to see it? Would you like to gaze into the eyes of destiny?'

'No. No, I don't. I quit, I renounce it. I renounce my right to the boy. I don't want to look destiny in the eyes, because I don't believe in it. Because I know that in order to unite two people, destiny is insufficient. Something more is necessary than destiny. I sneer at such destiny; I won't follow it like a blind man being led by the hand, uncomprehending and naive. This is my irrevocable decision, O Calanthe of Cintra.'

The queen stood up. She smiled. He was unable to guess what lay behind her smile.

'Let it be thus, Geralt of Rivia. Perhaps your destiny was precisely to renounce it and quit? I think that's exactly what it was. For you should know that if you had chosen, chosen correctly, you would see that the destiny you mock has been sneering at you.'

He looked into her glaring green eyes. She smiled. He could not decipher the smile.

There was a rosebush growing beside the summerhouse. He broke a stem and picked a flower, kneeled down, and proffered it to her, holding it in both hands, head bowed.

'Pity I didn't meet you earlier, White Hair,' she murmured, taking the rose from his hands. 'Rise.'

He stood up.

'Should you change your mind,' she said, lifting the rose up to her face. 'Should you decide . . . Come back to Cintra. I shall be waiting.

And your destiny will also be waiting. Perhaps not forever, but certainly for some time longer.'

'Farewell, Calanthe.'

'Farewell, Witcher. Look after yourself. I have . . . A moment ago I had a foreboding . . . A curious foreboding . . . that this is the last time I shall see you.'

'Farewell, O Queen.'

V

He awoke and discovered to his astonishment that the pain gnawing at his thigh had vanished. It also seemed that the throbbing swelling which was stretching the skin had stopped troubling him. He tried to reach it, touch it, but could not move. Before he realised that he was being held fast solely by the weight of the skins covering him, a cold, hideous dread ran down to his belly and dug into his guts like a hawk's talons. He clenched and relaxed his fingers, rhythmically, repeating in his head, no, no, I'm not . . .

Paralysed.

'You have woken.'

A statement, not a question. A quiet, but distinct, soft voice. A woman. Probably young. He turned his head and groaned, trying to raise himself up.

'Don't move. At least not so vigorously. Are you in pain?'

'Nnnn . . .' the coating sticking his lips together broke. 'Nnno. The wound isn't . . . My back . . .'

'Bedsores.' An unemotional, cool statement, which did not suit the soft alto voice. 'I shall remedy it. Here, drink this. Slowly, in small sips.'

The scent and taste of juniper dominated the liquid. An old method, he thought. Juniper or mint; both insignificant additives, only there to disguise the real ingredients. In spite of that he recognised sewant mushrooms, and possibly burdock. Yes, certainly burdock, burdock neutralises toxins, it purifies blood contaminated by gangrene or infection.

'Drink. Drink it all up. Not so fast or you'll choke.'

The medallion around his neck began to vibrate very gently. So there was also magic in the draught. He widened his pupils with difficulty. Now that she had raised his head he could examine her more

348

precisely. She was dainty. She was wearing men's clothing. Her face was small and pale in the darkness.

'Where are we?'

'In a tar makers' clearing.'

Indeed, resin could be smelled in the air. He heard voices coming from the campfire. Someone had just thrown on some brushwood, and flames shot upwards with a crackle. He looked again, making the most of the light. Her hair was tied back with a snakeskin band. Her hair . . .

A suffocating pain in his throat and sternum. Hands tightly clenched into fists.

Her hair was red, flame-red, and when lit by the glow of the bonfire seemed as red as vermilion.

'Are you in pain?' she asked, interpreting the emotion, but wrongly. 'Now . . . Just a moment . . .'

He sensed a sudden impact of warmth emanating from her hands, spreading over his back, flowing downwards to his buttocks.

'We will turn you over,' she said. 'Don't try by yourself. You are very debilitated. Hey, can someone help me?'

Steps from the bonfire, shadows, shapes. Somebody leaned over. It was Yurga.

'How are you feeling, sir? Any better?'

'Help me turn him over on his belly,' said the woman. 'Gently, slowly. That's right . . . Good. Thank you.'

He did not have to look at her anymore. Lying on his belly, he did not have to risk looking her in the eyes. He calmed down and overcame the shaking of his hands. She could sense it. He heard the clasps of her bag clinking, flacons and small porcelain jars knocking against each other. He heard her breath, felt the warmth of her thigh. She was kneeling just beside him.

'Was my wound,' he asked, unable to endure the silence, 'troublesome?'

'It was, a little,' and there was coldness in her voice. 'It can happen with bites. The nastiest kinds of wound. But you must be familiar with it, Witcher.'

She knows. She's digging around in my thoughts. Is she reading them? Probably not. And I know why. She's afraid.

'Yes, you must be familiar with it,' she repeated, clinking the glass vessels again. 'I saw a few scars on you . . . But I coped with them. I am, as you see, a sorceress. And a healer at the same time. It's my specialisation.'

That adds up, he thought. He did not say a word.

'To return to the wound,' she continued calmly, 'you ought to know that you were saved by your pulse; fourfold slower than a normal man's. Otherwise you wouldn't have survived, I can say with complete honesty. I saw what had been tied around your leg. It was meant to be a dressing, but it was a poor attempt.'

He was silent.

'Later,' she continued, pulling his shirt up as far as his neck, 'infection set in, which is usual for bite wounds. It has been arrested. Of course, you took the witcher's elixir? That helped a lot. Though I don't understand why you took hallucinogens at the same time. I was listening to your ravings, Geralt of Rivia.'

She *is* reading my mind, he thought. Or perhaps Yurga told her my name? Perhaps I was talking in my sleep under the influence of the Black Gull? Damned if I know . . . But knowing my name gives her nothing. Nothing. She doesn't know who I am. She has no idea who I am.

He felt her gently massage a cold, soothing ointment with the sharp smell of camphor into his back. Her hands were small and very soft.

'Forgive me for doing it the old way,' she said. 'I could have removed the bedsores using magic, but I strained myself a little treating the wound on your leg and feel none too good. I've bandaged the wound on your leg, as much as I am able, so now you're in no danger. But don't get up for the next few days. Even magically sutured blood vessels tend to burst, and you'd have hideous effusions. A scar will remain, of course. One more for your collection.'

'Thanks . . .' He pressed his cheek against the skins in order to distort his voice, disguise its unnatural sound. 'May I ask . . . Whom should I thank?'

She won't say, he thought. Or she'll lie.

'My name is Visenna.'

I know, he thought.

'I'm glad,' he said slowly, with his cheek still against the skins. 'I'm glad our paths have crossed, Visenna.'

'Why, it's chance,' she said coolly, pulling his shirt down over his back and covering him with the sheepskins. 'I received word from the customs officers that I was needed. If I'm needed, I come. It's a curious habit I have. Listen, I'll leave the ointment with the merchant; ask him to rub it on every morning and evening. He claims you saved his life, he can repay you like that.'

'And me? How can I repay you, Visenna?'

'Let's not talk about that. I don't take payment from witchers. Call it solidarity, if you will. Professional solidarity. And affection. As part of that affection some friendly advice or, if you wish, a healer's instructions: stop taking hallucinogens, Geralt. They have no healing power. None at all.'

'Thank you, Visenna. For your help and advice. Thank you . . . for everything.'

He dug his hand out from under the skins and found her knee. She shuddered, put her hand into his and squeezed it lightly. He cautiously released her fingers, and slid his down over her forearm.

Of course. The soft skin of a young woman. She shuddered even more strongly, but did not withdraw her arm. He brought his fingers back to her hand and joined his with hers.

The medallion on his neck vibrated and twitched.

'Thank you, Visenna,' he repeated, trying to control his voice. 'I'm glad our paths crossed.'

'Chance . . .' she said, but this time there was no coolness in her voice.

'Or perhaps destiny?' he asked, astonished, for the excitement and nervousness had suddenly evaporated from him completely. 'Do you believe in destiny, Visenna?'

'Yes,' she replied after a while. 'I do.'

'That people linked by destiny will always find each other?' he continued.

'Yes, I believe that too . . . What are you doing? Don't turn over . . .'

'I want to look into your face . . . Visenna. I want to look into your eyes. And you . . . You must look into mine.'

She made a movement as though about to spring up from her knees. But she remained beside him. He turned over slowly, lips twisting with pain. There was more light, someone had put some more wood on the fire.

She was not moving now. She simply moved her head to the side, offering her profile, but this time he clearly saw her mouth quivering. She tightened her fingers on his hand, powerfully.

He looked.

There was no similarity at all. She had an utterly different profile. A small nose. A narrow chin. She was silent. Then she suddenly leaned over him and looked him straight in the eye. From close up. Without a word.

'How do you like my enhanced eyes?' he asked calmly. 'Unusual, aren't they? Do you know, Visenna, what is done to witchers' eyes to improve them? Do you know it doesn't always work?'

'Stop it,' she said softly. 'Stop it, Geralt.'

'Geralt . . .' he suddenly felt something tearing in him. 'Vesemir gave me that name. Geralt of Rivia! I even learned to imitate a Rivian accent. Probably from an inner need to possess a homeland. Even if it was an invented one. Vesemir . . . gave me my name. Vesemir also revealed yours. Not very willingly.'

'Be quiet, Geralt. Be quiet.'

'You tell me today you believe in destiny. And back then . . . Did you believe back then? Oh, yes, you must have. You must have believed that destiny would bring us together. The fact you did nothing to quicken this encounter ought to be attributed to that.'

She was silent.

'I always wanted . . . I have pondered over what I would say to you, when we finally met. I've thought about the question I would ask you. I thought it would give me some sort of perverse pleasure . . .'

What sparkled on her cheek was a tear. Undoubtedly. He felt his throat constrict until it hurt. He felt fatigue. Drowsiness. Weakness.

'In the light of day . . .' he groaned. 'Tomorrow, in the sunshine, I'll look into your eyes, Visenna . . . And I'll ask you my question. Or perhaps I won't ask you, because it's too late. Destiny? Oh, yes, Yen was right. It's not sufficient to be destined for each other. Something more is needed . . . But tomorrow I'll look into your eyes . . . In the light of the sun . . .'

'No,' she said gently, quietly, velvety, in a voice which gnawed at, racked the layers of memory, memory which no longer existed. Which should never have existed, but had.

'Yes!' he protested. 'Yes. I want to —'

'No. Now you will fall asleep. And when you awake, you'll stop wanting. Why should we look at each other in the sunlight? What will it change? Nothing can now be reversed, nothing changed. What's the purpose of asking me questions, Geralt? Does knowing that I won't be able to answer give you some kind of perverse pleasure? What will mutual hurt give us? No, we won't look at each other in the daylight. Go to sleep, Geralt. And just between us, Vesemir did not give you that name. Although it doesn't change or reverse anything either, I'd like you to know that. Farewell and look after yourself. And don't try to look for me . . .'

'Visenna—'

'No, Geralt. Now you'll fall asleep. And I . . . I was a dream. Farewell.'

'No! Visenna!'

'Sleep.' There was a soft order in her velvety voice, breaking his will, tearing it like cloth. Warmth, suddenly emanating from her hands.

'Sleep.'

He slept.

VI

'Are we in Riverdell yet, Yurga?'

'Have been since yesterday, sir. Soon the River Yaruga and then my homeland. Look, even the horses are walking more jauntily, tossing their heads. They can sense home is near.'

'Home . . . Do you live in the city?'

'No, outside the walls.'

'Interesting,' the Witcher said, looking around. 'There's almost no trace of war damage. I had heard this land was devastated.'

'Well,' Yurga said. 'One thing we're not short of is ruins. Take a closer look – on almost every cottage, in every homestead, you can see the white timber of new joinery. And over there on the far bank, just look, it was even worse, everything was burned right down to the ground . . . Well, war's war, but life must go on. We endured the greatest turmoil when the Black Forces marched through our land. True enough, it looked then as though they'd turn everything here into a wasteland. Many of those who fled then never returned. But fresh people have settled in their place. Life must go on.'

'That's a fact,' Geralt muttered. 'Life must go on. It doesn't matter what happened. Life must go on . . .'

'You're right. Right, there you are, put them on. I've mended your britches, patched them up. They'll be good as new. It's just like this land, sir. It was rent by war, ploughed up as if by the iron of a harrow, ripped up, bloodied. But now it'll be good as new. And it will be even more fertile. Even those who rotted in the ground will serve the good and fertilise the soil. Presently it is hard to plough, because the fields are full of bones and ironware, but the earth can cope with iron too.'

'Are you afraid the Nilfgaardians, the Black Forces, will return? They found a way through the mountains once already . . .'

354

'Well, we're afeared. And what of it? Do we sit down and weep and tremble? Life must go on. And what will be, will be. What is destined can't be avoided, in any case.'

'Do you believe in destiny?'

'How can I not believe? After what I encountered on the bridge, in the wilderness, when you saved me from death? Oh, Witcher, sir, you'll see, my wife will fall at your feet . . .'

'Oh, come on. Frankly speaking, I have more to be grateful to you for. Back there on the bridge . . . That's my job, after all, Yurga, my trade. I mean, I protect people for money. Not out of the goodness of my heart. Admit it, Yurga, you've heard what people say about witchers. That no one knows who's worse; them or the monsters they kill—'

'That's not true, sir, and I don't know why you talk like that. What, don't I have eyes? You're cut from the same cloth as that healer.'

'Visenna . . .'

'She didn't tell us her name. But she followed right behind us, for she knew she was needed, caught us up in the evening, and took care of you at once, having barely dismounted. You see, sir, she took great pains over your leg, the air was crackling from all that magic, and we fled into the forest out of fear. And then there was blood pouring from her nose. I see it's not a simple thing, working magic. You see, she dressed your wound with such care, truly, like a—'

'Like a mother?' Geralt clenched his teeth.

'Aye. You've said it. And when you fell asleep . . .'

'Yes, Yurga?'

'She could barely stand up, she was as white as a sheet. But she came to check none of us needed any help. She healed the tar maker's hand, which had been crushed by a log. She didn't take a penny, and even left some medicine. No, Geralt, sir, I know what people say about Witchers and sorcerers in the world isn't all good. But not here. We, from Upper Sodden and the people from Riverdell, we know better. We owe too much to sorcerers not to know what they're like. Memories about them here aren't rumours and gossip, but hewn in stone. You'll see for yourself, just wait till we leave the copse. Anyway, you're sure to know better yourself. For that battle was talked about all over the world, and a year has barely passed. You must have heard.'

'I haven't been here for a year,' the Witcher muttered. 'I was in the North. But I heard . . . The second Battle of Sodden . . .'

'Precisely. You'll soon see the hill and the rock. We used to call that hill Kite Top, but now everybody calls it the Sorcerers' Peak or the Mountain of the Fourteen. For twenty-two of them stood on that hill, twenty-two sorcerers fought, and fourteen fell. It was a dreadful battle, sir. The earth reared up, fire poured from the sky like rain and lightning bolts raged . . . Many perished. But the sorcerers overcame the Black Forces, and broke the Power which was leading them. And fourteen of them perished in that battle. Fourteen laid down their lives . . . What, sir? What's the matter?'

'Nothing. Go on, Yurga.'

'The battle was dreadful, oh my, but were it not for those sorcerers on the hill, who knows, perhaps we wouldn't be talking here today, riding homeward, for that home wouldn't exist, nor me, and maybe not you either . . . Yes, it was thanks to the sorcerers. Fourteen of them perished defending us, the people of Sodden and Riverdell. Ha, certainly, others also fought there, soldiers and noblemen, and peasants, too. Whoever could, took up a pitchfork or an axe, or even a club . . . All of them fought valiantly and many fell. But the sorcerers . . . It's no feat for a soldier to fall, for that is his trade, after all, and life is short anyhow. But the sorcerers could have lived, as long they wished. And they didn't waver.'

'They didn't waver,' the Witcher repeated, rubbing his forehead with a hand. 'They didn't waver. And I was in the North . . .'

'What's the matter, sir?'

'Nothing.'

'Yes . . . So now we – everyone from around here – take flowers there, to that hill, and in May, at Beltane, a fire always burns. And it shall burn there forever and a day. And forever shall they be in people's memories, that fourteen. And living like that in memory is . . . is . . . something more! More, Geralt, sir!'

'You're right, Yurga.'

'Every child of ours knows the names of the fourteen, carved in the stone that stands on the top of the hill. Don't you believe me? Listen: Axel Raby, Triss Merigold, Atlan Kerk, Vanielle of Brugge, Dagobert of Vole—'

'Stop, Yurga.'

'What's the matter, sir? You're as pale as death!'

'It's nothing.'

VII

He walked uphill very slowly, cautiously, listening to the creaking of the sinews and muscles around the magically healed wound. Although it seemed to be completely healed, he continued to protect the leg and not risk resting all his body weight on it. It was hot and the scent of grass struck his head, pleasantly intoxicating him.

The obelisk was not standing in the centre of the hill's flat top, but was further back, beyond the circle of angular stones. Had he climbed up there just before sunset the shadow of the menhir falling on the circle would have marked the precise diameter, would have indicated the direction in which the faces of the sorcerers had been turned during the battle. Geralt looked in that direction, towards the boundless, undulating fields. If any bones of the fallen were still there – and there were for certain – they were covered by lush grass. A hawk was circling, describing a calm circle on outspread wings. The single moving point in a landscape transfixed in the searing heat.

The obelisk was wide at the base – five people would have had to link hands in order to encircle it. It was apparent that without the help of magic it could not have been hauled up onto the hill. The surface of the menhir, which was turned towards the stone circle, was smoothly worked; runic letters could be seen engraved on it.

The names of the fourteen who fell.

He moved slowly closer. Yurga had been right. Flowers lay at the foot of the obelisk – ordinary, wild flowers – poppies, lupins, mallows and forget-me-nots.

The names of the fourteen.

He read them slowly, from the top, and before him appeared the faces of those he had known.

The chestnut-haired Triss Merigold, cheerful, giggling for no reason, looking like a teenager. He had liked her. And she had liked him.

Lawdbor of Murivel, with whom he had almost fought in Vizima, when he had caught the sorcerer using delicate telekinesis to tamper with dice in a game.

Lytta Neyd, known as Coral. Her nickname derived from the colour of the lipstick she used. Lytta had once denounced him to King Belohun, so he went to the dungeon for a week. After being released he went to ask her why. When, still without knowing the reason, he had ended up in her bed, he spent another week there.

Old Gorazd, who had offered him a hundred marks to let him dissect his eyes, and a thousand for the chance to carry out a post mortem – 'not necessarily today' – as he had put it then.

Three names remained.

He heard a faint rustling behind him and turned around.

She was barefoot, in a simple, linen dress. She was wearing a garland woven from daisies on long, fair hair, falling freely onto her shoulders and back.

'Greetings,' he said.

She looked up at him with cold, blue eyes, but did not answer.

He noticed she was not suntanned. That was odd, then, at the end of the summer, when country girls were usually tanned bronze. Her face and uncovered shoulders had a slight golden sheen.

'Did you bring flowers?'

She smiled and lowered her eyelashes. He felt a chill. She passed him without a word and knelt at the foot of the menhir, touching the stone with her hand.

'I do not bring flowers,' she said, lifting her head. 'But the ones lying here are for me.'

He looked at her. She knelt so that she was concealing the last name engraved in the stone of the menhir from him. She was bright, unnaturally, luminously bright against the stone.

'Who are you?' he asked slowly.

She smiled and emanated cold.

'Don't you know?'

Yes, I do, he thought, gazing into the cold blue of her eyes. Yes, I think I do.

He was tranquil. He could not be anything else. Not anymore.

'I've always wondered what you look like, my lady.'

'You don't have to address me like that,' she answered softly. 'We've known each other for years, after all.'

'We have,' he agreed. 'They say you dog my footsteps.'

'I do. But you have never looked behind you. Until today. Today, you looked back for the first time.'

He was silent. He had nothing to say. He was weary.

'How . . . How will it happen?' he finally asked, cold and emotionless.

'I'll take you by the hand,' she said, looking him directly in the eyes. 'I'll take you by the hand and lead you through the meadow. Into the cold, wet fog.'

'And then? What is there, beyond the fog?'

'Nothing,' she smiled. 'There is nothing more.'

'You dogged my every footstep,' he said. 'But struck down others, those that I passed on my way. Why? I was meant to end up alone, wasn't I? So I would finally begin to be afraid? I'll tell you the truth. I was always afraid of you; always. I never looked behind me out of fear. Out of terror that I'd see you following me. I was always afraid, my life has passed in fear. I was afraid . . . until today.'

'Until today?'

'Yes. Until today. We're standing here, face to face, but I don't feel any fear. You've taken everything from me. You've also taken the fear from me.'

'Then why are your eyes full of fear, Geralt of Rivia? Your hands are trembling, you are pale. Why? Do you fear the last – fourteenth – name engraved on the obelisk so much? If you wish I shall speak that name.'

'You don't have to. I know what it is. The circle is closing, the snake is sinking its teeth into its own tail. That is how it must be. You and that name. And the flowers. For her and for me. The fourteenth name engraved in the stone, a name that I have spoken in the middle of the night and in the sunlight, during frosts and heat waves and rain. No, I'm not afraid to speak it now.'

'Then speak it.'

'Yennefer . . . Yennefer of Vengerberg.'

'And the flowers are mine.'

'Let us be done with this,' he said with effort. 'Take . . . Take me by the hand.'

She stood up and came closer, and he felt the coldness radiating from her; a sharp, penetrating cold.

'Not today,' she said. 'One day, yes. But not today.'

'You have taken everything from me—'

'No,' she interrupted. 'I do not take anything. I just take people by the hand. So that no one will be alone at that moment. Alone in the fog . . . We shall meet again, Geralt of Rivia. One day.'

He did not reply. She turned around slowly and walked away. Into the mist, which suddenly enveloped the hilltop, into the fog, which everything vanished into, into the white, wet fog, into which melted the obelisk, the flowers lying at its foot and the fourteen names engraved on it. There was nothing, only the fog and the wet grass under his feet, sparkling from drops of water which smelled intoxicating, heady, sweet, until his forehead ached, he began to forget and become weary . . .

'Geralt, sir! What's the matter? Did you fall asleep? I told you, you're weak. Why did you climb up to the top?'

'I fell asleep.' He wiped his face with his hand and blinked. 'I fell asleep, dammit . . . It's nothing, Yurga, it's this heat . . .'

'Aye, it's devilish hot . . . We ought to be going, sir. Come along, I'll aid you down the slope.'

'There's nothing wrong with me . . .'

'Nothing, nothing. Then I wonder why you're staggering. Why the hell did you go up the hill in such a heat? Wanted to read their names? I could have told you them all. What's the matter?'

'Nothing . . . Yurga . . . Do you really remember all the names?'

'Certainly.'

'I'll see what your memory's like . . . The last one. The fourteenth. What name is it?'

'What a doubter you are. You don't believe in anything. You want to find out if I'm lying? I told you, didn't I, that every youngster knows those names. The last one, you say? Well, the last one is Yoël Grethen of Carreras. Perhaps you knew him?'

Geralt rubbed his eyelid with his wrist. And he glanced at the menhir. At all the names.

'No,' he said. 'I didn't.'

VIII

'Geralt, sir?'

'Yes, Yurga?'

The merchant lowered his head and said nothing for some time, winding around a finger the remains of the thin strap with which he was repairing the Witcher's saddle. He finally straightened up and gently tapped the servant driving the cart on the back with his fist.

'Mount one of those spare horses, Pokvit. I'll drive. Sit behind me on the box, Geralt, sir. Why are you hanging around the cart, Pokvit? Go on, ride on! We want to talk here, we don't need your eyes!'

Roach, dawdling behind the cart, neighed, tugged at the tether, clearly envious of Pokvit's mare trotting down the highway.

Yurga clicked his tongue and tapped the horses lightly with the reins.

'Well,' he said hesitantly. 'It's like this, sir. I promised you . . . Back then on the bridge . . . I made a promise—'

'You needn't worry,' the Witcher quickly interrupted. 'It's not necessary, Yurga.'

'But it is,' the merchant said curtly. 'It's my word. Whatever I find at home but am not expecting is yours.'

'Give over. I don't want anything from you. We're quits.'

'No, sir. Should I find something like that at home it means it's destiny. For if you mock destiny, if you deceive it, then it will punish you severely.'

I know, thought the Witcher. I know.

'But . . . Geralt, sir . . .'

'What, Yurga?'

'I won't find anything at home I'm not expecting. Nothing, and for certain not what you were hoping for. Witcher, sir, hear this:

363

after the last child, my woman cannot have any more and whatever you're after, there won't be an infant at home. Seems to me you're out of luck.'

Geralt did not reply.

Yurga said nothing either. Roach snorted again and tossed her head.

'But I have two sons,' Yurga suddenly said quickly, looking ahead, towards the road. 'Two; healthy, strong and smart. I mean, I'll have to get them apprenticed somewhere. One, I thought, would learn to trade with me. But the other . . .'

Geralt said nothing.

'What do you say?' Yurga turned his head away, and looked at him. 'You demanded a promise on the bridge. You had in mind a child for your witcher's apprenticeship, and nothing else, didn't you? Why does that child have to be unexpected? Can it not be expected? I've two, so one of them could go for a witcher. It's a trade like any other. It ain't better or worse.'

'Are you certain,' Geralt said softly, 'it isn't worse?'

Yurga squinted.

'Protecting people, saving their lives, how do you judge that; bad or good? Those fourteen on the hill? You on that there bridge? What were you doing? Good or bad?'

'I don't know,' said Geralt with effort. 'I don't know, Yurga. Sometimes it seems to me that I know. And sometimes I have doubts. Would you like your son to have doubts like that?'

'Why not?' the merchant said gravely. 'He might as well. For it's a human and a good thing.'

'What?'

'Doubts. Only evil, sir, never has any. But no one can escape his destiny.'

The Witcher did not answer.

The highway curved beneath a high bluff, under some crooked birch trees, which by some miracle were hanging onto the vertical hillside. The birches had yellow leaves. Autumn, Geralt thought, it's autumn again. A river sparkled down below, the freshly-cut palisade of a watchtower shone white, the roofs of cottages, hewn stakes of the jetty. A windlass creaked. A ferry was reaching the bank, pushing a wave in front of it, shoving the water with its blunt prow, parting the sluggish straw and leaves in the dirty layer of dust floating on the surface. The ropes creaked as the ferrymen hauled them. The people thronged on the bank were clamouring. There was everything in the din: women screaming, men cursing, children crying, cattle lowing, horses neighing and sheep bleating. The monotonous, bass music of fear.

'Get away! Get away, get back, dammit!' yelled a horseman, head bandaged with a bloody rag. His horse, submerged up to its belly, thrashed around, lifting its fore hooves high and splashing water. Yelling and cries from the jetty – the shield bearers were brutally jostling the crowd, hitting out in all directions with the shafts of their spears.

'Get away from the ferry!' the horseman yelled, swinging his sword around. 'Soldiers only! Get away, afore I start cracking some skulls!'

Geralt pulled on his reins, holding back his mare, who was dancing near the edge of the ravine.

Heavily armoured men, weapons and armour clanging, galloped along the ravine, stirring up clouds of dust which obscured the shield bearers running in their wake.

'Geraaaalt!'

He looked down. A slim man in a cherry jerkin and a bonnet with an egret's feather was jumping up and down and waving his arms on an abandoned cart loaded with cages which had been shoved off the highway. Chickens and geese fluttered and squawked in the cages.

'Geraaalt! It's me!'

'Dandelion! Come here!'

'Get away, get away from the ferry!' roared the horseman with the bandaged head on the jetty. 'The ferry's for the army only! If you want to get to the far bank, scum, seize your axes and get into the forest, cobble together some rafts! The ferry's just for the army!'

'By the Gods, Geralt,' the poet panted, scrambling up the side of the ravine. His cherry jerkin was dotted, as though by snow, with birds' feathers. 'Do you see what's happening? The Sodden forces have surely lost the battle, and the retreat has begun. What am I saying? What retreat? It's a flight, simply a panicked flight! And we have to scarper, too, Geralt. To the Yaruga's far bank . . .'

'What are you doing here, Dandelion? How did you get here?'

'What am I doing?' the bard yelled. 'You want to know? I'm fleeing like everybody else, I was bumping along on that cart all day! Some whoreson stole my horse in the night! Geralt, I beg you, get me out of this hell! I tell you, the Nilfgaardians could be here any moment! Whoever doesn't get the Yaruga behind them will be slaughtered. Slaughtered, do you understand?'

'Don't panic, Dandelion.'

Below on the jetty, the neighing of horses being pulled onto the ferry by force and the clattering of hooves on the planks. Uproar. A seething mass. The splash of water after a cart was pushed into the river, the lowing of oxen holding their muzzles above the surface. Geralt looked on as the bundles and crates from the cart turned around in the current, banged against the side of the ferry and drifted away. Screaming, curses. In the ravine a cloud of dust, hoof beats.

'One at a time!' yelled the bandaged soldier, driving his horse into the crowd. 'Order, dammit! One at a time!'

'Geralt,' Dandelion groaned, seizing a stirrup. 'Do you see what's happening? We haven't a chance of getting on that ferry. The soldiers will get as many across on it as they can, and then they'll burn it so the Nilfgaardians won't be able to use it. That's how it's normally done, isn't it?'

'Agreed,' the Witcher nodded. 'That's how it's normally done. I don't understand, though, why the panic? What, is this the first war ever, have there never been any others? Just like usual, the kings' forces beat each other up and then the kings reach agreement, sign treaties and get plastered to celebrate. Nothing will really change for those having their ribs crushed on the jetty now. So why all this brutality?'

Dandelion looked at him intently, without releasing the stirrup.

'You must have lousy information, Geralt,' he said. 'Or you're unable to understand its significance. This isn't an ordinary war about succession to a throne or a small scrap of land. It's not a skirmish between two feudal lords, which peasants watch while leaning on their pitchforks.'

'What is it then? Enlighten me, because I really don't know what it's about. Just between you and I, it doesn't actually interest me that much, but please explain.'

'There's never been a war like this,' the bard said gravely. 'The Nilfgaard army are leaving scorched earth and bodies behind them. Entire fields of corpses. This is a war of destruction, total destruction. Nilfgaard against everyone. Cruelty—'

'There is and has never been a war without cruelty,' the Witcher interrupted. 'You're exaggerating, Dandelion. It's like it is by the ferry: that's how it's normally done. A kind of military tradition, I'd say. As long as the world has existed, armies marching through a country kill, plunder, burn and rape; though not necessarily in that order. As long as the world has existed, peasants have hidden in forests with their women and what they can carry, and when everything is over, return—'

'Not in this war, Geralt. After this war there won't be anybody or anything to return to. Nilfgaard is leaving smouldering embers behind it, the army is marching in a row and dragging everybody out. Scaffolds and stakes stretch for miles along the highways, smoke is rising into the sky across the entire horizon. You said there hasn't been anything like this since the world has existed? Well, you were right. Since the world has existed. Our world. For it looks as though the Nilfgaardians have come from beyond the mountains to destroy our world.'

'That makes no sense. Who would want to destroy the world? Wars aren't waged to destroy. Wars are waged for two reasons. One is power and the other is money.'

'Don't philosophise, Geralt! You won't change what's happening with philosophy! Why won't you listen? Why won't you see? Why don't you want to understand? Believe me, the Yaruga won't stop the Nilfgaardians. In the winter, when the river freezes over, they'll march on. I tell you, we must flee, flee to the North; they may not get that far. But even if they don't, our world will never be what it was. Geralt, don't leave me here! I'll never survive by myself! Don't leave me!'

'You must be insane, Dandelion,' the Witcher said, leaning over in the saddle. 'You must be insane with fear, if you could think I'd leave you. Give me your hand and jump up on the horse. There's nothing for you here, nor will you shove your way onto the ferry. I'll take you upstream and then we'll hunt for a boat or a ferry.'

'The Nilfgaardians will capture us! They're close now. Did you see those horsemen? They are clearly coming straight from the fighting. Let's ride downstream towards the mouth of the Ina.'

'Stop looking on the dark side. We'll slip through, you'll see. Crowds of people are heading downstream, it'll be the same at every ferry as it is here, they're sure to have nabbed all the boats too. We'll ride upstream, against the current. Don't worry, I'll get you across on a log if I have to.'

'The far bank's barely visible!'

'Don't whinge. I said I'd get you across.'

'What about you?'

'Hop up onto the horse. We'll talk on the way. Hey, not with that bloody sack! Do you want to break Roach's back?'

'Is it Roach? Roach was a bay, and she's a chestnut.'

'All of my horses are called Roach. You know that perfectly well; don't try to get round me. I said get rid of that sack. What's in it, dammit? Gold?'

'Manuscripts! Poems! And some vittles . . .'

'Throw it into the river. You can write some new poems. And I'll share my food with you.'

Dandelion made a forlorn face, but did not ponder long, and hurled the sack into the water. He jumped onto the horse and wriggled around, making a place for himself on the saddlebags, and grabbed the Witcher's belt.

'Time to go, time to go,' he urged anxiously. 'Let's not waste time, Geralt, we'll disappear into the forest, before—'

'Stop it, Dandelion. That panic of yours is beginning to affect Roach.'

'Don't mock. If you'd seen what I—'

'Shut up, dammit. Let's ride, I'd like to get you across before dusk.'

'Me? What about you?'

'I have matters to deal with on this side of the river.'

'You must be mad, Geralt. Do you have a death wish? What "matters"?'

'None of your business. I'm going to Cintra.'

'To Cintra? Cintra is no more.'

'What do you mean?'

'There is no Cintra. Just smouldering embers and piles of rubble. The Nilfgaardians—'

'Dismount, Dandelion.'

'What?'

'Get off!' The Witcher jerked around. The troubadour looked at his face and leaped from the horse onto the ground, took a step back and stumbled.

Geralt got off slowly. He threw the reins across the mare's head, stood for a moment undecided, and then wiped his face with a gloved hand. He sat down on the edge of a tree hollow, beneath a spreading dogwood bush with blood-red branches.

'Come here, Dandelion,' he said. 'Sit down. And tell me what's happened to Cintra. Everything.'

The poet sat down.

'The Nilfgaardians invaded across the passes,' he began after a moment's silence. 'There were thousands of them. They surrounded the Cintran army in the Marnadal valley. A battle was joined lasting the whole day, from dawn till dusk. The forces of Cintra fought courageously, but were decimated. The king fell, and then their queen—'

'Calanthe.'

'Yes. She headed off a stampede, didn't let them disperse, gathered anyone she was able to around herself and the standard. They fought their way through the encirclement and fell back across the river towards the city. Whoever was able to.'

'And Calanthe?'

'She defended the river crossing with a handful of knights, and shielded the retreat. They say she fought like a man, threw herself like a woman possessed into the greatest turmoil. They stabbed her with pikes as she charged the Nilfgaardian foot. She was transported to the city gravely wounded. What's in that canteen, Geralt?'

'Vodka. Want some?'

'What do you think?'

'Speak. Go on, Dandelion. Tell me everything.'

'The city didn't put up a fight. There was no siege, because there was no one to defend the walls. What was left of the knights and their families, the noblemen and the queen . . . They barricaded themselves in the castle. The Nilfgaardians captured the castle at once, their sorcerers pulverised the gate and some of the walls. Only the keep was being defended, clearly protected by spells, because it resisted the Nilfgaardian magic. In spite of that, the Nilfgaardians forced their way inside within four days. They didn't find anyone alive. Not a soul. The women had killed the children, the men had killed the women and then fallen on their swords or . . . What's the matter, Geralt?'

'Speak, Dandelion.'

'Or . . . like Calanthe . . . Headlong from the battlements, from the very top. They say she asked someone to . . . But no one would. So she crawled to the battlements and . . . Headfirst. They say dreadful things were done to her body. I don't want to . . . What's the matter?'

'Nothing. Dandelion . . . In Cintra there was a . . . little girl. Calanthe's granddaughter, she was around ten or eleven. Her name was Ciri. Did you hear anything about her?'

'No. But there was a terrible massacre in the city and the castle and almost no one got out alive. And nobody survived of those who defended the keep, I told you. And most of the women and children from the notable families were there.'

The Witcher said nothing.

'That Calanthe,' Dandelion asked. 'Did you know her?'

'Yes.'

'And the little girl you were asking about? Ciri?'

'I knew her too.'

The wind blew from the river, rippled the water, shook the trees and the leaves fell from the branches in a shimmering shower. Autumn, thought the Witcher, it's autumn again.

He stood up.

'Do you believe in destiny, Dandelion?'

The troubadour raised his head and looked at him with his eyes wide open.

'Why do you ask?'

'Answer.'

'Well . . . yes.'

'But did you know that destiny alone is not enough? That something more is necessary?'

'I don't understand.'

'You're not the only one. But that's how it is. Something more is needed. The problem is that . . . that I won't ever find out what.'

'What's the matter, Geralt?'

'Nothing, Dandelion. Come, get on. Let's go, we're wasting the day. Who knows how long it'll take us to find a boat, and we'll need a big one. I'm not leaving Roach, after all.'

'Are we crossing the river today?' the poet asked, happily.

'Yes. There's nothing for me on this side of the river.'

IX

'Yurga!'

'Darling!'

She ran from the gate – her hair escaping her headscarf, blowing around – stumbling and crying out. Yurga threw the halter to his servant, jumped down from the cart, ran to meet his wife, seized her around the waist, lifted her up and spun her, whirled her around.

'I'm home, my darling! I've returned!'

'Yurga!'

'I'm back! Hey, throw open the gates! The man of the house has returned!'

She was wet, smelling of soap suds. She had clearly been doing the laundry. He stood her on the ground, but she still did not release him, and remained clinging, trembling, warm.

'Lead me inside.'

'By the Gods, you've returned . . . I couldn't sleep at night . . . Yurga . . . I couldn't sleep at night—'

'I've returned. Oh, I've returned! And I've returned with riches! Do you see the cart? Hey, hurry, drive it in! Do you see the cart? I'm carrying enough goods to—'

'Yurga, what are goods to me, or a cart . . . You've returned . . . Healthy . . . In one piece—'

'I've returned wealthy, I tell you. You'll see directly—'

'Yurga? But who's that? That man in black? By the Gods, and with a sword—'

The merchant looked around. The Witcher had dismounted and was standing with his back to them, pretending to be adjusting the girth and saddlebags. He did not look at them, did not approach.

'I'll tell you later. Oh, but if it weren't for him . . . But where are the lads? Hale?'

372

'Yes, Yurga, they're hale. They went to the fields to shoot at crows, but the neighbours will tell them you're back. They'll soon rush home, the three of them—'

'Three? What do you mean, Goldencheeks? Were you—'

'No . . . But I must tell you something . . . You won't be cross?'

'Me? With you?'

'I've taken a lassie in, Yurga. I took her from the druids, you know, the ones who rescued children after the war? They gathered home-less and stray children in the forests . . . Barely alive . . . Yurga? Are you cross?'

Yurga held a hand to his forehead and looked back. The Witcher was walking slowly behind the cart, leading his horse. He was not looking at them, his head turned away.

'Yurga?'

'O, Gods,' the merchant groaned. 'O, Gods! Something I wasn't expecting! At home!'

'Don't take on, Yurga . . . You'll see, you'll like her. She's a clever lassie, pleasing, hardworking . . . A mite odd. She won't say where she's from, she weeps at once if you ask. So I don't. Yurga, you know I always wished for a daughter . . . What ails you?'

'Nothing,' he said softly. 'Nothing. Destiny. The whole way he was raving in his sleep, delirious ravings, nothing but destiny and destiny . . . By the Gods . . . It's not for the likes of us to understand. We can't mark what people like him think. What they dream about. It's not for us to understand . . .'

'Dad!'

'Nadbor! Sulik! How you've grown, a pair of young bulls! Well, come here, to me! Look alive . . .'

He broke off, seeing a small, very slim, mousy-haired creature walking slowly behind the boys. The little girl looked at him and he saw the huge eyes as green as spring grass, shining like two little stars. He saw the girl suddenly start, run . . . He heard her shrill, piercing cry.

'Geralt!'

The Witcher turned away from his horse with a swift, agile

movement and ran to meet her. Yurga stared open-mouthed. He had never thought a man could move so quickly.

They came together in the centre of the farmyard. The mousy-haired girl in a grey dress. And the white-haired Witcher with a sword on his back, all dressed in black leather, gleaming with silver. The Witcher bounding softly, the girl trotting, the Witcher on his knees, the girl's thin hands around his neck, the mousy hair on his shoulders. Goldencheeks shrieked softly. Yurga hugged his rosy-cheeked wife when she cried out softly, pulling her towards him without a word, and gathered up and hugged both boys.

'Geralt!' the little girl repeated, clinging to the Witcher's chest. 'You found me! I knew you would! I always knew! I knew you'd find me!'

'Ciri,' said the Witcher.

Yurga could not see his face hidden among the mousy hair. He saw hands in black gloves squeezing the girl's back and shoulders.

'You found me! Oh, Geralt! I was waiting all the time! For so very long . . . We'll be together now, won't we? Now we'll be together, won't we? Say it, Geralt! Forever! Say it!'

'Forever, Ciri.'

'It's like they said! Geralt! It's like they said! Am I your destiny? Say it! Am I your destiny?'

Yurga saw the Witcher's eyes. And was very astonished. He heard his wife's soft weeping, felt the trembling of her shoulders. He looked at the Witcher and waited, tensed, for his answer. He knew he would not understand it, but he waited for it. And heard it.

'You're more than that, Ciri. Much more.'

extras

orbit

meet the author

ANDRZEJ SAPKOWSKI was born in 1948, in Poland. He studied economy and business, but the success of his fantasy cycle about the sorcerer Geralt of Rivia turned him into a bestselling writer. He is now one of Poland's most famous and successful authors.

if you enjoyed
SWORD OF DESTINY
look out for

BLOOD OF ELVES
Book 1 of the Witcher Saga
by
Andrzej Sapkowski

The Witcher, Geralt of Rivia, becomes the guardian of Ciri, surviving heiress of a bloody revolution and prophesied savior of the world, in the first novel of the **New York Times** *bestselling series that inspired the Netflix show and the video games.*

For over a century, humans, dwarves, gnomes, and elves have lived together in relative peace. But times have changed, the uneasy peace is over, and now the races are fighting once again. The only good elf, it seems, is a dead elf.

Geralt of Rivia, the cunning assassin known as the Witcher, has been waiting for the birth of a prophesied child. This child has the power to change the world for good—or for evil.

As the threat of war hangs over the land and the child is hunted for her extraordinary powers, it will become Geralt's responsibility to protect them all—and the Witcher never accepts defeat.

CHAPTER ONE

The town was in flames.

The narrow streets leading to the moat and the first terrace belched smoke and embers, flames devouring the densely clustered thatched houses and licking at the castle walls. From the west, from the harbour gate, the screams and clamour of vicious battle and the dull blows of a battering ram smashing against the walls grew ever louder.

Their attackers had surrounded them unexpectedly, shattering the barricades which had been held by no more than a few soldiers, a handful of townsmen carrying halberds and some crossbowmen from the guild. Their horses, decked out in flowing black caparisons, flew over the barricades like spectres, their riders' bright, glistening blades sowing death amongst the fleeing defenders.

Ciri felt the knight who carried her before him on his saddle abruptly spur his horse. She heard his cry. "Hold on," he shouted. "Hold on!"

Other knights wearing the colours of Cintra overtook them, sparring, even in full flight, with the Nilfgaardians. Ciri

382

caught a glimpse of the skirmish from the corner of her eye – the crazed swirl of blue-gold and black cloaks amidst the clash of steel, the clatter of blades against shields, the neighing of horses—

Shouts. No, not shouts. Screams.

"Hold on!"

Fear. With every jolt, every jerk, every leap of the horse pain shot through her hands as she clutched at the reins. Her legs contracted painfully, unable to find support, her eyes watered from the smoke. The arm around her suffocated her, choking her, the force compressing her ribs. All around her screaming such as she had never before heard grew louder. What must one do to a man to make him scream so?

Fear. Overpowering, paralysing, choking fear.

Again the clash of iron, the grunts and snorts of the horses. The houses whirled around her and suddenly she could see windows belching fire where a moment before there'd been nothing but a muddy little street strewn with corpses and cluttered with the abandoned possessions of the fleeing population. All at once the knight at her back was wracked by a strange wheezing cough. Blood spurted over the hands grasping the reins. More screams. Arrows whistled past.

A fall, a shock, painful bruising against armour. Hooves pounded past her, a horse's belly and a frayed girth flashing by above her head, then another horse's belly and a flowing black caparison. Grunts of exertion, like a lumberjack's when chopping wood. But this isn't wood; it's iron against iron. A shout, muffled and dull, and something huge and black collapsed into the mud next to her with a splash, spurting blood. An armoured foot quivered, thrashed, goring the earth with an enormous spur.

A jerk. Some force plucked her up, pulled her onto another

saddle. *Hold on!* Again the bone-shaking speed, the mad gal-lop. Arms and legs desperately searching for support. The horse rears. *Hold on!* . . . There is no support. There is no . . . There is no . . . There is blood. The horse falls. It's impossible to jump aside, no way to break free, to escape the tight embrace of these chainmail-clad arms. There is no way to avoid the blood pouring onto her head and over her shoulders.

A jolt, the squelch of mud, a violent collision with the ground, horrifically still after the furious ride. The horse's harrowing wheezes and squeals as it tries to regain its feet. The pounding of horseshoes, fetlocks and hooves flashing past. Black caparisons and cloaks. Shouting.

The street is on fire, a roaring red wall of flame. Silhouetted before it, a rider towers over the flaming roofs, enormous. His black-caparisoned horse prances, tosses its head, neighs.

The rider stares down at her. Ciri sees his eyes gleaming through the slit in his huge helmet, framed by a bird of prey's wings. She sees the fire reflected in the broad blade of the sword held in his lowered hand.

The rider looks at her. Ciri is unable to move. The dead man's motionless arms wrapped around her waist hold her down. She is locked in place by something heavy and wet with blood, something which is lying across her thigh, pinning her to the ground.

And she is frozen in fear: a terrible fear which turns her entrails inside out, which deafens Ciri to the screams of the wounded horse, the roar of the blaze, the cries of dying people and the pounding drums. The only thing which exists, which counts, which still has any meaning, is fear. Fear embodied in the figure of a black knight wearing a helmet decorated with feathers frozen against the wall of raging, red flames.

The rider spurs his horse, the wings on his helmet fluttering as the bird of prey takes to flight, launching itself to attack its helpless victim, paralysed with fear. The bird – or maybe the knight – screeches terrifyingly, cruelly, triumphantly. A black horse, black armour, a black flowing cloak, and behind this – flames. A sea of flames.

Fear.

The bird shrieks. The wings beat, feathers slap against her face. *Fear!*

Help! Why doesn't anyone help me? Alone, weak, helpless – I can't move, can't force a sound from my constricted throat. Why does no one come to help me?

I'm terrified!

Eyes blaze through the slit in the huge winged helmet. The black cloak veils everything—

"Ciri!"

She woke, numb and drenched in sweat, with her scream – the scream which had woken her – still hanging in the air, still vibrating somewhere within her, beneath her breast-bone and burning against her parched throat. Her hands ached, clenched around the blanket; her back ached . . .

"Ciri. Calm down."

The night was dark and windy, the crowns of the surrounding pine trees rustling steadily and melodiously, their limbs and trunks creaking in the wind. There was no malevolent fire, no screams, only this gentle lullaby. Beside her the campfire flickered with light and warmth, its reflected flames glowing from harness buckles, gleaming red in the leather-wrapped and iron-banded hilt of a sword leaning against a saddle on the ground. There was no other fire and no other iron. The hand against her cheek smelled of leather and ashes. Not of blood.

"Geralt—"

"It was just a dream. A bad dream."

Ciri shuddered violently, curling her arms and legs up tight. A dream. Just a dream.

The campfire had already died down; the birch logs were red and luminous, occasionally crackling, giving off tiny spurts of blue flame which illuminated the white hair and sharp profile of the man wrapping a blanket and sheepskin around her.

"Geralt, I—"

"I'm right here. Sleep, Ciri. You have to rest. We've still a long way ahead of us."

I can hear music, she thought suddenly. *Amidst the rustling of the trees . . . there's music. Lute music. And voices. The Princess of Cintra . . . A child of destiny . . . A child of Elder Blood, the blood of elves. Geralt of Rivia, the White Wolf, and his destiny. No, no, that's a legend. A poet's invention. The princess is dead. She was killed in the town streets while trying to escape . . .*

Hold on . . . ! Hold . . .

"Geralt?"

"What, Ciri?"

"What did he do to me? What happened? What did he . . . do to me?"

"Who?"

"The knight . . . The black knight with feathers on his helmet . . . I can't remember anything. He shouted . . . and looked at me. I can't remember what happened. Only that I was frightened . . . I was so frightened . . ."

The man leaned over her, the flame of the campfire sparkling in his eyes. They were strange eyes. Very strange. Ciri had been frightened of them, she hadn't liked meeting his gaze. But that had been a long time ago. A very long time ago.

"I can't remember anything," she whispered, searching

for his hand, as tough and coarse as raw wood. "The black knight—"

"It was a dream. Sleep peacefully. It won't come back."

Ciri had heard such reassurances in the past. They had been repeated to her endlessly; many, many times she had been offered comforting words when her screams had woken her during the night. But this time it was different. Now she believed it. Because it was Geralt of Rivia, the White Wolf, the Witcher, who said it. The man who was her destiny. The one for whom she was destined. Geralt the Witcher, who had found her surrounded by war, death and despair, who had taken her with him and promised they would never part.

She fell asleep holding tight to his hand.

The bard finished the song. Tilting his head a little he repeated the ballad's refrain on his lute, delicately, softly, a single tone higher than the apprentice accompanying him.

No one said a word. Nothing but the subsiding music and the whispering leaves and squeaking boughs of the enormous oak could be heard. Then, all of a sudden, a goat tethered to one of the carts which circled the ancient tree bleated lengthily. At that moment, as if given a signal, one of the men seated in the large semi-circular audience stood up. Throwing his cobalt blue cloak with gold braid trim back over his shoulder, he gave a stiff, dignified bow.

"Thank you, Master Dandelion," he said, his voice resonant without being loud. "Allow me, Radcliffe of Oxenfurt, Master of the Arcana, to express what I am sure is the opinion of every-one here present and utter words of gratitude and appreciation for your fine art and skill."

The wizard ran his gaze over those assembled – an audi-ence of well over a hundred people – seated on the ground, on carts, or standing in a tight semi-circle facing the foot of the oak. They nodded and whispered amongst themselves. Several people began to applaud while others greeted the singer with upraised hands. Women, touched by the music, sniffed and wiped their eyes on whatever came to hand, which differed according to their standing, profession and wealth: peasant women used their forearms or the backs of their hands, merchants' wives dabbed their eyes with linen handkerchiefs while elves and noblewomen used kerchiefs of the finest tight-woven cotton, and Baron Vilibert's three daughters, who had, along with the rest of his retinue, halted their falcon hunt to attend the famous troubadour's performance, blew their noses loudly and sonorously into elegant mould-green cashmere scarves.

"It would not be an exaggeration to say," continued the wizard, "that you have moved us deeply, Master Dandelion. You have prompted us to reflection and thought; you have stirred our hearts. Allow me to express our gratitude, and our respect."

The troubadour stood and took a bow, sweeping the heron feather pinned to his fashionable hat across his knees. His apprentice broke off his playing, grinned and bowed too, until Dandelion glared at him sternly and snapped something under his breath. The boy lowered his head and returned to softly strumming his lute strings.

The assembly stirred to life. The merchants travelling in the caravan whispered amongst themselves and then rolled a sizable cask of beer out to the foot of the oak tree. Wizard Radcliffe lost himself in quiet conversation with Baron Vilibert. Having blown their noses, the baron's daughters gazed at Dandelion in adoration – which went entirely unnoticed by the bard, engrossed as he was in smiling, winking and flashing his teeth at a haughty, silent group of roving elves, and at one of them in particular: a dark-haired, large-eyed beauty sporting a tiny ermine cap. Dandelion had rivals for her attention – the elf, with her huge eyes and beautiful toque hat, had caught his audience's interest as well, and a number of knights, students and goliards were paying court to her with their eyes. The elf clearly enjoyed the attention, picking at the lace cuffs of her chemise and fluttering her eyelashes, but the group of elves with her surrounded her on all sides, not bothering to hide their antipathy towards her admirers.

The glade beneath Bleobheris, the great oak, was a place of frequent rallies, a well-known travellers' resting place and meeting ground for wanderers, and was famous for its tolerance and openness. The druids protecting the ancient tree called it the Seat of Friendship and willingly welcomed all comers. But even during an event as exceptional as the world-famous troubadour's just-concluded performance the travellers kept to themselves, remaining in clearly delineated groups. Elves stayed with elves. Dwarfish craftsmen gathered with their kin, who were often hired to protect the merchant caravans and were armed to the teeth. Their groups tolerated at best the gnome miners and halfling farmers who camped beside them. All non-humans were uniformly distant towards humans. The humans repaid in kind, but were not seen to mix amongst themselves either. Nobility looked down on the merchants and travelling salesmen with open scorn, while soldiers and mercenaries distanced themselves from shepherds and their reeking sheepskins. The few wizards and their disciples kept themselves entirely apart from the others, and bestowed their arrogance on everyone in equal parts. A tight-knit, dark and silent group of peasants lurked in the background. Resembling a forest with their rakes, pitchforks and flails poking above their heads, they were ignored by all and sundry.

The exception, as ever, was the children. Freed from the constraints of silence which had been enforced during the bard's performance, the children dashed into the woods with wild cries, and enthusiastically immersed themselves in a game whose rules were incomprehensible to all those who had bidden farewell to the happy years of childhood. Children of elves, dwarves, halflings, gnomes, half-elves, quarter-elves and toddlers of mysterious provenance neither knew nor recognised racial or social divisions. At least, not yet.

"Indeed!" shouted one of the knights present in the glade, who was as thin as a beanpole and wearing a red and black tunic emblazoned with three lions passant. "The wizard speaks the truth! The ballads were beautiful. Upon my word, honourable Dandelion, if you ever pass near Baldhorn, my lord's castle, stop by without a moment's hesitation. You will be welcomed like a prince— What am I saying? Welcomed like King Vizimir himself! I swear on my sword, I have heard many a minstrel, but none even came close to being your equal, master. Accept the respect and tributes those of us born to knighthood, and those of us appointed to the position, pay to your skills!"

Flawlessly sensing the opportune moment, the troubadour winked at his apprentice. The boy set his lute aside and picked up a little casket which served as a collection box for the audience's more measurable expressions of appreciation. He hesitated, ran his eyes over the crowd, then replaced the little casket and grabbed a large bucket standing nearby. Master Dandelion bestowed an approving smile on the young man for his prudence.

"Master!" shouted a sizeable woman sitting on a cart, the sides of which were painted with a sign for "Vera Loewenhaupt and Sons," and which was full of wickerwork. Her sons, nowhere to be seen, were no doubt busy wasting away their mother's hard-earned fortune. "Master Dandelion, what is this? Are you going to leave us in suspense? That can't be the end of your ballad? Sing to us of what happened next!"

"Songs and ballads" – the musician bowed – "never end, dear lady, because poetry is eternal and immortal, it knows no beginning, it knows no end—"

"But what happened next?" The tradeswoman didn't give up, generously rattling coins into the bucket Dandelion's apprentice held out to her. "At least tell us about it, even if you have no wish to sing of it. Your songs mention no names, but we know the witcher you sing of is no other than the famous Geralt of Rivia, and the enchantress for whom he burns with love is the equally famous Yennefer. And the Child Surprise, destined for the witcher and sworn to him from birth, is Cirilla, the unfortunate Princess of Cintra, the town destroyed by the Invaders. Am I right?"

Dandelion smiled, remaining enigmatic and aloof. "I sing of universal matters, my dear, generous lady," he stated. "Of emotions which anyone can experience. Not about specific people."

"Oh, come on!" yelled a voice from the crowd. "Everyone knows those songs are about Geralt the Witcher!"

"Yes, yes!" squealed Baron Vilibert's daughters in chorus, drying their sodden scarves. "Sing on, Master Dandelion! What happened next? Did the witcher and Yennefer the Enchantress find each other in the end? And did they love each other? Were they happy? We want to know!"

"Enough!" roared the dwarf leader with a growl in his throat, shaking his mighty waist-length red beard. "It's crap – all these princesses, sorceresses, destiny, love and women's fanciful tales. If you'll pardon the expression, great poet, it's all lies, just a poetic invention to make the story prettier and more touching. But of the deeds of war – the massacre and plunder of Cintra, the battles of Marnadal and Sodden – you did sing that mightily, Dandelion! There's no regrets in parting with silver for such a song, a joy to a warrior's heart! And I, Sheldon Skaggs, declare there's not an ounce of lies in what you say – and I can tell the lies from the truth because I was there at Sodden. I stood against the Nilfgaard invaders with an axe in my hand…"

"I, Donimir of Troy," shouted the thin knight with three lions passant blazoned across his tunic, "was at both battles of Sodden! But I did not see you there, sir dwarf!"

"No doubt because you were looking after the supply train!" Sheldon Skaggs retorted. "While I was in the front line where things got hot!"

"Mind your tongue, beardy!" said Donimir of Troy flushing, hitching up his sword belt. "And who you're speaking to!"

"Have a care yourself!" The dwarf whacked his palm against the axe wedged in his belt, turned to his companions and grinned. "Did you see him there? Frigging knight! See his coat of arms? Ha! Three lions on a shield? Two shitting and the third snarling!"

"Peace, peace!" A grey-haired druid in a white cloak averted trouble with a sharp, authoritative voice. "This is not fitting, gentlemen! Not here, under Bleobheris' crown, an oak older than all the disputes and quarrels of the world! And not in Poet Dandelion's presence, from whose ballads we ought to learn of love, not contention."

"Quite so!" a short, fat priest with a face glistening with sweat seconded the druid. "You look but have no eyes, you listen but have deaf ears. Because divine love is not in you, you are like empty barrels—"

"Speaking of barrels," squeaked a long-nosed gnome from his cart, painted with a sign for "Iron hardware, manufacture and sale", "roll another out, guildsmen! Poet Dandelion's throat is surely dry – and ours too, from all these emotions!"

if you enjoyed
SWORD OF DESTINY

look out for

THE TOWER OF FOOLS
Book One of the Hussite Trilogy

by

Andrzej Sapkowski

Andrzej Sapkowski, winner of the World Fantasy Award for Lifetime Achievement, created an international phenomenon with his New York Times *bestselling Witcher series. Now he introduces readers to a new hero: Reynevan, a young alchemist and healer journeying across a war-torn land.*

When a thoughtless indiscretion finds Reinmar of Bielau caught in the crosshairs of a powerful noble family, he is forced to flee his home.

extras

*But once he passes beyond the city walls, he finds that
there are dangers ahead as well as behind. Pursued by
dark forces both human and mystic, Reynevan finds
himself in the* Narrenturm, *the Tower of Fools, a medieval
asylum for the mad—or for those who dare to think
differently and challenge the prevailing order.*

*Gloria Patri, et Filio et Spiritui sancto.
Sicut erat in principio, et nunc, et semper
et in saecula saeculorum, Amen.
Alleluia!*

As the monks concluded the Gloria, Reynevan, kissing the
back of Adèle of Stercza's neck, placed his hand beneath her
orchard of pomegranates, engrossed, mad, like a young hart
skipping upon the mountains to his beloved...

A mailed fist struck the door, which thudded open with such
force that the lock was torn off the frame and shot through
the window like a meteor. Adèle screamed shrilly as the Stercza
brothers burst into the chamber.

Reynevan tumbled out of bed, positioning it between himself and the intruders, grabbed his clothes and began to hurriedly put them on. He largely succeeded, but only because
the brothers Stercza had directed their frontal attack at their
sister-in-law.

"You vile harlot!" bellowed Morold of Stercza, dragging a
naked Adèle from the bedclothes.

"Wanton whore!" chimed in Wittich, his older brother, while Wolfher—next oldest after Adèle's husband Gelfrad—did not even open his mouth, for pale fury had deprived him of speech. He struck Adèle hard in the face. The Burgundian screamed. Wolfher struck her again, this time backhanded.

"Don't you dare hit her, Stercza!" yelled Reynevan, but his voice broke and trembled with fear and a paralysing feeling of impotence, caused by his trousers being round his knees. "Don't you dare!"

His cry achieved its effect, although not the way he had intended. Wolfher and Wittich, momentarily forgetting their adulterous sister-in-law, pounced on Reynevan, raining down a hail of punches and kicks on the boy. He cowered under the blows, but rather than defend or protect himself, he stubbornly pulled on his trousers as though they were some kind of magical armour. Out of the corner of one eye, he saw Wittich drawing a knife. Adèle screamed.

"Don't," Wolfher snapped at his brother. "Not here!"

Reynevan managed to get onto his knees. Wittich, face white with fury, jumped at him and punched him, throwing him to the floor again. Adèle let out a piercing scream, which broke off as Morold struck her in the face and pulled her hair.

"Don't you dare..." Reynevan groaned "...hit her, you scoundrels!"

"Bastard!" yelled Wittich. "Just you wait!"

Wittich leaped forward, punched and kicked once and twice. Wolfher stopped him at the third.

"Not here," Wolfher repeated calmly, but it was a baleful calm. "Into the courtyard with him. We'll take him to Bierutów. That slut, too."

"I'm innocent!" wailed Adèle of Stercza. "He bewitched me! Enchanted me! He's a sorcerer! *Sorcier! Diab—*"

Morold silenced her with another punch. "Hold your tongue, trollop," he growled. "You'll get the chance to scream. Just wait awhile."

"Don't you *dare* hit her!" yelled Reynevan.

"We'll give you a chance to scream, too, little rooster," Wolfher added, still menacingly calm. "Come on, out with him."

The Stercza brothers threw Reynevan down the garret's steep stairs and the boy tumbled onto the landing, splintering part of the wooden balustrade. Before he could get up, they seized him again and threw him out into the courtyard, onto sand strewn with steaming piles of horse shit.

"Well, well, well," said Nicolaus of Stercza, the youngest of the brothers, barely a stripling, who was holding the horses. "Look who's stopped by. Could it be Reinmar of Bielawa?"

"The scholarly braggart Bielawa," snorted Jentsch of Knobelsdorf, known as Eagle Owl, a comrade and relative of the Sterczas. "The arrogant know-all Bielawa!"

"Shitty poet," added Dieter Haxt, another friend of the family. "Bloody Abélard!"

"And to prove to him we're well read, too," said Wolfher as he descended the stairs, "we'll do to him what they did to Abélard when he was caught with Héloïse. Well, Bielawa? How do you fancy being a capon?"

"Go fuck yourself, Stercza."

"What? What?" Although it seemed impossible, Wolfher Stercza had turned even paler. "The rooster still has the audacity to open his beak? To crow? The bullwhip, Jentsch!"

"Don't you dare beat him!" Adèle called impotently as she was led down the stairs, now clothed, albeit incompletely. "Don't you dare! Or I'll tell everyone what you are like! That you courted me yourself, pawed me and tried to debauch me behind your brother's back! That you swore vengeance on me if I spurned you! Which is why you are so...so..."

She couldn't find the German word and the entire tirade fell apart. Wolfher just laughed.

"Verily!" he mocked. "People will listen to the French-woman, the lewd strumpet. The bullwhip, Eagle Owl!"

The courtyard was suddenly awash with black Augustinian habits.

"What is happening here?" shouted the venerable Prior Erasmus Steinkeller, a bony and sallow old man. "Christians, what are you doing?"

"Begone!" bellowed Wolfher, cracking the bullwhip. "Begone, shaven-heads, hurry off to your prayer books! Don't interfere in knightly affairs, or woe betide you, blackbacks!"

"Good Lord." The prior put his liver-spotted hands together. "Forgive them, for they know not what they do. *In nomine Patris, et Filii—*"

"Morold, Wittich!" roared Wolfher. "Bring the harlot here! Jentsch, Dieter, bind her paramour!"

"Or perhaps," snarled Stefan Rotkirch, another friend of the family who had been silent until then, "we'll drag him behind a horse a little?"

"We could. But first, we'll give him a flogging!"

Wolfher aimed a blow with the horsewhip at the still-prone Reynevan but did not connect, as his wrist was seized by Brother Innocent, nicknamed "Brother Insolent" by his fellow friars, whose impressive height and build were apparent despite his humble monkish stoop. His vicelike grip held Wolfher's arm motionless.

Stercza swore coarsely, jerked himself away and gave the monk a hard shove. But he might as well have shoved the tower in Oleśnica Castle for all the effect it had. Brother Innocent didn't budge an inch. He shoved Wolfher back, propelling him halfway across the courtyard and dumping him in a pile of muck.

For a moment, there was silence. And then they all rushed the huge monk. Eagle Owl, the first to attack, was punched in the teeth and tumbled across the sand. Morold of Stercza took a thump to the ear and staggered off to one side, staring vacantly. The others swarmed over the Augustinian like ants, raining blows on the monk's huge form. Brother Insolent retaliated just as savagely and in a distinctly unchristian way, quite at odds with Saint Augustine's rule of humility.

The sight enraged the old prior. He flushed like a beetroot, roared like a lion and rushed into the fray, striking left and right with heavy blows of his rosewood crucifix.

"*Pax!*" he bellowed as he struck. "*Pax! Vobiscum!* Love thy neighbour! *Proximum tuum! Sicut te ipsum!* Whoresons!"

Dieter Haxt punched him hard. The old man was flung over backwards and his sandals flew up, describing pretty trajectories in the air. The Augustinians cried out and several of them charged into battle, unable to restrain themselves. The courtyard was seething in earnest.

Wolfher of Stercza, who had been shoved out of the confusion, drew a short sword and brandished it—bloodshed looked inevitable. But Reynevan, who had finally managed to stand up, whacked him in the back of the head with the handle of the bullwhip he had picked up. Stercza held his head and turned around, only for Reynevan to lash him across the face. As Wolfher fell to the ground, Reynevan rushed towards the horses.

"Adèle! Here! To me!"

Adèle didn't even budge, and the indifference painted on her face was alarming. Reynevan leaped into the saddle. The horse neighed and fidgeted.

"Adèèèèèèle!"

Morold, Wittich, Haxt and Eagle Owl were now running towards him. Reynevan reined the horse around, whistled piercingly and spurred it hard, making for the gate.

"After him!" yelled Wolfher. "To your horses and get after him!"

Reynevan's first thought was to head towards Saint Mary's Gate and out of the town into the woods, but the stretch of Cattle Street leading to the gate was totally crammed with wagons. Furthermore, the horse, urged on and frightened by the cries of an unfamiliar rider, was showing great individual initiative, so before he knew it, Reynevan was hurtling along at a gallop towards the town square, splashing mud and scattering passers-by. He didn't have to look back to know the others were hot on his heels given the thudding of hooves, the neighing of horses, the angry roaring of the Sterczas and the furious yelling of people being jostled.

He jabbed the horse to a full gallop with his heels, hitting and knocking over a baker carrying a basket. A shower of loaves and pastries flew into the mud, soon to be trodden beneath the hooves of the Sterczas' horses. Reynevan didn't even look back, more concerned with what was ahead of him than behind. A cart piled high with faggots of brushwood loomed up before his eyes. The cart was blocking almost the entire street, the rest of which was occupied by a group of half-clothed urchins, kneeling down and busily digging something extremely engrossing out of the muck.

"We have you, Bielawa!" thundered Wolfher from behind, also seeing the obstruction.

Reynevan's horse was racing so swiftly there was no chance of stopping it. He pressed himself against its mane and closed his eyes. As a result, he didn't see the half-naked children scatter with the speed and grace of rats. He didn't look back, so nor did he see a peasant in a sheepskin jerkin turn around, somewhat stupefied, as he hauled a cart into the road. Nor did he see the Sterczas riding broadside into the cart. Nor Jentsch of Knobelsdorf soaring from the saddle and sweeping half of the faggots from the cart with his body.

Reynevan galloped down Saint John's Street, between the town hall and the burgermeister's house, hurtling at full speed into Oleśnica's huge and crowded town square. Pandemonium erupted. Aiming for the southern frontage and the squat, square tower of the Oława Gate visible above it, Reynevan galloped through the crowds, leaving havoc behind him. Townsfolk yelled and pigs squealed, as overturned stalls and benches showered a hail of household goods and foodstuffs of every kind in all directions. Clouds of feathers flew everywhere as the Sterczas—hot on Reynevan's heels—added to the destruction.

Reynevan's horse, frightened by a goose flying past its nose, recoiled and hurtled into a fish stall, shattering crates and bursting open barrels. The enraged fishmonger made a great swipe with a keep net, missing Reynevan but striking the horse's rump. The horse whinnied and slewed sideways, upending a stall selling thread and ribbons, and only a miracle prevented Reynevan from falling. Out of the corner of one eye, he saw the stallholder running after him brandishing a huge cleaver (serving God only knew what purpose in the haberdashery trade). Spitting out some goose feathers stuck to his lips, he brought the horse under control and galloped through the shambles, knowing that the Oława Gate was very close.

"I'll tear your balls off, Bielawa!" Wolfher of Stercza roared from behind. "I'll tear them off and stuff them down your throat!"

"Kiss my arse!"

Only four men were chasing him now—Rotkirch had been pulled from his horse and was being roughed up by some infuriated market traders.

Reynevan darted like an arrow down an avenue of animal carcasses suspended by their legs. Most of the butchers leaped back in alarm, but one carrying a large haunch of beef on one shoulder tumbled under the hooves of Wittich's horse, which took fright, reared up and was ploughed into by Wolfher's horse. Wittich flew from the saddle straight onto the meat stall, nose-first into livers, lights and kidneys, and was then landed on by Wolfher. His foot was caught in the stirrup and before he could free himself, he had destroyed a large number of stalls and covered himself in mud and blood.

At the last moment, Reynevan quickly lowered his head over the horse's neck to duck under a wooden sign with a piglet's head painted on it. Dieter Haxt, who was bearing down on him, wasn't quick enough and the cheerfully grinning piglet slammed into his forehead. Dieter flew from the saddle and crashed into a pile of refuse, frightening some cats. Reynevan turned around. Now only Nicolaus of Stercza was keeping up with him.

Reynevan shot out of the chaos at a full gallop and into a small square where some tanners were working. As a frame hung with wet hides loomed up before him, he urged his horse to jump. It did. And Reynevan didn't fall off. Another miracle.

Nicolaus wasn't as lucky. His horse skidded to a halt in front of the frame and collided with it, slipping on the mud and scraps of meat and fat. The youngest Stercza shot over his horse's head, with very unfortunate results. He flew belly-first right onto a scythe used for scraping leather which the tanners had left propped up against the frame.

At first, Nicolaus had no idea what had happened. He got

up from the ground, caught hold of his horse, and only when it snorted and stepped back did his knees sag and buckle beneath him. Still not really knowing what was happening, the youngest Stercza slid across the mud after the panicked horse, which was still moving back and snorting. Finally, as he released the reins and tried to get to his feet again, he realised something was wrong and looked down at his midriff.

And screamed.

He dropped to his knees in the middle of a rapidly spreading pool of blood.

Dieter Haxt rode up, reined in his horse and dismounted. A moment later, Wolfher and Wittich followed suit.

Nicolaus sat down heavily. Looked at his belly again. Screamed and then burst into tears. His eyes began to glaze over as the blood gushing from him mingled with the blood of the oxen and hogs butchered that morning.

"Nicolaaaaus!" yelled Wolfher.

Nicolaus of Stercza coughed and choked. And died.

"You are dead, Reinmar of Bielawa!" Wolfher of Stercza, pale with fury, bellowed towards the gate. "I'll catch you, kill you, destroy you. Exterminate you and your entire viperous family. Your entire viperous family, do you hear?"

Reynevan didn't. Amid the thud of horseshoes on the bridge planks, he was leaving Oleśnica and dashing south, straight for the Wrocław highway.

orbit

Follow us:

 /orbitbooksUS

 /orbitbooks

 /orbitbooks

Join our mailing list
to receive alerts on our
latest releases and deals.

orbitbooks.net

Enter our monthly
giveaway for the chance
to win some epic prizes.

orbitloot.com

ANDRZEJ SAPKOWSKI, WINNER OF THE WORLD
FANTASY AWARD FOR LIFETIME ACHIEVEMENT,
CREATED AN INTERNATIONAL PHENOMENON WITH HIS
NEW YORK TIMES BESTSELLING WITCHER SERIES. *THE
SWORD OF DESTINY* IS A COLLECTION OF UNMISSABLE
TALES SET IN THE EPIC FANTASY UNIVERSE THAT INSPIRED
THE NETFLIX SHOW AND THE HIT VIDEO GAMES.

Geralt is a witcher, a man whose magic powers,
enhanced by long training and a mysterious elixir,
have made him a brilliant fighter and a merciless
assassin. Yet he is no ordinary murderer. His targets
are the monsters and vile fiends that ravage the
land and attack the innocent.

SWORD OF DESTINY follows the adventures
of Geralt as he battles monsters, demons,
and prejudices alike....

Praise for The Witcher series:

"A BREATH OF FRESH AIR IN A WELL-WORN
GENRE. DON'T MISS IT!"
—*Fantasy Book Review*

"LIKE MIÉVILLE AND GAIMAN, SAPKOWSKI
TAKES THE OLD AND MAKES IT NEW."
—*Foundation*

ALSO AVAILABLE FROM

AUDIO

www.orbitbooks.net

COVER ILLUSTRATION BY BARTŁOMIEJ GAWEŁ,
PAWEŁ MIELNICZUK, MARCIN BŁASZCZAK,
ARKADIUSZ MATYSZEWSKI, MARIAN CHOMIAK
COVER DESIGN BY LAUREN PANEPINTO
COVER © 2015 HACHETTE BOOK GROUP, INC.

U.S. $17.99 / $22.99 CAN.

ISBN 978-0-316-38970-9

51799

9 780316 389709